Spearfield's Daughter

Jon Cleary

William Morrow and Company, Inc.
New York • 1983

Library of Congress Cataloging in Publication Data

Cleary, Jon, 1917-
   Spearfield's daughter.

   1. Vietnamese Conflict, 1961-1975—Fiction.
I. Title.
PR9619.3.C54S74   1983   823   82-14542
ISBN 0-688-01736-3

Printed in the United States of America

FIRST U.S. EDITION

1 2 3 4 5 6 7 8 9 10

FOR BENJAMIN

Spearfield's Daughter

ONE

'You're Sylvester Spearfield's daughter, aren't you?'

'Occasionally.'

Cleo Spearfield knew she was being unnecessarily rude to the war correspondent from Melbourne. But he, a crude chauvinist, was accustomed to being snubbed by women and just grinned and walked on, satisfied that he had put her in her place.

Tom Border looked after the Australian, then back at her. 'Remind me never to ask you a question like that. Who is your father, anyway?'

'Nobody. Go on with what you were saying.'

Tom appraised her with a stare, then seemed to mentally shrug and went on with his thesis: 'Wars are only benefit games for the generals. The poor grunts who have to fight the wars are necessary, but no career-minded man above the rank of colonel ever says they're not expendable.'

'I'm tired of all your male cynicism.'

'That's because you're female, sentimental and compassionate. You also have a very nice swagger to your ass. Why did you come to the war, Cleo old girl?'

'Because the mums back home in Australia are beginning to worry about their boys in a war that seems to be going all wrong. I thought I might be able to get at some of the truth.'

But that, in itself, was only some of the truth. She had come to Vietnam to escape being Sylvester Spearfield's daughter and to find her own name, if not fame.

Her father, who saw himself as everyone's guiding light and sometimes blinded himself with his own luminance, had once said to her, 'Come to me when you've finished university. Whatever you want to do, I'm sure to know someone. Just don't go into politics.'

She knew he had given the same advice to her two brothers, who had listened to him and then gone into dentistry and meteorology, as if realizing the futility of competing against a famous father in his own field. Sylvester Spearfield had never been Prime Minister of Australia, but there were Prime Ministers who would never be remembered as long as the flamboyant Senator from New South Wales, the ex-trade union organizer who had risen to be a politician for whom even his old opponents, top management, now had a grudging but sincere admiration.

'Afraid of the competition, Dad?' At both convent school and university she had already established a reputation as a radical. But all the newspaper reports on her activities called her her father's daughter ... *Cleo Spearfield, daughter of the radical Senator, yesterday* ...

Her father had let out the belly-laugh that the election crowds had once loved. Television had killed the belly-laugh as a campaign weapon and Sylvester had had difficulty in coming to terms with the living-room smile. 'You'd lose your deposit every time you ran against me, sweetheart. I'll still be in Parliament when your kids, my grandkids, are old enough to vote.'

'You could retire and let me take your seat.'

Her father had shaken his head with its long thick thatch. He had worn his hair long ever since he had gone into politics, liking to be thought of as one of the good old-time politicians, a man from Federation days, though he hadn't been born when Australia became a nation. But fashion had caught up with him and now he was surrounded by others with long hair.

'I'm not interested in creating a dynasty. You might turn out to be better than me. Then who'd remember me? I'd just be known as Cleo Spearfield's father.'

Which would serve him right, thought his daughter. She had decided then that she was going to be better than her

8

father, but in another field. When she graduated and got a job on the *Sydney Morning Post,* he had reacted with mock disgust.

'Whatever happened to the radical Cleo? How the hell did you con a conservative rag like the *Post* into taking you on?'

'I think they're trying to prove they're not as reactionary as they really are. They're also probably being spitefully funny, having the radical daughter of a radical Labour Senator on their women's page.'

'On the women's page, eh? Try and subvert the blue-rinse set, sweetheart. Good luck.'

But she hadn't subverted the blue-rinse set; within three months she had been moved off the women's page and on to general reporting. Within a year she had got her by-line, but all the readers knew she was her father's daughter. She had longed to be Cleo Brown or Smith: Spearfield was too distinctive.

Now, in 1968, she had decided to put distance, if nothing else, between herself and her father. She had applied to be sent to the *Post*'s London office, but they had turned her down. Then she had taken the plunge: 'Send me to Vietnam. There's no other Australian woman in the field there. Let me go and give the woman's view.'

The *Post* had never had a woman war correspondent; it did not even have a woman covering the small political wars in Canberra. But it had surprised her, after sitting on her application for two weeks. The editor had said, 'All right, but don't get yourself killed. And we want nothing radical, Cleo, none of your old anti-war stuff from your university days. Just good objective reporting.'

Now Tom Border was saying, 'The moms back home in America are also worrying about their boys in the war that's going wrong every goddam day. But if ever we gentlemen – and ladies –' he bowed his head '– of the press told them the truth, they'd think we were un-American. The generals certainly would.'

They were sitting on the terrace of the Continental Hotel. Above their heads the loudspeakers attached to the columns

9

were blaring, taking all the mystery out of the Beatles' *Magical Mystery Tour*. Out on the streets Saigon flowed, scampered, jerked past like a back-projection scene that wasn't quite in synchronization with what went on inside one's head. Cleo had been here in Vietnam a month and she had begun to wonder if she would ever get any part of this war and this country into focus. She knew that many of the men, the press correspondents as well as the GIs, stoned themselves out of focus. Drugs, opium pills, cocaine, heroin, had become standard equipment, like a chow-tin or an M-16 rifle. The Australian officers had told her there was much less drug-taking amongst their men than amongst the Americans, but they had been guarded and she had wondered whether they were lying or trying not to be too critical of the Americans. She hadn't pursued the question, however, and that had been when she had started to dodge the truth. She sipped her vermouth cassis and wondered how much more of the truth she would ignore before she went home.

'I'm going up to An Bai tomorrow. You want to come?'

As if he were asking her to a movie or a picnic. Tom Border had been in Vietnam over a year and soon he would be going home, to be replaced by another correspondent who would arrive full of curiosity, looking for the truth, and would gradually become cynical and stoned and would wait only for *his* replacement. Though, come to think of it, she had never seen Tom stoned or even drunk, and never heard him mention that he took pills or smoked an opium pipe.

'I was going anyway.'

'You're gutsy, Cleo old girl. You could sit here in Saigon on that beautiful ass of yours, like so many of the guys who don't have beautiful asses, and write about the war from what they tell us at the Five O'Clock Follies. You swagger –'

'I do not!' But she knew she did: she had inherited her father's walk. Swaggering Sylvester, a newspaper had once called him, and he had let out the belly-laugh and swaggered even more.

'You do, old girl. In that custom-tailored combat suit of yours, I have trouble distinguishing you from General

10

Westmoreland. You and he are easily the two best-dressed Beautiful People this town has seen.'

Which was more than could be said for him. No matter what he was dressed in, his clothes always seemed to fit him like a catcher's glove, as if he had bought them in anticipation of middle-age spread. He was tall and bony and he might be handsome in twenty years' time, when the bone in his face would be an advantage; he talked a lot, but she had noticed that his eyes often did not match his words, that they had a withdrawn look, as if his thoughts were a long way from his mouth. He was the correspondent for a small chain of Mid-West newspapers and she knew already that she would miss him when he went home next month.

'But you're gutsy and that makes you okay. I wish *I* could make you.'

'Forget it, Tom. I didn't come here to climb into bed with the first feller who asked me.'

'I'll bet I'm not the first who's asked you. I mean that as a compliment.' He had a slow smile which gave him a certain charm missed by those who saw only his usual sober, watchful face.

She had been invited to bed by at least two dozen men. There had been a brigadier-general who had sounded as if he were doing her a favour and dropping his rank; several colonels, a major, half a dozen captains and assorted press correspondents from Australia, the United States, Britain, France, Germany and Italy; and a huge jet-black man from Nigeria, whose role she never did learn, who had suggested they go to bed and discuss the death of colonialism. She was not the only woman correspondent in Saigon and she was not the best-looking, but she was the newest and she had the most eye-catching figure. She had made a mistake having her suits made for her by the tailor on Tu Do; accustomed to making *ao dais* for the bar girls, he had assumed that she, too, wanted something tight that revealed her figure. Her looks were striking rather than beautiful; men would always gaze at her for there was a vibrancy about her that was more than just the flash of good white teeth and dark blue eyes. Though she

11

didn't know it, being only twenty-three, she had the sort of looks that would attract attention all her life. And would be both a blessing and a curse.

She saw Pierre Cain coming across the square, dodging gracefully through the swarms of piranha-like Hondas. He came up on to the terrace, saw her and Tom, came along to their table and stood waiting to be asked to sit down. Part French, part Annamese, he had the best formal manners of each.

'Sit down, Pierre,' said Tom. 'You're the best traffic-dodger I've ever seen. Twice there I thought one of those cowboys had got you.'

Cain smiled. 'We have an old superstition in Annam –' He spoke as if Annam still existed, as if the present situation were only transitory, and Annam would tomorrow be again as it always had been. In his mind he still lived in Indo-China, no matter what the foreigners now called it. 'If a man is haunted, all he has to do is take the evil spirit close to a motorcycle or an automobile and it will be run down.'

'What happens if the evil spirit gives you a push and you're the one who's run down?'

Cain smiled again. 'Then you are no longer haunted.'

'Are you haunted now, Pierre?' said Cleo.

He shrugged, turned away to order some mineral water, then looked back at them. 'I have some disappointing news. No correspondents are being allowed into the An Bai area tomorrow.'

Tom Border gave a Gallic shrug; but Cleo was angry. 'Why not, for God's sake? Isn't that where they've had all the trouble with the VC? Are they afraid we might get hurt or something? Is that it?' She was afraid, but she would not admit it, not to men, even two men as sympathetic as Tom Border and Pierre Cain. 'What's gone wrong this time?'

'They are bringing out our men and replacing them – it is to be an all-American operation.' He said it without bitterness or shame, as if it were natural to accept that this was now an almost all-American war. He was a liaison officer

12

between the US and Vietnamese commands and had learned the diplomacy of swallowing one's pride.

Cleo looked at Tom, who said, 'There you are, old girl. Nobody wants us.'

'I don't believe it. We were told only yesterday we could go up there...'

'Brigadier-General Brisson –' Cain always gave everyone his exact rank; he had been an accountant in Hué before the war had swallowed him up – 'I'm afraid he's cancelled everything that was promised yesterday. He's in charge of the An Bai operation. He says there will be no transport available for the press.'

Cleo knew Roger Brisson; he was the brigadier-general who had invited her to bed. She had met him two days after her arrival in Saigon, at a reception at the American embassy for a party of US Congressmen come to visit the war. There had been few other correspondents there and none of the women from the press; nobody was interested in writing stories about anyone from Washington. But she was new and had gone along, to learn nothing except that General Brisson thought he was God's gift to women and the war effort.

He had taken her to dinner at the Caravelle Hotel, where he had shown he knew his way through a wine list as well as through a tactical plan. Outside, the White Mice, the Vietnamese police, paraded up and down, keeping the war at a safe distance. Come Armageddon, there will still be generals who will find time to dine properly.

'Cleo? Is that a nickname?'

'No, it's short for Cleopatra. My mother was a romantic, she saw me growing up to sail my barge down the Murrumbidgee, conquering all before me.' Brigid Spearfield had been a country girl and all her reference points had been country towns, rivers, anywhere in the bush that helped her shut her mind against the city, which she had never accepted.

'The Murrumbidgee?' Roger Brisson wondered if he had brought some sort of kook to dinner. Saigon was full of them, scores of them coming in and claiming to be representatives of the press. He decided it was time to get her out of public view into a more private place. 'We'll go back to my quarters after dinner.'

'Is that an invitation to go to bed with you?'

'Yes.' He always gave a direct answer to a direct question; it meant that down the chain of command there was never any confusion. Or should not be. 'You could do far worse than me, but not any better. Not in this town.'

He was handsome, trim and fit; the twenty years' difference between them didn't worry either of them. But Cleo knew the bed would be crowded, his ego would keep getting between them. 'No, thank you.'

He looked at her as if she should be put on a charge-sheet for conduct prejudicial to military order and good discipline. 'You may be glad of my civilized company, you won't find any of that amongst the press corps. That is, if you stay long enough. I don't believe women have much stamina for war.'

'You may well be right,' she had said, though she wondered what sort of answer Martha Gellhorn or Marguerite Higgins would have given him. Gellhorn who had been covering the Spanish Civil War when Brisson was not yet in high school and who was still writing about war; and Higgins who had slogged her way through Korea with the best of the men and died from a tropical disease picked up right here in Vietnam. 'But some of us don't find that disgraceful, General.'

The evening had ended shortly after that. He had abruptly remembered that he had to attend a conference – there was a war to be won. She had seen him only once since then, going past in a Jeep across Lam Son Square; he had looked at her and through her, then turned and stared straight ahead. She had wanted to jeer and boo, something she would have done on campus in her university days. But anti-war demonstrations were out of place in Saigon.

'Well, I'm going *somewhere* tomorrow,' she told Cain and Tom. 'Where else can I get a ride to?'

'Attagirl,' said Tom; then looked at Cain. 'Send her somewhere healthy, Pierre. We don't want to lose her.'

'I'll think of somewhere.' Cain raised his glass of mineral water and drank their health. Then he looked at the label on

14

the bottle the waiter had left. 'Vichy water. Do you think they bottle treachery?'

But that had been another war, ending the year she was born, and Vichy meant nothing to Cleo.

2

She sat on her pack on the edge of the air-strip and listened to the obscenities, wondering when the English language had become so inadequate that nothing but four-letter words would do to describe everything from the war to the weather. Four-letter words had been very fashionable back on campus, as if the students of the day had been proving that education was a barrel of nightsoil, as her father would have called it. She had always had an aversion to such language and if she had not been such a radical in other matters she would have been called a prig by her fellow students. But whatever the language back on campus, she had heard nothing like the conversation of these American grunts.

'The war's nothing but fucking shit, I tell you.' He was nineteen and back home in Chappell, Nebraska, his mother would probably have told him to wash out his mouth with soap. 'Only them motherfuckers back in Washington won't admit it.'

'I come out here to fight for the fucking gooks and all the fucking gooks done was fucking run away.'

'Sensible motherfuckers. I been reading about the fucking wisdom of the East.'

'Wisdom is shit, man. I'm fucking wise to all that fucking wisdom.'

I can't write any of this, Cleo thought, not for the mums back home. She wondered how the grunts would describe the war to their mothers when, and if, they got back home.

The crew of the Chinook helicopter were polite young men, careful of their language in front of her. The co-pilot, brash and boyish, a Saturday night hero back home in Denver who had become a real hero and didn't want to know

15

about it, winked at her and invited her to sit up front in the jump-seat just behind him and the pilot. The big helicopter was ferrying supplies to an Australian company in the hills – one that was operating quite separately from the main Australian force.

The American captain at the press centre at JUSPAO (some day she would get all the initials worked out; acronyms had become another obscenity) had worked on her like a used car salesman. 'Honestly, Miss Spearfield, this is the story for you. The Aussies are doing a fantastic job up there – you ought to tell the folks back home all about it.' She had been suspicious of his hard sell, wanting to question him about An Bai. But in the end she had decided that perhaps he was right. After all, the *Sydney Morning Post* had sent her here to write about the Australian war effort. The mums back home in Sydney wouldn't care about what was happening in An Bai.

They were flying through heavy rain, the rotors above them spinning it off in a thick spray; looking up, Cleo had the image that they were flying under a giant circular saw. It was cold here in the bubble and she was glad she had worn her sweater; the four crewmen back in the hold of the chopper had whistled at her, but she had long ago accepted that as part of the pleasure and irritation of being a woman. Unconsciously she leaned back in her seat, lifting her bosom, and the pilot looked back at her out of the corner of his eye.

'Don't do that, miss. It's hard enough as it is flying this bird.'

She relaxed, smiled. 'Sorry.' She had to shout to make him hear, so that put an end to any flirtation, even if she had felt like it, which she didn't. She leaned close to him and bellowed in his ear: 'Which way is An Bai?'

He nodded to the right. 'Somewhere down there. All these gook villages look the same from up here.'

'Can we go back that way?'

'What for, for crissakes? I'm not a fucking taxi pilot.' Up till now he had been careful with his language.

She saw the sudden anger in his face and then recognized the other signs. The young-old eyes, the grey-yellow pallor

16

like that of an elderly, sick man: he was twenty-three years old, but his birthdays stretched behind him like memorials rather than celebrations. Some other pilots, the adventurers, the rebels, might have instantly swung off course to take her down to An Bai. But Lieutenant Hurd, unlike Joe Puzio, the co-pilot, was a career man, even if he was thoroughly disillusioned by his first war.

She sat back, careful to keep her bosom down, and looked out through the rain-cracked perspex bubble at the green, dream-like countryside up ahead. The whole of Vietnam had become a dream, and a bad one. She had come here excited by her first big adventure; now, only a month later, she had begun to hate the war. It was a different hatred from that she had felt during the demonstrations back home against Australia's becoming involved in Vietnam; this was anger and disgust about the *actual* war, the death and maiming in the abstract. So far she had seen virtually no real action; it was almost as if the Viet Cong had retreated to make *her* war more comfortable. But she had seen the bags on the air-strips, like the rubbish of war, all tagged with the names of this week's garbage: Jeffrey T. Partridge, Mortimer Wineburg, Lester O. Schwabe. She had used the simile of the garbage bags in her first story, then crossed it out. The mums back home did not want to be told that their dead sons resembled rubbish.

Suddenly the helicopter lurched to one side and Cleo saw rather than heard the pilot swear. He swung the chopper in a wide arc, steeply banking; Cleo felt the canvas seat-belt slicing into her. Her stomach seemed to roll around inside her; she thought she was going to vomit. Something hit the floor beneath her with a jarring bump and the chopper bounced. There was a loud crack and the bubble on the pilot's side burst; it seemed to disintegrate in slow motion. Then she saw Lieutenant Hurd shake his head and the blood began to spurt out of the wound in his throat.

The chopper wobbled, began to swing through the air up, down and around, a Big Dipper ride on no rails. Cleo sat petrified, wanting to be sick but with her stomach never in

17

the right place to throw up. Then she heard Lieutenant Puzio yelling at her, jerking his head at Hurd. He got the chopper on an even keel, but it seemed to be bumping its way over a rough road of rain-filled air. She tore off her scarf, a Lanvin piece of silk given her as a going-away present by her sister-in-law Cheryl, just the thing for this year's combat zone. She strained against the canvas straps, reached across, wrenched off the pilot's helmet and awkwardly wrapped the scarf round his throat. He was slumped in his seat and made no response. Lieutenant Puzio nodded his thanks without looking at her, peering ahead through the rain which was now beating in through the shattered bubble. The helicopter was still pitching, dropping lower and lower towards the rice paddies that lay like great sheets of mottled glass below them.

Then Cleo saw the three Chinooks rising from beyond a long straggling village to their right. They swung away through the curtain of rain like giant fat turkeys that had learned to fly; as they disappeared Lieutenant Puzio took the chopper towards the village. The helicopter went in sideways above the village; Cleo saw the flower of flame suddenly bloom out of the roof of a hut below her. She saw villagers running in panic to get away from the crashing helicopter; then she realized the chopper was not going to crash and that Joe Puzio was putting it down safely. She saw the soldiers running after the villagers, who were now falling over and lying still in the mud. Lieutenant Puzio put the helicopter down with a bump and switched off the motors; Lieutenant Hurd fell forward and hung in his belting. Cleo had never seen a dead man before, not one who had been alive only a minute ago, and she shut her eyes and waited to be sick, but nothing came up out of her dry, constricted throat.

Then a mud-drenched sergeant appeared outside the shattered bubble, his wild-eyed thin face like a skull under the bowl of his helmet. 'What the fuck are you doing here? Get the fuck outa here!'

Puzio shook his head, dumb with shock, and pointed weakly at the dead pilot. Cleo could hear the harsh bursts of automatic rifle fire behind the crackling roar of the flaming huts; the whole village was now on fire, dark clouds of smoke wreathing up to merge with the low rain-clouds. She saw bodies lying in the mud of the long streets, all of them villagers: men, women and children. And she heard the screams behind the rifle fire and then she was sick. She tore off her seat-belt, dived across the lap of the dead pilot and vomited into the mud beside the boots of the sergeant as he came round to her side.

He waited till she had finished, then he put his M-16 into her white face. 'Don't move outa this fucking chopper, you hear me? That goes for you jerks, too.' He swung round on the crewmen who were about to jump out of the side door of the Chinook. 'This ain't none of your fucking business, you unnerstand? Don't move or I tell you, I'll blow your fucking heads off! Alla you!' He looked back at Cleo, then he swung away and went running down the street, slipping and sliding in the mud as he dodged corpses, yelling back without turning round, 'It ain't none of your fucking business!'

Cleo fumbled for a handkerchief, wiped her mouth. She eased herself back from Lieutenant Hurd, not wanting to look at him, but everywhere she looked, there were dead. She saw a woman run out from between two burning huts, hands held over her smoking hair; a soldier came out from between the huts and put her out of her pain and misery and her life with a short burst from his carbine. Then he looked across at the helicopter, grinned and waved and ran back between the huts.

'Oh Jesus!' said one of the crewmen in the open door of the Chinook. 'Someone tell me this ain't happening!'

'They're stoned outa their fucking heads,' said the man beside him. 'They gotta be.' Then he looked back inside the helicopter at Cleo. 'You gonna write a story about this?'

She found her voice, which she had begun to fear had left her forever. 'Where are we?' But she knew, as if she could see signposts all down the long, corpse-strewn street; they were in An Bai, where Brigadier-General Brisson had wanted no correspondents. 'How do we get out of here?'

'How's everything up front?' They were still standing in

19

the doorway of the Chinook, like workers waiting in some loading dock for a truck to arrive.

'Lieutenant Hurd is dead, I think.' She didn't look at him as she turned back to Puzio. 'Are you all right?'

He had put his hand inside his shirt, taken it out and was staring at the blood on it. He looked across at her as if he had been insulted by what had happened to him. 'I got a hole in my side –' Then he winced and fell forward.

Cleo grabbed him, pulling him upright, screaming for one of the crewmen to come forward. She could feel herself panicking: the war was stifling her with its dead, packing them in around her.

One of the crewmen suddenly appeared behind her. He was short and fat and looked like a middle-aged cab driver; but he was twenty-four years old and a rich man's son from Cleveland, Ohio. She leaned away while he squeezed his bulk over her to look at Lieutenant Puzio. Then he sat back and looked as if he were about to cry.

'He's dead, too. Christ, what a day!' He looked out past her as if he were commenting on the weather. 'Just shit, that's all.'

'Can you fly this thing?'

He looked at her in surprise, as if she had asked him if he himself could fly. 'I can fly it if it'll go. But I dunno if it will – that ground-fire hit us pretty hard. They spattered us with real shit then.'

'I think it's worth a try.' She could hear herself talking, like listening to someone else in another room. 'I think they might come back and kill us, too.'

'Jesus, why would they wanna do that?' The other three men were crammed in behind the fat man. The youngest had spoken, nineteen and more afraid of something he didn't understand than all the other deaths he had seen. 'We're Americans, like them – we're on the same side, for crissake!'

'I dunno I want to be on their side,' said the fat one. 'I saw a coupla guys like this once before, not a whole goddam company, but a coupla grunts, they went around shooting every slopehead in sight. I got outa there so quick...'

20

'You don't look like no slopehead.' But no one laughed, not even the young man who said it, thin-faced behind his gold-rimmed glasses, looking young enough to be arrested for trespassing in a pornographic adult area.

Cleo leaned over Lieutenant Hurd, touching him carefully as if afraid she might hurt him, looked down the street and saw half a dozen men coming up towards the helicopter, walking slowly with their carbines swinging back and forth in front of them, looking for game they had missed in the first beating. The huts blazed on either side of them, the flames too bright in the grey day, like botched technicolor; the smoke was a thick black cloud lying like a dark, heaving roof over their heads. They picked their way carefully amongst the bodies clad in black pyjamas lying in the mud, but more as if they thought the corpses might be booby-trapped than out of respect for the dead. She would remember the scene for the rest of her life, the Inferno in which the good had suddenly become the devils.

The fat crewman abruptly pushed into the bubble and began fumbling with the seat-belts. Cleo, all at once feeling useless and female, her physical strength not enough to cope with what had to be done, crept back, pushing her way through the other crewmen into the hold of the chopper. The crewmen were struggling and swearing; then Lieutenant Hurd's body was dragged from the cockpit. A few moments later Lieutenant Puzio's body followed it; the corpses were stacked in beside the supplies of rations, ammunition, clothing. The youngest crewman blessed himself and lowered his head for a quick prayer; then he came and stood beside Cleo in the doorway of the hold. He was blinking rapidly and she thought he was going to jump out of the helicopter and run down towards the soldiers coming up the street.

There was a moan from the motor, then the clattering sound that Cleo was still not comfortable with: she was always waiting for the rotor blades to break off and fly away. The rotors began to whirl slowly, spinning the rain away like a giant agricultural spray. Looking down the street she saw the soldiers break into a run as the helicopter began to lift off.

21

The rotors were spinning swiftly now, but the Chinook rose as if it were climbing through invisible mud.

The helicopter lurched and Cleo grabbed at a strap and hung on. She saw one of the soldiers stop running, raise his M-16 and aim it at the Chinook. She shrank back, turning her head away, not wanting to die with a bullet in her face. The young crewman stood in front of her, holding on to the side of the doorway for dear life, and screamed obscenities at the soldiers. Then the Chinook swung away, suddenly gaining speed, and carved its way up through the rain. Cleo made herself look back and down, saw An Bai disappearing like a nightmare into the mist of rain and smoke, saw the soldiers standing in the middle of the street amongst the corpses, waving to her like the decent, friendly kids they once must have been.

'Jesus,' said the young crewman; his shout was a whisper of despair in her ear; there was no obscenity now but that of the scene below. 'Whatever happened to us?'

3

'There was no incident today at An Bai,' said the briefing officer. 'It was just a routine change-over. Turning to the Bu Dop area, the body count for today was –'

'Excuse me, Major.' Cleo could feel all the other correspondents looking at her, bored and irritated that she was going to stretch out the baloney. Most of the correspondents in Saigon no longer came to the daily briefing, the Five O'Clock Follies; it was accepted that JUSPAO and MACV (some day she would write an ABC of the American forces) were fighting a different war from that out in the field. She saw two of the women correspondents, the French girl whose name she could never remember and the Italian woman who saw the war only in terms of politics; both of them nodded encouragingly to her, taking her side in the other war between the sexes. She looked back at the briefing officer.

'Major, I was there in An Bai today – it was no routine change-over –'

'General Brisson himself was there supervising the change-over. There was no incident of any kind, Miss Spearfield. There is enough happening in the war without the press manufacturing stories –'

Even the male correspondents laughed at that. Cleo, suddenly losing control, shouted, 'Why don't you listen to the bloody truth for once? I tell you, I saw –'

'Who's that?' said an American voice. 'I've just landed here.'

'Her name's Spearfield,' said an Australian voice. 'Her old man's a big-shot politician back home, he's dead against the war. She trades on his name.'

She turned round ready to kill the correspondent from the Melbourne newspaper. He was fat and bearded and always wore dark glasses, even at night; it was rumoured he had once worn them down a coal mine. He grinned at her and gave her a mock thumbs-up sign.

'Attagirl, Cleo. Daddy would be proud of you.'

She measured the distance, worked her mouth, then spat. The spittle landed on one of the dark lenses. Then she turned back to the major.

'I repeat, Major, why don't you tell the truth for a change? Let's see General Brisson so I can ask him face to face –'

Then a strong hand pulled her down into her seat. She turned angrily to see who had done it: Tom Border sat beside her. 'I just came in, Cleo old girl. Take it easy, you're not going to get anywhere with that guy up there. They say there was no incident at An Bai, there was no incident at An Bai. It's not the first time. This is the most incident-free war you're ever likely to cover. Come and I'll buy you dinner.'

She wanted to struggle with him to stay where she was; but all at once she realized it was useless. As she went out of the big press room the major was once more giving the body count for the day. She closed her eyes, saw the pyjama-clad bodies in the mud of the village; she stumbled and Tom straightened her with a firm grip on her elbow. She opened

23

her eyes and one of the male correspondents, sitting on the end of a row, smiled and shook his head at her.

'Write the story, honey, then see if they'll print it back home. It's a waste of time, I tell you from experience.'

She was still angry and upset when she and Tom reached L'Amiral restaurant. The Indian money-sellers were going past on their way to their temple; the Catholics were heading for evening Mass at the cathedral. Prayers would be offered for another day of survival, another day of profit. She felt herself surrounded by corruption, caked with it as if with mud.

'You know, I'd never tasted wine till I came out here, even during the year I spent in Europe. I was just a beer and bourbon man.' Tom ordered a bottle of Meursault with the same careless confidence as he might have ordered a Schlitz or a Jack Daniels. ''Nam has been quite an education for me.'

'Meaning it should be for me?'

She had recovered enough to put on a new face and comb her hair. She remembered that her mother had always frowned on women who did their hair or repaired their make-up at the dinner table or in restaurants; but Brigid Spearfield was dead now, her world of small conventions dead with her. Maybe mine, too, thought Cleo: at least *something* she had believed in had died today.

'Cleo, every guy who has been here a year, two years, whatever, has got a story like yours. I've got my own. I saw four dinks, villagers, no one knew for certain if they were VCs, taken up in a chopper with their hands tied behind their backs and pushed out, maybe from a thousand feet, I don't know. All I know is they seemed to take forever to fall. I was on the ground and I couldn't believe what I was seeing.'

'But that was probably some local commander, a captain or a lieutenant, someone who'd gone round the bend or was stoned. But today – it was *planned*, it must have been. If General Brisson was there, then he'd okayed the massacre. Why did they suddenly cancel all transport for us?'

'It's not the first time. We're only Priority 3 when it comes to transport. Look –' he leaned forward across the table, all

at once tense and concerned, 'I can guess what happened –
I *believe* you. But it's like Jack Martin said to you back there
in the press room – no editor is ever going to print the truth.
They prefer to believe the mullarkey they get from their
bureaux in Washington – they think we're all junkies out
here or alcoholics –'

'My paper will print it. It doesn't always believe what
Washington says –'

He sat back, relaxed and cynical again. 'Well, good luck.
But didn't your late Prime Minister, the one who was
drowned, say "All the way with LBJ"? I just hope for your
sake that your editor doesn't subscribe to that. Now eat up
your *croustade de langoustes*.' His accent was terrible, Missouri
Provençal. 'I'm going to take you to bed tonight and comfort
you. I don't think you should be left alone.'

Before she could answer that, Pierre Cain came into the
restaurant with his wife. She was small and beautiful, an
Annamese, with a look of sad dignity about her, as if she had
lost everything that had meant anything to her but would
never let her grief be public. Cain seated his wife at a table,
told a waiter to attend to her, then came across to Cleo and
Tom. As ever, he stood waiting as if he dare not sit down
until invited. But this time, when Tom reached for a chair,
he shook his head.

'This will only take a moment – I don't like to desert my
wife for too long. She is afraid of being alone –' Cleo looked
at Tom, but Cain missed her glance. 'Miss Spearfield, I heard
what happened out at An Bai today, that you were there. Are
you going to write the story?'

She hesitated, then nodded. 'Yes.'

'Please do. But I have to warn you – if you do, your visa
will be withdrawn and you'll have to leave. Our government
does everything the Americans ask.'

'Do you think I should write the story, Pierre?'

It was his turn to hesitate, then he nodded. 'It should be
written by someone. This is my country – I don't think we
should be the victims of both the Communists and the Americans.'

25

He bowed and went across the restaurant to his wife. As she ate her dinner, for which she now had no taste, Cleo looked across at them sitting stiffly opposite each other like strangers. Then she saw Madame Cain's hand slide across the table and press her husband's. It was only a small gesture, one that Cleo had seen dozens of times in restaurants in Sydney; but this time she wanted to weep. She bent her head, feeling the tears in her eyes.

'Something wrong?' said Tom.

'I'm feeling female, sentimental and compassionate.' She looked up at him and wiped her eyes with her napkin. 'A cynic like you wouldn't understand.'

He looked at her, then across at the Cains, then back at her. 'I can understand people still being in love after twenty or thirty years. My folks still are. Only thing is, they've been luckier than those two over there. When things are like they are with the Cains, maybe all they have is each other. I don't think they have any kids.'

It was almost as if she were looking at him for the first time. She had seen him virtually every day since she had been here and she had appreciated his company; though he talked about wanting to take her to bed, he had never made a physical pass at her; he had never come at her as strongly and bluntly as some of the other men with time on their hands in Saigon. Sometimes his cynicism annoyed her, but it was no worse than that of most of the other correspondents; God knows, in a year's time, if she stayed here that long, she might be just as bad. She knew nothing of what he sent back to the chain of newspapers in the American Mid-West. She realized all at once that she knew nothing at all about him, that behind the withdrawn eyes was a total stranger.

'Who are you, Tom? What are you?'

He smiled, sipped his wine. 'A Budweiser boy with pretensions maybe, I don't know. I'm American provincial, right out of the mould. My dad's people and my mother's, too, came down the Wilderness Road out of Kentucky into Missouri nearly one hudred and fifty years ago. Dad's a farmer, not a big one, but we've always lived comfortable. The farm's outside a little town called Friendship in south-west Missouri and about the only excitement it's ever known is when a tornado goes through every couple of years or so.'

'You came straight from there to *here*?'

'No. I went up to the University of Missouri, did journalism. I got a job on the Kansas City *Star*. I left there after a year and went to New York and the *New York Times* gave me a six months' trial. At the end of it we parted company with no hard feelings on my part and no feelings at all on theirs – I was just another hick from the sticks who hadn't made it. After that I just drifted – I even went to Europe for a year. Maybe that's what I really am, a drifter. A newspaper bum. There are a lot of us. You only have to look around here in Saigon. A guy down at JUSPAO told me there are over 600 accredited correspondents in 'Nam. There's got to be a pretty fair number of bums amongst them, guys just chasing a story, any story.'

'I don't think you're like that. I mean, you're not out here just chasing a story.'

'Why am I here?' He was smiling, but the eyes were darkly watchful.

'The same reason I am. You wanted to *know*.'

He put his big bony hand on hers. 'I could love you, Cleo old girl.' He was still smiling and now the eyes had lightened. 'Even with all your swagger.'

She knew there was no swagger in her tonight. 'Are you married?'

He shook his head. 'I got close a couple of times. But they were both homebodies, a girl in Friendship and one in Kansas City. If I'd married either of them and settled down and then one day come home and complained I'd got itchy feet, she'd have gone out and bought a jar of Foot Balm. I don't think you'd do that.'

She didn't answer that. What he had described would have fitted her own situation; there were two lovers back home in Sydney who had not understood why she had refused the security each had offered her. Even her father, the one-time drifter, the political bum, had hinted he would like her to settle down, be near him whenever he wanted to call on her.

'Where do you live? I mean here in Saigon?'

'I thought you'd never ask.' Then he looked at her seriously. 'Are you sure you want to come with me?'

She smiled, put her hand on his; she was full of such affectionate gestures. They were a weakness: men read more into them than she intended. 'Tom, I don't think you really want to go to bed with me. You're scared.' She saw his eyes narrow, as if he had been hit; she was instantly sorry, for she did not like hurting people. She lifted his hand, kissed it as a penance. It was always the same: she dug her own quicksands, trying to compensate for her mistakes. 'I'm sorry. I didn't mean that.'

He had a two-room apartment in a dilapidated villa ten minutes by taxi from the restaurant. A French lawyer had owned the villa, but that had been in the days of French Indo-China; a dead flame tree stood in the front garden like a shattered memorial to what had once been. All the windows were covered with thick wire mesh and a guard, a young Vietnamese, stood at the front gates, a rifle slung over his shoulder.

'The other guys who live here are chopper pilots, Americans. A couple of times the VC came around with their calling card. Grenades. You scared?'

She smiled and suddenly he laughed, the first time she had heard a full laugh from him. He put his arm round her and they went upstairs to his apartment. She looked around it, but there was nothing in it to identify him. She wondered if all the other rooms in his drifter's existence had been as bare.

She was surprised at his technique in bed; she had expected him to be smoother. He had apparently learned to make love at an unarmed combat school; he reduced foreplay to a ten-second dash. She rolled out from beneath him.

'I'm not an obstacle course. God knows, I'm trying to make myself easy for you. Here, let me show you ...'

'I don't like the woman on top.'

28

'That's just American male chauvinism.'

'What about Aussie men?'

'They're different. They just think it's pervy for the girl to be on top. *Lie still!*'

But it wasn't satisfactory at all. The love-making was more acrobatic than passionate; like a couple of kangaroos trying to be human, she thought. She lay back after it and stared at the stained and cracked ceiling. Neither of them said anything and after a while she got up and dressed. He still lay in bed, watching her.

'That's ruined everything, hasn't it?' he said at last.

'Between us? Not necessarily. I just don't think we'll be going to bed again, that's all.'

'I'm out of practice. I haven't had a woman since I came out here. I don't fancy the bar girls, getting the clap –'

'Get dressed and take me back to the Continental. I don't like wandering around on my own at night.'

He was not the sort to make conversation to cover awkward silences. They sat without talking during the taxi ride back to the hotel, but when they reached it he got out and paid off the taxi driver.

'It's goodnight here, Tom, not up in my room. Tonight was my fault as much as yours.'

She had the sense of guilt that she always had when she allowed a man to make love to her; she hadn't entirely thrown off the influence of the nuns at the convent. She had been in love, or imagined herself to be, with each man at the moment; afterwards she had not been disillusioned with the man but with herself. She had been *looking* for love, not falling in love; the men had not been to blame for falling short of her dreams. She had never believed that sex was a way of leading to love; she knew enough to be able to separate sensation from emotion. But, like her mother, she was a romantic and tonight, suddenly and (she thought) inexplicably, she had felt romantic. And all Tom Border had wanted was a roll in the hay.

'I'm going into the bar.'

'Don't get drunk on my account, Tom.'

He smiled, the old Tom Border again: withdrawn, watchful. 'Just a glass of Budweiser, to remind me of home. Good-night, Cleo old girl. Like you say, it was nobody's fault.'

She was about to say, *That wasn't what I said*; but didn't. Never argue about your mistakes, her father, the politician, had said.

'I'll see you tomorrow, Tom.'

4

She dreamed that night of her home street in Coogee back in Sydney, with black-clad corpses lying in the roadway and faintly familiar figures (boys she had once known?) stand-ing over them with guns. She woke in a sweat and it took her a long time to go back to sleep again. She wondered if dreams like this had first started the GIs on the need to get stoned.

In the morning she learned that Tom had gone up to Danang. She wondered where he would go from there and hoped he wouldn't go looking for the worst of the war. Not with only three weeks to go before he went home for a visit to the farm outside – where was it? Where the only excitement was an occasional tornado.

She felt a sense of loss and wondered why: for God's sake, she hadn't been in love with him! The loudspeakers on the Continental terrace were playing a Rolling Stones number, *2,000 Light Years From Home*, Mick Jagger sending his comfort on a nice safe plastic disc. She got up and went looking for more evidence of what had happened at An Bai yesterday. But she might just as well have gone looking for true love amongst the bars.

She asked to see General Brisson and was told he was up-country; that afternoon she saw him in his Jeep going down Tu Do Street. She tried to find out which company from what regiment had gone into An Bai yesterday; but even that information wasn't available. It took her two days to write her story and she had the sense not to cable it; she went down to the post office and mailed it special delivery. Then she went back to the Continental and waited; at night she had more nightmares, but after three nights they were gone; put away at the back of her mind for future torture. She was relieved and pleased that she did not feel she needed an opium pill.

She found after a day or two that she was also waiting for Tom Border to come back. But he didn't and at the end of the week she learned he had been wounded in a Marines action up beyond Danang, not badly but enough to have him sent out on a plane going to Tokyo. She felt annoyed that he had gone without saying goodbye to her; but she went up to her room and wrote him a short note. She said she hoped he wasn't badly wounded and would soon be well enough to go on drifting. She did not know where to send the letter and she would not go to the press office to ask the address of the head office of the chain of newspapers he represented. In the end she addressed it simply: Tom Border, care of Friendship, Missouri.

Next day she got a cable from the *Sydney Morning Post* recalling her.

5

'They won't print my story, Dad – that's why I've resigned!'

'Sweetheart, what did you expect? I believe your story and I'm sure the *Post* believes it. But they back the Government, they back the war. They couldn't print subversive stuff like yours. It would be like asking Old Jack Pack to vote Labour.' John Pack was the fifth generation of the family that owned the *Post*. 'Go and ask them for your job back, tell 'em you had second thoughts.'

'God Almighty, how can you suggest such a thing? I'm not a bloody politician, I can't compromise like you –'

He was not hurt by her remark, he had been too long in politics to be wounded by insults. The fun of politics for him was the insults; they were part of the masochism. Or so he said with the belly-laugh.

31

'Sweetheart, things like you describe happen in all wars.'
He had not fought in World War Two. He had been in
Parliament then, in his first term; he had also had a bad back,
a heritage of his days as a sheep-shearer, and the army had
rejected him. There were times when he regretted he had not
gone to the war: he still dreamed of being a real hero, more
than just a warrior with words. There had been snide remarks
by Government members during the Vietnam debates about
his never having seen a shot fired in anger, and those insults
had hurt. 'I remember an incident in New Guinea during
World War Two. I heard about it, but none of us ever
bothered to check it because it put our fellers in a bad light.
They were supposed to have bayoneted something like a
hundred wounded Japs rather than take them prisoner. They
could have shot them, but they preferred to bayonet them.
That was hushed up because God was supposed to be on our
side and no Aussie mum wanted to be told her son was a
murderer.'

She was prepared to believe anything about men: she was
blind with rage and frustration. It was men who had killed
her story. 'That was over twenty years ago, before I was
born. You men have always been fighting dirty wars . . . This
is *now*, the war that's going on right *now*!'

He could see it was pointless arguing with her. He, like
most politicians, knew when an argument was lost. 'All right.
What are you going to do, then?'

They were in the house where she had been born, in
Coogee, looking down towards the beach. Her mother, feeling
secure in suburbia, had never wanted to leave here, at least
not unless she could move back to the even better security of
the bush. Her father, safe in a Labour seat (when he had
been a Member of the House and not yet in the Senate), had
always said he would never desert the voters who had given
him his start. He ignored the fact that, as time went on, a lot
of his voters prospered, moved to more affluent districts and
began to vote for the other party. The house had none of the
flamboyance of Sylvester: it was like Brigid Spearfield, solid,
modest, a small fortress against the sins and temptations of a

larger world. Not that much sin and temptation passed up and down the streets of Coogee.

'I'm going to London.' Where sin and temptation abounded, but that was not the reason for her going.

That surprised him. He had always supposed that she would want to stay close to home, to be comforted and supported. She was a radical like himself, of course, but radicalism in women never lasted. 'Oh ... well, I guess it's a good idea to see as much as you can before you marry and settle down. You want an introduction to anyone? Harold Wilson? He'd know someone in Fleet Street.'

'No, Dad. I want to do it on my own.' *Before I marry and settle down*, but she didn't add that, afraid of the bitter sarcasm on her tongue.

'Well, I suppose so. I did.'

'No, you didn't. You had Mum.'

He had the grace to look ashamed. 'Do you think I've forgotten? Well, good luck, sweetheart. I hope the Poms appreciate you. How long will you be away?'

'I don't know, Dad. I'm ambitious. Some day I may own Fleet Street.' She laughed as she said it: still, it was a nice dream. One that had come to her only last night, the shaft of light on the road to London.

The Senate was in session in Canberra when she left Sydney for London and her father could not get away. He phoned her, wished her goodbye. Perhaps it was a bad connection ('Connections are always bad between Canberra and Sydney,' he had once said, but he had meant it in another context), but his voice seemed to break. He hung up hurriedly, saying he had just heard the division bells ring. She put the phone slowly back in its cradle and let the tears come. She felt guilty: as much as anything else, she was running away from him, from his name and what passed for fame in politics. She wondered if he had guessed.

Her brothers and sisters-in-law came to the airport to see her off. Her brothers, Alexander and Perry, short for Pericles (heroes both; or so her mother had hoped when she had christened them), hugged her to their beer bellies, the Great

33

Australian Profile as she called it, and wished her the best of Aussie luck; in their own way they had tried to escape from their father by being as ordinary and plebeian as they could be. Her sisters-in-law, Madge and Cheryl, kissed her and, she sensed, envied her. They had both married young and if sin and temptation ever crossed their paths it would be in the form of some footballsy stud from the Leagues club, not a boulevardier from some Gomorrah like London, Paris or Rome.

Madge, the quiet sensible one, said, 'I won't wish you the best of Aussie luck. I wouldn't wish that on anyone.'

Perry, who wasn't her husband, laughed and slapped Madge on the rump. 'You girls don't know when you're well off.'

Cheryl said, 'If you get into trouble, Cleo love, enjoy it. That's the best I can wish you.'

Suddenly she loved her sisters-in-law: us women against the male world. But she knew they were not women's libbers; and neither was she really. Men just goaded them into sounding that way.

Alexander, her elder brother, took her to the gate that led to Passport Control. 'Don't think too harshly of Dad for not being here to say goodbye.'

She looked at him in surprise. 'Of course I don't. He's been like this all our lives, hasn't he? We shouldn't have chosen a politician for a father.'

'No, this is different. He really wanted to be here. I talked to him last night – he called me. He didn't want you to think that he didn't care about you going away for so long. You're going away at the wrong time.'

'What do you mean?'

'He still thinks he has a chance of toppling Gough Whitlam as Leader. If he did, he'd be Prime Minister at the next election.'

Then I'm going away at absolutely the right time.

'He's got to be there in Canberra every minute, just in case Whitlam slips up.'

'Do you think he has a chance?'

34

Alex, vague and soft, more like his mother than his father, shrugged. 'I hope so, for his sake. When you have as much ambition as he has . . .'

'I'm ambitious, too, Alex.'

'Then I hope you're never disappointed.' Then he smiled and kissed her on the cheek. 'The best of Aussie luck, Sis.'

She went through into Passport Control. She showed her passport, then took her first step into the future. There was no turning back now, she had stepped off a cliff. It was a lovely feeling – almost, she guessed, like sky-diving. Her parachute, she hoped, would be her talent.

TWO

1

November is not a good month in which to land in London. No sensible invaders, Celts, Romans, Anglo-Saxons, Danes, Normans, or American tourists ever chose any time but summer to start their conquest of Britain; some summers, of course, *seemed* like November, but at least the invaders had chosen the proper time of the year. Cleo chose the worst of all possible times.

Snow covered the whole of eastern and northern Britain; London looked as if it had been dressed for a Dickens Christmas. A razor-sharp wind blew in from the Russian iceworks; ducks waltzed drunkenly on frozen ponds; mini-skirts and hot pants suddenly were, if not out of fashion, out of sight under long heavy coats. Noses were red and fingertips blue and permissive love, a recently-revived English custom, suffered a sharp set-back: it is difficult to be uninhibitedly orgiastic in front of a one-bar radiator.

In the United States Richard Nixon had been elected President and in England Enid Blyton had died; black crêpe was hung in Democratic wardrooms and in Kensington nurseries. The year was ending on the same gloomy note that had pervaded all the preceding months. In years to come people then in their youth would look back on that decade as the Swinging Sixties, forgetting the black periods. That year Martin Luther King and Robert Kennedy had been assassinated, American youth was protesting about being drafted for a war it didn't believe in, the Russians had invaded Czechoslovakia, an earthquake had killed 12,000 non-

36

swingers in Iran. Cleo wondered why she had left the sunny bliss of ignorance that was the Australian climate. True, there had been anti-war demonstrations back home, but most of the population put on their sun-glasses, put their transistors to their ears, sank their lips into beer-foam, saw no evil, heard no evil, spoke no evil.

She found a bed-sitting-room in a street off the Gloucester Road and for the first time in her life felt lonely. All at once she missed her mother. Brigid Spearfield had died in Cleo's last year at the Brigidine Convent, where the nuns had thought how lucky Cleo was to have a mother named after their patron saint and how discouraging it was for them to have such a female devil as a pupil. Cleo had cried for two days after her mother's death; then she had put her grief away inside her with her memories of her mother and got on with living. Now, in the dark, depressing flat she put the photo of Brigid on the chipped mantelpiece and wished that the serenely cheerful face could speak to her. She wanted someone to tell her she had done the right thing. There was no guarantee that Brigid, the least adventurous of women, would have told her that, but at least she would have offered her comfort. Brigid had always been very good at that. It only struck Cleo now, after she had got over the self-pity that had engulfed her, that there might have been times when Brigid herself would have welcomed some comfort, someone to tell her that she had done the right thing in always making herself subservient to Sylvester's ambitions.

Cleo went looking for work in Fleet Street. She was a little disappointed in the Street itself; somehow she had expected it to be wider, an avenue suggesting the power and influence it exerted. The buildings were unprepossessing but for the Law Courts at the western end; she hated the *Daily Express*'s art deco home and the Greek-Egyptian (as if the architect had been looking both ways at once) *Daily Telegraph* building. The worst of all was the *Daily Examiner*'s which looked as if it had started out to be a cathedral, decided to be a bank and finished up a barracks. She was only saved from total disillusionment with the Street when she went into the tiny courts hidden like cubby-holes for the affronted aesthetes off the main thoroughfare. She felt herself brushed by the ghosts of Johnson, Boswell and Dickens and decided to give Fleet Street another chance.

She knew a few Australian journalists working in London, but she did not go to them for advice or contacts. She was determined to make it on her own; if she was going to be independent, the flag had to be planted right at the start. The Fleet Street editors were unimpressed by this, though.

'There are too many Aussies working in the Street already. You're a bloody Mafia.'

'What makes you think you should start at the top? Try one of the provincial papers, start there like most of us did.'

'My dear girl, this is *The Times*. We haven't had a colonies correspondent since the turn of the century.'

'I don't want to be a bloody colonies correspondent! I want to write about *here* – Britain!'

The Times man had smiled, showed his Oxbridge politeness. 'I was pulling your very attractive leg, Miss Spearfield. Why don't you try the *Telegraph*? They could do with a little Antipodean iconoclasm.'

She did not want to work for a newspaper that needed Antipodean iconoclasm. She got a job as a temporary secretary, but proved more temporary than her employer or she had anticipated. She left after one day when the employer, fired by her bosom and an electric radiator too close to his crotch, made a proposition to her that had nothing to do with the business of Thrackle and Gump, customs agents.

She had saved very little money in Sydney. After her mother had died, she had had the house almost to herself, since her father spent most of his time travelling or in Canberra. There had been no need to think of the rent or the gas and electricity bills or of putting something by for a rainy day. She had arrived in London with only a little over five hundred pounds. One hundred of which had gone in a bond on the flat. She began to wonder what the newspapers back home would say when it was learned that Sylvester Spearfield's daughter had joined the dole queue in Britain.

38

The girl in the next-door flat was an actress who, as she said, divided her time between being on the boards and being on her knees.

'When I'm not in a play or doing a bit on telly, I clean house for what I like to think is a select clientele. People in Mayfair. The only thing select about some of them is their address, but I can charge them a bit more than the usual.'

Her name was Pat Hamer, she came from Leeds and the Yorkshire accent came and went like a faint echo on a moorland wind. She was dark and pretty and had iron in her; she would never allow herself to be melted down for soap operas; she would play Lady Macbeth some day. In the meantime she played one-line parts as a maid in farces at the Whitehall Theatre. She and Cleo shared baked beans on toast in each other's rooms and each, secretly, wondered at the gutsy ambition of the other.

'Bluddy hell,' Pat said one day, 'I missed out on a fantastic part today, right up my street. A prostitute from Leeds with a heart of solid brass. But the director had seen me in that bluddy thing at the Whitehall. All he could see me as was a maid in a short skirt with me boom showing.' When she was angry or disappointed, Leeds came to London. 'So it's back to bluddy house-cleaning again. How's it going with you, luv?'

'Bluddy awful,' said Cleo, making a passable imitation of the accent. 'If only I could latch on to a story that everyone else has missed ... I'm thinking of going out and inventing one. How'd you like to be The Secret Mistress of a Royal Duke Who Tells All?'

'Nobody back home would believe it. My dad's a Communist shop steward.'

Christmas came and went, the gloom only relieved by a phone call from her father. 'How are you, sweetheart? We're all missing you back here. We had Christmas dinner at Alex and Madge's, all of us, Perry and Cheryl and the kids. We had it beside the pool. It's been a marvellous day, a bit hot, but I suppose you wouldn't mind some of that now, eh?'

Why did he have to be so bloody hearty and cheerful? Did he think she was one of his voters? She looked out of her grimy window at a grim, grimy day; London was wrapped in dark clouds, snow and ice lay under a tree in the garden opposite like a mockery of fallen summer blossom. Her small radiator glowed in the gloomy room, looking no warmer than a neon sign on an Arctic highway.

'Has Fleet Street opened its arms to you yet?'

'Not yet, Dad.' It was better to be honest; he would guess the truth from her voice anyway. She was cold and lonely and miserable and she could not disguise the fact, even at 12,000 miles. She hated all those bastards beside their pools back in Sydney and she hoped every one of them would develop incurable sun cancers. 'But the stars chart in the *Daily Mirror* says things will be better for Scorpios in 1969.'

'Stars charts are like political opinion polls, always just wide of the mark. But hang in there – isn't that the expression they use these days? If I can help at all ... Harold Wilson? Or maybe Rupert Murdoch?'

'No, Dad. When I really need help, I'll cable you for the money to come home.'

'That's my girl. Keep trying, sweetheart.' But somewhere between Sydney and London his voice seemed to break. 'Merry Christmas and a Happy New Year.'

She cried her eyes out, wiped them, put on some make-up and went out to a pub. From there she almost went home with a sentimental doctor from Adelaide who was doing a post-graduate course at Bart's. But he, too, lived in a bed-sit and abruptly she did not want to be made love to in a lumpy single bed in a chill room with stained wallpaper and the smell of last night's warmed-up TV dinner hanging in the air. If she was going to let herself be seduced as a comfort, she should at least ask for a double room at the Savoy or Claridges. She thanked the doctor for his invitation and went home to the Gloucester Road.

She said prayers that night, the first for a long time, and wished she had gone to Midnight Mass last night. It would have pleased her mother, if Brigid was in a place to know of

40

such things. Still, she went to bed feeling virtuous, even if it was only the cold that had kept her pants on.

2

Pat Hamer had gone back to Leeds for Christmas. She returned the day after New Year's Day, went back to her house-cleaning chores and a week later knocked on Cleo's door.

'Cleo, I think I've heard a story that might interest you. You know you're always hearing about the poor being evicted? Do you think there'd be a story about the rich being kicked out of their home? My Red dad would say serves them bluddy well right, but you may think different.'

Cleo wasn't immediately excited by the prospects of the story. 'What's it all about?'

'I didn't get all of it. I was out in the hall dusting when I heard Mrs Dysen, that's the woman I work for Tuesdays, talking about it on the phone. She lives in Curzon Street and it seems that just down the street from her there are two old ladies who have lived in this house all their lives, born and bred there in fact. Now they're to be kicked out because Bolingbroke's, the gambling club next door to them, wants the house.'

Cleo did not want to look ungrateful, but she had to act very hard to look enthusiastic. Pat, the actress, was taken in by it. 'It sounds a marvellous idea! What's the address? I'll get around there right away!'

But first she phoned the features editor of the *Daily Examiner*. 'Mr Brearly, the *Examiner* always likes stories about how the other half, the richer half, lives. Would you be interested in how the rich react to eviction?'

'Are they titled rich?' The *Examiner*, owned as it was by a lord, loved titles in its columns. The peerage and appendages who could not make *The Times* or the *Daily Telegraph* could always rely on a line or two in the *Examiner*. 'We could take a para. for Gideon's Diary.'

41

'Not the Diary, Mr Brearly.' Gideon's Diary was a social gossip column, a waste basket of trivia. This story might turn out to be no more than trivial, but she did not want it reduced to a short paragraph before she had written it. 'I'll do it as a feature or nothing.'

'You have cheek, Miss Spearfield. Okay, go ahead, but I promise you nothing. If it's any good, it'll need pictures.'

'If it's any good, you'll be rushing round there to take pictures.'

'Where?'

'Ah, that would be telling, Mr Brearly.'

He chuckled. 'You Aussies never trust us Poms, do you? When can I have it?'

She rugged herself up against the January cold. She wore her fake fur coat and her fake fur hat, all that she could afford, but she had enough style to make fake look like an endangered species. She did her best to look elegant; or at least not too unrefined to be knocking on the door of the rich, albeit about-to-be-evicted rich. The house in Curzon Street was itself elegant, a town house built in the days of gracious living and leisurely pursuits when society was not divided into halves, the rich and the poor, but into two per cent and *them*. The two per cent had lived hereabouts, standing on their doorsteps and turning west to breathe the then country air of Hyde Park, turning east to get a nose-wrinkling sniff of *them*. Cleo was surprised to find that the small brass knocker on the front door was shaped like a woman's breast. She put that down to the whim of some eighteenth-century blade who had, at least, had the taste not to ornament his door with a pair of knockers.

A maid opened the door and Cleo told her she was from the *Daily Examiner*. 'I should like to see Miss St Martin – either of them.'

'Miss St Martin, both of them, never have visitors without an appointment.' She shut the door in Cleo's face.

Cleo stood there unperturbed. She had had doors shut in her face before; if journalists were not so nimble, they would be recognizable by their broken noses. Then, as she went down the few ice-covered steps to the frozen pavement, a taxi drew up at the kerb. An elderly woman in a mink coat and hat got out and immediately skidded across the pavement towards Cleo, who stepped out and threw her arms round her. Both of them thumped up against the iron railings that stopped people, on days like this, from plunging headlong into the basement area. They stood there in their furs, clutching each other like a couple of lesbian bears. Then Cleo burst out laughing.

'We must look a great pair. Just as well we didn't finish up on our bottoms.'

The old lady straightened her hat, which had fallen down over one eye, and clung gingerly to the railings. 'Thank you, my dear. I wonder if you would give this money to the driver, please? I dare not trust myself on that ice again.'

Cleo paid the taxi driver, who had remained in his seat watching the performance: he was one of *them*. Then she went back and helped the elderly woman up the steps to the front door. 'Would you be Miss St Martin? I'd like to talk to you, if you could spare me a few minutes. I'm Cleo Spearfield, from the *Daily Examiner*.'

Miss St Martin suddenly lost her warm smile, as if the ice had run up her thin legs and frozen any hospitality she might have been about to offer. 'I'm grateful to you for saving me from a nasty fall, Miss Spearfield. But I never talk to newspaper people.'

'Miss St Martin, I understand you're about to lose the lease on this house, where you've lived all your life. I think that's scandalous and so does my editor.' She was becoming proprietary towards the *Examiner*; there was no one in sight to deny her. 'Perhaps we could help you in your fight against your landlord's callousness.'

Something like a gleam of humour suddenly appeared in Miss St Martin's eye. She put her key in the door, opened it and stepped into the hallway. She stood there for a moment with her back to Cleo, then looked over her shoulder, her hat slipping forward over one eye again. 'Why not? Your employer, Lord Cruze, used to be a - a friend of ours. Come in, my dear. We'll have tea.'

Cleo stepped into luxurious elegance such as she had not expected. She had read that the English upper classes now lived in rather shabby refinement, as if tatty surroundings were now the proper mark of good breeding. There was nothing tatty about the St Martin household. While Miss St Martin slipped off her boots and put on some shoes from the closet, Cleo looked about her. The hall was hung with ornately framed mirrors, the walls papered with green silk. A wide doorway, its folding doors swept back, led into a double drawing-room where the walls were papered with yellow silk. Regency-striped, green and yellow silk drapes hung at the windows; all the chairs and couches were covered in silk. Highly polished antique tables were placed strategically about the room and in one corner stood a grand piano. There were more mirrors, all ornately framed, on the walls; but only a single painting, that of a voluptuous nude lying on what looked to be a replica of one of the room's couches. As she sat down Cleo looked back through the doorway and saw that another wide doorway opened into a similar room on the other side of the hall. It was a moment before she realized that the Misses St Martin must live in *two* houses. It was not going to be easy to write so sympathetically about two rich old ladies being thrown out of two houses.

'I am Dorothy St Martin,' said that lady. 'Take off your coat, my dear. My, you do have a fine figure. And you're only a reporter?'

'On newspapers you don't get promoted on your figure,' said Cleo. 'Well, perhaps you do, but I've never tried it that way.'

Miss St Martin rang for the maid, ordered tea, then arranged herself on a chair. 'Now what can we do for you? Or what can you do for us?'

'Well –' Cleo looked around her. 'Do you also own the house next door?'

'Through there? Oh yes. But not the one on this side – that belongs to Bolingbroke's. My sister and I bought that one there right after the war. *Our* war,' she said, and Cleo marked the sign of the times: the generations now had their own wars. 'World War One. Or rather our dear father bought it for us. But we are to lose that, too. The lease on it runs out at the same time as the lease on this one.'

'There are just you and your sister? It's a lot of accommodation for just the two of you.' She looked around again, at the tables and the grand piano. 'Do you run some sort of club? A bridge club or a musical society?'

'Good heavens, no. This is a bordello,' said Miss St Martin and smiled towards the doorway. 'This is my sister Miss Rose.'

Cleo thought for a moment that she had double vision. The Misses St Martin were identical twins, even to the way they dressed: cream blouses buttoned to the throat, cashmere cardigans, severely cut skirts, sensible shoes, a single strand of pearls. Cleo tried not to stare as she was introduced to Miss Rose, and then sat back on her chair. She remembered what she had just heard.

'A bordello? A brothel?'

'We never use that word, Miss Spearfield.' Miss Rose's voice was identical to that of her sister, soft and cultured. 'We like to think that the difference between a bordello such as ours and a brothel is the difference between the Rolls-Royce showrooms in Berkeley Square and the second-hand car showrooms on the Euston Road.'

Cleo had had no experience of London car showrooms; nor, for that matter, of bordellos or brothels. 'I had no idea –'

'Are you sure you are from the *Daily Examiner?*' said Miss Dorothy; then explained to her sister: 'She works for John Cruze.'

'We never see him nowadays.'

Cleo didn't know Lord Cruze and wasn't to be sidetracked by talk of him. 'I'm new to London –'

'I thought I recognized the accent,' said Miss Rose. 'One hears it on television when tennis players and cricketers are interviewed.'

'You've never had any Australian – clients here?'

'Not clients, my dear. Guests. Tea? Milk and sugar?' said Miss Dorothy as the maid wheeled in a small serving-cart. 'No, we have never had any Australians. We are very selective.'

'Perhaps you should apologize for that, Dorothy. Miss Spearfield looks offended.'

Cleo took her cup and saucer and chose a French pastry from the silver tray. 'No, I always defend women's right to be selective.'

'Are you in favour of women's liberation?' said Miss Dorothy. 'We're not. Two of our girls specialize in bondage.'

Cleo felt giddy; the cup rattled in its saucer. Pat Hamer must have set her up for this; it was some great practical joke. The Misses St Martin were probably some retired music hall act and had sneaked into this great house to perpetrate the deception. But then commonsense returned: it was all too elaborate to be a joke played on an out-of-work journalist. Cleo tried hard to retain her commonsense, but it was like trying to keep one's foothold on a tightrope.

'Why don't you allow Australians in?'

'Oh, it's not just Australians. This is an *English* establishment and we keep it exclusively English. We did have a Scottish duke once and we have had a French ambassador – a little *entente cordiale* –'

'There was also that gentleman from Boston,' said Miss Rose. 'He came from one of the best families. We understand his forbears had fought on *our* side in the American Revolution.'

Cleo put down her cup and saucer, planted her feet firmly on the thick carpet and tried to sound patient and rational. 'Miss St Martin, both of you, how can you expect me to write a story about such an establishment and get public sympathy on your side so that you won't be evicted?'

'Miss Spearfield –' Miss Dorothy wiped her lips delicately with a lace napkin, 'we don't expect anything. We didn't invite you here.'

Cleo saw her mistake. 'I'm sorry. But – well, to tell you the truth, I didn't expect anything like this.'

46

'Your editor would have known about us. All the news-papers do. But they never mention us because they know our guests are foundation members of what I believe is now called The Establishment. Not all of them were that, I suppose – your employer, for instance. Are you sure you are from the *Daily Examiner*? I hope you haven't lied to us, Miss Spearfield. My sister and I are great respecters of the truth.'

Cleo was waiting to be shown the door; but the Misses St Martin continued to sip their tea and nibble at the French pastries. They were giving her another chance. So she told the truth. 'If I can write a good story on you, a sympathetic one, the *Examiner* will run it. And, I hope, they may offer me a job. I need one.'

'We could offer you a position,' said Miss Rose, running what Cleo now recognized as an expert eye over her. 'But we are intending to retire.'

'You're going to sell the – the bordello? Is that why you want the lease renewed?'

'Not at all. Our family has lived in this house, *this* one, for one hundred and ninety-eight years. We have had two ninety nine-year leases on it. We are now seventy years old – though we'd rather you didn't mention our age – and we should like to die in the house, as our parents and their parents and *their* parents did. We should then like to bequeath the house to a nephew, so that the St Martin line may continue in it. The estate that owns the freehold knows what sort of place we have been running – indeed, some of the scions of the family that own the estate have been our guests. But now they want to evict us and sell the new lease to that gambling club next door. The new lease will be considerably more expensive than the old one, but we can afford it. We feel it is nothing but rank discrimination. They are objecting – after all these years, mind you – that we may continue to run our bordello. We have no such intention, but what if we did? What is the difference between catering for a gentleman's physical needs and his gambling needs? Moreover, from what we have observed, not all the clients of Bolingbroke's are gentle-men.'

47

Cleo suddenly saw her angle; but would the *Examiner* buy it? It was a tabloid and it ran pictures of bosomy, scantily-clad girls, but it was not the *News of the World*, it did not run stories on brothel-keepers. Or even on bordello ladies.

'How did you get into this – do you mind if I call it a business? – in the first place?'

'We started during the war, the last war – *your* war –'

'Not mine. Mine was, *is*, the Vietnam war.'

Miss Dorothy shook her head at the continuity of war. 'Well, we started when we learned that some of our gentle-men friends, senior officers, were finding it difficult to meet the proper feminine company. All the girls, even those from good families, were chasing the Americans. So we did some recruiting –' she smiled at her choice of words '– and we found some very attractive young ladies who were willing to work for us. There were occasions when, if a buzz-bomb had dropped on our two houses, it would have eliminated half the brass of the British army.' The sisters smiled at each other, mirror images of genteel glee. 'If the Germans had only known where to aim!'

'But how did you know – well, how did you know what to provide?'

'We had been to Paris in the 1920s,' said Miss Rose. 'We sneaked away from our parents, we were rather naughty as young girls, and persuaded a French gentleman we knew to take us to one of the Paris bordellos. We never forgot what we saw.'

Miss Dorothy fanned herself with the lace napkin at the memory. 'We used that establishment as our model, but we tried to make ours more tasteful.'

'More English?' said Cleo.

'Exactly,' said Miss Rose. 'Nothing as obvious as red plush. The French do tend to overdo things when it comes to sex.'

'Please, Rose,' said Miss Dorothy, as if her sister had used a dirty word.

Cleo burst out laughing, and the sisters joined in. They could laugh at their gentility; it was part of their act, part of

48

what they sold to English gentlemen who had physical needs. Cleo asked for more tea, began to take notes.

An hour later she left the Misses St Martin. 'That was the nicest time I've had since I landed in London.'

'You must come and have tea with us again,' said Miss Rose. 'We'd invite you to supper, but you have such a fine figure, some of our guests might mistake you for one of our girls.'

'If the *Examiner* doesn't buy my story, I may be back.'

'I was joking, my dear. We are closing our establishment at the end of the month. After that we shall devote ourselves to our church work.'

I'm having my leg pulled this time. 'Church work?'

'Oh yes. We go to Mass every Sunday down at Farm Street. The Jesuit fathers look on us as their most devout sinners. They'll be delighted when we give up sin.'

3

'It's marvellous,' said the *Examiner*'s features editor. 'But Felicity Kidson, our women's editor, wants to run it on her page. She'll give you a whole page with pictures. She's just discovered women's rights, God help us.'

'I'd like it run it as is, Mr Brearly,' said Cleo. 'I don't want the mickey taken out of those two nice old ladies.'

'That's the point - Felicity will run it exactly as you've written it.' He was a tiny man with a mop of grey hair who seemed to live in a continual miasma of cigarette smoke. He would like to have visited the Misses St Martin's bordello, but Cleo's story had already told him he would not qualify as a guest. 'I don't think our readers will give your nice old ladies as much sympathy as you seem to think. Let's face it, they're snobs. But the Mayfair Estates people won't like it, not since they've known about the brothel –'

'Bordello.'

'Okay, bordello. I didn't know there was a difference. Since they've known all about the bordello and done nothing about it.'

'I'll play down the snob angle and play up the bit about only English clients. It probably won't help the *Examiner's* Scottish edition, but you Poms will love it.'

'Now you're taking the mickey out of us.'

Which was exactly what Felicity Kidson said when Cleo went in to meet her. 'But I don't mind that at all, darling. I think we English like having the mickey taken out of us, so long as it's not vicious. It proves we have a sense of humour about ourselves. Would you like a job with me?'

'I was hoping you'd say that. Yes, I'd like very much to work for the *Examiner*.'

She had not wanted to work on the women's page, but it would be a start. It hurt her to think that she was having to start all over again, but this was England and England had always made foreigners start at the bottom. Except, of course, its imported kings.

'I have only one rule,' said Felicity. 'I am the boss lady and don't ever forget it.' She smiled, not taking the sting out of the remark, just polishing it. 'I know all about you ambitious Aussies.'

'I'm surprised you're offering me the job.'

'I like to live dangerously.' She flicked a gentle finger at the single red rose in the glass on her desk. 'Good luck, darling.'

4

That evening Cleo took Pat Hamer to dinner. 'Dress up, Pat. We'll go to the Mirabelle.'

'Luv, that costs the earth! Please don't go off your head. Let's go to a steak house.'

'I owe you the best, Patricia. When you get your star part with the Old Vic, you can take me out for a champagne dinner.'

'Are we going to have champagne, too? Wait till I write and tell my dad about it. He'll die of shame.'

They went to the Mirabelle, two good-looking girls who got admiring glances from the stout, balding businessmen who stole surreptitious looks at them while their bouffant-haired wives weren't attending.

'They think we're a couple of tarts,' said Pat. Then, 'Oh migord! There's Mrs Dysen, one of the ladies I clean for!'

Mrs Dysen, a formidable woman under her blonde helmet of hair, saw Pat and reared back as if she had just been pierced in a joust. Her face cracked in a mix of grimace and smile, then she turned her head away and took a sip of water, as if recovering from an unexpected assault.

'There goes *that* job,' said Pat.

But it did not matter. A week later she got a job with a company going on tour before coming into the West End. She gave up her bed-sit and said goodbye to Cleo and the two of them wished each other all the luck in the world. Cleo gave up her own bed-sit, went looking for something better and found it in South Kensington. Recklessly she took a year's lease on it with an option for a further year, leaving herself with exactly nine pounds to get her through to her first *Examiner* pay day. But she knew, as only the truly ambitious can tell themselves, that from now on she was safe from the dole queue. Though it was only the beginning of February even the sun broke through. True, it did only shine for an hour, as if it had come by to see if Britain was still there, but it was an omen.

Then a small package was delivered from Cartier in Bond Street. In it was a gold pen and a note written in a copperplate hand: 'A small thanks for your splendid story. Our lease has been renewed for another 99 years. Do come and have tea with us again.'

The year looked as if it was going to be a good one. She rang home and told her father so. 'I'm on my way, Dad.'

'Good for you, sweetheart.' But he sounded disappointed, as if he had lost something or someone.

51

THREE

John Cruze, Lord Cruze of Chalfont St Aidan, was tired of
the Swinging Sixties. He wondered why he had bothered to
go to tonight's party at the country house of Saul Petty; it
had made him feel *old*, a state of mind that he tried to avoid
as much as he did the thought of cancer. Everyone at the
party, with the exception of himself and the host, had either
been under twenty-five, or if they weren't, had tried to *look*
under twenty-five. He thought there was nothing more pathetic than middle-aged swingers: they might try to put the
clock back but their faces showed the true time. Tonight
there had been men of his own age, fifty, pillars of the City
looking decidedly shaky on their Twisting legs, the creaking
of their bones competing with the clanging of the gold chains
and medallions round their necks; there had been so many
gold medals, he had felt he was at some geriatrics' Olympiad.
There had also been their wives and mistresses, dressed in
Chelsea boutique clothes that made them look as if they had
looted their daughters' wardrobes. The girls under twenty-
five, in hot pants and mini-skirts, had worn make-up that
wouldn't have looked odd on a tribe of New Guinea hillmen;
he reckoned there must have been enough mascara on display
that night to have painted the hull of the *QE2*. Their escorts,
hipless, chestless, shoulderless, the new fashion, looked as if
they had been dressed by Cecil Beaton for the girls' parts in
a revival of the Gaiety Girls; he had never seen so many
ruffles. The band, six hipless, chestless, shoulderless hairy
wrecks, all wearing dark glasses against the glare of the

Chinese lanterns strung around the terrace of the house, were playing so loudly, it sounded as if they were also playing for a party in Brighton, some fifty miles away.

'You were bloody sour this evening,' said Felicity Kidson. 'You didn't move out of your chair, just sat there like the bloody Archbishop of Canterbury all night.'

'I'm bloody sour now. I thought that was the Archbishop of Canterbury you were dancing with, till I saw it was Saul. What's he doing, getting dressed up like that at his age?'

The glass partition of the Rolls-Royce Phantom was up and Sid Cromwell, the chauffeur, could not hear their conversation. Lord Cruze never worried what his servants thought about his actions, that would have put too much of a curb on his sex life; but he had never learned to ignore them when he conversed in front of them. Which was another reminder that he was not a true aristocrat, just another life peer.

'I don't know how Saul – he's what? Seventy-seven? – gets a kick out of something like tonight's bedlam. I noticed he wasn't wearing his hearing-aid.'

Felicity sighed and sank back into her long bright-red feather boa. She was wearing white satin jodhpurs, white boots and a sequined blue silk shirt open to the bottom button; with her bright red boa, he privately thought she looked like a French hairdresser on his way to an international rugby match; but he had given up making any comment on the way she dressed these days. Beside her, in his black tie and dinner jacket, he sometimes felt like an undertaker on night duty. He knew he was narrow-minded about trendiness, homosexuality, unisexuality, women's liberation and all the other aberrations that had broken out during that decade, but he could not help it. Like so many men who had started out as crooks, he had a narrow moral outlook in many ways.

He glanced sideways at her, still sour, and wondered what she would say in the morning when she got the farewell bunch of white roses. He always said farewell to his mistresses, whether of short or long standing, with white roses; they got red ones right up to the final bunch. He knew that his method of ending an affair was no secret, but he liked it that way: it meant that he did not have to write any farewell notes. He never put anything on paper to a woman.

'You're getting old and crotchety, Jack. That was an absolutely *fantastic* party tonight.' She was thirty-eight back-pedalling to eighteen. Unlike the other editors on his newspapers, she featured as much copy about herself as she did about other people. She had become a celebrity (a word he hated: he had written a memo to all his editors that it was never to be used in any of the Cruze Organization's chain of papers), the trendiest of the trendies. She had been his mistress for three years, but the affair had started before she had begun wearing mini-skirts and putting more mascara on her face than Theda Bara.

'You look like Theda Bara.'

'Who's she, for Christ's sake?' She hadn't started swearing till she was thirty-seven; had had a modest tongue to match the cashmere cardigan and small diamond pin she had worn in those days. Now she came to the office wearing kaftans and yards of beads, looking as if she was the editor of *Harper's Souk*. 'Oh, *her*. You and your old film stars. Personally, I thought I looked more like Joan Crawford in *Our Dancing Daughters*. That was the effect I was after.'

'You missed by a mile.'

He owned one of the best private collections of silent films in the country. Other rich men collected paintings or porcelain or antique furniture, learned about Correggio or *pâte tendre*, Sèvres or Riesener; he was an authority on Griffith and Ince, Milton Sills and Vilma Banky. He had gone to see his first film when he was five years old, a Jack Hoxie Western, a print of which he now owned; ever since then films had been his escape from his preoccupation with money and power. He had never looked on sex as an escape: it was only another way of showing his power over women. He seduced his women with his money and power, which was a quicker method than that of lesser, poorer men. Once upon a time he had invested in charm, having no money or power, but the girls of those days had not been impressed and decided he was no Ronald Colman or William Powell. In any event, girls in that year were looking for Clark Gables, a type in short supply in the villages of Buckinghamshire.

The car drew up outside Felicity's block of flats in Chelsea; she had moved here last year from Hampstead. 'I want to be right in the middle of the action,' she had said and waltzed up and down the King's Road tearing off her cardigan and brassière. Or so he had imagined: he came here only on rare occasions and never before midnight.

'Coming up, darling? I'm still high.'

He waited for her to lasso him with the red feather boa: she was so damned gay, a debutante on the verge of the menopause. 'Goodnight. Don't trip over your boa.'

He didn't look back as the car drove away, but he knew she would be standing on the kerb staring after him, getting the message. But she was as tough as he was; she would go up to her flat and empty a vase and wait for the arrival of the white roses. He felt no regret or guilt, he had never told her he loved her or promised her anything. It had been the same with her as it had been with all the others since Emma had left him twenty years ago.

He pressed a button and the glass between him and Sid Cromwell slid down. 'Sid, see about some roses for Miss Kidson first thing in the morning. White ones.'

'Big or little bunch, m'Lord?'

'Big.' After all she had lasted three years, even if there had been others at the same time.

Up front Sid Cromwell smiled to himself, made no comment. He had worked for Lord Cruze for fifteen years, from the very day the Boss had bought the *Examiner*, and since then he had sent enough bloody roses, red and white, to stock the Chelsea Flower Show. He saw himself as the Boss's executioner, but at a safe distance: he was never close enough, when the women's heads were chopped off, to see their tears or whatever it was women did when they got the shove. He had felt sorry for some of them, especially the young ones; but he was not sorry to see Miss Kidson go. She had begun to make the Boss look ridiculous and Sid Cromwell, a working man with a proper sense of class, did not like to see lords lose their dignity.

He'd go to the florist first thing in the morning and order a small bunch of white roses, maybe just half a dozen. The Boss wouldn't know and Sid Cromwell felt he was entitled to make his own comment. Old-fashioned enough to believe in the dignity of lords, he also did not believe in career women.

2

'Who are you?' said Lord Cruze.

'I'm Cleo Spearfield. I work on the *Examiner*, my Lord.'

He eyed her from under a hairy brow. She had not said *m'Lord*, making it sound like one word as it should be sounded: she had said *my Lord*, stretching the two words into what sounded suspiciously like a send-up of him. He recognized the accent, remembered her by-line: another Australian come to Britain to take the mickey out of the Poms. He knew the name of every by-lined journalist on his papers, but he never went near the offices, neither to Fleet Street nor to the offices of the provincial papers; people might work for him for five, ten years, maybe more, and never be anything but faceless names to him. But he read every word they wrote and it did not take him long to size up their talent, their attitude and their prejudices. This one was an iconoclast, a word that never appeared in the plain-English pages of a tabloid like the *Examiner*.

'Who sent you?'

'Miss Kidson.'

The bitch. She had sent the Hatchet Lady to do a job on him. He knew the reputation and nickname that Miss Spearfield had earned for herself in Fleet Street over the past six months. Felicity had probably already resigned, was already talking to the *Mirror* or the *Express*; but before she relinquished control of her women's page, relying on his boast that he never killed a story that his editors wanted to run, she

56

would feature Miss Spearfield's demolition of him. It would create a one-day sensation in Fleet Street, the home of sensation, and it would do him no real harm. But it would satisfy Felicity's urge for revenge. He smiled, perversely pleased that Felicity felt *something*.

'Have you come to write something on me?'

'Just the Horse Show in general, my Lord.'

'No photos of me, you understand.'

It was an iron rule that no pictures of him ever appeared in his newspapers. He had his vanities, but seeing his picture spread across his own papers was not one of them. Besides, he knew he didn't photograph well. He always looked shorter than he actually was, which was five feet seven; and his square face seemed to broaden in a camera's lens, so that he looked as if he had a flat-topped head. His brows, heavy enough as they were, thickened into hairy awnings that left his eyes in shadow. Photographs made him look evil, and he wasn't that at all, though not everyone took him at his word.

'You look very smart, my Lord.' Her face was very straight.

Her face was also damned attractive, he thought, taking another look at her. Not beautiful; but some of the most beautiful women he had known had been the dullest company and the worst lovers. Those eyes, those cheekbones, that almost-black hair cut in a bob with thick bangs: he always thought of it as the French look, because French apache dancers in his silent films always looked like that. But he doubted that this one would allow herself to be tossed about the floor as the women had been in the apache dances. She had a magnificent figure and she wasn't dressed like a rebel teenager. Her legs were excellent, though she wasn't advertising them; her skirt came down to her knees, leaving you hoping she might lift it to show you more. Under his driving-apron things began to stir, an old stallion sighting another filly.

'You look very smart, too.'

'I always dress for the occasion, my Lord.' She glanced around at the crowd at this horse and carriage show. 'I've got the right legs for mini-skirts, but I don't think the Queen would like them. Mini-skirts, I mean, not my legs. The Duke might, but not the Queen.'

He wished she would not keep calling him *my Lord*. 'Besides good legs, you also have a good opinion of yourself.'

'It's the old Australian inferiority complex, my Lord. We always tend to over-compensate.'

She looked the last person in the world to have an inferiority complex, Australian or not. But then his two grooms appeared and told him his number was about to be called. He got up on to the front seat of the four-wheeled carriage and was handed the reins of the four-horse team. Then the two grooms clambered up into the rear seat, took their places and waited while he adjusted the reins in his left hand.

'Good luck, my Lord. This is the dressage, isn't it?' There was no sign of any tongue in her cheek, but he knew she was laughing at him.

'Yes.' Then he could have applied the long carriage-whip to himself when he heard himself say, 'It shows how much control I have over those who work for me.'

'The horses, you mean?'

'Of course.' Damn it, why was he letting her upset him so?

When he had got his peerage five years ago he had looked around for a recreation that would give him more respectability in the eyes of those who still thought he was a *nouveau riche* upstart, yet another of the postwar Goths who were trying to take over Britain. He had power, through his newspapers, and he was accepted by those who thought power had its own respectability: politicians, financiers, union officials and the bosses of the London gangs. But he had not been accepted by the real Establishment, the old money that had had its own power long before the press barons, Northcliffe, Rothermere and Beaverbrook, created their fiefdoms. So he had studied his own newspapers and magazines; amongst the latter, the social journals had pointed the way. Horses: at certain times of the year the real Establishment was surrounded by horses, up to their hocks in breeding and manure. He could not ride well enough to hunt or play polo; if he was going to get involved with horses, he had to find some way to avoid throwing his leg over them. He bought two carriages, a phaeton and a four-wheeled dog-cart, and had them sent to his country estate. He engaged a coachman to instruct him and had been pleased to find that he was a natural driver – 'One should drive a horse like one handles a woman, m'Lord. You have the right sort of hands for it.' Some of his women, he thought, would have been amused to hear that.

He had practised for a year, learning everything there was to know about driving show horses, and then had entered his first show. Typically, he had started at the top, at the Royal Windsor. Also typically, he had won, beating the Duke of Edinburgh into second place. He had not been invited to Windsor Castle or Buckingham Palace on the strength of the win, but one of the lesser dukes had patted his winning horses, then given Cruze an encouraging nod. 'Well done, old chap. Jolly good show.' It was almost as much a welcome as being admitted to the Order of the Garter.

He was accepted now. His horses were one of the three best teams in the country: *they* would have been invited to the Castle or the Palace if they could have been seated at table. In their stead, he had been invited and now he had no worries about his acceptance. Of course he was not and never would be a full member of the Establishment. He had enough horse-sense to realize that.

He settled his bowler firmly on his head, spread his driving-apron neatly about his legs and flexed his fingers inside the yellow gloves. He sat stiffly in his seat, the whip held at the proper angle in his right hand, all ready to go, Phaethon in a bowler hat. But he knew he was no Greek god and out of the corner of his eye he could see Miss Spearfield smiling at him, tongue well in cheek now.

When his number was called he started the horses off too fast. His left hand was all thumbs; the two lead horses and the two wheelers behind them felt in his hand as if they might gallop off in different directions. He got them under control while he stood at the Halt for inspection by the judges, but he knew he had already lost points. Then he started them off

59

on the Walk, but they could feel the tension in his hand; he lost more points on that section. Behind him he could feel the restlessness of his grooms, though he knew they would be sitting as stiffly formal as always. He put the horses into the Working Trot, still trying to take the tension out of his fingers. But the reins – near-lead over his left forefinger; off-lead between forefinger and middle finger; near-wheel between the same fingers and under the off-lead rein; off-wheel between middle and third fingers – felt as tangled and unresponsive as spaghetti. When he put the horses into the Collected Trot he knew at once that he had not got it right. They should have had their necks raised, should be taking shorter steps, but he could see that they all seemed to have their heads at different levels and he could feel the off-lead horse, with a longer stride, pulling slightly to one side. He finished the course doing the Extended Trot and the Rein Back, but he knew he had never driven so badly.

He had no control over the horses, but worse, he had lost control of himself.

3

Cleo's story appeared in the *Examiner* two days later, as if she had taken her time taking aim and getting her shots right. It was written tongue-in-cheek, a gentle horse-laugh at the horsey set. Cruze was mentioned only once, in the last line: 'Lord Cruze was amongst the also-rans.'

He rang Quentin Massey-Folkes, the *Examiner*'s editor. 'I want to see that Miss Spearfield. Tell her to come to lunch at the flat tomorrow, one o'clock sharp.'

Massey-Folkes had a name that should have had him working on *The Times* or the *Tatler*, but he was a tabloid man, happy with big headlines and near-nudes on Page Three. He had known Cruze when the latter had been no more than a knight and a new one at that; he had never called him Sir John and now he never called him *m'Lord*, except in front of underlings. 'Jack, you're not going to fire

60

her, are you? That's one of the best stories she's ever done. I've just offered her the job as women's editor. Felicity has resigned. But I suppose you know that?'

'I guessed she might,' he said cryptically; he knew his affairs were gossip fodder at the *Examiner*. 'Are you trying to turn the women's page into *Private Eye* or something? No wonder she's called the Hatchet Lady. I think the Duke will horse-whip me next time he sees me.'

'Jack, she's one of the best writers I've got. If I let her go, someone else will grab her – Rupert Murdoch would take her on like a shot. Better to have her on our side than agin us. Our readers can take her, Jack. They're not all Bible-bashing Empire Loyalists.'

'Keep going, I may put her in your job.' But he smiled to himself. Quentin was the only one he ever allowed to rib him and then only when they were alone. He had no close men friends and he needed someone to play court jester and devil's advocate. Quentin Massey-Folkes, cynical enough to be either or both, fitted the bill. 'No wonder Beaverbrook sacked you when you were on the *Express*. Send the girl over, Quent. What did Felicity say when she resigned?'

'Just that she'd had a better offer.'

'She would.' He descended to the level of the court jester: 'They all do.'

'How would I know, Jack? I've been married for twenty-two years. But I don't think we'll miss her.' Meaning both of them, the editor and the lover.

'No.'

He wondered, though. He had been troubled lately by empty hours, something he had not experienced since those weeks immediately after Emma had left him. He hung up the phone and looked across his bedroom into the mirror-wall. There sat his best company, on a replica of the bed that had provided so much company; but he had begun to wonder if it was enough, if himself and the bed were slowly emptying. Mirrors, too often, are empty of comfort.

At first glance Cleo was impressed by the flat. Then, as she continued to look around, she realized that this was an interior decorator's exercise, like the advertisements one saw in Harrods' ground floor display section; she would not have been surprised to find price labels still hanging on the chairs and couches. Lord Cruze had written a blank cheque and the interior decorator had given him a blank residence but not a home.

There were two levels to the flat, with a staircase curving down from the upper level into the huge drawing-room. The western wall of that room was all glass through which one could see Green Park like a mural. Slantwise across the park was Buckingham Palace, the Royal Standard fluttering in the breeze like regal washing: the Queen was at home.

'What are you thinking?'

'Does the Queen ever wave to anyone who lives on this side of the park?'

'Is that why you came to England, to poke fun at us?'

'No. I came here thinking I might climb to the top in Fleet Street. Be a sort of Rupert Murdoch in drag, if you like.' She sipped her sherry, smiling at her own naïveté. 'But there's never been a woman at the top in Fleet Street, has there? Certainly not on the *Examiner*. It's the journal for the male chauvinist.'

'Do you usually tell your bosses what you think of their papers?'

He led her into the dining-room. There was a long dining-table with twenty chairs (she did a quick count); they sat at one end and the empty chairs stretched away down the table like unwanted guests. A blunt-faced cheerful woman brought in helpings of potted shrimps, beamed at His Lordship, cast Cleo a critical glance, then disappeared back into the kitchen.

'I told my last one what I thought.' She smiled at the memory; the *Sydney Morning Post* had been another male chauvinist domain. 'After I'd resigned, of course.'

'Are you thinking of resigning from the *Examiner*?'

'Not immediately, my Lord.'

'You pronounce it m'Lord, all one word.'

'I know.' Then she smiled, a friendly smile that, against his will, brought an answering smile from himself. 'I'm sorry, Lord Cruze. I have been taking the mickey out of you. But that seemed the safest way of having to face you. I knew why Felicity Kidson sent me to do that story on the horse show. You're not half as forbidding as I'd been led to believe.'

'I can be when it's necessary. We'll have the main course now, Mrs Cromwell.' Cleo's potted shrimps were whipped away by Mrs Cromwell, who appeared to be both cook and maid. 'Mrs Cromwell doesn't like to be delayed in serving her main course.'

'His Lordship likes his liver and bacon just so,' Mrs Cromwell explained to Cleo. 'How do you like yours?'

'Just the bacon will do. I'm afraid I don't like liver.'

'It's better for you than bacon,' said Mrs Cromwell, who had no time for food-pickers and fancy diets, and marched back through the swing door to her kitchen.

'Well,' said Cleo, 'it seems I'm rubbing everyone up the wrong way today. My father always said I'd never succeed as a politician.'

'Is he in politics in Australia?'

It was like being asked if God was in Heaven. She felt light-headed at being released from her father's shadow. 'He's a Federal Senator.'

'Spearfield? Oh, *that* one. The one who wants to do away with the monarchy?'

'Only as far as Australia is concerned.'

'I don't take much interest in Australian politics.'

'Who does?'

That had been brought home to her in the nine months she had been in London. The British, convinced that all Australians were beer-swilling, loud-mouthed anarchists, evidently believed that the Antipodes took care of themselves without benefit of government or politicians. They had heard of Sir Robert Menzies, but only because he had come to England every year to have tea with the Queen and watch

63

the cricket. They looked upon him as *their* representative Down Under.

Mrs Cromwell brought in the main course, one bacon-and-liver with fried potatoes, one bacon-without-liver and a double helping of potatoes. *Haute cuisine* would never stick its Froggy nose into her kitchen. 'Just so's you won't go hungry, miss.'

She went out again and Cruze said, 'Mrs Cromwell and her husband, my chauffeur, come from my home village Chalfont St Aidan. That's in Bucks.'

'I know. I looked up your obit. It's already written, but I suppose you know that. They up-date it every six months.'

'I hope they don't let your poison pen up-date it next time.'

She smiled, feeling more at ease with him than she had expected. She knew his reputation, though that hadn't been in the obituary: how he could be as ruthless as he could be loyal to his staff. Men such as Quentin Massey-Folkes had worked for him for years; others had worked for him for weeks, even days. She knew, too, how ruthless he could be with his women, though she had heard nothing of his loyalty to them. She had been studying him carefully during their fencing, was a little surprised by her growing interest in him. He was interesting, of course, for what he was: one of the most powerful and influential newspaper barons in Britain, indeed in Europe. But her interest was more in him as a man: she wanted to peel away the public image and look at the Emperor without his clothes.

She was beginning to see what Felicity Kidson (and a score of other women, if the stories were true) had seen in him. Physically he had little to recommend him. He was short, looked as if he might be muscular, had greying curly hair and a face that only escaped homely anonymity because of the thick eyebrows and the military moustache. He appeared to do nothing to try to improve his appearance with tailoring; she would learn that he only dressed well when he was appearing in horse shows. Now he looked like the product of a London laundry catering to the transient tourist trade:

shirt ironed by a cold corrugated iron; suit pressed by hand but no iron; a tie so shiny it looked as if it had been polished rather than cleaned. But something (energy? power? She knew enough to know they were not the same thing) gleamed in him.

'Yes, I come from Bucks,' he said. 'The way the papers tell it, even my own, you'd think all the self-made men in this country came from the north country or are Jews from the Mile End Road. I'm a grammar school boy from the Home Counties. My father was a solicitor's clerk and my mother wanted to be a teacher. I got my ambition from her. She had a crippled leg, infantile paralysis as they called it in her day, but she never let it handicap her. She was handicapped enough being a woman. That's why I always see that women are given an opportunity on my papers.'

'That's not quite true.' The bacon had been over-cooked, as if Mrs Cromwell was putting her in her place for refusing the liver; it crackled in her mouth like verbal bullets. 'You only give them a go on the women's pages.'

He looked at her over a forkful of liver; it put more iron into one, so they said. Not that he felt he needed it. 'You don't want to be editor of the women's page?'

'No.'

'What do you want?' He chewed on the liver: it *tasted* like iron. This girl was upsetting him again.

'I'd like my own column.' The last of the bacon crackled between this teeth. She noticed that Mrs Cromwell hadn't cooked His Lordship's bacon as crisp as this. 'The female answer to Bernard Levin.'

'The *Examiner* doesn't have those sort of readers.'

'I know. I just dragged his name out of the air. I don't want to write about politics or music. But I'd like to go out and find my own stories, instead of being told what to write.'

'You can write what you like as women's editor. Within reason,' he added, careful of the hatchet.

'No. The women's page isn't where I want my stuff to be. I want to be read by men, too.' Especially by men, since they thought they ran the world as well as it could be run.

65

He swallowed the liver, which had suddenly proved hard to chew. 'I never interfere with what Massey-Folkes wants to do.'

That wasn't what she had heard. Men had been fired on notes that came from this flat or from the country house in Bucks. 'I shouldn't want you to. Actually, I think Quentin would give me my column if he can find someone else to be women's editor.'

'*Quentin?*'

She smiled. 'It's all perfectly innocent. He likes my legs, but that's all there is to it. He likes my copy better.'

'Well, he's the –' he almost said 'the boss' but he knew she wouldn't believe it. 'He runs the paper. There's just one thing. If he gives you your column, you don't come to any horse shows and write any more of your guff. Understand? You ready for coffee? I never eat sweets at lunch.'

'Oh. I was looking forward to bread-and-butter pudding or tapioca custard. I'd heard you believe in sensible food.'

'There you go, more guff.' But he smiled and wondered if she liked roses.

FOUR

'As one who was there myself for a while, I'd like to know, Mrs Roux, how an older woman feels being at the top?'

Cleo knew the questioner. She was a red-head, had been Miss Something-or-other and was a movable ornament, like rented plastic flowers, at receptions and parties around town. It was rumoured that she earned extra money as a lay-by for pop stars on the road; to certain golfing show business stars she was known as the British Open. When her legs were together she wrote occasional interviews for one of the celebrity-orientated weeklies.

'Who are you, young lady?' said Claudine Roux.

'Rhonda Buick. I was Miss Galaxy 1963.' She was a fading star now, she knew, but she never used metaphors like that in her stories. She would have been a nice moral girl if she had been plain.

'My belated congratulations. I'm afraid I missed that – would you call it an event?'

'It was for me,' said poor Miss Buick, laying her head on the block.

'I'm sure it was. Anything would be.'

My God, thought Cleo, and they call *me* the Hatchet Lady. She decided then that she would ask no questions at this press conference. She had only come to it because she had wanted to see what a First Lady of the Press was like. That was how the hand-out had billed her: Mrs Claudine Roux, First Lady of the New York Press. Mrs Roux had come to London after buying a British publishing house and the press conference had been called for her to explain why. Americans buying British publishing houses was on a plundering par with their buying British castles or bridges. Or so the man from *The Times* seemed to think.

'You're wrong, young man. English literature is part of the American heritage and I see this as an investment in our common heritage –' It was glib, but Claudine Roux had an imperious dignity about her that would have stopped even a man from *The Times* from accusing her of such a thing.

Cleo lost interest. She knew as well as anyone that no reporter or columnist ever got a real story out of a press conference; but, when she had called the Connaught Hotel to ask for a private interview, Mrs Roux's secretary had said that Mrs Roux never gave such interviews. So Cleo, wanting a look at a woman who owned one of the most influential newspapers in the United States, had come to the press conference. Cats, she thought, may look at queens as well as kings.

Then, getting up to move quietly out of the room, she saw Tom Border standing by the door. It seemed to her that she caught her breath, but she put it down to indigestion; she had rushed her lunch to get here. There was no reason why she should be surprised or excited to see Tom. He had said he was a drifter and drifters turned up anywhere.

He gave her the old slow smile when she took his arm and pulled her out of the room. 'I saw you in there. I was waiting for you to jump up and go for the Old Lady.'

'It was like the Five O'Clock Follies in Saigon. She wasn't saying anything I wanted to hear. What are you doing here – passing through?'

'I got in yesterday.' He didn't appear to have changed, he looked as much as ever like bones in a bag. 'I'm joining the *New York Courier*'s bureau here in London.'

'You work for Mrs Roux? Oh, you're just the man I want! Come and I'll buy you a drink.'

The press conference had been held in the publishing house in Bedford Square. Cleo found a nearby pub, almost empty, and they took their drinks to a corner table. She looked at him and felt a complexity of emotions that she hadn't expected.

'I wrote you a note after I heard you'd been wounded.'

'I got it.' He sipped his beer, tasting it as if he were a connoisseur. 'I like English beer, even when it's warm. I didn't answer your note, Cleo old girl. There didn't seem much point.'

'How's your wound? Where were you hit?'

'In the ass.' He grinned. 'I was running away. It left a nice scar, but not one I can show off. You're showing no scars.' He looked at her sideways, as if she might contradict him.

'No visible ones.' She had none at all, or none that she was aware of. But women like to hold an ace, or a scar, up their sleeve; it comes in handy during their martyrdom season. Or so she had heard her father, a self-proclaimed expert on women, say. 'But this is a tough town. The English aren't as civilized as they like to think.'

'You've done all right. Your own column – we all dream about that. Are you married or anything?'

'No. You?'

He shook his head, gave the same slow smile. 'When I went back to Friendship to convalesce, my mother had the girls lined up. But I heard the clack of faraway typewriters –'

'You always had a flair for the lousy poetic phrase.'

They both smiled, all at once comfortable again with each other. 'I went to New York and got a job on the *Courier*. Two weeks ago they offered me the job in the London bureau. They're cutting down on staff and they wanted a single man, one they could push around Europe at a moment's notice. The *Courier* isn't making the money it used to.'

'I thought Mrs Roux was one of the richest women in New York?'

'She is. But her money doesn't come from the *Courier*. It's a sort of family hobby. Her great-grandfather bought it a hundred years ago for a song.'

She wondered what a song had been worth a hundred years ago, but didn't ask. Though ambitious, she had no real interest in money in actual cash terms; a million or two either way, in today's terms, meant nothing to her. Which showed that, though not rich, she could think rich.

'Some hobby, to be able to have all that influence.'

'It doesn't have as much as it used to. Tell you the truth, it's a bit fuddy duddy. It's rather like working for the Yale Club's house magazine. But don't quote me.'

'I shan't, if you'll get me an interview with Mrs Roux.'

He looked at his empty glass. 'I knew you weren't plying me with beer for nothing. I'll try, but I have no influence with the Old Lady. I've never actually had a word with her. The Empress never gets down as far as the kitchen staff. They call her The Empress back in the New York office.'

They talked for another half hour, then he said, 'How about dinner tonight?'

'I'm sorry, Tom. I already have a date. But some other time.'

If he was disappointed, he hid it well; he still had the same withdrawn look. 'I'll see what I can do for you with the Old Lady.'

'The Old Lady – I got the impression that phrase doesn't fit her.'

'It's a generic term for all bosses. Don't you call Lord Cruze the Old Man?'

2

'Jack –' At their first dinner together, their second meal, he had told her to drop the *m'Lord*. 'I'm going to Northern Ireland at the weekend. I want to interview Bernadette Devlin.'

'She'll be coming to London, interview her here. There's a chance you'll get hurt over there in Ulster.' He let his steak and kidney pie get cold; he was truly concerned for her. 'I'll tell Quentin not to let you go.'

They were having dinner, their second, in the flat. So far he had not gone out in public with her; in private his behaviour had been impeccable. She felt safe, felt she was not being tested for the role of mistress. It was an employer-employee relationship; she knew that Massey-Folkes and some of the other senior executives came here occasionally for lunch or dinner. She did wonder, however, if Felicity Kidson had come here originally on the same basis.

She pushed a piece of kidney aside and looked for some steak in the pie. Mrs Cromwell was still defending the barricades of English cooking; all over Britain another French revolution was taking place but Mrs Cromwell was standing fast. All them trendies could cook what they liked, but she knew what was best.

'Jack, please don't interfere. I know whom I want to interview and where. I don't want to talk to Miss Devlin in the security of Westminster. I want to see what she's like back in her own bailiwick.'

'You take a lot for granted, talking to me like that. Eat your dinner.'

She resented his abrupt tone. 'Am I keeping Mrs Cromwell waiting again?'

He glowered at her from under the hairy brows. 'Dammit, you do everything you can to rub me up the wrong way. Why can't you get the chip off your shoulder? I don't care a damn where you interview the Devlin woman, so long as it's safe. I don't think you'll be safe in Ulster, not if the IRA knows you're working for me.'

She softened, apologized. 'I appreciate your concern for me. Nevertheless, I'm going to Ulster.'

'Dammit, you're stubborn!'

Later, after Mrs Cromwell had joined her husband in bed in the servants' quarters beyond the kitchen, he led Cleo upstairs to his library. 'I'll show you some films. Did you ever see Rudolph Valentino?'

'He was a little before my time.' She was amused. Did he see himself as the Sheik of Green Park?

The library was a big room, two of the walls lined to the ceiling with books. A small projection box was built into the third wall and a cinema screen came down out of the ceiling to cover the drapes on the fourth wall. She looked at the

71

books while he loaded the projector. If he had read only half of what was on the shelves, he was well-read. The social as well as the political philosophers were there; there was history, biography and travel. There was no fiction, none at all: evidently he got all that from his silent films.

They watched *Monsieur Beaucaire*. She wanted to laugh at the flaring nostrils and the flashing eyes, but a glance at Cruze in the darkened room told her it would be the wrong thing to do. It was as if he were looking at home movies, a fantasy of his childhood. He lived in a past that was not his own, an escapism that had been created for his parents' generation. The film finished and he sat for a while, neither looking at her nor saying anything. Then he got up and went into the projection box. She sat in the darkness, wondering why he was taking so long to turn on the lights. Surely he wasn't going to run another Valentino film?

Then a single light came on and she turned round. He stood by a door that she hadn't noticed before, a section of the bookshelves that opened into his bedroom. He wore only his socks and suspenders.

'Great balls –' she said, and for a split second His Lordship was flattered, '– of fire! What are you doing?'

'Getting ready for bed.' He stood on one leg while he wrestled to undo a suspender.

She played dumb, a lady of the silent screen. 'If you wanted me to leave, why didn't you just wind the clock and put the cat out?'

'All the clocks are electric and I don't have a cat. Take your clothes off.'

Oh my God, he does think he's the Sheik! 'Jack, put your clothes back on. You're old enough to be my father.'

'Let me give you some fatherly advice – don't ever say that to a man!' He stood there in fury and one sock. 'Dammit, who do you think you are?'

She was glad his eyes weren't flashing and his nostrils flaring; she didn't want to laugh if she could avoid it. 'I know who I'm not. I'm not someone who goes to bed with the Boss – it's not in my contract.'

72

'You don't have a contract!'

'I do, you know. I got Quentin to give me one, just to cover any syndication rights. I never dreamed syndication would be something like this.'

His member quivered with fury, like an irate conductor's baton; she would have been happier with the flaring nostrils and flashing eyes. Then he turned and went into the bedroom, slamming the door behind him. Books tumbled out of the shelves: *The Wisdom of Confucius* lay at her feet. Confucius he say ... she couldn't remember what Confucius had said, but guessed he would never have allowed himself to be rejected in just his socks and nothing else. She knew Jack Cruze would never forgive her for that. But it had been his own fault.

She let herself out of the flat and went home to her own place in South Kensington. She went to bed laughing. Women have no pity for men who make themselves look ridiculous in private or public. They prefer to do the demolition themselves.

3

She had a one-bedroom flat in a mansion block that still had a majority of older, conservative residents. The porter in the entrance lobby looked as if he might have been at Mafeking; the agents seemed to have put him there against an invasion of the swingers who were taking over South Kensington. Some of the older residents, those who were still capable of it, had their discreet affairs; and the porter turned a half-shut eye to strangers, male or female, who might sneak out in the early morning. So long as they *looked* respectable and didn't flaunt themselves, he didn't care what went on upstairs. A bit of breeding never hurt what the upper classes wanted to have on the side.

He had never thought of Miss Spearfield, being Australian, as upper class, but he was impressed when the big Rolls-Royce drew up outside and the chauffeur came in with a box of red roses. 'Will you see Miss Spearfield gets these right away?'

'Will she know who they're from?' Meaning he'd like to know.

'She'll know,' said Sid Cromwell, ready for another campaign at the florist's.

There was no note or card in the box, but when Cleo opened it and saw the red roses she did indeed know.

4

'No, Mr Border, I do not give exclusive interviews. I hated that press conference yesterday, but Farquhars thought it politic that I should hold it. I don't know that it achieved anything. All the cheap papers referred to me as the rich American heiress, as if I were still twenty-one.'

Claudine Roux was scrutinizing Tom Border while she talked to him. She was not over-impressed by what she saw; she did not like untidy men, or untidy women for that matter. But she liked his watchful eyes – they would miss nothing from here to any horizon – and though he was not handsome now he might be in years to come. She liked the thought of that, though not directly connecting the thought with him; looks were always more interesting when they were backed up by experience. She was sixty and still beautiful and though she admired the beauty of the young she did not yearn to be young again herself. There were, of course, *some* drawbacks to being older ... but she never thought of herself as old and would have sacked Tom Border on the spot had she known he referred to her as the Old Lady.

'I think Miss Spearfield might be more discreet than that.' Tom was not sure he could make such a promise. He had looked up some of Cleo's pieces and 'discreet' was in fact the last word he would have applied to them. But he wanted to get her her interview, if it was possible. He felt he owed her something, though he wasn't sure what.

'Mr Border, I read the English newspapers, even tabloids

74

like the *Examiner*. Miss Spearfield uses her little axe more frequently than Lizzie Borden did.'

Tom stood up, shrugged. 'Maybe you're right, Mrs Roux.'

'I usually am, Mr Border. What are you doing this evening?'

Tom hung on to his eyebrows. 'Well – nothing, I guess.'

'Don't look so shocked. I'm not in the habit of soliciting young men, certainly not those who work for me. I have to go to a dinner this evening and I prefer to choose my own partner rather than being burdened with some bore.'

He chanced a half-smile: 'You don't think I'd be a bore?'

'I shouldn't have asked you if I'd thought that. But you're not very gallant, Mr Border. You're not rushing to accept my invitation.'

'I'm sorry, Mrs Roux. My mother would be ashamed of me – she brought me up to have proper respect for ladies.'

'Old as well as young?'

'Both,' he said gallantly.

'Never forget older women, Mr Border. Often all some of them have to look forward to is small courtesies.' She did not include herself in that group. She would always expect more than small courtesies – and get them.

She had not met Tom Border until yesterday, though she had seen his by-line in her paper. Although she owned the largest bundle of stock in the *Courier*, she never interfered with the paper below board level and knew none of the staff except the top executives. Empresses, she had read (she had read a great deal about empresses, and felt she understood Catherine the Great, Elizabeth of Austria and Carlotta of Mexico), never concerned themselves with the palace drains. She thought the *Courier* just occasionally published sewage, but then so did all newspapers, even the *New York Times*. She hated muck-raking and after reading a scandalous story in the *Courier* always brought the matter up at board meetings.

'You are a good reporter, Mr Border.'

'I think so, Mrs Roux. I say that modestly, of course.'

'Of course. How else could you say it?' They smiled at each other, the empress and the new young man at court. But she did not have Catherine the Great's appetite for young lovers. New York in the second half of the twentieth century was not Moscow in the eighteenth century. That other empress had not had to suffer syndicated gossips, just those at court. 'Do you have a dinner suit?'

Tom hadn't worn anything even semi-formal since his high school graduation. 'No, but I guess I can hire one.'

'Do, and get one that fits you better than that sack you're wearing. Be here at the Connaught at seven forty-five. Sharp.'

'Yes, ma'am. May I ask where we're going for dinner? I like to be briefed.'

'To Lord Cruze's.'

5

'I don't mind an occasional bleeding heart leader writer,' said Cruze, 'but I don't want a haemophiliac.'

'Jack, dear boy, if you weren't so short yourself,' said the Tory shadow minister, 'you wouldn't care a damn about the Little People.'

'Women give rape a bad name,' said the homosexual writer who had been raped only by critics.

Cleo and Tom, deaf to the sometimes soggy soufflé of conversation being passed round the dinner table, looked across at each other. Each had been surprised to see the other with their respective boss; even more, they were both shocked, puritanism welling up as it does in all lapsed Christians. One did not go out with one's boss, especially when the boss was so much older.

Later, in the drawing-room, Tom came and sat beside Cleo. He looked uncomfortable in the well-tailored dinner jacket: he needed room to move within his clothes. 'You look beautiful tonight, Cleo old girl.'

She was in white, a virginal suggestion spoiled by the exposure of her bosom. 'So do you, positively suave. Did you get that from Moss Bros? I thought so. You should get them to dress you all the time. Is that in honour of the Old Lady?'

He smiled, shook his head, sipped his brandy. He had had no experience of life at this level and he was enjoying himself. Maybe he should try for a life as a rich drifter.

'If I didn't know you better, I'd think you were jealous. I'm jealous of Lord Cruze.'

'There's no need to be. I'm just here to keep a chair warm till he finds another mistress.' She hoped she sounded convincing.

'He couldn't find a more beautiful ass to keep a chair warm.'

'I hope you two are not discussing me,' said Claudine Roux, sitting down opposite them.

'Not at all,' said Cleo, wondering how much she had heard.

She had not noticed if Mrs Roux's ass was beautiful, but the rest of her certainly was. Back home in Australia, where the harsh sunlight rarely allowed a woman's beauty to last beyond middle age, she had never really looked to see if there were truly beautiful women amongst the elderly. She also had the fault of all youth, of setting a low age limit for beautiful women or handsome men. Secure in flesh and mind and the present tense, she did not bother herself with how she would look in the future.

'Lord Cruze has just been extolling your virtues,' said Claudine.

'Singular as well as plural, I hope?'

Claudine smiled, polishing her shield: she liked fencing with the young. 'I've never believed that virtue has its own reward. Some celibate priest coined that one. Don't be shocked, Mr Border. I'm not advocating permissiveness, just a little moderate immorality when the occasion calls for it.'

'How does one recognize the occasion?' said Cleo.

'My dear, I'm sure you'd know it. Get me some more coffee, would you, Mr Border?' She looked after Tom as he moved away, then turned back to Cleo. 'You and Mr Border obviously know each other. Where did you meet?'

'In Vietnam.'

77

'Really? What were you doing there?'

'Protecting my virtue, mostly. When I wasn't doing that, I was covering the war.'

'Indeed?' She looked at Cleo with new interest, taking her out of the revealing white dress and putting her in combat-dress; though, of course, the white dinner-gown was also combat-dress for a different, undeclared war. 'Did you ever meet my brother? General Brisson.'

Cleo almost ruined the white gown; her coffee cup rattled in its saucer. 'Yes. Yes, I had dinner with him once.'

'Only once? Then you must have kept your virtue. Oh, I know my brother, Miss Spearfield. My sister-in-law calls his diversions his "supply troops". I hope you were not one of them.'

'No, Mrs Roux, I was not.' She put some ice into her voice.

'I'm sorry. I've offended you.'

Claudine's apology was sincere. She attacked more often than she intended; those who knew her would have laughed if she had claimed that it was a form of defence. But it was, had been ever since her father and her husband, both arrogant men, had died and left her in charge of the Brisson empire. She had never expected to be the empress, only the consort. Until Pierre Brisson and Henri Roux had died in the same plane crash twenty years ago, she had been content to be what everyone saw her as: the beautiful but dutiful daughter and wife, doting mother of an only son born in her late thirties because Henri had not wanted children before then, loving sister of an only brother who had had a brilliant if chequered career at West Point. Suddenly faced with responsibility after Roger had refused to leave the army and come home and run the empire, she had put up sharp pointed defences, an irony-railed fence. She had always had a sharp tongue, but only Henri had known of it, though he had never listened.

'You shouldn't jump to conclusions, Mrs Roux. You've been studying me all evening. I'm sure you think I'm one of Lord Cruze's supply troops. I'm not. No more than Mr Border is one of yours.'

78

'*Touché*,' said Claudine and took her coffee from Tom as he came back. 'Miss Spearfield and I are getting on so well. She knew my brother, General Brisson, in Vietnam.'

'Yes?' Tom looked at Cleo out of the corner of his eye.

'Mrs Roux knows his faults,' said Cleo blandly. 'How he likes to dally.'

'Yes.' Tom kept his composure and his curiosity tight inside the well-fitting jacket.

Then Lord Cruze, having given enough time to his other guests, came over to join them. He sat on the edge of a chair, tie awry, jacket open, shirt creeping out of his trousers. Claudine looked at him with distaste and admiration: she had learned to do both living with Henri.

'I heard you talking with the French ambassador,' Cruze said. 'You speak French fluently. I never thought Americans were good linguists.'

'We think the same about the English,' said Claudine, wondering why she was raising the American flag; she rarely did that at home. 'My parents were French, Jack. My brother and I were born in France. My husband was French. It sort of runs in and out of the family.'

'I thought your family had been in America for generations. Somehow one doesn't think of the French as immigrants.'

'The French never think of themselves as immigrants, Jack. Other nationalities, yes, but never the French. Some of my ancestors owned plantations in Louisiana, owned them before the Louisiana Purchase. But each time a woman in the family found herself pregnant, she went back to France to have the child. It just so happened that my mother and I both married Frenchmen who later became American citizens. Reluctantly, I believe. My husband, for instance, pulled the blinds down on July the Fourth but let off fireworks on Bastille Day.'

Cruze envied people who could trace their families, and especially family influence, back through generations. He had tried tracing the Cruze and Brown families and had given up at his great-grandfather on each side: a family tree

79

of shrivelled nonentities was not what he was looking for. He had got more pleasure, as a junior bank clerk, tracing the bank manager's signature.

He looked at the American sitting beside Cleo. He hadn't missed their glances at each other across the dinner table and he wondered if he had competition here. 'What do you think of Britain, Mr Border?'

'I'm still feeling my way, sir. They tell me London isn't Britain, just as New York isn't America. I'm going to start in the worst part, over in Belfast, and work my way back. I'm going there, this weekend.'

Cleo sat up, and glanced at Cruze. 'I'm going there, too. But Lord Cruze has been trying to talk me out of it. He doesn't think women should expose themselves –' she lifted the front of her dress, caught Claudine's eye and smiled, '– to danger.'

'It's no place for women,' said Cruze. 'The information I have is that it's going to get very dirty over there. Like your Vietnam.'

'No, never like Vietnam,' said Tom and looked sideways again at Cleo.

'Well, we'll see,' said Cleo. 'We'll go to Belfast together, Tom, and compare notes. You can look after me for Lord Cruze.'

The two men looked at each other and smiled, but Cruze's smile was tight and Tom's tentative. Each of them was surprised at his own sudden jealousy.

'The young,' said Claudine, 'they seem to enjoy war.'

Oh my God, thought Cleo, if you only knew who did enjoy it!

6

The guests had gone and Cruze, tie off and collar loosened, sat in the drawing-room having a night-cap with Cleo. The extra staff who had come in to help Mrs Cromwell had also gone; the Cromwells themselves were in bed. The huge flat was silent, and across Green Park Cleo heard a police car ringing its way down Constitution Hill. The bell had no real urgency about it, any more than would a carload of carillonists ting-a-linging their drunken way home. Soon, she had heard, all the cars would be equipped with sirens, bringing the city's tension properly up to date.

'Would you like to see a film?' Cruze had not felt so uncertain of himself with a woman in years.

'I'm too tired for Valentino, Jack.'

'How about Hoot Gibson?' He grinned, then looked at her carefully, as he might at a new executive he was about to employ. 'You were a beautiful hostess tonight.'

'Was that what I was – the hostess?' She looked at him just as carefully, not looking for employment.

'Would you like to be?'

'Is that a proposal or a proposition?'

She stood up, straightening her dress over her hips. She wished now that she had worn a looser, less revealing gown; she had put it on without thinking about the possible consequences. She liked to show off her figure and she knew that men liked to look at it. But she had been naïve tonight. The women at the dinner party, all older than she, had read more into the tight, revealing gown than had occurred to her. She had advertised herself as Jack Cruze's latest girl.

'Dammit!' But he swallowed his annoyance and changed the subject. 'Are you still going to Belfast? With that fellow what's-his-name?'

'Tom Border. You never forget names, Jack.'

'Is there something between you and him?'

She found her wrap, draped it round her shoulders. 'He asked exactly the same about you. The answer in both cases is No. Call me a taxi, please, Jack.'

She had refused to allow him to send Sid Cromwell to pick her up and had told him at the same time that she was not to be driven home. To have accepted the Rolls-Royce as her transport would somehow have been, in her eyes, an acceptance of her role as more than just his dinner partner. Going home by taxi declared her independence.

He didn't argue. He rang downstairs to the night porter, then opened the front door of the flat and took her hand. 'You're bloody annoying, Cleo. We could be good friends.'

'I thought we were.' Then she relented, kissed him on the cheek. 'Goodnight, Jack. Don't take me for granted, that's all I ask.'

FIVE

'No, Miss Devlin won't be letting herself give interviews to rags like the *Examiner*. Now if you were from *The Times* or the *Guardian*...'

'How about the *New York Courier*?'

'Ah, we'd have to think about that, wouldn't we? Boston and Brooklyn, we know about our support there, but New York...'

He was an old man, too old for war. But war had been his life if not his profession; he had fought in the Troubles, killed his share of Black-and-Tans. The young men were itching to take over, but he was one of those hanging on, protecting his authority as much as his fierce nationalism. He wore a cloth cap instead of a red-banded army cap, but he was just like the British generals had been in World War One. Tom Border had made a study of generals.

'I don't think you should judge me on what paper I work for,' said Cleo. 'For all you know, I may be very sympathetic to Miss Devlin and the IRA.'

'You may be that, too. But there's no evidence, is there, not from your paper. No, Miss Devlin, she's saving herself to talk to the British press in London. She's a very intelligent lass, that one.' He tried to keep the surprise out of his voice, wondering why so many sensible fellers had voted for the girl. 'Maybe you'd like to interview me. I knew all the big fellers, De Valera, Michael Collins, all them fellers.' He lived in the past, the battles had become a romance in his misted memory. 'It was different then,' he added, pathetically.

Cleo and Tom left him, went out into the street and walked down past the narrow houses, grey and drab even in the August sunshine. They were aware of people watching them; lace curtains moved like white eyelids. On a street corner a group of youths stood still as Cleo and Tom came up to them; the intruders, for that was what they knew they were, had to step into the gutter to get by. They had come to the wrong address, in more ways than one.

'That guy was one of the Old Guard,' said Tom. 'We should have gone looking for the young ones. Who gave you his name?'

'He rang me himself at the hotel, told me to come and see him first. I suppose someone at the hotel told him I was there but forgot to say what paper I was from.'

'Why didn't you get in touch with Bernadette Devlin direct?'

'I tried that, but she's not in Belfast this weekend, she's somewhere out in the country, they said.'

They came out of the side street, turned down the Falls Road, and were looking vainly for a taxi when they heard shouting and banging of drums. Coming up the road, spread right across it like a slow dark tide, was a procession; at its head marched two drummers and behind them, banging away to the same rhythm, was a line of youths with dustbin lids. A banner waved above the crowd, but the two young men holding the poles were marching too close together and the message on the banner sagged in on itself like a strangled shout.

'Here come the Young Turks,' said Cleo.

'Oh Jesus,' said Tom, looking the other way.

At the end of the block on which they stood a barricade was hastily being dragged into place. Police, the Royal Ulster Constabulary in glistening helmets and with plastic shields held up like a loose wall, were lining up behind the barricade. Behind them were the B-Specials, the civilian militia, their stiff-peaked caps held hard down on their heads by chin-straps, their pick-handle batons held at the ready. The silence at that end of the road was an eerie contrast to the shouting

84

and banging of drums and lids, now louder still, from the other end.

Cleo suddenly realized they were in the middle of a rapidly diminishing no-man's land. She looked wildly around for escape; then banged on the front door immediately behind her. But she could have been thumping on the door of an empty house: the door remained shut, the lace curtains at the windows didn't move. The crowd, turning now into a mob as its anger and noise grew, was less than fifty yards away.

Two youths suddenly appeared on the roof of a house across the street. One of them swung his arm and a bottle, trailing a tiny wisp of smoke, flew through the air towards the barricades. The distance was too great; the Molotov cocktail hit one of several cars parked along the road. Instantly flames spread around the car; it seemed only a moment before it blew up with a roar. The car behind it caught fire, then the one in front of it. Then the air was full of smoke and stones and bottles and single spiked railings hurled as spears.

Tom dragged Cleo back into the shallow doorway and stood in front of her; the door knocker, a clenched fist, was hard against the back of her head. The mob swept past, its faces all one face, distorted by hate and fury and the pent-up frustration of generations. None of the men seemed to see Cleo and Tom; the mob pressed them against the door like a surging river. Tom turned his back on it, held Cleo tightly in his arms, his legs braced so that they would not be forced to their knees by the raging crowd.

He twisted his head, saw the armoured car with its water-cannon come through a gap in the barricade. The jets of water sprayed the burning cars, then turned on the mob as the first line of youths swept on it.

Another Molotov cocktail hurtled through the air, hit the armoured car and burst; there was a scream as one of the youths was splashed and he flung up his hands to his face. Then the first shot was fired and the mob's yelling suddenly stopped; bullets were not part of the game. For a moment

85

Cleo and Tom had the feeling that they had all at once gone deaf; there seemed to be no sound in the packed, smoking street. Then there was a sudden single roar, a horrible sound coming out of a wounded bull's throat; Tom saw a big youth break from the front of the crowd and run towards the barricade. He drew back his arm and hurled a spiked railing with all his strength; the RUC policeman on the other side of the barricade could not have seen it coming. His shield was too low; the spear went into his throat. Then there were two more shots; the big youth suddenly stopped and sat down, then fell over and lay still. Another volley of shots, and the RUC came out from behind the barricade and began to move down the road, their shields now glinting in the sun like unbreakable windows. Behind them the B-Specials, some wielding their pick-handles, modern-day shillelaghs, others brandishing pistols, crowded in support.

The noise was deafening, the air thick with acrid smoke from the burning cars, the roadway strewn with men wounded by bricks or bullets. The mob retreated, still throwing anything that came to hand; a large stone hit the wall just beside Tom and Cleo, missing them by inches. The police and the militia pressed forward slowly and relentlessly. They went past Cleo and Tom and a policeman turned his face behind his shield and looked at them, unsurprised and without curiosity.

'I'd get out of here if I was you,' he said in a matter-of-fact tone and went on, raising his shield deftly to fend off a flying stone. He was embarking on a long war, but he didn't know it.

Behind the RUC and the B-Specials Cleo saw the armoured car still trying to put out the burning vehicles with its water-cannon. A truck came round its side and moved slowly down the street behind the police and militia. Crouched on the platform on its roof was a cameraman. The truck went by and Cleo saw the BBC insignia on its side.

'Oh God,' she said, 'not them again!'

No matter what she and Tom wrote, and they had been in the thick of today's story, nothing would compare with the colour and immediacy of the television coverage. It had been the same in Vietnam. War had become a home movie.

<h2 style="text-align:center">2</h2>

Cleo wrote her story and phoned it to London. She wrote it well and she knew it would be on Page One as the main news story and not as her column. But she also knew that when it appeared tomorrow morning it would be stale news.

'Everyone will have seen it all this evening. Who'll read my stuff?'

'Cleo old girl, TV is only illustrated headlines. There is still a majority of people who want background, some real depth to their news. You can give them that when you do your column.'

She shook her head. 'It's not enough. For me, I mean.'

They were having a late dinner in the dining-room of their hotel. Most of the other diners had gone and the staff hovered in the background, wanting to go home or to the pubs; anywhere where they could discuss this afternoon's riot. Six men had been killed and at least twenty badly hurt. The staff was a mixture of Protestant and Catholic, so there was no discussion within the hotel. Jobs, for the moment, were more important than sympathies.

Something in her voice made Tom look hard at her. Stirring her coffee, intent on her own disappointment and chagrin, it was a moment or two before she looked up and saw him staring at her.

'What's the matter?'

'You said that as if what happened this afternoon wasn't so important.'

'Of course it was. And tragic, too. But I'm talking about me – about you, too. If TV is going to take our stories away from us, who's going to read us? We'll just be reduced to comment for people who have more time than they know what to do with. Retired people, people out of work, academics.'

'Cleo, academics don't read the *Examiner* unless they're doing a paper on the tastes of the lower orders. But the other ones you mentioned – don't you think they need to be informed? And the politicians read the columns, even those in the *Examiner*, I guess.'

'You're a journalist snob. You keep talking about the *Examiner* as if it were a paper for morons. It has the second largest daily circulation in this country. No matter what you Americans may think, there aren't four million morons in this country.'

Tom didn't debate that point. At times, when depressed, he felt the world was populated entirely by morons, including himself. There had been no intelligence in the Falls Road this afternoon, only emotion.

'Is that all you're concerned with? How many people read your stuff?'

She put her spoon carefully back in the saucer and returned his stare. Without knowing it, he was asking her why she had come all this way from Australia. She had not been untouched by what had happened this afternoon; she saw the tragedy beginning to stretch down the years ahead; she could understand the grief in the homes of the men who had been killed. But there was more: her own life was not going to be spent in the streets of Belfast. All the reasons for her seeming selfishness were too complex to explain to him now, though.

'Yes.' She knew she sounded too blunt.

He leaned back in his chair, threw up a hand, looked from side to side as if hoping someone might interrupt them. The head waiter started forward hopefully, but Tom looked right through him, then back at Cleo.

'You are too much, Cleo, too much for me. I hadn't realized it before – all that sparks you is ambition. The news, any goddam thing at all that happens, is just a stepping-stone for you.'

'I'm a newspaperwoman.'

'Yes. But you're an awful lot more than that. I think in a way you're a lot like Claudine Roux.'

The comparison hadn't occurred to her. 'I'm flattered.'

'It wasn't meant to be flattery. I told you we call her The Empress. Empresses chop heads off. Or they did.'

She laughed, but felt uncomfortable. Women like to look into mirrors, but not when held up by men, particularly men they like. 'Whose head is in danger? Yours?'

He shook his head, as if to prove how securely it was attached to the rest of him. 'I'm not important enough. No, you'll go for heads bigger than mine.'

'Lord Cruze's?' She was still laughing, but it was becoming harder.

'Who knows? You have plenty of time.'

She stopped laughing. 'You should take a look at yourself some time. You accuse me of being self-centred. What about you? What's a drifter but a self-centred bum, someone who moves on every time he looks as if he might have to become involved in something. How long are you going to remember those dead boys in the street this afternoon?'

He stared at her: she had held a mirror up to him. It was cracked, but he recognized enough of himself. Abruptly he signalled for the head waiter. The latter dived forward like a magpie, stiff white breast buckling as he bent over with the bill.

'Separate bills, please,' said Cleo.

'No,' said Tom. 'It's my treat, while I can afford to do it.'

She had been idly thinking that if he asked her to bed tonight, she would have gone with him. She stood up, angry and hurt, and walked out while he was still signing the bill. He caught up with her out in the lobby.

'You're angry,' he said. 'Well, goddam it, so am I!'

'What the hell have you got to be angry about?'

'Because you've let me down. I once said you were female, sentimental and compassionate. All you are now is female.'

She was surprised at his bitterness even while she was angry with him. She wondered how the relationship between them had suddenly gone sour; she might have explained herself better to him had he been a stranger. She admitted the truth of what he had said, or part of it: she *was* ambitious. But lovers, or people on the verge of love, have no time for immediate explanations. The sad fact was that neither she nor Tom realized they were on the verge of love. They thought it was a quarrel between journalists, who prefer facts to rumours of feeling.

'Oh my God, you really are a male chauvinist, aren't you?'

'It's no worse than an ambitious women's libber.'

They were arguing in jargon and she knew it. She spun round and went quickly towards the lifts at the end of the lobby. But the lifts were on some upper floor and tantalizingly kept her waiting: the lift attendants were all men. She was still furious, but while she waited impatiently reason crept back, prodding her. She had been foolish; but so had he. She would hold out a friendly hand, try to explain herself to him. She turned round, all at once reasonable and forgiving.

But he had gone. The revolving front door spun like a runaway wheel.

3

She went back to London next day after the reception clerk had told her that Mr Border had left on the early morning plane. Bernadette Devlin came in from wherever she had been in the country and gave a press conference on yesterday's riot; but Cleo did not go to it, left it to the *Examiner's* local stringer. The conference was held in the hotel and when she saw the television cameras going into the big public room set aside for the mass interview, she lost interest. One couldn't blame Miss Devlin, she would get better exposure on television than in all the newspapers combined. Sincere anger always looks more convincing on a screen than on the printed page.

When she got back to London she went to her flat before going to the office. The porter met her at the lobby door. 'There was more flowers for you this morning, Miss Spearfield. I give 'em to your cleaning lady to put in water. Roses need lots of water.'

He was no gardening expert, he was just wondering who

owned the Rolls-Royce that had brought the roses. He had noted the number plate, JC-1. It wasn't the Archbishop of Westminster's number plate though he wouldn't be surprised if the Archbishop did ride around in a Rolls; he was firmly convinced that the Catholic Church had more money than it knew what to do with. JC-1 ... then suddenly it clicked: Jesus Christ, John Cruze! Lord Cruze, Miss Spearfield's boss! He beamed at her with new respect.

Cleo saw the recognition in his eye. 'I won them at bingo, Mr Wood. A year's supply, once a week.'

There had been six boxes of roses in two weeks, but he made no mention of that. 'Pity you didn't win the money, miss.'

'Mr Wood, do you watch television very much?'

'Every chance I get, miss.' He looked puzzled. 'The news, documentaries, fillums, *Coronation Street*, Benny Hill. The missus often says she doesn't know what we did before the telly came.'

She knew he read the *Examiner*; she had seen it in his tiny office. 'Do you read the papers?'

'Only the sports pages, miss.' And the gossip columns, to see if any of *his* people were mentioned. But he was diplomatic, if a little late: 'Oh, your column, too. Never miss that.'

He must have missed her by-line on the Page One story this morning. Or he hadn't read it, had got all he wanted to know from last night's telly.

'You going to be on the telly, miss?'

'I might, Mr Wood. You never know.'

Once in her flat she took her time over a bath, read her mail as if looking for secret messages between the lines, changed the fresh water of the bunch of roses for more fresh water, inspected the flat to see how the cleaning lady had rearranged the dust this time, did everything she could to put off what she knew she was going to do anyway. Then at last she picked up the phone and dialled the number of the Fleet Street bureau of the *New York Courier*.

'Mr Border? I'm sorry. You've just missed him. He's going to the Continent ... No, he'll be away some weeks, I understand. You may be able to reach him at our Paris bureau . . .'

She hung up. She wasn't going to chase him to Paris, not even by phone. She felt a certain relief at the same time as she felt let down. No, more than let down: empty. As if she had thrown away – what? A chance of happiness? But wasn't she happy enough as she was? She hadn't come all this way, had she, to have her happiness depend on a man who hadn't even told her he loved her? Was she in love with him or did she just want to convince him that she wasn't *all* ambition? She asked herself questions, being her own devil's advocate, which meant she didn't want any honest answers.

She went to the office, early enough to catch Massey-Folkes before he started the afternoon editorial conference. He was in his glass-walled office; he believed every editor should be a goldfish in a bowl. Or anyway, a shark. He was tall, bald and when he stood up always hunched over; fifteen years of working for a short boss had taught him physical diplomacy. When he straightened up in the presence of those under him they knew they were in for a blast. He didn't rise at all when Cleo came into his office, but gave her his big buck-toothed smile.

'Good story, Cleo my love. It had a nice feel to it.' Feel was something he always looked for in a story, though he had never defined what he felt.

'Quentin –' She sat down, looked at him across his meticulously neat desk. It struck her that he could have been a Civil Service Permanent Secretary had he not been such an anarchist. 'The Cruze Organization owns some television shares, doesn't it?'

'Fifteen per cent of United TV. United held the Monday to Friday franchise for the London area. 'Before you go any further, love – there are never any stories, except favourable ones, on United. Those are orders from His Nibs.'

'I thought he was supposed never to interfere with what you ran?'

'Don't be naïve, Cleo. He's not going to have one of his employees writing crap about the golden goose, not when he

92

owns fifteen per cent of the goose. Forget it. Much as my secret Marxist heart would love it, I'm not running any of your hatchet work on the ill-gotten, print-your-own-money returns from commercial television!'

'Quentin, I don't want to *write* – I want to *appear*. On TV, preferably on United.'

'You'd have to talk to the United people about that – I can ring up someone there and put in a word for you. Their women's hour is pretty bloody, so my wife tells me –'

'I'm not interested in the women's hour. I'm after my own spot on *Scope*.' *Scope* was a hard-hitting, big-budget weekly news magazine that had a top rating. It had made stars of two of its reporters; the third spot was usually reserved for a guest reporter. 'I could handle it. Even with my Australian accent.'

'You're fishing for compliments. You know you have the sexiest voice since –' But he couldn't remember the last sexy voice that had seduced him. Not his wife's: she still sounded as if she were keeping goal for the Roedean hockey team.

'Since Theda Bara?'

'Did she have a sexy voice? Maybe you'd better ask His Nibs. That was what you were going to do all along, weren't you?'

'Yes.' Now she had made her decision, she felt no shame; or had immunized herself against it. She sat back in her chair, showing Massey-Folkes the legs he admired. 'He's sending me red roses.'

'Before we go any further – are you thinking of giving up your column?'

'No, of course not. I won't desert you, Quentin.'

'Good. Now, are you talking to me as your editor or your surrogate father?' He had two daughters and he'd have skinned them alive if they'd accepted red roses from Jack Cruze. At the same time he wondered what Jack had that he didn't, except, of course, money and power.

'Both.' She would never have asked her own father for advice on such a topic.

He sighed, looked out through the glass wall into the big

93

newsroom, saw the various editors gathering to descend on him. Tomorrow's paper seemed suddenly unimportant; he would rather sit here and admire her legs and give her fatherly advice.

'He demands payment, Cleo. You'll never be the only one. Felicity lasted the longest, but even she never had a monopoly on him. He had a wife once, you know.'

'No, I didn't know.'

'She left him after a year, no kids. I don't even know if they were ever divorced. I could find out, but that's his business. I never met her. She lives somewhere in East Anglia, Suffolk or somewhere. He still looks after her, I mean sees that she still lives comfortably. But he never goes near her or talks to her. I don't know why she left him, but ever since that he's had all the women his money could buy.'

'That's nasty, Quentin. To him and to me.'

'You asked me, Cleo. All I'm saying is, if you want to set your price, make it high. And see you get more of a golden handshake than just a bunch of white roses.'

She stood up; the attempt at immunization had failed and she felt shame. 'Do me a favour, Quentin. Whatever I decide to do, don't talk about me to the other men.'

He looked out at the other editors ogling him through the glass wall. 'I'd never do that, Cleo. If ever you want more advice...'

She smiled, but it was an effort. 'You could never have run the women's page.'

'You'd be surprised. There are still a lot of women who prefer a man's advice, no matter how wrong it might be. You're all masochists.'

4

'That garden down there was designed by Capability Brown,' said Cruze. 'I used to sneak up here when I was a kid down in the village and pinch eggs out of the birds' nests. I'd sit up in that big elm over there and look at the house and

94

one day I decided that some day I'd own it. I was twelve or thirteen, I think.'

'You're kidding.'

He looked at her as if she were a child, or stupid. 'You told me at lunch you're ambitious. I thought you'd understand. You don't have to be over twenty-one to be ambitious. I knew I wanted to be rich when I was about twelve years old. Setting myself to make a million pounds, or two million, wasn't any good – after your first million, you're not rich till you've made ten, fifty million. So I set this house as my target. When I could afford to buy it and have enough money to run it, I'd settle for being rich. Everything that's come after it has been incidental.'

'Except the power.'

He lowered the hairy eyebrows, looked at her sideways. 'Except the power. What's your target?'

He had been away in the United States for the past five days. The Cruze Organization had a quarter-share in timber plantations and a pulp mill in the Carolinas and twice a year he went over to Charleston, one of his favourite cities, to talk with his American partners. When he had returned to London yesterday Cleo had called him at the flat and asked if she could see him.

'I'm going down to St Aidan's House,' he had said. 'You want to join me for the weekend?'

He had noticed the hesitation on the line, but had waited. He had learned to be patient; up to a point, that is. He would have been patient only up to a point with God Himself.

Then she had said, 'All right, Jack. Do I need to bring a dinner dress? I mean, am I playing hostess again?'

'No, there'll be just you and me. For Saturday anyway. Maybe on Sunday I'll have people in for lunch –' He never had a free weekend entirely to himself and he would have been worried if he had. Kings like to be reminded that they reign. 'I'll send Sid Cromwell to pick you up at your flat.'

Again there had been the slight hesitation, then she had said, 'All right.'

He had known then that she had passed a fork in her road.

95

He did not worry about his own road: he was too far down it now to worry about whether he took the right or the wrong fork. Or so he thought.

Now she was hesitating again and he repeated, 'What's your target?'

'Jack, I want to go into television. I'll keep on with my column, but I want one of the spots on *Scope*.'

They were walking along the top of the hill behind the big house. In the distance, beyond the oaks and beeches that were a green battlement at the southern end of the great park, the Norman tower of a church rose up as a marker of where the village of Chalfont St Aidan stood. Beyond it a black umbrella of storm was opening up and the humidity in the air could be felt being pushed ahead of it. He liked to sweat; it reminded him there was still juice in him. He had heard somewhere that the sweat glands dried out the older one got, but he had never bothered to check it. He turned a blind eye and a blank mind to the thought of growing old.

'I don't interfere –'

'Jack, did you come all the way to where you are without once asking someone to interfere for you?'

'All the way.' He didn't need to boast; he knew it was true. Then he relented, because he didn't want to sound smug in front of her. 'But I trod on a lot of people, kicked them in the knackers, caught them when they weren't looking. The only thing I didn't do was stab 'em in the back. I'm not that sort.'

'That could happen to you some day. Be stabbed in the back, I mean.'

'Who by?' He smiled and took her hand. 'By you? Come on, we'd better get back to the house or we're going to get a wet tail.'

They hurried down the winding path, suddenly stopping as thunder hit them like shellfire. The air was stifling now and the light had become unnervingly bright, a last explosion before the storm extinguished it. The trees were strangely green and the long dry grass on the side of the hill had the brilliance of a mustard field. Then they saw the church tower disappear in the silvery rain and abruptly the light began to

96

race towards them, contracting across the park as it surrendered to the darkness of the storm. They began to run.

They reached the house a moment before the rain pelted down. They dashed into the conservatory, and stood getting their breath, looking up at the rain trying to shatter the glass roof above them. They were both sweating, standing there amongst the palms and shrubs and creepers like lovers in a green jungle.

He put his hand on her arm and she turned towards him. For a moment it seemed to him that she turned her head away to look over her shoulder, as if she were taking a last look at something or someone. Then she put her lips to his and he tasted the sweet salt of her.

5

He might have got where he was by treading on people, kicking them in the knackers, catching them when they weren't looking; but he was not a bull-at-a-gate lover in bed. Which surprised Cleo. Of all places, bed was where she had expected him to be brutal, proving his power where all men thought it counted.

Afterwards he got up and walked naked about the big bedroom. He had some conceit about his physical condition. He would not have won any Mr Universe contest or even been invited to pose with one of the voluptuous girls on Page Three of the *Examiner*, but he knew that he looked good for a fifty-year-old. He had muscular shoulders, a broad chest, a flat stomach and better than average bedroom equipment. Cleo thought he looked slightly ridiculous strutting about the room like a pole vaulter warming up for a second jump, but she had passed the point (the fork in the road) where she was going to laugh at him any more. She would laugh *with* him, or try to sound as if she were.

The storm had passed and the sun had come out again, streaming in through the windows. He paused by one of the windows and, looking out, said, 'If I talk to them at United,

97

how do I know you'll produce the goods? There is more to being a good TV presenter than just sitting in front of a camera. Even I know that.'

He had never been in a television studio, refusing all invitations to interviews. He had been flattered when John Freeman had wanted him, a representative of the new tycoons, for the *Face to Face* series, to be one with the likes of King Hussein of Jordan and Stirling Moss, a national hero; but he had resisted the invitation and as time had passed it had become accepted that he would never appear on television. He might walk naked in front of the woman, any woman, he had in his bedroom, but there were parts of himself he never wanted exposed.

She sat up against the pillows, the sheet drawn up over her breasts. He noticed that all women, except the cheap brazen ones, always showed a little late modesty after making love. He was never sure whether it was guilt for their shamelessness minutes before or whether it was coquetry, another start to another session. She didn't smoke, which pleased him, and he saw her reach into her handbag and take out something and pop it into her mouth.

'What's that? The Pill?'

'I take that in the mornings. This is just a peppermint.'

He laughed, came back and sat down on the side of the bed. The Pill had been a great boon to men as well as women: it made life so much easier, less worrisome. Quentin Massey-Folkes had wanted to run an editorial in the *Examiner* protesting against Pope Paul's encyclical against the Pill; he had borrowed a heading for it, Paul's Epistle to the Fallopians. But Cruze had vetoed that; he didn't want to get into a war with the Catholic Church, no matter how good it might be for circulation.

'We don't want to get you pregnant.'

'We?' But she smiled and put her hand on his. 'Well, I suppose it is a double act.'

'You're asking me to do a double act with you in this TV business. If I say anything to them at United, they're going to link my name with yours.'

'I always had the idea that that sort of thing didn't worry you. Everyone at the *Examiner* linked you with Felicity.'

'That was different. She was women's editor before I took up with her. I never gave her any extra clout on the paper.'

'I'm not asking you to give me any clout at United.' But that wasn't true and she knew it. She had to be honest, even if devious: 'Well yes, I guess I am. But they'll kick me out if I'm no good. I'd kick myself out. I'd never make a fool of myself just to get to the top.'

'No, I don't think you would. Television, more than any other business I can think of, has people at the top who are fools. I don't mean the executives, they're as shrewd as they come, I mean the performers. They fool themselves that they have talent and they haven't. They don't last long, they come and go like English tennis players or heavyweight boxers, but for a while they think they've made it. Newspapers could never stand the turnover they have in television.'

'You sound as if you hold TV in contempt.'

'I do.'

'Why did you invest in it, then?'

'Because I knew it would make money for me easier than anything else I've ever invested in. They came to me, told me what return I could expect and I gave them the money they asked for. Let me tell you something –'

'Put a robe on, Jack, or get back into bed. I find it a bit disconcerting talking to the Boss with his Old Feller staring me in the eye.'

'Old Feller? Where did you get that expression?'

'I used to hear my father using it with my brothers.'

He got into bed and she pulled the sheet up to his chest and tucked it in around him. They were like an old married couple. But neither of them thought of that. 'Now tell me something ...'

He wasn't sure why he wanted to tell her about himself. He did not think he was in love with her, but he had not felt so confidential since he had first fallen in love with Emma. The love-making had been as good as he had ever experienced; but there had been something more to the feeling of being with her. She excited him as few women had, but there was more to her than sexual excitement. He had met ambitious women before, in and out of his bed, so it was not just that that they had in common. He wondered if it was because he had found her a good listener. He had had other women who listened, or had seemed to, but he had discovered as time went by that they hadn't listened at all. No, he didn't know why he felt he wanted to share confidences with her; except that she invited them. For all her swagger and her eye to the main chance, there was a sympathetic warmth about her that she could not hide even if she tried.

'I've always known where and how to make money. My father died in 1935, when I was sixteen. He'd never had any money to spare, he was a solicitor's clerk and I'm afraid that was all he ever wanted to be. If he had any dreams, he never told me. It was my mother who gave me books to read about men who'd made good. Rockefeller and Carnegie in America, Selfridge in this country. She gave me other books, history, Shakespeare, Dickens, but I knew what I liked most. She got me a job in a bank in Aylesbury and told me I'd learn more about money there than in any books.'

Mrs Cruze sounded like a robber baroness. But all Cleo said was, 'It must have been nice to have such an encouraging mother.'

He looked sideways at her. 'I know what you're thinking. No, my mother wasn't greedy, a money-grubber like that American woman Hetty Green. She wanted me to have something better than she and my father had had. The only talent I had was with figures – I always topped the class in mathematics at school. I wasn't going to get rich, or even comfortable, as a lawyer or a writer or a university don. The only thing to do was put me where the money was and see how other people made theirs.'

'Did she trust you? I mean, did she think you would make your money honestly?'

'Yes, she did.' He was silent for a while, eyebrows drawn down in a deep frown. Conscience rarely troubled him and when it did he was at a loss at what to do about it; it was like a social disease one didn't mention in polite company. But he mentioned it now: 'I never told her how I made my first profits. I saw that the bank's richest customers all owned property. So I embezzled £200 of the bank's money –'

'You *were* good at figures, weren't you?' She was wrapped in a sheet, but she tried not to sound like Justice. At least she was not blindfolded.

He grinned, all at once completely comfortable with her. 'I was also a good forger – I had to forge the manager's signature. The bank never found out. I went out and bought a plot of land for £150 and three months later sold it for £400. I put the £200 back into the bank's accounts and nobody was any the wiser. And I had £250, my first capital. By 1939 I'd left the bank and gone to work for estate agents in London. I had £2,000 capital by then, all from buying and selling property, and I used to stay back at the office at night and go through the firm's books looking for bargains in property. When war broke out I was on my way.'

She had put her hand up and was idly stroking the back of his neck. She felt comfortable with him now, comfortable with herself, was not troubled by conscience. She had made a commitment and found to her surprise that she had got more than she had hoped for. She liked being made love to by him, the man old enough to be her father.

'What a pity Hitler interrupted you.'

Hitler had caused only a brief interruption in his career. But he had told her enough of his knavery; confidences, like flattery, could be taken too far. He did not tell her how he had immediately volunteered for the army, not out of patriotism but because he knew he would be deferred because he was the sole supporter of his widowed mother. He had volunteered because even then, at the start of a war that might last as long as the Great War or even longer, he was looking well ahead: when he eventually became successful he did not want to be branded as a man who had dodged war service. He was duly deferred and posted to a reserved occupation in a food factory, where he made more money on the black market selling the factory's products. He had seen it as stealing

101

from the rich, the government, to give (well, sell) to the middle classes; he would have sold to the poor, if they had had enough money to pay his prices. He did, however, work hard at the factory and by the end of the war was assistant general manager and was awarded an MBE. A year after the end of the war he bought the factory with the profits from selling its products on the black market, going back to the bank where he had started his career for the extra finance he needed for the purchase. He would like to have told her that bit, since she had a sense of humour, but he thought he would keep that until he was more certain of her.

'Hitler interrupted everyone,' he said piously. 'When the war was over I went into army disposals. I sold everything the army no longer wanted – blankets, jerry-cans, lorries, guns – everything. I made a packet and I was on my way. My mother died in 1950 –'

She made a sympathetic noise. She wanted to ask him about his wife; but didn't. She had the feeling that he was going to give bits of himself to her, piecemeal, and she was prepared to wait. Naked though he was, she was beginning to realize she had never met a man who had so many layers to him.

'I bought my first newspaper, a suburban one down in Kent, in 1951. Two years later I bought my first provincial paper. By then I knew I wanted something more than just money. Now let me tell you something –'

'Yes?' She was patient with him. In a way he was like her father, every lesson had to be prefaced by stories of his own experience.

'If you're going to get to the top, never fool yourself. I mean don't kid yourself you're honest when you're not, don't have a double standard about scruples. The way television, commercial TV, is going, the only criterion will be how much money a programme makes. That's why I invested in it – you should think the same way. You may make a reputation, get a little fame, but nobody in television is ever going to go down in history. The picture lasts only as long as you see it on the screen and even when they make tapes they eventually destroy them. In the end all that will count is how much money you made out of it.'

She did not agree with him, but she didn't argue. He had the obsession she had heard from other men in the newspaper game, the reporters and columnists and editors: TV pictures would never last as long as the printed word. She thought she knew the power of television; she wanted to be part of it. But she felt uneasy at how easily she was accepting his cynical approach. She knew she could not be like that, never. She drew the sheet closer round her, feeling a little chill.

'Would you mind if I finished up rich? Met you on your own terms?'

He smiled, sure of himself. 'I've been to bed with rich women. It makes no difference under the sheets.'

Rich men, poor men, it made no difference: they all liked to boast of their conquests. She wondered if she should tell him of her fortnightly teas with the Misses St Martin. Or hadn't he thought of his visits to their girls as conquests?

'Will you talk to them at United then?'

'Yes,' he said and all at once felt uncharacteristically nervous: he had come to what looked like a fork in the road, an unexpected one. 'But I hate to interfere –'

'Interfere with me,' she said, knowing the value of vulgarity in bed.

6

When she had arrived at St Aidan's House on Saturday morning she had been shown to a guest-room by Mrs Cromwell. On Saturday night she slept with Jack Cruze in the big master bedroom. She was wakened on Sunday morning by the drapes being hauled back and sunlight flooding her in the huge bed. She rolled over, blinked at the silhouette against the glare.

'Please, Jack –'

'His Lordship's gone over to Chequers – the Prime

Minister called him first thing this morning. Time to get up, I've got me housework to do. The maid's sick.'

'A house this size and there's only one maid besides yourself?'

'His Lordship don't like too many people around him. They come in and clean the house during the week, when he ain't here. It's the way he's always been. He likes his privacy about his private affairs.' She trod on the word *affairs*, squashed it flat.

'Could you give me a little time to wake up, Mrs Cromwell?' It had been a disturbed night, with Jack waking her up as if to let her know what the latest score was. But she hadn't minded. She had been a year without sex and she had been hungry for it. 'Then I'd like to have a bath.'

Mrs Cromwell was bounding around the room, bending and straightening like a fussy hen, picking up His Lordship's clothes where he had dropped them, fluffing up cushions in chairs. 'Do you want some fresh flowers in here? Some don't like flowers in a bedroom.'

Cleo sat up, pulling the sheet up around her. 'You don't seem surprised I'm here. Do you approve or not?'

'It ain't my place to approve or disapprove. You're not the first and you won't be the last. His Lordship's always been very keen on the leg-over. All men are. My Sid used to be the same – still is, I suppose. He just don't have the stamina any more. The working classes wear out quicker, I suppose. You want me to bring all your clothes in here?'

'Yes, please.'

She was moving in, though she did not know for how long. All she could hope was that she did not fool herself.

After she had bathed and dressed she toured the house and grounds. The house was larger than anything she had ever seen as a guest. It had been built during the Restoration and added to over the next hundred years; it displayed all the rational comfort and order of that period. She wandered through the long halls, admired the Mortlake tapestries, ran her hands almost sensuously over the Grinling Gibbons carvings, stopped by windows to admire again the landscaping by Capability Brown. In the huge library she found books on the family who had built the house; they had not been king-makers but they had known the uses of power. She wondered if Jack had known the family's history when, as a twelve-year-old, he had dreamed of owning this house some day.

She walked down through the park, stood at the end of the long avenue of beeches and looked back up at the house. Her first impression was not of the power that had once, and still, resided in the great house, but of the peacefulness of the park that surrounded it. Yesterday's storm had cleared the air and sounds travelled smoothly on it: the tolling of the church bell in the distant village, the hum of a car going up a nearby lane, the song of a thrush somewhere beyond the beeches. Money could buy this sort of peace; and if one were powerful, one probably needed this occasional escape. She felt strangely at ease, but she knew the mood could not last, a thought which unsettled her. She wondered if, given the circum-stances, she could spend her life in such peaceful surround-ings, insulated against the storms and stresses of the outside world. And decided she couldn't.

She was too much her father's daughter. He had never settled for peace and security, as Brigid had wanted him to: they would have killed him as inevitably as some terminal disease. They might not kill her, but they would render her unhappy and useless. She had become Jack Cruze's mistress, but she could not settle for being that alone.

He drove up the avenue as she began to walk back towards the house, in a scruffy-looking estate van. She got in beside him and kissed him like a good wife, or good mistress. He smiled in satisfaction, proud of himself.

'You look proud of yourself. Is that because the Prime Minister sent for you?'

'No, it's because of you.' He meant it. He could not remem-ber feeling like this since he had first fallen in love with Emma. 'You like it here, don't you? We'll come down here as often as we can make it.'

'Every chance we get.' Then she said, 'Will you speak to them at United tomorrow?'

'You never let up, do you?' But he was in high good humour. The PM had asked him for advice this morning; last night he had enjoyed more physical and emotional satisfaction than he had thought he was still capable of. He would give her anything she asked for. If he could give the PM what he asked for, the least he could do for Cleo, the best of them all since Emma, was to give her the same. 'I'll ring them first thing in the morning. Just one thing – don't make a fool of yourself.'

'I'll let you be the watchdog.'

'I shall be.' He felt immensely protective towards her, like a true lover. Or father: but he put that thought out of his mind at once.

SIX

1

Across the Channel, in the Dordogne in France, Claudine Roux looked steadily at her brother, who had always fooled himself.

'Roger, I heard rumours about a cover-up in Vietnam last year. You were supposed to be involved.'

'Where did you hear that claptrap?'

Roger Brisson spread some Périgord *foie gras* on toast, poured himself another glass of the estate's Monbazillac. He appreciated the rich life, which is not always so with the rich who have inherited it; he savoured everything it offered, like a poor man who had won a lottery. It was one of his few endearing qualities, if indulgence is endearing. He sometimes regretted the wilfulness that had made him choose the army as a career, but now he saw the army as a proper discipline, one that he needed. He had joined the army against the wishes of his father and almost solely for that reason. But there had been another, lesser reason: in one of the rare moments when he had looked at himself objectively, he had decided that, as the wild playboy he then was, he had been heading for disaster. He had no confidence that he could reform himself; in a reckless moment he had chosen the army to do it for him. There had been times at West Point when he had been on the verge of resigning; ironically and perversely it had been his father's continued resentment of his choosing an army career that had kept him in it. He had served in the Korean War, distinguishing himself for his leadership and his bravery under fire. His father had eventually come to accept

107

him as a soldier with a future and, without ever mentioning the surrender, withdrawn his objection to Roger's army career. By then it was too late for him to resign from the army; he needed it more than it needed him. It was the only institution that would not indulge him as the rest of his small world, his family, his wife and his friends, had done.

'You know what rumours are like in wartime. They're as numerous as bullets.'

'Don't lie to me, Roger.' Since she had become head of the family, Claudine had become more domineering than their mother had ever been. But he tolerated her with good humour, she had relieved him of responsibilities heavier and more boring than the army laid on him. 'Did something go wrong out there?'

'No.'

He had been called before the GOC and asked to explain why he had ordered the cleaning out of An Bai – the word 'massacre' had not been used.

'You were stupid, Roger,' the GOC had said. 'Maybe the village *was* a nest of VCs –'

'That was what Intelligence told us.'

'Okay, so it was. But we don't kill women and kids –'

Contrary to what the briefing officer had been told to tell the press conference, he had not been in An Bai on the day. He wished he had been: he might have been able to prevent what had happened. But it had been no more than a company action, it had not needed the presence of a brigadier-general.

'My orders were misunderstood. The troops, I'm told, were stoned out of their minds. They were meant to eliminate all the men, that was all.'

'You know enough to issue orders that can't be misunderstood. Your officers couldn't have been stoned out of their minds when you gave them the orders. It's a foul-up, Roger, but we'll straighten it out. Just lie low till we get you something Stateside. We don't want the goddam media making anything out of this.'

'What do I do now?'

108

'We'll move you to a base area. No announcement, but if anyone from the media asks, it'll be for health reasons.'

'I'd rather go back Stateside, if it's going to be like that.'

'That would only raise questions – you haven't been out here long enough to have completed your tour. You'll stay. But the men in the An Bai operation will be split up and posted either Stateside or to Europe. They may talk individually, but it's unlikely. Let's hope to Christ they don't. No soldier would want to boast that he gunned down women and children.'

'They're not soldiers, they're draftees. Nobody knows what they'll talk about or who to.'

'Well, we'll just have to trust to luck and some good old American decency. I don't want any report written, nothing at all. There was no action at all at An Bai on that day, understand?'

'Yes, sir. How long do you think it will be before I can go back Stateside?'

'I don't know. It could be another year. In the meantime be an inconspicuous base commander. I guess that will be a pain in the ass to a fighting man, but that's the way it's got to be. You made a mistake, Roger. You fought dirty in a dirty war and forgot to camouflage it.'

So he had gone to a base area, had dodged the media correspondents and spent a miserable twelve months. He learned that the Australian girl, Cleo Spearfield, had asked awkward questions at a briefing, but JUSPAO had stalled her; then her newspaper had recalled her and as the months went by he relaxed, felt safer from investigation. The only jarring note had been a visit one day from Major Pierre Cain.

'I thought you might like to know, sir – they are rebuilding An Bai.'

'Oh?' He kept his composure; he had always been a good actor. 'I'm glad to hear of any rebuilding that goes on in your country, Major. It's a change from demolition.'

'Yes, isn't it?' Cain, too, was a good actor; and he had inherited a bland, inscrutable look from his Annamese mother. He continued in French, 'I must warn you, General.

109

Certain of my countrymen know what happened at An Bai.'

Roger Brisson's French was as fluent as Cain's. 'Major, that matter was taken out of my hands. I know nothing about it.'

'Of course not, General. Still, I thought you'd like to know about the rebuilding of An Bai. The problem is, they have to move in a whole new community. There are no survivors of the old one.'

Cain saluted and left. Roger's aide, who spoke only English and that not always well, said, 'Was he giving you some shit, sir?'

'No,' said Roger. 'He was just recommending a new book by Racine.'

'Never heard of him, sir.'

Roger had felt safe with his tongue-in-cheek joke. Safer than he had felt in his conversation with Major Cain.

Then at long last his transfer came through; not Stateside as he had expected, but command of a division in NATO. He was promoted out of the way, a solution not necessarily confined to the army. He applied for two weeks' furlough before taking up his command and now here he was at the Brisson château near Souillac, enjoying the rich life till Claudine had tried to spoil it. He had been surprised and annoyed to find her here when he had arrived.

'I've been promoted to major-general and I'm on my way to my new command – it's as simple as that. I suppose you got your rumour from one of your newspaper friends.'

'I got it from one of your Pentagon friends. He didn't say what it was, just that you had been promoted out of harm's way.'

'Some friend. Who was it?'

'Never mind, we'll forget it.' She did not believe in pressing people, especially blood relatives, who did not want to talk. She was an empress who would never have used the rack: it only distorted the truth as well as the victims on it. She sipped her wine. 'They tell me this is going to be an excellent vintage year. Not much quantity, but top quality. A relief, after last year.'

They were lunching on the terrace that looked down the steep hill to the tree-lined Dordogne River in the narrow valley. Down there the campers' tents were huddled together like canvas tenements, everyone having a dogged holiday. August was the month when the French fled the congestion of their cities and towns to crowd together along rivers and down on the Riviera and on the beaches of Brittany and Normandy. A month of it, then they would go home, having proved their individualism. Up here on the terrace the two Americans, proud of their French blood, sat in splendid isolation.

The Brisson estate had been in the family for six centuries, since the reign of the quarrelsome and undistinguished Louis X. Survival had been a Brisson talent and the family had succeeded in choosing the right side, or at least in not antagonizing too much the wrong side in the wars and struggles of the succeeding centuries. Like the present-day French, they had been down south on what passed for a fourteenth-century vacation when the Black Prince of England had massacred the citizens of Limoges. In 1789, hearing rumours from Paris, they had abruptly become the most generous *seigneurs* for miles around, raising wages, kissing workers' babies, cutting down on all ostentation. Then, when they saw from the writing on the château's walls, the first samples of *graffiti* they had ever seen, that the peasants were not impressed, they took the hint and set a record time for the coach journey from Souillac to Bordeaux. There they had boarded a ship, hiding themselves in wine casks, thinking of themselves as vintage quality, and escaped to England. Unimpressed by the English who were unimpressed by them, they had sailed on from there to Louisiana, where an adventurous member of the family had already established a plantation.

The Souillac branch of the family hated the colony and the constant quarrels amongst the Americans and the British and the Spaniards and had been relieved and delighted when Napoleon invited them back in 1802. Since then the family had chosen the right side to vote for, but its fortunes and numbers had dwindled until finally one of the Louisiana

111

Brissons had come home. Members of the family were still scattered around France, like semi-precious stones, but the one remaining jewel was Claudine, who had inherited the estate from her father. She was la Comtesse, but she never used the title outside the estate. Comtesses were ten centimes a dozen.

'Why are you over here at this time of year?' asked Roger. 'You usually don't come till October.'

'I've bought Farquhar Press, the London publishers.'

'Whatever for? You're always buying headaches.'

'I have only two headaches, Roger. You and the *Courier*.' She had a third, her son Alain, but she never confessed to anyone that he troubled her. 'Ah, Louise!'

Louise Brisson half ran out on to the terrace; she always seemed to be running, as if chasing invisible buses. Her friends back in New York referred to her as a long-suffering wife, but there was no hint of suffering on her amiable, pretty face. Twenty years ago she had landed the catch of the season; she still enjoyed him, if only seasonally. She had always seen what a vain, philandering man Roger was, but she had thought that all he needed to bring out the hidden character in him was a good discerning woman; the first cave-woman had told herself the same thing as she recovered consciousness after the first blow with a club. As time went by Louise was discerning enough to see that there was no hidden character; it was all there on the handsome glittering surface. She had sensibly settled for less when she told herself there was no more, and never would be.

'I've been over in Brive, ferreting around in a little shop there.'

She was a collector, of anything and everything; it was mostly junk, but she never admitted as much. Her home at Sands Point on Long Island was a museum of trivia and it delighted her; she felt herself surrounded by bits of other people's lives and that helped soothe her secret loneliness. *Objets d'art*, antique furniture, paintings: she never felt that *they* were bits of people's lives. She would rather have had a jar of Rembrandt's brushes than one of his paintings. She was the despair of her sister-in-law, but it never worried her. She certainly would not care to be surrounded by any bit of Claudine's life.

'You should never be allowed out of America,' said Claudine. 'This foreign air goes to your head.'

Louise had no French blood, but each time she came to France she was more French than the French. She dropped into a chair, spread her legs as if practising for the can-can. 'Roger, *chéri*, pour me some wine. Oh, isn't it a marvellous day! On days like this I just want to sing and make love!'

'Don't attempt both at the same time,' said Claudine. 'It might produce a hernia.'

Roger smiled indulgently at his wife. He loved her sincerely and always had, but he knew he could not resist the lure of other, younger women. He had never formed any permanent, or even semi-permanent, relationship with the latter: they came and went like recruits in boot camp, and he always enjoyed coming home to Louise. She was a perfect soldier's perfect wife, a solidly established base to fall back on. Strategy and tactics were as important for a good marriage as for a good war.

Louise returned his smile, raised her glass to him. 'I'm just glad to have you home from that dreadful war, darling.'

'I understand we have no chance of winning it,' said Claudine.

'That's not true,' said Roger.

But he did not want to talk about the war, not if Claudine had heard rumours from Washington, even if they were stale rumours a year old. He now regretted what had happened and admitted that he had been over-zealous. An Bai had been a festering sore for almost a year before he had ordered the attack on it; it was known that it harboured Viet Cong, though Intelligence had not been able to determine exactly how many. Villagers had been brought in and interrogated, but it had been like asking questions of statues. Frustrated, angered by an ambush that Intelligence thought had originated from VCs working out of the village, he had ordered the cleanout operation. His orders *had* been imprecise: he had

113

meant all adult males to be eliminated, not the whole of the population. Something had got out of hand: maybe his orders had been misunderstood, maybe all the troops had been so stoned that the massacre had become just a party for them. He had interviewed the lieutenant in charge of the operation, who had not been on drugs. The lieutenant had been distressed to the point of collapse at what had happened and had insisted he had done everything he could to stop his men in their indiscriminate killing but had been unsuccessful. He, a junior officer who would have received his orders down the chain of command, had not queried those orders at the interview; he seemed more concerned with protecting his men from the consequences of what they had done while under the influence of drugs. If he had later queried the orders, when he had calmed down and was able to look at the whole mess in perspective, it seemed that he had kept his queries to himself. He, unlike the grunts under him, had been a career man; maybe someone higher up had talked him into the proper priorities. Roger did not know and had never gone back to enquire. He had turned his back on what had happened and hoped the lid would never be lifted again on what had been dumped in the latrine.

'I'm on furlough. Let's forget the war,' he said. 'How's the *Courier* doing? You said it was a headache.'

'It's not doing well at all, it's lost money for the last five years. I don't know what the solution is, except to turn it into a tabloid and hope for the best. Which I would never do. While I was in London I looked at successful papers there, ones like the *Mirror* and the *Examiner*. I'd never let the *Courier* sink to that level.'

'Personally,' said Louise, 'I'm going to miss the *Daily News* while we're here in Europe.'

'Why don't you sell the *Courier* then?'

Roger had never taken much interest in the family fortune. Each year his dividends came to him with a statement of the family holdings' finances; he looked at the figures on the dividend cheque and rarely, if ever, read past the first page of the financial statement. All he knew was that each year

114

the cheque was bigger than the previous year's and that, as far as he was concerned, meant he did not have to worry. He was possibly the richest man in the US armed forces, but to talk about it or even think about it would be shameful. He had his standards. West Point, the home of so many impoverished officers, had taught him those.

Claudine looked at him as if he had suggested that she should sell herself. 'If you bothered to look at the paper's constitution and refresh your memory, you would know that we cannot sell our stock unless there is a one hundred per cent takeover bid for the *Courier*. Father wrote in that clause when the paper went public forty years ago. He wanted us to have the controlling interest or be out of it altogether, so that if it should be turned into a cheap rag, our name would no longer be associated with it.'

'What are the stock holdings?' Louise, a wealthy man's daughter, had no interest in money other than the spending of it.

Claudine wondered how she could be related to two such irresponsible fools. She herself had never worshipped money, though she had a proper respect for it. One could be as well bred in financial etiquette as in anything else.

'I have thirty-five per cent and Roger has ten per cent of the *Courier* – we hold those through the holding company. The other fifty-five per cent is owned by general stockholders, none of whom, as far as I can remember, has more than ten per cent.'

'Then if the paper is such a loser, why don't you get all those stockholders together and suggest you look for a buyer?' Louise's eyes sparkled with her idea, as if she had just discovered the secret of alchemy.

Spenders, thought Claudine, have orgasms of piety when they suddenly have a thrifty notion. 'If you can find a buyer, I'll do that. So far I don't think we could even give it away. Haven't you noticed how many New York papers have died in the last twenty years? The *Herald Tribune*, the *World-Telegram*, the *Journal-American*. Father would be sick to his stomach if he could come back and see what has happened.'

115

Pierre Brisson had loved his newspaper and the newspaper world. 'I had a faint hope that I might be able to persuade Lord Cruze to buy it lock, stock and barrel, but he just shook his head and said it wasn't his cup of tea. The English seem to do all their thinking over cups of tea.'

'Lord Cruze? The man who owns the *Examiner?*' Louise might not worry herself about money but she knew who had it. 'But he'd turn the *Courier* into the sort of cheap paper you're talking about. A snappy tabloid,' she said, sounding almost wistful for such a thing in the family.

'I shouldn't care, if he bought us out completely. Then I could turn my back on it.' Claudine had a back for turning: all empresses have them. 'Well, where are you going to live in Germany?'

'Somewhere around Heidelberg,' said Louise. 'The army has a house for us, but I thought I'd look for something better. You know what army houses are like.'

Claudine didn't; she did not believe in slumming. 'It's a pity you are not further south. There are some pretty villas in Baden-Baden.'

Despite his love of the rich life, Roger smiled at the two women. 'I don't want to get on the front pages of the tabloids. The *Daily News* would have a field day if it learned an American divisional commander was trying to live like Mad Ludwig of Bavaria.'

'Very sensible,' Claudine conceded. 'None of the Brissons has ever been on the front pages. We should not start spoiling the record.'

No, thought Roger. So don't encourage rumours by listening to them and repeating them.

2

Louise found a very attractive house on the hills behind Heidelberg, half an hour's drive from Roger's divisional headquarters. The rent was three times what the army allowed its senior officers, but that was no problem for Louise.

The house did not compare with any of the castles of the mad King of Bavaria, but it had hints of Rococo style that did not seem entirely appropriate for a United States army general. Pearl-handled pistols might be an accepted adornment, though Roger had more taste than that; and a personally designed, braid-encrusted cap might be tolerated on a top general. But a copy of the Amalienburg at Munich was not a setting from which an American general should emerge each morning. But emerge from it each morning Roger did, and to hell with what his driver or his aide or the local natives thought. He was happy, as always, to be back with Louise and she was happy, too.

One of the first correspondents to interview Roger when he took up his appointment was Tom Border, who was on roving assignment.

'I'd rather you didn't write a piece on me, Mr Border. It would look too much like using the family paper for self-advertisement.'

Tom thought self-advertisement would never have worried Major-General Brisson. 'I just thought you might like to make a comparison between a command here and the one you had in Vietnam.'

'Were you in Vietnam?' He had never been friendly with the press out there, even before An Bai. 'Not with the *Courier*?'

'No, sir, not with the *Courier*. But I was out there for over a year. All through '68.'

Roger was suddenly aware that he might have stepped into a minefield. For the first time he looked carefully at this bony, untidy young man, noted the withdrawn look in the dark eyes. Was he imagining it or did so many of today's young have that withdrawn, prove-it-to-me look? Even his nephew Alain had been wearing it last time he had seen him. Youth was growing too thoughtful; it had been different when he was young. Yet he knew he could not be more than fourteen or fifteen years older than this Tom Border.

'One can't compare it, Mr Border.' What he meant was that if war came to Europe, it would be a nice clean war, the enemy easily recognizable. The Russians would never wear

117

black pyjamas, try to look like coolies, be your laundry-boy during the day and your killer at night. 'I really do think it would be better if you interviewed someone else in my command. Someone who doesn't have an interest in a newspaper,' he added with his famous charming smile.

'I'm sure I can find someone like that, General. But you're unique – there's no other divisional commander here who's had combat experience in Vietnam. There are some GIs but no commanders.'

'Well, maybe you can get something from those GIs.' That was a mistake, he realized at once. He had no idea where the men who had taken part in the An Bai operation had been posted. They could be here in Germany, walking booby traps. 'Look, I'll have my aide take you around the division. You can write anything you like, but keep me out of it except for naming me as divisional commander. Spare me my blushes.' He had not blushed since his nurse had tickled his testicles when he was six months old.

Tom Border declined the offer and went off wondering if General Brisson was troubled now by what had happened at An Bai a year ago. But he could not pursue that line, not if he wanted to go on working for the *Courier*. He was enjoying the freedom that the *Courier*'s roving assignment gave him and though the expenses were not what the *New York Times* and *Time* men got, it was more than the Mid-West chain had paid him. He would pay the bill to Truth when it faced him, but he was not at this stage going looking for it. He had been corrupted by an expense account.

He thought of Cleo more often than he cared to. On his second day in Paris he had seen a dark-haired girl with marvellous hips swaggering down the Champs Elysées and he had followed her, an apology on the tip of his tongue. He was both disappointed and relieved when the girl turned round and he saw that she wasn't Cleo. It was that day that he decided to go to Germany: Paris was too close to London. Lovers are more haunted by the living than by ghosts.

SEVEN

1

'I like that swaggering walk of yours,' said Roy Holden, the producer. 'It denotes confidence and that's what we want on this programme.'

Cleo had grown tired of being told that she swaggered. She never did it consciously; it was just the way her body moved. It was the way her father walked but she hated to see him swaggering down the street, like a riverboat gambler turned politician, confidence oozing out of him. She had confidence, but she did not like to think it oozed out of her.

'Having told you that, I don't want you to start exaggerating your walk.' Holden had played rugby for Oxford and wore his club pullover at all times, summer and winter, not to boast of his Blue but to hint to strangers that he hadn't always been fat and lazy-looking. He had a pleasant plump face and a kind heart, which he attempted to hide since kind hearts, in television, were supposed to belong solely to compères of quiz programmes. 'After all, this is supposed to be a serious programme.'

'I thought it *was* a serious programme.'

'No, love. *Panorama* is serious – *Scope* is only meant to *sound* serious. We package information, wrap it up nicely so that the low-brow and the middle-brow viewer can ease his confidence that he hasn't devoted all his viewing time to watching Morecambe and Wise and *Bless This House*. But it's flimflam, Cleo, nothing more. We show it on Sunday night, but I don't know anyone who has gone out on Monday morning to mount a crusade on anything we've shown. That's another thing –'

119

'What?'

'We have to work on your delivery. You say show-en, like most Australians – you all love to throw in a free syllable. And you speak too fast, most of you. I think the Australian drawl is a myth, except on certain words. Most of you *gabble*. And we can't have gabble, not when we're talking down to the masses.'

'Is that what you do on *Scope*?'

'Not only on *Scope*. We don't want any fancy phrases, leave that to the trendy writers in the *Sunday Times* colour mag. Dull stuff is what we want, no long sentences and no polysyllables. Plenty of pauses – we'll fill those in with visuals. And you have to hit certain key words. You must *never* overestimate the *public*'s attention span. The public like to hear the word *public* – it makes them feel we recognize them.'

Cleo had heard a lot of cynicism in Fleet Street, but here at the Kennington studios of United Television it seemed to hang in the air like pollution. Or perhaps it was only in the offices of *Scope*. She had noticed a certain cynicism in the staff's welcome to her when she had arrived to start her two weeks' training. When her training was finished she was to be given a small guest spot for the first two weeks, then she was to be one of the three permanent reporters on the series. The spot for a guest reporter was to be eliminated; she had no doubt that she would be resented by those who had regularly filled the guest spots; they were all men and no man liked being put out of a job by a woman, especially one with what she had to sell.

Lord Cruze's name had never been mentioned, but she was sure that everybody knew whose favourite she was. She had her own cynical amusement at the thought. A man on his way to the top could sleep around and it was looked upon as no more than the deserved fruits of his success. If a woman with the same ambitions went to bed it was taken for granted that it was a means to an end.

She took to television at once. She was totally unafraid of it. She could ignore it when necessary, confide in it, treat it

120

as an accomplice in a joke: which meant that she accepted the audience as her partner. On the Monday morning after her first programme the television critics in Fleet Street swallowed their natural jealousy and lauded her. She was not an overnight star, but she glimmered enough to belong to the sixth magnitude in television's constellation.

Jack Cruze, against his own inclinations, was delighted with her success. 'But it means you're going to be recognized in public from now on.'

'You mean you don't want to be seen with me in public from now on.'

He worked his eyebrows in a facial shrug. 'Well, I do like to be discreet.'

'Jack, everyone in Fleet Street knows about us by now.'

'Well, yes . . . But I don't think the general public wants to know, does it?'

'Jack, I shan't embarrass you. If the general public stops me in the street and asks me, I'll say we're just good friends.'

'There you go, more guff.' But he kissed her, since they were in his flat and protected from the general public, and he felt proud and pleased and in love. So far he had not confessed that latter feeling to her.

2

A month after Claudine arrived back in New York there were widespread demonstrations throughout the country against the war in Vietnam. The *Courier* ran editorials backing the Administration's pursuit of the war; but Claudine knew now that the war, if not lost, could not be won. She would not, however, have tolerated the *Courier*'s saying so.

Her son Alain came home from Montana where he had been working on a ranch. The sight of him thrilled her as it always did: she was beautiful herself and she deserved to have such a handsome son. But he did look scruffy, as if he had just come straight from a cattle round-up and had not stopped to bathe or change. In the elegance of the

121

Roux penthouse he looked very much out of place, a cowboy hippy.

'You look marvellous,' she told him. 'Healthier than I've ever seen you look. Life on the ranch suits you.'

'That's what I'd like to do eventually. If it's all right with you, I'd like to take the place over.' The ranch, on the Yellowstone River, was part of the Brisson holdings, purchased by Henri Roux at the end of World War Two. Claudine had been there once, but was not at home there. 'A little more experience and I could manage it okay.'

'Why have you come home then? You've only been out there since mid-summer.'

'I'm home for just a few days. The guys from Yale are putting together a group for next Saturday's demonstration. I want to be with them.'

She knew about the demonstration, the biggest, its organizers hoped, that New York had ever seen. 'That's ridiculous! Leaving your job, coming all this way ... If you wanted to protest, why couldn't you have done it in Montana?'

'Stay out of the way, you mean? Keep the family name in the background? Don't worry, Mother – no one is going to pick me out of the thousands who'll be there on Saturday. It will be the size of the crowd that will count, not the names amongst it.'

Though handsome, he might be overlooked in a crowd, she thought. He was slim and only medium height and could be overshadowed by bigger, burlier men; but she knew he would not allow that. His vitality would draw attention to him; there was a restlessness about him that attracted the eye. He got up now and began to pace about the apartment.

'The war's over, Mother. Or it should be. Nixon and Kissinger are trying to find a way out – we're going to push them. America's lost its first war and we're prepared to admit it.'

'I'm glad your uncle isn't here to hear you say that.' Not that she really cared two hoots for Roger's feelings.

'Uncle Roger is intelligent. He knows what's what. But of course he's like all the intelligent generals – there are a few of them – he can't admit the truth. Not if he wants to stay in the army.'

'I don't think we should discuss it. I just wish you had stayed in Montana, that's all.'

He came over and kissed her. 'Mother, you're getting old.'

'I am not!'

'Yes, you are. You're shutting your mind to everything you disagree with. That's a sign of getting old.'

'You young are so free with all your wisdom.' She smiled and kissed him in return. But he had wounded her.

An hour later, bathed and changed and (thank God, she thought) looking more presentable, he went out to visit friends. After he had gone she went out on to the terrace of the penthouse. This apartment building was one of the older ones on Fifth Avenue, built long before they had been called condominiums. The Brisson family had owned the penthouse ever since the building had been put up in 1910 and Claudine had always loved it; just as she loved New York, or anyway, Manhattan. She looked down the Avenue towards the lights coming on in the buildings along Central Park South; sometimes, she thought, they looked like electric gulls nesting on a long cliff-face. Further downtown, in a narrow gap between the skyscrapers (she still used the term; which, perhaps, did make her old), she could see the floodlit radio tower on top of the *Courier* building. The *Courier* owned a radio station which, unlike the newspaper in the building beneath it, continually returned a substantial profit. From this terrace she could also see several of the office buildings that belonged to the holding company. Her father and her husband, for all their faults, had left her an empire worthy of her.

She went back into the apartment, paused in front of one of the mirrors in the huge living-room. It was called the living-room by the maids, but it was too big for mere living in, unless it was meant to accommodate a ballet troupe or a commune of interior decorators. It was a transplanted Paris salon of the Empire period; it had been her mother's choice and Claudine had not changed it. She had never been one to assert her personality with possessions; she had been born to

123

the best and she was content with it. Particularly with the mirrors, of which there were four in the room: she thought of them as truly French, designed to compliment any woman who looked into them. She looked into one of them now, deciding that Alain, like so many of the young, did not know what age really was.

But all at once she felt lonely.

3

'The Americans always do things so much bigger, if not always better. Even their demonstrations.' Roy Holden looked out on the huge crowd in Central Park with smiling approval, as if the Sermon on the Mount was being re-staged for television. 'I was here to cover the civil rights marches and demonstrations. Tremendous! They made the Aldermaston marches and the Tariq Ali demos look like bus queues.'

New York, without the demonstration, had already thrilled Cleo; it was everything she had expected it to be. As the BOAC plane had come in over Manhattan she had pressed her face against the window like a child window-shopping at Christmas. In the shining October air the city did actually seem to glitter, as she had read so many times that it did; almost as if the city council sent helicopters out each morning to spray the buildings with decorative sparkle. She felt a certain excitement, was tempted to become an instant immigrant. But Tom Border had told her it was a tough town, far tougher than London. She was doing well enough where she was and she should settle for what she had.

She had been surprised when Holden, who produced her segment of *Scope*, had come to her and told her they were going to New York. 'The other two units are already committed. So it's us, love. I told Simon you could do it –' Simon Pally was the executive producer. 'You can, can't you?'

'Of course.' She had done three shows and already she felt a veteran.

124

He hugged her with a fat arm. 'Cleo, I love your confidence. In anyone else I'd think it was conceit, but with you it's not. You really don't let anything faze you, do you?'

Ah Roy, if you only knew. There had been a mild argument with Jack. He had complained that since she had been a television reporter as well as a newspaper columnist, he was seeing too little of her. She had been surprised at how possessive he had sounded, as if she had been his mistress for years instead of weeks. She had been fazed then, by his jealousy.

'Jack, what about you? Your time-table is just as busy as mine. More. If you're not in your office you're in the House of Lords or you're somewhere on the Continent –'

'I'm back here in the flat most nights. Every night, almost. That's when I want to see you. But you're gallivanting all over the place with these young chaps –'

'Is that what's worrying you? That I'm with *young* chaps? God, you're so unsure of yourself –' That sounded funny even in her own ears.

He had looked at her in genuine astonishment. Then he had burst out laughing and she had taken advantage of the moment to end the argument. She laughed, too, then kissed him and pressed herself against him. She was learning what a mistress could use.

'Relax. The young chaps never get any of that.'

He had held her to him: possessively? No, lovingly. But she did not expect love from him, at least not a declaration of it. 'Cleo, I miss you when you're away. I wouldn't have spoken to them at United if I'd known you were going to be gallivanting –'

She kissed him again. 'I'll be all yours for thirteen weeks in summer. We can gallivant anywhere you like then.'

'Summer? Another nine bloody months. I'm not going to put up with it for that long –'

She gently got out of his arms. 'Jack, we can always call it off –'

That frightened him, but he was experienced enough not to show it. He had been frightened before, once or twice in business, once with a woman. He kept his voice steady: 'No,

125

we shouldn't want to do that. We enjoy each other too much to break it off – you're the best thing that's happened to me in ages –' There: she couldn't expect more of a declaration than that. 'No, we'll work it out.'

She felt suddenly suspicious. 'Jack, you won't go to United and interfere, will you? That *would* finish it for us.'

He had had that in mind; but he saw the fierce, if controlled, antagonism in her. 'Of course not. We'll just – we'll see each other every moment you're free. Spend all our time together.'

'I'm not going to move in with you, Jack.'

That was something he had *not* had in mind. But for a moment he considered it, then discarded the temptation. None of the others had ever been invited to live with him: you could take commitment just so far. 'All right, I know how independent you are. We'll work it out. Take care in New York. The place is full of muggers, they tell me.'

'I'll have all the young chaps to look after me. They're very protective of me.' It was the wrong thing to say. You could joke with young lovers about other young men, but not with an older lover. She had to go back into his arms, kiss him again. She suddenly felt very protective of him, or anyway of his ego. 'Let's go to bed.'

Now she was in Central Park, being protected by the young chaps in the crew as the vast crowd milled about them. There was much noise and movement, but so far no violence; the police, on foot and on horseback, had kept to the very fringes of the crowd. Banners waved in the air; they reminded Cleo of battle flags she had seen in medieval tapestries. But these were not battle flags, unless this was a war against war. Girls and boys, often looking like sisters in their identical dress and long hair and granny glasses, presented single flowers to the young policemen, who smiled and took them but watched warily, made cautious by the very size of the crowd. The older policemen, who had seen a war or two, did their best to look patient and understanding; but some of them wondered whatever had happened to patriotism, what was happening to America. A small group of middle-aged men, wearing Legionnaire caps, stood under a big American flag; they looked out of place, pathetically brave, like Indians in a July the Fourth carnival. Young blacks wandered amongst the crowd, skirting the policemen with cold suspicion whenever they happened upon them. But that was another war, one already won on paper if not in fact.

'I thought there'd be more Negroes,' said Cleo.

'Negro is a taboo word, love. Blacks is what they are. They've stayed away because they think they're cannon fodder anyway, no matter what war is being fought. I shouldn't mention them, Cleo. That's an American family argument, not ours. I don't think we should look like holier-than-thou Limeys. Stick to the theme, that these kids are against the war in Vietnam. You'll find plenty of articulate talking heads.'

Cleo recognized many of the articulate talking heads, the hippy radicals who had been featured so much even on British television. She looked for someone new, looked again and again at the dark-haired young man weaving, side-stepping, like a rugby fly-half, in and out of a group whose banner said, in neat Baskerville lettering, that it was from Yale. He seemed to be keeping everyone laughing, had enough energy to win a war on his own. Or stop one.

She pushed her way towards the Yale group, spoke to a girl who looked the archetypal American college girl, like someone held over from the Fifties: short blonde hair, sweater, skirt, long socks and saddle shoes, Sandra Dee outfitted for battle.

'Who is that chap, the one in the yellow sweater?'

In the noise of the crowd Cleo thought the girl said Al Roo. The girl shouted, 'You're English, right? You want to interview him? Hey, Al!'

Alain Roux danced rather than pushed his way through the crush, put his arm round the girl, kissed her on the cheek and laughed at Cleo. 'A convert to the cause? Where you from?'

'London,' she shouted; then gave up, backed out of the crowd, beckoning to him as she went. He looked at the blonde, laughed again and followed Cleo. When he caught up with her they were on the outskirts of the crowd and the noise. She said, 'I'm from United Television in London – a programme called *Scope*. I'd like to interview you.'

'Why me? All the names are here –' But he took her arm, helped her up a slope and found a spot where they could imagine the illusion that they had some privacy. He held out his hand. 'Hi, I'm Alain Roux. R-o-u-x.'

'Cleo Spearfield.' Then his name penetrated, as if the sound of it had been delayed by the noise below them. 'Roux? Would you be any relation to Mrs Claudine Roux of the *New York Courier*?'

He sighed, though she didn't hear it, and looked away from her. He had never felt burdened by his name till the last two years at Yale. Then the strident support of the *Courier* for the war in Vietnam had been embarrassing amongst the men who were his friends; having an uncle who was a gung-ho general had not helped either. He had always been proud of his Brisson heritage; he had majored in History and developed a sense of it. The Roux heritage was respectable but only middle class: he would never admit it to anyone, but like his mother he was a snob. But since nobody, not even his mother, had yet discovered the fact, he was liked by everyone, even inferiors.

He looked back at Cleo. 'Does that make any difference?'

'No. Well, yes, I suppose it does. I know your uncle, General Brisson ... May I interview you or not?'

'If I say no, will you mention that I was here?' He gestured at the crowd, a hundred thousand or more.

'I think in that crowd you can be as anonymous as you wish.' In her column she might state that amongst those present were ... but on television you never mentioned just names, you had to show faces. To be amongst those present in front of a television camera was to be on the cutting-room floor.

Suddenly he laughed: he had a full-bellied laugh. It reminded her of her father's, though it was not as practised. 'Okay, get your camera up here. Ask me anything you want.'

128

She asked him all the usual questions: why are you against the war, what do you hope to achieve with this demonstration, what is your solution to the problem of the war? She got the usual answers: there was nothing new to be said. The slogans at home were as war-torn as the soldiers abroad.

Then she said, 'Your uncle, General Brisson, has been quoted as saying that the only acceptable end to the war is an American victory.'

Alain winced only slightly. 'My uncle is a professional soldier, doing his duty. But this is a political war, not a military one.'

'Some people would say that all wars are political.'

'Or religious. But they still have to be fought by ordinary men who have to be led by professionals.' He knew he must sound as if he did not totally condemn the Pentagon and he wondered what his friends would say if they came up the slope to hear him. He was ambivalent in his feelings towards his uncle, but he was not going to attack him in public. Brissons just did not do that to each other.

'The *Courier*, of which your family is the biggest stockholder, is very much for the war.'

'I don't write the editorials for the *Courier*. I wish I could, but that's not the way it works on newspapers. I'm sure you don't write the commercials that pay for this programme, right? But you'd like to, right?'

She would ban all pet food commercials, all close-ups of dogs golloping their chunky meals, of cats licking their lips like Chinese emperors who had just executed another hundred enemies. But United Television's programme directors would tell her to mind her own business. 'I take it you haven't been drafted, Mr Roux?'

'I got a deferment to finish my course. I got this yesterday.' He reached into his pocket, took out an envelope; it was so perfect it looked staged: 'It's my draft notice. I have to report next week.'

'Will you report? Or will you dodge the draft?'

'I think that's between me and the draft board.' He

laughed, not at her but straight into the camera, as if his only audience were the youth of the world.

'Cut!' said Roy Holden. 'Marvellous, Mr Roux! We'll use all of that. Maybe we'll come and do an epilogue when you're in the stockade or wherever they'll put you.'

Alain laughed again, but Cleo watching him, saw that this time the laugh was a little forced. 'I'll send you a postcard.'

As he turned to go back down the slope to rejoin the Yale group Cleo said, 'Would you have dinner with me tonight if you're free?'

He looked at her, eyebrows raised. 'That's a switch.'

'I don't have any designs on you. I'd just like to talk to you.'

'Sure, I'll be glad to. Will you call for me?'

She smiled, liking him, a young chap. 'I'll do that. Whereabouts? I don't know New York at all.'

He gave her the address on Fifth Avenue. 'I'll be waiting for you downstairs. I don't think you should meet my mother until I know what your intentions are.'

Cleo, for reasons she didn't bother to examine right then, did not mention she had already met Claudine Roux. 'Eight o'clock. I'll let you choose the restaurant. *Scope* will be paying, so no expense spared.'

'Oh, to have an expense account,' said he, too rich to have one.

He was waiting under the canopy outside the apartment building when she drew up in the cab. He suggested a restaurant on Lexington Avenue. 'It's one of the few truly French places in New York. The food's so good the proprietor won't serve you any drinks that deaden the taste buds. Only aperitifs, nothing else. My mother goes there when she wants a quiet meal alone.'

'Will she be there this evening?'

'She's at the Met. She appears there regularly. She's one of their non-singing prima donnas.'

The restaurant was intimate, a bijou establishment where Cleo could see Claudine Roux coming in alone and yet not seeming alone: the staff would pay court to her all evening

The food was as good as Alain had promised, a change from Mrs Cromwell's sensible dinners. Cleo had had far too many of them in the past few months and had begun to wonder if *her* taste buds had been deadened.

'Do you get on well with your mother?'

'Well enough. We have the usual thing between the generations these days. I mean we argue about the war, things like that. What about you and your mother?'

'My mother's dead.'

'Oh. Your father?'

'We never argue. Dad's always right, so my brothers and I just agree with him. It's easier.'

'What does he do? Is he in newspapers or TV?'

'He's a politician.'

'Oh God.' She noticed that he didn't swear, or at least hadn't done so in front of her. She wondered if that was the influence of Yale or his mother. 'They're the worst sort, aren't they?'

'Not necessarily.' She had to defend the absent Sylvester. She knew that, for all his faults and egotism, he would defend her to strangers. 'There are worse.'

'For instance?'

She had to think. 'Self-made men, the achievers. The ones who can't understand why their kids don't want all the material things. My father isn't like that.'

'Do you want all the material things?' He seemed unaware of his smug position, the heir to the throne.

'Yes, a few of them. I'm no idealist, if that's what you're looking for.'

He shook his head. 'No, I don't think I am. That blonde girl this afternoon – Joan Temple. We talk about it, but we've decided we're from the wrong side of the tracks to be idealists. Both our families have too much money. Oh, I know,' he said, reading the unspoken remark on her face, 'money should be no barrier. But it is, when it's all tied up the way our money is.' She looked at him, saying nothing, and after a while he nodded. 'Okay, I want it both ways. Now you think I'm a hypocrite.'

131

'Not at all. I want it both ways, too. I'd like to be a £50,000-a-year idealist. That way, when I got to Heaven, I'd be seated with only the best. I'm an élitist idealist.'

He raised his glass to her, a Corton-Clois du Roi '61, ideal for élitists. 'The best sort. Now where do we go after dinner? Your place or mine?'

'We go our separate ways. I'll put you in a taxi and pay the fare and tell the driver to see you get home safely.'

'Do you have a boy-friend or a husband?' He had noticed she wore no wedding ring, but that meant nothing these days.

'Yes.' Jack would be flattered to be called a boy. 'Your mother has met him. Lord Cruze.'

He laughed, full-bellied; the intimacy of the place was shattered. The head waiter looked towards them reproachfully, but Alain didn't see him. 'Really? Oh boy, can you pick 'em!'

'Do you know him?'

'Only what I've read about him in *Time* and *Newsweek*. He's the successor to Lord Beaverbrook, isn't he?'

'He wouldn't like that. He thinks he's an original.'

'Is he? I mean for you?'

After a pause: 'Yes.'

He had stopped laughing and was watching her. At last he said, 'Why did you have dinner with me? I really thought this was going to lead to bed.'

The thought tempted her for the moment. 'I don't know. I just wanted to have dinner with a young chap.'

He was sharp, like his mother. 'Lord Cruze is a bit ancient?'

It was her turn to laugh. 'Not quite. He's fifty, fifty-one – I'm not sure. You may not believe it, but men at that age are not past their prime. Righto, don't ask,' she said, reading the unspoken remark on *his* face. 'I'm not going to discuss what he's like as a lover. We get on very well together.'

'But ...'

'Well, yes. But ...' She changed course. 'I didn't tell you before – I've met your mother. At Lord Cruze's. I was quite impressed by her – she's a formidable lady. I wanted to see what sort of son she'd raised.'

He wasn't offended: he had become accustomed to being examined as part of his mother's handiwork. 'Are you planning to do something on her? You'll never get anywhere near her, you know. Not for TV.'

'I'm not planning anything. I just wanted to see what was behind the First Lady of the New York press – that's what they called her in London.'

'Do you have that ambition? To be a First Lady?' He *was* sharp.

She liked him enough to be honest with him. 'Yes.'

'Well, good luck.' He sounded as if he felt sorry for her. 'Are you impressed with my mother's son?'

'Yes. You're a credit to her, if that's not too much of a put-down on you.'

He smiled; he had remarkable resilience. 'No, I see what you mean. Mother is, as you say, a formidable lady. But she's also a very good mother. It can happen, you know. Is that what you want to be eventually? A formidable lady and a good mother?'

'Did you take feminine psychology at Yale?' She paid the bill with her American Express card. She wondered if the accounts department of United Television would query why she had to take out a rich woman's son. 'I don't know about the formidable lady bit. I think your mother has more steel in her than I have. I mean that as a compliment.'

'Maybe.' He was flattered that she thought he understood feminine psychology. He'd seen no evidence of it himself, not with the girls he had known. 'There's still time for you to develop it. The Empress didn't always have it.'

His mother was the Empress to him, too. But Cleo made no comment.

When Cleo got back to her hotel on East 39th Street there was a message that Lord Cruze had called. She looked at her watch, saw that it would be two o'clock in the morning in England, decided not to call him and went to bed. At six o'clock the phone rang.

'I rang you twice last night. Where were you?'

'Jack, I'm only half-awake. Don't start on some sort of inquisition.'

There was a pause, then: 'Sorry. But I missed you. I thought you might have called back.'

'By the time I got in, it was too late. I didn't want to wake you.'

'Where were you then, that it was so late?'

'It was late *your* time, not here. I'd been out to dinner.'

'Who with?'

This is ridiculous, she thought; but kept her tongue under control. 'With Alain Roux, Mrs Roux's son. I interviewed him.'

'What's he like?'

Young, handsome . . . 'A bit like his mother. A snob, I think.'

'Did you see her?'

'No. Do you want me to?' She didn't know why she said that, except perhaps to put some edge to her tongue.

He caught the sarcasm. 'There you go again . . . When will you be back?'

'We're flying out tomorrow night.'

'Have dinner with me Monday night.'

'All right. But Jack – this time let's go to a French restaurant. I've gone off sensible English food.'

'Just so long as you haven't gone off Englishmen.' He laughed, but at 3,500 miles he sounded as if there was static in his throat.

5

On Sunday morning Alain told his mother that he had had dinner with Cleo. 'She sent you her regards.'

'How did you meet her?'

'She interviewed me.'

'What about? Us?'

'No, the war and the demonstration.'

'She did that at dinner? For her column?'

'No, the dinner was private, just social. She did the interview yesterday afternoon for her TV programme.'

'What did you tell her?'

'The same as I've told you. That I'm against it.'

They were at breakfast in the small breakfast-room that looked out on to the terrace. Claudine was having her usual croissant and coffee; but Alain was eating ranch style. She saw him gorging himself on bacon and eggs and brown hash (from a supermarket freezer for the metropolitan cowboy) and it only increased her annoyance with him.

'You should have been more discreet. God knows what the British will make of such a thing. Their newspapers love to snipe at us – they've never forgiven us for the War of Independence. I suppose it's the same with their television.'

'Are you afraid they'll snipe at us Brissons?' Both of them always thought of themselves as Brissons.

'We've kept our name out of the papers and off television. Up till now, that is.'

He played her at her own game: 'Okay, Mother, let's not discuss it. Oh –' He took his draft notice out of his hip pocket and laid it on the table. 'I got that on Friday.'

She knew at once what it was, though she had never seen one before. 'Why didn't you tell me then?'

'I wanted to think about it.' He ate a mouthful of bacon and egg, chewing on it with an abstracted expression on his face, as if he were having breakfast alone and he was wondering what he would do with this free Sunday. Then he swallowed and looked across at her. 'I'm going to go.'

'Where? Canada or wherever they all go? Sweden?'

'There's no war in Canada or Sweden.' He smiled, being patient with her. 'No, I'm not going to be a draft dodger. I'm going to Vietnam, if that's where they're going to send me. I'll bring you back the truth of what's going on out there.'

She didn't want the truth, not if he had to risk his life to bring it to her. 'When will you be going?'

'Pretty soon. They don't waste any time. I shan't go back to Montana, I'll report straight from here.' Then he pushed his plate away from him and looked directly at her. 'I don't know if I'm doing the right thing. But it would hurt you more if I did split for Canada, wouldn't it?'

No, it would not: but she could not separate her public image from her private self. She wondered how some mothers could proudly send their sons off to war, as the *Courier* editorials were always obliquely suggesting. 'I have friends – perhaps we could have you posted to some army post here at home –'

She was surprised at the anger in his face; but all he said was, 'No, Mother. No string-pulling.'

Later, when he had gone out, she went into her bedroom, shut her door against interruption by one of the maids, and wept. It was the first time she had shed tears since his birth.

That evening she went to Mass at St Patrick's Cathedral and prayed for his safe return. She went home confident that God had listened to her. She didn't ask much of Him, but when she did she expected service.

Alain reported with his draft, but found he was not expected to join the other draftees going to boot camp. He was being sent south to another camp to start an Intelligence course.

'How do I rate that, sir? I thought I should learn first how the army works.'

'You've done six months ROTC, okay?'

'Yes, sir.'

'Then that oughta give you an idea how the army works.' But the captain behind the desk, battle-scarred with cynicism as much as anything else, looked up at him. 'You also got an

136

uncle, General Brisson, right? I guess he told you all you need to know, right?'

Alain knew then that strings had been pulled after all, not by his uncle but by his mother. 'I'd rather go to boot camp first, sir. I did that ROTC bit when I first went to college. I dropped out – they said I'd never make officer material.'

'They don't say anything here about making you an officer down at this course. All it says here is that's where you gotta report. Here's your ticket. North Carolina oughta be pretty nice this time of year. Give my regards to your uncle, if you ever see him.'

Alain didn't blame the captain for his attitude. 'I'll do that, sir.'

He thought of calling his mother, blasting her for pulling the strings as she had done, then decided it would be a waste of time. She would tell him she didn't want to discuss it.

In the train taking him south he looked out at the countryside, grey-green, faded red and brown, like a tinted etching, under the fall sky. A small town went by: a white church steeple, a neon sign above a tavern, tattered bunting flapping in the wind above a used car lot. A man on a horse (a horse? Alain tried to look back, but the man was already gone from view) waited at the railroad crossing like someone from another era: a messenger who had arrived too late, he thought. *Oh Christ, do the messages ever get through in time?* He was twenty-two years old and he was beginning to think that no one ever listened to him, least of all his mother.

He began, for the first time, to think of dying in Vietnam. Up till now the thought had not occurred to him, but now all at once he was frightened by it.

A girl stood in the aisle beside him. 'Is this seat taken?'

'No.' She was no knock-out, but she was attractive and looked cheerful. 'It's all yours.'

She sat down, arranged herself as some women do, as if taking a long lease on where they've planted their bottoms. Then she looked at him. 'I was watching you from across the aisle, I was in that window seat there. You looked lonely. Sort of sad. You're going into the army, aren't you?'

137

He looked at her with a spark of interest. 'How did you know? You're pretty perceptive.'

'I just know. I study boys your age, the ones who have to go to the war. What were you thinking about? Your folks, your girl-friend?'

'Me.' All at once she was a nuisance. 'Actually, I was thinking about being killed.'

'You shouldn't. Think about living. Jesus will take care of you.' She put her hand in the large cloth bag on her lap, then handed him a booklet. 'He takes care of all of us. It's all here, in this book.'

'Do you ride the trains looking for guys like me?' He said it facetiously.

'Yes,' she replied, seriously.

Suddenly, against his whole nature, he wanted to shout at her, be cruel to her. What made her think Jesus had all the answers? The priests at his prep school had lost him years ago; their messages had never got through. He had run away from them and now, out of kindness, he got up to run away from this busybody.

'What's your name, miss?'

'Lola Ann Fluegler.'

'Well, Lola Ann, when I meet up with Jesus, I'll tell Him you're busy spreading His word. But if you should be talking to Him, ask Him why He doesn't stop the goddam war.'

'It's a war against Communism, against the Anti-Christ.'

Oh God, he thought, how old is she? The same age as myself, younger? What would she be like in middle age? Still riding trains, looking for young men to fight the Anti-Christ?

His anger all at once ran out of him. 'I'm sorry, Lola Ann. Some day you're going to be sadder than me.'

He went down the aisle, his legs abruptly weak, hardly holding him up against the swaying of the train. He wondered if, after all, he might be killed, if at some crossing in Vietnam the pale horseman, Death, would be waiting for him with the final message of all.

7

He went to Vietnam three months later, in February 1970. Within a week he learned from the grunts, the men who were fighting it, that the truth was that the war could not be won. Two weeks later he was wounded, when the Jeep in which he was travelling hit a land-mine. The two men with him were killed and he sustained wounds to his knee that meant he would limp for the rest of his life. The doctors and nurses in the field hospital were surprised that he could laugh about it.

'It could have been worse,' he told them. 'I was looking for a horseman with a message.'

They guessed he must have been stoned out of his mind when he went into action.

EIGHT

1

The Sixties went out and the Seventies came in. Politicians, economists, philosophers, fashion designers and astrologers were asked for their opinions on the decade ahead. They were all cautious and the man in the street suffered from platitude sickness.

Over the next year Cleo became more and more well-known. If Cleo Spearfield wasn't exactly a household name, like Bird's Eye fish fingers or Spillers dog food, it did conjure up a face and figure for millions of television viewers. Her column was moved to a more prominent place in the *Examiner* and occasionally the paper featured her picture on its billboards. She was herself at last, her own woman, no longer Sylvester Spearfield's daughter. She was still Lord Cruze's mistress, but such a distinction was not the subject of common gossip in the households of Britain.

The fantasy of the Swinging Sixties died away, like a slowing swing in a children's playground when everyone has grown up and moved on. A few still struggled to keep alive the euphoria: boutiques, bistros and pop bands; but it was like Paris of the Twenties, kept going for the tourists rushing to experience it before the Depression of the Thirties took root. No one expected another Depression in Britain, something like that could never happen again, but a certain exhaustion had set in. The British had been too long out of training to become marathon hedonists.

Labour went out of power to be replaced by the Tories and Mr Heath. The latter, a bachelor, an organist and a racing yachtsman, three pursuits the voters didn't expect from their Prime Ministers, came in with a lot of goodwill from everyone but the far Left and the old guard Right. As time went by he would find that the middle ground in politics is often where the shooting range is just right from both extremes.

Cleo and Jack Cruze's relationship settled into a sort of freelance marriage: there was no contract but both kept working at their alliance. Cruze continued to win events at horse shows, Cleo's presence no longer tangling his reins; the male members of the horse set gave Cleo mental pats on her flanks and told each other she was a fine mare. She played hostess at the Cruze dinner parties, even persuading Mrs Cromwell to experiment a little with the menus: Mrs C. went so far as to make her raspberry flan with French pastry but that was as far as she was prepared to stray beyond national boundaries. Sometimes, in the quiet hour after such dinner parties, Cleo marvelled at her own ease amongst the company Jack had invited; hostessing, like prostitution, is a trade for which some have a talent and some don't. She charmed ambassadors and Cabinet ministers and tycoons, if not always their wives, and held her own in the dinner table conversation; that was something she had inherited from her father, something for which she did not resent him. She and Jack went to Antibes in the summer and joined a Greek shipowner for a Mediterranean cruise on his steam yacht; she appeared on deck in a bikini and the Greek at the wheel almost ran the yacht straight into Italy, so blinded was he by lust. Jack Cruze, stomach tucked in, muscles painfully bulged, felt pride as he saw the young chaps gloating over her. He told himself his money hadn't bought her, just made a down payment: now she loved him for himself. Though so far she hadn't said so in so many words.

The war ground on in Vietnam: everyone seemed to know it was finished but no one knew how to stop it. Edward Kennedy, shaking the waters of Chappaquiddick from himself, began to be heard again; Irish Indians once more began circling the White House. President Nixon retreated from America, the country held at bay by a two-man wall,

141

Haldeman and Erlichman. Americans turned to a television star for a guide to what to believe: Walter Cronkite became the American Pope.

'I'd love to have that sort of influence.' Cleo and Cruze were sitting in his study looking at a CBS clip featured in a *Panorama* programme on the American scene.

'Forget it.' Jack Cruze was at ease, in pyjamas, dressing gown and slippers. Cleo had begun buying his clothes for him, but Turnbull and Asser, when told for whom she was buying, had cut their labels out of their shirts and pyjamas and gowns: they knew a poor advertisement when they heard of him. 'You're too good-looking to be influential. If ever a woman is going to have that sort of influence in this country, she's got to be the homely, motherly sort. Like they have in detergent commercials. You come on the screen and half the men in the country say, I wonder what she's like in bed? They're not listening to you because they want to be re-assured.'

'What about the women? Maybe I could influence them.'

He shook his head. 'They like you, I think. But if you and Mrs Whitehouse ran against each other in a by-election, she'd romp in.' Mrs Whitehouse had come to prominence in the past couple of years, leading a detergent crusade against smut on television. 'She's married and doesn't shove her chest out the way you do.'

'My chest would have nothing to do with it.'

'Let me tell you about breasts. When I bought the *Examiner* it was a dull newspaper that backed the Liberal Party and sold about as many copies as the Libs had paid-up members. The English have always loved tits, so I gave 'em to them. In brassières, of course – that was 1955, remember. You couldn't have Anthony Eden and bare tits on the same page. Circulation doubled in a year, trebled within five years. I don't know whether the Libs continued to buy the paper, but the Labour voters came in from all over the country. The average British working man loves tits and bums more than he does the Welfare State – give him a choice of Raquel Welch for a weekend and a top pension for life and see what he takes. In

1964 we backed Labour to win – I'm a Tory, but I knew who the *Examiner*'s readers were going to vote for. On election day we featured a girl with the biggest tits in London, a Labour rosette on each nipple and that was all. People laughed and the intellectual Labourites, the dons from the universities, said it was disgusting. But it helped Labour win. In the New Year's Honours List a little while later Harold Wilson gave me my life peerage. He still calls me Lord Tits when we're alone.'

'Well, if I put a Union Jack on each breast –' she hated the word *tit*, but let him use it, 'maybe they'll vote for me.'

'You missed my point. They didn't vote for the girl with the tits. They all knew what she was, a come-on for them to buy the *Examiner*. She was part of the ballyhoo of the campaign, but it was what we said in the editorial that counted with them. If we'd run a picture of Mary Wilson, as nice a woman as you can find, with rosettes on her tits, Labour would have been swamped. Be satisfied with what you've achieved so far, Cleo. You're the best-looking reporter in this country, but you're no female messiah.'

Don't tell me what I should do! But she didn't say that, just got up and switched off the television set. 'I'm going down to my flat. I have some reading to do.'

He had bought her a flat in this building and she had moved into it, against her better judgement. It was nowhere near as large as his duplex, but it was bigger than the flat in the mansion block in South Kensington, and it looked out on to Green Park, a view she found both attractive and restful. She knew that he had never bought a flat for any of his previous mistresses, though he had paid the rent for some; he had certainly never brought any of them to live in the same building as himself. It was tantamount to asking her to live with him, a proposal of some sort of marriage, and she had realized that, by her acceptance, it had been a commitment for both of them. Much more, she suspected, than either of them had bargained for when she had first gone to bed with him that weekend at St Aidan's House.

'What sort of reading?' On the nights when they did not

143

sleep together he liked her to stay up here with him until he was ready to say goodnight.

'I'm going to Hamburg tomorrow. *Scope* is doing a piece on the NATO exercises.'

'Dammit, you're off again! I wanted us to go down to Antibes. I've rented a yacht.' He had never bought a yacht because, with their high running costs, he had never been convinced they were a sound capital investment. He still counted the pounds, if not the pennies.

'You didn't tell me.'

'I'm telling you now. It was meant as a surprise.'

'Jack, you should know me by now – I'm not the sort of girl who's thrilled by surprises.'

'You're too bloody phlegmatic.'

She didn't think she was, but she let him have that one. 'Anyhow, I'm a working girl. I can't just buzz off whenever I feel like it. Or whenever *you* feel like it,' she added with some asperity. 'I wish you'd get that into your baronial head.'

'Don't start calling me *my Lord* or we'll have a ding-dong argument.' There hadn't been any real arguments, just mild rows that left a sour note for no more than an hour or overnight, the sort of aperient that married couples occasionally use to clear the air. 'You're always trying to prove your bloody independence.'

'You mean I'm not independent?'

'Of course you bloody well are!' He had to force the words out but he knew he could not argue with her as he had with the others. He had never been afraid of losing any of them. 'But sometimes you act as if you have to hit me over the head with it.'

If she had, she had not done it intentionally; but she realized at once that it did no harm to let him think so. She recognized a worried lover, the best kind for an independent-minded woman to have.

'Jack –' They never used any terms of endearment, except in the frenzy of sex; it was almost as if they felt that was some sort of public troth. 'You know what my work means to me. I'm not giving it up, no matter what.'

144

No matter what? But he was afraid to ask. 'All right, I'll phone Antibes and call it off. But I wish you'd let me know what you're doing. It seems to me that I have to fit into your spare moments.'

He sounded pathetic, like a neglected wife. Her sense of humour came to the rescue. She laughed, went to him and kissed him. 'I'll be back on Friday afternoon. Take me to Paris for a dirty weekend.'

'How can I? You have to be here in London for your bloody telecast.' He held her to him, loving her but still unable to tell her. 'You bugger up my feelings, Cleo. There's nothing worse than an ambitious woman.'

She stayed in his arms, though he didn't deserve even that much. 'What about an ambitious man? Do you think we women can handle them better than the other way round?'

No: Emma hadn't been able to handle him. 'Maybe you women are more adaptable. I suppose there are faults on both sides –'

'But women's are bigger faults? I mean, if they're ambitious.'

He kissed her on the cheek; he knew he couldn't win this argument. Not tonight, anyway. 'Have breakfast with me. Better still, stay up here tonight.'

'I have my period.' She hadn't; but it was better than saying she had a headache. 'I'll be up here at seven-thirty for breakfast. I have to be at the airport at nine-thirty.'

She went downstairs to her flat. She felt comfortable in it, if not completely at home. Jack had presented it to her complete and ready, as another surprise; she had had to furnish nothing, indeed had been left no room for any of her larger possessions. The same decorator who had designed the duplex had been engaged for this flat; it had the same anonymous taste, less masculine than Jack's but not feminine. The decorator, never having met Cleo, had played safe. The flat was sexless; a home, she thought, for a kewpie doll.

She was reading newspaper clippings that the *Scope* researchers had collected for her, underlining certain sections with a red pencil, when the phone rang. It was Sylvester, at eight-thirty in the morning in Canberra, ready for another day's fray in Parliament. He had always been more lively, more enthusiastic for the day, in the national capital than at home in Sydney. Brigid, who knew her man better than he realized, had once said that he had his own blood bank down at Canberra, in Parliament House.

'Sweetheart! I've been neglecting you!' She felt like a long-lost voter. 'You know how I hate to write letters –'

Neither of them was a regular letter-writer. 'It's good to hear you, Dad. Everything's all right, isn't it?'

'Everything's great, except we still have those same nongs in government. But we'll toss them out next time ... Madge is having another baby. So's Cheryl. I'll soon have a team of bloody grandkids – it's not going to be any good for my image –'

'What image is that, Dad? Has the Labour Women's League been courting you with scones again?'

He had his women friends, but he had never discussed them with any of his children. 'Sweetheart, I'm coming to London! The end of this week – I was going to drop in on you and surprise you. Then I thought I'd better not.' Everyone wanted to surprise her; as if she were a child. 'It's the usual politicians' junket – it's my turn this time. Don't quote me, but what I'm supposed to do I could do with a couple of airmail letters. But what the taxpayer doesn't know, he won't vote against ...'

'Dad, what's happened to you? Where's all that idealism gone?'

'I wouldn't have accepted the trip, sweetheart, if it hadn't meant I could see you for free.' But he laughed when he said it; the belly-laugh boomed down the wire, as if Australia itself had exploded with mirth. 'I'll be in London for a week. I've missed you, sweetheart.'

'I've missed you, Dad.' She had, too. She looked forward to their reunion, on equal terms at last. Though she could never tell him so. 'Let me know when you're arriving. I'll be at Heathrow.'

Only when she hung up the phone did it occur to her that

146

something she had put out of her mind was now unavoidable. She would have to introduce Jack Cruze to her father. She felt a little like she had done the first time she had gone to Confession at the age of seven. Even then the priest had been surprised at what she had to tell.

2

Tom Border had watched Cleo's rise from far and near; yet never near enough for her to notice him. He had avoided her, not as he would have avoided the plague but with a sense of sweet torture. He had read somewhere (he couldn't remember where: all the philosophers, like astrologers, were so contradictory) that love was the passion of an idle mind. At times he allowed his mind to idle, just to agonize with his love for Cleo. He found other women to distract him – if not his mind, then his crotch. There was a girl in London, one in Paris, one in Rome, one in Bonn: after all, he was a foreign correspondent, though he engaged in no correspondence with any of them. That, though he did not know it, he had in common with Lord Cruze.

He knew she was now Cruze's mistress; Fleet Street gossip penetrated even the foreign news bureaus. Especially the foreign bureaus – foreigners loved the dirt of England. He felt a sharp stab of jealousy every time he thought of her and Cruze together; fortunately, no pictures of them together ever appeared, not even in *Private Eye*. He could not have stood actually seeing them together: the thought was bad enough.

He was standing at the reception desk in the Vier Jahreszeiten Hotel in Hamburg when the voice he knew better than his own (for we all have a defensive tin ear to our own voices) said, 'If I buy you a drink, can we be friends?'

She had not changed in looks, except to appear more sophisticated; he had watched her every week he had been in London, so he had not forgotten a single feature or expression. He gave her his slow smile, which was very much out of rhythm with his heart. He felt like a callow schoolboy, but tried not to sound like one.

'It's your turn to shout. I'll have a beer.'

'Ah, you haven't changed.' She put her hand in his and led him across the lobby into the lounge. He did not allow himself to read too much into this gesture; he remembered how affectionate she had always been. But he had to force himself to let her hand go when they sat down. 'Tom, you look great! You're so – spruce-looking!'

If he was spruce-looking it was unintentional. He looked down at the pin-striped navy blue suit he had bought in the middle-class mayhem of a Harrods sale; it did indeed fit him better than anything else he owned. His blue button-down shirt and black knitted tie, having just been put on, had not yet had time to become untidy.

'I'll accept that. But you look better than spruce, Cleo old girl.'

'How's that? Give me a word.'

He hesitated, then decided on the truth: 'Successful?'

She ordered a beer for him and white wine for herself; then looked back at him after the waiter had gone away. 'I'm successful, yes. I just wish it didn't show so blatantly. I haven't forgotten that you said I was blatantly ambitious.'

She was still ambitious: he could see that. But all he said was, 'Let's just be nice and friendly to each other. What are you doing here?'

'Covering the NATO exercises.'

'Me, too. Did you know our friend General Brisson is coming up here for them? I met him last year down at Heidelberg. He's put Vietnam behind him.'

'I suppose that's natural. We are all, all of us, always putting things behind us.'

'Have you put it behind you? Vietnam, I mean. An Bai.'

She sipped her wine, wrinkling her nose: it was too sweet for her taste. She signalled the waiter and told him to bring her something drier. Tom noticed how she handled the small situation: quietly, adroitly, not making the waiter feel that he had made the mistake. In Saigon she had always been too

148

solicitous of the waiters, as if she had been a visiting trade union official bent on showing she was no better than the workers; there had been others, some of the army personnel, white Australians through and through, who had known no other way but to shout at and abuse them. Tom had come to know that some men, and women, would never learn how to deal with a waiter: the trouble would always be with themselves. He had learned exactly what the relationship should be, when to be personal, when to be firm, and good waiters appreciated the fine line that was drawn. He was not always successful himself, but Cleo, he saw, knew now how to draw that line.

'Yes,' she said, 'there's no point in remembering what happened at An Bai. It's been buried, probably deeper than the people who were massacred. No one in Britain would be remotely interested if I wrote a word about it. No, if I meet General Brisson I'll be as charming as I can possibly be. I'd like him on *Scope* if I could get him. He's so damned handsome and dashing in his uniform, we could re-run the programme on *Women's Hour* and the ladies would gush.'

He drank his beer, liking it: German beer had guts to it. 'You haven't become a women's libber, thank God. You wouldn't have said that about *Women's Hour* ... Brisson is staying with the British GOC at a villa down near Luneburg. You want to drive out with me this afternoon and see if we can see him?'

She hesitated. 'I'm not sure what Roy Holden, my producer, had in mind for me. He and the crew are at another hotel.'

He smiled. 'What are you doing here? Don't you slum with your producer and his crew?'

'Normally, yes. But I want a column out of this trip, too. I want to do a piece on how the burghers of Hamburg live, the rich ones. I don't know whether you're aware of it, but this was the only city in Germany that gave Hitler the cold shoulder. He came here only once, in 1933, and he never came back. The Allies fire-bombed the city – I've seen photos of what it was like. I just want to do a piece on the sort of

149

people who rebuilt it, if they are the real descendants of the Hamburgers who were part of the Hanseatic League. Anyhow,' she said, looking around her, feeling at ease and showing it, 'I always treat myself to the best, now that I can afford it. Or when the *Examiner* pays. In any case, what about you? What are you doing here?'

'The same. I'm treating myself – or anyway, partly. The *Courier* is paying about two-thirds of the cheque – they're still tight with their expenses. But if you come down to Luneburg with me, I'll even rent a Mercedes, instead of my usual Volkswagen.'

'I'll come.' She made up her mind abruptly. She not only put Vietnam out of her mind, but Jack Cruze, too. Which was harder: but she managed it. She had put Tom out of her mind, but now he was back and she was not going to give herself a headache trying to forget him. Not today, anyway.

3

In an apartment in Polsdorf, one of the better districts in Hamburg, the guerrillas were going over their plans. Conspiracy, more often than not, is a pursuit of the middle classes; as if the poor had neither the time nor the stamina for it. These four conspirators, two young men and two girls, were all university educated and came of families which put social standing as necessary for entry into a Hamburger's heaven. The parents planned dinner parties while their sons and daughters made ready for destruction.

'Brisson plays golf every chance he gets.' Kurt was the leader of the group. He had long dark hair and thin patrician features; he would not have been out of place in a painting of Florentine conspirators. 'He is playing a round this afternoon with the British general.'

'Kurt –' She was young, nineteen, careless of her looks, dressed like the boys in shirt and jeans; there was an intensity about her that might have worried older, more experienced anarchists. Her Marxist lecturer at the university had tried

150

to tell her that revolutions were better led by middle-aged revolutionaries, but she didn't believe a word of it; experience only weakened the spirit of anarchy. She believed there had not been enough women revolutionaries: she would join Emma Goldman and La Passionara in legend. 'The golf course is too open. We'll never get away ...' But she said it without fear, she invited death as another lover. 'He'll have bodyguards.'

'Of course he will. So will the English general, Thorpe. It would be good if we could kidnap them both, but that may not be possible. All right, we forget the golf course. We attack just after they leave General Thorpe's villa. Two streets away, out of sight of the guard at the villa. Here.'

They all looked at the map, then the second young man straightened up. He was short and stocky and had blond hair cut short, almost *en brosse*; thirty-five years before, he would have been featured on posters for Hitler's Youth Movement. His father was a colonel in the Wehrmacht and he had inherited his father's military mind.

'I know that street in that village. It is too wide for our purpose. The military driver would be able to swing his car round ours —'

'But we need a wide street so that we can have a clear escape route, don't we?'

The second girl did not want to die for the cause or any other reason. She was blonde and plumply pretty and was in the movement because she was in love with Kurt. She left the table — she had no interest in maps — drifted to the window and looked out. On the other side of the street two well-dressed women came out of a *konditorei*, looking as sleek as the cream cakes they had just eaten, and stopped by a boutique to look in at the Missoni knits in the window. That was her world and she wondered if she had left it forever. Less than half a mile from here her mother would be sitting at a window in the apartment on Harvest Weg bemoaning the loss of her other two daughters, Trudi's sisters, both of whom had married overseas: one in Brazil and one across the Alstersee. Her mother was like that: the wrong side of the city's

151

lake was overseas. So far her mother knew nothing of her devotion to Kurt: she was still on the right side of the Alster-see.

Kurt came and stood beside her, put his arm round her. 'We'll escape, darling. We'll celebrate in bed tonight.'

Rosa, the younger girl, looked at them with contempt. 'Stop that crap! Let's get back to what we have to do...'

They argued for another hour, true anarchists, but in the end Kurt prevailed. Leaders are necessary, if only to be blamed for everyone else's mistakes.

'We take him here then,' said Kurt, pointing on the map again, almost jabbing his finger through it. He had spent hours planning the kidnapping and now damned Gerd, with his damned military mentality, had created argument. 'Then we demand the ransom this evening. Five million marks.'

'We'll be rich,' said Trudi, with a bourgeois beam.

'Oh God,' said Rosa. 'It's not the money. We want it to finance other operations. But the object, the real point, is to show them that their generals are expendable. Like all leaders!'

'I was only joking,' said Trudi, but she hadn't been.

Gerd said nothing, only wondered why Kurt should throw his life away on this dumb blonde.

4

'We can only guess at the Russians' intentions,' said Roger Brisson, trying not to sound like a political general. But then so many of his colleagues were sounding political these days. From West Point to White House there were no longer any log cabins as a starting point. 'But we must be prepared. Does that sound too profound?'

He gave Cleo his smile, ignoring Tom Border. As soon as the two reporters had come into this sitting-room in the villa of the British commander, General Thorpe, he had sensed that the real interview, even if it never got into words, was with the Australian girl. Border could be fobbed off with the

152

usual non-committal platitudes. He began by trying one on Cleo, but he could see that it hadn't gone down. So he tried his famous smile.

'It doesn't sound very original, General,' said Cleo, 'but perhaps the politicians in Washington don't like originality in their generals?'

Come off it, Cleo! Tom looked hard at her, trying to warn her not to ruin *his* interview. After all, he'd set up this meeting.

But Cleo didn't glance at him, just went blithely on as if he were not in the room with her and General Brisson: 'You see, General, I suspect that politicians and generals live in two different worlds, that too often they are fighting different wars. Or is that too profound?'

Oh, what a smart-ass bitch she was! He wondered with part of his mind what she would have been like had he got her into his bed that night in Saigon. 'Not *too* profound, Miss Spearfield. Nonetheless, it is true. If the politicians had allowed the generals to finish off World War Two in Europe as the generals wanted, there might have been no need for NATO and I should not be here on these exercises. You won't quote me, of course?' He smiled again.

'Of course not,' said Cleo and gave him a smile in return.

God Almighty, Tom thought, all these goddam teeth! It was like looking at courting crocodiles.

'General,' he said, 'if I may get a word in –'

'In a moment, Tom,' said Cleo. She was in command here. GOC: Good Old Cleo. 'General Brisson, do you think the politicians or the generals are right in Vietnam?'

'No comment,' said Roger, the smile gone as if some rookie had insulted him.

'That's the real war right now, General. Surely you have some comment on it?'

Roger looked out of the window. Joe Thorpe was in the garden, pruning the last of his roses. Was he ever plagued by questioning reporters, did he have things he wanted to forget about Palestine, Malaya, Ulster? 'I prefer to leave questions like that to the men out there fighting the war.'

'Are you glad you are no longer there?'

153

'Are you, Miss Spearfield?' He knew it was a dangerous question as soon as he asked it.

'Very glad, General. I'm still haunted by dreams of what I saw at An Bai.'

She's lying, he thought: she means I should be the one who's haunted. He stood up abruptly. 'I'm sorry, I have to go.'

Tom said, 'But, General –'

'I'm sorry, Mr Border. I'm afraid Miss Spearfield has taken up your time as well as mine.'

When they were outside in the Mercedes Tom said, 'For crissakes, Cleo, did you have to lay it on as thick as that?'

'I couldn't stand his bloody smugness! I came down here with a perfectly open mind –'

'Like hell you did. I should have known better ... Where the hell are we?' He was driving blindly, had swung the car out of the villa's gates without thinking about which road to take back to Hamburg.

'You're going in the wrong direction. That sign back there said to Luneburg. Simmer down, Tom. I'm not going to write anything about An Bai, I told you that. But he sounded so damned superior and sure of himself, I just had to let him know that I, for one, hadn't forgotten what happened out there in Vietnam.'

'You let him know all right. Now shut up while I find a place to turn round.'

5

As they came down the steps of the villa Roger said to his aide, 'No more press interviews, Rod. Especially with that damned Miss Spearfield.'

'No, sir.' But Lieutenant Hill wondered why his boss should be so vehement about Miss Spearfield, who had looked quite a doll.

'I never talk to 'em,' said General Thorpe, short and thin, a red-headed terrier who bared his teeth at every newspaper johnny who came within a hundred yards of him. 'Damned nuisance, all of them. What's your handicap?'

That damned woman Spearfield . . . 'Eh? Oh, eight.'

'Jolly good,' said General Thorpe, whose handicap was eighteen. 'I hope you don't play for money?'

'Never.'

'Jolly good,' said Thorpe, who knew how rich his guest was.

He and Roger got into a staff car; in the front seat were a driver and an armed corporal. Hill and General Thorpe's aide got into a second car; they also had a driver and an armed guard. The tiny convoy pulled out of the garden of the villa; everyone in the cars was relaxed, including the two guards. Picnic duty like this was part of the perks of working on the staff of a GOC.

'I was here in '45,' said Thorpe. 'When the Jerries surrendered on Luneburg Heath. I was a young subaltern on Monty's staff.' That had been a good war, the last decent show of any real size. He felt sympathy for the American johnnies, trying to salvage something from the Vietnam show. 'We're promised good weather for tomorrow. October is my favourite month. All the damned tourists have gone home and are back at work. One can enjoy the countryside.'

'How do the local farmers feel about the manoeuvres? I guess we'll be tearing up a lot of their land tomorrow.'

'Farmers will always complain. It's in their nature. I always tell 'em their land will be cut up a damn sight worse if the Russkis ever come this far.'

A block ahead, on a side street, Trudi sat at the wheel of the stolen van. She had her blonde hair tucked up under a woollen cap and she was wearing dark glasses and was trembling with fear. Ahead of her, across the intersection, she could see the other stolen vehicle, the BMW, parked in the continuation of this side street. Dark glasses, or fear, blurred her vision and she could not distinguish Kurt, Gerd and Rosa in the BMW. But they were there and she wished that they weren't. She would rather that they had been delayed on their way to this rendezvous, so that she could have got out

155

of the van and walked away from this crazy, dangerous adventure.

Tom Border and Cleo, now on the right road back to Hamburg, came down the street. The mood between them had eased again but they were still a little wary of each other; they, too, were on manoeuvres of a sort. Night manoeuvres still lay ahead of them.

'Let me take you to dinner this evening. And no talk about An Bai or Saigon –' He still remembered the night in Saigon, his own An Bai when he had massacred his chances with her.

'I have to have dinner with the *Scope* crew. But afterwards?' She was stepping off a cliff, or anyway an embankment, but she could not help herself.

They were halfway down the wide residential street, Cleo looking out and admiring the comfortable houses with their window boxes and the solid front doors with their highly polished door knockers that caught the sun like small golden explosions, when the blue van shot out from the side street, narrowly missing the army staff car that had just gone past. It braked to a skidding halt right in front of the second staff car, then swung sideways as the staff car hit it. At the same moment a white BMW came out from the opposite direction and jerked to a stop beside the crashed staff car. Two men, both hooded, one carrying a pistol and the other a sub-machine-gun, jumped out of the BMW.

'Jesus!' Tom slammed on the brakes of the Mercedes, throwing Cleo forward; she threw out both hands and held herself off the dashboard. 'That's Brisson in that staff car!'

Then, above the hum of the Mercedes' engine, they heard the gunfire. The first staff car had pulled up and a uniformed soldier and two young men in sweaters and slacks were tumbling out of it. The soldier ran back towards the smash, firing his sub-machine-gun. The driver of the van jumped out and began to run blindly down the street, as if just wanting to get away from the shooting. The driver of the first staff car leaned on the car's bonnet, took careful aim with his pistol as if he were on a firing range, and dropped the running figure. As Trudi stumbled the dark glasses fell off

156

and she plunged face forward into the kerb, ruining her pretty face forever, though she would never know.

Cleo and Tom sat and watched the ambush; it seemed to Cleo to last for two or three minutes, but it was no more than ten or fifteen seconds. The guard in the crashed staff car, blood pouring from his face, was sitting side-on in his seat, spraying the white BMW with a narrow arc of fire. The driver of the BMW had dropped out of sight; then Tom and Cleo saw the door open on the blind side and the driver fell out on to the roadway. The guard in the staff car suddenly slumped back against the driver beside him, his sub-machine-gun pointing upwards. His finger was caught in the trigger-guard and bullets shot into the air above the houses opposite. A front door had opened and was abruptly slammed shut. Somewhere a woman was screaming, but Cleo couldn't see anyone.

The two hooded men from the BMW now came back round the van, backing away from the smash. One of them turned and shot the driver of the first staff car as the latter took aim again; the other, with the sub-machine-gun, shot the two young men in sweaters and slacks and the remaining guard. Then both of them ran across the road towards the Mercedes, the driver of the BMW, now on her feet, running after them. One of the men snatched open the rear door of the Mercedes, jumped in and put his Luger pistol against Tom's head.

'Drive!' he said in German.

The other two ambushers clambered into the Mercedes as Tom, white-faced and clumsy, gunned the motor without putting the car into gear. The pistol barrel was thumped against his head and Cleo, struggling to wake from this horrible dream, waited for the top of his skull to be blown off. At last he got the car in gear and it shot forward and raced down the street.

In the rear seat Rosa lay back and cursed obscenely, beat-ing her fists against the upholstery of the seat. Beside her Kurt and Gerd were silent, masked dummies with live guns in their trembling hands.

157

Tom drove the car as he was directed, at a steady seventy kilometres an hour, so that he would not be picked up for speeding. Kurt and Gerd were now in the rear seat beside Rosa and all three of them, still hooded, were hunched over so that as little as possible of them was visible to any passing motorist. But Tom and Cleo knew, without looking back, that their guns were still pointed at the back of their necks.

The Mercedes went out of the village along the main road leading north towards Hamburg. Then it turned off on to a side road and soon came to a track that led into a thick copse. Parked in the middle of the wood was a black van. Tom and Cleo were ordered out of the Mercedes and into the back of the van. Cleo stumbled in her high heels on the rough ground and Kurt, still on edge at how things had gone wrong, still shocked by Trudi's death, hit her across the back with a clenched fist.

'Cut that out!' said Tom, but Gerd hit him on the side of the head with the barrel of his Schmeisser. Tom, dazed, fell face first into the back of the van. Gerd pushed him right in, jumped in and pulled a black cotton sack over Tom's head. Then he turned and dragged Cleo in after him.

'There's no sack for you,' he barked in English. 'Pull your sweater up over your head. Do it!'

Cleo had hesitated, but at the tension in his voice she hastily slipped off her jacket and pulled her sweater up from the bottom, slipping her arms out and rolling it up over her shoulders so that it turned inside out and became an inverted hood. Gerd looked at her breasts in the flimsy lace brassière, but women had never interested him sexually. Part, if only a small part, of his rejection of his parents' society was their convention of who should love and live with whom. He loved Kurt, but so far had managed to hide it, even from Kurt.

Kurt and Rosa took off their hoods, got into the front seat of the van and two minutes later they were back on the main road, heading north again. Then they headed west along a side road and a little later turned off on to a track that led up to a farmhouse hidden amongst some trees on the crest of a slight rise.

The farm belonged to Kurt's parents. They did not work the farm themselves but rented out the fields to a neighbouring farmer; the farmhouse was no more than a summer or weekend retreat from Kurt's father's crowded life as a Hamburg lawyer. His parents at present were in London; they were to be away a week, plenty of time in which to hold General Brisson here and collect the ransom money. But everything had gone wrong and Kurt had driven here almost automatically, as if he could not start thinking again until he was back in familiar surroundings. He had spent his boyhood vacations here when his life had been happy and uncomplicated, and the only anarchy he had subscribed to was that of a child's temper.

He ran the van into the barn beside the house; then Cleo and Tom, still unable to see where they were, were taken into the house, led up some steep stairs and pushed into a room. Then the sack was removed from Tom's head and Cleo was told to pull her sweater down.

Kurt, Gerd and Rosa were still hooded, all dressed alike in dark sweaters and jeans. Cleo had seen countless pictures of terrorists, bank robbers, kidnappers: there was a uniform now for criminals. Even the guns looked familiar: the Schmeisser and the Luger had become standard issue, at least for European terrorists.

'Do not attempt to escape, it will be useless.' Kurt stood under the single light in the bedroom and pointed with his Luger at the boarded-up window. 'The shutters are also bolted on the outside. If you give no trouble, you will be all right.'

'Who are you?' said Rosa. They all spoke English, Cleo noted. Continental education was preparing its youth for all contingencies: the Common Market, international terrorism ... 'Are you tourists?'

Tom realized that the girl had recovered, though the men

159

still seemed tense and nervous. She might be the leader of the gang before the day was out, if she was not already.

'No, we're not tourists –' But his tongue had got away from him. It would have been better to have claimed to be no more than tourists.

'Who are you, then?'

Tom looked at Cleo and shrugged. 'My name is Border, I'm with the *New York Courier*. Miss Spearfield is with the London *Daily Examiner*.'

Rosa ignored Tom then, looked at Cleo with interest. 'Lord Cruze's newspaper?'

Cleo, still very conscious of the guns trained on them, was having difficulty in holding herself together. She had been afraid but never cowardly in Vietnam; this was different, the threat here was more personal than the random mine in a roadway. The odds were shorter; these guns could not miss if they were fired.

'Yes.' Her voice was as dry as a crow's.

Rosa lifted her hood above her mouth and spat. She was given to theatrical expressions, but this time she just looked comical. Cleo wanted to smile, but her mouth wouldn't work itself into the right shape.

'The capitalist pig, one of the worst!'

Oh Christ, thought Tom, here we go with the jargon. 'Miss Spearfield only works for him, she doesn't necessarily believe in everything Lord Cruze does.'

'What about your paper, the – *Courier*? Is it a capitalist rag?'

'No,' said Tom, taking a risk, 'it's a liberal, left-wing rag.'

'What are you doing here? Were you going to cover the NATO manoeuvres?'

'Yes. But so is Tass, I'm sure.'

'Tass! You're all the same, none of you ever tells the truth.' Some day there would be a newspaper telling the real truth, an anarchist daily with no editor, every journalist free to write what he believed in. She dreamed of what she would create, but shut the word *leadership* out of her mind. 'You

160

both must be important journalists, if your newspapers sent you all this way.'

Discretion overcame vanity: Cleo found her voice: 'Not really. We're just staff hacks.'

Rosa looked at her. 'Why would they send a woman to cover military manoeuvres? You must be more than just a staff writer.'

'No,' said Cleo; so much for making a name for herself. 'That's all I am.'

'You're a liar.' Gerd spoke for the first time since they had entered the house. 'What did you say your name was?'

Cleo all at once felt the burden of her name again; but this time her father was far away, and would mean nothing to these people. 'Cleo Spearfield.'

'Does that mean anything to you?' Rosa said to Gerd.

'I was in England in April. She has her own column in the *Examiner*. And she is on television, the programme called *Scope*.' They were speaking German to each other now. 'We should go downstairs and talk. This one could be worth some money. Not as much as General Brisson, but some.'

Kurt looked at Cleo and Tom, said in English, 'Behave yourselves and you will not be harmed. Now, give us everything in your pockets. And your handbag, Miss Spearfield.'

Cleo's handbag and everything from Tom's pockets were put into the hood that had covered Tom's head. Kurt handed it to Rosa, who immediately passed it on to Gerd.

'We shall bring you some food in a little while,' said Kurt, and nodded at Rosa. 'She will prepare it.'

'No,' said Rosa. 'There will be no women's role. We shall all prepare the meal.'

'Don't let's argue in front of them!' Gerd snapped in German and led Kurt and Rosa out of the room.

The door was shut and locked from the outside. Tom, his legs suddenly going, sat down on the side of the double bed and looked up at Cleo. 'Are you all right?'

She shook her head, sat down on the one chair in the room. 'No. I feel I want to cry and be sick. They're crazy, all three of them. What were they trying to do?'

161

'I don't know. Either kill or kidnap Brisson or Thorpe. They mentioned Brisson's name when they were talking in German.'

She said nothing, but looked around the room. It was comfortable and tastefully furnished in heavy provincial furniture, but there were bare spots on the walls where pictures had been removed. There was nothing in the room to identify the owners except the furniture. She determined she would commit it all to memory, down to every detail. Then she looked back at Tom.

'We seem to get together only when we're in trouble.'

7

Lord Cruze got the ransom demand twenty-four hours after the story of the ambush had been front page news round the world. Generals Brisson and Thorpe, with generals' luck, had been unhurt; but both aides, a driver and a guard, had been killed. One of the terrorists had also been killed and since been identified as the daughter of a prominent Hamburg family. The kidnapping of Cleo and Tom had been secondary paragraphs in the main story, as if the sub-editors felt that reporters should not be news in themselves. They did not merit a headline till the ransom demand was received.

'Two million Deutsche Marks! £250,000 roughly.'

'That's just for Cleo,' said the finance manager of the *Examiner*, keeping his profit and loss columns separate. 'They don't mention the American, Border. I don't think he should be debited against us.'

'They could be throwing him in free. Or perhaps they're going to ask the *Courier* for a separate ransom.' Jack Cruze had never felt less in control of a situation; or of himself. He felt sick and weak, exhausted by worry and a sleepless night. 'Has anyone been in touch with Cleo's family in Australia?'

'I called her father as soon as the story came in,' said Massey-Folkes. 'He said he'd get on a plane immediately.'

'Do we pay the ransom?' asked Dunlop, the finance man-

162

ager. 'The German police have asked us to hold off for twenty-four hours.'

'Of course we bloody well pay it!' Cruze wanted to tell the German police to mind their own business; Cleo was his responsibility, not theirs. 'As soon as we get their instructions...'

'I think one of us should go over to Hamburg,' said Massey-Folkes. 'I'll go, if you like.'

'All right, go over this afternoon. I'll come across as soon as Cleo's father arrives. I'll bring him with me. You'd better co-ordinate things with the German police. But tell them we'll pay the ransom. I don't care a bugger about whether the kidnappers are caught, all we want is Cleo back safe and unharmed.'

'And Tom Border, too,' said Massey-Folkes, hoping the boss was not going to go to pieces. He had never seen him like this before. But then he had not been around when Jack and his wife had broken up.

'Of course.' But Cruze had not given a thought to Tom Border, had done his best not to think about why he and Cleo should have been together. She had mentioned nothing about Border's being in Hamburg when she had said she was going there.

He had come into the *Examiner*'s offices to discuss the ransom demand and to lay down the law as to how the story was to be handled. The kidnappers, if they were in a position to see copies of the *Examiner*, were not to be angered by what was said in either the news or editorial columns. When the conference was over he went downstairs and out into Fleet Street where Sid Cromwell drew up a moment later in the Rolls-Royce. Several photographers appeared, none of them from the *Examiner*, and for the first time in fifteen years Lord Cruze was photographed in his own domain. It was not as bad as being photographed with Cleo, but it still annoyed him.

He went back to the flat, where Mrs Cromwell hovered over him like a nurse. There were countless phone calls, all intercepted by his secretary, Miss Viner, but it did not escape

Jack Cruze that his closest true sympathizers were two women in his employ and Quentin Massey-Folkes; he had no family to lean on. He half expected, half hoped, for a call from Emma, but none came.

'I think you should eat something, m'Lord,' said Mrs Cromwell. 'A little onion soup.'

'French onion soup?' He tried the small joke as much for his own sake as in the hope of a smile from her.

'English onion soup.' There were limits.

'In that case I'll try some. Just a small bowl of it. Ask Jenny to come in here.'

Miss Viner was trim, homely in face and figure, smart in her dress and manner and had been with His Lordship for eighteen years. He knew she had an opinion on his women, but she never gave a hint of what it was.

'Jenny, if nothing happens overnight, I'll be at Heathrow in the morning to meet Senator Spearfield. Have the company plane ready to fly us straight to Hamburg. Book us two suites at the Four Seasons.' He could not pronounce German and he gave the Vier Jahreszeiten its English name. He wished he were fluent in languages; he was not going to enjoy dealing with the Germans, police or kidnappers, through an interpreter. 'Better make it three. We'll hold one for Miss Spearfield when we get her back.'

'Should I stay here overnight? Just in case . . .'

It would be the first time she ever had; he was sure she had remembered that. 'Have Mrs Cromwell get the guest-room ready for you. And tell her you'll have dinner with me.'

She folded her notebook shut, stood up and, it seemed to him, marched out of the room. The bloody Sergeant-Major, he had once called her. But she was what he wanted right now, someone to keep his own self-discipline in line. He felt like weeping, as if he had already lost Cleo forever. Abruptly he cursed her for leaving him to go to Germany, for exposing herself to danger. From now on he would protect her, never let her out of his sight.

Miss Viner came back into the room. 'There is a Miss

164

Dorothy St Martin on the telephone. She says she is a friend of Miss Spearfield's.'

'St Martin?'

'I think she is one of those women who ran that brothel in Curzon Street.' Miss Viner knew every story that had run in the *Examiner*; she was a walking morgue of facts.

He said nothing for a moment; the last thing he wanted was to hear voices from the past, except for Emma's. Then he nodded, got up and went to the phone. 'Miss St Martin? This is Lord Cruze.'

'Hello, Jack,' said the soft voice at the other end of the line. 'Rosa and I have never called you before. But we were worried about Miss Spearfield.'

'That's kind of you. But I didn't know you knew her that well.'

'Well, perhaps not *well*. But once a fortnight, regularly, she's been to have tea with us. She treats us as her lucky charms, says we got her started in Fleet Street. She's a fine young woman, Jack.'

'Yes.' Cleo had never told him she was a friend of the St Martin women. Christ, he thought, what secrets have they exchanged over the teacups?

'We're having a Mass said for her safe return.'

He thought Masses were said only for the dead, but he couldn't hear himself saying that. 'Thank you. How have you and Rose been?'

'We miss the old days, Jack. But then at our age I suppose one always misses what we once had, don't you think?' She spoke as if she included him in her age group, which he resented. He wanted to resent her calling at all, but he could not blame her for that: she had done it with the best of intentions. There had been a time when he had called her, for his own intentions.

'Give my best to Rosa,' he said and hung up.

165

Sylvester Spearfield arrived at Heathrow the following morning, worn out by worry and the long journey. But most of his life had been a public appearance and he had an old actor's resilience. He tried to suggest that he had reserves of strength, that he was bearing up well, as he shook hands with Lord Cruze.

'This is good of you,' he said. 'I know a lot of bosses who wouldn't go to this trouble.'

'I have a plane waiting,' said Cruze, not yet ready to confess that he was not here in his capacity as Cleo's boss. 'Are you up to another two hours' flight to Hamburg?'

'Maybe I can have a kip while we're flying. Have you had any more news?'

'None. I've arranged for the ransom money to be waiting for me when we get there. We'll pay it, no questions asked.'

They flew to Hamburg in the DH-104 Dove, each of them quiet, Jack Cruze staring out of the window at the bright morning, Sylvester lying back with his eyes shut but half opening them to watch the Englishman when the latter had his head turned away. They were careful of each other: Jack because he was wondering what Cleo's father knew of him and Cleo; Sylvester because, steeped in all his old prejudices, he was wondering why a boss was personally going to all this trouble over an employee. He had noticed that no one else but the plane's crew, no personnel manager or PR man, was travelling with them.

When they reached the hotel in Hamburg, Quentin Massey-Folkes was waiting for them. 'No news yet, Mr Spearfield.' He wasn't sure whether Senator was a title Australians cared about; Americans did, but they loved all titles that put them above the herd. 'As an editor I can't tell you that no news is good news. We just have to hope for the best.'

'Have the police any leads?' said Jack Cruze.

Massey-Folkes shook his head. 'They're trying to trace the personal movements of the dead girl, the kidnapper who was killed. They know her name and her family, but so far they've drawn a blank trying to find out whom she got around with. She left home six months ago and her parents hadn't heard anything of her until the police got in touch with them. I gather her mother's totally uncooperative, and refuses to believe her daughter had anything to do with the gang.'

'How did they identify her?'

'She had a St Christopher's medal in her purse with her name on it. Evidently even anarchists like a little spiritual help.' He explained to Sylvester: 'The kidnappers, in their ransom note, call themselves Universal Anarchy.'

'It sounds like a trade organization.' But Sylvester didn't really mean it as a joke.

'Do you want to meet the police, Jack?' This was no time for '*m'Lord*'. 'I didn't tell them you were coming.'

'Let it go for the time being. Senator Spearfield would like to get some rest first. I'll come along to your suite, Senator, and make sure they've looked after you properly.'

'Anywhere I can stretch out will do. And forget the "Senator". Sylvester is good enough, if it's not too much a mouthful. Some people shorten it to Sylver, with a *y*. And I'll probably be silver-haired by the time this is over.'

He was not used to the sort of luxury suite he was shown into by the assistant manager, but he said nothing; in politics you took the perks as they came. But this, he knew, was no perquisite: this was something more. He turned round as Jack Cruze, having dismissed the assistant manager, closed the suite door and stood with his back to it.

'Do you know about Cleo and me?'

'What?' But he knew at once, if too late.

'We're – well, I suppose the word is lovers. Some people might call her my mistress, but she's more than that to me.'

Sylvester looked at the grey-haired man who, today, looked as old as himself (though he had not looked in a mirror, so he did not know how old *he* suddenly looked). He thought of Cleo as he had last seen her, young and ripe, a girl for a young man. What had happened that she had sold (there couldn't be any other word for it) herself to this man?

167

'Jesus wept! No. No, I hadn't a clue. How long's it been going on?'

Going on: the phrase made him angry, but he kept himself under control. Couldn't Spearfield see that he loved his daughter? 'Over a year. Eighteen months, I suppose. It happened gradually. There was no – no starting date.'

Shock had given Sylvester revived energy; he kept looking around him as if caged. 'Christ Almighty, man, you're as old as I am!'

'I'm fifty-one.'

'Old enough to be her bloody father! Jesus, I'm only fifty-eight!' Then he slowed down, tried to concentrate on the man standing on the other side of the big room. A future son-in-law? He couldn't grasp the idea. He took a deep breath, then sighed, shaking his head, waving a helpless, resigned hand. 'I don't know why I'm blaming you. I suppose she went into it with her eyes open.'

'I think you know your daughter well enough –'

'I don't know that I do. Do you have any kids? Who knows what they think these days?'

'I don't have any children.'

'Well, I suppose that helps. It'd be bloody embarrassing for you, having a girl-friend the same age as your daughter or son. Are you married or divorced or what?'

Jack Cruze hesitated only a moment; but Sylvester caught it. 'I'm married, but we're separated. Have been for twenty years.'

'But not divorced? Your wife won't give you one?'

Again the slight hesitation: again Sylvester noticed it. He had spent too many years on the floors of the House and the Senate to miss the change of gears in a man's mind. 'No.'

'Well, that makes it promising for Cleo, doesn't it? Aaah!' It was like a stifled cry of pain. Suddenly he sat down, the last thirty-six hours falling on him with a weight he couldn't bear. 'Leave me alone, Cruze. I'll have a sleep. Maybe I'll feel better when I wake up.'

'I'll wake you if we get any news.'

He went out of the suite and Sylvester lifted himself and

168

crossed to the bed, pulled back the coverlet and lay down without taking off his clothes. He loosened his tie and lay on his back, his eyes closed but his mind still wide open. He was both angry and sad at what Cruze had told him; then, as his mind started to close in, reason told him he was concerned about the wrong thing. Cleo was in much more danger than just being involved with the wrong man. He fell asleep, too exhausted even to dream. Which was his only relief.

9

Claudine had rung Roger from New York. 'You're all right? You're not hurt?'

'No, Joe Thorpe and I got out okay. I lost Rod Hill, my aide –'

'I know, it was on the wire. How's Louise? I think you should go back to Heidelberg, be with her after what's happened. She's had a dreadful shock. We all have –'

'Claudine, Louise is an army wife – she's been through this sort of thing before –'

'Not an attempted assassination or kidnapping or whatever those crazies had in mind! I think –'

'Claudine, let the army run its own affairs – *please*. Apart from having to stay on here for the manoeuvres, I can't run back home while Tom Border and that girl Spearfield are still missing.'

'No, I suppose not. What are you doing to get them back?'

'Personally, I'm doing nothing. This isn't an army matter. The German police are handling it. I understand Lord Cruze has agreed to pay the ransom, though that hasn't been made public yet. If they ask for more money, I hope you'll contribute some. I mean the company.'

'Of course, Roger –' She loved him, even though he could be a trial at times. 'Take care. I'll get in touch with Jack Cruze and tell him we'll pay half the ransom.' Then she repeated, 'Take care.'

He promised that he would, and hung up. But take care

against whom? He was still suffering from the shock of what had happened, but he had managed to hide it. There might have been no shock at all if he had been expecting such an attack; but he had been totally unprepared for it. In Vietnam it had been different: there, you worked on the premise that the enemy surrounded you, could even be in your own house. But here the war had become just play-acting: the enemy was hundreds of miles to the east. Or so he thought until that blue van had come out of the side street, then the white BMW, and the bullets had come smashing into the staff car – then he had realized there was more than one enemy. Only a miracle had saved him and Joe Thorpe: perhaps he should say a prayer of thanks. Then he decided against it. God would know a hypocrite when he heard one.

The manoeuvres would start tomorrow. Six thousand men, a hundred tanks, guns, trucks, missile-carriers: he had the wild, mad idea that they should all be used to devastate the countryside, to bring the kidnappers out into the open. But he knew what could happen when an operation went too far. The wrong people could be killed.

Then, and the thought horrified him with its callous efficacy, he wondered if that would not solve his major problem.

10

Their captivity dragged on into the third day. They had slept together in the double bed without making love; or, as Cleo would have put it in her convent school days, without going all the way. They had slept in their underwear and despite the hopelessness of their situation (or because of it) the urge for sex had been strong in both of them.

Gerd had brought them a meal five hours after they had been locked up. In that time they had had plenty of opportunity to inspect their cell and to realize there was little or no chance of escape. The boards across the window were set into the outer frame, then screwed down and the heads of the screws filed flat. The door was a stout one, a real country door not a plywood one, and there were two locks to it. There was a small fireplace in the room, but the chimney was far too narrow for any escape that way.

'Why couldn't you have been one of those skinny fashion models? I could have hoisted you up the chimney.'

The meal tray had been taken away by Kurt (Rosa was doing no woman's work: she was downstairs cleaning the guns) and it was time for bed. Cleo was exhausted physically and emotionally; she knew she would sleep the sleep of the dead. She knew in her heart that she was dead anyway: the gang below were not going to allow her and Tom to go free. She took off her sweater and skirt and got into bed.

'I'll sleep in the chair,' Tom said.

'No. I want some comfort.' That was all she was thinking of at the moment.

He undressed, all but his shorts, switched out the light and got in beside her. A thin ribbon of light from the light out on the landing lay under the door, but in their mental state the darkness seemed complete. Hesitantly he lifted his arm and was pleased when, without hesitation, she put her head in the crook of it. They lay like two people who had been going to bed together for years, for whom sex was only a Friday or Saturday night entertainment.

'Today's Tuesday,' she said. 'The manoeuvres start to-morrow. Maybe they'll have the army out looking for us.'

'Maybe.' He wasn't hopeful. He had had experience of the army's interest in newsmen when he had been in Vietnam. 'We could be miles from where the army is. I lost track of time when they put that sack over my head. I couldn't tell whether we travelled twenty miles or a hundred.'

'It wasn't far, not that far. I looked at my watch when they brought us up here. We couldn't have been travelling for more than an hour. And they didn't drive too fast.'

'Probably the same as when they had me driving the Merc. They didn't want to attract attention. Maybe everything will work out okay.' He pressed her shoulder, felt the satin of her skin.

'Tom –' She could feel the muscles of his arm beneath her

171

neck, felt their hard edge against her cheek. He was still bony, but he was also more muscular than she had remembered. Or perhaps all young men were. 'When we get out of this, let's be friends. Don't let's avoid each other.'

He said nothing for a moment, then he felt for her chin with his free hand and lifted her face. He kissed her on the lips, and was not surprised when they opened under his. He moved his body against hers, turning sideways so that she could feel what was happening to him. She felt him, all right: young men and old were all hard there, given these circumstances. She rolled over on her back, lifting her elbow to hold it against his ribs so that he would not think she was offering him an invitation.

'You'd better get up and let the night air get to the Old Feller.'

'To the what?'

'*That* . . . We can't, Tom. Not with them down there in the room below. They'd come up to watch.'

It was some relief and pleasure to know that she might have let him make love to her had they not been where they were. He lay back and laughed softly. 'You're right. They'd hear us. There's an old saying down where I come from. There's no humpin' without bumpin'.'

'Delicately put. Do you think you can sleep without trying to stick it into me?'

'Delicately put. I'll try. Do you want to put a pillow between us? Bundling, they used to call it.'

'It might be better.' She pulled a pillow down between them. In the darkness she could not see him, but unerringly she found his lips when she raised herself and leaned over the pillow to kiss him. 'Goodnight, Tom. Another time. I promise.'

But in the darkness she wondered if she was mistaking affection for love, confusing gratitude for his just being there with a feeling that she needed him permanently. Emotion was heightened by fear; and she was afraid. To declare, as much to herself as to him, that she was in love with him might not stand up to examination in other circumstances. More-

172

over, she didn't want a repetition of what had happened in Saigon. Nonetheless, during the night, her hand found its way over the pillow and took his. In a way, even if in her sleep, it was a declaration. He was awake and took her hand, but he was cautious enough not to read too much into it. Women asleep are no more readable than women awake: not by a man afraid of commitment.

In the morning they looked at each other and smiled, as if they had been through some sort of test. 'I slept like a log,' she said.

'Me, too.' But he hadn't. He had slept fitfully and woken an hour before her with an erection, which hadn't improved his state of mind. He had lain awhile, then got out of bed and dressed in the dark. When he heard her stir he had turned on the light.

'I want to go to the bathroom,' she said. 'That's the first thing I do in the morning.'

'Me, too.' They were married, if only in exchanging small early morning intimacies like honeymooners after the first night. 'I'll rouse the staff.'

He thumped on the door and a minute later Rosa, hooded and holding the Luger, opened it. She grunted good morning and, in turn, led Cleo and Tom to the small bathroom along the narrow hallway. Each of them did their usual morning business, washed themselves and cleaned their teeth with their fingers. Tom had a little trouble urinating; he had heard of men who suffered from shy penises in public lavatories and couldn't pass water with someone standing beside them. Those guys were lucky: he had a hooded dame with a Luger standing three feet from him outside the open bathroom door. Finally his bladder won out.

The small routine in the bathroom, as ordinary as anything they did on any morning except that they were covered by a gun, set them on an even keel for the rest of what the day had to offer. Going back along the hallway Cleo looked for some identification, but even here the pictures had been removed from the walls. She did not know it but Gerd, of the military mind, had thought of everything.

173

Gerd brought them breakfast, then, with the Schmeisser in his lap, sat and watched them while they ate. Inside his hood his own face was as strained as the faces of his prisoners. But he sat so quietly, so anonymous in his mask, that he looked as unfeeling as a robot.

'What are you planning to do with us?' Tom was eating ham and cheese spread on rough bread.

'We are holding you for ransom. Well, Miss Spearfield ... We know who she is. She should be worth a lot of money.'

'Not as much as the two generals you tried to kidnap,' said Cleo. 'Or had you intended just to kill them?'

'If we'd intended to kill them, we could have done it without any trouble.' That was what he had advised originally: kill the American general, then threaten further assassinations if a ransom was not paid. That way there would not have been all the mess and inconvenience of having to keep prisoners. But Kurt and Rosa had been all for the big immediate action. 'You are a substitute, Miss Spearfield. You're not English, are you?'

'No, Australian.'

'Why do you bother yourself with European affairs? Why did you leave Australia? It is a simple country, is it not?'

What would they say to that in Canberra, where they all took themselves so seriously? 'Yes,' she said, 'but I was ambitious. Just like you and your friends.'

Gerd's ambitions were wilting, but the mask hid his pessimism.

'What are your aims?' asked Cleo. 'I mean, what do you hope to achieve by what you've done?'

'What makes you think we are political?' Rosa stood in the doorway with her Luger. She had heard the voices and, suspicious as always, had come upstairs.

Cleo laid a piece of cheese on a round of bread. She was keeping control of herself, trying to ignore the guns, by being deliberately normal. 'Then you're just mercenaries? Ordinary kidnappers?'

The two hoods, eyes as blank as owls', looked at each other.

174

'No,' said Rosa, 'we have aims, but they are not political. Politicians have ruined the world.'

Dear Dad: listen to this ... 'If it wasn't them, it would be someone else ruining it. You had Hitler.'

'A madman,' said Rosa, and spat. Her hood fluttered.

'Then you're anarchists?' said Tom.

'Yes!' The hood fluttered again, as if a bird were caught in it. 'All governments are a conspiracy!'

'Bakunin? I've read him. As I remember it, he retired disillusioned with everything, including his own connections.'

'Not true!' Rosa threatened to blow the hood off her head.

'They are baiting you,' Gerd told Rosa in German. 'Let us be calm. We have to live together, with them as well as with each other. Who knows, perhaps we can convert them to be our propagandists?'

He was suffering from his own disillusionment. The operation was not going to succeed; he could feel it in his bones, the military bones of his father. Kurt, who had gone into Hamburg to phone the London *Examiner* from the central railway station to ask if the ransom would be paid, was already going to pieces over the death of Trudi. No matter how Rosa might rant about the stupidity and fallibility of love, it was a mortar that held people together. It had held Gerd to Kurt and he despaired now to see his loved one falling apart.

'People can run their own lives,' said Rosa, who still had to control her own. She ignored Gerd, and continued to speak in English to the representatives of the enemy: 'Government and politicians are not necessary. A co-operation of labour, that's all that is necessary. You worship all the wrong things – property, wealth, position. I can tell by the way you dress.'

'It's that Harrods suit,' Cleo said to Tom, and the two anarchists wondered why their prisoners smiled at each other.

'Don't laugh at us!' Rosa's hood fluttered again; the Luger wavered in her furious hand. 'We should kill you! You're worth nothing –'

175

'That's enough!' Gerd stood up, picked up the tray with the breakfast only half eaten. He was looking at Cleo and Tom, but he spoke to Rosa. 'We'll talk some other time.'

He backed out, pushing Rosa ahead of him with his elbow. He could feel the aggression in her, but she had the sense to wait until they were downstairs before she attacked him.

'You are too soft! You damned queers are all the same!'

He almost hit her then; but he had never hit a woman and he was not going to start now. She was like all women, and had the fixed idea that men like himself were afraid to fight; most men thought the same though there were some in Hamburg who knew different, having been bested by him in brawls. He sighed, suddenly feeling pity for her. She was like himself, defeated, and she was striking out in every direction in her frustration. All at once he yearned for Kurt to hurry back, wanted to be comforted just by his presence.

'Shut your stupid mouth,' he said quietly, turning his back on her. 'You should grow up, Rosa.'

She raised the Luger, aimed it at the back of his head. Then reason came back, the blindness of rage disappeared. She lowered the pistol, spun round and went out into the kitchen. He heard her rattling dishes, doing the washing-up from last night's supper. He smiled, but he knew enough not to go to the doorway of the kitchen and let her see the smile or make some comment.

Up in the bedroom Cleo and Tom had heard the muffled voices, through the thick rug on the floor, raised in fierce argument. The row was in German, but the sounds of disagreement do not need translation.

'They're fighting between themselves,' said Tom. 'That's a good sign.'

'Is it?' said Cleo. 'What if she shoots him and then comes up and kills us? She's itching to use that gun.'

'The female of the species . . .' But it was just an idle remark, because he could think of nothing better to say.

The day dragged on. They heard the third kidnapper come back and the atmosphere downstairs seemed to improve:

once they heard a laugh. They were given a meal in the middle of the day and again at seven o'clock, brought each time by Gerd. They recognized that he was the most sympathetic of the three kidnappers, though they hadn't seen the leader since the first day they had been brought here.

They went to bed that night with the pillow between them again. They kissed goodnight and Tom kissed her breasts through the lace of her brassière. For a moment she was tempted to remove the brassière, but stopped herself. She was not going to have another disastrous attempt at love-making with him; she was an uninhibited lover, given to notions of delight when she felt like expressing them; she could not be mute if she tried. She remembered when she had lost her virginity at sixteen, on the living-room floor in the big house in Bellevue Hill in Sydney, with a pillow under her and the boy from Riverview, the Jesuit school, on top of her. Her ears had been as erect as the boy's penis as she had listened, above his panting, for his parents to come downstairs from their bedroom and demand to know what was going on. Though your senses might desert you at the climax of passion, they were with you up till that moment. She was not going to make love to Tom with ears cocked.

'No further?' said Tom with male hopefulness.

They're all the same, she thought: once they're worked up, they're deaf from the balls up. 'It wouldn't work, Tom. It would be even worse than – that other time.'

He turned over and eventually went to sleep. It wasn't easy, not with a standard between his legs.

On the third day they were woken when the tanks clattered into the yard outside the farmhouse.

11

Gerd was standing at the kitchen window putting water in the coffee pot when he saw the four tanks and the Jeep coming up the track from the neighbouring field. He had been looking out at the early morning with that idle curiosity

177

of the half-awake, noting that a wind had risen during the night and the line of oak trees down the main track to the road were leaning slightly to one side, like a corps of arthritic ballet dancers. Birds and leaves were indistinguishable as they flew before the wind and over to the right he could see, beyond the rim of a hill, dust rising from what was probably a newly ploughed field. Then he saw the Jeep, followed by the tanks trailing their trains of dust, come over the skyline of the hill, dip down and begin to come up the track towards the farmhouse.

He shouted to Kurt and Rosa, not moving from the window, and in a few moments they came scrambling down the stairs, half-dressed but each of them carrying a Luger. His own Schmeisser lay on the draining board beside the sink, but he hadn't picked it up and still held the coffee pot in his hand. A sub-machine-gun would be of no use against the firepower in those tanks.

'Jesus Christ!' Kurt was tucking his shirt into his trousers, pulling on a sweater. 'What are they doing here?'

'How did they get on to us?' Rosa had pulled on her sweater and jeans but forgotten her shoes.

'Who said they know anything about us?' Gerd said. 'Go outside, Kurt, and ask them what they want. Go on, you live here. Leave your gun.'

Kurt hesitated, then went to the kitchen door. There he paused, looked at the Luger in his hand as if wondering what he had intended doing with it, put it down on a chair and went out into the yard, closing the door behind him. Rosa moved to one side of the window, her pistol held ready. Gerd remained at the window, the coffee pot still in his hand, the Schmeisser still on the draining board like something left over from last night's washing-up.

Out in the yard the American lieutenant, young and blond, more German-looking than Kurt, got out of the Jeep and smiled tentatively at the angry young man who had come out of the farmhouse. He said in German, 'Good morning. You're expecting us, I hope?'

Kurt was puzzled. Why should the army have been sent

178

and not the police? He regretted leaving his Luger inside the house; they were going to take him without his being able to put up a fight. The wind whipped his long dark hair about his face as he stood with his feet braced apart: he looked wild enough to take them all on with bare hands.

'Did you need so many tanks? How many of us did you think there were?'

It was the American's turn to look puzzled. 'Are you Herr Hauser? Do you live here?'

'Yes.' Kurt began to see a little light, though it illuminated nothing.

'Did you not receive the letter telling you we should be using your farm as an observation post during our exercises? Only for today,' the American added apologetically. His parents were German, but he had been born in America and he was beginning to hate the idea of being the liaison officer between the NATO forces and the civilian population. He had always believed that his father's countrymen were militaristic, but none of the farmers and villagers he had met so far had welcomed the intrusion of these military manoeuvres. 'We shall be gone this evening.'

Kurt said, 'When was the letter sent?'

'Oh, at least a month ago.'

'Then my father would have received it, but he forgot to tell me about it. He is away in England at present.' Kurt felt only a degree of relief. The army had not come to arrest him, Gerd and Rosa, but their presence was going to be dangerous. 'Do you have to set up your observation post here near the house? My – my girl friend is not well.'

The lieutenant looked towards the house, saw the other young man at the kitchen window. Then he looked up at the sergeant in the turret of the lead tank. 'What are your instructions, Sergeant?'

'We got to keep the tanks under cover in these trees, Lieutenant.' He nodded towards the trees that sheltered two sides of the yard. 'I can't see anywheres else we can put 'em. We got to hold 'em under cover till Blue headquarters call for us.'

179

'I'm sorry,' Kurt said in English, 'but you will have to go further down the hill, away from the house.'

The lieutenant looked embarrassed. 'I'm afraid that's not possible, Herr Hauser.'

'What sort of army is it that can't improvise?'

'Oh shit.' The sergeant was a ten-year veteran and he had no time for civilians; they only got in the way. 'That's just great coming from a German. When did you guys ever improvise anything?'

In the kitchen Gerd and Rosa could only catch snatches of the conversation. The tanks had switched off their engines, but the wind was plucking at the voices, tearing words away. 'What do they want?' Rosa said.

'They want to stay here for the day, I think.' Gerd wished he had gone out to the yard with Kurt. He wanted to protect him, he looked so thin and vulnerable out there, the wind tearing at him and the tanks looming over him as if ready to crush him. Their venture was doomed anyway, all he wanted was to see that he and Kurt got out alive. 'If we can keep them out of the house –'

'They can't stay here! Kurt should be on his way now to collect the ransom money. Are we supposed to look after them?'

Gerd smiled, though he felt no humour at all. 'I think the army can look after itself.'

Upstairs Cleo and Tom, both fully dressed now, could hear nothing of the conversation in the yard. They had heard the tanks arrive, then there was silence when the engines were switched off, but for the wind. They could hear nothing from downstairs and they wondered where the kidnappers had gone. The wind moaned down the chimney like a child's taunt.

'Are you sure they were tanks?'

'I know the sound of a goddam tank!' Tom was tense, one eye on the door, waiting for the kidnappers to burst in and kill them before whoever it was outside could break into the house to rescue them. 'There must have been three or four of them. They're still out there – I didn't hear them go away.'

180

'What do we do? Do we start yelling?'

Then, without waiting for a yes from him, Cleo began thumping on the boards across the window, shouting for help at the top of her voice.

Down in the kitchen Gerd reacted at once. He dropped the coffee pot, spun round and raced out of the kitchen. He was halfway up the narrow stairs when he remembered he had no gun; he plunged back down to the kitchen, grabbed Kurt's Luger from the chair by the door and ran back upstairs. He could feel the panic in his fingers as he fumbled with the two locks, then he had hurled the door back and stood in the doorway. The Luger was aimed at Cleo, who had turned to face him, mouth wide open for the scream stuck in her throat.

'Come out from behind the door, Herr Border,' ordered Gerd, 'or I shall shoot Fräulein Spearfield.'

Tom stepped sheepishly from behind the door. He was surprised at how heroic he had intended to be; but he was relieved the German had anticipated him. He had enough steel in him to say, 'If you shoot, they'll hear you out in the yard. You wouldn't want that.'

'Do you want to take the risk?' Gerd said to Cleo. He had forgotten to put on his hood, but the fact didn't worry him. Everything was finished and he knew he and the others would be dead before the day was out. All at once he felt sorry for his parents, felt their shame, and wished he could die anonymous.

'I don't believe you're a killer.' Cleo was surprised at her own calmness; but even before she uttered it she knew the truth of her remark. 'Your girl friend, maybe. But not you.'

Gerd lowered the Luger. 'Then perhaps you are fortunate that it was I who came up here –'

Then he heard the Schmeisser go off in the kitchen below.

At a command post three miles away Roger Brisson looked up from his map case as his new aide, Lieutenant Johns, came running across from the radio truck.

'There's trouble at a farm further up the road, General! Some crazy dame with a machine-gun has opened up on four of our tanks and a Jeep. Three of our guys are dead!'

In less than five minutes Roger was at the Hauser farm. His driver pulled up the Jeep at the bottom of the rise and Roger and Johns jumped out and, keeping low, made their way up to the three tanks that had withdrawn to a dip in the hill just below the farmyard.

A sergeant scrambled out of one of the tanks and saluted Roger. 'Sergeant Knudsen, General. There's some bitch in the house with a Schmeisser or something like it, sir. She opened up when Lieutenant Dorten got into an argument with the son of the owner of the farm. Lieutenant Dorten's dead, I think, and so are his driver and Sergeant Leeds up there in the lead tank. I think the driver is wounded, too. He must be, otherwise he'd have got his tank outa there.'

'Someone in the tank is still alive.' Roger took a cautious look up into the farmyard. 'They're firing back at the house. What's going on in the house, anyway?'

'I dunno, sir. The young guy, the owner's son, he run back into the house soon's the shooting started. There's a second guy in there, too. That makes three at least. There may be more. I heard some yelling, sounded like a woman's voice, just before that crazy dame opened up. She's gotta be crazy, sir. Who else'd take on four tanks with a Schmeisser or whatever she's got?'

There was a sudden light *boom!* and a cloud of smoke billowed up beside the tank in the farmyard and then was whipped away by the wind. 'They have something else – that was a grenade! What's that tank man using?'

'I'm not sure, sir. Could be a pistol or a carbine, I dunno. What do we do, sir? We can close up these three tanks and just bulldoze our way in.'

'Hold it a minute,' said Roger. 'Do we have a loud-hailer here?'

'No, sir. We weren't expecting anything like this.'

Inside the house Kurt, Rosa and Gerd were moving from room to room downstairs, sneaking looks out of the windows to see if they were being surrounded. Gerd, taught by his father that a good army always had reserves to fall back on, had stock-piled extra guns and several dozen grenades; they were in boxes that had been brought to the farm four days ago. They had been reserves for the future, not to be used, he had thought, for perhaps months or even years. But Rosa had already ripped the lids off the boxes, and stood like a mad child amongst a Christmas arsenal of gifts.

'If we can hold out till dark –'

Even Kurt was shocked by her stupid optimism. 'For God's sake – that won't be for another twelve or fourteen hours!'

'Don't listen to her.' Gerd, coming back from a rear room, paused in the kitchen doorway. The man in the tank in the farmyard was letting off the occasional shot, but they were all standing back out of the line of fire. The glass in the kitchen window was already shattered and the wind blew in with the last of the smoke from the grenade hurled by Rosa. 'I think we should surrender, Kurt. It's useless.'

'That's all we should expect from a cowardly queer!' Rosa was more of a man than either of them; she was determined to prove it. She fired another burst at the tank as if that were some sort of proof. 'Let him go out if he wants, Kurt –'

Kurt paid no attention to her. He looked at Gerd and shrugged; he no longer cared, and wished now that he had stayed out in the yard and given himself up to the tank men. He knew how Gerd felt about him, but there was nothing he could do about it: he could never love a man the way he had loved Trudi. 'It's up to you, Gerd. If you want to stay alive . . .'

Gerd stared at him, reading Kurt's rejection of him in the dark handsome face. It had always been a useless dream: it would never have worked, anyway. 'No, I'll stay.'

Outside the house, down in the dip behind the three tanks,

183

Lieutenant Johns, a devotee of crime novels if not of military manuals, had an idea: 'General, do you think those crazies up there could be the gang that held you up on Tuesday?'

'Could be.' The thought had already occurred to Roger. He had kept in constant touch with the police during the manoeuvres, concerned for the safety of Cleo Spearfield and Tom Border even while the dark side of his mind considered the advantages of Cleo's not surviving. What if she and Border were held prisoner in the farmhouse? The callous thought of what could happen if the house was razed came back; again he was horrified at what the urge for self-survival could suggest. Then he saw the gun turret on the tank in the yard turning slowly towards the house. 'Good God, what's he going to do? Stop him, Sergeant, he's going to shell the house!'

'I can't contact him, General.' Sergeant Knudsen looked unperturbed: let the fucking crazies in the house get what was coming to them. 'His radio's out.'

Roger watched with sickening dismay as he saw the gun's barrel line up on the kitchen window. Then the barrel recoiled, he heard the sound of the shot and saw the shell turn the window opening into a gaping jagged hole.

Rosa had stepped out of the kitchen, gone to the back of the house to check that they were still safe from that direction. Gerd had stepped into the kitchen, had put out a hand towards Kurt. Then Kurt seemed to grow bigger as did the room itself; there was a tremendous roar that both blinded and deafened Gerd, and then Kurt fell on him in a bloody embrace. They died locked together as they had never been in life.

Up in the bedroom Tom held Cleo to him as they heard the giant roar beneath them and felt the house shake with the explosion. When the firing had started downstairs their blond captor, as if he no longer cared about them, had run out of the bedroom, leaving the door wide open behind him. Cleo had started for it at once, but Tom had grabbed her as he heard the gunfire shattering the windows in the rooms below.

'Stay here!' he had yelled above the din. 'We'll be chopped in half if we go down there!'

He had pulled her back into the bedroom, then gone out on to the landing and looked down the stairs. He could smell the cordite and hear the shouts of the three kidnappers. Someone (it sounded to him like the blond man) was shouting abuse at Rosa: he understood none of the abuse but caught the girl's name. She was screaming as if berserk, her yelling punctuated as she kept firing at whoever was out in the yard. He took a tentative step down the stairs, then jumped back as bullets thudded into the bottom of the stairs and splinters flew like spent yellow cartridges.

He went back into the bedroom, took Cleo in his arms and pulled her down on the floor away from the outer wall. They lay there for what seemed an hour but was no more than ten minutes, while the battle went on below them. Occasionally the firing stopped and the kidnappers' voices drifted up the stairs. Neither of them understood what was being said, but it was obvious that the gang was divided amongst itself.

They heard the small explosion out in the yard. Then a minute later there was the tremendous explosion from below as the shell crashed into the house. Smoke and dust billowed up the stairs; then Rosa, wild-eyed and bloody, the Schmeisser held in the crook of her arm, staggered into the room. She shook her head, as if trying to clear her eyes of whatever was blinding them: smoke, dust, disillusion. She didn't see Cleo and Tom, was unaware of them almost at her feet as they crouched behind the door. She whimpered with pain, anger, it was impossible to tell; then she let out an animal scream of rage and sprayed the bed and the far wall with bullets from the Schmeisser. The gun fell abruptly silent as the magazine ran out. In that moment Tom, letting go of Cleo, slammed the door against Rosa. She fell back on to the landing and Tom, jerking open the door again, went after her. He landed on top of her, hit her with all his strength, and she went limp beneath him. He picked up the empty Schmeisser, not knowing what he intended doing with it, crouched on one knee and aimed it down the stairs.

185

He heard Cleo, right behind him, say, 'General Brisson – what a nice surprise!'

Part of his own shocked mind registered the coolness of Cleo's voice; but he knew it was an act, a prop to prevent her collapsing. He was more shocked, as he stared down at Roger Brisson standing in the settling dust and smoke at the bottom of the stairs, at the look on the general's face – the look of a man also about to collapse.

NINE

'Sweetheart!' Sylvester embraced Cleo as he had not embraced her since she was a child. He was crying, and soon the tears came to her own eyes and she clung to him. They were weakened at discovering how much they loved each other. 'I've been praying – more bloody Hail Marys than I've said in years!'

He held her to him, comforting her; it was the best he had felt since Brigid had been alive. 'When they didn't come to pick up the money, I thought that was – never mind. You're safe. Thank God for the US Army, eh?' He smiled at her, trying to get her to smile. 'But don't quote me to the Labour Party back home, eh?'

Jack Cruze and Tom Border and Roger Brisson and a hundred police, soldiers and reporters stood in a circle round them, but Cleo was alone with her father. 'I didn't know you were here – I thought you'd still be back home – Oh, Dad!'

Then she eased herself away from him, wiped her eyes and saw Jack for the first time. She looked at her father and realized at once that he knew about her and Jack. Suddenly she was glad of the crowd around them: she could not have gone straight from her father's arms into Jack's, not in front of him. She turned to Jack and put out her hand.

'Thanks for coming, Lord Cruze.'

Cameras were aimed, lights flared; but in tomorrow's papers they would look only like close friends, or employer and employee enjoying the best of labour relations. Jack winked at her, glad for his own sake that she hadn't made public their real relationship. 'It's good to have you back with us, Cleo. You're all right?'

She nodded. 'Both of us. Me and Tom Border.'

'Good,' he said, but she noticed he didn't glance at Tom.

Then Roger Brisson came forward. In helmet and combat dress he looked dashing and formidable, a general who had just won a major battle. But Tom Border, standing to one side, still remembered the look on Brisson's face an hour earlier, when he had looked like a general who had surrendered rather than won.

'I must be going, Miss Spearfield. The police are going to escort you and Mr Border back to Hamburg. It's their business, after all.'

'I'm glad you and your men were on hand, General. Thank your men, please. Especially that man in the tank who blew up the kitchen without hurting me or Mr Border.' She had a woman's faith in the accuracy of weapons and that of the men who fired them.

'Yes,' said Roger and kept his face straight and sober. 'I'm sorry you were subjected to all this. It was meant for General Thorpe and me, but you were the unfortunate substitutes. I don't know how we can compensate, but if there is any way...'

A year of your pay will do, plus your dividends, thought Tom. But no one was asking him. He was a *Courier* man, part of the family. But before he left, Roger did come across to him and shake his hand.

'You have a story now, Mr Border. A big one.'

'May I say that you directed the rescue operation, General?'

'No,' said Roger, face straight again. 'That would take credit away from the men responsible. Talk to Sergeant Knudsen.'

'I'll do that, sir. You'd still rather I didn't mention you?'

'Only if you have to, Mr Border. Good luck. I hope the *Courier* gives you a bonus for what you've been through. It's quite a story.'

'I didn't do it for the story,' said Tom.

188

Roger knew when he'd said the wrong thing. 'No. Well, good luck,' he said again, lost for words.

And he went off once more to the manoeuvres, turning his mind back to fighting the Russians. They were a diversion for generals as well as politicians.

A policeman came up and handed Cleo her handbag. 'We found this in the rubble of the kitchen, Fräulein.'

It was a crocodile-skin bag that Jack had given her. She brushed it free of grit and dust, opened it and took out the purse, compact and crocodile-skin wallet containing her passport and other papers: Jack had given her the compact and wallet. She found the St Martin sisters' gift, the gold pen, at the bottom of the bag.

'Everything's here,' she said with some surprise.

'They weren't purse pinchers,' said Jack. 'They were asking a quarter of a million pounds for you.'

'They undervalued you, sweetheart,' said Sylvester and put his arm round her again.

Going back to Hamburg in the Mercedes 600 that Jack had rented Sylvester and Cleo sat in the rear seat and Jack and Tom in the jump seats. Tom had hung back as everyone had got into the big car, but Cleo turned back and insisted that he ride with them. He sat beside Jack Cruze and could feel the Englishman's antagonism and suspicion as plainly as he had felt the kidnapper's pistol against his head in the other rented Mercedes three days ago. It was Sylvester, the politician, who knew how to melt the ice in an atmosphere.

'You both must be absolutely buggered.'

Cleo pressed his hand, smiled at Jack and Tom. 'That's the standard of language in Canberra. They don't allow for any ambiguity.'

Tom said, 'Buggered has several meanings where I come from.'

Like performers in a television sketch they all looked at Jack for his line, but he was contributing nothing. He was not dense to the situation, he knew the chatter was nothing more than a life-raft for their emotions. Soon a reaction would set in with Cleo and the American beside him, but he

189

couldn't help them put it off. His own reaction had already occurred.

'Well –' said Sylvester, and for once was lost for further words. But the silence in the car was too stiff and after a while he said, 'So the two fellers who kidnapped you are dead. What will they do about the girl?'

'They've taken her to some prison hospital.' Jack at last made his contribution, but his voice was awkward and a little harsh. He had two rivals in this car and that had never happened to him before, not for the affections of a woman.

'Do they have the death sentence in Germany?' Cleo looked at Tom.

He shrugged. 'I don't know. Right now I don't care.' He had never hated anyone until he met the girl who had tried to kill him and Cleo. 'She deserves everything she gets.'

'That's right,' said Jack, but didn't look at him. Instead he looked at Cleo, wondering what he would have done if he had found her dead.

Cleo gazed at the two men who loved her, then turned to her father: his was the easiest love to bear. 'Let's go straight back to London.'

'That would be nice, sweetheart. Unfortunately, you can't. The police want to interview you. I think you should have a good rest, see the coppers late this afternoon, then we'll have dinner tonight. We'll go back to London first thing tomorrow. That okay, Jack?'

'A good idea,' said Jack, but he wondered how soon he was going to have Cleo to himself.

'You'll have to excuse me,' said Tom. 'I've got to file my story as soon as we get back to Hamburg. I'll see the cops after that, then I have to go down to Paris, to our bureau there. I'll take a rain-check on the dinner.' He looked at Cleo.

'I wish you'd stay,' she said, avoiding looking at Jack.

'Another time,' he said, and she heard the echo of her own voice. 'I promise.'

The car drew up outside the Vier Jahreszeiten and Tom said goodbye to Sylvester and Jack with the stiff formality of a diplomat at a failed summit meeting. Then he said to Cleo, 'How do you feel?'

'No swagger, none at all.'

'You'll get it back.'

Police had got out of the escorting cars; newspaper reporters and television cameramen had appeared like magicians' assistants, though without a puff of melodramatic smoke. A senior police officer spoke to Jack Cruze, naming a time when he wanted to see Cleo and Tom.

While Jack's attention was distracted, Cleo pressed Tom's hand and whispered, 'Yes, another time. Call me.'

'Sure,' he said, but took his hand out of hers and gave it to Sylvester. 'Take care of her, Mr Spearfield.'

'I will,' said Sylvester, but already knew how difficult it was going to be.

Jack came back into the small circle, hesitated, then put out his hand to Tom. 'Good luck, Mr Border. I hope they give your story the spread it deserves.'

'See they do the same for Cleo in the *Examiner*.' He couldn't bring himself to say *m'Lord* or *Your Lordship*. It wasn't just that he was an American. He was a rival in love.

He left them at once and went up into the hotel, as if he were the only one staying there and they were dropping him off. Cleo posed for more pictures, including some by the *Scope* cameramen, she was hugged and kissed and welcomed back by Roy Holden, then she and her father and Jack Cruze went up into the hotel. The manager himself took them up to their suites.

'I've moved you and Senator Spearfield, Lord Cruze. You now have three adjoining suites looking out on the lake. I'll put someone in the corridor to see that you are not disturbed.'

Cleo said, 'Roy Holden will probably want to come up –'

'No,' said Jack with authority. 'Nobody comes up.'

'That's right,' said Sylvester, but he realized he had no authority here, not even with his daughter.

The manager left and the three of them were alone. Cleo decided she was not going to sleep on the situation; it would

191

be worse than a spiked mattress. Better that it was faced now than later. 'You know about me and Jack, Dad?'

'Yes.'

It struck her that both men looked uncomfortable. Either she was too tired or she didn't care – she wasn't sure which – but for the present she felt no discomfort at all now that the subject was out into the open.

'Well, you'd have known sooner or later. I was going to tell you when you came to London.'

'I'd rather have found out that way.' He noticed that she did not ask if he approved – he guessed his disapproval was plain enough. 'But you get some rest now. I'll see you at dinner.'

He kissed her and left, without another word to Jack. The latter had stood like a callow young suitor who had been told by a much older man that he was no longer welcome in his house. But when the door closed behind Sylvester he moved quickly to Cleo, took her in his arms and held her so tightly that she had difficulty in breathing. She didn't protest, aware of the emotion she could feel trembling inside him. But she wondered that there was no tremor in herself.

At last he let her go, though he kept his hands on her arms as he stood back from her. His eyes were glistening and he looked older than she had ever seen him look, old and exhausted. 'The money was supposed to be picked up at seven-thirty this morning. When they didn't put in an appearance, I –' He let her go, took out a handkerchief and wiped his eyes, 'I felt like it was the end of everything. Then the police came and told us you were out there at that farm...'

Suddenly she, too, was exhausted. 'Tell me about it at dinner, Jack. I'm worn out.'

'Of course.' He kissed her again, gently this time, holding her as if he thought she might crumble in his hand. 'Sleep as long as you like. The police can wait.'

When he had gone she undressed and got into bed. She looked around the big room, comparing the luxury of it with the bedroom she had shared with Tom the past three days. Another time, she thought. She was crying when she fell asleep, not for the immediate past but for the future. Tom wouldn't call, she was sure of that.

2

She, Sylvester and Jack went back to London next day in the *Examiner*'s plane. She had been interviewed by the police and told that she would be required to come back to Germany as a material witness when Rosa Fuchs was brought to trial; she had promised she would do so, but already she knew she would be looking for some way to avoid it when the time came. Now the danger was over, now that she and Tom had come out of it unharmed, she had no feelings at all towards the surviving kidnapper. She did not hate Rosa Fuchs nor did she feel any pity for her. Psychologists wrote that often a love–hate relationship grew between prisoners and their kidnappers; but that hadn't happened with her. Let the law take its course: she just wished she did not have to be a part of it.

The night before they left for home she had had dinner with her father and Jack and each of the men had done his best to keep the mood light, to shield her from the friction between them. She could see the strain in both of them and she knew it was not just a hangover from her kidnapping; but she didn't raise the subject of herself and Jack again, just divided her attention equally between him and Sylvester. She acted out her role as a journalist, saying she had to get all the facts for the story Quentin Massey-Folkes would be waiting for on her return to London. It was a role easier to play, for the couple of hours of the dinner, than daughter or mistress.

'The money was left in a suitcase in a locker at the main railway station,' Jack said. 'It was an obvious place and the police had it staked out. But they were going to pick it up in the morning rush hour and the chap who phoned us told us that if their pick-up man was followed and arrested, you and Border would be – well, you know what they would have done. They were that sort.'

'The girl would have killed us,' said Cleo. 'I don't know about Kurt Hauser – we didn't know him. The other one, Gerd Silber, I don't think he would have touched us. Were the police going to follow the pick-up man?'

'Yes,' said Sylvester, 'but we talked them out of it. They were pretty reluctant, but I can see their point. There comes a time when you have to say no to these sort of ransom demands, I mean when they're terrorists like this lot. Only thing is, when it's someone of your own who's been kidnapped you don't care about law and order and justice and all that.'

'Did they ask the *New York Courier* for extra money for Tom? I'd just like to know if Mrs Roux was as generous as you were for me, Jack.'

'She rang me and said she would put up half the money. I told her we'd talk about it after the event.'

'In the event, we saved you a quarter of a million quid. We'll let him pay for dinner, Dad.'

It was the only time during dinner when they all smiled at each other.

They went back to London and Sylvester moved in to stay with Cleo in her flat. He looked around at the furnishings, saw that they were much more luxurious than anything in the house back in Coogee; then he walked to the big window and looked out at Green Park, now a green and gold park in the autumn sunlight. She waited for him to say something.

At last he said, 'You've got a beautiful view.'

'What does that mean? That that's all I've got?' She went and stood beside him, but they were looking at each other now rather than at the view. 'What upsets you so much, Dad? That Jack's so rich or that he's so much older than me? Do you think I'm just a gold-digger?'

'I haven't heard that word since I was a kid. Are you?' Then she saw the pain in his face at his own remark. He

194

turned away to look out of the window again. 'I didn't mean that, sweetheart.'

She wasn't sure that he hadn't meant it; she gave him the benefit of the doubt. 'He actually loves me, Dad. I'm not just his kept woman. Oh, he's given me this flat, but I pay for everything else. I don't get an allowance or anything like that. I make good money –'

'More than me, I understand, much more. I asked him. You're a real success and I'm glad for you – that's what you came to London for. But – I don't know, maybe I'm old-fashioned. I just wish I had your mother to talk to, to see what she'd think of it. He's old enough to be your father.'

'I hope you didn't tell him that.'

'I did. It was the obvious thing to say.'

'He wouldn't have thought so.' She rolled her eyes in mock dismay.

Suddenly he laughed, not the belly-laugh but more like a gasping sigh of mirth. 'Righto, you know your own mind. But I asked him a few other questions, too. We had a lot of time together while we were waiting to find out what was happening to you and Tom Border. He has a wife, do you know that? Have you ever met her?'

'No. She lives somewhere in the country. We've never talked about her.'

He threw up his hands in one of his old theatrical gestures; but he was playing to a constituency of only one. 'Christ Almighty, sweetheart, you're breaking up a marriage –'

'I'm not. The marriage is finished. I don't like you thinking I'd do that –'

'All right, I apologize. But hell, what sort of future have you got with him? Do you just go on being his – his –'

'Mistress is the word, Dad. It's the one I like better than any of the others, even girl friend.'

'Okay, mistress. Do you go on like that till she dies? He told me she won't give him a divorce. And what about Tom Border? What is there between you and him?'

'Nothing,' she lied. 'What makes you think there is?'

'Sweetheart, I've been reading politicians' faces for more

195

years than I care to remember. If you can read those, every-one else's is an open book. That young bloke –' almost un-intentionally he emphasized *young* '– he's head over heels in love with you. And you know it.'

She had always known how politically shrewd he was; no one in Australia had a better reputation in that regard. But with the conceit of women, especially young women, she had never credited him with much shrewdness in affairs of the heart. She had assumed he had closed his eyes and his mind to such things, had always left that to her mother and not bothered to interest himself after Brigid had died. She had seen him woo women voters, old and young, with all the charm of a political Casanova; but he had never hinted that he might know anything of what was in the electorate of their hearts, that he cared that they might be in love or in need of love. It set her back to realize that he had read her as easily as he might have read Hansard.

'Tom goes his own way. He's not interested in marrying a career woman.'

'Did he say that? You two must have had plenty of time to talk about things while you were at that farm.'

Now that she came to think about it, they had talked about surprisingly little: at least about themselves. They had skirted the subject of love in the same way they had avoided the subject of their possible death.

'He's never mentioned marriage. He thinks I'm too am-bitious. All you men are the same.'

That was a mistake and he picked it up at once. 'Lord Cruze, too. I got the idea he'd like you to settle down and be – well, settled down.'

'Be just his kept woman, you mean. Yes, he would. But I'm not going to accept that. Times have changed, Dad. Mar-riage isn't the be-all and end-all of a woman's life. It wasn't the be-all and end-all of your life. Mum always had to share you with the Labour Party. She said she sometimes felt she was in bed with the whole Labour Caucus, Ben Chifley, Arthur Calwell, Uncle Tom Cobley and all.'

'I know,' he admitted. 'She told me that often enough. We

196

had our rows about it. But we both believed in marriage, in our own. We were happy in it, one way and another. That's all I want for you, sweetheart. To be happy.'

She kissed him: it was the easiest answer. She was not happy now but she couldn't tell him so.

He stayed for two weeks. She hardly saw him in the last week. He was busy on political business with the other members of the all-party delegation that had arrived from Canberra; they made mental notes for reports that would never be written. Canberra talked to Westminster and vice versa, though Westminster gave only half an ear to the ex-colonials, since it believed that no worthwhile word had come from Down Under since Captain Cook had delivered his report two hundred years before. Both sides, however, agreed that you could never teach the voters anything; though that, too, was never recorded. A senator from Washington sat in as an observer on the conference and agreed with what was implied if not stated: that between elections none was so dumb as a voter and even at election time his intelligence was borrowed from the representative he intended to elect. Cleo, out of deference as a daughter and not as a voter, refrained from writing a column on the parliamentary conference.

She had written her story on the kidnapping and Massey-Folkes had spread it across two pages of the *Examiner*. She went on *Scope* on the Sunday night following her and Tom's rescue and told the story again, this time using the angle of rising terrorism in Europe; Roy Holden had put together enough visuals, from film by his own crew and from library stock, to make it a good feature. She narrated everything without dramatics but still made it sound like the greatest adventure since World War Two; the television critic on the *Daily Express*, a first-class chauvinist, headed his review, 'An Evening at Home with Pearl White.' Nonetheless, it topped the ratings for that week. The viewers sat in the small forts of their living-rooms and bed-sits and looked at a real live heroine being modest about her escape from death and thought how nice it was that she was British, even if at one

197

remove. The male viewers had their fantasies about being locked up with her for three days in a farmhouse bedroom; no pictures of Tom Border were shown and she mentioned his name only once; Roy Holden and Simon Pally, the producers, wanted only one star and she their very own. The female viewers noted that she was as well-dressed as on all her other appearances, looked for broken fingernails in the occasional close-ups of her hands and commented that if she had indeed been in any real danger it had left no blemishes on her. Men like their real-life heroines to look like the unreal goddesses of films; women prefer their heroines to be reasonable facsimiles of themselves. Goddesses need not necessarily have feet of clay but they are more believable if they have thick ankles. When Cleo got up and walked away from the camera with her swaggering walk the male viewers went with her into an imaginary bedroom. The women were already on their way to the bathroom or to the kitchen to make a cup of tea.

On the morning of Sylvester's departure Cleo borrowed the Rolls-Royce and had Sid Cromwell drive her and him out to Heathrow. He had said goodbye to Jack Cruze the night before. They shook hands like two retired middleweights who wished they were thirty years younger and they had another referee.

'Look after her,' Sylvester had said and tried to make it sound like a threat. But he knew his voice would be faint from 12,000 miles away.

'Of course,' said Jack, who, in any case, had not expected any parental blessing.

'I don't know when I'll next be over,' said Sylvester. 'Unless there's a wedding.'

Cleo, the referee, called *Time!* Or rather, she said, 'It's late. It's time we turned in.'

At Heathrow next morning Cleo took her father up to the VIP room. 'Did Jack Cruze arrange this?'

'Yes.' She didn't tell him that she also got this treatment each time she travelled. VIPs don't necessarily have to be important: it is enough to be a celebrity.

'Well, I guess you're a VIP yourself now. Do you need him to get you this sort of treatment?'

But she knew what he meant: do you need him, period, question mark. 'Possibly not. Dad, let me work it out myself. I have a good life here. And though you may not believe it, Jack is part of it.'

He gave up; but his surrender was grudging. 'If he offered to marry you, I'd find it easier to take . . . Righto, sweetheart. Like I said, all I want is for you to be happy. A father can never guarantee that for his kids. Not even a good one.'

'You've always been a good father.' She believed it at that moment.

He shook his head. 'No. You were lucky, and so was I – you had a good mother . . . Will you be coming home for a visit?'

'Some time, I'm not sure when. Maybe after the next elections, to help you celebrate Labour's win.'

'That could be another two years. But we'll win, all right.'

'Where will Gough Whitlam put you in the Cabinet?'

'God knows. He's as unpredictable as the wind. That's what some of them call him, The Educated Wind.' Cleo knew there was no back-stabbing to equal that in the Labour Party. Whitlam, the Party leader, would some day look like the dummy target in a knife-throwing school. 'I've got my eye on Foreign Affairs. I fancy myself as a foreign affairs expert now.'

She was wistfully sympathetic. 'But you still dream of being Prime Minister?'

He laughed, but it was one for the voters, canned and on tap. 'I gave up that dream when I went into the Senate. I just couldn't stand the in-fighting any more in the Party. I settled for the comfort of the Senate.'

It was the first time he had ever confessed to her that he was no longer ambitious for the top post. She should have realized it long ago, but she had been too concerned with her own ambitions. She had been so intent on getting out from under his shadow she had not noticed that the shadow had shortened.

199

'You hadn't noticed, had you?' he chided her gently. 'You're like most people – you make up your mind about a person and most of you never bother to change it unless he or she does something harmful to you. The majority of people are lazy about their opinions.'

Lazy or myopic: she wasn't sure which. 'I'll say some Hail Marys that you get the Foreign Affairs job.'

'You still pray?' She didn't, except when in danger; but she nodded. 'That would please your mother. I prayed myself while I was sitting in that hotel in Hamburg.'

Then it was time for him to go. They kissed and embraced. He held her as if he were a dying man, as if he would never see her again; but she made no comment, just hugged him to her. She was weeping when he went out of the room, but she managed to hold the tears until his back was turned.

She stayed that night with Jack in the penthouse flat. Their love-making at first was awkward, as if they were making up after a major row; but when she was finally aroused she gave herself up to him completely. Her one worry after it, when he lay asleep beside her and she lay wide awake listening to the traffic in Piccadilly and down Constitution Hill, was whether she had been trying to convince him or herself that nothing had changed. As she fell asleep she heard a police car going along Piccadilly, its bells ringing their warning.

3

Tom Border lay that same night in a bed with his Parisian girl friend. She was a stewardess with Air France, a girl seemingly always on the wing, even when off-duty. She was the ideal solace for a man in love with another woman: she asked no questions, made no demands, took each day (and night) as it came. Her name was Simone and, though she didn't know it, she was a smaller edition of Cleo. Her ambition, too, was smaller: all she wanted out of life was to enjoy it.

Tom, while in Paris, shared an apartment with an older man, Bill Dickey, who had lived in Paris for years and worked

200

for the American embassy. He seemed to spend more than half his time out of Paris and Tom sometimes wondered if he was a CIA man; but he never asked, was just thankful that he could have the apartment to himself so often. It was on a narrow street off the Boulevard Saint-Germain, in a building that had once been a mansion and was now a warren of small apartments, though the rooms were big. The rent was high, which was why Bill Dickey was glad to have a co-tenant.

In the morning Tom got up while Simone was still asleep and went out onto the tiny balcony and looked down in to the street. The opposite side of the street had no mansions, converted or otherwise; it was a row of apartment buildings above narrow-fronted shops. The baker's shop directly opposite was already open and he imagined he could smell the fresh bread he could see in the shop's window. A girl came out of the baker's and walked down the street, a long loaf held over her shoulder like a rifle; she looked jaunty, as if she had just spent a marvellous night and wanted everyone to know about it. Paris was the city for love: or so all the poets and writers who came from other places said. He knew it wasn't true. Love, and lovers, suffered just as many bruises in this city as in any other.

Simone, wrapped in a blanket, came to the door and looked over his shoulder. 'You want to go after her? The one with the bread?' She always spoke English, except when she was making love, because she said his French gave her a headache. 'Was it my fault that last night was not very good?' She didn't say it accusingly: she aimed to please.

'No, *chérie*.' He always tried to throw in a few French words to show he was trying. But he had the Mid-West ear for foreign languages and he knew he would never be a linguist, not even in bed where incoherence disguised the poor accent. 'That was my fault.'

'You probably were thinking of your dreadful experience.' She had a genuinely sympathetic nature, not one taught her by Air France. He appreciated her caring for him, for not all the French cared about foreigners, especially Americans. 'I once had a lover, a pilot, who escaped from a terrible crash – he was no good for six months afterwards.'

'As a pilot?'

'No, idiot, as a lover.'

'I'm sure you cured him, *chérie*.'

'No. He became very faithful to his wife and she cured him. It was very touching and I was happy for him.' She was happy for all her lovers when they were happy, whether because of her or some other woman. She was totally without jealousy, which meant she was only in love with herself. But that didn't spoil her charm and Tom knew that some day she would fall in love with someone other than herself and be as jealous and miserably happy as himself.

'Simone, I'm going back to New York.' He had made up his mind in the early hours of the morning, the thought dawning on him as the sun came up that he had to put an ocean between himself and Cleo.

'Ah, darling, that will complicate things.' She flew regularly on the Paris–New York run, and had lovers on both sides of the Atlantic.

He grinned and understood, felt no jealousy at all. They were perfect partners for love-making if not for love. 'We'll have dinner tonight at Le Grand Véfour. A farewell dinner.'

'You're going so soon?' Then she added with French thriftiness, 'But Le Grand Véfour? That is too expensive.'

She had never thought that he should spend money on her to get her favours. He kissed her and she let the blanket drop. Across the street the baker, who had come to his door to see what sort of day it would be, looked up and saw the American in his pyjamas and the naked girl embracing. It was going to be a good day, at least for those two, and he went back into his shop satisfied.

Simone went home to her widowed mother and Tom went into the *Courier*'s bureau office just off the Boulevard de la Madeleine. The *Courier*'s principal stockholder might own a chateäu in the Dordogne and stay in Paris at the George V, but the Parisian employees of the paper worked in what Tom thought of as pre-Revolution squalor. Chuck Nevin, the bureau chief, had been there since the end of World War Two and sometimes sounded as if he might have been there much longer, might have interviewed Danton and Marat. He had the dark eye-pouches of a liverish Frenchman and an air of knowing there was nothing new in the world, that all the news he sent back to New York was only a re-hash of history.

'You want to go home? Well, I'll have to talk to New York. What'll I tell them?'

'Tell them I'm afraid that friends of those German kidnappers will come after me. Especially when I give evidence against that Rosa Fuchs.'

Nevin didn't believe him; but he nodded his head. He would not have wanted to go through what Border had been through and he could not blame the younger man for using it as an excuse, even if there was another reason for his wanting to go home. 'They can't say no to that. Head office couldn't afford to pay compensation to your folks if you were bumped off while working. Of course if you were bumped off in your own time...'

'Chuck, you're too cynical even for me.'

'It's the only way to live with the Frogs.'

'You wouldn't want to live anywhere else but Paris.'

'True.' Chuck Nevin had a French wife and five French children, all of whom were anti-American. 'How soon do you want to go home?'

'As soon as possible.'

'As soon as I can get a replacement. But God and the New York office protect me from young guys wanting to come over here and be the next Hemingway.'

Tom took Simone to dinner at Le Grand Véfour, he in his Harrods suit, she looking chic and beautiful and heart-achingly like Cleo in a Seventh Avenue Givenchy copy she had bought in New York. He said, 'Have you always worn your hair like that?'

'No. I was going to change it back to my old style, till you told me you liked it this way.'

'Well, you can change it now, when I'm gone. Pull your

203

bangs back.' She pushed them back and was another girl, a stranger. But he said gallantly, 'You look beautiful either way.'

'Ah, *chéri*, you said that like a philosopher, not like a lover.'

'That's my new role.' Diderot, another philosopher, had dined here, might even have sat at this very table. He looked around him, felt himself surrounded by ghosts, something he had never felt in the inexpensive restaurants he frequented in New York. 'Philosophers live longer.'

'Do you want to live so long?'

'Yes.' Long enough for Jack Cruze to die and leave Cleo free.

4

Claudine Roux went to Heidelberg to see Roger and to comfort Louise. She sometimes acted, Louise thought, as if she were the Commander-in-Chief; but she never mentioned the thought to Claudine or even Roger. Claudine would not have taken it as a jibe but as the proper analogy to her role in the Brisson family.

'You were very fortunate, Roger,' Claudine said, at home at once in the villa outside Heidelberg. She had looked around admiringly when she had arrived. Whatever else one might say about Louise, she had taste and knew the proper surroundings for a Brisson. 'This may not be the last attempt on your life. I think you should ask for a new posting, preferably back to the United States. Don't you agree, Louise?'

'I think that's up to Roger.' Louise did not look forward to a Stateside posting. Army bases in the United States were dreary places and, as the alternative, she did not want to be left alone on Long Island, hoping that Roger could get home every second or third weekend. She liked the present posting, even if Roger was in danger. She had learned to live with the thought of his being in danger, but she could not live with army wives on a US home base. 'They are going to tighten security about him.'

'I don't want to come home yet,' said Roger, and Louise looked at him gratefully, though she knew he was only thinking of himself. 'I'm doing a good job here, Claudine, and I think they realize it back in Washington.'

Claudine, seeing his ambition, was as surprised as if he had told her he was going over to the Russians or the Democrats. The army had always been his career, but she had always looked upon it as a self-imposed discipline where his natural brilliance would see that he was always one step above where the real discipline started. To hear him hint now, if only obliquely, that he aspired to something higher than the command of a division, surprised and pleased her.

'How much longer do you need to stay here to impress them? They don't promote you posthumously, do they?' She always called a spade a spade, even a grave-digger's one.

Louise put her hand to her breast, though she knew her heart was not beating any faster. 'Don't talk like that, Claudine! Roger will outlive both of us.'

'Possibly,' said Claudine, meaning *possibly you but not me*. 'But a posting to the Pentagon would be safer and would bring him to much closer attention.'

'Hands off, Claudine,' said Roger, recognizing his sister's mind already at work. 'No string-pulling.'

'I don't run the Pentagon. You flatter me.' But she liked the flattery and thought it not so far-fetched. She had had Army Secretaries and generals to dinner and not just for their conversation. She polished brass till the generals were dazzled by their own shine. 'No, I think you'll get it on your own merits, if you apply yourself.'

'Get what?' Louise said. Roger never told her any military intelligence, she had to pick it up from *Time* and *Newsweek*. 'Roger, you're not thinking of the Presidency?'

It seemed at that time that every other general was. Still, her ambition surprised both Roger and Claudine. They looked at her with new respect, though both thought she should have known better. Roger said, 'Darling, I could never run for

President. I had a French father and I was born in France.'

'Oh, of course. I forgot.' Louise thought the Constitution was a piece of bureaucracy designed to hold the truly good men down. 'Well, what then?'

'There are lots of things,' said Roger, cautious now. He stood up, tall, handsome and commanding. He would make a wonderful President, thought both Claudine and Louise, their agreement showing in their faces. Roger was the only honest assessor of himself in the room; he knew he would never make even a good President. He had never been able to scratch any back but his own, and recent Presidents had proved that back-scratching between the White House and Congress was as necessary as a deficit Budget. He was no longer fooling himself as he once had. 'Let's have lunch. How is Alain these days?'

'His leg has mended, but he still has his limp.'

'Is he bitter about Vietnam?'

'If he is, he says nothing. He's started work on the *Courier*.'

'What as?' said Louise. She adored Alain, her only nephew. 'I always thought he wasn't interested in the paper.'

'He would now like to be editor some day. I should like that. In all the time we have owned the *Courier*, no Brisson has ever actually run the paper.'

'Everyone's on their way to the top,' said Louise and led the way into lunch. She sat at the top of the table, the only time she ever out-ranked the Brissons.

On the way back to New York Claudine stopped off in Paris to buy some clothes. She had worn Chanel dresses and suits since she had been old enough to choose her own wardrobe; her taste had always been classical, she had never had any time for the extravagances of Dior, Courrèges and some of the recent outlandish English designers. Coco Chanel had died this year and Claudine bought a dozen suits as a memorial to her favourite designer. And to ward off the thought that she herself might die before the classical gave way entirely to the bizarre.

From the George V she rang Chuck Nevin at the *Courier* bureau. 'Everything satisfactory, M. Nevin?'

Chuck Nevin had spent twenty-five years learning not to say no to such a question. His own salary and expenses were good and he was not going to fight for those who worked for less. Live and let live as best they could, was his motto. He admired Marie Antoinette and thought Claudine was a reasonable facsimile thereof. 'Everything is fine, Mme Roux.'

They always spoke French to each other, their only intimacy. 'How is M. Border after his ordeal?'

'He's here in Paris, Madame. He is going back to work in New York.'

'When?'

'The day after tomorrow.'

'Tell him to wait till Friday. He can travel back with me. I should like to talk to him.'

'Madame, he'll be travelling economy class. It's the paper's policy.'

'He'll be travelling first class with me, M. Nevin. Please arrange it. Tell him to look smart. He does tend to think he's covering Skid Row.'

Tom, looking reasonably smart, called for Claudine at the George V in the limousine Chuck Nevin had ordered. He got out, inclined his head in a small bow and handed her into the car with a reasonable imitation of Gallic gallantry. She looked at him in his Harrods suit and nodded approvingly.

'Much better, Mr Border. Clothes do make the man.'

'Make him what, Mrs Roux?'

She cut a slice off him with the side of her eye. 'Don't be smart with me, young man.'

'I thought that was what you wanted me to be. Smart.'

He was going home, saying goodbye to his one true love, though she did not know it. He was drunk with regrets and, like all drunks, careless of the future. He was drifting towards being a drifter again.

But he knew when he was being churlish and at once said, 'I apologize, Mrs Roux. I got out of the wrong side of the bed this morning.'

'Did you have a row with your girl friend on the other side

of the bed?' She gave him a thin smile. 'I know what news-papermen are like, Mr Border. I don't keep company with them, but I know their habits and their morals. They are one of the few professions that parade their peccadilloes. They are like small boys smoking in the street.'

'I slept alone last night, Mrs Roux.' Simone had left for New York yesterday morning. 'No, I think I must be getting old. There was a time when I could leave a place, even home in Missouri, without any regrets.'

'Why are you coming back to New York then? Mr Nevin told me it was your own request. Or were you really afraid that some other terrorists might come after you?'

He had considered the possibility but decided that Rosa Fuchs's colleagues, if she had any left, would not waste their time and lives on him. But he said, feeling dishonest, 'I was thinking of the others in the *Courier*'s office. There was a faint chance someone else might get killed . . .'

'Are you going to write a book about your experiences? Most journalists do.'

He had already had offers from three publishers: terrorism was a good theme that year. 'I don't think so. I may write a novel.'

'You don't sound enthusiastic. Are you a lazy man, Mr Border?'

He grinned. 'Will you sack me if I say yes?'

'No. I don't admire lazy men, but some of them have a better sense of perspective than the achievers. Men on the run often don't see what they pass by.'

At Orly airport the TWA ground staff and cabin crew treated Claudine as if she were the First Lady, if only for the day. Some of the staff and crew recognized Tom, when they saw his name, as a recent hero in Germany and thought how nice it was for Mme Roux to be so solicitous of one of her employees as to allow him to travel with her. That Claudine hardly gave him a glance until they were settled in their seats in the plane escaped the notice of the TWA staff. It is difficult to be watchful when being trampled underfoot.

'You have a way with you, Mrs Roux,' said Tom.

208

She didn't miss his irony. 'I know what you people call me – The Empress. The role suits me and pleases me. The airline staff like a little hauteur now and again, so long as one smiles while treading on them. They must get bored with an airplane full of *hoi polloi*.'

'I have a stewardess friend who told me exactly that. She thought *égalité* should never have become airborne. I gather it isn't on Air France.'

'I think you and I may have an enjoyable trip, Mr Border. Now have some champagne and listen to me. No, miss,' she said to the stewardess hovering over them, 'we'll have *champagne*, not Californian bubbly. One can take patriotism too far.'

When Tom's glass was filled he lifted it to Claudine, but had the sense not to say 'To you, Empress', though the words trembled on the end of his tongue.

'I don't know what position you will be taking over when you get back to New York –'

'I'm hoping they may find a place for me on the editorial page. I kid myself I know something about foreign affairs now.'

'I may be able to help you there.' Now that Alain was working on the *Courier* she intended to take more interest in what went on below board level. 'It would suit me to have you in the office every day instead of running around the country gathering news. My son Alain has just gone to work on the paper.'

'Yes, Chuck Nevin told me.'

'What sort of tutor do you think you could be? Allowing for your laziness.'

'There'd be better men on the paper than me at that sort of thing. Some of the older guys.'

'I don't think my son has much respect for some of the older – guys.' She disliked slang. But she was asking a favour of him and she was willing to come down to his level for the moment. 'There would be more rapport between my son and you.'

He had never met Alain Roux and he wondered how much

his mother's son he was. There would be no rapport between himself and a little emperor. But if he could not get on with Alain Roux, he could always drift on. He had never worked in California and the *Los Angeles Times* was now one of the better papers in the nation. California was full of crazies, but so far none of them was a terrorist.

'I guess it's up to your son, Mrs Roux. If he thinks I could help him ...'

'Thank you.' She finished her champagne, handed her glass to one of TWA's scullery maids. Travelling by plane was one of her major dislikes and she wondered why men and women chose such jobs. She gave the stewardess a queenly smile to alleviate the girl's hardship. 'You may serve our dinner now.'

'Soon, Mrs Roux.' The stewardess was from Kansas City, where they hung the title Empress only on prize cows. 'They've had to go back for the smoked salmon. They left it at Orly.'

The girl passed on and Tom hung his head as he laughed silently. Then he looked sideways at Claudine. 'No rapport there, Mrs Roux.'

'I should have her head.' But then she smiled, descending to the lower levels. 'My son is not like me, Mr Border, if that should be worrying you. He has an unhealthy respect for democracy.'

Tom wondered if she was right about her son. He doubted very much her ideas of democracy were those of the majority of the Republic.

He turned away and looked out of the window. They were flying at 33,000 feet above a carpet of cloud; yesterday, a red streak in the sky, rested on the horizon ahead of them. He looked down, but he had no idea whether England was below them or behind them. He said goodbye to Cleo from a great height, but was sad, not condescending.

TEN

Cleo waited two weeks to hear from Tom, then she called the Paris office of the *Courier* and was told that Mr Border had returned to New York. She was hurt and disappointed; but she didn't blame him too much. She had an innate sense of fairness, an aberration most women succeed in avoiding, and she knew she could offer him no more than he was prepared to offer her. But she was upset, which brought on her period early, which in turn upset Jack Cruze. He liked to keep love-making to a schedule, like the rest of his life. It was a sign of approaching age, but he would not admit that.

The new year, 1971, came in. It was the centenary year of the publication of Lewis Carroll's *Alice Through the Looking Glass*, an event that Quentin Massey-Folkes laid down for editorial comment when the exact date came; but Cleo looked hard at her own looking glass and found no entry there. It seemed that she had come to a dead end. She began to wonder where she would be ten years hence, then dismissed the thought. She wrote a column asking at what stage the young started thinking beyond next week. The young, too busy with today, didn't answer.

In March she went to Hamburg for the trial of Rosa Fuchs. Roger Brisson, as a serving officer of a foreign army, had been excused from appearing, but he sent a deposition. Cleo arrived the night before the trial was to begin, booked into the Vier Jahreszeiten and waited for Tom to arrive. But he did not put in an appearance and next morning she drove to the court with Quentin Massey-Folkes and the *Examiner*'s lawyer, David Dibdin.

'I can't intervene for you, Miss Spearfield,' Dibdin told her in the car. He had a prominent belly, chins to spare and a razor-sharp mind. 'But the Hamburg lawyer we have engaged for you is the best. He may not even have to intervene, the case is so straightforward.'

'Not for me it isn't,' said Cleo. 'I'd rather forget the whole thing.'

Massey-Folkes pressed her hand. 'We'll get you out of here as soon as possible.'

'I'm glad you came, Quent, but you shouldn't have. You don't look well.'

'A few days away from the office is all I need. It's my wife who isn't looking well, knowing I'm in your company.'

Cleo looked at Dibdin. 'He's the heaviest-handed flirt I know.'

But she had great affection for Massey-Folkes and, though she was grateful for his company, she worried about how he looked. He appeared to have lost weight and there was a tiredness to him that was too apparent to be ignored.

Tom Border was waiting at the court. He gave her the old slow smile and put out his hand, like an old acquaintance rather than a man in love.

'Cleo old girl, you look great. As usual.'

He looked like the old Tom, a bag of bones held together at the top by a loosely knotted tie. 'I thought you weren't coming.'

'I couldn't leave you to face this on your own.'

Security in the court was so efficiently tight it was frightening. It seemed to Cleo that the German authorities were as afraid of the past as of the future. They were shutting out all the extremists: Nazis, Communists, anarchists. They were also shutting out the democracy, or at least that was what some of the banned would-be spectators shouted outside the court.

Rosa Fuchs was brought into court and at first Cleo didn't recognize her. The long hair was neatly done in a chignon, she wore a plain grey dress that showed off her figure, and her face, classically beautiful, was discreetly made up. Either

212

she had an astute lawyer or she had rejoined the bourgeoisie against which she had rebelled.

She made no retraction of her aims, refused to answer when asked if there were other members besides Kurt Hauser and Gerd Silber involved in the attempted kidnapping of Generals Brisson and Thorpe; but she was unfailingly polite, the model of a decorous terrorist.

Cleo and Tom, fortunately, were called on the first day. The German authorities, with an eye to a bad international press, were eager to have the foreign witnesses out of the way as soon as possible. Cleo and Tom were told that they could return to London and New York, with the proviso that they must return immediately if required in Hamburg. As she left the court Cleo looked across at Rosa Fuchs. The girl was staring at her, cold hatred in the beautiful blue eyes.

Outside the court she told Massey-Folkes and Dibdin that she would see them back at the hotel. 'I think you'd better stay with us, Cleo,' said Massey-Folkes. 'Just in case. The Boss sent me to keep an eye on you, remember.'

She saw the logic of the suggestion. 'Righto. But I'd like Tom Border to come back with us. We'll have dinner together.'

'I think we should go back to London immediately,' said Dibdin. 'We can't expect the German police to guard you for another night while you enjoy the town.'

Cleo turned as Tom came across towards the three of them. Police stood close to them and newspaper photographers and television cameramen hovered on flashes of light; it was no background at all for lovers to kiss and make up. Though what was there to make up? she wondered.

'Are you going straight back to New York or coming to London first?'

'Straight back to New York.' He was pleasant and friendly, but she could almost see the defences he had built up. She was in love, but not blindly so. 'I'm catching tonight's plane.'

'Where are you staying?'

'At the Atlantic.' The *Courier* was treating him well, though the paper had known the Germans would help with the tab.

213

He had chosen the Atlantic because he had guessed she would be at the Vier Jahreszeiten.

'Can you drop me off at my hotel?' She ignored the frowns of Massey-Folkes and Dibdin.

'If you don't mind riding with my escort.' He was gracious, if reluctant.

The escort sat up front with the driver, stiffly formal both of them; Cleo and Tom sat in the back of the BMW with almost equal stiffness. Cleo suddenly felt a prisoner, of her emotions if nothing else. She should have ridden back to the hotel with Massey-Folkes and Dibdin.

She said bluntly, beating her way out of herself, 'Why did you go back to America so abruptly? Not even a word.'

He was just as blunt. 'Where's Lord Cruze? I thought he'd be here to bolster your nerve. That wasn't easy in the court today.'

'The German police advised him not to come. They thought I was enough of a security risk on my own.' She knew that Jack had been relieved when the advice had come through from Hamburg. Not that he was afraid of terrorists, just publicity. He did not want to be shot, in her company, by photographers. 'Why did you go back?'

He was more constrained by her attitude than by the presence of the two Germans up front, both of whom spoke English. He looked out of the car at the Alstersee, a lake of chopped blue ice under the March wind. All of a sudden he leaned forward and tapped the driver on the shoulder.

'Pull up there by the Lombard bridge, please. Fräulein Spearfield and I want a few words alone.'

The driver looked at the escorting policeman, who said, 'It is not permitted, Herr Border.'

'It is permitted,' said Tom. 'I'm an American citizen and your government has placed no restriction on my movements. I'll take the responsibility.'

'But if something should happen –'

'I'll feel it more than you, believe me. Five minutes, Sergeant, that's all we need.'

The police car pulled up and Tom helped Cleo out and

214

walked with her, hand on her elbow, to the middle of the bridge that separated the two lakes that made up the Alstersee, the Aussenalster and the Binnenalster. The wind whipped at them as if to further fray their emotions.

'There was no point in prolonging the agony, Cleo – that was why I went back to New York. You're Lord Cruze's girl, no matter what.'

'Don't you think you might have asked me about that?'

'I didn't need to. You're married to your career on the *Examiner* and that TV programme of yours – that's almost the same as being married to Cruze. It's all tied in together.'

She looked back at the main part of the city, at the pale green copper domes, steeples and roofs, like faded pistachio icing on buildings that suggested the solidity of granite cliffs. Yet twenty-five years ago the city had been in ruins. She wondered what the lovers of Hamburg, standing here in those days and looking back at the jagged skyline, had thought of their future.

'I don't love him,' she admitted. 'I've found that out.'

'I guessed that. But you're not going to say goodbye to him, Cleo. I just didn't want to hang around in Europe till he died.'

'If I came to America – ?'

The thought tempted him. A ferry came out from beneath his feet, from under the bridge. It was almost empty, a lone passenger standing at the bow, gazing fixedly ahead of him like an explorer looking for a new horizon. Then the man threw up his arms, as if whatever thoughts or hopes he had were fruitless, and went back inside out of the wind.

'What would you do in New York? I don't think I could keep up with you, Cleo. You have more drive than I'll ever have. You've got more ambition than just to be Tom Border's missus.'

She had never really looked at the incompatibility between them; there had been no need to, since there had been no commitment. She began to believe now that he might always be a drifter. 'What are you doing now? Are you going back to Vietnam for the end of the war – when it happens?'

He shook his head. 'I've put Vietnam out of my mind. Some day America will want to do that – I'm just ahead of the rest of them.'

'So what are you doing?'

'I'm writing special features and the occasional editorial.' He had also become tutor and friend to Alain Roux, but he didn't think that would interest her. In his spare hours he was writing a novel, but he did not mention that to her either: he was not sure how much of her was in the book. He said almost defensively rather than with pride, 'I'm doing all right.'

'I'm sure you are. I think you're better than you let yourself be.'

'Lack of ambition.' He grinned; but it was no joke. Then he took her gloved hand and lifted it to his lips; he had learned a few things living in Paris. 'It's goodbye, Cleo. There's nothing else to say.'

'Oh Tom!' But she didn't break down. She clutched his hand as they walked back to the police car. 'Shall we try again in ten years' time?'

He smiled. 'Let's do that.'

It was all very civilized, which is no way for true lovers to act. The policeman and the driver, relieved that their charges were still unharmed, welcomed them back as if they were greeting State dignitaries. The drove on to the Vier Jahreszeiten.

As the car pulled up Cleo leaned close to Tom and kissed him on the lips. He held her shoulder but didn't pull her to him. He could hold a naked girl in his arms on a balcony in Paris but he couldn't embrace his real love in the back seat of a Hamburg police car. He returned her kiss, but there was a moratorium on any passion between them. Perhaps in ten years . . . Another time, she had said.

'Take care,' he said.

'You, too.' And felt suddenly lonely. There were more things to be afraid of than terrorists.

In June, on a bright summer's day when all the British looked smugly at the foreign tourists who made rude remarks about Britain's weather, Quentin Massey-Folkes resigned as editor of the *Examiner*. He was dying, of cancer, but Jack Cruze refused to let this be discussed. He would have barred obituaries from the *Examiner* except that they made such good reading for the living. For all the living except himself, that is.

Cleo had watched with agony the deterioration of Massey-Folkes. She had deep affection for him and thought he deserved to die gracefully and at his leisure. It almost hurt her to see how affected Jack was by Quentin's illness.

Jack had not been easy to get on with since her return from Germany in March. There may have been a change in her own attitude; she didn't know and preferred not to examine herself too deeply. Jack had known that Tom Border had been in Hamburg, but he made no mention of him at all. They bickered more often, an occupational hazard for those who live together; but they did not live together, and she saw the possibility of such a state of affairs looking fainter and fainter. The same thought had occurred to Jack, for he became more and more possessive.

'You can forget your column for July and August,' he had said to her in mid-May. 'We're going on a cruise to the Dodecanese Islands. You and I alone most of the way, but we'll pick up a few people at Piraeus. I've rented a yacht, a big one. A hundred-and-twenty-footer.'

The size meant nothing to her; she was in a mood that day to have refused the *QE2*. 'Two months is too long for my column to be out of the paper.'

'All right, you can send it from the yacht.'

'What will I write about? I write for ordinary people, not silvertails.' Silvertails was one of her father's favourite expressions; he used it for everyone making more money than himself. It went down well with the voters back home, ninety-nine per cent of whom aspired to be silvertails. She had introduced the word into her column and a Socialist MP at Westminster had paid her the ultimate compliment of using it in the Commons.

'The poor like to read about the rich,' said the silvertail in the room with her.

'I don't deny that. But only if I'm writing about them from the outside – taking the mickey out of them, if you like. They're not going to be happy about me living *la dolce vita* with you on the back end of a boat, especially a hundred-and-twenty-footer. They might buy you and me in a rowing boat on Staines reservoir, but I think that's about as far as they'd go.'

'There you go again. I try to do things to please you.'

'Jack, a little consultation would help. You're trying to run my *life*.'

'I'm trying to protect you from yourself. All you think about is your damned work. You haven't stopped since you came back from Hamburg in March, you don't even seem to want to take time to think. Every time I suggest something, you're busy.'

'We see each other at least three nights a week'

'It's not enough!' His temper was rising.

'Well, that's too bloody bad!' She lost her own temper, something she had rarely done with him in the past. 'My life's my own – I don't belong to you – not yet.'

Then he hit her. She had seen the suppressed violence in him before, something he seemed to keep under control as if he were afraid of what it would do to him as much as to someone else. She had seen it break out of him only once, when he thrashed at a fractious horse with his whip. There had been only the two furious lashes, then he had stopped, trembling as much as the whipped horse. Now he hit her across the face, jerking her head sideways with the force of his open hand.

She staggered back, blinded by shock more than by the sudden sting across her cheek. Then she picked up the small battery-run carriage clock on a table against one wall and hurled it at him. Fortunately she was still stunned and her aim was not good; otherwise she might have killed him. It struck him a glancing blow on top of the head and crashed to the floor on the far side of the room. He staggered back, one hand clutching his head, as taken aback by her violence as she had been by his.

She left him then, sailing out of his flat in full fury, all swagger gone, an Amazon who had given more than she had got. She slammed the front door and, to add to his own fury, the security alarm was somehow triggered and bells began ringing. Sid and Mrs Cromwell came running from the kitchen and the hall porter burst out of the lift and banged on the front door. Jack Cruze, blood running from the cut on his head but soaking into his thick hair, told them to get the bloody bells fixed, then stamped upstairs to his study. Sid Cromwell picked up the smashed clock and nodded appreciatively; Miss Spearfield had given the Boss the time of day in a way he probably had not expected but had certainly deserved. Sid knew his boss's failings better than Jack did himself.

Upstairs in the library Jack got out a print of Greta Garbo in *Flesh and the Devil,* and lost himself in a fantasy of the woman who had been the dream goddess of his youth. The cut on his head had stopped bleeding, but there was a bump under the grey curls and he had a slight headache. When he went to bed he fell into another dream; Cleo was both flesh and the devil. He woke in the morning gritty-eyed, his headache worse. Erotic dreams are too exotic a course for a man in his fifties.

He sent her a dozen red roses and she called him at lunchtime, making him wait and suffer. 'All right, Jack, I forgive you. But don't ever hit me again or that's the end between us.'

'I'm sorry. I shouldn't have lost my temper like that. It won't happen again.'

That night she slept with him in the penthouse flat and he woke next morning with fresh eyes and a clear head. Which proved to him that the actual exercise was far better than the fantasy, if only to induce sleep. But you never tell your loved one she is as good as Valium.

A week later she played hostess at a dinner in the flat. There were sixteen guests, which virtually split the dinner into two parties. Jack sat at one end of the long table and she at the other. The guest of honour was a Sheik from one of the Trucial States; his wife was safely back home in the harem, so he brought Rhonda Buick, the ex-beauty queen. She was introduced as his public relations adviser, but it was obvious there were also private relations between them. The Sheik sat on Cleo's right and was polite, but his eyes kept straying down the table to where Miss Buick sat with Jack Cruze.

'I hope Miss Buick has made things smooth for you here in London,' said Cleo.

'Oh yes, yes. Very smooth. English women have many talents.'

'Thank you,' said Cleo being English for the evening. She supposed that, in a way, she was no better than Rhonda Buick. She looked down the table at Jack, who employed her, though he didn't think she made things smooth for him. Then she turned to the man on her left. 'What about the talents of American women, Mr Kibler?'

Jerome Kibler was a New York banker, small, dapper and burdened with a giggle which made a low joke of high finance. But since he had got out of the army twenty-six years ago, coming out as a paymaster sergeant who had spent the war studying the stock market, confident that God, the Allies and Wall Street would win, he had piled dollar upon dollar and now sat on a heap where virtually everyone but the men at the very top in Wall Street, men on old heaps of money, looked up at him. He was Jewish and a friend of the Sheik, whose investments he supervised in the United States.

'American men are frightened of their women's talents.' His laugh turned into a giggle, as it always did.

'Are you all afraid of the Women's Liberation movement? What do you think of all this bra-burning?'

'We're advising our clients to sell their stock in Maidenform.' Again the giggle. It was a pity he couldn't control it, because he was a nice, intelligent man and Cleo liked him at once. 'No, seriously, we think it's a good thing. Or anyway I do. The Women's Lib thing, I mean, not the bra-burning. In my own bank we're promoting women to top positions. I think we're ahead of most banks in that respect.'

The Sheik shook his head. 'You are buying trouble, Jerry. I hope I shan't have to deal with a woman when I come to New York next time.'

'Oh, I'm sure Mr Kibler will protect you against that danger,' said Cleo.

The Sheik was not dense, just bigoted. He smiled, light winking on the gold at each corner of his mouth. 'I come from an old-fashioned society, Miss Spearfield. If I were younger and not the ruler of my country, perhaps I could be more liberal.'

'What about the Sheik at the other end of the table?' said Kibler and didn't giggle. 'What does he think about liberated women?'

Impulsively Cleo put a hand on his and laughed. 'Mr Kibler, Lord Cruze could take over from Sheik Abdullah tomorrow and the women in that man's country would never know the difference.'

The Sheik and Kibler laughed and all three looked down the table at Jack. His stare was frozen, and Cleo frowned, wondering what was on his mind; then she realized her hand was still on Jerry Kibler's. Oh God, she thought, this is ridiculous. He was now even jealous of their dinner guests.

Perversely she looked directly at Kibler, widened her smile as if she were trying to wrap him in it and said, 'Mr Kibler, would you have lunch with me tomorrow? I'd like to do a column on the place of women in the world of banking.'

'I'd be delighted. But let me take you. I like to keep a few of the old conventions.'

She didn't argue. She had only suggested having lunch with him to annoy Jack, another old convention.

Afterwards, over coffee in the drawing-room, Cleo said to Rhonda Buick, 'Business seems to be improving. The PR business, I mean.'

221

Miss Buick, wide-eyed and innocent of all but major crimes said, 'I know what you mean, Cleo. We're both getting on, you know. You just woke up earlier than I did to the fact that older men are more reliable than young guys with their payments.'

'What *is* the going rate at the harem?'

'I'll let you know,' said Miss Buick, spooning sugar into her coffee and her smile. 'You may be out of a job some day.'

They parted the best of enemies. Miss Buick left early with the Sheik, warning him of the heavy day he had tomorrow. He went eagerly, as if looking forward to a heavy night.

Later, when the last guests had gone out of the door, Jack said at once, 'What was going on between you and Jerry Kibler?'

'He's taking me to lunch tomorrow. We're going to talk about women in banking.'

'Is that all you're going to talk about?'

'Goodnight, Jack.' She went out of the flat, slamming the door behind her but this time not setting off any alarm.

Except in him. He opened the door to call her back, but the landing outside was already empty; she must have gone down the stairs without waiting for the lift. He closed the door and went into his bedroom, undressed and got into bed. Billie Dove, Lilian Tashman, even Garbo could not comfort him tonight. He knew that at times lately he had been acting like a jealous youth, someone with no experience of women, but he could not help himself. He had learned to live with the absence of Emma, but she had been gone more than twenty years now; in less time one learns to live without a leg or both legs. Even an hour's absence by Cleo was like trying to live without his head. He used that analogy rather than *without his heart*. He was head over heels in love but still not romantic.

In the morning he called Emma, but Emma's housekeeper answered the phone, went away and came back to say that Lady Cruze could not come to the phone; she was otherwise engaged. He slammed the phone down as if it were a bludgeon across the back of Emma's neck.

222

He and Cleo made up again. She did her column on women in banking and Jerry Kibler read it, rang her to say he liked it, giggled at some of her remarks and went back to New York, asking her to look him up if ever she came to America again. She said she would and forgot him.

Then Quentin Massey-Folkes resigned. Cleo was in the *Examiner*'s news-room on his last day there. She could have written her column at home, but she went into the office on the three days when her column appeared and wrote it there; sitting at a small desk in a far corner of the big room. It was her way of showing that she still considered herself part of the paper's staff. Whether the rest of the staff appreciated her presence, she did not know, but no one sneered at her and she thought, or hoped, she had not lost her early popularity. She had swagger and confidence, but, as far as she knew, no one had ever accused her of having a big head.

She finished her column, handed it to a boy to take to the features editor, who was still Joe Brearly, the man who had given her her first job on the paper. Then she walked down the long room and into Quentin's office.

He looked like a dim reproduction of himself; thin, grey, all life gone from his eyes. She wanted to cry, but knew he would be angry if she did.

'I'm going down to the West Country, to a cottage I always meant to retire to. I'll be out of the way there.'

'Jack's going to miss you. We all are. The paper won't be the same without you, Quent.'

'I should hope not.' He had never been burdened with false modesty. 'I've been here more years than anyone else, except some of the chaps in printing. I made it what it is. I hope you've learned a thing or two from me.'

'I have. Who's taking over from you?'

He shrugged; it seemed a major effort, he looked so weak. 'I've talked to half a dozen chaps for Jack. I don't think any of them is right. Well, maybe they're right for the paper – I don't know whether they're right for the Boss. He's not the easiest man to work for.'

They exchanged smiles. 'What about Joe Brearly?'

'He doesn't want the job. He says he could never handle Jack.'

'What about me?' She had been thinking about it for the past twenty-four hours. It would bind her even more closely to Jack, but that couldn't be helped; she had come to Fleet Street to get to the top and this was the opportunity. 'I can handle him.'

For a moment there was a spark of the old Quentin in the thin grey face. 'Do you think you could do it? Ah, but why am I asking? If the Queen asked you to take over from her, you'd be up there on the throne like a shot.' Then he shook his head and subsided. 'No, it wouldn't work, Cleo. There are too many men on the staff who think they've paid their dues and could do a better job than any woman. There's never been a woman editor of a newspaper in Britain and those chaps wouldn't stand by and let you, an Aussie to boot, be the first.'

'You're wrong in saying there's never been a woman editor. The first editor of the first daily paper in England, the *Courant*, was a woman. That was in 1700. She didn't last long, but she was the editor. It's time there was another one.'

He smiled shrewdly. 'I knew about that woman, but I didn't think you would. You'd really like the job, wouldn't you? Well, try your luck with Jack. I can't back you, Cleo. It wouldn't be fair to some of the chaps I've worked with all these years. Between you and me, I don't think any one of them would be any better than you. But you're untried, Cleo. You've never even sat on a subs' desk, you've never made up a page –'

She looked out through the big glass wall at the newsroom. She could see the reporters at their desks getting into gear to report tomorrow's news. Some of them were typing, with their backs hunched, necks craned, in the posture of those who had never learned to touch-type; others sprawled in their chairs reading notes or other newspapers, the younger ones being studiously casual as if they had not yet quite fitted into their roles. On the sub-editors' desk older men were sharpening their blue pencils, sharpening their teeth as they prepared to teach the young reporters how to write terse, readable prose. Two or three men were grouped around the various editors' desks: the metropolitan desk, the provincial, the foreign. Copy boys sat at the far end of the room like cattle dogs waiting to be whistled up. Though the evening rush had yet to start, the huge room already had its own vibrancy, the sort of atmosphere that almost no other industry had. Because it *was* an industry: the production of news. And there were few products that had to be produced and sold so quickly.

The newsroom was only part of it. There were the circulation department, the advertising department, finance, personnel; and there was the printing department, the engine-room of the whole paper, where the printers, a race apart, grouped in the quaintly named union chapel, ruled as in another country. Journalists have the conceit that *they* are the paper, but without the other departments their typewriters would be just a battery of unheeded clacking.

She looked back at Quentin. 'I think I'll ask Jack to try me.'

She did, that evening. She would have done better, perhaps, if she had asked him to marry her, though she would have got the same answer.

'No! Every bloody paper in the country, even *The Times*, would run something snide about Cruze making a present of the *Examiner* to his girl-friend –'

'Is that all you're afraid of?'

'No!' He was spearing her with exclamation marks. 'I'm more afraid you'd make a mess of the paper! You know nothing about editing –'

'Men have been promoted to editor without editing experience. Or is it that you don't trust a woman?'

'You're too young. If you were ten years older, maybe –'

'Hugh Cudlipp was only twenty-four when he was made editor of the *Sunday Pictorial*.'

'He'd had years of experience.' He made it sound as if Cudlipp had started editing letter-blocks in his cradle. 'No, I'm not giving you the job. The subject's closed.'

She did not lose her temper this time; she had half-expected the refusal. She had asked him down to her flat for dinner; she felt safer on her own ground. She had had dinner sent across from the Stafford Hotel opposite; she knew she was a poor cook, though Jack, with his palate, would not have been too critical. She had not wanted to do battle with him on a stomach fortified only by Mrs Cromwell's cooking. Mrs C. served Brussels sprouts and peas with everything, which would have made for windy argument.

'Does that mean I've gone as far as I can on the *Examiner*?'

'What does that mean?'

'Just what I said.'

'Has someone else offered you a job? Murdoch or Max Aitken?'

She put down her spoon and sat back in her chair, giving her exasperation full rein. 'Why do you always look for a rival? No, no one has offered me a job – though I'm sure I could get one if I wanted it. All I asked is, have I gone as far as I can go on the *Examiner*?'

'For a few years, yes.'

'Well then, maybe I will look around to see what else is on offer.' The threat came off the top of her head, taking flight of its own accord.

He pushed his plate away from him: there was nothing as good as bread-and-butter pudding, not even chocolate velvet. 'What do you want me to offer you? Maybe you can have one of the magazines.'

'I don't want to go onto a magazine. Every second week another story on the Royals. Or How to Bring Up Baby in the Seventies. Or Forty-seven Ways to Cook a Brussels Sprout.' Forty-six ways of which would be thrown out by Mrs Cromwell. 'Jack, I'm at a dead end. Oh, a very comfortable dead end, I'll admit that – a lot of women would give their eye-teeth and a lot more to be where I am. But I'm going to become very stale if I have to go on doing the same thing for the next ten years, till you think I'm old and experienced enough to edit the *Examiner*.'

'You could give up newspaper work altogether. And television, too.'

'And do what?' But she knew.

'I could take more time off and we could travel. I'd like to compete in more horse shows, some of the big ones in America, for instance. I could buy a yacht and we could spend more time cruising. There's a lot of the world I've only lately realized I've never seen. The out-of-the-way places. Machu Pichu, for instance. The Himalayas –'

'Woy Woy.'

'Of course.' Then he said, 'Where's that?'

It was a village back home in Australia, north of Sydney and still clouded by the joke it had been in her father's youth when everyone had thought of it as a weekend retreat for drunken fishermen. It was now a respectable retirement retreat, but it was not Machu Pichu. She ignored his question and said, 'Jack, you're talking about what *you* want to do for the next ten years. You'd better get some extra stickers for me, because you make me sound like baggage.'

He threw up his hands: for a moment she saw her father. 'There you go! Always trying to put me in the wrong. We'd *share* all I've been talking about.'

'Who would I be? Your travelling companion? Your very good friend?'

He kept his hands on the table this time, did not say *There you go again*. Instead he said very quietly, 'What would you like to be?'

Then she found she couldn't say '*Your wife*'. Instead she said, 'Jack, what I want is not to be taken for granted. I've got no hold on you at all. If I gave up everything to be whatever I'd be, your travelling companion or your good friend or whatever other people would call me, and then in two or three years' time, or five or ten, if we fell out – where would I be? In my thirties, starting all over again. I have no idea what the competition will be like in two or three years, let alone ten. I might find it very hard to make it.'

'You wouldn't have to worry, I mean financially. I'll set up a trust for you.'

227

'No, Jack, it's not the money.' She said it honestly.

He got up, poured coffee for both of them from the percolator on a side table. He brought hers, kissed the top of her head, then sat down opposite her again. It was a small round table but, it struck her all at once, he still gave the impression that he was sitting at the head of it. Like the chairman of the board.

'I could try for a Mexican divorce and we could be married.'

He had never mentioned marriage before, nor had she. It had been a subject, like death, to be avoided. But she was not unprepared for it. 'What would your wife think of that?'

'Not much. She's a Catholic, a strict one. They never recognize divorce at all. You should know that, you're a Catholic.'

A poor one. 'Does English law recognize a Mexican divorce?'

'I don't know, I'd have to get my lawyers to check that. But we'd find a way –'

But lawyers were not going to make up her mind for her. She did not want to be Lady Cruze II, not if it meant he remained chairman of a board of two. She loved him, but not wholly; it was as if he were several men and she had love for only one of them. Also, a shadow on her conscience, there were the more than occasional thoughts of Tom. She thought she truly loved him, but there were moments when she wondered if he, too, were not several men. Perhaps her love was true only for not being tested.

'Would I keep working?'

'Why should you want to? You'd be my wife.' *Enough for any woman*: she could read the extra words in his face.

'I'll think about it.'

'Do that.' He sounded as if he were suggesting another merger. He can be so bloody unromantic, she thought: one of several men she didn't love.

But she had little time to think about being Lady Cruze II. Quentin Massey-Folkes died two days after leaving the office, before he had even set out for the cottage in the West Country. It was as if the *Examiner* had been his life raft; he slipped from it and was gone. Coming back from the funeral in the Rolls-Royce Jack broke down and Cleo put her arm round him and comforted him. She saw Sid Cromwell look at her in the driving mirror and nod approvingly.

At last Jack recovered, wiped his eyes and sat back. 'I'm going to miss him.'

'I know that,' she said, and wanted to cry. But tears never comforted tears, not even if one took turns: they just made grief seem sentimental. Quentin had been a father-figure to her, but never one whose shadow blotted her out. 'We'll all miss him.'

'Back to the flat, m'Lord?' said Sid Cromwell.

But Cleo got in first. 'No, drop me at the *Examiner*, Sid.'

'Take the day off,' said Jack. 'I want someone to talk to.'

'Later. First, I'm going back to the office to write Quentin's obituary. If Guy Tallon says anything –' Tallon, an old *Examiner* hand, had already been appointed editor '– I'll tell him you okayed it.'

'I'd like to write it myself.'

'You stick to your last, I'll stick to mine.'

She had never written an obituary before. Her thoughts were maudlin and fulsome, but she didn't put those ones on paper. Massey-Folkes would have thrown out such a piece, no matter who the subject was; his ghost would come back and tear the place apart if such a column was written on himself. So she wrote with the ghost behind her and it was the best piece she had ever written. For once, the readers in the suburbs and provinces might understand that a man, with all the virtues and faults of all men, had sat in the editor's chair, that he had not been some god of cynicism and manipulation.

'That's him exactly as he was,' said Guy Tallon. He was

short and plump and cheerful and he would never be the editor that his predecessor had been; but he knew it and that was his saving grace. 'I shan't touch a word of it. Quent would have loved it. No bull in it. He hated bull.'

'Don't put my name to it,' said Cleo. 'I think it should be a tribute from all of us.'

Tallon gave her a look that said he was seeing a new side to her. He didn't like career women because he was afraid of them; especially career women who slept with the Boss. He had never allowed himself to think there might be any modesty in Cleo. She might not be so difficult to work with, after all.

'I think the Boss will like it.'

'He'd better,' she said and smiled at him. But she would never take him into her confidence as she had Quentin.

With the death of Massey-Folkes it was almost as if Jack had decided that his and Cleo's future need not be discussed again. A new editor had been appointed, things would go on just as before. It was a deliberate ploy on his part. Though Emma had never changed hers, he liked to believe that if women's minds were not disturbed they would eventually be influenced by the stronger minds about them. He had no doubt which was the stronger mind of his and Cleo's: hers was just stubborn. Life, like his own mind, went on unchanged. There were dinners, horse shows, a quick trip to Nice for a three-day cruise with the Greek ship-owner; Cleo was given notice of what was going to happen but was never consulted. She said nothing, treating her resentment as if it were a social disease she wanted hidden from him. She was tired of argument because she was not sure what her own argument should be. Jack, had he known, would have said she was being a typical woman. Which, for better or worse, would have crystallized her argument into a Waterford vase thrown at his head. The vase always held the red roses and she would have thrown the roses, too.

Cleo now felt strongly that her career, indeed her life, was at a standstill. *Scope*, coming back after the summer break, held its place in the ratings and, Roy Holden told her, she was now looked upon as the Number One reporter – 'but don't tell the other chaps.' Her column, even to her own eyes, sometimes seemed a little tired, but the fan mail, for and against the subjects she raised in it, was just as big as ever. She began, however, to wonder how long she could go on before she turned into a well-paid hack.

Christmas came and went, spent at St Aidan's House. Jack gave her a mink coat, something she had previously refused to accept: it had seemed to her too much the uniform of a kept woman. This Christmas he wouldn't take no as an answer and she surrendered to the luxury of the coat; her soul, she told herself, was still her own but now it would be warmer. She bought him, with the advice of his coachman, a new set of harness; but if she had hinted that she wanted to put a rein on him, he gave no response. He still laid down their programme, the year ahead was all his.

On a cold March day in 1972 she went to have tea with the Misses St Martin. Last year she had gone regularly once a fortnight to have a little tea, a little chat with them; this year she had been only once, her spare time taken up with Jack. They understood, they had told her when she had phoned them: Jack had always been a demanding man.

'What did you mean when you said Jack had always been demanding?'

They were having tea in the rear drawing-room which faced out on to the tiny garden. The house had remained unchanged except that the painting of the nude girl had been replaced by a Turner seascape. It was as if the St Martin sisters, too old now for the pleasures of the flesh, did not want to be reminded of them. The sensuality of Turner's colours was enough for them.

'Not with us,' said Dorothy. 'I didn't mean with us. We never tolerated that sort of client. Not that he was a client of ours for very long.'

'No more than two or three times,' said Rose. She was a lady, but she had a madam's memory for figures. One didn't run a successful brothel, or bordello, with loose housekeeping. 'Then he met Emma.'

231

Cleo kept her cup steady in its saucer. 'Emma? Lady Cruze?'

'Of course.' Dorothy offered the plate of petits-fours. 'Do take one. We've never mentioned her when you have been here before – you never did, so we thought perhaps we shouldn't. Come to think of it, we've never said much about Jack Cruze.'

'We've always been discreet about our clients,' said Rose. 'We had to be, with the gentlemen we had here. Though Jack, of course, is more than a client. He'd prefer to forget why he first came to our house, I'm sure.'

'Did he meet Emma here?'

'Of course, where else?'

'She was one of your girls?'

'Good heavens, no!' The St Martin sisters sang a chorus. 'She is our niece.'

Cleo put down her cup and saucer and left the petit-four untouched on her plate. She knew that all the men she worked with thought she was coldly calculating: *they* had foresight, but she was calculating. None of them knew how often she worked on impulse: 'Do you think she would see me if I went down to visit her?'

The two sisters looked at each other, then back at her. 'Why should you want to do that?'

'Because very soon I have to make a decision about – well, about the rest of my life, I suppose.'

'Has Jack asked you to marry him?'

'In a way. He's suggested he get a Mexican divorce.'

Dorothy St Martin sighed, put down her cup and saucer, wiped her lips delicately with the lace napkin. She knew the demands of men's carnality and had catered for them; certain sins were forgivable. But she did not believe a man should be relieved of his sacred vows, not when it meant hurting her favourite niece. She used her religion to excuse herself her own inability to forgive.

'Does he love you?'

'Yes.' She said it with certainty and without conceit.

'Do you love him?' said Rose.

232

My surrogate mothers, Cleo thought, two ex-bordello-keepers. 'Yes and no. Or does that make me sound as if I don't know my own mind?'

'Yes,' said Dorothy. 'But so many women in love are like that. Men, too. Being in love isn't a cut-and-dried state of mind.'

'She reads a lot,' Rose explained with a smile. 'Colette, Elizabeth Bowen, Germaine Greer, Marjorie Proops. You, too, but you never write much about love, do you?'

'I've never dared to,' said Cleo. She had made notes on it: Love is an Illusory Fact, Love is a Factual Illusion, Love is a Race from Go to Woe. But her readers would have contradicted her no matter what she had written. There were more ways of being in love than Cupid, who was never very bright anyway, could have counted. 'Were you ever in love?'

'Of course!' They looked at her as if she had asked them if they were kind to animals. They were female and English and only English men doubted their capacity for love. 'Both of us. Twice.'

'What happened?'

'War happened,' said Dorothy. 'Both of us lost our young men in 1918, at Amiens. They were brothers.'

'We fell in love again. They were not brothers, but they might well have been. They were both cads.' Rose mopped up the crumbs of her petits-fours with her cake-fork. 'After that, it hardly seemed worthwhile trying again.'

Cleo felt unutterably sad for both of them. And wondered if, in years to come, she would remember Tom as these two old women remembered their dead heroes and their cads.

'Would you marry Jack if he got – a Mexican divorce?' Dorothy said it as if it were a sin just to utter it.

'I don't know. That's why I'd like to see Emma. It might clarify the confusion I'm in.'

'Or make it worse.' But the sisters looked at each other. 'Should we?'

'I'll understand if she says no,' said Cleo, airborne now as she had taken the plunge.

'Telephone her,' Dorothy said to Rose and the latter, with

an encouraging smile to Cleo, rose and went out of the room. 'Rose has a better way with her than I have. I tend to land on other people's feelings feet first.'

'I don't believe that. You have a heart of gold.'

'All bordello-keepers are supposed to have one of those,' said Dorothy. 'It isn't true. One would be out of business within a month.'

'How are the priests down at Farm Street?' It was a non-sequitur that could have slandered the Jesuits, though slander has never been a hair-shirt to them.

'Delightful men. We had three of them to tea last week.'

Cleo looked up at the Turner on the wall, wondered what the priests would have thought of the previous occupant of the space. Then Rose came back, all smiles.

'She will see you. She suggests tomorrow, if that would suit you. Tea at four.'

Tea at four, the meeting of the estranged wife and the current mistress: it was all so – lady-like? Cleo took out her gold pen and wrote down the address Rose gave her. Then she held up the pen.

'It's been my lucky charm.'

'May it continue to be,' said Dorothy; then added, 'Be kind to Emma. Life hasn't been easy for her.'

'Should you tell me something about her?'

Again the sisters looked at each other. Then Rose said, 'I think you should form your own impression. But you do know she is crippled?'

Cleo was shocked. 'Jack's told me nothing about her.'

Dorothy sighed at the perfidy and callousness of men. 'She will tell you how it happened, if she wishes to. Good luck, my dear.'

4

Cleo still had no car of her own, but rented one whenever she needed it. She usually rented one of the more expensive ones, a Volvo or sometimes a Jaguar, something to fit her image of a successful columnist and one of the smaller TV stars; the British aristocracy might turn its back on ostentation, but the middle and working classes liked to judge a bestseller by its cover. Today, however, she was not going to flaunt her success, whether in her career or with Jack, in front of Emma Cruze, for whom life had not been easy. She drove down to Suffolk in a Ford Escort.

It was the sort of day when she still pined for the climate of Sydney. A cold wind blew in from the east: Siberia, it seemed, was just across the Channel. The buds on the fruit trees were pale, as if it were still too early for any colour; cows stood miserably in the fields, facing west like mournful refugees at a border. A man sat on a tractor in the corner of the field, as if he had ploughed himself into it and didn't know how to get out; crows cawed at him with the mocking laughter of dying consumptives. It was appropriate weather for going in cold on another man's wife.

Preston St William was in Constable country, a village that seemed hardly to have changed since the painter's day. A few bungalows and a row of Victorian workmen's cottages stood on the outskirts, but they didn't belong, and looked like newcomers waiting to age enough to be admitted to the old people's home. Preston St William had been here when the medieval wool trade with Flanders had been at its height; it had been here, under other names, when the Romans and the Normans had come up from the coast. It struck her that she had never been to this part of England before and she wondered if, by some sort of hypnosis, Jack had kept it out of her mind.

Malton Hall was sixteenth-century: half-timbered, with a tile roof that rippled in places like a tent disturbed by breeze, it made an anachronism of the Rolls-Royce standing outside the front door. Life might not have been easy for Emma Cruze, but it looked as if it might have been worse. Cleo drove the Ford Escort up the gravelled drive and parked behind the big black car.

The front door was opened by a housekeeper. In other circumstances she might have been warm and cheerful; today she gave Cleo a cold, suspicious eye. She could have been an East Anglian cousin to Mrs Cromwell: she knew a kept woman when she opened the door to one.

'Lady Cruze is expecting you,' she said in a voice that suggested Cleo might also be the mistress of one of the Four Horsemen of the Apocalypse.

Emma Cruze sat in a wheelchair in a low-ceilinged sitting-room that looked out on to a large garden still recovering from winter. A fire burned in the big brick fireplace and the colours of the furniture and drapes gave added warmth to the room. But Emma herself, like her housekeeper, was cool.

'You look exactly like you do on television, Miss Spearfield.'

'How's that, Lady Cruze?' It was odd to be calling someone Lady Cruze. There had been occasions when hotel clerks and restaurant waiters in foreign cities had slipped up, when she had been with Jack, and called *her* Lady Cruze.

'As if you own the camera.'

'I don't feel any sense of ownership today.'

'Not even of my husband?'

'If I felt that, I don't think I'd be here, do you?'

They were studying each other, opponents at the ladies' fencing school; there would be no name-calling or hair-pulling, just neat blood-letting thrusts. Emma had the advantage: she had seen the exterior Cleo Spearfield on the television screen, got an insight into her mind through her column; now she was waiting to see what morals the girl had. She had been waiting twenty years for some woman to come demanding Jack's freedom.

Cleo had to start from scratch. She had had no idea what Emma would look like and she had been surprised at the beauty of the older woman. A niece of the two good-looking St Martin sisters could be expected to have some looks: but Emma had not expected that an embittered, neglected and crippled woman could still retain her beauty the way Emma had. Certainly there was a frailness to her beauty, as if Emma sat inside a thin, delicate mask; certainly her almost-white

hair made her look older than she could possibly be. But
Emma Cruze had not allowed herself to forget what she once
must have been, a very beautiful girl.

The housekeeper brought tea. There were small sandwiches, scones and strawberry jam, a cream sponge cake, all
on a silver tray and with cups and saucers and plates of
delicate china. Emma said, pouring tea, 'Afternoon tea is my
favourite meal of the day. Do you have to watch your figure?'

'A little – I put it on here and there. Do you have to watch
yours?' Then she stumbled as she took her foot out of her
mouth: 'I'm sorry. I didn't mean –'

'Don't be embarrassed by the wheelchair, Miss Spearfield.
I no longer am. Though I suppose it is easier for me. Did Jack
tell you that I was a cripple?'

'No, your aunts did.' She felt she was somehow betraying
Jack. But he should have told her more about Emma.

'Did he tell you anything about me?'

'Nothing.'

'Did you ever enquire?'

'No.'

'That's strange. Most mistresses, most *women*, would want
to know about a man's wife, why he wasn't living with her,
who'd left whom. Why didn't you want to know, Miss Spearfield?'

'I'm not quite sure. Cowardice, perhaps. I don't really
know everything about Jack himself and I suppose I should
after three years. Something but not everything.'

'I was married to him only a year. So perhaps you know as
much about him as I do.'

'I don't think so.' She said it gently, almost as a compliment.

Emma cut the cream sponge cake. 'Does he still like what
he calls good plain food? He never did have any taste, in food
I mean. In his women, yes.'

'Thank you,' said Cleo, taking the slice of cake.

Emma broke her cake with a silver fork. Cleo noticed she
had beautiful hands, almost the hands of a young girl: as if,
with her heart and legs crippled, she had concentrated on

237

keeping young something that had remained unhurt. 'I suppose I do know Jack better than most women, even though I haven't seen him in ten years. Yes, he used to visit me, once a year. Ten years ago I told him not to come again. But I've been studying him, at a distance. We women don't always see our men clearly when we're in bed with them. Is he still demanding in bed?'

'Demanding?' It wasn't the word but the question itself that threw Cleo off-balance. She had not expected Emma to speak as frankly as this. But then she was the niece of two bordello-keepers, so why not? 'He likes making love, if that's what you mean.'

'That's what I mean. I never minded – he was like a boy, trying to prove his stamina.'

'But he was much younger then . . . He's still the same. But, Lady Cruze, I didn't come down here to talk about that.'

'No, you didn't, of course. Strange, the way we talk today, as if we're all trying to prove we're uninhibited by convention. Twenty, even ten years ago I wouldn't have mentioned the subject. I suppose it's because I watch a lot of television – the BBC plays seem to be courses in bedroom technique. I sometimes wonder if the producers and directors of such plays aren't very successful with women in their private lives.' For the first time she smiled, a pleasant expression that took years off her face. 'Don't misjudge me. I'm not a frustrated middle-aged woman with a dirty raincoat. You'd never catch me wheeling myself into those sex cinemas I read about in Soho.'

Cleo wondered what a woman in her physical circumstances did to relieve any sexual feelings she might have. Abruptly, to put the thought out of her mind, she said, 'Did you love him?'

The smile remained on her face, as if she had forgotten it. 'Yes, I did. Very much. But I wouldn't have if I'd remained with him.'

'Why not?'

She put down the half-eaten cake, looked out through the leaded windows at the garden. Tiny buds showed on a willow, like pale green tears; a bed of crocuses was a single patch of colour, like half-buried Christmas crackers. In the far distance a church tower showed above a barbed-wire frieze of tree branches. Wind-streaked clouds smeared the sky like strokes from a dry brush.

'You know, John Constable lived not far from here. I have two of his paintings. I live very comfortably, as you can see. A lovely house, good furniture, paintings, books, the car you saw outside. Jack has always looked after me that way. Anything I asked for, I could have. All he wanted in return was a divorce. Which I never gave him.' She turned back to look at Cleo. 'Never will.'

'Because of your religion?'

'Partly. Are you Catholic? Yes, you are. I remember you mentioned it once in your column, something about the Pope's banning the Pill. But you're not a strict one?'

'No, not even a good one. But why did you say religion was only part of the reason for not giving Jack a divorce?'

She sat looking at Cleo for several moments. The atmosphere between them had softened; they were not friends, but they were edging away from being rivals. Or enemies. 'I shouldn't want Jack to ruin another woman's life the way he tried to ruin mine. Oh, I don't mean this.' She tapped the arm of the wheelchair. 'He wasn't to blame for that. I thought so at the time and accused him of it, but I was wrong.'

'What happened? Or would you rather not talk about it?'

Again there was the long silence, then she said, 'No, I'll tell you about it. Jack seems to be more serious about you than he was about any of the others. And I don't believe my aunts would have allowed you to come down here if they didn't think you were – decent? Is that a word one can use about a woman? There are decent chaps, but I don't think I've ever heard anyone mention a decent woman.'

'Men don't expect women to be decent, not in that sense.'

'No.' They were slowly reaching out for agreement, even if only on subjects that were so general and meant nothing to their immediate relationship. 'I met Jack when I'd just turned twenty-one. My father was in the Indian army, then

239

after India's independence he went out and joined the East African Rifles in Kenya. I was educated at a convent school here in England and my aunts would look after me in mid-term hols or whenever there wasn't enough time to fly out to join my father – my mother died when I was seven. I knew by the time I was fifteen what sort of place my aunts ran, but for some reason I wasn't shocked – it made me a sort of heroine in the dormitory with the other girls. The nuns would have died if they'd known what we used to talk about after lights out.'

'I gather nuns are a bit more broad-minded these days. They have to be to survive.'

'Probably. Well, after I'd left school I went out to live with my father in Kenya. Then he died, just before I turned twenty-one – that was in 1949, if you're interested in how old I am.' She absent-mindedly ran a hand over her white hair, as if to say to take no notice of it. 'I came back to England and I met Jack. No, not at my aunts' house. They took me to a reception at the Dorchester and Jack was there. It was love at first sight for both of us. Do you believe in love at first sight?'

'Not quite. I think I'm what you'd call a myopic romantic. I like a second look at a man.'

'Perhaps I'd have done better with your experience. I'm sorry, I didn't mean that to sound so bitchy. I was utterly *in*experienced in men. There was plenty of social life in Kenya, but I'd never found it very exciting and I never wanted to get myself involved with any young man there, in case I had to settle down with him and remain there forever. I never wanted to be a planter's or a soldier's wife.'

'Then I can imagine you falling for Jack the way you did. He was already successful then, wasn't he?'

'Not the way he is today, but yes, he was successful. He also had a rough charm and something else – vitality?'

'Yes, he has that. Still.'

Emma poured herself another cup of tea, but left unfinished the cake on her plate. 'Well, we married three months after we met. I thought I was going to have the most marvellous life any girl could have. But it never turned out like that, not at all. Even on our honeymoon he started *managing* me.'

Suddenly Cleo knew why she had come. All during the drive down she had been telling herself she only wanted to see who and what Emma Cruze was. But no: she had come to see if she could stop herself from making the same mistake that Emma had. She settled back in her chair while Emma went on unravelling the life she had had with Jack Cruze.

'He was so – *possessive*. I thought at first I might be wrong. I'd lived a life in which no one, neither my mother nor my father, had ever tried to run it the way Jack did. Of course the nuns tried to run it, but that was just school discipline. But everything with Jack had to fit in with him. I wasn't even allowed to go shopping on my own without telling him.'

'He's almost as bad, but not quite. But then I'm not married to him.'

'Perhaps that makes the difference. You have a career of your own, too. I never did. I was just his *possession*.' It was as if she had not thought of the word before: she paused, as if to underline it. 'He became jealous, fanatically so. Is he like that with you?'

'Fanatically? No, I don't think so. But I've never really given him any reason to be.' Nothing had happened with Tom Border, so why should Jack be fanatically jealous? Women and politicians: they could be selective about the degree of their sins. Her mother, a politician's woman, had told her that.

'Is he jealous at all?' Emma was beginning to read the nuances in Cleo's voice.

'Ye-es.' Then she said, 'He is possessive. I think that's why I'm here. To find out if he was like that with you.'

'He was. After six months we began to fight about it – he had a dreadful temper in those days. I wanted to have a child, but I kept putting it off because I knew he'd – possess it, too.' She was still speaking calmly, but her hands had disappeared beneath the cashmere rug over her legs and Cleo could only imagine how agitated they might be. 'Then one night we had a dreadful fight. He hit me, I thought he was going to kill me ... Has he ever hit you?'

'Only once. I threw a clock at him. I think it shocked him more than hurt him. He's never been violent with me since, but it's still there in him. The violence, I mean.'

'Perhaps I should have done the same. I'd wanted to go away for a week to Biarritz with my aunts and he refused, said he wouldn't let me out of his sight with *them*. When he hit me I stormed out of the house – that sounds melodramatic, but it's what I did. It was a dreadful night and I ran out into the rain and thunder and lightning –' She stopped and, unexpectedly, smiled. 'It was like a scene from one of his silent films, he'd already started his library of them then. Except there was all the dreadful noise of the storm. I got into one of the estate cars, he'd just bought St Aidan's House, and I started off for London – I was going to my aunts. I didn't see the tree that had fallen across the road in the storm, not till the last moment. I woke up in hospital four hours later, my back broken and my legs crippled forever. They didn't use the word paraplegic then, not the way they do now. Not in English county hospitals, anyway. They told me in nice undiplomatic language that I was a cripple and I'd never walk again. I blamed Jack for it and I refused to forgive him – I wouldn't even let him see me. Not for three months, after I'd left the hospital and was in a convalescent home. By then I knew he wasn't to blame, not for my being crippled. He came to see me and he was crippled – emotionally. Then he started talking about what he was going to do for me and I realized it was going to be the same all over again, only worse. Because I should *have* to let him organize my life. So I said I was never coming back to him and that was that. It was the hardest decision I've ever had to make and for a year or two I thought I'd made a mistake. But then I came to know it was the right decision, the only one.'

She suddenly looked exhausted. Cleo wondered how long it had been since Emma had talked as long and as frankly about what had happened to ruin her life. She said gently, 'And you still don't regret it?'

Emma took her hands out from under the rug. There were weals across the back of them, as if her fingers had been clawing at them; but now they rested calmly in her lap. 'No. I couldn't have held him, not the way I am. He'd have had other women and I just could not have stood being so close to him and knowing about them. At least down here I only hear about them. I don't smell their perfume on him, I don't smell *them*.' The hands tightened, the voice hardened vulgarly for a moment. Then she relaxed, looked gently at Cleo. 'I'm sorry. That's insulting to you.'

'If you had still been living with him, I should never have –' Her voice trailed off: it was not easy to give a name to oneself in front of the wife. 'It's insulting too, I suppose – but while you were out of sight, you were out of mind.'

'Will you stay with him?' *Now you've met me . . .*

'I shan't marry him, if that's what you mean.' Side-stepping the question, something women don't mind between themselves though they abhor it between themselves and a man. 'I'll become a good Catholic, tell him I could never recognize a Mexican divorce.'

'One shouldn't use one's religion like that.' She was truly devout, not socially pious.

'The Church bends any of its own rules to keep another – it happens with all institutions. I think God laughs sometimes at the things done in his name.'

'Are you really so cynical? I can never tell from your column.'

Cleo smiled, completely at ease with her now. 'Not really. But in a man's world, how else does a woman survive? I grew up in a man's world, politics, and now I'm working in another, the newspaper business. Even Dorothy Dix had to put her tongue in her cheek occasionally.'

'Will you tell Jack you've been down to see me?'

She had always been honest with him. 'Yes.'

Emma took her to the front door, wheeling her chair with skill. 'One becomes good at it after so much practice. Jack used to make silly men's jokes about women drivers ... I suppose I was bad the night I crashed into the tree.'

'Can you drive that?' Cleo nodded at the Rolls-Royce.

'No. Mrs Goodlet, my housekeeper, drives me. There's an elevator contraption that lifts my chair into the car. I don't sit in the house all day. We even drive to the South of France every summer for a fortnight. Jack takes care of everything – he was never mean. Part of his trouble is, I think, that he doesn't really know how to use the power of money.'

'Have you told him that? I have. I've tried to tell him that people are not corporations.'

'He'll never learn.' Emma held out her hand. 'I'm glad we met. But I don't think we should meet again. We should only finish up hating each other.'

Cleo put the question carefully: 'Do you hate Jack?'

She hesitated. 'Let's say I haven't forgiven him. Perhaps that is just as bad.'

5

That was Wednesday. Cleo waited till Saturday to tell Jack she had been down to Suffolk. In those three days she pondered on the bitterness that, no matter how well controlled and camouflaged, still lingered in Emma. She believed that everyone, even a saint, was capable of bitterness; a seasoning of wormwood was good for the soul, cleaning out the caries of sweet sympathy. She wondered if, as time and her relationship with Jack went on, she too would become bitter. The prospect filled her with apprehension.

· But she wasn't apprehensive about telling him that she had seen Emma. She was blunt: 'I went down to see your wife last Wednesday.'

''You *what?*'

They were at St Aidan's House, where it had all begun. They were walking in the park in the early spring sun. The weather had suddenly warmed in the past two days and colour had begun to appear in the pale green park. Windflowers, wood anemones, lay like flecks of old snow in the lee of shrubs; blossom cloaked a pear tree, turning it into a pale pyramid. A grass snake, lured by the con man sun, crossed the path up ahead, a green shiver across the eye. It's the wrong season, Cleo thought: spring was a beginning, not an end.

'I had to lay a ghost to rest, Jack.' That was not true: she was no longer being honest with him. Emma had never haunted her. But then she added, 'She's been your ghost.'

He was making an effort to control himself. Women did the damnedest things: which, of course, made them women as much as their sex organs. 'You should have told me.'

'I just have,' she said, woman-like.

'No, before.'

'You'd have told me to mind my own business. Or worse, gone down with me.'

'How did you get on with her?'

'Beautifully,' she said, putting the knife in.

He sighed, as if wounded. 'I knew you would. You're a little alike.'

'No, we're not. That's only because you think all women are a little alike. I don't think Emma ever had any ambition, for one thing. She'd have made you a very good wife, a better one than I would, if you'd treated her as a wife.'

'Did she tell you I treated her as anything else?' He was wary: God knew what women talked about when they were together. Maybe not even God knew.

'Yes.' She would not tell him that Emma had told her of his hitting her. That was something between man and wife and Emma, perhaps, had gone further than she intended in telling her about it. 'She said she was your *possession*. I can understand that. You'd like me to be the same.'

'That's all bull!' He tramped through a patch of crocuses, killing spring. She could see the violence in him now, more aware of it than ever before because now she was looking for it. 'Christ Almighty, I love you, don't you understand that? I loved her, too.'

'I didn't say you didn't. Your intentions are the best – but only for you. You'd never give me any independence, Jack.'

245

'You're bloody independent enough now. Why would it change?'

'If I became Lady Cruze – could I call myself that after a Mexican divorce? We'd have to ask Debrett about that.' The title had no appeal to her. The name Cruze would be a bigger cloud, throw a deeper shadow, than Spearfield once had. 'If I married you, would you let me go on with my column, still appear on *Scope*? No, you wouldn't. You've said so. So there would go my independence.'

'You'd have another sort of independence. You'd have all the money you want to do anything you want. I could set up a charity trust, you could run that.'

She was too shrewd for him. 'Jack, you'd be setting it up for yourself. You'd be its biggest beneficiary.'

'There you go again!'

They tramped round the park, arguing all the way and getting nowhere. She had made up her mind she wouldn't marry him, no matter what; but she did not know what else she was going to do. If she was to break off their relationship altogether, then she would have to leave the *Examiner*; Felicity Kidson had done that and now was women's editor of a rival newspaper. Cleo knew she would have little trouble in taking her column to another paper; the job on *Scope* would also be safe. But she would still be within reach of Jack, she would always stand the chance of running into him. The world, she had learned, above a certain level was just a collection of small exclusive parishes; only the vast poor and the drifting loner could escape those constricting circles. If she was to escape from Jack she would have to leave everything she had achieved in the three and a half years she had been in Britain. She had had to sacrifice nothing material to escape from being Sylvester Spearfield's daughter.

They had to go to dinner that evening at a neighbouring country house. As they drove through the soft twilight the mood between them was not soft; but she was more at ease with herself than he was with her or himself. But they would not embarrass their hosts, they would wear their good manners like cloaks.

246

Their host was a retired ambassador who had served in Moscow and Cairo and done a stint in Canberra as High Commissioner; he showed more scars from Canberra, because there he had been amongst the Commonwealth family. He was small and soft-voiced and big-eared, a wise rabbit.

'Welcome, Cleo. You're the only reason we invited Jack, you know.'

Cleo gave Jack a brilliant loving smile. It was a marvellous imitation and he gave her a reflection of it. 'I'd never get anywhere without her, Hugo.'

All the other guests were retired ambassadors and their wives. Jack and Cleo were the only two non-Foreign Office people there; Cleo felt very foreign. The world was taken apart, a dissection of another collection of parishes, this time foreign capitals; then the ex-diplomats, no longer having to be diplomatic, put it together again, gerrymandering the world as they thought it should be. It was the sort of dinner party Cleo loved and knew she would miss.

'Kissinger is too thick-skinned. He wouldn't be stung if he were lost in a beehive.'

'I think we should invite Lee Kuan Yew to come and take over Westminster. After all, we used to invite foreign kings to take us over. Lee would have everyone in place in no time.'

'He'd deport half the academics. He can't stand beards.' They stroked their small moustaches, those who had them, and the cleanshaven ran their fingers down satisfactorily smooth cheeks.

'Good riddance.' Diplomats are suspicious of university staffs. Until, of course, they retire and are invited to become vice-chancellors.

'Take no notice of the men, Cleo,' said the hostess, all *crêpe de chine* and a yard wide. She had run a tight embassy in Moscow and Cairo and Canberra, running her husband with an equally tight rein. The Russians and the Arabs, behind her back, had called her The Gunboat, the Australians Big Bertha. 'They're enjoying their retirement. They no longer have to compromise.'

247

'What do newspaper barons do when they retire?' Jack and the other men were in another room with their port and brandy and cigars, and another wife, ex-Peru and Spain, felt free to ask. Cleo was the youngest woman there and they looked at her with the wary envy of women who had learned to cloak their real feelings for sake of Queen and Country.

'Jack never discusses retirement. I think he's already discussing whom the *Examiner* should back for Prime Minister in 2001.'

They all warmed to her: they liked a woman who didn't take her husband (well, her lover) too seriously. Then the conversation turned to gossip. The world was their suburb, embassies the parish pump: world figures were caught with their pants down, their ladies in their underwear. It was the sort of gossip Cleo would miss when she left Jack.

Going home he said, as if reading her mind, 'You enjoy all that, don't you?'

'Yes.'

'So do I. The young fellow from the village – I often wonder if they know where I came from?'

'They'd know. But I don't think it would matter.'

'No, I suppose not. I'm safe.' He said it without thinking as if he had not heard what his secret tongue, the one that spoke to himself, had betrayed.

She looked sideways at him in the dimness of the car. He was staring straight ahead as they came up through the High Street of Chalfont St Aidan; but he did not turn his head as they passed through the village under the midnight moon. He was seeing the village of thirty-five years ago and the boy in the bright sunshine of youth who, even then, had paid a down payment, if only ambition, on the big house on the hill.

'Safe from what?'

He came back out of the past. 'What? Oh, nothing.'

But he had opened wider a chink into which she had peered before. For all his outward self-assurance, it seemed that he had built himself on sand. He instructed his newspapers to deride class-consciousness and suffered from it himself, like a weak chest. He had not gone to a right school or a

248

right university; his education had been at the University of Experience, which grants no degrees, so no cap and gown can be worn. He went in through the front doors of the great houses in the land, but he knew where the back doors would be, something some of the owners would only hazily know. Even tonight, in the house where there was no real money, only privilege and connections, he had still felt an outsider. He had, Cleo realized, come back to live in Chalfont St Aidan because that was where he felt safest. The villagers, who knew where he had come from, would never let him feel that he was looked down upon.

They slept together that night, but did not make love. She said she was tired and he did not persist. They went to sleep lying on their sides, her back tucked into his front and his arm resting on her hip. Once, during the night, she woke with a start when his arm tightened convulsively on her, as if she had tried to slip away from him.

6

She finished her contract with United Television at the end of May and Simon Pally, the executive producer, offered her a new two-year contract with more money.

'You're worth it, Cleo. We want to protect our investment.'

'I'll think about it, Simon.'

'Someone else isn't laying bait for you?' He was a pale middle-aged man who had started in black-and-white television and seemed afraid of colour: he always dressed in grey and wore a black tie, as if in mourning for the early days of the BBC. But he knew the public taste as if he had taken it apart with a scalpel. '*Panorama?*'

'I'm not *Panorama* stuff, you know that. Robin Day would throttle himself with one of his bow-ties before he'd work with me. No, it's just that I want to think about the future. I'll let you know in plenty of time, Simon. Don't worry.'

'You're not thinking of getting married or anything, are you?' He was circumspect enough not to add, *to Lord Cruze.*

She laughed. It was the practised laugh of the television interviewer, almost as good as her father's belly-laugh. 'Whatever gave you that idea?'

But it struck her that maybe a lot of people expected her to marry Jack Cruze sooner or later.

Jack, realizing he was not going to be able to entice her on the two months' cruise to the Dodecanese, cancelled the rented yacht. He knew when to cut his losses and he was not a man to waste money; he could pay millions for a company but he hated to see even a hundred pounds go down the drain for nothing. As a compromise Cleo went with him to St Tropez for two weeks, to a villa lent Jack by the Greek shipowner who had taken them on a cruise on his yacht last summer. It was another example of the parish relationships that Cleo had come to note: some people lent a lawn-mower, others lent a Mediterranean villa. Good neighbourliness was all relative.

The villa was on the hill above the town, surrounded by a high wall and giving Jack all the privacy he demanded. He came out of the house one morning and found Cleo sunbathing topless beside the pool. The sight went to his head.

'Put your top on! You'll give the garden boy a bloody hernia if he sees you!'

She sat up and pulled on her shirt. 'Jack, he can go down to the beach and see a hundred girls lying there topless. If he wants to swim out to the point he can see Brigitte Bardot lying there in the altogether –'

'I don't care a damn about Bardot and those other girls. While you're with me you're not going to flaunt your tits –'

'I'd rather you called them something else,' she said coldly through the perspiration that covered her. 'And not boobs.'

It was just another of their small rows, but they were becoming increasingly regular. There were diversions and they saved the days and occasionally the nights. Jack spent half an hour on the phone every day to London; Cleo was tempted to sneak that half-hour to tan her bosom whole but decided it was not worth another row. They ate each evening

250

in the villa, none of your good plain food but excellent dishes prepared by the ship-owner's French chef; Jack made his concession towards *entente* and made a pretence of liking the *haute* muck. After dinner they would stroll down to the town and pretend they were not noticed amongst the hordes of people promenading up and down the quay, most of whom only looked at other people to see the reflection of themselves in the passing eyes. Cleo made a mental note for her column: St Tropez seemed to be evenly divided between exhibitionists and voyeurs. The exhibitionists sat on the after-decks of their yachts, sipping drinks and looking bored by the voyeurs; the voyeurs strolled up and down looking bored by the exhibitionists. Cleo had the feeling that at any moment both sides would suddenly change places, but that phenomenon never happened. She, for her part, was bored and only slightly amused by the poor theatre of the whole scene. Jack just sneered that he had never seen such a bunch of narcissistic poofs, tarts and layabouts; they were a good argument for Communism. Fortunately none of the poofs, tarts and layabouts heard him: Cleo feared they both might have finished up in the harbour.

She did notice the number of older men squiring very young women, many of the men older than Jack, the girls younger than herself. Jack noticed it, too; but neither of them made any comment on it. Though their relationship was now showing dents and bruises, neither of them wanted to cheapen it by comparing it to what they saw. But Cleo wondered how many of the young men at the tables along the quay looked at Jack's grey hair and made snide remarks.

On their third night along the quay a young man rose from where he was sitting with four other bucks and came towards Cleo and Jack. He was a beautiful young animal and he knew it and pretended to be nothing else. He was dressed all in brilliant white, as if he had stepped off the front of a packet of washing powder; he was so darkly tanned he might have been sprayed with mahogany floor stain. His trousers were so tight his sex equipment bulged like a misplaced goitre; his shirt was open to the waist, showing a gold chain and

251

medallion that Jack thought wouldn't have been out of place round the neck of a lord mayor. His looks were dazzling, his smile a night-time glare and his conceit vividly splendent. He made Jack sick.

'M'sieu, when you have finished walking your daughter, may I take over?'

Cleo knew it was a joke, an insulting one; she could see the other four expensively-dressed louts grinning in the background. It was probably a routine with them, each one of them dared to take his turn at taking the mickey out of the older men. It had been going on since humans had come out of the caves and started promenading.

Then she saw Jack boil up and she knew he was going to hit the youth. She stepped in front of him and looked directly into the dark mocking face and the mouthful of teeth inviting someone to smash them. She could feel the itch in her own fist.

'Piss off, smart-arse,' she said in the best lady-like accent she could manage. 'When I want to play with little boys, I'll let you know. Now go back to playing with yourself, if you can find it.'

She took Jack's arm, feeling the violence still trembling in him, and without being too apparent steered him on their way along the quay. The buck was standing where they had left him, the smile still on his face but looking now like a boxer's slipped mouthguard; some passers-by, those who spoke English, had heard Cleo and were laughing at him. At their table his four companions were also laughing: there is no team loyalty amongst *boulevardiers*. He had just been castrated, if only for the moment, and they were laughing at him as someone laughs at a comic who slips on a banana skin, glad that it hadn't happened to them.

'I'd have killed the young bugger!' But Jack was subsiding as she discreetly pressed his arm. 'Who do those young shits think they are?'

'Watch your language.'

'What about yours?' Then he laughed and she felt all the violence go out of him as if he had been flushed of it. He even

252

tried to joke against himself: 'I don't think I'd like a daughter of mine using language like that.'

She squeezed his arm, had the sense and sensitivity not to say, *Righto, Dad.*

They had declared a truce in the bedroom; so they fought each other in the love act each night. A week of it, every night, sometimes twice a day, began to wear Cleo more than Jack. She now had to pretend she enjoyed going to bed with him. Sometimes she did enjoy it; but more often than not it was now a concession, as if she had become a bored but dutiful wife. She despised herself, felt she was now doing it only for the favours he bestowed on her. Which, since she had a conscience, made it harder for her to be ardent. Meanwhile, during the day she wore dark glasses to hide her tired eyes and Jack was as clear-eyed as any Indian scout in *The Covered Wagon.*

If he noticed her faked ardour, he made no mention of it. He could not cut his losses with her; he would be bankrupt if he let her go. So he made love with all the vigour he could muster, as if, trying to avoid misery, he might die on top of her. Sometimes, after she had reversed their positions and ridden him, he would lie in the dim room and be content to die there and then.

They went back to London after two weeks. The world had gone on while they were away, not missing either of them. Cleo went back to writing her column. She went through the last fortnight's papers looking for items that might be worth commenting on, but saw nothing that would make a column. The Australian cricket team was in England again; there had been a break-in at Democratic Party headquarters at a complex called Watergate in Washington; Evonne Goolagong was preparing to defend her Wimbledon title. So, stuck for want of a subject, she wrote a satirical piece on St Tropez and got some complimentary fan mail from a Tass correspondent. It was the doldrums season and she began to wish she had stayed longer in St Tropez or even gone to the Dodecanese. She even thought of a quick trip home to Australia, but that would probably only cause another argument with Jack.

He now wanted to see her every night. Since the death of Massey-Folkes he had felt a loneliness that, despite his attempts to fight it, persisted like a stubborn cold. He had a hundred acquaintances, but, since the death of Quentin, no friends. He had never totally unburdened himself to Quentin, but he realized now that, obliquely but deliberately, he had taken most of his problems to the cynical, amiable editor. Quentin had listened and, also obliquely, given advice. Their friendship had been deeper than Jack realized till Quentin was gone.

The second week in July he went off to Charleston, South Carolina, on business. He tried to persuade Cleo to go with him and she was tempted; then she said no, deciding that a week alone to think about him would be more productive than a week with him. She went to the airport with him and they kissed goodbye like loving husband and wife.

He had been gone three days when Alain Roux turned up on her doorstep, literally. Bligh, the hall porter, called from downstairs on the Saturday morning. 'Miss Spearfield, there is a Mr Alain –' he paused, as if he were reading from a visiting card, 'Roux, R-o-u-x, down here to see you.'

She was still in a robe, but she had already bathed and her face and hair were done. She looked in the mirror beside the phone, then said, 'Please ask him to come up.' Then she wondered why she had looked in the mirror.

She opened the door to him and even in the first few moments saw how he had changed in the two and a half years since she had seen him last. The college boy had gone; in his place was an older man, though still young. But the restlessness had disappeared; he walked now to a different pace. Then she saw the silver-topped walking stick.

'You have an unlisted number, otherwise I'd have called you. But I'm staying over the road at the Stafford. They know I'm from the *Courier* and I happen to have the same waiter serving me who serves you and Lord Cruze. He mentioned that the famous Miss Spearfield often dines there. So . . .'

'I'll have to speak to him. Sending strange men to pound on my door. Come in, Alain. Can I take your stick?'

'I better keep it. I get a bit shaky in the leg when I'm walking on a surface I'm not used to.'

'Oh. Stupid –' She chided herself. 'Was that from Vietnam? Tom Border did mention you'd been wounded –'

He had noticed her discomfiture. 'Don't let it bother you, Cleo. I've got used to it. Mother thinks it makes me look distinguished. I'm the only distinguished-looking junior sub-editor on the *New York Courier*.' There was no bitter self-pity in his voice. He sat down and looked around. 'A very nice place. From what Mother said, I always thought the English lived rather tattily. But Mother's a snob.'

'So were you.'

'I've got worse.' He smiled and for the first time she saw the lines in his face. Pain had left its mark on him and she saw that the wound in his leg had spread: his hopes had been irreparably damaged, his soul scarred. He saw the concern on her face and the quick second glance at the leg stuck straight out in front of him. He tapped it with the stick. 'Please ignore it, Cleo. I've got over it. There are a lot of things I wanted to do that I'll never be able to do – I was aiming some day to climb Everest, did I tell you that? I was also a very good fancy skater, not Olympic class but still pretty good. No skating now, no mountain-climbing. I got pretty sour about losing all that. Then I looked at guys in wheelchairs, paraplegics and quadriplegics –'

'I know someone like that, a paraplegic.'

'Yes, well, they have it far worse than I've got it. *I complained because I had no shoes, till I met a man who had no feet.* So please don't let's mention it again, okay? Now get dressed. I have tickets for the Centre Court at Wimbledon, we'll see the women's final.'

'I have a press ticket – ' She had intended going to Wimbledon. She was no tennis fan, no sports fan at all; the fervour of crowds for their team or favourite to win only amused her; sport for her was something one did for exercise. But Evonne Goolagong was playing Billie Jean King and, feeling a welling of nationalism, as if someone had waved a bunch of gum-leaves under her nose, she had decided to go and wish the best of Aussie luck to the young Australian girl.

'Forget work,' Alain said, misunderstanding her. 'You're my guest for the day. I was your guest in New York, remember? Get dressed while I order a car. We'll go down to Maidenhead for lunch first.'

Jack had left her the Rolls-Royce and Sid Cromwell, but she decided she would give Sid the day off and rang him in the penthouse flat to tell him so. It was partly goodwill, a *de facto* employer being generous to the worker; but she knew that it was also circumspection, that she did not want Sid wondering why she was going out with another man, a young man at that, while the boss was away. There would be no harm in what she was doing, but it was better that no harm might be suspected.

So she let Alain order a chauffeur-driven car while she got ready. She didn't dress hurriedly but took her time, telling herself that she was not going to rush and give him the impression that she was eager to go out with him. She also, however, took her time about making the most of her face and hair and choosing her wardrobe. She wore a Givenchy silk suit that was both casual and dressy, open-toed Italian sandals and a handbag to match with a Givenchy silk scarf tied to the handle. Just what any girl would throw on for a rushed invitation to lunch at a Wimpy bar and a run round the roller-skating rink afterwards.

They drove out into the country in the hired Daimler and from the moment they had turned out of St James's Place Cleo felt no guilt: it was as if while in her flat she had been aware of Jack jealously watching her. Even as they were driving down Piccadilly, still within sight of the western side of the apartment building, she was relaxed. By the time they were on the M4 motorway she hadn't a care or another beau in the world. Alain, though she didn't tell him so, was her boy friend for the day.

Ah, but there *was* another beau ... Over lunch at the restaurant on the river Alain said, 'Did you know Tom Border has written a novel?'

'I never hear from Tom.' She said it non-committally, as if Tom were no more than another journalist she had met on their working rounds.

'Oh. I thought after that experience you two had –' But if he suspected there might have been more between them, he gave no further hint of it. 'Well, he's written a novel based on that.'

'Am I in it?' she asked cautiously, as if afraid of libel. Or worse: like having Tom tell the world he loved her.

'I don't know, I haven't read it. But it's been accepted by Exeter House – that's the publishing house we own. They've given him a twenty-five-thousand-dollar advance, which is pretty good for a first novel. Farquhars are doing it over here. It'll be out next spring. The chief editor at Exeter told me they expect big things of it. The paperback rights are going up for auction and the book clubs and Hollywood are already asking to look at it.'

'Good for Tom. I hope success doesn't spoil him.'

'I don't think so.' He gave her a quick glance, then went back to his Dover sole. 'I've never met anyone so laid back as Tom. As if he really doesn't care about the world or what it thinks of him!'

'Does that sort of attitude suit a stuffy newspaper like the *Courier*?'

He put a hand to his breast. 'You've just stabbed the Brisson family pride. Mother thinks the *Courier* is the only honest paper in America.'

'It may well be. But it's still stuffy, isn't it?'

'Stuffy as hell.'

'Why don't you do something about it?'

'I'm still too far down the totem-pole. But some day ...' Then he lifted his wine glass. 'You're the best-looking woman in this restaurant, do you know that? Maybe not the most beautiful, but easily the best-looking.'

'Is there a difference?'

'In a man's eyes, yes.'

He put his hand on hers and she lifted her glass and poured a little cold wine on it. 'Cool down, sport.'

He grinned, licking the wine from the back of his hand. 'You're laid back, too, aren't you?'

Not really, not when Tom was mentioned. 'Laid back, but not to be laid.'

'Oh, clev-*er*. You've been saving that up for someone like me.'

But he was not put out, he was enjoying being with her too much. He had gone across to her flat this morning looking for no more than a good-looking girl, one he remembered with some good feeling, to take out for the day. Now he was falling in love; or at least he had stumbled and had yet to regain his balance. The walking stick would be no help to him.

They drove back up to Wimbledon, took their seats, excellent ones, amongst the crowd on the Centre Court. The two women players came out, the champion looking relaxed and carefree, the challenger looking determined and tense. Cleo, ambitious in everything except sport felt her sympathy go out for Goolagong, not because she was an Australian but because she seemed as if she had put the match in its proper perspective: it was only a game, it was not the end of the world. Of course if she lost there would be people back home who would hint that you could never rely on an aboriginal, he or she could never be expected to respect the things that counted. Whereas King, coming from the United States which had a proper sense of values, knew that achievement was everything. All at once Cleo thought that Tom had an aboriginal's approach to life: he would rather go walkabout than climb the ladder ...

Goolagong tried hard, laughed and shook her head at her own mistakes; but on the day King was the better player, knew she was going to win. Australians in the crowd groaned and grew morose as their heroine went down; but Cleo felt only sympathy for the aboriginal girl of whom too much was expected. Goolagong would be disappointed at losing, but tomorrow she would be laughing again, while on the other side of the world Australia would go into another of its depressions at losing a sporting event. King, meanwhile, would already be practising for the next tournament.

'I'm sorry, I shouldn't be so jubilant,' said Alain. 'I'm waving the damned flag too much. But Billie Jean was good, wasn't she?'

Have I been like Billie Jean? Cleo wondered. For four years now she had been an achiever. But once she had been as carefree as Evonne, had laughed and looked on tomorrow as another day distinct from today: life then had been a dream, but not an ambitious one. She was still an achiever, still aiming for the title; but what title? Certainly not Lady Cruze. Editor of the *Examiner*? Yes, but Jack would not allow that for another ten years, if ever. She was on the Centre Court of Fleet Street with no racquet and no balls ... That, of course, was the trouble. She would have had no problem if she had had balls.

'Cleo?'

'What? Oh sorry. I – I was thinking I might do a piece on Evonne.'

'Why not on the winner? Or are you being chauvinistic?' Then he pressed her hand. 'I'm sorry, I'm rubbing it in.'

'Are you going to do a piece on Billie Jean?' She glanced up and saw a television cameraman, looking for reaction now the action on court was over, aiming his camera at her. Her first reaction was to smile: but she wasn't on *Scope* now.

'No, we have our own man here somewhere. I'm on vacation, like I told you. I go over to Germany tomorrow, to Heidelberg, to spend a few days with my uncle and aunt. Then I'm going down to Italy. I haven't been there since I was a kid, with my mother. Would you like to come with me?'

She saw the question was serious, but she managed to laugh it off. 'My editor wouldn't give me the time off.' Neither would Jack, the boss.

They made their way through the crowd to the car park, not waiting to see the men's doubles. People recognized her and gave her hesitant friendly smiles, as if afraid of being rebuffed for their intrusion; she smiled back, liking the attention. She had geared the pace of her stride to that of his limp. Instinctively she walked on his stick side, as if to ward off people who might bump against him and whip the stick from under him. He had looked so handsome and young and alive when sitting beside her in the car, at lunch and in the tennis stadium. But now he was a young man with so much of his life behind him and the handsome brow was furrowed as if he felt vulnerable in the crowd.

'Dinner?' he said.

'Yes.' She almost said *Of course*, as if it were the most natural thing that they should finish the day in such a way. She had been surprised at how much she had enjoyed his company; she could not remember having given him a single thought since she had seen him last. But he made no demands on her, he was not possessive, he was just attentive and charming. And young. 'There's a place called the White Tower – if we mention my name we might get in –'

'Your choice. I chose the restaurant in New York. How will eight o'clock do? This –' he tapped his leg '– gets a bit tired when I've been on it all day. I'll have a bath and a nap.'

They got out of the car and stood beside each other for a moment. She looked at him, grateful for the day, then she made one of her old affectionate gestures and touched him on the cheek. 'It's been a lovely day.'

He smiled, kissed the back of her hand. 'I'll pick you up at eight.'

Then he limped across to the Stafford. She watched him go, then went up to her flat. She opened the front door and went in and at once felt there was someone else there in the flat. It was a most peculiar feeling, like hearing a silent whisper in one's head.

'Jack?'

There was no answer and, when she went through the other rooms, no sign of anyone. She went back to the front door to check for marks, to see if someone had somehow forced their way in; there were no marks at all. She closed the door, locking it; then went through the flat again, checking if anything was missing; but nothing was. Finally she rang down to the hall porter.

'Mr Bligh, has Lord Cruze returned?'

'Not as I know, miss. I was away for a coupla hours this afternoon, I just this minute got back –'

'Is anyone else in the building?'

'No, miss. Everyone's gone away for the weekend. You're the only one home.'

'Thank you, Mr Bligh.'

She put down the phone, then dialled the penthouse number. She let the phone ring, but there was no answer. She replaced it, then dialled St Aidan's House.

'Lord Cruze's residence.'

'Who's that?'

'It's the coachman. There's no one else here –'

'Tim, this is Miss Spearfield. Is Lord Cruze there?'

'No, miss. He's in America, isn't he?' His puzzlement was plain even over the phone. 'I come up here today to do some work on the carriages, His Lordship wants to drive 'em next weekend –'

She hung up, annoyed at herself for her unease. It was guilt she had felt, not a presence in the flat. She had wondered why Sid or Mrs Cromwell hadn't answered the phone either in the penthouse flat or down at St Aidan's House. Then she remembered that Sid had told her, when she had given him the day off, that he and the missus would go out to Chalfont St Aidan and visit their son and daughter-in-law. They would stay at the big house tonight and come back to London tomorrow afternoon, if that was all right with her. His Lordship, Sid had said, would be in Monday and he'd be out at Heathrow to pick him up. All that had been in the back of her mind, like loose change in a purse, when she had come in the front door. But something, conscience or fear of Jack's finding out she had been with Alain, had warned her that she was not to take advantage of being unobserved.

She bathed, lay on her bed for a couple of hours, then got up and dressed. She made herself up even more carefully than she had this morning, chose her dress with an eye to what it would do for her figure; she was not going out tonight amongst older people, she would not be expected to be modest about what she had to show. The dress was the one she had worn to her first dinner party as hostess for Jack; she had not dressed for a date with such anticipation in far too long. It struck her that she had never had the opportunity to dress like this for a dinner with Tom.

Alain had kept the Daimler and the driver. He was waiting beside the car as the hall porter opened the front doors for Cleo. As she came down the steps to him he whistled softly. 'As I used to say in my uncouth college days – wow-*eee*!'

Bligh had come down the steps to help them both into the car. He was an ex-army sergeant who had once known his way round a lot of women but was now confined to barracks by a commanding wife. Looking at Miss Spearfield he wished he was a young recruit again, a rich one. 'Have a nice evening, miss. You've got your front door key? I go off this evening at ten.'

'Yes, thank you, Bligh.'

As they drove away Alain said, 'You have a conquest back there. Hasn't he seen you dressed up like this before?'

If Bligh had, he'd kept his enthusiasm from showing. But then, dressed up, she had always been going out with His Lordship.

The White Tower was crowded, mostly, it seemed, with American film people. She recognized several whom she had interviewed and nodded to the wife of a director on whom she had based a column. The wife, with the wife of a writer, had founded the 'You, too, Club' ('Will you come to dinner next week, Mr X? Oh, and you, too, Mrs X'); Cleo had written the column with some relish, working off the last of her resentment at being overshadowed. It had brought a flood of mail, all from women; and a sour question from Jack as to whether she now thought she was a spokesman (he wouldn't say spokeswoman or spokesperson) for some radical feminist group. The film director's wife gave her a wink and a wide smile, but it was difficult to tell whether she was still pleased about the column or whether she was complimenting Cleo on having a new, younger man for the evening. It occurred to Cleo that though all the other diners in the restaurant probably knew the Roux or Brisson name, none of them recognized Alain. He was heir to more money and lasting influence than any of them, but none of them knew him.

It was an enjoyable evening. Alain was charming and entertaining and discreetly revealing about the Brisson family; he was loyal to his mother, but he knew everyone was interested in her. Cleo, forgetting she was a columnist, listened avidly and with enjoyment; it was a pleasure to hear about another parish. She found her old affectionate gestures creeping back; she had, at Jack's jealous insistence, stopped touching other people. But twice during the evening she put a hand on Alain's to emphasize a point; the second time he turned his hand over under hers and she let her fingers entwine in his. When they walked out of the restaurant they were hand in hand.

Going home in the car she knew she would let him stay with her tonight if he suggested it. She had bathed in the freedom of the evening; there had been no bickering, no demanding, no jealousy. And she had been excited by the fact that he was *young*: despite his crippled leg he was in his animal prime, he was ripe with sexuality. She wanted to go to bed with him.

She had put Jack out of her mind, no mean feat. But ... 'One thing I like about you, you haven't talked about other girls. You don't boast of your conquests, do you?'

'I try not to. What ever happens between me and a girl is something just between us.'

Good. Then Tom wouldn't know ... 'You haven't mentioned that girl, the blonde in New York – Joan someone-or-other?'

'Joan Temple. She's married and has a baby.' He had let her hand go as they had got into the car, but now he took it again. 'No strings.'

She could take that any way she wanted: he had no strings tying him or there would be no strings attached to whatever happened tonight. She chose to take it the latter way. He would be gone tomorrow, to Heidelberg and his uncle and aunt, and she could make it her one and only fling since she

263

had met Jack. A one night stand, good enough for a woman if it was good enough for a man.

In the narrow street between the hotel and the apartment building he dismissed the car and took her up the steps to the front doors. 'I better see you up to your flat, if the porter's gone off duty.'

Going up in the lift he kissed her hand but made no attempt to embrace her. They were both confident now of what was going to happen, there was no need to rush things. But when she opened the front door of her flat he dropped his walking stick, put his arms round her and pulled her to him. She put her arms round his neck and pressed his face almost savagely against hers.

Then the light in the living-room was switched on.

7

Jack Cruze had arrived in Charleston impatient to get his business done and be on the plane again for home. Perhaps because of his impatience he managed to convince himself that he was not suffering from jet lag; he got down to business immediately on arrival. He called Cleo late that evening and, as usual, woke her up in the early hours of the morning. As usual he was profuse in his apologies, but he knew he could not have waited another couple of hours to speak to her. He finished his business two days ahead of schedule, declined an invitation by his American associates to spend the weekend in the Carolina country; he decided he would not call Cleo but would surprise her by arriving home early. He did not realize that jealousy influenced him in not giving her any warning. He had no reason to suspect that she might see another man, but he wanted to be certain. He wore a hair-shirt with no more style than he did something from Turnbull and Asser.

He flew up from Charleston to New York, stayed the night there and flew out on an early morning flight for London. He arrived at Heathrow to find no Sid Cromwell though he had asked the airline to contact Sid and instruct him to be at the airport. He caught a taxi, the first time he had ridden in one in more years than he could remember, and his mood, which had grown worse across the Atlantic, was not improved by the garrulity of the taxi driver. When he arrived at St James's Place he was tired to the point of exhaustion, deeply irritable and prey to thoughts as yet not clearly defined. He wanted to find Cleo waiting for him with open arms, then everything would be fine.

There was no Bligh on duty in the lobby; he had to let himself in with his own key. He dumped his bag in the lift and went up to Cleo's floor. There was no answer to his ring on her front door, so he found his key to the door and opened it. He went in, calling her name almost like a child coming home; but the flat was empty. He could feel rage welling up inside him, the unreasonable fury of someone who expected everything to be exactly as he desired it: the welcome mat out, the bed turned down, Cleo in place. He stamped out of the flat, slamming the door, and went up to the penthouse. His mood worsened even further when he found there was no Sid or Mrs Cromwell there, that he was alone.

He took some aspirin for the headache that had taken hold of him after he had slammed out of Cleo's flat, lay down on his bed without turning back the silk coverlet and tried to fall asleep; but couldn't. He got up, wandered about the big bedroom, going to the window and looking out into Green Park, as if he might see Cleo walking there, feeling as lonely and neglected as he felt.

He turned back, saw the television set and switched it on. He had no interest in sport other than his horse shows; but Wimbledon was as much a social event as a sporting one; who knows, with that Goolagong girl playing today, perhaps Cleo had gone down to Wimbledon to wave her Aussie flag or do a piece on the aboriginal girl. If she was down there, it might please her if he could talk with her about the women's final, especially if Goolagong won.

But Goolagong hadn't won; the match was over. The camera was roving over the spectators; amongst the crowd he saw several men from the City and their wives. Then the camera paused, Cleo looked directly into it, straight at *him*. Then she turned away, smiled at the handsome young man who sat beside her holding her hand. The camera moved on, but Jack saw only a blur of colour, a screen full of distorted images, a writhing mangle of twisting lines like a coloured X-ray of guts in agony. He switched the set off with such fury that the knob came off in his hand.

He sat down heavily on the bed, only half-believing what he had seen; yet jealousy had always told him that it was possible. Who was the man she was with? He had never seen him before. Was he just a young stud she had picked up for the day, were there others? He stabbed himself with thoughts; it was too early yet for anything more lethal. He lay back on the bed, praying that sleep would drown him, but he might as well have prayed for total amnesia.

He would certainly never remember how he passed the time till he found himself in the kitchen making a cup of tea. The kitchen looked out on St James's Place. The street was narrow, the buildings crowding in on it; sound floated up as if out of a funnel. He heard a car drive up, then the sound of the car door being shut, then Cleo's laugh. He leaned out of the window and looked down. She was standing beside a Daimler with the young man from Wimbledon. She put her hand to the young man's cheek and he took her hand and kissed it. Then he said, 'I'll pick you up at eight,' and limped across to the hotel opposite, walking with the aid of a stick. A bloody cripple! Jack leaned against the sink, the cup and saucer rattling in his trembling hands.

He was still standing there, his mind clouded with fuming jealousy, when his private phone rang in the drawing-room. He straightened up, took one step towards the kitchen door to go through into the main part of the flat, then stopped. He had never felt like this before, not even when Emma had run away from him; there had been no other man then. Love is a mutual selfishness and selfishness now took him over like a seizure. He remained rigid in the kitchen doorway, eyes shut, face distorted as he tried to shut his ears against the phone and the voice he knew was waiting to speak at the other end; for he was certain that it could be no one else, no one else existed but Cleo and the young man across the street. Then the ringing stopped and he opened his eyes, his face easing like a man who had just been released from torture.

He went slowly into the main part of the flat and up to his bedroom. He sat down in a chair and gazed out at Green Park; but saw nothing of what was there. He knew he had lost Cleo; he had felt her slipping away from him over the past few months, ever since she had come back from the trial in Hamburg in March. Several times he had thought of hiring a private investigator to trail her to see if she was secretly meeting another man; but he had resisted the temptation, afraid of what she would do or say if she found out. But she was no longer his and he wondered who was the new man in her life. It wasn't the American Tom Border, he had checked only a month ago that Border was working in New York, had not left there since his return from Hamburg in March. So who was the new man, the young man with the limp and the walking stick?

In the next two hours the phone rang three times; but he did not answer it. He had no idea whether it was Cleo calling or someone else: it really didn't matter. Just before eight he got up and went downstairs and out into the kitchen again. He was at the window, neck craned so that he could look directly down into the street, when Cleo came out, was greeted by the young man and got into the Daimler and was driven away. He had held his breath, almost as if afraid that he might be heard down there in the street. Now he let it out and it was like a long moan of pain.

He went back upstairs to his study, poured himself a brandy and sat down again. He wished he had someone he could call: his mother, Quentin Massey-Folkes; but he had no one. He had another brandy, then he got up, closed the curtains and got out a copy of George O'Brien in *The Iron Horse*. He did not want to torture himself with fantasies tonight about Garbo or Crawford or Del Rio; he wanted escapism and the John Ford Western gave him that. But the film didn't last long enough: he wanted the Iron Horse to carry him across the prairies for hours, maybe forever.

When the film ended he switched on the lights and had another brandy. His head had begun to ache again, his eyes felt as if he had washed them with sand. He sat sunk in a depth of despair that he had never known before. He had known grief at his mother's death, and shock and anger and a sense of loss when Emma had left him; but he had never known anything like this; he felt old, as if this time it was too late to start again. The exhaustion of the trip and the jet lag did not help; he had run from Marathon only to find that his news was a joke, the war had been lost, not won. Emotions curdled within him, as if he were slowly decaying from the inside. When he at last stood up his mind had ceased to think clearly: he was looking only for an end to it all.

He got the pistol from the locked bottom drawer of his desk. He had bought it three years ago, on the advice of Quentin, when a crazed Biafran, fired by an editorial in the *Examiner* on the war then going on in Africa, had threatened to kill him. It was a Colt .45 automatic and it had never been fired, at least not by him; he had put it away in the drawer and never looked at it again till now. He loaded it from the box of cartridges he had bought at the same time. He did it all with the stiff slow movements of an automaton that had not been properly programmed.

He went down in the lift with the same stiff measured movements and let himself into Cleo's flat. He turned on the light in the living-room, put a chair just inside the doorway that faced the entrance; then he turned out the light and sat down in the chair, the automatic resting on his lap. He had no idea what time it was, but he had all the time left in the world. Because his world was going to end very soon.

He dozed off once or twice, but at once snapped awake again. He had forgotten the other man, he felt no jealousy now, just a terrible depression that everything should end this way. Yet it was the only way.

He heard the key in the lock and he sat up, raising the gun. The door opened and he saw Cleo and the man silhouetted against the light on the landing. Something told him to give her one more chance: if she closed the door in the man's face, he would forgive her. The two of them stood there for a moment, then the man dropped his walking stick and took Cleo in his arms. She responded, pulling the man's face down onto hers. Then Jack reached across and switched on the living-room light.

He lifted the gun and pulled the trigger. He would never know whether his aim was bad or whether at the last moment he did not want to kill Cleo. There was a loud crack, but Cleo didn't fall. She let out a cry and put her hand to her side. Then Jack turned the gun up under his chin and pulled the trigger again. This time it jammed.

He looked down at it angrily, strained his finger on the trigger; then he fell out of the chair and slumped unconscious on the floor. Cleo, still holding her side, walked unsteadily into the room and sat down on the couch. She looked at the inert Jack dumbly, unable to believe what had happened.

Then Alain, standing over Jack, his bent leg making him look like a man ready to run away, said, 'Are you all right?'

She looked down at her side: a faint stain was showing where she had pressed the dress against the wound. 'I think it just nicked me.'

Alain bent down awkwardly and picked up the gun. Then he limped to the couch and sat down beside her. 'Take your dress off.'

She slipped the dress over her head with less pain than she had expected. The bullet had just nicked her side at the bottom of the rib cage. 'I'm all right. Where did the bullet go?'

'Never mind about that – it's probably in the door or the wall.' He looked down at the still unconscious Jack. 'Jesus Christ – *why*? It's Lord Cruze, isn't it?'

Cleo, in her underwear now but unaware of it, dropped to her knees beside Jack. No longer worried about herself, she was worried about him; she feared that he might have had a stroke. He was breathing heavily, like a man coming out of a fit; she rolled him over on his back and put a cushion under his head. She slapped his face gently, took the glass of water Alain had got from the kitchen and tried to force it between the pale lips; but Jack gave no response. Then she stood up.

'I'll call his doctor. You'd better get out of here.'

'Don't be crazy! I'm not going to leave you alone with him!'

'I'll be all right. Please, Alain – go! If I need you, I can always come and get you. And don't say a word about what's happened. Nothing, you understand?'

He went to protest, then changed his mind. He saw that she was in control of herself and the situation; for the time being it was better to let her have her own way. 'Okay, but I'll wait outside the hotel till the doctor comes, just in case. You better put something on that side of yours – I wouldn't let the doc see it, just in case he wants to know the truth of what happened. What are you going to tell him anyway?'

She was already at the phone. 'Just that Jack collapsed ... Dr Hynd, thank God, you're in town! Could you come over immediately – Lord Cruze has just had an attack. I don't know – it could be his heart –'

Dr Hynd lived above his rooms in Sloane Street; she knew he would be here in less than ten minutes. She pushed Alain towards the front door, kissed him quickly on the cheek as she would one of her brothers; though she was in her underwear, sex had never been further from her mind than now. 'I'll talk to you in the morning, first thing. And remember – not a word – you weren't even here.'

'Do you want me to take the gun?'

'No, leave it here. I'll hide it somewhere.' She was suddenly thankful that the building was empty, that no one in any of the other flats had heard the gun go off.

She closed the door on Alain, went to the bathroom, put some disinfectant on the small wound on her side, put a Band-Aid on it, went into her bedroom and put on a robe. She put the gun in a drawer of her dressing-table, then went back into the living-room. She sank on to the floor beside Jack, staring at him as if at a stranger; she shook her head in disbelief at what he had done. She stroked his forehead, pushing the grey curly hair back from it, thinking to herself how old and ill he looked, an inmate of the concentration camp of his own possessive jealous nature.

Jack regained consciousness just as Dr Hynd arrived. The latter, big and bluff, was not the best medical practitioner in London but he was discreet; he knew there were more forms of exposure than being adrift on a raft in the Atlantic. He had Cleo help him lift Jack on to the couch, then he made an examination.

'Have you had an attack like this before, Lord Cruze?'

Jack flicked a glance at Cleo before he answered. 'No. It's probably just overwork. Is it my heart?'

'I don't think so,' said Hynd, but he had made the wrong diagnosis. 'Medically, there's no such thing, but you may have had what used to be called a brainstorm. Do you still have a headache?'

Jack nodded, then winced. Other than for the one quick glance at her, he was ignoring Cleo. She was content for the moment to be ignored. She had her own headache, though it was mental and emotional.

'It's probably just a combination of things – exhaustion, jet lag, worry. And you're getting on –' That was not very discreet. 'Stay in bed tomorrow and I'll come round and see you again. Then we'll put you through some tests on Monday.'

'We'll see.'

'No, *I'll* see.' Hynd had his rich patients and knew when to pamper them; but he also had authority and knew when to use it. 'I'm the doctor. We'll have tests done on Monday.'

When Hynd left Cleo and Jack at last looked directly at each other. She waited for him to say the first word and at last he said, 'I'm sorry.'

She was still fragile inside at the horror of what he had intended doing. She had known nothing of his having a gun; using it was the ultimate violence that she never expected. She could only dimly remember, as if her vision had been fragmented at the moment, the shot aimed at her; but, painfully sharply, she could still see him as he put the gun up under his chin and pulled the trigger. There had been no second shot that she heard, but in her mind there had been an explosion that still echoed.

'I'm sorry, too – that you would even think of doing such a thing.'

'It was like Hynd said – a brainstorm. I don't know what got into me.' But he did, though he was not going to make any confession of it. 'Who was that fellow?'

'A friend.' She did not know how successful she might be, but she knew she had to keep Alain's name out of it. Not to protect the Roux or Brisson names, but to protect him.

'Have you been seeing him while my back's been turned?'

'No. Your back hasn't been turned that much. Don't let's argue, Jack. You're going up to bed.'

He stood up, tottered a little but waved her away when she moved to help him. 'I'll be all right. Don't bother to come up –'

'Stop telling me what to do!' She could feel hysteria bubbling in her, reaction beginning to set in. 'I'll come up and sleep in the study, just in case –'

'In case what?' But abruptly he wanted no more argument. Depression settled on him like a fog, all he wanted to do was sleep and forget.

They went up in the lift, not speaking to each other, no contact at all between them other than the wariness in their eyes. She went ahead of him up to the main bedroom, turned down the coverlet and sheets while he stood and watched her listlessly, ready to succumb to the exhaustion and misery that weighed him down.

'There you are. Goodnight, Jack. I'll be downstairs, not in the study. There's a bigger couch down there.'

She went past him without touching him. He took off his clothes, let them lie where he dropped them and fell into bed. He was weeping when he fell asleep.

Cleo did not sleep easily, though the long couch was comfortable enough. She rose early, went up to see that Jack was still asleep, then went downstairs to her own flat and called Alain in the Stafford.

'Sorry to wake you –'

'I've been awake most of the night worrying about you.'

'Everything's all right. I don't want you to come across to the flat – just leave for Germany as you planned. He doesn't know who you are and I'm not going to tell him. All I ask is that you never mention to anyone, *anyone*, what happened last night.'

'You don't owe him anything, Cleo. Not after what he tried to do.' He wanted to stay, to be by her side and protect her. But he knew she had no feeling for him other than yesterday's friendship, the warmth of a pleasant date that would have taken them to bed but no further. There was nothing in her voice to suggest that he meant anything more to her. 'The man's crazy –'

'No.' Crazy with jealousy, perhaps; but that was between her and Jack and she was not going to burden Alain with it. 'I can handle it, Alain. Please leave today. And it would be best if you didn't write or phone me. Maybe we can have dinner again some time in New York.'

'Will you be coming to New York?'

'Possibly.' But she knew she wouldn't be. 'Goodbye, Alain.'

She hung up and went back upstairs to the penthouse. She made tea and toast for herself in Mrs Cromwell's kitchen, ate it, then went up to the bedroom. Jack was still asleep. She went downstairs again and called St Aidan's House. Sid Cromwell answered.

'Sid, Lord Cruze is back. You and Mrs Cromwell had better return at once. He hasn't been well and he needs to stay in bed for a day or two.'

'We'll be there as soon as we can. How bad is His Lordship?'

'All he needs is some rest.' And some adjustment of thinking.

Dr Hynd arrived at nine o'clock, woke Jack and examined him again. 'There's an improvement. Go back to sleep, stay in bed for the rest of the day. We'll be doing the tests at ten tomorrow morning.'

Then Cleo and Jack were alone again and certain things

273

had to be said. But Cleo could not bring herself to say them: she was cowardly, she was going to retreat under cover of silence. 'Go back to sleep. Sid and Mrs Cromwell should be here soon.'

'What are you going to do?'

'Pack. Go back to sleep.'

'Cleo – where's the gun?'

'I'll get rid of it.'

'Will you forgive me?'

She was at the door, at a safe distance. 'Yes – in time.'

Then she went out quickly and down to her fat again. She looked for the bullet that had been fired, something she had forgotten to do, and found it lodged in the door-jamb; it took her ten minutes to prise it out with a skewer and screwdriver from the kitchen. She put it and the gun in a plastic bag and took it into the bedroom. She packed four suitcases, mostly with clothes; she was surprised, when she came to take inventory, how little else she owned. A few books, a couple of paintings: everything else had been provided by the decorator with Jack's money. She took the mink coat out of the closet and laid it on the bed; on it she put her jewel-box containing everything that Jack had bought her in the way of jewelry. Mrs Cromwell, besides doing the penthouse, came down each Monday morning to collect the laundry: she could be trusted to see that the coat and the jewelry went upstairs to their rightful owner.

She rang downstairs to Bligh and asked him to call her a taxi, then to come up and pick up her bags.

Five minutes later she took a last look around the flat, saying goodbye to a life. She went out of the front door, closing it quietly behind her for the last time. Downstairs she got into the taxi and Bligh said, 'Where to, Miss Spearfield?'

She had to lie to him, was sorry that she could not even say goodbye to him and thank him for his attentions while she had lived here; it was the same with Sid and Mrs Cromwell. Even the staff miss out in a family row. She would send him and the Cromwells huge tips, which is more spendable than kind words. 'To Paddington Station.'

But once they were out of St James's Place she leaned forward and told the taxi driver, 'I've changed my mind, driver. Heathrow.'

'A woman's privilege, miss.' The driver laughed. He had recognized his passenger: 'You ever done a column on that, like? The missus, she's allus telling me I oughta take notice about what you say. She says you ought be required reading, like, for every man in Britain. Does your boss ever read you?'

'Occasionally.' But he always mis-read her, or had lately.

At Heathrow Qantas told her she was fortunate. There were no first class seats left on the 747 going out at 1730, but there was one left in first class in the 707 leaving at 1700. She would have preferred the comfort of the bigger plane, but refugees can't be choosers. It had not occurred to her that she might not get on a plane. She began to understand for the first time in a long while how pampered she had been in the past three years: when *Scope* or the *Examiner* had not been making her bookings for her, she had been flying in Jack's private plane. Well, that was all over now.

She paid for her ticket and her excess baggage with her credit card, wondering, as she did so, how people had run away at weekends before credit cards were invented. She had exactly six pounds nine shillings in her wallet; thank God for American Express, saviour of fugitive women. 'You have quite a while to wait, Miss Spearfield. Would you care to go up to the VIP room?'

No, that too was all over. 'No, you have a Captain's Club Room, haven't you? I'll go up there.'

But first she went for a walk. She found a waste bin and, like a terrorist planting a bomb, casting sly glances right and left of her, she dropped the plastic bag containing the gun and bullet into it. Then she went up to the Qantas private room and, collect, phoned her father at his flat in Canberra.

'Dad, could you come up to Sydney Tuesday morning? I'm coming home.'

'Great, sweetheart! A holiday or work?'

'Neither, Dad. I'm coming home.' There was an echo on the line: she heard her voice repeat *coming home*.

275

Even at that distance, over a bad connection, he did not miss the nuance in her voice. 'Righto, sweetheart, we'll talk about it when you get home. Have a good trip.'

The day dragged, as only airport time can. Then at last departure time approached. Half an hour before she was called to board the plane, she went down to one of the gift shops.

'Do you take orders for Interflora? I'd like a dozen white roses sent to Lord Cruze at this address.'

It was the cruellest thing she had ever done and she felt ashamed of the satisfaction it gave her.

ELEVEN

1

'Oh yes, you're Senator Spearfield's daughter, aren't you?'

Back to taws, Cleo thought; but she smiled. 'Yes. I'm to write special releases, stuff like that.'

'Well, I'm sure we'll find something for you to do.' She was an old-timer, a woman who had been in Labour politics all her life but never given the opportunity to run for office. She knew her place, in the kitchen of elections, and she resented all these young trendies who were coming in to take over the Party. Especially this one, who looked as if she should be working for some silvertail Liberal.

It was November 1972; Cleo had been home almost five months. She had returned with a mixture of feelings; had she been too hasty, what sort of future did she have in Australia? Her father and her brothers and her sisters-in-law had greeted her as if she were indeed Cleopatra, home after having put Caesar in his place; they weren't indiscreet enough to say so in so many words, but there was no mistaking the impression that their welcome home had an extra level of meaning to it. Australia was the place to be and to hell with the Poms.

'There'll be an election soon and we're going to romp in,' her father said. 'Australia's going to take off like a rocket. You've come home just in time, sweetheart. You'll be in on the ground floor.'

'Doing what?'

'Anything you like. They'll be looking for someone like you. The newspapers, TV, even government if you like.

There's going to be a lot of openings in government when we get in.'

There had been no openings in newspapers or television, at least not wide, well-paying ones. The *Sydney Morning Post* offered her a job on its women's pages at less than half the *Examiner* had been paying her in London. She was interviewed on two talk shows on commercial channels and was both annoyed and amused at how she was cut down to size by the producers' assistants and floor managers, some of whom sounded as if their voices had just broken. Television in Australia was only sixteen years old and it seemed to her that, on the floor anyway, it was being run by sixteen year-olds. It was her first experience of the local assassination syndrome, the cutting down of tall poppies. It had not occurred to her that she should be such a tall poppy as would need cutting down.

She made enquiries about working in television. The executives whom she saw were all polite but wary of her; it did not take her long to recognize that they were afraid of her. Not of her personally but of her experience. She was talking to men who had little talent, who had come into television on the ground floor, bringing their own ladders with them to higher floors. They had come from newspapers, radio, everywhere, it seemed, but television. They had built their little fortresses and they were not going to be white-anted by someone with top talent and wide experience. They were polite and they offered her jobs at salaries that were insulting, hoping she would refuse; just as politely, she thanked them for the offers and went away, hoping they would all drop dead. Later she heard stories of other expatriates who had come home, met the same treatment and gone away again.

Sydney had changed even in the time she had been away. Everywhere she looked there seemed to be the skeletons of new buildings. It was not a frontier town, its citizens were too fat and comfort-loving for that, but it gave the impression of being on the edge of an uncharted future. Beyond the boundaries of the city itself Australia stretched away with a vastness that Cleo, never an Outback girl, still failed to comprehend. Despite all her father's and his friends' optimism, she doubted if the continent would ever be conquered even in her lifetime. Now that she was home, she did not feel at home. She could not come to terms with Australia.

One day in September she had been driving up Pacific Highway on Sydney's North Shore with Cheryl, her sister-in-law. The sky was cloudless, the wattle hung like golden smoke in gardens and for the moment she understood why so many people would never want to leave here; she remembered how in English winters she had pined for such a day as this. But there were more climates than just the weather.

Perry, her dentist brother, had found gold in other places besides his patients' mouths; he had made a small fortune on the stock exchange, much to the disgust of Sylvester, who had an old Labour man's dislike and suspicion of speculative investors. Perry and Cheryl now owned a house on half an acre in Killara, a weekender at Palm Beach and a half-interest in a vineyard at Mudgee; they also owned a Mercedes and a Jaguar E-type. On this spring day Cleo and Cheryl were in the white E-type with the hood down.

They pulled up at traffic lights at Crows Nest and a council truck pulled up alongside them. In it were half a dozen council workers in blue work singlets, shorts and floppy terry-towelling hats. They stared down at the two well-dressed women in the expensive car.

Then one of them spat over the side of the truck and said in a dry flat voice, 'What's it like to be down to your last hundred thousand, love?'

Cheryl stared straight ahead, but Cleo looked up at him, threw back her head and let go one of her father's belly-laughs. The lights turned green, the council worker winked at her and the truck drove on. Cheryl gunned the E-type and swept ahead of it.

'You shouldn't take any notice of them! They only resent what some people have got for themselves.'

'Cheryl, that's the nicest put-down I've had since I came home. I don't mind that sort of crack – somehow, to me, it's *Australian*. I prefer it to some of the other put-downs I've had.

279

That chap might have been envious, but I don't think he was malicious. He's probably thinking, good luck to 'em.'

'Maybe –' Cheryl, still unaccustomed to the money they had almost suddenly acquired, was continually looking for people who might take it away from them. Tax men, revolutionaries, burglars: she had acquired a host of enemies. She had changed the subject: 'What are you going to do, Cleo? You've been home over two months now.'

'I really don't know.' Cleo had stopped laughing. She had been surprised in the change in Perry and Cheryl while she had been away and she did not feel entirely at ease with them. She had never despised money but she had never worshipped it. Each time she had been to their house, for dinner or a Sunday barbecue, the conversation had seemed to consist of no other subjects but investment tips, tax evasion schemes and retirement funds. She had already noticed that when her father was in Sydney from Canberra he declined invitations to Killara if Perry and Cheryl were having any of their friends to the house. 'I'll find something.'

'How are you off for money? Perry told me to ask you –'

'Does he want to give me an investment tip?' But that was too pointed a lance and she smiled to blunt it. 'I'm all right. I brought a bit back with me.'

She had made no investments while she had lived in London, mainly because she had never been investment-minded. She had been surprised when she had written her bank, after her return home, and found out how much, despite high taxation, she had managed to save. Once again it occurred to her how pampered she had been, how much Jack had protected her from the day-to-day worries. Bills had been taken care of, transport provided: she had been wrong, though she had not lied, when she had told Sylvester she was not Jack's kept woman. She had not paid her way as much as she had thought.

'I'll be all right,' she told Cheryl. 'I just want to make sure I settle into the right job.'

She was living at home in the family house in Coogee, having it to herself most of the time. She had bought herself a second-hand Mini; that had been her major expense since coming back. She felt that she was drifting and, though she had not sat down and planned anything definite, she was throwing down no anchors. Not yet.

Jack had traced her to the house in Coogee and phoned her there. She remarked to herself that he had not written: he still would put nothing on paper to a woman. She was not disturbed when he rang her; she had expected a call sooner or later. A bunch of red roses had preceded the call, but she did not thank him for them or even mention them.

'I wish you'd come back,' he said. 'We could make a new start.'

'It's all over, Jack.' Distance lent civility to their voices.

'You can have anything you wish, if you come back.'

The editorship of the *Examiner*? But she said, 'That's not the point. It's just that we're finished. I wish you'd accept that –'

'I can't!'

She felt sorry for him; but that was all. 'Goodbye, Jack. Please don't call me again.'

But he did, twice more; she hung up on him as soon as she heard his voice. Red roses came every day for a week; then abruptly there were no more deliveries, no more phone calls. But he hovered there on the horizon of her mind, just over the edge of the world, like a storm that had once buffeted her and might come again. She knew his power, that of his money and influence but, worst of all, of his jealousy. She only began to relax as the weeks went by and he did not turn up on the doorstep of the house in Coogee.

Then a Federal election was announced. Sylvester came up from Canberra blown up with promises to the voters and his own optimism. Labour had been twenty-three years in the wilderness: God, though not a recognized member of the Party, had promised to work an eighth day. 'I think your mother, up there, has had a word in His ear. The Party can use you, too, sweetheart. I've talked to Gough Whitlam.'

'Dad, what do I know about recent Australian politics?' Now that she was home she was ashamed how little she had been interested in Australia while she had been away. Her sole interest had been Cleo Spearfield, another country altogether.

'You'll catch on in no time. We're going to waltz in, Cleo. The country has had twenty-three years of those other bastards – it's yelling out for a change.'

She worked well within the Party organization, because she had always been able to work with people. None of them was jealous of her, except some of the older women; but even those loosened up with her when she let drop hints that she was not interested in going to Canberra after Labour had won. She was still not sure where she would be going, but she knew she was not going anywhere where she would once more be just Sylvester Spearfield's daughter.

Sylvester was in his element during the campaign. There was an interest in the election such as Australia had not seen since the war; Cleo sometimes felt she was writing press releases for the Second Coming. She met Gough Whitlam and was impressed by the man; he was vain and intellectually arrogant, but he had a presence the look of a leader. The younger Party workers began to talk as if he could walk on water; the older ones, the Irish Catholics, muttered about sacrilege but worked just as hard, just in case he was The Lord. They knew that if they didn't, God might forget the Apostles who had spent twenty-three years in the wilderness of the electorates. There is no desert like a party district branch that does not have a sitting member in Parliament.

Cleo discovered, or re-discovered, that all was not sweet accord in the Party. Labour never needed outside enemies; it bred its own within the ranks. It knew it could do nothing about the enmities, so, being politically wise, it boasted that they were a measure of its true reform philosophy. The Liberals, who were conservative and not liberal, had their own dissensions, but pretended they were gentlemen and did their knifing in locked sound-proofed rooms. It was politics in any democracy in the world: only the accent was different.

On a warm December Sunday evening Labour came back into power. It seemed that three-quarters of the country got drunk on beer, wine and euphoria; the other quarter drank hemlock. All the family had gathered in the family home in Coogee to watch the results on television. Alexander and Madge, Labour down to Alex's red socks, floated about as if Utopia were just outside the garden gate. Perry and Cheryl, who had voted Liberal, afraid of capital gains tax and all the other secret Labour heresies, were there, wearing the smiles of Pompeians who had just bought a villa on Vesuvius for the view.

Alex, whose beer-belly now made him look pregnant, put his arm round Cleo's shoulders and looked across at their father. 'I'm more pleased for him than I am for the Party. He's waited what seems like forever for this.'

'What's he going to get out of it?' She remembered Sylvester's confession in London that he had long ago given up dreaming of being Prime Minister. 'Now that I've been working at headquarters, I've learned a few things. He's not a front runner for any of the plum jobs.'

Alex looked at her. 'You're kidding.'

'I'm not. And I think Dad knows it now.'

'Oh Christ!' Alex shook his head, and looked as if he were about to weep into his beer. He was a meteorologist, accustomed to sudden changes, but he had taken the political weather for granted. 'All that bloody effort over the years – they'll give him more than the crumbs, surely!'

Sylvester came across to them, belly-laughing as if there were still votes to be won. 'I wish your mother were here – I'd have crowned her Queen tonight!' And he a republican.

Cleo looked at him, feeling sorry for him: she knew that he knew that all he was going to get would be the crumbs. She would never know what had happened and she would never ask him. Somewhere along the years he had made the wrong friends and the wrong enemies.

'Congratulations, Dad,' she said and kissed him.

A month later he got the very minor Ministry for Power, which gave him no power at all. He came home from Canberra and sat out on the back verandah and looked down at the surf rolling in on to Coogee beach. Back in the days when the

283

family had all lived here, there had been a makeshift billiards room on this verandah. Sylvester and the boys had put up fibro walls at one end of the verandah; the walls had been too close to the table and certain shots had to be played with the billiard cue at an acute angle. But it had been another point round which the family had congregated, a green baize field where they had played out their friendly rivalries.

Now the billiards table was long gone, as was the family cohesion. The fibro walls had been taken down and a bougainvillea allowed to run riot. It blazed like a purple bushfire and the sun, reflected from it, gave his face and head a violet hue. He looks Roman, Cleo thought, with that profile and that head. But he was not the noblest Roman nor the happiest, not today.

'I should have expected it,' he said. 'The writing's been on the wall, but I guess I've become illiterate.'

'Don't joke, Dad. There's no need to.'

'We haven't done too well, either of us, have we? We're both back almost where we started from.'

'Not quite. People didn't know you when you first started. They do now.'

He was preoccupied with his own disappointment; he didn't pay her the compliment of saying she, too, was well-known now. Or perhaps he knew that back here in Australia she was still known only as his daughter.

'Do you want to come to Canberra?' he said. 'There'll be good jobs going and the pay will be good.'

'On your staff?'

'If you want to. But it would look better if you worked for someone else. The voters can't spell nepotism, but they know it when they see it.'

'No, thanks.' His shadow would be much smaller, but she did not want to stand in it.

'What are you going to do, then?'

She had asked herself the same question for the past three months and the answer had come to her last night. It seemed to her that the answers to all her problems came to her suddenly, not thought out but like instinctive movements for

284

survival. She had gone to London almost on a whim, she had come home on the spur of a horrifying moment ... Coming home as she had, there had been no time to think about what she expected from her return. She had arrived back without expectations; so now her disappointment was minimal. She had shied away from any involvement with men; one of her old lovers had rung her up and taken her out, but it had been like spending an evening with a boring stranger. There had been men at her brothers' dinner parties and barbecu s, with her sisters-in-law working hard as match-makers, but none of the men had appealed to her. She had met one man, a journalist who worked for the Labour Party during the campaign, and he had been attractive; then she had realized he reminded her of Tom, and that sort of substitution held no future. She was going to run away again.

'There's a government information office in New York. Could you get me a job there?'

He looked at her with pain. 'Sweetheart, when are you going to settle down? You're what – twenty-seven? I don't mean settle down and have kids – I don't know that you're that sort.'

She didn't know herself. She liked her small nephews and nieces and got on well with them, but she had never really thought about having children of her own. It was something that Jack had never brought up.

'But get yourself a decent job,' Sylvester said. 'Something with a future.'

'I thought I had that in London. For a while, anyway.' She had told him no more than that she had left Jack, that she had taken his advice and decided that Jack was too old for her. Because she had taken his advice, he had not queried her any more on the break-up. No one likes his good advice watered down by other reasons. 'No, Dad, I want to go to New York.'

He could recognize his own stubbornness in her. He sighed. 'All right, I'll see what I can do. But you can't keep running round the world –'

She was glad he didn't say *keep running away*. He, or his

fame, had been the original reason for her escaping; but she had never resented him for it. But he was now a spent force, like the forgotten gold medal winners of two or three Olympics ago. She said very gently, 'Dad, you kept running on the Canberra treadmill for years.'

He nodded. 'I know what you mean – what did it get me? But I'd like you to achieve your ambition, whatever it is. I wouldn't want to see two of us disappointed.'

She stood up and kissed him on top of his head. 'At least your hair is still thick. No bald patch.'

He laughed, almost the old belly-laugh. 'Well, that's something. I'll keep an eye out to see if Gough loses any on top.'

'You'll have to stand on a chair.' The new Prime Minister was six feet four, or 193 centimetres. She still could not get accustomed to the new metric table and always laughed when she read that the police were looking for a bank robber 165 centimetres tall. It conjured up an image of a midget criminal standing on his toes to look over a bank counter and threaten the teller, who had to lean forward to find out what the hold-up man wanted. 'Put your trunks on and we'll go down for a swim.'

They hadn't swum together since she had been at school. They were both strong swimmers and they went out beyond the breakers and floated on the swell, shutting their eyes against the sun and their minds against their futures. At last they caught a wave and came surging back to the beach, but it was the surf that drove them in, not their hopes.

They stood drying themselves while the surfies, all muscle and bleached hair, looked at the good sort with the boobs and the good sort looked at her father and saw the signs of approaching age. His hair was thick, but his muscles no longer were; she saw the crêpe under his upper arms, the slight sagging of what had once been a massive chest. She wanted to weep for him, seeing him already at the end of his life. Suddenly she leaned across and kissed him on the cheek; he smiled, not embarrassed or surprised, and squeezed her bare shoulder. The surfies turned away in disgust, wondering why a doll like her wasted herself on such an ossified oldie.

They did not recognize Sylvester and even if they had would not have been impressed. Politicians were the pits, man.

'We'll go out for dinner tonight,' Sylvester said. 'Over to Doyle's.'

They ate that evening in the restaurant on the harbour foreshore. Cleo had oysters and John Dory, still the best seafood she had ever tasted, and a bottle of Hunter Valley white at a price that made European wines bottled gold. Sylvester looked at her as she watched the lights flickering on the harbour waters.

'You really want to leave all this? There's no better place in the world to live.'

'It's not enough, Dad. But some day I suppose I'll come home to it. Most people seem to.'

'You won't if you get to the top in New York.'

'I'm only going over there to work for the information office.'

'Don't kid me, sweetheart. I don't know what you have in mind, maybe you don't even know yourself. But you're not going to settle for being a government hack.'

Two couples stopped by their table and the men congratulated Sylvester on getting the Ministry of Power. Sylvester thanked them without irony, then said, putting the two women's minds at rest, 'This is my daughter Cleo.'

'Really?' said one of the women, brown and lean as a whippet, already having put the young girl and the old man to bed together. 'You don't look like your father.'

'He's male,' said Cleo. 'It always makes a difference.'

When the couples, bruised, moved on, Sylvester said, 'That was a bit rugged, wasn't it?'

'They thought I was your girl friend.'

'What's wrong with that? I'm not *that* old.'

'Don't start sounding like Jack Cruze.'

He let out the belly-laugh and those other diners who had recognized him said, 'There's old Sylvester, happy as Larry as usual.'

A week later he came home and said to Cleo, 'There's a vacancy in the office in New York, but it's what they call a locally-engaged post. You'll have to pay your own way to New York and all it pays is the minimum New York union rates. But it will give you an American C-1 visa, which means you can stay in the States for as long as you work for a foreign government. It's not much, sweetheart, but it was the best I could do. Everybody and his cousin are down in Canberra looking for a job. It's not only jobs for the boys, but for the girls and hermaphrodites.'

'I'll take it. If I pay my own way to New York, no one can say there was any nepotism.'

A month later she left Sydney, stepping off another cliff but knowing this time she could glide. As she went through Passport Control she was swaggering, but it was unintentional. Life, as they say, is but a dream. She was out of practice, but she had not forgotten how to dream.

Sylvester had come to the airport to say goodbye. He watched her go, tears in his eyes, his own dreams now ashes in his skull.

2

Half a world away Jack Cruze had given up dreaming. For weeks he had nourished the hope that Cleo would come to her senses, which meant she would come back to him. He complained about the stubbornness of women, but was always surprised and annoyed by it. When Christmas came he looked hopefully for a card from her; the Queen sent him one, and the Prime Minister and the presidents of half a dozen countries; even the Governor-General of Australia, whom he had never met, sent him one. But not Cleo. He gave up then and looked around for another woman, this time one who had no career or ambition. He chose a divorced countess, closer to his own age, passionate but too indolent to be trendy or ambitious, the failings of his last two mistresses. But often during the night, after he had made love to the countess, he thought of Cleo. In the morning the countess would receive a dozen red roses. She thought they meant he loved her,

288

something that meant nothing to her. She was not to know he sent them as a penance.

He was as engrossed in his business affairs as he had ever been. He continued with his show driving, winning more competitions than he lost. The countess, who, she had told him, had lost her virginity falling off a point-to-point rider and had never since liked the horse scene, never attended the shows with him. Which didn't displease him, since she would have spoiled one of the few pleasures he had left.

He was still troubled by the memory of the attempted murder and suicide. After the shock of finding out that Cleo had disappeared, there had been the equally devastating, if delayed, shock at what he had tried to do. He had gone down to Cleo's flat and searched for the gun but had not found it; that had troubled him, then he had credited Cleo with the good sense to get rid of it. He had rung the Stafford and, using his old Buckinghamshire accent, posed as a taxi driver: he had picked up a young American at the hotel, a man with a limp and a walking stick who had left a parcel in his taxi. Oh yes, that would be Mr Roux, who had left that morning for the Continent. He had asked them to spell the name and they had: R-o-u-x, Mr Alain Roux. He had thanked them, said he would bring the parcel to the hotel and hung up. Alain Roux, Claudine's son, the young chap Cleo had had dinner with in New York – how long ago? It didn't matter. Obviously they had kept in touch with each other, though reason told him they could not have met often, if at all.

Alain Roux would have to be watched, listened for. He knew too much, he had been a witness to attempted murder and suicide. The young could not be expected to keep their mouths shut: Jack was convinced of that, it was against the nature of the young. In his own youth he had been as close-mouthed as a lockjawed ant-eater, but one was always different from today's generation; it was necessary to believe that, otherwise one lost confidence in oneself. But how was he to check that Alain Roux did not talk? All he could do was watch for the more obvious hints, such as gossip in American papers, where the law of libel was so much looser than here in Britain. Or for subtler hints, such as how Claudine treated him when next he saw her; but perhaps the wisest course there was to stay out of her way. For the next three months he waited for the bomb to go off (or the gun to be fired again, from across the Atlantic); but no sound was heard, no libel published. Yet he knew he would always have Alain Roux to fear.

On the other side of the Atlantic Alain kept his secret. He had had a father who never listened to him and he had a mother who preferred not to discuss awkward questions. He had grown up in an atmosphere where he learned to keep things to himself: he had a treasure-box of small secrets, like a hobby of which he was secretly ashamed. It was no effort to keep to himself what had happened in London. Besides, he was half in love with Cleo; he did not want to endanger his chances with her, in case he fell the other half. He was both honourable and selfish: he wanted to protect Cleo for himself. He was no different from other men in love, or halfway there.

So he said nothing to anyone, and guessed that Lord Cruze probably hated him more than he hated Cleo.

3

'I used to read your stuff in the *Examiner*, when I worked in London.' Stewart Norway was thin and wiry, had black curly hair, glasses and a shy friendly smile that hid one of the sharpest minds in Australian journalism. He was no government hack but, when asked, had taken this job as bureau chief because, if only for a time, he wanted to sell his country instead of newspapers. He would have laughed if anyone had called him a patriot, but that was what he was. It was becoming fashionable back home now to be patriotic and nationalistic, but he had been that way all his life. 'Unfortunately, you won't be able to write like that in this job. Frankly, Cleo, I was surprised when you wrote and said you wanted to come here.'

'I'll be frank, too. It was the only way I could get a long-term visa. But I'll give you my best, I promise. There's just one thing – I'd like to write outside stuff, in my own time. The cost of living here in New York isn't cheap.'

'I wish I could pay you more, but Canberra doesn't believe the natives should be spoiled. Because you're locally engaged, even though you've come all the way from Australia, you're looked upon as a native. Okay, you can write outside stuff, just so long as you don't get the bureau into bother. Where are you living?'

'For the time being, at a women's hotel downtown. They don't allow men above the ground floor. Lesbians are okay, but not men.'

Though he had been in newspapers all his life, Stew Norway was a little strait-laced. He was uncomfortable with talk about lesbians, even from such an obviously heterosexual girl as Cleo. At least he hoped she was heterosexual. You never knew these days, not with so many closet doors flying open like trapdoors.

The bureau was small, part of the Australian government offices in Rockefeller Center on Fifth Avenue. The rest of the staff were friendly but wary of Cleo; they knew who she had been in London and, like Stew Norway, they could not understand why she had taken the job. But within a week they found that she was friendly to them, had no airs and worked hard. Only the latter made her suspect: why work so hard for so little pay? They were all Americans, but they had learned the Australian suspicion of someone who appeared to like work.

She waited till she had been in New York two weeks, till she had got her bearings on herself as well as the city, before she called the *Courier*. Or rather, called the *Courier* to ask for Tom Border.

'Tom? This is Cleo.'

There was a noise at the other end of the phone as if he had sat down suddenly on an air cushion; or on his own lungs. 'Cleo! Are you in New York? What the hell are you doing here?'

'Working.' She explained where she was, but not why.

But he asked, 'Why, for God's sake? A government job?' He was not old, but he had an old newspaperman's suspicion of working for a government. 'Your father's not the Consul-General, is he?'

She laughed at the idea. 'Dad – *here*? He'd set Australian-American relations back two hundred years. Can we have dinner or something?'

There was a slight hesitation, then he said, 'Are you free now? Where are you – in Rockefeller Center? There's a café downstairs, looks out on to the ice rink. We'll have tea, be English.'

That was the last thing she wanted to be: afternoon tea had been a ritual with Jack. 'Lovely. Half an hour?'

She told Stew Norway that she had an old friend on the *Courier* who might be a good contact for placement of pieces on Australia. It was strange, after all this time, to have to account to someone for her absence from the office, but she played the game strictly according to the rules. She didn't want anyone in the office thinking that she thought herself above them. Privately she thought she was, but she was a modest egotist.

She was waiting in the café by the ice rink when Tom arrived. If that made her seem eager to see him, she didn't care. He squeezed her hand, bent down and kissed her cheek, then sat down opposite her. They ordered tea and English muffins and strawberry jam and when it was brought England was as far away as ever; Europeans can imitate English habits, but Americans, more closely related, just fail. The tea was brewed from tea bags, the muffins tasted like doughnuts and the strawberry jam was a jelly. Mrs Cromwell would have declared war.

They skated round themselves as delicately as the skaters outside were going round the rink. 'What did you think of Rosa Fuchs's sentence?'

That had been months ago, before she had left London to go home. 'In a way I was glad they didn't sentence her to death. That would have worried me.'

'Yes,' he said, but didn't sound convinced. 'Life

imprisonment – I think I'd rather they hanged me. I sometimes think the anti-capital punishment people are more concerned with their own feelings than they are for the prisoners'.'

'I couldn't care less about Rosa Fuchs,' she said emphatically, meaning *let's talk about us.*

'Well, fancy you being here! Are you liking it?'

'Very much.' Especially right now.

He waited for her to go on, but she didn't. He looked out
at the rink, at a girl in a bright red costume who floated like
a firebird about the ice. He had never skated, the ice on the
ponds down home had rarely been thick enough, and he
envied the grace and sense of freedom that skaters could
suggest. He looked back at Cleo

'Can you skate?'

'No. The only sport I was any good at was surfing. I did a
lot of that while I was home this summer.' They were like
strangers on a train, sharing a meal in the restaurant car. At
last she said, 'I hear you've written a novel.'

He nodded. 'It's based pretty loosely on a kidnapping in
Germany some time ago.'

'Am I in it?' Hoping she was.

Some authors delight in talking about their books, written
or unwritten: the Irish are masters at the latter. Others are
secretive or just embarrassed, as if they were being asked to
write their own reviews. Which all writers, shy or otherwise,
would love to do.

'I'm not sure. I guess there are bits and pieces of you in
it.'

'Physical bits and pieces? Or something else of me?' Then
she smiled and put her hand on his and some of the constraint
between them fell away. 'No, don't tell me. I'll read it. When
does it come out?'

'Two weeks' time.'

'How do they think it will go?' She said nothing about
Alain and what he had told her about the book.

His grin was almost an *aw shucks* one: he couldn't boast, not
to her. 'I can't quite believe it. It – ' he said *it*, – not *I*, 'it's got
both a Literary Guild and a Readers Digest Condensed Books

293

choice. Exeter House, they're my publishers, are doing a first printing of 100,000. We've sold the paperback rights –' He paused.

'Well, go on. I never get embarrassed when money's mentioned.'

'Half a million dollars, of which I get half. Exeter gets the other half, as the hardback publisher.' He sounded as if he were trying to excuse himself having so much money.

'Movies?'

'It's been bought by an independent producer who's going to make it for Universal.'

'How much?'

'Two hundred and fifty thousand. Plus what I'll get for doing the screenplay. That's what I wanted to tell you ...'

But she had sat back, at last letting all her surprise and pleasure for him come out of her in a wide gasping smile. 'Tom – I'm thrilled for you! God, how successful can you be? And you're sitting there like nothing's happened to you, still trying to sound like the Budweiser boy from the bush ... Look at you, still in your Harrods' sale suit! And that same old topcoat! Couldn't you have even tried to look successful, just for my sake? No, you come here in disguise, trying to make me feel sorry for you –'

'Cleo, shut up, please.' He was smiling, pleased that she was so obviously pleased for him. Then the smile died: 'I have to tell you something –'

'No, tell me over dinner tonight. I have to get back to the office – no, really. I'm a *worker*. This isn't like working on a newspaper –'

'Cleo old girl –' He held her by the wrist. 'I can't take you to dinner tonight – I have a date. And I'm leaving for California in the morning. You were lucky to catch me at the *Courier*. I was there cleaning out my desk.'

She could feel him hurting her wrist, so strong was the pressure of his grip. She could feel the emotion in him and she stopped being gay and pleased, for him or for herself. She knew at once that everything was not as she had hoped.

'I can't get out of going to California – I start work on the

294

script next Monday. But that's not the real reason I can't have dinner with you tonight. Cleo, there's a girl . . .'

She gently eased her wrist out of his grip. 'Well, I suppose there had to be. I don't know why, somehow I never saw you settled down – ' It struck her that their roles had been reversed. He was the success now; she was the drifter. For she had really been nothing else for the past eight months. 'But you're not a drifter any more, are you?'

'No,' he said. 'I'm a married man.'

4

Tom settled into the seat beside Simone, smiled at her as she took his hand. 'I hate flying when I'm not working,' she said. 'I have too much time to think about what might happen.'

'TWA have guaranteed me personally that they will deliver us safely to Los Angeles.' He looked sideways at her, loving her but not in the same way as he still loved Cleo.

He was sardonically amused at what had happened. The drifter who had avoided commitment for so long had at last drifted into marriage.

'I'm so happy for you, *chéri.*' He could feel her nails digging into his palm; she never held back on any of her feelings. 'I've been saying prayers that everything will turn out just so well in Hollywood. That you have no fights with the producer, that you write a wonderful screenplay, that – '

'That you and I are not spoiled by it all.' He squeezed her hand, but not hard enough to hurt her. He had hurt her enough, though so far she did not know it.

He had never told her about his feelings for Cleo. After he had returned from Hamburg almost twelve months ago he had been determined to put Cleo out of his mind. Once, in a desperately low mood, he had been tempted to write her, but had resisted the temptation; heavy hearts use heavy pens and he did not want Cleo feeling sorry for him. He had settled down to finishing his novel; but that had filled in only another month. Then Simone had rung him.

'Tom, I have two whole days in New York and no one to talk to.'

He had been more than just glad to see her again. She was still with Air France but no longer with the New York boy friend; he had been a pilot, but Tom had never asked with which airline. Perhaps he had been transferred to another base, he may even have crashed; Tom didn't bother to enquire. That was how it had always been between him and Simone: no questions asked, no lies told.

Then the first week in July she had called to say that her mother had died and she would not be coming to New York that week. When she did arrive two weeks later there was a difference in her; he had never seen her sad and it gave a new depth to her. She turned to him for comfort and he gave it, because he had a natural sympathy for those in need of it. At first he had thought he was no more than her American comforter; then he realized she looked on him as her only one. She was like him: she had dozens of acquaintances but no close friends. Each time he met her he noticed the growing difference in her: she was as content to be with him as she had once been eager to go to bed with him.

In the last week in that same month he had learned of Cleo's leaving the *Examiner*.

'Have you heard the news?' Alain Roux said one morning in the *Courier*'s newsroom. 'Your friend Cleo Spearfield has left the *Examiner* in London.'

'What do you mean – left?'

'Up and left.' Alain had returned only the day before from his vacation in Europe. He looked so tanned and fit that when he was standing still the walking stick seemed to be an affectation.

'Has she gone to another paper?'

'I don't think so. She's just disappeared.'

'Where'd you get all this?'

'On the grapevine.'

Alain's grapevine had been no more than a telephone cable; he had been the grape-picker. Against Cleo's warning, though she had given him her unlisted number on his insistence, he had called her from Heidelberg on the Monday morning; there had been no answer from the flat. He had bought all the English newspapers to see if there was any mention of her or Lord Cruze; there had been none. He had not enjoyed his four days with Roger and Louise; he had been too distracted by the memory of what had happened in London. But he had been polite and grateful for their efforts to entertain him; then he had gone on to Italy. There he continued to buy the English newspapers every day, but still there was nothing about Cleo or Lord Cruze. He began to wonder if there had been a reconciliation. He had heard his mother, wise in such observations, say that most women were gluttons for punishment when it came to men. He doubted if that were true, especially in the case of Cleo.

The day before he left Rome for New York he called the flat once more, again got no answer. Then he called the *Examiner*, was told by the switch girl that Miss Spearfield was no longer with them. He hesitated, then took a risk.

'May I speak to the features editor? My name is Roux. I'm with the *New York Courier*.'

Joe Brearly came on the line. 'What's it about, Mr Roux?'

'I've been asked to look for some features we could buy for the *Courier*. Miss Spearfield's name came up. We couldn't use all her stuff, most of it would be too local, but some of it ...'

'She's no longer with us, Mr Roux.'

'Oh. Well, maybe I could deal direct with her. Do you know where she's gone?'

There was a slight pause on the line. 'I'm afraid not, Mr Roux.'

'She's not retiring or marrying or anything like that?'

There was a coughing laugh. 'You'd better ask her, Mr Roux. If you can find her.'

He hadn't tried any further to find her. She was obviously safe; and he was not concerned with how Lord Cruze was. The man was patently a megalomaniac in love as well as in business; he would not have cared if Cruze had indeed suffered a stroke or a heart attack. Just so long as he caused no further harm to Cleo.

But he told none of this to Tom Border, who was not a close enough friend of Cleo's to be told any more. 'She's just retired, I guess. Maybe she's gone somewhere to write a book, like you.'

'Yeah, maybe.' They were both cautious, without either of them seeing it in the other. 'Well, she'd have a lot of material.'

'I guess so.' *More than you realize, Tom.* 'How's your own book going?'

'Looking good.'

Tom had no phone number for Cleo other than at the *Examiner*, but he knew it would be useless to call her there. He thought of writing her care of the *Examiner* in the hope that the letter would be sent on; then he wondered what he had to say beyond what he had said on the Lombard bridge in Hamburg. So he had waited, hoping that she would write him; but he heard nothing. Wherever she had gone, she had not taken any thoughts of him with her. He had his pride, which, along with reason and commonsense, is one of the banes of lovers.

Then things began to happen with his novel. Success glimmered on the horizon, then rose in a blaze. It did not go to his head; instead it went to his heart. He suddenly found he wanted someone to share it with; and Simone was the natural one, because she was at hand. His parents and his sister wrote from Missouri to tell him how pleased they were for him; they asked for nothing because, he knew, it would not occur to them. He went home to Friendship for a weekend; on the spur of the moment, because she had three days off in New York, he took Simone with him. He took his mother a Cartier bracelet and his sister a gold watch; he went to Abercrombie and Fitch and bought his father an English sporting rifle. They berated him for his extravagance, but were delighted with the gifts. They were more delighted with Simone.

'Is it serious?' his mother asked him. Olive Border was a countrywoman, as bony as her son but with a certain beauty that appealed to men who did not like chocolate box looks; she had her own morals, but realized that Tom lived by a different set. He and Simone would sleep in different rooms in her house, but she did not care how they slept in New York. 'I've read that Frenchwomen make good wives, but Frenchmen make lousy husbands.'

'You've been reading *Playboy* again. I wish you'd give up those centrefolds, Mom – '

Simone had watched the interplay in the Border family; the only child of a widow, she had had none of that. There was a surrounding warmth here that she had never known; her mother had loved her and she had loved her mother, but two people do not make a family circle. She had liked Clem Border and he had been captivated by her.

'Bring her down here again, Tom,' he had said when Tom and Simone were leaving. 'I've always been suspicious of the French. But a man would have to be tetched to be suspicious of Simone. Is it serious between you?'

Tom had embraced his father. Clem Border was a plain man whose best feature was the honesty that shone out of his long lean face; with most people, even women, that was enough. 'You're getting to be as bad as Mom, trying to match-make.'

'I've never tried it with any of the others your mother lined up for you. But that girl's got something different.'

'It's only because you've never seen a French girl before. All weekend you've been waiting for her to do the can-can.'

Tom had looked across at Simone saying goodbye to his mother and sister. Paris-born-and-bred, she looked at home with this Mid-West farm family; he saw that it was more than the commercial *bonhomie* that she had been taught as a stewardess. The French had come down through here in the late seventeenth and early eighteenth centuries, but only as traders; the explorer Du Tisne had been through here at much the same time. But there was no French influence around Friendship now; none other than what Simone was exerting. She was doing it without effort, so easy did she feel with his family, and he was sure she was not doing it deliberately. There was no calculation about Simone. She met everyone on the same terms. The family had already married her, if he hadn't.

299

He married her in December, the week before Christmas. By then he no longer thought about Cleo, though sometimes he had to put the thought of her out of his mind. He had not heard from her and he could only guess where she might be. The week before he and Simone married there was a small item in the *Courier* that a new government had been returned in Australia and he thought of her then and wondered if she had been home to celebrate her father's triumph. But by then he and Simone were part of each other's life, even if subject to Air France schedules. By then, too, he knew he was going to be rich. Not rich by Brisson standards, but good enough.

'You must get someone to look after your money,' Simone had said and he knew that she did not mean herself.

'I've never met anyone thriftier than you.'

'You need someone who *understands* money.'

'I think you understand it. I'd trust you with it.'

She was suddenly ahead of him, though she hadn't meant to be. 'Tom, are you proposing to me?'

He was as surprised as she was; but he had the grace not to show it. He could show the French a thing or two when it came to gallantry. 'I guess I am,' he said with laconic Missouri courtliness. 'What do you say?'

'I am Catholic,' she said. 'It would be for keeps.'

Ah, the Catholics, he thought: who else uses sin the way they do? She had been sleeping with him for almost three years now; but all that had been only a venial sin in her eyes. Now she was warning him she would never commit the mortal sin of divorce.

But he was wrong: she was only warning him that she was not interested in a trial marriage. She had told him she was a Catholic because she wanted to be married by a priest in a church. 'My mother would have wanted it, *chéri*. I do not want to be married at City Hall. That is too much like asking for a certificate, like being naturalized or something. I do not want to be naturalized a wife.'

'I'm Baptist, or I was. I don't think it'll upset my folks too much if I'm not married a Baptist. Would you like to go out

300

to Friendship to be married? I used to go to high school with the guy who's now the local priest, a nice guy named Tony Briano.'

So they were married. She loved him and he almost loved her; he liked her and he was happy with her and that, more often than not, is good enough. Cleo, who had never given him happiness, only dreams of it, faded more and more in his memory. Until yesterday.

And now he and Simone were bound for Hollywood, where everything, including happiness, was make-believe.

'We'll make out,' he said and prayed that they would.

TWELVE

1

Over the next six months history, as it so often does, wrote its small messages; newspaper headlines wrote the messages large, but copy-editors are never remembered as historians. One large message was that oil was never going to be cheap again, though no one at the time realized just what an effect the raising of oil prices would have on the world's economy. The man in the street was concerned only with the state of his own economy and he hated those Arab sons-of-bitches who were going to make him pay a cent or two more for a gallon of gasoline.

Cleo had no car and so no worries about paying more for gasoline. But she needed more money. She had moved out of the women's hotel into a tiny apartment above a delicatessen on Second Avenue. It was noisy and dark, but it was clean and the rent was reasonable if one thought in terms of ransom money; but she was in the gut, if not the heart, of New York. In peak hour the traffic crawled past and, if she was home by then, she would look out from her second-storey window at the morose citizens heading for what purgatory that time of day offered them. They would look at each other, she with interest, wondering why all New Yorkers should look so unhappy, and they with suspicion, wondering if the smiling dame at the window was on the game. Once a youth waved to her and she waved back; but the bus driver, a misanthrope like most of his passengers, picked up speed and took the youth away before romance could blossom. Cleo figured it was safe to fall in love with boys in passing buses; there was no commitment there, the bus schedules didn't allow for it. In the meantime New York, and America, had to be conquered.

And more money was needed if that was to be done. Her bureau salary was not enough to live on in this location; and she was determined she was not going to move off Manhattan. Her capital was shrinking and she reckoned (though she was a poor reckoner when it came to money) that it would all be gone in another few months. Immigrants from Eastern Europe had landed in America with far less than she had and had fought their way upwards, some even reaching the top. But she had been spoiled by the three years of success in London; she had grown soft, taking luxury for granted. She was not prepared to sell apples or herrings from a sidewalk barrow. Australians, like the French, never see themselves as immigrants.

She looked at the *Courier* and decided it would never buy any of the freelance articles that she might write. The paper was duller and stodgier than she had imagined; it was like reading soggy sponge cake. Besides, she did not want to renew her acquaintance with Alain. Then she went to see an agent.

Gus Green was an ex-newspaperman, short, fat and in his late sixties, a ball of energy kept going by the momentum he had built up over the years. He had an office that looked out on to Times Square and a reputation that stood up to any looking into. He was not the biggest agent in New York but he was one of the best.

'I'm on the wrong side of town for all the publishers, but this is where I like to be, even with all the pimps and pushers and hookers who've taken over Times Square. So you want to conquer New York, eh?' She hadn't said so, but she guessed he said that to all his new clients. 'So did I, so did I. I came here from Chicago fifty years ago. It was summer, I wore a ten-dollar seersucker suit, a Sears Roebuck panama hat, I was eighteen years old and I was going to conquer the *World*. The *World* was the paper everyone wanted to work for in those days. They started me at twenty bucks a week and I

303

couldn't believe I was being *paid* to work in New York. I was a newspaperman right up till the end of the war, WW Two. Then I decided I wanted to meet a classier lot of people, the wife was always complaining she never met anyone but newspaper bums. So, Christ forgive me, I chose book publishers and magazine editors, better dressed bums, that's all, says the wife. I make more money, but I work twice as hard and I still miss everything that goes on in the city room just before the paper goes to press. A big book generates excitement, but it's nothing to what I used to get out of a big story breaking. Don't you miss what you used to have on the *Examiner?*'

'I didn't mention anything about working for the London *Examiner,*' she said cautiously.

'Miss Spearfield, I *know* you. How many dames in the world are called Cleo Spearfield? I been going to London twice a year for Christ knows how long – I used to read your column. I don't want to know why you're here working for peanuts for the Australian government, but don't expect me not to recognize you. If I'm going to handle you, if you'll forgive the expression, I'm going to sell you as Cleo Spearfield, not as Jane Doe or whatever other name you had in mind.'

'I hadn't thought of using any name but my own.'

'Good, then I got something to sell. Who sent you to me, by the way? Tom Border?'

She stiffened, retreated into herself. 'I didn't know Mr Border knew you.'

'I represent him, didn't you know that?' He pushed a book across his book-littered desk. 'Have you read it?'

The book, *The Guns of Chance*, had been out several months, but she had resisted the urge to buy it and read it, afraid, for no reason she could name, that she might find herself in it, even though it was fiction. The book was in every bookstore window in the city; Brentano's and Scribners and Doubleday had featured blown-up photographs of Tom. She had decided that when, if, she fell in love again it would be better to fall for someone anonymous, a man whose face would never be made public. A CIA agent or a tax collector or a socialist Presidential candidate from Arizona.

'No. It was an experience I don't want to relive.' Meaning taking too long to make up her mind about Tom. She had cried herself to sleep the night after he had told her he was married, realizing there in the darkness of the night and her own bitter disappointment how much she had loved him.

'Yeah, I can understand that,' said Gus Green, meaning something else but wondering if Miss Spearfield had any ideas about libel. He would have to re-read the book and see what Tom had said about his heroine.

'Perhaps if you represent Mr Border it would be better if I went to another agent ...'

Gus Green waved her back into her chair, though she hadn't risen from it. 'Look – can I call you Cleo? – I don't know what's with you and Tom. It's none of my business. And his business, I mean *business* business, isn't yours and yours isn't his. I make myself clear? You'll be my client and no other client on my list need ever meet you or you meet them. It'll just be you, me, editors and publishers. Now what do you want to write and who for?'

She was at the bottom again. She could not afford to spurn a helping hand, not even one that charged her ten per cent commission for saving her from poverty. 'I have a couple of ideas that might interest *International*.'

'Good choice.'

International was a magazine, so it advertised, for intelligent women one step ahead of trends. It featured articles on sex, clothes, sexy clothes, where to go for sex and what clothes to wear, travel, how to enjoy sex while travelling, beauty, how sex improved beauty, how to prepare for sex in (God, dare we mention it?) old age. There were no articles on cookery, unless it was the odd piece on how to concoct an aphrodisiac, and the only articles on housekeeping featured advice on how to furnish a bedroom that would turn a man on. It published editions in six other countries besides the United States and its circulation suggested that the world was in danger of being

305

over-run by intelligent women hell-bent on sex. The women's liberation movement was applying to the courts to have it banned as obscene, pornographic and seditious.

'Tongue-in-cheek stuff about sex.'

'We'd have to see how they react to that,' said Gus Green doubtfully. 'They think sex is holier than motherhood. I don't think they'd buy heresy. Anyhow, let's try 'em.'

Next day he called her at the bureau. '*International* would like to see you – they know your work. You want me to come with you?'

'They're an all-women staff, aren't they? I think you might be embarrassed, Mr Green, especially when we start to talk about sex.'

'I'd only be embarrassed because I'm too old to do much about it. Okay, see 'em on your own. But don't talk money, let me do that.'

Cleo went in to see Stewart Norway. 'Stew, I'd like a couple of hours off this afternoon. I have an appointment over at *International*.'

He was a generous man. 'Cleo, it embarrasses me, being your boss. You do work that's worth so much more than we can pay you. So long as you get done whatever has to be done, take all the time you like.'

'Stew, I could fall in love with you if you weren't so plain and middle-aged and married.'

'Geez, I got close, didn't I?'

She went out, revising her idea that all Australian men, including her father and her brothers, were male chauvinists. Stew Norway was not the sort of man who would ever be written about in the pages of *International*, but a lot of intelligent women, tired of trying to stay one step ahead of trends, would have found him a comfort.

The offices of *International* were in Rockefeller Center; Cleo had only to cross from one building to another. The address of the bureau and the magazine might be the same, but they were countries apart. The office of the bureau was strictly functional, designed to discourage loitering, as if afraid that too much information about Australia might leak out. The magazine's offices were strictly sensual, designed to lure, a bordello (but not a brothel) of publishing.

Francine Tobin, the executive editor, fitted her magazine's format. She was in her thirties, intelligent, beautiful (if manufactured) and discreetly suggested that she was interested in sex. She wore a hat in her office, a wide-brimmed felt with the brim turned up in front, as if she were facing a gale that had struck no one else. Cleo had once read about the Queen Bees of American business, women executives above a certain level, who always wore hats in their offices, like bishops' mitres. But that, Cleo thought, had been back in the Fifties.

'What did you have in mind, Cleo?'

There were two other women in the office, younger than Francine, both hatless, and everyone was on first name terms as soon as Cleo came in the door. Just like back home, Cleo thought, amongst the boys in the pub. Delia and P.J., the latter of which Cleo took to stand for two first names, were in their late twenties and looked like ex-models who had read the wrinkles in their untouched photos and wisely gone into another career.

'I'd like to do a piece about the gigolos, the studs, along the French Riviera. Tongue in cheek.'

Francine looked at Delia and P.J. 'Can we take a little tongue in cheek?'

'Why not?' said P.J., stroking a long finger down a still flawless cheek. But she had laughter wrinkles round her eyes and Cleo liked her. 'We keep telling our readers they're intelligent.'

'Do you know the Riviera?' said Delia, who, Cleo guessed, would some day wear a hat in this office.

'Intimately. But not the studs – I only know them from observation.'

'Could you work in something about the older men? I understand there are lots of older men available there, ones with more money than the young guys.' Francine's beautifully made-up face was beautifully blank.

Cleo could feel Delia and P.J. freeze, just as they had once done before the cameras. Somehow all three of them knew about Jack. They were waiting for her to let her hair down, give them the dirt on what turned on an English lord.

'The Greeks and South Americans, you mean? Yes, I can work something in.'

'Good,' said Francine, disappointed but not showing a trace of it. 'Well, let's discuss some angles . . .'

Next day Gus Green rang Cleo. 'Okay, go to work. I've got you two thousand dollars. They pay more, but you'll have to work up to it. Who knows, some day you may write a book and I'll make you a fortune, like I did for Tom Border.'

2

Cleo wrote her piece, quickly as she always did, and *International* loved it and the promptness with which it was delivered. They took out an article that had been scheduled and substituted hers. It is now history that in the autumn of 1973 hordes of intelligent, one-step-ahead-of-the-trend women converged on the French Riviera to study the gigolos and bucks they had been warned against. The gigolos and bucks, tongues in cheeks, wrote Cleo thank-you notes.

P.J., whose full name was Pia Jane Lagerlof, called her up a week after the article was accepted and invited her to lunch.

'We want you to do two more pieces for us, Cleo. You have a fresh approach. You take people down a peg or two, but you're not offensive. That's fresh for *us*, anyway. Between you and me, we tend to cut the balls off of anyone we're ragging. Well, anyway. We'd like something in the same vein, as the gold-digger said to the sugar daddy.'

Cleo laughed and shook her head. 'Your similes aren't much better than your syntax.'

P.J. grinned. 'I was hired for my looks originally. When I gave up modelling, they signed me on as assistant to the beauty editor. They were bowled over when they found out I had a B.A. in Eng Lit, from Barnard.'

'What about Francine and Delia?' She was interested in

the opportunities for women in this city, how they got them and what use they made of them. Soon, she hoped, she would be taking her first step out onto the same battlefield.

'Francine has been in magazines or advertising ever since she got out of some tacky little college in the Dakotas somewhere. There are no flies on Francine, as you probably noticed. There *is* blood on her spike heels, but we never mention that ... Delia is an ex-model like me. She wouldn't know a parenthetical clause from a bull's ass, but she knows where she's going – right into Francine's chair, some day. She also knows what our readers like, so she leaves the syntax and the parenthetical clauses to me. On top of all that she knows that in this town nice people, especially nice women, come last. Why am I telling you all this? What do you do for men?'

'What's Delia like on non-sequiturs? You're not bad. What do I do for men? At present, nothing.'

'See anything here you like?'

They were in a restaurant in Rockefeller Center, one of those whose prices were more digestible if one was on an expense account. Cleo was still becoming accustomed to the glossier and wider spread of affluence here in New York compared to London or Sydney. There was more visible money here. The diners in this crowded restaurant might be up to their necks in debt in private, but they were ordering from the menu with no public sign of pain. There were restaurants like this in London and Sydney, but they were smaller and would not have been as crowded. There certainly would not have been as many women present, not at lunch.

'There are guys from NBC and *Time*, a few from advertising, some bankers – '

'What about the women?'

P.J. cocked an eyebrow. 'You're not a dyke?'

Cleo laughed. 'No, I'm straight. But I can't get over the number of women in this city who look as if they've got it made. In business, I mean. This really is the world capital for career women.'

'You might do a piece on that for us. But enough about

309

business. I get the feeling you could be getting more out of this town than you are. I mean after office hours.'

'I don't rush into things.'

A man stopped by their table to say hello to P.J. He was tall and heavily built, with the thick rubbery skin that Cleo had come to notice on some healthy American men, as if the flesh were applied freshly each morning over their bones. He was dressed in a dark flannel suit and wore a button-down shirt with a silk tie. He looked as if he wore it as a uniform each day, but was at ease in it. He said a few words to P.J., gave Cleo a charming smile and a quick appraising look and passed on.

'He's with Socony, in finance or something. He's just going through his second divorce, he's marvellous in bed, so I'm told, and I wouldn't get into the hay with him, or the sand, if I was alone with him on a desert isle. He's the worst sort, he *talks*. A girl goes to bed with him, every guy in the Yale Club knows about it the next day. You have to watch out, Cleo. American men say that we women have cut their balls off, but they've only got themselves to blame. I don't think women are natural castrators, do you?'

It was surgery she had never contemplated, at least not knowingly. 'Do you have a man?'

P.J. nodded and looked sad, an expression that lay oddly on her vivacious, beautiful face. 'He's married, unfortunately. I see him from Monday to Friday, then he goes home to his wife in Philadelphia and I feel as guilty as hell all week-end. I go to church on Sunday and pray for forgiveness for breaking up a happy home, then on Monday he comes back and I welcome him with open arms and open legs. I'm disgusting, really.'

Cleo made no comment, but wondered if she would open her arms (and her legs) to Tom if he wanted to see her Monday to Friday. But knew that she wouldn't, not while he was happily married to – Simone? She had only dimly taken in the name of his wife when he had mentioned it.

'I'm a very moral girl, actually,' said P.J. 'My father is an Episcopalian minister up in New Hampshire and I respect everything he believes in. I think the Ten Commandments make much better reading than anything we ever print in *International*. Unfortunately, I have a body that's not moral at all and I'm in love with a married man.'

'P.J., why are you telling me all this? I'm a perfect – well, an imperfect stranger – '

'I honestly don't know, Cleo. Yes, I do.' She blinked and Cleo was shocked to see the shine of tears in the beautiful blue eyes. 'I just saw my man across the room there – he's gone now. He was having lunch with his wife.'

Oh God, Cleo thought, don't let Tom come back to New York. Let him settle forever in California with his wife, let him take her to lunch there, let me never see them together.

Cleo accepted the commission to write two more articles and Gus Green, delighted with his new client, had her price raised. She was no longer on the breadline, albeit it had been fancy bread, and she felt a re-awakening of her ambitions. She took an excursion trip round Manhattan Island and looked at what she might some day conquer. She felt a certain trepidation: there were battlements to be scaled, certain of the taller buildings stood like castle keeps. Had she the talent to batter down the gates? How many other would-be knights and Joans of Arc had arrived here and failed, they and their descendants still trapped in the moats of the Lower East Side or up in Spanish Harlem? She knew the geography of the city, though she had seen very little of it. All she had to learn and conquer was the climate.

She worked diligently at the bureau, writing pieces about Australia, telling Americans more than they really wanted to know about Down Under. She did articles, short and long, on the Barrier Reef, the revival of the arts under the Labour government, the terrors of funnel-web spiders, the gastronomic delights of the pavlova, the lamington and the iced vo-vo (that one done tongue in cheek but taken seriously by American readers, who were so ignorant of Australia they believed anything they read) and the honoured place of racehorses in the Australian pantheon. But while she dispensed information about her own country she began to learn

311

all that she could about the country she had, she had now decided, come to conquer.

She learned a few things about American men. She went out occasionally with P.J. on a double date and soon caught on that P.J.'s married lover was quite happy with the arrangement as it stood and had no intention of making an honest woman of P.J. Cleo never raised the matter with P.J. because she also caught on that the latter was so in love she was ready to settle for any arrangement her married man suggested. For her own part Cleo enjoyed herself with a couple of the dates P.J. brought along but none of them interested her enough for any regular dating. One night, feeling in need of sex, she went to bed with her date for that night, an editor from one of the larger publishers. He treated her as if she were a tyro writer, editing everything she attempted in their love-making and imposing his own format on the exercise. When he rang her the next morning she sent him a rejection slip.

Time and the seasons slipped by. She went up to New Hampshire with P.J. for Christmas, but felt an intruder in the Lagerlof family. The night before she left Manhattan she called her father and her brothers and sisters-in-law and felt worse for hearing their voices. She felt homesick, something she had told herself she would never feel.

'How are things, sweetheart?'

'Fine, Dad.' She had a sizeable income now from her magazine pieces. But she hadn't come to America just to make money. 'How are things with you?'

'Fine.' But she knew at once that they were lying to each other. 'I've been hoping I might get over to see you, but Gough seems to be the one who's doing all the travelling these days. No chance of you coming home?'

'Not yet awhile.' She was homesick but going home would be no cure.

'Well, good luck for 1974, sweetheart. Who knows, we may both be on top at the end of the year.'

Another six months went by. Her bank account grew, but she seemed to be standing still; she might finish up a rich fossil. She had moments of panic when it seemed that the years, her best years, were going down the drain like water. Then one hot steamy day in mid-summer Stewart Norway called her into his office.

'Cleo, I've got some bad news. I'm going to have to put you off. Canberra has decided it will spend more money here and they're sending over another journalist. I recommended they appoint you from here, since you were on the spot, but I'm afraid the job had already been promised to someone back home. You know what politics are like.'

'That means I lose my visa?' She knew at once what it meant.

'I'm afraid so. I'll see what I can do about getting you an extension, but I think it would be for six months at the most.'

Her first reaction was to call her father and ask him to do something. She knew that he could; he might have lost out on a senior Cabinet post, but he still had clout in the Party. But the word would get out that he had used his influence and once again she would be back where she had started: Senator Spearfield's daughter, the girl who had to use her father to keep her job.

'How long before you sack me, Stew?'

He looked most unhappy. 'I wish you could think of a better way of putting it, love. I'm not sacking you. Canberra has put a gun at my head and told me I have to let you go. So don't say I'm sacking you. I'll tell them I can't let you go under a month. You make an application for a change of visa and I'll see what I can do about backing you up. But it will only be for a limited period and that's not good enough, right? You're hoping you can settle here. That's what you've got in mind, isn't it?'

'Yes. How would you like to come back in your old age and find I owned New York?'

He shook his head in mock wonder. 'Normally, ambitious women give me a pain in the neck – ' He grinned his slightly buck-toothed smile. 'I know, I'm a typical Aussie male chauvinist. But you ... Well, I'd like to see you get to the top. I don't think you'd stomp over a man to get there.'

313

'Don't flatter me, Stew. There are some men back in Canberra I'd stomp on if I could get to them.'

But she realized now that this time she had been pushed off the cliff. She had been teetering on the edge for too long, almost as if she had lost her courage or her ambition. She had been shaken, as a stopped watch might be, and got going again.

She went to see Gus Green and explained her problem. 'I'm staying here, Gus, no matter what. I'll be a wetback if I have to, I'll swim across the East River and back. I can't get immigrant status – the Australian quota is filled for the next seven years or something.'

'I've had other clients who have had the same problem. You got to marry a US citizen – you don't want that, do you? I'd marry you myself, if it wasn't for the wife – or you got to work for some organization that says it needs you here. Or you can get some Congressman to put through private legislation. You know a Congressman?'

'No.' She sat for a moment or two in silence, then she said reluctantly, because she did not like the thought that had slipped into her mind, 'But I know an organization that I might be able to persuade that it needs me. Or anyway someone in the organization.'

Gus Green chewed a fat lip. 'Cleo, don't sell yourself. To some guy, I mean. I've seen too many dames go the wrong route doing that.'

I've seen this one go the same route. 'I'll be careful, Gus. I'll be dealing with a gentleman.'

'Who said you could trust one of them?' said Gus Green, who'd never claimed to be a gentleman.

She rang Alain at the *Courier*. She thought he was going to jump through the phone at her. 'Cleo! For crying out loud – where the hell are you? Here in *New York*! How about dinner tonight?'

Well, at least he was free if he could offer her dinner on the spur of the moment. 'Alain, this is business. I'm after a job.'

He had been laughing at the other end of the phone, but abruptly he sobered. 'There's something wrong?'

314

'In a way.'

'Lord Cruze? I still haven't forgiven the son-of-a-bitch –'

'No, Alain, it's not him. It's the US government.'

'Oh *them*!' He laughed again. 'So long as you're not involved in Watergate, we can help you there. So how about dinner? Oh hell – I've just remembered. You see? You've made me forget what day of the week it is. I have to go out to the country with my mother.'

'Well, it can wait till next week –'

'No, wait a minute. You sound worried. If Uncle Sam is on your back you can't spend all weekend worrying about him. Come out to the country with me. It's a house party. I'll tell Mother you're my date.'

She didn't want to face Claudine Roux, not while she was about to ask Claudine's son for a job on the *Courier*. 'No, I think it would be better if I waited till you come back to town –'

But he wouldn't hear of that. 'Cleo, I can't wait that long to see you! Good Christ –' he suddenly sounded passionate, as if the memory of two years still burned in him '– I haven't seen you since ... No, you're coming out to Souillac.' She didn't catch the name properly and she thought it was probably Indian; somehow she could not see Claudine in Indian territory. 'Where do I pick you up? There's no dressing-up – it's just casual –'

She gave in. 'Alain, your mother hasn't been casual since she was in diapers and I doubt if she was then.'

He laughed, sounding like the college boy she had met oh, so many years ago. Time and the world were slipping by: maybe he was right, she couldn't afford to waste even a weekend.

He picked her up in an Aston-Martin convertible, one with automatic transmission: a sports car designed not to exclude cripples. He didn't get out of the car when he drew up outside the delicatessen; she was watching for him and waved to him from her window when she saw him. She went down to him, dumped her case in the back seat and climbed in beside him. She leaned across and kissed him on the cheek, all at once glad to see him. He'd been an old friend, if only for one day.

'Where's your mother? You're not luring me into the country for what you hope will be an illicit weekend, are you?'

'She went out to the house at lunchtime.' He put a hand on her arm, looked at her carefully. She had dressed casually but with care, not just for him but for his mother. She had always believed that, outside of the bedroom, all women dressed for the approval of other women. 'You look great. No visible scars.'

'No invisible ones, either.' But that wasn't true: but then he was talking about Jack, not Tom.

They went through the Lincoln Tunnel into New Jersey and headed north up Route 3. It struck Cleo that this was the first time, in the seventeen months she had been here, she had been into this part of New Jersey; maybe Claudine Roux did live in Indian territory after all. As they drove along through the warm summer's day they exchanged notes on what each of them had been doing for the past two years. Alain was hurt when he learned that she had been in New York since February of last year.

'Hell, why didn't you get in touch with me before this?'

'Alain, I almost got you into a lot of trouble last time we met. I didn't know what had happened to you in the meantime. You might have married –'

He shook his head. 'There have been some near-misses, but no missus.'

'Well, I just stayed away, that's all. I've always been half-afraid that Jack might pop up again.'

'What would you do if he did?'

'I don't know.' She changed the subject: 'I'm ashamed to say I only called you because I want help. I want to stay in America.'

He listened while she explained her position. 'You want to stay permanently?'

'That's a pretty permanent term. Maybe. I don't know. But probably.' She dared not tell him about ambition. Jack

316

had understood, even if he hadn't liked it; but Tom never had and probably never would. 'I'd like a job on the *Courier*. If they can give me a job and fix me a visa . . .' Then all at once she wanted to get out of the car, go back to Manhattan, try some other way of sneaking into America. 'I'm sorry. I'm bludging on you.'

'Bludging?'

If she was going to remain in America she would have to start speaking the language. 'Back home it means – well, bumming on someone.'

He had turned off on to a side road that climbed and dipped through rolling hills. She caught glimpses of small lakes, large houses, woods that looked as if they might have been delivered gift-wrapped. She had seen enough of such areas in England, Germany and France with Jack to know she was entering rich territory. There would be no Indians hereabouts, only Claudine Roux, who might be more warlike than Geronimo, especially when she found out what message had been brought by the Aston-Martin stagecoach.

'My dear Cleo –' He had never called her that before and it sounded a little affected. She hoped he was not going to grow pompous as he grew older. 'I don't have any official pull at the *Courier*, any clout. I've been promoted since I saw you last, but I'm still only the assistant features editor. But I'm also the son of the chairwoman and publisher and, if Mother dies before me, which I'm beginning to doubt, I'll some day be the biggest stockholder. I very rarely get the opportunity to do anyone a favour, I mean do something that will mean something to them. So don't think you're – bludging? If you are, I couldn't be more pleased. You'll get a job on the *Courier* and you'll get your visa, I promise.'

3

Claudine was not expecting Alain to bring a guest, especially Cleo Spearfield. Her guest list was evenly divided between the sexes and now Alain had upset the balance; what was

317

worse, he had upset her. She greeted Cleo politely, then on a pretext took Alain aside.

'Alain, you know how I detest unexpected guests –'

'Mother, *please*. Just for once let's have a lopsided table. Cleo is my friend and I asked her.'

'I didn't know you knew her well enough to call her a friend.'

'She is now. You didn't ask me who I wanted as my weekend partner – whom did you get, anyway?'

'Polly Jensen, of course. You've taken her out –'

'Twice, that's all.'

'How many times have you taken Miss Spearfield out?'

'Once, in London a couple of years ago.'

'Was that when she broke up with Lord Cruze and disappeared from London?'

He looked at her sharply. 'You don't miss much, do you? You're a gossip-monger, Mother.'

'No, I take in gossip, I never dispense it. *That's* a gossip-monger. What I've just said about Miss Spearfield is fact, not gossip. Was that when you took her out? Did you cause the break-up between her and Lord Cruze?'

He laughed nervously; fortunately it came out as a scoff. 'I think you have far too much faith in the Brisson charm. I'm not Uncle Roger.'

'Thank God for that,' said Claudine and went back to Cleo.

They studied each other behind the cane-brake of their smiles, each lying in ambush for the other. They had not met in several years, but neither could see much change in the other. Claudine, Cleo noted, was remarkable: some women age suddenly when they move into their sixties, but Claudine seemed to have put a stop to the years. Claudine, on the other hand, noted that Cleo was no longer a girl but a woman and therefore more formidable.

'Miss Spearfield –'

'Mrs Roux, I'd prefer it if you called me Cleo.'

'Of course. Did you come by barge?'

I should have stayed in Manhattan, I should never have called

318

Alain. 'Only across the Hudson River. Or Nile West, as I like to think of it.'

Claudine smiled, thinking that perhaps the weekend would not be so bad after all. 'Do you breed asps as a hobby?'

Float the barge, Alexas, we return to the Second Avenue deli palace this night.

Then Claudine relented, took Cleo's arm. 'Welcome to Souillac. I think you and I, if no one else, may have a splendid weekend.'

None of the other guests had yet arrived. When Claudine went away to give instructions to the servants, Cleo walked out to stand on the large terrace that fronted the huge house. The sky was still bright and the countryside sloped away below the house in a soft pattern of light and dark green, more restful on the eyes than any darkened room on Second Avenue. She suddenly realized that the angles, the glittering planes and the harsh light of Manhattan had been battering at her for too long. She took off her dark glasses and let the green wash over her.

'What's the matter?' Alain had come out to stand beside her.

'I just remembered a couple of lines of poetry I once used in my column. A Welsh poet named Davies. *I stare at dewdrops till they close their eyes/ I stare at grass till all the world is green.* I hadn't realized how tired I am, even my eyes.'

'You don't want to sleep all weekend?'

'And miss all this?' She gestured at the house and the acres in which it stood. It was as big as St Aidan House, but she doubted that it had been built by king-makers.

'Great-grandfather Brisson built it,' said Alain. 'We're only about fifteen or twenty miles across the State line from Tuxedo Park.'

'Tuxedo Park?'

'It's a social resort, or was.' He wondered how much she knew about the class structure in America. He had always known the upper levels, but had only come to know the many gradations when he had gone to work on the *Courier*. But now he was talking about one of the top levels: 'It was built by

319

Pierre Lorillard – the Fifth, I think. He was one of the tobacco Lorillards. The first Lorillard, Pierre One, was the first man ever to be called a millionaire. Incidentally, we never use that word around the family. Mother thinks it's vulgar.'

'Oh, so do I.' He had sounded for a moment as if he, too, thought it was vulgar.

'No mickey-taking. Anyhow, Pierre Five built Tuxedo Park over there in New York State as a resort for the Four Hundred. You've heard of the Four Hundred?'

'Who hasn't?' Ninety-five per cent of the world's population, perhaps: but now was not the time to nit-pick.

'You could only join the Tuxedo Park Club by invitation. Great-grandfather declined his invitation – he was a bigger snob than Mother. He felt that any society that allowed a figure as high as four hundred to be classed as its élite had no sense of values. So he built Souillac, which is named after the region where the family originally came from in France. That was back in 1895 and he never invited more than twenty or thirty of the Four Hundred here. The standards have gone down since then, of course.'

'Of course. Or why should I be here?'

He smiled and took her hand. 'Actually, I feel you've raised the standards about ten notches.'

After she had showered and changed Cleo quietly, almost surreptitiously, inspected the mansion. It was too large and forbidding to have any charm. The architect, brought over from France, had been bemused by his assignment. Trying to marry both sides of the Atlantic, he had only succeeded in putting a scaled-down version of Versailles to bed with one of the more formidable New York armouries. Cleo gave up counting the rooms when she reached thirty; to anyone brought up in a four-bedroomed house, anything larger is not a home. She sidled along the panelled corridors, climbed the wide staircases, opened doors on rooms that had more taste and better proportions than the exterior of the house suggested. She was still unconcerned with possessions of her own, but, despite the experience of her years in England, she

320

still had some awe of what the rich possessed. As the real estate agents say, you can move people out of the suburbs but you can't take the suburbs out of the people.

She opened one wide heavy door and found herself in a billiards room. She supposed Americans would call it a pool room, though that suggested shady characters looking for suckers to be conned into a game where they'd lose their shirts. No shirts would be lost in this room. She could imagine the side bets, maybe a hundred dollars or even a thousand; but the real bets would have been placed on things far beyond this room, on mergers and takeovers and the floating of new ventures. The green baize table would be a substitute board table. She could see Alain's father or grandfather, cue in hand, as chairman of the board. She remembered the games she had played with her father in the makeshift billiards room on the back verandah in Coogee. There had been no side bets there, only a warm friendly rivalry as she and her brothers tried to beat the self-acknowledged family champion.

She ran her hand over the cues in the rack, then looked around for some balls but could see none. Perhaps over the weekend she might challenge Alain to a game. All at once she felt a nostalgia for what the family had once had on the back verandah in Coogee. She went out, closing the door on the feeling as well as on the room.

She finished her inspection of the great house. It had brought home to her the real wealth of the Brissons. They were like all the old rich: they would never show their bank balances, not even under pain of death, but erected their houses like billboards of their position. Immodesty has to break out even amongst the well-bred.

Friday night had to be swum through; Cleo knew now that she had fallen into a deeper pool than she had anticipated. Alain would not be the only one to have a say in whether she got a job on the *Courier* and, more importantly, sponsored her for a visa. The final say would be Claudine's.

Ten of the weekend guests had arrived by seven o'clock. With Alain and his mother and herself, Cleo could see thirteen sitting down to dinner: the weekend began to look worse and worse. She always told everyone she was not superstitious, but the Celt in her knew better.

The guests were a mixed lot, but not too mixed; they all looked as if they came from the same bank. This was not the assortment she had seen at Jack Cruze's weekends or his dinner parties, when ambassadors and Cabinet ministers and trade union officials and film and theatre stars had, if not rubbed shoulders, then rubbed each other up the wrong way. That was not likely to happen with this lot, she thought. There were no outsiders here, except herself, no social climbers: she might be an outsider, but she was not one of *that* sort. The guests, she decided, fitted together like cogs, well oiled by money and the certainty of their own position.

'This is Polly Jensen,' said Claudine and brought forward a slim blonde like a couturière introducing a new creation; Cleo had the feeling it was all so stage-managed that she would not have been surprised if Polly Jensen had pirouetted to show herself off. 'An *old* friend of Alain's. They went to nursery school together. This is Cleo Spearfield, a new friend. From Australia.' She made it sound like Darkest Africa before the Empire builders had switched on the lights. 'You must play tennis together tomorrow.'

'You play tennis, of course?' said Polly Jensen as Claudine left them to tear each other down. 'Australians are such good tennis players. We had John Newcombe staying with us for a weekend early this summer. He worked on my backhand.'

Bully for Newcombe. He'd have to give up his own career if he wanted to work on mine. 'I'm afraid surfing is my sport.' There was no surf within miles, thank God. 'But I'll enjoy watching you and your backhand.'

A tall distinguished-looking man interrupted them before carnage could begin. 'I'm Polly's father, Stephen. Alain's been telling me about you, Miss Spearfield. I remember reading your column when I was in London. Are you going to join the *Courier*? Between you and me, it could do with a little livening up. I say that as a stockholder.'

The name Jensen clicked. Cleo remembered that this man was one of the top bankers in the United States, one of the movers and shakers whom Washington listened to. She looked at him with interest, since he was looking at her in the same way, and wondered if he could move and shake to get her an extended visa; that would relieve her of any obligation to Claudine Roux, if the latter decided to help at all. Then she saw the deeper look in Mr Jensen's eye and decided against asking even the smallest favour of him. As Gus Green would have said, that was the wrong route, one she had taken before. Stephen Jensen would be almost exactly the same age as Jack Cruze.

'I'm still looking around, Mr Jensen. I haven't decided yet what I'll do.'

'If I can help, please do call me. I think you should fit very well into the public relations field.'

'And into a bikini,' said Polly Jensen and walked away.

Her father looked after her with benign irritation. 'My daughter thinks I should never compliment a woman younger than myself. Have you anything against older men, Miss Spearfield?'

Only their age and their possessiveness and their jealousy . . . 'I get on very well with my father, Mr Jensen.'

'*Touché*,' said Stephen Jensen, who knew a rapier when it nicked him. He flicked his grey moustache with one finger, like a gesture of appreciation. 'I've been told by my colleagues who have been Down Under that Australians know how to take care of themselves.'

'It's the aboriginal blood in us,' said Cleo and saw that Jensen was not sure whether she was joking or not. He looked at her almost-black hair before he hesitatingly smiled.

Just before dinner the last two guests arrived, saving the embarrassment of thirteen at table. Louise Brisson came in on the run and Roger marched in behind her. Oh God, Cleo thought, now the weekend really has gone down the drain!

Roger, casting a military eye over the terrain, saw Cleo at once. His face was blank for a moment and he glanced at Claudine, as if wondering what sort of joke was being played on him. Then, a soldier who believed in attack, he advanced on Cleo, all teeth blazing.

323

'Miss Spearfield, what a delightful surprise! Are you over from London on business?'

'I left London almost two years ago, General. I'm thinking of settling in America.'

It might have been Brezhnev telling him he had the same intention.

'Are you home on leave, General?'

'No, I've finished my tour of duty in Europe. I'm glad to see you're fully recovered from your ordeal.'

The ordeal with Jack was the one from which she wasn't fully recovered; but he wasn't referring to that. 'It seems almost like ancient history now.'

'Yes, I suppose so much happens in today's world that history becomes ancient much quicker.' He took a gamble: 'It seems only a year ago that we were so concerned with Vietnam. Now it's Watergate and President Nixon and his tapes.'

'I wouldn't comment on that, General. America's dirty linen is its own business.'

'I agree. But the rest of the world is hanging over the back fence in malicious delight . . . Oh, you haven't met my wife, have you? Louise, this is Miss Spearfield. You know, the Luneburg business –'

He said it as if it was something he had just taken out of a military file. Louise nodded briskly and Cleo wondered if all senior officers' wives had their husbands' careers neatly docketed. But Louise's smile was genuine and Cleo at once liked her.

'I'm in your debt, Miss Spearfield. Roger and I owe you a great deal. You and that other reporter, what's-his-name, should never have been put in such a situation. But if they hadn't taken you and what's-his-name, they might have persisted with trying to kill Roger.'

'Well, we're all safe in America now.' Cleo hadn't meant to sound sarcastic; she saw Roger's face tighten. 'All's well that ends well, as they say.'

'Shakespeare,' said Louise.

That's right, what's-his-name. Then Cleo realized she should not be so critical of Louise Brisson. The woman was on edge, was so highly strung that at any moment something in her might snap. Had there been a husband-and-wife argument on the way here to Souillac?

But Louise had learned the lessons of military discipline, she would not break down in public. She smiled again, but now Cleo could see that it was forced. 'I must have a quick shower. Claudine hates to have dinner kept waiting. We'll talk later, Miss Spearfield.'

The two of them left her and Alain limped across to her. 'I'd forgotten you'd met Uncle Roger. He hasn't changed. I noticed he made a bee-line for the best-looking woman in the room as soon as he came in.'

'I think he's too much of a gentleman to flirt in front of your aunt.'

'He used to be. The gossip now is that he's not as discreet as he used to be. These older guys –' Then he thumped his stick on the floor. 'Sorry. That wasn't very discreet, was it?'

She put her hand on his arm; after all, he looked like being the only friend she might have all weekend. 'Stick by me and I'll forget you said that.'

'I've spoken to Mother about you coming to work for the paper.'

'What did she say?'

'That it would be a decision for the editor – that's Jake Lintas. We don't have the sort of set-up they have at *The Times*, where there seem to be editors for everything – they practise federalism over there. Jake Lintas is editor and what he says goes.'

'Could he get me the necessary visa?'

'He might have to come back to Mother for that. Jake ran a series last year criticizing the Immigration Service for not doing its job down on the Mexican border. Jake's an isolationist racist, he'd close the doors to all immigrants, especially anyone who isn't a WASP.'

'Well, I'm white,' said Cleo ruefully. 'So you may have to ask your mother to help me?'

He laughed. 'Don't look so glum. They don't call her The Empress for nothing.'

Maybe not, but that didn't mean she would go out of her way to help an Australian serf.

Despite feeling that she was very much the outsider, Cleo enjoyed dinner. For one thing, the food was excellent. It was neither the bland tasteless American food that was served in most restaurants nor was it the good sensible food that Mrs Cromwell had foisted on the Cruze dinner parties; there was a French flair to it and the wines were French. The conversation was as interesting as the food, though purely American: Watergate and the White House Praetorian Guard were the subjects. Both items were now history and the real subject was how long Richard Nixon would continue to hold on to the Presidency; the House Judiciary Committee had just passed its first article of impeachment. Cleo had very early caught on that she was amongst dyed-in-the-sable Republicans, Old Guard conservatives who had little if any time for the upstart President from California and his home state henchmen. There was no sympathy at all for Nixon, only well-bred fury that the Presidency itself had been tainted.

'It's worse than the Harding days,' said a lawyer named Halstead, a tall square-faced man who reminded Cleo of pictures of George Washington. He had a deep sonorous voice and sounded as if he were relaying an opinion from the Supreme Court. 'Even Truman –' he got the name out as if it made his tongue bleed to pronounce it '– even he wasn't as bad as this.'

'It shows the dangers of too much ambition,' said a man named Kirkland. He was short and spry and reminded Cleo of the grooms she had seen at horse shows in England; but if he spent his time around horses it was certainly not curry-combing them or sweeping up their manure. He had the air of a man who would never need ambition, who had been born to a position that totally satisfied him. 'As Shakespeare said, By that sin fell the angels. And Nixon has never been an angel.'

'Do you have political corruption in Australia, Miss

Spearfield?' The woman across from Cleo had the look of a lesser monarch, the sort one found on the edges of group photographs of British royal weddings. In her own home she might be queen, but here she played second viola to Claudine. Cleo knew she had a husband somewhere along the table, but she was one of those women who can look unrelated to their husbands even in a bridge four. 'Or are you like the British?'

Everyone craned forward to look at Cleo. This is how Bennilong must have felt, she thought, the first aborigine taken to England in 1792. But what could she tell them about tribal customs in Canberra? 'We have it at State level, but not at Federal level. The letters I get from my father –'

'Her father is a Senator,' Claudine interposed as if trying to give Cleo some semblance of respectability.

'– one would think that Canberra is all angels and none of them will ever fall. But then Dad is a member of the Labour government.'

'Are you a socialist?' said Alain, grinning widely; but everyone at the table held their breath.

'Only on May Day. We run up the Red Flag on the front lawn.'

Everyone relaxed; she was only joking, of course. Cleo looked towards the bottom of the table and saw Roger smiling quietly at her. He winked and she almost bit her dessert spoon in surprise. Then she became aware of Louise watching her; she hazarded a tentative smile across the table, like a peace offering. Louise remained hard-faced for a moment, then her features relaxed and she smiled. I pity her, Cleo thought. Louise Brisson would never hate anyone, not her husband nor his women. She would always resort to hope and the blind eye, the marriage counsellors of the desperate.

After dinner, in a drawing-room that made the one in the penthouse flat in St James's Place look like an ante-room, Cleo did her best to stay away from Roger Brisson. The room was so big that she could take evasive action and she kept on the move. At last Alain caught up with her.

'Stand still a while,' he said, leaning on his stick. 'I can't chase women the way I used to.'

327

'I'm trying to stay ahead of your uncle. He has a look in his eye.'

'You're okay now. He's looking at Polly. He really is getting beyond a joke. I don't know how Aunt Louise puts up with him.'

'That's because you're not a woman in love.'

'I'm a man in love.' He smiled as he said it, but he was deadly serious.

'Don't rush me, Alain. It could be a long weekend.'

'Okay.' He was prepared to take his time; or anyway a day or two. He looked over his shoulder as the other guests began to drift out of the room. 'Well, we better join them.'

'Where are we going?'

'To the billiards room. Mother is an expert pool player.'

'You're pulling my leg.'

'I wish I were stroking it,' he said, showing that his college days were not so far in the past. 'No, Mother really is very good at pool. She thinks that it and croquet are the only two ball games a woman of her age can play with dignity.'

'You can be pretty undignified bending over a billiard-table for a shot down the side cushion.'

He glanced at her in surprise. 'You sound as if you know something about it.'

'I used to play it with my father when I was a schoolgirl. My mother had a pianola, a player-piano, and Dad his billiard-table. It was his only relaxation, that and surfing.'

'Are you any good?'

'I was the Brigidine Convent champion three years running.' No other girls at school played billiards.

Alain grinned. 'Don't say anything. We'll do some hustling. I'll back you to beat Mother.'

'No!' She had no idea how good Claudine might be; and she had not played a game herself in ten years. The billiard-table back home had been sold, along with the pianola, when her mother had died. If she were lucky enough to beat Claudine, she could imagine Claudine's revenge. A call would be made to Washington and Cleo Spearfield, pool hustler, would be deported as an undesirable.

But Alain had already limped ahead into the big billiards room. 'Mother, I have a contender for the championship. I have a hundred dollars that says my protégée, the Down Under Ladies Champ-een, can give you a licking at pool.' He turned back to Cleo, who stood in the doorway wishing she were in Manhattan or, better still, Coogee. 'I have to tell you, Cleo, that Mother was offered the Paul Newman part in *The Hustler*, but refused because it would have ruined her amateur status. However, like all good amateurs, she does take under the table payments and bets on the side.'

'Are you an amateur, Cleo?' said Claudine, chalking the end of a cue as if she were sharpening a pikestaff.

'In everything,' said Cleo, deciding she was on her way out and she might as well go out with a swagger.

'I'll bet,' said Polly Jensen and offered her a cue held up like a one-fingered salute.

Dear God, Cleo prayed, do you help pool hustlers? Let me be a champ-een just for tonight, another Walter or Horace Lindrum or that American, Willie what's-his-name. Hoppe. She took the cue and began to chalk it. She looked across at Claudine and somehow managed a smile.

'I haven't played in years. I had to sell my table to buy my barge.'

The others missed the joke, but Claudine didn't. Cleo realized all at once that Claudine enjoyed opponents more than she did her friends; if things did not get nasty, she might even be invited back to Souillac. She decided that she would play as well as she possibly could, that Claudine would dismiss her as not worth bothering about if she gave Claudine a walk-over victory.

'You never played with Lord Cruze?' It was the first time Claudine had mentioned him. 'But no, I don't think Jack would have the patience for this. Shall we play snooker or pool? Perhaps we better play snooker, you'll feel more at home with that.'

The other guests had come out of the drawing-room looking like the embers of a dinner party that had died; they

329

would rather go to bed than indulge their hostess by playing her favourite game. But now they glowed again and some of the men even made small side bets amongst themselves; the women bet on Claudine, if only to show Cleo that, in more ways than one, she was a long-shot. Roger set up the fifteen coloured balls and smiled down the table at Cleo.

'I have ten dollars on you, Cleo.'

Cleo didn't look at Louise or Claudine, but added more chalk to her cue. She had worn the wrong dress for leaning over a billiard-table; it was low-cut and she was wearing no brassière. Even as she bent over to take the first shot and split the pyramid of balls she could see that Roger, facing her, was smiling as if he had already got back fifty cents of his ten dollars.

Claudine had a moderate-sized bust, but it was properly supported and she was wearing a dress with a turtle-neck, as if she had dressed for billiards and not dinner. She played with brisk, decorous skill, an empress hustler, despatching the balls as if she were *ordering* them to fall into the pockets. Cleo, troubled by her extruding bosom, still trying to narrow her concentration on to the table and the balls, played a mixture of poor and brilliant shots. The game, however, was close and at last came down to the point where Cleo was left with the pink and the black to be sunk if she was to win. It was a difficult shot, the pink almost hidden behind the black. If she did not hit it properly, there was a fifty-fifty chance that neither of the balls would go into a pocket and Claudine would be left with a choice of shot to win.

Cleo looked at the angle, then across at Claudine on the other side of the table. The older woman was watching her unsmilingly: I'm being tested in some way, Cleo thought. She knew now that Claudine was a far better player than she would ever be; it was only luck that had enabled her to make such a close game of it. Claudine was waiting for her to play safe.

She bent over the table, ignoring her exposed bosom; her breasts could fall out on the table so long as they didn't get in the way of her cue. She lined up the shot, focused on the cue ball, then hit it cleanly and crisply. It shot across the green baize, caromed off the side cushion, feathered the black ball and knocked the pink smartly into an end pocket.

'Great shot!'

Everyone round the table clapped, but Cleo looked neither at them nor at Claudine. She moved round, saw that the cue ball and the black were lined up perfectly for a simple hit into a side pocket. She made the shot with all the authority of the Lindrums or Willie Hoppe polishing off a game. She straightened up, feeling her breasts settling comfortably back into her dress like two spectators who had been on tenterhooks, and looked at Claudine.

'Well played,' said Claudine. 'You're not afraid to take risks.'

4

Cleo slept well, convinced now that she had passed her test with Claudine. Someone tapped on her door during the night and whispered her name; but she came only half-awake, didn't respond and went back to sleep immediately. She had locked her door, against whom she was not sure (Alain? Roger? Stephen Jensen, who admired younger women?), and she knew it was a strong, thick door, making her safe against seducers and rapists. She woke refreshed and lay for a while listening to the birds in the tree outside her window. I'd like a house in the country some day, she thought, somewhere quiet and peaceful to retreat to. Another ambition: but it reminded her too much of Jack and St Aidan's House and she put it out of her mind.

She showered, dressed in slacks and shirt and went downstairs to breakfast, though Claudine had told everyone they could have breakfast served in their rooms if they wished. She wished at once that she had accepted the suggestion.

Roger Brisson was sitting alone at the large round table in the sun-drenched room where two servants, both black, one a young girl, the other a grey-haired man, were serving

331

breakfast. Roger stood up and pulled out a chair right beside him.

'I think breakfast conversation should be quiet and intimate. I hate hearty breakfast tables. I always avoided breakfast in the mess for that reason. You look splendid this morning, a real champion.'

'I'm sure your sister looks just as good, if not better. She let me win last night.'

'You still had to risk that last shot. It's always the last shot or two that counts.'

'What about in a duel? I should think it would be the first shot that would count there.'

'If it's a good first shot, it should also be the last. I can recommend the home-made sausages. Cyrus's wife makes them herself. Cyrus has been with the family since – how long?'

'Nineteen twenty-nine I come here, sir. As a gardener's boy.'

'Ellie is his granddaughter.' The girl smiled shyly at Cleo. Then she and her grandfather went out of the room and Roger said, 'Old family retainers. There aren't many of them left.'

'Claudine must be a good mistress or they wouldn't stay.'

He buttered her with a smile. 'You'll find out. I gather you're going to work for the *Courier*.'

'Nothing is decided yet. I still have to be okayed by Mr Lintas, the editor.'

'It's been decided without Mr Lintas. I talked to Claudine last night.'

Do I adopt the blunt approach or do I wait patiently until he tells me? She chose the first approach, remembering how blunt he had been with his invitation for her to go to bed with him in Saigon.

'General –'

'Roger. I'm out of uniform or hadn't you noticed?'

She had noticed; but his mufti dress was as elegant as his uniform. Even casually dressed, he looked as uncreased as a *New Yorker* ad. 'Roger – why are you interesting yourself so

332

much in me? And don't give me any flirtatious bull. I hate that worse than even hearty breakfast conversation.'

Louise had asked him the same question in bed last night. He had not given an answer then and he was not going to give one now, at least not a direct one. When he had entered the house last night and seen Cleo, he had realized at once that she was far too close to home for comfort; indeed she was *in* the home, which gave him a great deal of discomfort. He still felt a raw guilt about what had happened at An Bai six years ago and, since his own memory of it was so vivid, he assumed Cleo's was just as indelible. He knew he would never have to go back to Vietnam; though nobody admitted it, he knew the war there was lost. He could not turn his back on Cleo; so he had adopted the only other approach he knew, to court her. An enemy in sight is less dangerous than one that can't be seen: that had been a major lesson in Vietnam. Clausewitz may not have written such a dictum, but Clausewitz had never fought in the jungle and had fought few, if any, women.

'Don't get me wrong. I have no influence with my sister when it comes to running the paper. *Her* paper. But if you are going to be – in the family, as it were –'

'I'm just a friend of Alain's, I'm not in the family.'

'Well, let's say you're more in the family than Mr Lintas. He's never been invited to Souillac. So if you are going to be coming here, isn't it better I greet you as a friend of the family than as a newspaperwoman?'

'That's what I'll be when I next come here. That is, if I'm invited after I go to work for the *Courier*.'

'I'm sure Alain will see that you are. He's very smitten with you.'

Smitten: it was a word she thought had gone out with the Victorian novels. Roger was going too far in his effort to be on his best behaviour. 'We're just friends.'

'So let's you and I be friends, too.' He put no double meaning behind the words and, reluctantly, she accepted them at their face value. But she felt uneasy and knew she would have to watch him, not be smitten by him.

Later, when the morning grew hot, she changed into a bikini and went out to the large pool at the side of the house. Some of the other guests were already there, the women soaking up the sun, the men trying to find some of the lost grace of their youth in the water. She took off the towelling robe she had found in her room and, even behind their dark glasses, saw the women's eyes swivel towards her. She always had mixed feelings about her figure; she liked men to admire it, but she did not like women to be envious of it or resent it. She pulled on her bathing cap, walked quickly to the side of the pool and dived in.

She swam two lengths of the pool, with the easy graceful stroke that had always come naturally to her, even as a child. When she paused, holding on to the tiled edge of the pool, Alain surfaced beside her.

'Did you sleep well? I came along during the night to see how you were, but got no answer.'

'I heard your knock.' She was glad it had been he and not one of the other men. 'What did you have in mind if I hadn't been sleeping well? Never mind, don't answer.'

Then Stephen Jensen swam up beside them. Immersion in water likens older men to the ape: it does not improve their looks. Last night Jensen's grey hair had looked sleek and thick; now it hung down in long strands about his ears and his scalp on top was clearly visible. When he lifted an arm out of the water to grasp the side of the pool Cleo could see the loose skin on his under arm. His moustache hung down from his upper lip like a sprig of wet Spanish moss and his eyes were red from the chlorine in the water. There is no one with less romantic potential than a water-soaked roué.

'You will have to watch her, Alain. Any girl who swims like Cleo will be welcome at any pool from Newport to Palm Beach.'

'In future,' said Alain, 'I'm only going to invite her out here in the winter.'

They were discussing her like judges at some beauty contest. She was about to say something sharp, when a shadow loomed over them and Claudine said, 'Cleo, may we have a

334

few words together? No, you stay there, Alain. I want to talk to Cleo alone.'

Cleo pulled herself out of the water, feeling Alain pat her hip comfortingly as she did so. She was glad he had not patted her bottom, not in front of his mother. She picked up her towel, quickly wiped the water from herself, then went to don the robe.

'Leave it off if you want to sunbathe. I don't mind.' Claudine wore a long-sleeved shirt, slacks and a large straw hat. She led the way to a table and chairs under a sun-umbrella and gestured to Cleo to lie down on a lounge in the sun. 'I soaked up the sun when I was young, but at thirty-five I decided I did not want to look like an over-baked croissant in my old age. When I am old,' she said, stopping any suggestion that she might already be that, 'I hope I shan't look much worse than I do now.'

'You look beautiful now,' said Cleo sincerely.

'I know, but thank you for the compliment. You look beautiful, too. You have a certain animal beauty, an intelligent animal. Well, that's enough mutual admiration. So you want to come and work for my newspaper?'

'Yes. I gather Alain has explained my visa situation.' Cleo smeared herself with lotion, put on her dark glasses. 'I'll be frank, Mrs Roux. I want to do as well in America as I did in England.'

'You sound as ambitious as Richard Nixon must have been.'

'Possibly. But I don't want to find myself owing debts to anyone. In the end that was why I left Lord Cruze.' That wasn't strictly true, but it seemed to be the best way of getting Jack into the conversation and out of it quickly. Claudine was sure to raise his name sooner or later.

'I wondered what had happened there.' Claudine seemed satisfied with the explanation. 'What is your relationship with Alain?'

Cleo smiled. 'You mean what are my intentions? Honourable.'

Claudine smiled in return, but behind her dark glasses her

eyes were serious. 'He is my only child, all I have. He has had enough disappointment in life, with that leg of his. Don't encourage him if you then intend disappointing him.'

Cleo wondered if all American mothers were as protective of their sons as soon as they brought home a girl. Or had Alain told his mother more than he had told her? 'I came to America for a career, not to look for a lover or a husband.' That, too, wasn't strictly true. She had come looking for Tom, though she had not admitted it to herself till after she had arrived in New York. 'I don't think Alain has any ideas about marrying me.'

'I should not try to stop him if he did, he's old enough to make his own mistakes. I just don't think it would work.'

'Why not?' Even a girl with no ambition to marry doesn't like to be dismissed offhand.

'Cleo, you want to go further than the altar and mother-hood. I think you and I are very much alike. If I hadn't been born to what I am, I'd have found some other way of getting to the top. I don't think I'd have settled for marriage as the way.' She stood up. 'I'll see that you get a visa. We'll ask for one for two years. Will that be long enough?'

'To sink or swim? Yes, I think so. Thank you, Mrs Roux.'

Cleo stayed in the sun for another hour. From the nearby tennis court she could hear shouts and laughter; Polly Jensen was there working on her backhand. Alain had got out of the pool and wandered across to watch the tennis; then he looked back and saw that his mother had left Cleo. He limped across and sat down in a chair beside Cleo. She looked once at his crippled leg, the first time she had seen it exposed, then she ignored it and looked at the rest of him. She could feel the sun insinuating itself into her, warming the juices, as Jack used to say. Claudine had called her a beautiful animal and she let the image float through her lazy mind; with a job and visa assured, the tension had gone out of her. She had had no sex in too long; she had relieved her hunger with masturbation, but she had never found that a sufficient substitute for a man; she had never been her own best friend in bed. She looked at Alain from behind her dark glasses and saw that, apart from his leg, he too was a beautiful animal. He had muscular shoulders and arms, a slim waist and a promising bulge in his swim trunks. Drugged by the sun, she found her intentions towards him were strictly dishonourable.

'What did you tell your mother about you and me?'

'Nothing. Well, yes – I told her I liked you as much as any girl I've met. Is she holding that against you?'

'No, I'm getting on much better with her than I'd expected. But don't let's get serious, Alain. I have a long way to go before I find out if I've done the right thing coming to America.' She was sure she had done the right thing, but to say so might give him more encouragement than she wanted.

'We'll play it day by day,' he said. 'And maybe the occasional night by night.'

He still had his college boy repartee. He would be very different from Jack.

That evening after dinner there was a movie instead of billiards. No silent film with Rudolph Valentino fluttering his eyelids at Agnes Ayres; Cleo knew she would have had to walk out on such a reminder of other, best forgotten evenings. Instead they all sat and watched Yves Montand and Romy Schneider in a French film with sub-titles. Claudine and Alain and the Brissons and some of the other guests laughed at jokes in the dialogue that hadn't been translated, and once again Cleo lamented her lack of languages. But she was pleased to see that Polly Jensen, who had given her cool stares and nary a word all day, had put on glasses to read the subtitles. There is a certain joy in malice that makes it one of the more pleasurable sins.

The movie was sentimental, but the French always lace their sentiment with astringency, which makes foreigners think the French are hard-headed and above the saccharine. Alain reached for Cleo's hand in the dark and she let him hold it, silently promising him more later. The sun had gone down, mostly to her loins.

He came to her room that night after everyone had gone to bed. Her room was at the end of a corridor, with no one occupying the room next to her. It occurred to her then that

337

Alain had, somehow, engineered her location; but when he came, she was glad of the near-isolation. She remembered something Tom had said: there's no humpin' without bumpin'. Then she put Tom out of her mind and, only stopping short of screaming aloud when her climax came, enjoyed the love-making without restraint. Alain was a practised lover, but if he was proud of his talent he had the modesty not to mention it. He made love to her twice, she made love to him once: which wasn't a bad night's pleasure, she thought, for a girl out of practice. He went back to his own room, limping as much from exhaustion as from his leg, and she went to sleep. Her last thought, lost and forgotten as soon as she fell asleep, was that she had been given another visa to a country of one, Alain.

THIRTEEN

Over the past year or more things had not gone as well as Tom Border had expected. Hollywood had turned out to be less than he and Simone had hoped for. Like so many novelists he had thought writing for the screen would be easy. He had filled pages of yellow paper with what he thought was witty, well-turned dialogue, only to have the producer and the director blue-pencil it as no newsroom copy editor had ever worked on his stuff.

'Half of today's movie audiences are deaf from listening to rock music, so they never hear any of the dialogue.' The producer had been forty years in the movie business, which he insisted was a business and none of your film-is-an-art crap. 'Ninety-five per cent of the other half wouldn't know Oscar Wilde from Oscar Fishbein, who's my bookie. So wit is wasted on 'em.'

'That leaves two and a half per cent. What about them?'

'They go to Woody Allen pictures. We're not making this movie for them. I dunno what you had in mind when you wrote your book, Tom, but it's basically a thriller and that's what we bought. You can't thrill people outa their pants with witty dialogue. Try again, will you, Tom?'

Tom knew he was probably being given more chances than most writers. He had learned that novelists still had a certain standing with most producers, as if writing novels was more difficult than writing films, though he was finding the opposite true. He had been given his own bungalow, small though it was, and not a room in the writers' building. The studio had a vast parking lot where everyone below a certain executive level had to park and pay for the privilege; but Tom had his own parking space, free, outside his bungalow. He was pampered, but it didn't help his writing the screenplay.

At the end of six weeks the producer, with best wishes for the future, patted him on the back and let him go; as Tom moved out of his bungalow, the associate producer was already moving in. When Tom went out to get into his rented car, a studio sign-writer was painting out his name and had a stencil ready to substitute the new occupant's name.

'You don't waste any time,' said Tom, not feeling in the least witty today.

'That's life, buddy.' The man was old enough to have grown up with *buddy* and, Tom imagined, even *twenty-three skidoo*. His coveralls creaked with years of paint. 'You come, you go. The only writers permanent around here are us guys that paint the names.' He wiped his brush over the last *r* of Border. That's all I am now, thought Tom, a blank space. 'So long, buddy. Try TV. They don't put your name on a sign if you're a TV writer, they put a meter there.'

The wit of studio sign-writers: did he go to see Woody Allen movies? 'Watch out. I'd hate to run over your brush.'

'Up yours, buddy,' said the man.

Tom went home to the apartment he and Simone had rented on Wilshire Boulevard in Westwood. It had once belonged to Rita Hayworth and Simone said she could still feel the essence of glamour in the place. But not today. She threw her arms round Tom and let fly a stream of French abuse about Hollywood producers that would have earned her *Cahiers du Cinema*'s critic-of-the-year award. Tom was glad of her comfort and even the mere fact that she was *there*; he would have hated to come back to an empty apartment, even one full of the essence of Rita Hayworth. He might still be a drifter, but he had become less of a loner. Simone's attention and devotion to him had spoiled him, had brought home to him the disadvantages of being self-reliant, especially in cooking a meal, doing one's laundry and shopping for

340

groceries. He loved her, but still felt guilty, since he sometimes felt he loved her only for her services. He would never love her as he had loved Cleo.

Simone gave up abusing Hollywood producers, which is as self-defeating as trying to flatter certain movie stars, and became practical. '*Chéri*, we have a six months' lease on the apartment. It will cost us money to break it.'

'Thrifty. How did French girls ever get a reputation for being sexy?'

'We're thrifty in bed, too. Haven't you ever noticed how long I make our love-making last? No, chéri, I'm being serious. We have money, lots of it, but I am not going to see it wasted. We shall stay on here till the lease is up and you will write.'

'What?'

'Something. Another book, magazine articles. Something. You will go to work tomorrow morning. I'm not going to let you sit around and be sorry for yourself.'

'I've never felt sorry for myself.' But he had; immediately after he had left Cleo in the cafe in Rockefeller Center. But that was all behind him. 'What are we going to do between now and tomorrow morning?'

'Go to bed and make thrifty love. Then tonight you can take me to dinner at Chasen's.'

'They don't have thrifty prices there.'

'It will be our last fling. Tomorrow I start being a very thrifty French housewife.'

He did not start another book; he discovered he did not have another book in him, not then. He called Gus Green, who wasted no time on sympathy over losing the script job but got him a commission for two pieces for *Playboy*. He wrote them and *Playboy* paid for them but didn't ask for any more from him. He did a couple of pieces for the *Los Angeles Times*, but he was writing mechanically and he knew it and he got no pleasure at all from it. If he was going to write for newspapers he wanted to be back in the atmosphere of a newspaper office. But he could not bring himself to ask for a job on the *Times*, not while he was supposed to be a highly

341

successful novelist. *The Guns of Chance* was still on the bestseller list. Reporters on the *Times* would not welcome another reporter whose royalty cheques made their weekly pay envelopes look like food stamps.

When the lease ran out they left for Paris, stopping over for a few days in Missouri, where Tom's parents almost smothered Simone in their delight with her. Simone asked them to come visit her and Tom when they were settled in Paris and they said they would, which surprised Tom. All his life his father had said there was no point in travelling when you could get everything in Missouri or, if you were really stuck, next door in Kansas.

But Tom and Simone did not settle down in Paris. He was suddenly restless, the old drifter again. His British publishers were bringing out the paperback edition of his novel; they asked him to come to Britain to promote it and he accepted. They mentioned that it was about to be published in Australia and New Zealand and on the spur of the moment he asked would they like him to go out there and promote it. So he and Simone went to Australia, where Tom sought some of the essence of Cleo and found none. He saw Senator Spearfield's name in a newspaper and the name Spearfield was like a stab in his breast. His publishers' Australian office overwhelmed him with hospitality, but it also worked him into exhaustion and he was glad to leave Australia for New Zealand. There the pattern was repeated and he boarded the Air New Zealand flight for Tahiti with relief.

'You were looking for something, weren't you?' said Simone. 'What?'

He shrugged. He really didn't know, unless he had been looking for the ghost of a girl who had long since fled her homeland. 'What would you think about staying in Tahiti for six months?'

'Gauguin wrote a book when he lived there. Perhaps you can, too.' She wanted him to be a writer, thinking that was what he wanted.

But Tahiti produced no book. At the end of six months they moved on, drifting. Tom said he wanted to see all the

342

places he had read about: they went to South America, to Machu Pichu, then to Rio de Janeiro. At last Simone put her foot down. Or said she wanted to, in Paris.

'I have had enough of all this, *chéri*. All we are doing is spending money. Neither of us is enjoying himself.'

He agreed. 'Okay, we'll go back to Paris and settle down. I've got an idea for a novel, I think. It's a love story.'

'You and me?' She was only half-joking: she wanted to be in a book written by him.

'Maybe. I'll see how it works out.' He was half-afraid to write it. The story was still only vague in his mind, but the wrong girl kept coming into his mind as the heroine. 'It'll be set in Paris, about a rich American and a young French girl.'

'It *is* you and me. Oh *chéri* –' She took him to bed and made thrifty love.

Two weeks later they flew to Paris. Their drifting, each of them hoped without saying anything to the other, was over.

Paris in October, Tom always thought, was the perfect marriage of time and place. Paris in the spring had its moments but autumn had always been his favourite season, no matter where he was. They rented an apartment on the Left Bank with a view of the Seine. Simone screamed *bleu merde* at the rent and beat the landlord down ten per cent, something no foreigner could ever have done. What would I do without her? Tom wondered. And had no answer.

Then he settled down to write a novel about the love-hate relationship between a young French girl and a much older rich American, told from the viewpoint of a young artist waiting, with mixed feelings, in the background.

2

Cleo had started work at the *Courier* on the day that Richard Nixon vacated the White House. It was an awkward day for a foreigner to move into an American newsroom. Somehow Cleo felt a sense of shame, as if she should have known better than to choose today to start.

'You'll be on police rounds, Miss Spearfield.'

Jake Lintas looked more like a banker than the stereotype of a newspaperman. He was stout, always impeccably dressed, wore a homburg to the office, never had a hair out of place on his sleek head; he did not wear his jacket in his office, but he never rolled up his sleeves and protected his cuffs with old-fashioned paper cuffs which he ordered by the dozen pairs from somewhere in Vermont. He tried to give the impression that news should not happen till he was ready for it, but never showed any fluster if the news did break too fast.

'I've never been a crime reporter, Mr Lintas.'

'You'll learn. If you want to write about this city, you'll get all the education you want down in the police shack. Here is our style book. You will notice that all women are referred to as Mrs or Miss. I don't allow words in this newspaper that can't be pronounced.'

'You mean Ms?'

'Exactly.' He had let her know at once that he had no time for Women's Liberation and their aberrations. She was unsure just how much time he had for her personally, but he had made no attempt to welcome her.

She presented herself to the city editor, Carl Fishburg. A once lean reporter, he had become fat and sour at his desk; he envied the men who were able to get out and about. More importantly, with his promotion he had lost his by-line, the seal that every newspaperman worked for. He was better paid and he had authority, but he was now anonymous.

'Hal Rainer will show you the ropes.' Carl Fishburg also did not sound welcoming.

Hal Rainer, thin-nosed and bald-headed, looked like a studious city-bred eagle. He was fifty years old, came from Denver, Colorado, and hated New York but could never leave it.

'It's like some girl you fall for. You know she's a whore, but because she's giving you a free lay you think she loves you.' He talked to all the women on the *Courier*, of whom there were not too many, as if they were men; a newspaper was a man's world, or should be, and he made no concessions.

344

'I came here like Lochinvar out of the West, got a job on the *Brooklyn Eagle* and I thought I had it made. I was gonna be the new Heywood Broun, the new Ring Lardner. Those names mean anything to you?'

'I've heard of them.'

'You sound doubtful. Never sound like that in front of a New York newspaperman. They are gods in our pantheon.'

'What happened to you? Did they pull you up at the pantheon door?'

'I never got within sight of it. I found out I was a facts man, not an ideas man. I had a skull full of fancy phrases, but my typewriter refused to use them. I became a police reporter and I got a life sentence. I never write a word unless I got to and I've worn out three re-write men. All I console myself with is that I know more about crime than even the Mafia. I believe you knew Tom Border?'

The question so surprised her she thought there was something behind it. 'Yes. We were kidnapped together.'

'Yeah, I know. He was a nice guy, Tom. Pity he wrote a book, he'll never write anything decent again.' Then he seemed to put Tom out of his mind. 'Well, this is the shack. A little seedy, but it's our home away from home.'

The police shack was two rooms above a bail bond store on a narrow street at the back of Police Headquarters in downtown Manhattan. Tattered and yellowed sheets torn from newspapers were stuck to the walls, New York tapestries, stories of major crimes long forgotten: criminals fade almost as fast from memory as their victims. An embittered newspaper reporter had scrawled a message for history on a wall: *TV news is for the eyes and ears of idiots.* There were other less caustic messages, some of them yellowed and torn, some of them dated: on 11/3/48 Nita wanted Hal Rainer to call her urgently.

'Did you ever call her?' Cleo asked.

'I can't remember who she was.'

The grimy windows were open to give the inmates a choice of suffocating from the pollution outside or the smoky fug inside. The half dozen other reporters in the rooms seemed

345

to have dressed down to their surroundings; Hal Rainer himself looked as if he had come from a welfare handout. American crime, Cleo decided, must be scruffy. She had had little experience of British crime and none at all of Australian.

Over the next few months she began to widen her American education, beginning at the bottom of the moral scale. She found more cynicism than she had ever known back in Britain or Australia; but she had moved in different circles there, where the cynicism had been more refined and therefore to be taken for sophisticated wisdom. She was still appalled, however, at some of the stories she had to write.

'Don't waste your sympathy,' said Hal Rainer. 'Most of the time all we are writing about is the shit of human nature.'

'You should be teaching philosophy at Yale or Harvard.'

'Two posts I've applied for over the years.'

The two of them, the sleek once-successful girl and the scruffy middle-aged man who had never made it, had reached a compatibility where they could kid each other without offence. He never made a pass at her, not even in a joking word, never complimented her on how she might look; he treated her as he might another man. Which, she realized, was his way of complimenting her.

But she knew she was on probation as far as the paper was concerned. The *Courier* had obtained a working visa for her but it was valid only for so long as she continued to work for the paper. She soon realized that Jake Lintas saw no reason why she should be working for the paper at all; but The Empress had sent down instructions and he had obeyed them. But giving Cleo a job did not mean he had to treat her with any favouritism; he had a certain autonomy and he jealously guarded it. Cleo was just one of the reporters and if she wanted to rise higher she would have to prove she had something more than the others.

'How are you making out?' said Alain.

She went out with him once a week, never on the same night, rationing him as well as herself. He wanted to spend all his free time with her; he was in love with her and she knew it, but so far he had not told her so. She went to bed with him but not on a regular weekly basis; she was trying, in not very subtle ways, to let him know that she was not to be taken for granted. He accepted the situation because, the more he came to know her, the more he came to know that she had an ambition that might override any other inclination she might have. He was not absolutely sure that that would occur, but it scared him and so he held back and settled for what she was willing to give him. He had never before been involved with a really ambitious woman.

'I'm getting impatient. Every time I try to give a lift to anything I've written, the guys on the copy desk wipe it out. You were right – the *Courier* really is a stuffy sheet.'

'That's Jake Lintas. But Mother and the board would never get rid of him. They're afraid they'd get someone who'd turn it into another *Daily News*.'

'That formula works.'

'Not for the *Courier*. Not while Mother runs the board.'

She went home with him to his apartment on the floor below his mother's penthouse. They made love under his mother's feet. There was humpin' with bumpin' and no restraint: it is an acoustical fact that the squeak of bedsprings does not travel upwards. Cleo did cry out in ecstasy but no one heard her: the inventor of double-glazed windows was not a man afraid of the cold but one who had a wife given to knock-off-siren whoops of joy. Afterwards Cleo went into the bathroom and showered, then looked at herself in the wall-length mirror.

'Perfect,' said Alain, naked, leaning against the door-jamb. When he leaned on the proper side his crippled leg was not apparent. 'Girls with a body like yours should never be allowed to dress.'

Outside, though it was only November, sleet was falling. 'Just the weather for getting around like that. My nipples would stand out like six-inch spikes.'

'What a wonderful way to be stabbed to death.' He put his hand to his bare chest.

I wish he'd grow up all the way, she thought. She looked at herself again in the mirror. She did mild exercises every morning, walked to and from the office every day, watched

347

her diet: it all paid off, there was no sign yet of any erosion. She looked at her hair, still worn short and with bangs. 'I may change my hair style.'

'No,' he said emphatically. 'It's you. Cleo Spearfield.'

'Being me isn't amounting to much. Jake Lintas still hasn't given me my by-line.'

'Changing your hair style won't get you a by-line. It'll come.' He wished it wouldn't. He would like her to fail, give up all ambition and be his wife, take up the by-line of Mrs Alain Roux.

'It had better happen soon. I think Jake is just letting me work out my visa time.'

Christmas came and went. She spent it at Souillac with Alain and his mother and Roger and Louise Brisson; which was a mistake. It suggested she was family, or almost; and Claudine, without being rude, made it clear that the family, like Fort Knox, was not easily broken into. Presents were exchanged on Christmas morning and Cleo was discreet enough to make her gifts to Alain and Claudine modest ones.

Claudine recognized the discretion and wondered whether Cleo was shrewd or was not seriously interested in Alain. She was disturbed by the gift Alain gave Cleo, an expensive gold bracelet, but she said nothing. Then she and Cleo exchanged looks above the gift when the latter opened the velvet box, and she was reassured. The girl also thought the gift was too expensive.

Alain, for his part, enthused about Cleo's gift to him, a Mark Cross wallet, as if it were a five-piece set of Vuitton luggage. Do restrain yourself, his mother told him silently, or· soon you'll be on your knees before her.

Cleo had tried to call her father before leaving Manhattan, but all the lines to Australia had been busy. With Claudine's permission she called him from Souillac on Christmas night.

'How are you, Dad?'

The belly-laugh floated across the world, sounding in her ears as sweet as bell-song. 'Sweetheart, you know better than to ask.'

Then she remembered his old advice: never ask an Aussie

how he is because he'll bloody well tell you, at great length.

'Righto, what sort of Christmas did you have?'

'We had dinner up at Perry's,' he said, his voice coming and going on the wire. 'Roast turkey, plum pudding, all the English stuff. We were in our cossies beside the pool – it was bloody hot. We should have our heads read, all this sticking to tradition.'

Cossie: she hadn't heard the word in ages. Nobody even used *bathing costume* any more; but Sylvester still put on his cossie to go for a swim. Suddenly she wanted to weep, loving him so much that she actually felt a physical pain in her chest; but she knew, too, that she wanted to weep for the child she had once been, when her mother had been alive and all the family had been together, unspoiled by ambition, careless of possessions, just happy in the traditional Christmas spirit.

'How are things down in Canberra?'

'The bloom has worn off, Cleo. We're beginning to stumble around like a lot of blind chooks –' *Chooks*: chickens. *Oh Dad, go on speaking Australian to me!* 'Gough's still in charge, but he's got a few no-hopers he should sack. We've got more trendies in Canberra than you'd find in an arcade of boutiques –' His voice died away, lost across the snows of America, the winds of the Pacific; or just lost in the bitter climate of himself? Then he came back, laughing the old belly-laugh: 'Don't worry. I'll still be here when all the trendy professors are back in their universities. Nobody will remember them, but I'll bet Sylvester Spearfield will be. What do you reckon?'

He sounded pathetic, wanting reassurance from *her*. 'I'll bet on it.'

'Hooroo, sweetheart. Take care.'

'Hooroo, Dad.' She did weep then. 'Have a happy 1975.'

That evening she heard on the news that a cyclone, the worst in Australian memory, had hit Darwin in the far north. She hoped that it was not an omen for her father and the old-timers in the Labour Party.

Alain drove her back to Manhattan late that night. In the morning when she went downstairs to the delicatessen to buy milk, the owner, Mr Kugel, brought out a dozen red roses.

349

'They came Christmas Eve, just after you left. No note, nothing. I kept them in water for you.' He was thin, looked as if he had been boned, had a blotchy complexion like sliced salami; but he was kind and friendly and believed red roses from anonymous admirers should be kept from dying. 'They must of cost a fortune, this time of year.'

'Thank you, Mr Kugel.' She took the roses, knowing that the man who had sent them could well afford them. It did not occur to her that Alain might have sent them: they smelled of Jack Cruze. 'Did you have a nice Christmas?'

'I'm Jewish, what's to celebrate?' But he smiled. He liked pretty girls, even Christian ones. 'May the roses last. They become you.'

She went upstairs, wrapped the roses in brown paper, put on her topcoat and went for a walk. She passed an old black woman, stopped and gave her the roses. The old woman looked at her first with suspicion, then with surprise, then with puzzlement. But Cleo had already left her and walked on. She wondered how Jack had discovered her address and thought that she would immediately have to look for a new apartment. Then she realized that he would know she worked for the *Courier* and it would not matter where she lived. She passed a Catholic church, paused, then went in and prayed that Jack would not follow up the signal of the red roses. She came out feeling guilty: she only talked to God when she wanted a favour of Him.

In late January she applied to *The Times*, the *News* and the *Post* for a position; but none of them wanted a foreigner, not if they had to go to the extent of guaranteeing her for a work visa. It seemed that it was to be the *Courier* or *International* and no other choice.

3

She had been working on the *Courier* a year when she began to worry that she was getting nowhere. She had a good salary and she was still earning money on the outside with articles

350

in various magazines; she kept waiting for Jake Lintas to crack down on her outside work, but so far he had made no move. On the paper itself she was being held down by men much older than herself who were hidebound by their prejudice against women; they laughed at Women's Liberation and knew that God, who was a man, would eventually convince them of their foolishness. Books by Friedan, Millett or Greer, if they were reviewed at all in the book columns, were always reviewed by men and invariably panned. The mood of the editorial staff was that one had only to look at Washington where, though men had fouled up the White House, women, quite properly, were not trusted with running the country. What was good enough for the country was good enough for the *Courier*. They conveniently overlooked the fact that they themselves worked for a publisher who was a woman. Like most people afflicted with the cataracts of prejudice, they looked down, never up.

News came in every day, some of it turning into history; but Cleo never felt she was contributing to any story that would last beyond tomorrow's edition. She had lost interest in what was going on in Vietnam; though she had had experience of it, no editor ever asked her opinion of it. Television had taken over Vietnam: as someone wrote, war was now in the living-room.

Alone in her apartment one Saturday night, she was watching the news when she saw a familiar face turn and stare at her from the screen. Pierre Cain, out of uniform, looking almost ragged in unpressed shirt and trousers, stood in line outside the US embassy in Saigon amongst a crowd of other would-be refugees. There was no sign of Madame Cain. The major, sad- and bitter-faced, stared at the camera, accusing – whom? Cleo suddenly felt a sharp stab of guilt. She was not responsible for his and his country's plight; but she, too, had deserted him. Out of sight, out of mind ...

She sat down at once and wrote him care of JUSPAO, unable to think of anywhere else he might be traced. She offered to help him in any way she could, asked after Madame Cain, finished by saying how much she regretted the way the

351

war had gone. She went out immediately and posted the letter, as if Pierre Cain had to be rescued before daylight. But then the weeks went by and she never heard from him. Guilt still troubled her, but it slowly faded. Life, meaning her own, had to go on.

She took two weeks' vacation and went to Miami. It was the wrong time of the year to go to Florida, Alain told her: wait till Christmas and he would take her down to the Brisson house at Palm Beach. But she wanted to get away from him as much as from New York; she wanted to swim in the ocean, lie on the sand and think. If she was to remain in America she would need to do a lot of thinking.

She did not like Miami, but was fascinated by it; or rather, by the people she saw there. It seemed that everyone wore dark glasses; she felt she was in a city of walking skulls. Though it was a vacation city only the very young seemed to be enjoying themselves. Everyone else walked around with the same expressions she had seen on the faces of New Yorkers. America, she decided, was as worried as herself.

On her third day in the city a Senate Crime Commission came to town. Educating herself in America, she had been reading recent American history as well as past; she now remembered reading snippets on the Kefauver inquiry into crime in the 1950s. That had quietened organized crime down for a few years; it hadn't lessened it, it had just become less visible. Now, with Richard Nixon gone and Gerald Ford in office, a new moral tone was taking over Washington. The nation was about to be cleaned up again.

Cleo, restless with herself after only three days, called Jake Lintas in New York. 'I'd like to cover the inquiry –'

'We're taking the wire services on it.'

'Mr Lintas –' They were still formal with each other, keeping each other at a distance. 'I'll be working in my own time. If the paper doesn't use my stuff, it'll have lost nothing. I'll just have lost a few days of my vacation.'

'Go ahead,' he said abruptly and hung up.

Cleo had never seen a Senate committee at work. Her first

impression was of circus performers, out of costume, milling around looking for a ring-master; hadn't she read somewhere that Ringling Bros came to Florida for the winter? This was another circus out of season. The committee members, counsel, witnesses, spectators all seemed to be enjoying themselves, determined to be informal, as if organized crime were a sport and not a killing business. But gradually a pattern was imposed on the proceedings; the patient questions, repeated with only a little variation, dampened the jovial air. Frowns began to appear on the brows of witnesses and spectators alike, crime was no longer a game.

Cleo put it all down, writing her piece as she used to write her column in the *Examiner*, tongue-in-cheek but cattle-prod in hand. She called the *Courier* and, instead of asking for the re-write desk, asked to be put through to one of the typists she had got to know.

'Annie, do me a favour. Take this down exactly as I dictate it, please. Then put it on the copy desk with my name in caps at the top.'

Annie Rivkin had worked for the *Courier* for twenty years and hated all the men who worked on it. 'Go ahead, honey. I already got your name in red at the top.'

An hour later Alain called her at her hotel. He had been working on the copy desk for the past three months and her gamble, about which he knew nothing, had paid off. 'It goes in exactly as is, Cleo. You were lucky – it came to me on the copy desk, not one of the other guys. I didn't touch a word. I took it in to Jake Lintas and persuaded him he had to run it. With a by-line.'

'You do too much for me, Alain. But I love you for it.'

'I wish you did,' he said quietly. 'Goodnight, Cleo.'

On her first day at the inquiry a small, slim young man had sat beside her, nodded hello but said nothing else, then proceeded to make copious notes in a thick notebook in the quickest shorthand she had ever seen. She wondered why he didn't use a tape-recorder, he seemed intent on getting so much down; then she wondered if he didn't want to be overheard and further wondered why. At each adjournment

353

during the day the young man disappeared, never once stopping to swap comments with the other reporters.

On the second day Cleo found herself again sitting next to the young man. She introduced herself and after a slight hesitation he said, 'Tony Rossano.'

'What paper?'

Again there was the slight hesitation. '*Il Corriere.*'

'*The Courier?*'

'It's not the same as your paper, Miss Spearfield.' Rossano's small smile seemed to hurt him. 'It's an Italian-language paper in Philadelphia. Excuse me.'

He got up immediately and moved away and never came back to the reporters' table. Cleo watched him each day, busily scribbling away in his notebook, but he was always on the far side of the big room, talking to no one, clad in an armour of concentration. Only once did he let the armour open, almost like lifting a visor. Cleo, intrigued by him, watching him when the proceedings before the committee grew dull, saw him once look up and nod at someone in the main body of the room. Cleo followed the direction of Rossano's gaze, but couldn't be sure whom the young man had nodded to. But the nod was meant for one of four men, all lawyers, seated behind the principal witness of the day, a one-time leading member of the old Anastasia gang in New Jersey and now claiming to be retired and respectable. Cleo wondered if Tony Rossano was working for someone else besides *Il Corriere.*

Then after four days the Senate committee moved on, to do another show in another town. Once again Cleo had the feeling of watching a circus going through its paces and its itinerary, but she didn't make that comment in her piece on the last day. She was still a visitor in the country, still on a visa that could be withdrawn. She kept her tongue out of her cheek, at least on that point.

She did not stay in Miami for the full two weeks. She went out to dinner twice with men from the reporters' table; both men, one from Atlanta and the other from St Louis, tried to get her into bed while she was still digesting her dinner. The man from St Louis, who had a brewery belly like her brother Alex's, began pawing her while she was having her dessert.

'I never go to bed on a full stomach,' she said, gathering up her handbag. 'And yours is fuller than most I've seen.'

She went back to New York the following day. Jake Lintas greeted her with grudging praise for her stories and Alain greeted her with almost effusive delight for her mere return. She went to bed with him on the first night, but refused to stay till morning, the first time he had asked her to do so. She did not want Claudine to come down from the penthouse and discover her having breakfast there. She had an old-fashioned respect for a mother's sensitivities. She also had an old-fashioned idea that if you stayed the night with a man it suggested some form of commitment; going to bed with him for an hour or two could be classed as a social engagement. She smiled at her own hypocrisy, but hypocrisy is a comfort when there is nothing else to fall back on.

She now had a by-line, but Jake Lintas still stubbornly kept her on police rounds. She knew she was being victimized, but there was nothing she could do about it; neither Carl Fishburg nor any of the other editors would go to bat for her. She did not complain to either of the Roux, Alain or Claudine, though she was doubtful if the former could do anything for her or that the latter would want to. She was on a treadmill, with the months slipping by like a moving diorama that moved faster than the treadmill.

One night in November, at 11.30, her phone rang. It was Stewart Norway. 'Sorry to call you so late, Cleo. But I thought you'd be interested in the news – I've just had a phone call from Canberra. Kerr, the Governor-General, has just sacked the Whitlam government.'

She thanked him for the news; but he knew her thanks was hollow and he understood. He was a Labour voter and she could imagine him lying awake all night seething at the political crime that had just been committed in Canberra. She herself lay for a while trying to focus her feelings. She was surprised, but not shocked or aghast, as Stew Norway had been; unlike him, she did not know when or even if she would ever return to Australia. It was almost as if news had come in on the press wires of a revolution in a foreign country.

At last she called the operator and asked for her father's number in Canberra. It was an hour before she got through; the lines to Canberra, it seemed, were being burnt out. Then her father came on the line, his voice as clear as if he were sitting beside her. Which she wished he were.

'I've just heard the news, Dad. What happened?'

'John Kerr has just kicked us out.'

'Were you expecting anything like that?'

'Hell, no! We've had a crisis here in the Senate, but I don't think any of us expected it to blow up like this. Gough came back from seeing Kerr looking like a stunned mullet.' *Ah Dad, don't speak Australian tonight. It needs more than that. Be Roman . . .* But she could think of no Latin, always her worst subject, to fit the occasion. 'There's to be an election next month.'

'Will you win it?'

'We'll waltz in, sweetheart. The ordinary voter's not going to let Kerr and Mal Fraser get away with this. Gough's come up with a great phrase – *Maintain the rage!* That's all we have to do, maintain the rage.'

But then the line became bad, his voice faded. Was he talking into the wind? she wondered. She wished him good luck and hung up. She had a moment of guilt, felt that she should jump on a plane and fly out to comfort him; in the old days he would have had Brigid to stand by him. Then she told herself he was an old campaigner; any man who had been in the Australian Labour Party for forty years had seen more battles than any of the generals from the war colleges of the world. Her brothers, even Perry the conservative who would vote in the secrecy of the ballot booth for Malcolm Fraser, would do their best to keep up his spirits. Sylvester himself would already be polishing his rhetoric, the politician's weaponry, practising the belly-laugh, getting ready to go out on the hustings, the battleground he had always enjoyed more than Parliament. He'll survive, she thought, and at last dropped off to sleep.

Contrary to Sylvester's expectations, in the December elections Labour did not waltz back in. The voters, far from maintaining the rage, an emotional state that the average Australian can only achieve politically when drunk, sent Labour into the wilderness again with a landslide defeat. Sylvester himself was returned to the Senate, but, as he told Cleo on the phone, he felt no personal victory.

'One of the press gallery reporters asked me for a comment. I tried to be like Gough, he's good on the Latin tags, but I couldn't. In the end all I could give him was *Up you, Jack*.'

Cicero might have made a similar remark, but there had been no press gallery in the Roman Senate. 'That was good enough, Dad. Be Australian all the way.'

Cleo went back to her own problems of trying to get off the treadmill. Then the Senate crime inquiry came to New York, the climax of its investigations. Cleo and Hal Rainer went down to the Foley Square courthouse to cover the proceedings.

'It's just a repeat,' said Hal, 'like a TV re-run. Twenty-four, twenty-five years ago I saw the same thing when the Kefauver committee came to town. Even this dame they've got on the stand today, Billie Locke, she's like a re-run. She could be Virginia Hill's daughter. Hill, she was Bugsy Siegel's girl friend, she's still around somewhere.'

'Well, I suppose crime is like everything else. The more things change et cetera, et cetera.'

'I couldn't have said it better myself, unless I'd said it in French, which I can't. Frank Costello was the Big Fish back in those days. That was the first time they'd televised anything like that. Frank said he wouldn't appear on camera and he won his point. The TV directors had to satisfy themselves with focusing their cameras on his hands. For a week there Costello's hands were famous. Palmists tried to read them, manicurists criticized the work on the cuticles, Liz Arden wanted to buy the commercial time on the TV broadcasts. It was all a lot of hoopla and all it added up to was that Kefauver got to run for the Democratic nomination in '52 and finished up out of the money. The Syndicate didn't lay any bets on him.'

As Cleo and Hal arrived in the crowded, faded, shabby courtroom the principal witness for the day was just taking the stand. Billie Locke was draped in furs ('silver mink,' Cleo whispered to Hal, 'The Empress would write her off at once for wearing that during the day') and wore a tight-fitting purple hat, like a Twenties cloche. She looked older than Cleo had expected, more than the thirty-two she was supposed to be, and the life she had led was stamped there on her face like faded immigration seals. She had red hair and bright green eyes and a smile like a whore welcoming a Shriners' parade. Billie Locke had come to town from Saratoga and, being a lady or anyway an ex-lady, she had kept the gentlemen waiting.

Cleo was fascinated by the woman and her performance. She was a gangster's moll, as outdated as the phrase itself might be; Cleo had seen the likes of her in 1930s movies in the *Late Late Show*, played by Glenda Farrell or Claire Trevor; but here she was, real. Cleo wandered round the crowded room. She had never seen such a fascinated audience, certainly not down at the Miami hearings; they'd be asking the tough-talking woman for her autograph before she left the court. Billie Locke talked, but told the committee nothing; she was a fallen angel who, she claimed, still had her innocence. All her gentlemen friends had been exactly that, real gentlemen.

'They weren't gangsters or racketeers or all them dreadful things you're calling 'em ...' The green eyes blinked, she was blinded by her own attempt at honesty.

Then Cleo saw Tony Rossano, face as impassive as it had been down in Miami, seemingly no more impressed by Billie Locke than were the committee members. He was scribbling away with the same mechanical fury as he had shown at the previous hearing; Cleo wondered if he had followed the inquiry at its dozen or more stops throughout the country.

Crumbs, she thought, he must be writing a book. Then she got her idea.

She squeezed Hal's shoulder, nodded goodbye and threaded her way out of the court. She stood in the corridor and waited. At last Billie Locke had finished her testimony and was coming out of the court. She came out on a wave of reporters and photographers. She stopped, swung her fist and one of the reporters fell back holding his jaw. Then she shouted, 'You fucking shits, I hope an H-bomb falls on every fucking one of you!' and was gone, leaving behind a mixed smell of perfume and brimstone. Women are hell, Sylvester Spearfield had once said, but had asked not to be quoted.

Cleo pushed her way through the crowd, picked Tony Rossano up from the floor. The other newsmen had trampled over him, going after Billie Locke, on heat for another quote, even though the four-letter words would never get into print. Rossano was still holding his jaw, still dazed, and for a moment he didn't recognize Cleo.

'Cleo Spearfield, from the *Courier*. Miami, remember? What did you say to her that made her slug you?'

'None of your business,' said Rossano, working his jaw to see if the lady had broken it.

'Righto, none of my business. But I'd like to put a proposition to you, Mr Rossano. You work for an Italian-language newspaper. Most of the mobsters who've been before the committee, they've been Italian. That must upset a lot of honest, hard-working Italians, being tarred with that sort of brush. How would you like to do a piece for the *Courier* on what the Italian community at large thinks of the Italian gangsters?'

'Get fucked,' said Rossano, no respecter of ladies, and he, too, was gone.

Cleo stood for a moment, then she hurried after the thin young man, keeping him in sight but not catching up with him. She would never know what made her follow Rossano; perhaps it was the instinct of a reporter scenting a story. She had learned a lot in the company of Hal Rainer.

Out in the square she saw Rossano get into a cab. She

359

quickly looked around, saw another one cruising towards her and hailed it. As she got in she said, 'Follow that cab,' and immediately felt like an amateur actor doing a bad audition.

Even the cab driver wasn't impressed. 'You didn't say that line very well, lady. You want more snap to it, y'know what I mean? Follow that cab!' His face was as battered-looking as his cab; his voice and its engine had the same grating quality. 'You one of them undercover women cops or something?'

'No, I'm a reporter.'

'Hey, we're on a story, are we? I'm your man, lady. I drove Walter Winchell a coupla times back in the old days. I once even picked up Damon Runyon, just the once, he was a guy didn't talk much, y'know what I mean?'

He talked all the way uptown; but he was a good driver and he never lost sight of the cab in front. At last he pulled up.

'Well, there he goes, into Gracie Park. You want me to wait?'

Cleo told him yes, gave him some money and jumped out of the cab and hurried into the park. She cast a quick glance at Gracie Mansion, the Mayor's residence, but Rossano was not heading towards it. He sat down on a bench and gazed out at the East River and an empty garbage scow making its way up towards Hell's Gate. He looked no different from the dozen or so other people in the park, the two or three tourists, the young mothers with their children, the old men soaking up what might be the last spring sun of their lives. Up by the Mayor's mansion a young man was taking photographs.

Cleo kept in the background, waiting and watching; she *knew* that Rossano had not come up here to look at the view or get over his aching jaw. The Italian had been sitting there about five minutes when two men, both dressed in dark suits and grey fedoras, came into the park. They passed close to Cleo and she saw that the shorter of the two fancied himself as a smart dresser; the bigger man was a bargain basement copy. They went down the path to the bench where Rossano sat. He stood up, the three of them shook hands formally,

360

then they all sat down and looked out at the river; the newcomers might have been property developers and Rossano a real estate salesman who was going to sell them Long Island across the river. But after a minute or two Rossano took out his notebook and began to read from his shorthand notes.

Cleo was too far away to hear anything. She debated whether she should stay here, whether to follow Rossano and the two strangers when they left; then decided she could spend the rest of the day running around for no result and very little information. Then she saw that the youth who had been taking pictures of Gracie Mansion had moved close to her.

She walked along to him. 'Do you have a telescopic lens?'

'Sure.' He was about twenty, plain and thin as a blank signpost; acne had been at him like borers. He was festooned with cameras and lenses, he was ready to shoot the world. 'What you want shot? Shoot!'

Crumbs, thought Cleo: New York was full of characters today. 'See those three men down there on the bench? Could you get me some shots of them?'

'Hey, what are you with that accent you got? You from the United Nations or anything? Those guys Commie spies or something?'

'No, I'm from the *New York Courier*. Get me those pix and I'll take you downtown, develop everything else you've taken today and give you fifty bucks. Okay? Shoot!'

She guessed he had never sold a photograph in his life; he seemed to think fifty dollars was more than enough. He took six photos, never once attracting the attention of Rossano and his companions on the bench. Going back downtown in the cab he introduced himself: 'George Hurlstone, I come from upstate, near Rochester. I been crazy about photography ever since I was a kid. You got any vacancies on the *Courier*, eh?'

'It's a tough town, kid,' said the cab driver. 'Let me tell you –'

The two of them had a dialogue all the way down to the

Courier's office. Cleo hurried George Hurlstone up to the picture editor, Bill Puskas, argued fifty dollars out of petty cash, said goodbye to Hurlstone and waited for Bill Puskas to bring her the pictures.

'Jesus, was that kid hard to get rid of! He's gonna be a pain in the ass, you believe me ... Well, there they are. They're not great, but maybe they're good enough.'

Cleo had already talked to Carl Fishburg, who had shown neither much interest nor enthusiasm. 'Look, Carl, I don't think this guy Rossano is a reporter – I think he's covering the inquiry for someone unconnected with newspapers. What if it's some Syndicate boss who's so far been unnamed? I want to show these pix around, maybe someone will recognize either or both of the two strangers –'

It was Hal Rainer who recognized the smaller of the two men, the smart dresser. 'It's Frank Apollo – I'd know him anywhere. He comes from Kansas City – he went down there from Chicago, I dunno, ten or twelve years ago. I was out there on a story about the old-time bootleggers. He wasn't big-time in those days, but what I hear, he's got things going for him out there now.'

Carl Fishburg now began to take an interest in the story. 'Okay, a week, no more. Both of you work on it. No running all around the country. Whatever you dig up, you gotta dig up right here in New York. You want to go anywhere else, you go on your own time and your own expenses.'

'They'd have loved you over at *Life* magazine,' said Cleo. 'You'd have had them photographing the world with a Box Brownie.'

'If the pix were in focus ...' said Fishburg, unsmiling.

'I'll stick with Rossano,' Cleo told Hal. 'You try and find out what connection Apollo has with any of the Mob.'

'I'm still not sure what we're after.'

'It's a hunch, Hal, nothing more. I think there's a nigger in the woodpile –'

'Hold it! Ain't no niggers in this country no more, you Aussie white trash.'

'A racist figure of speech.' She knew Hal was no racist, but like a lot of old-time newspapermen he had difficulty in not using phrases that had become clichés with him but were now taboo. He was the same with so-called sexist terms: he never used *chairperson* or *spokesperson* and the copy editors, acting under a recent reluctant order from Jake Lintas, another old-timer, were constantly correcting his copy.

'Right,' said Hal. 'Now what were you saying about the wop?'

'I think there's someone who's hoping the Syndicate, or whatever it's called these days, will collapse under the pressure of the hearings. It might be Frank Apollo or it might be someone bigger than him. We may get nothing, not even worth a line, but all we'll have wasted will be some *Courier* time. The trouble with the *Courier* has been that it's never wasted a day or a dollar, never gambled on a story. I'm gambling now.'

Over the next two days Cleo tried to nail down Rossano. But he was too shifty and slick and disappeared every time she approached him. Hal Rainer, using the phone to Kansas City and contacts in New York, had more luck.

'Our friend Mr Apollo was one of Billie Locke's boy friends when she first went up to Chicago from her hometown somewhere down in Oklahoma. He didn't last long, but evidently he's always had a yen for her. He's running a fairly big operation out in K.C. and around there, but he's out of favour with the Syndicate, they want nothing to do with him. Whether he wants to be in or out, I don't know. But in K.C., so I'm told, he thinks he's the Mid-West's answer to Al Capone.'

'That dates him a bit, doesn't it?'

'That may be the reason the Syndicate doesn't want anything to do with him. Now they're all trying so goddam hard to look respectable.'

'I think we need to have an interview with Mr Apollo.'

'Sure. I'd like to do an exclusive with the Queen of England, too. Come to think of it, the Queen might be more agreeable.'

'We're going down to Foley Square and you and I are

363

going to box in Rossano. I'll take him from one side and you from the other. He's not going to get away this time.'

Tony Rossano did his best to get away, but didn't succeed. Sour and dark-faced, he went out between Cleo and Hal Rainer into the grey drizzle of the Square. 'I could call up the Guild. You're harassing another reporter –'

'I've checked, Mr Rossano,' said Cleo. 'You don't belong to the Guild. You're not even on the staff of *Il Corriere*, they've never heard of you. We're not harassing you. All we want is an interview with Frank Apollo.'

'Frank who? You're fucking crazy. Look, I'm going back inside there –'

'Frank Apollo, from Kansas City. We have a picture of you and him taken up in Gracie Park ... Hold it. We're not planning to run it. But we know Mr Apollo is in town and we'd like a word with him. We're not gunning for him –'

Rossano smiled then: like a brat pulling wings off a butterfly. 'That's funny, that is –'

'A figure of speech,' said Cleo and gave a side smile to Hal Rainer. 'Tell Mr Apollo that we'd like an interview. Just half an hour at any place he cares to name. We're going to do a piece on him anyway, and he might prefer to see we get our facts right. You know how stories turn out when the writers never bother to check their facts. Call me at the *Courier*. No later than five today.'

Going back to the *Courier* in a cab, Hal said, 'What are we going to write if Apollo won't see us?'

'Nothing. What have we got that would make a story? But Apollo doesn't know that.'

'You're a natural-born newspaperman, my girl. Conniving, nefarious, underhanded. You're also a very tough lady. I'd give fifty bucks to see you in the same ring as Billie Locke.'

'I wouldn't last one round with her.' She didn't think of herself as tough and didn't want others to think so.

Rossano's call came at five o'clock, dead on, as if he had been deliberately waiting to pick up the phone wherever he was. 'Mr Apollo will see you on one condition. That you

364

don't mention he is here in New York. You'll interview him as if you had gone out to Kansas City.'

'Agreed,' said Cleo. 'Where and when do we meet him?'

'I'll pick you up outside the *Courier*, front entrance, at nine o'clock.'

When Hal heard the arrangements he said, 'We'll have a photographer follow us, just in case.'

'In case of what?'

'In case we get bumped off. The *Courier* will have an exclusive on our corpses. That should satisfy Carl Fishburg.'

'That's a horrible joke.' But she wondered if Hal Rainer, who had had much more experience of gangsters than she had, really was joking.

Rossano picked them up in a cab right on nine o'clock: he seemed to be a stickler for punctuality. He hardly spoke on the ride across and uptown. At last the cab pulled up and Cleo looked out.

'The Tower of London?' She knew it to be a newly opened restaurant, expensive, exclusive and specializing in English food; but she had never been here before. 'What's a nice Italian boy doing in a place like this?'

Rossano said goodnight and the cab drove off. Hal said, 'I wonder why he's not taking us in to introduce us?'

'It looks safe enough. At least it's not a dark alley.'

The Tower of London had a Beefeater on the door, an out-of-work actor who did a passable English accent. The decor was not meant to suggest the dingy dungeons of the Tower; the decorator had excelled himself in making incarceration look attractive. Red silk drapes hung from the fake barred windows; there was thick pile carpeting on the floor woven to look like rushes; the carved oak chairs were upholstered with thick leather cushions for Park Avenue behinds not accustomed to corporal punishment in public. The waiters, fortunately, were not dressed in period costume: Luigi, Vito and Pasquale would not have been varlets in the original Tower, not even as guest workers.

Frank Apollo sat at a table in the rear, put there by the snobish maître d'hôtel who knew a foreigner when he

365

saw one. With Apollo was the man who had accompanied him to Gracie Park to meet Rossano. He was introduced as Paul Sirio, 'my legal adviser'. Mr Sirio didn't say a word during the rest of the dinner, which, Cleo reckoned, must have set some sort of record for a lawyer and his legal advice.

Apollo was in silk: grey silk suit, white-on-white silk shirt, silk silver tie; Cleo looked for a spring of mulberry in his lapel. Minus twenty pounds he might have been handsome; as it was, his face was round and bland, except for the eyes. If there were such things as lean eyes, Apollo had them. They would tirelessly be seeking opportunities and enemies, he accepted that his world would be divided equally between them. Cleo doubted that he would have any friends.

'You like English food? Tony Rossano recommended this place to me.' He had a soft, rough voice. 'I don't like the pasta. All the time, everyone think Italians eat nothing but the pasta. The best food is the English roast and beef and the Yukshire pudding. Is better for you than all that pasta. Now what you want? Don't forget we're in Kansas City, not here.' His smile had a certain charm to it if one didn't look at his eyes. 'You ask the questions, I give you the answers. Maybe.'

Hal attacked the roast beef and left the questions to Cleo. 'You weren't called to the hearings in Kansas City, Mr Apollo, nor in Chicago, though you've had business dealings there for some years.'

'Not in Chicago.' Apollo glanced at Sirio, but the legal adviser didn't seem to think that was a statement that might incriminate him. 'I ain't had any business there, eight, ten years. In K.C. I'm in legitimate business, dry cleaning, parking lots, things like that. Why would the committee wanna call me, a legitimate businessman? They don't call David Rockefeller from the Chase Manhattan, right?'

Cleo cut into the Yorkshire pudding, which defied her knife as if it were Malayan rubber. 'Mr Rockefeller isn't an ex-boy friend of Miss Billie Locke.'

'You done your homework.' Apollo was still amiable. 'She was some dame, y'know that? She coulda been real class, she hadn't got mixed up with some of them bums she knows.'

366

Cleo gave up on the Yorkshire pudding. 'Mr Apollo, why are you unpopular with the Syndicate?'

'Unpopular? You don't like your Yukshire pudding? Gimme.' He speared the pudding and transferred it to his own plate. 'They don't like me because I wanna be my own boss in my own terr'tory.'

'In the dry cleaning and parking lot territory?'

Apollo smiled again, unoffended. ''At's right. You see, Miss Spearfield, I wanna be one of the Good People –'

'The Mafia,' said Hal as Cleo looked blank.

'What's the Mafia, Mr Rainer? We call ourselves the Good People, sometimes the old men call us the Honoured Society. I wanna be one of 'em, but I don't wanna be told what I can do in my own terr'tory.'

As the dinner progressed it began to dawn on Cleo that Apollo had granted this interview out of vanity. The man was laying himself open to a declaration of war by the Syndicate if he allowed himself to be quoted on what he had said so far; the Syndicate or the Mafia, or the Honoured Society or the Good People did not like men who talked to outsiders. Apollo wanted his name in the papers along with all those Big Names that had featured at the hearings. He was not the first man whose vanity had made him stupid.

'You wouldn't volunteer to give evidence before the committee?'

Apollo looked at Sirio, then at his plate. Suddenly he pushed the plate away from him, gulped down his wine as if he had all at once become very thirsty. 'Depends. Some of these guys, the ones everybody sees in the papers and on TV ... A man, he's got a right to earn a living in his own terr'tory, right?'

Hal said, 'You mean the Syndicate is trying to muscle in on Kansas City?'

'You know K.C., Mr Rainer? You know what a nice quiet place it could be, if people mind their own business? You want dessert, some nice bread-and-butter pudding?'

Shades of Jack, thought Cleo. What would he say if he saw whom I'm was eating good sensible food with?

'Those guys, no names but you know who I mean, they stay outa K.C., I got a nice business terr'tory. But they're greedy . . .' He sounded sorry for himself. He was in the right place, the Tower of London: no one in the original Tower had ever been ecstatic.

The restaurant had begun to empty now; it was the hour between the early diners and the theatre crowd who would come in for a late supper. The Beefeater came in the front door and stood there; a man in a dark topcoat and hat stood behind him. The man looked over the Beefeater's shoulder, as if deciding whether he liked the look of the restaurant, then said something to someone behind him. Two other men, also in topcoats, hats pulled low on their foreheads, suddenly stepped out of the alcove beside the front door. They came down towards the rear of the restaurant, not running but walking swiftly, taking the sub-machine-guns from under their coats as they did so. The few diners still in the restaurant looked up at them, but didn't take in what was about to happen.

Apollo and Sirio, facing the front door, suddenly stood up. Cleo looked back over her shoulder and saw the guns; she hurled herself sideways, knocking Hal off his chair. The two of them sprawled on the floor and the brief hail of bullets went over them and into the chests of Frank Apollo and Paul Sirio. Both men teetered back, then Sirio crumpled to the floor. Apollo remained on his feet for a moment, one hand raised as if in protest to the two gunmen; then he fell face forward into the bread-and-butter custard that had just been brought by the waiter. Cleo, lying on the floor beneath the table, saw one of the gunmen look at her and Hal, then point his gun at her. She waited to die, mind and body paralysed. Then the other man shook his head and both turned and went back up to the front door, moving their guns back and forth across the restaurant, like cleaners waving brooms and telling the tardy diners it was time to go home. They joined the man at the front door and went out without a backward glance. The Beefeater, the guardian of the Tower, fainted in a red, ruffled heap like a rooster overcome at having just missed the axe.

Hal Rainer got up from the floor, helped Cleo to her feet. 'Thanks. I'd have got some of that in the back of the head if you hadn't –' Then he looked at Apollo lying face down in the bloodstained bread-and-butter custard. 'Well, we got a story. Not the one we came looking for –'

'Better,' said Cleo, alive and no longer afraid of dying.

Then she looked at Frank Apollo and wanted to be sick. She turned away and, apart from her heaving stomach, felt nothing. Pity was something you didn't waste in certain terr'tories.

5

The killing of Apollo and his henchman, the legal adviser whose only advice, it turned out, was the gun in the armpit holster that he did not get out in time, was a Page One story in every newspaper in town. Under Cleo's and Hal's joint by-line in the *Courier* it ran over to a further two full columns on Page Two. The photographer who had followed them up from the *Courier* and had been fretting to his driver about wasted time, had got the only pictures of the bodies that appeared in any New York paper. Hal had rung the police and ambulance before any of the restaurant staff or guests had got over their shock; then he had stood by the phone to see that no smart waiter, anxious to earn an extra buck or two, rang any rival newspaper. By the time other photographers did arrive on the scene the bodies were already covered with tablecloths and on stretchers waiting to be wheeled out to the ambulance. Jake Lintas, conservative as always, had demurred about running the graphic pictures, but Carl Fishburg and Bill Puskas convinced him they were too good to throw out.

The story, as Cleo and Hal told it, meant the recall before the Senate committee of all the leading figures of the past week. But the mobsters denied any knowledge of Frank Apollo; to hear them tell it, they lived in a Garden of Eden where all they knew was innocence. In the end the police decided the killers were out-of-towners, probably sent in from Chicago. The one thing that worried Cleo was that Tony Rossano had disappeared and she began to wonder if it was he who had set up the killing of Apollo and Sirio, hoping that she and Hal might be killed in the crossfire.

'The thought occurred to me, too,' said Hal.

'Does it make you sweat?'

'Naturally.' Then he put his hand on her arm, one of the few times he ever had; he kept gestures of affection to a minimum. 'Don't worry, girl. He won't come back.'

Claudine did not like the way the story had been featured, but she made no complaint to Jake Lintas. She did, however, bring it up at the next board meeting. 'It sold a few extra copies for a week or so, but sales have dropped back again.'

'Maybe we should run more stories like it,' said Stephen Jensen.

'One can't keep manufacturing sensations day after day.'

'Mr Lintas doesn't even seem capable of manufacturing *news*. If I may suggest it, Claudine, I think you should spend more time as publisher and less as chairman of the board.'

Lately, she had noticed, Stephen had begun to show a degree of opposition to her. Several years ago she had had an affair with him that had lasted a year, one that they had discreetly kept from their respective children and their friends. She had terminated it when she had discovered that he was having another affair with a much younger woman at the same time. She had complimented him on his stamina, since her own appetite had not been diminished by her age, and told him to concentrate it on the other woman. Since then she had had no lover, though she still felt the urge for one occasionally and remembered Stephen's talents with some satisfaction. But she had never loved him, nor he her. Nonetheless, she had never expected him to start opposing her, at least in business, the way he had been for several months.

'I am satisfied with the way Mr Lintas is running things. There is something else that causes me more concern. I am told that someone has been buying up stock in the paper.

370

Something like twenty per cent has already changed hands. Who is buying and, more importantly, for the moment anyway, who is selling?'

There were seven other board members besides Claudine and Jensen, all men, all around Claudine's age. Glances passed round the table like mice looking for a way out of a maze. Then one man said, 'I was going to bring it up later in the meeting. I've sold my stock. I have my letter here and my resignation from the board.'

'Which I'll accept unread, Charles,' said Claudine, as if through a mouthful of dry ice. 'Whom have you sold to?'

'To be honest, I'm not sure. I think it's just a front company. I feel bad about this –'

'As you should,' said Claudine.

'– but part of the deal was that I told no one until the stock had changed hands. The price was too good to ignore, Claudine.'

'I shan't ask you what you got, that would only bring me down to your mercenary level. Why didn't you come to me and see if I would buy the stock if you were so eager to get out?'

'Would you have paid me five dollars above the current market price?' The man, fat and florid, seemed to be growing bigger and redder with Claudine's curtness. He knew he had done an unethical thing, but business was business and any offer that got him out of the newspaper business had its own absolution.

'No,' said Claudine; then looked around the table. 'Has anyone else sold his stock?'

A tall bald-headed man said, 'As you know, Claudine, I have no stock of my own. I am here representing the Hilliard family. We received an offer and I recommended they accept it. The price was the same as Charles got.'

'I'll accept your resignation too, David. Anyone else?'

Two other men, one a lawyer, the other a banker, each of them representing outside stockholders, said, yes, they had sold out. She was far from being as composed as she looked; she was deeply shocked. She knew that certain members of the board had been very dissatisfied with the paper's performance over the past few years; she was as aware as they that newspapers were dying all over the United States. If the stockholders wanted to sell out, she had expected they would warn her. Instead, they had presented her with a *fait accompli*.

She looked at Stephen Jensen, her only real friend on the board. He shook his head at her unspoken query. 'They made me an offer, Claudine, but I declined it. I wasn't being entirely altruistic or honourable. I just figured that anyone who wanted to pay almost fifteen per cent above the market price for a stock that hasn't moved in three years must be either crazy or he knows something I don't know. I don't think you should be so critical of Charles and the others. They've held their stock in the *Courier* for God knows how many years and I think they've been very patient and long suffering.'

'I hope their suffering is relieved now,' said Claudine, sounding like Florence Nightingale burning herself on her lamp. 'Exactly how much stock has gone to this mysterious buyer?'

'Twenty-two per cent. Enough to give them at least two seats on the board, if they ask for them.'

'Well, we'll wait and let them make the approach.' She wasn't going down the road to meet the tumbrils.

'I wonder if it's laundered money from the Mafia?' Jensen said. 'Or is it just coincidence that the bids started right after the *Courier* featured that story on the Apollo killing?'

The thought troubled Claudine, but she still looked calm. 'I'd have no gangster sitting on this board.'

'You wouldn't have a gangster,' said Jensen. 'He would probably be a perfectly respectable lawyer. Respectable on the surface, anyway.'

Two nights later Claudine had Alain and Cleo to dinner in the penthouse and told them of the sales of stock. 'Stephen Jensen has raised the possibility of its being Mafia money that has bought into the paper. You may regret having pursued that Apollo story, Cleo.'

372

'I think that's unfair, Mother,' said Alain.

'Do you think so?' Claudine looked at Cleo.

This was the first time Cleo had been invited up to the penthouse. It was almost as if Claudine had kept her at arm's length, out of her own private territory; Souillac might be the palace, but palaces have always been accessible. Cleo had been apprehensive about coming here tonight, wondering if, in her autocratic way, Claudine was going to tell her that she could now marry into the family.

'I don't think they would go to all that expense just to shut me up, Mrs Roux.'

'I wasn't suggesting that,' said Claudine. 'Please don't be so vain. What I am suggesting is that their attention may have been drawn to the *Courier* by your story, they learned there were certain people willing to sell their stock, and they bought. I am told they launder their dirty money through many channels. Radio stations, television stations, motion picture studios. Why not a newspaper?'

'The other three make money, newspapers don't,' said Alain. 'Not the *Courier*, anyway.'

'Perhaps they were looking for a tax loss,' said Claudine. 'Well, we shall just have to wait and see.'

Cleo went home that night, declining to stay with Alain in his apartment. She had a disturbed night's sleep, wondering if she had indeed drawn the Mafia's attention to the easy entry into the *Courier*. She could not see herself working for the killers of Frank Apollo, no matter how remote they might be from the paper's boardroom.

She would have been even more disturbed if she had known who the real buyer was, but Claudine kept that information from her to suit her own convenience.

Two nights after she had had Alain and Cleo to dinner, Claudine got a phone call. 'Claudine? It's Jack Cruze. I'd like to come and see you.'

They hadn't seen each other in she had forgotten how many years and here he was inviting himself up as if he were a regular visitor. 'What is it, Jack – business? I never bring business into my home. I'll meet you at the *Courier* –'

373

'No, Claudine, I don't want to go near the *Courier*. Though you have obviously guessed why I want to see you. I own twenty-two per cent of you now.'

'Not me,' said Claudine, wholly owned by herself. 'The paper perhaps. But not me, Jack. To think I thought you might be the Mafia!'

He sounded puzzled. 'The Mafia?'

'Never mind. But what you have done was underhanded and unfriendly. It's not the way I conduct business.'

'Only because you employ lawyers to do the dirty work for you. You may like to turn a blind eye to all of it, but ninety per cent of business is underhand and unfriendly.'

'What a world you must live in.'

'The same as you, Claudine, only I don't wear blinkers.'

No one had ever accused her of that before. 'Where are you?'

'At the Pierre.'

'Come up now. Don't bring anyone with you, Jack. No lawyers or accountants, just yourself.'

When he arrived it took her, a normally quick observer, several minutes to notice that he had changed. He had aged, the years had crept up and smeared their marks on him; but she hadn't seen him in too long and she knew how quickly some people could age once they had passed a certain milestone. The major change in him, however, was a certain hesitancy with her, something she had never expected. He was one man she had never awed.

'I'm going down to Charleston – you ever been there? I come over regularly – I try to miss New York. I like the South –'

'Out with it, Jack. You're beating about the bush, that's not your style. Why have you bought *Courier* stock and why did you pay so much for it?'

He seemed to relax when he saw that she was going to lead; as if they were dancers whose polka had become creaky through lack of practice. 'First, my name is never to be mentioned. *I* didn't buy the stock, not personally. It was bought by a Bahamian company.'

'I know that, Jack. If you want to play charades for tax purposes, all right –'

'It's not just for tax purposes. There are private reasons.' He pulled at his collar and his tie slid round towards one ear. He was as untidy as she remembered him, a walking laundry heap. 'I want two places on the board. One of them will be filled by Jerry Kibler, the banker – you know him. The other place I want kept open till I've talked to the person I have in mind.'

She had a flash of intuition. But she was too well bred to flash anything, even her intuition. She said blandly, 'That's your private reason for keeping your name out of the matter?'

'Yes.' Then he grinned and abruptly looked years younger. 'Claudine, why didn't you and I marry? We could have turned the Atlantic into our own little pond, you on one side and me on the other.'

'Marriages with that much distance between the partners never work.' Then she led again: 'It's Miss Spearfield, isn't it?'

He did not move for a moment; then he relaxed, glad to be led again. 'Yes. I suppose you think there's no fool like an old fool.'

'I never thought of you as old, Jack.' But the way she said it, it didn't sound like a compliment. 'Foolish, yes. But Miss Spearfield seems to have that effect on a number of men.'

He squinted at her from under the heavy brows. 'She hasn't been playing around. She's been going out with only the one chap.'

'My son. Have you been having her watched?'

He shrugged uncomfortably. 'Just for business reasons.'

'Of course. Have you been having me watched for the same reasons?'

'I've had Jerry Kibler watching the *Courier*.' He looked into the drink in his hand, a large Scotch and soda. 'Claudine, I'm in love with the girl, have been for seven damned years now. We had a bust-up about four years ago and I tried to get over it, put her out of my mind –'

'I know. I heard about you and your countess and the

several others since her. You do choose them from the top, don't you?'

'You know that isn't hard for a man in my position, with my money. So long as I don't look like King Kong and pick my nose at the table, there are always women willing to go out with me. It's the magnetism of power.'

'You have a becoming modesty, too, that I'm sure appeals to that sort of woman.' But she wasn't interested in his women on the other side of the Atlantic. She was concerned with the one closer to home: 'What do you have in mind for Miss Spearfield?'

He looked again at his drink. Claudine had noticed that he had barely touched it. 'I haven't seen her in four years, except once. I was here in New York on business a year or so ago. I knew she was working at the *Courier* and I went down and stood on the opposite side of the street hoping to catch a glimpse of her. Like a bloody schoolboy. I did that once when I was fourteen and thought I was in love with the headmaster's daughter. Cleo came out of the building with some chap, another reporter I suppose, got into a taxi and off she went. I got dizzy, I thought I was going to keel over. I don't know whether you've ever felt like that about anyone.'

'Jack, I really don't want to know about your love affairs.' She had once felt like he had, but that had been when she was in love with her husband in the first years of their marriage. 'What have you got in mind for her with the *Courier*?'

'I have to talk to her first.' He was suddenly embarrassed at how much he had revealed of himself. 'She may give me the bum's rush, as you Americans say.'

'Not this American. But she may, indeed.'

The matter of Cleo Spearfield, she could see, was becoming complicated. She knew that Alain was still seeing her, still carrying a torch (how that dates me, she thought, glad that she hadn't voiced the phrase); they were probably going to bed together, but Cleo still appeared independent. She did not want Cleo as a daughter-in-law; even married, the girl would always be independent, at least of her. If Jack Cruze persuaded Cleo to take up with him again, that would solve the possible problem of Alain's marrying her. But there would be other problems. Jack hadn't bought the *Courier* stock as an investment, he had bought it as a gift, a peace offering.

'Well, let me know when you've come to an understanding with her. She is a very good newspaperwoman, my son tells me.'

'I'm glad to hear of it. She takes risks, though – we used to argue about that. I read about that gangster killing. She was lucky to come out of that unscathed. She gives me heartburn.'

'I don't think she'll change. Now you can take me out to dinner. I have a very good French place where I go regularly.'

'Delighted,' he said unenthusiastically. 'But I like plain cooking myself.'

'They can boil you an egg,' she said and gathered up him, her wrap and her handbag and swept out of the apartment. As their elevator went down, the other elevator rose, carrying with it Cleo and Alain on their way to bed before dinner. It was an old French custom, *cinq à sept*, but neither Claudine, the French-American mother, nor Jack, the English ex-lover, would have been happy if they had known where the objects of their concern were heading.

FOURTEEN

1

Cleo had bought a copy of Tom's new novel, *The Vacant Mirror*, the day it appeared in the stores and began reading it that night, getting halfway through it before she fell asleep at two in the morning. Though the names had been changed to protect the guilty, she recognized herself, Jack and Tom. It had taken Tom eighteen months to write, but she did not know that. He had suffered enough writer's block to have turned him illiterate; but he had always returned to the typewriter, determined to get the story, like a sweetly painful abscess, out of himself. Nevertheless, the book was slight, which was what the critics said during the next couple of weeks; but it might have been a whole library, so heavily did it press down on Cleo. She felt miserable for a week and Alain hopefully asked her if she was pregnant. He was willing and eager to marry her and any reason, even an honourable one, would do.

'Of course not!' She had never snapped at him before; now she gave him a verbal whack. 'What gave you that idea?'

'You've got the mopes. You've hardly looked at me in the office.'

She took his hand, kissed it: the old affectionate gestures that betrayed her. It wasn't his fault she didn't love him. 'I'm just a bit homesick, that's all. I'll be all right in a day or two.'

'No, something else is worrying you.' Alain had come to know her better than she knew.

Something else besides her lost love was worrying her: 'Yes, it's my visa. It's up in a couple of weeks. I've asked Jake

378

Lintas if the paper is going to renew my contract, but he just keeps hedging. The old bastard would like to see me deported.'

'They can't do that! Look, don't *worry* – I'll get Mother to fix Jake. Why didn't you tell me about this sooner? It just never crossed my mind – I don't know, I just sort of take it for granted that you *belong* here –'

'The US government doesn't.' Then she realized he had mentioned Claudine. 'No, don't go to your mother.'

'Why not? She can have it all fixed without any trouble –'

I don't want to owe her any favours. 'No, leave it for a day or two. I'll bail up Jake.'

But Jake Lintas chose to go on vacation before she could confront him. She went to Carl Fishburg, to the personnel manager; but neither of them felt he could do anything, sympathetic though they tried to sound. She was not the only woman on the staff, but she began to feel that she might as well be. It was as if, with the increasing strength of the women's liberation movement, the male citadel of the *Courier* had raised the drawbridge. They were not going to leave themselves open to attack by a Trojan mare.

'I wouldn't worry, honey,' said Annie Rivkin from the typing pool. 'In another year or two the paper's going to be dead and buried. They'll bury all these guys with them and good riddance ... I already got my eye on a job over at CBS. You oughta get into TV, honey, that's where the money is.'

Alain went to his mother. 'Cleo *needs* that visa. The paper can't let her go – there isn't a better writer working for us –'

'You know I never interfere with the running of the paper. Mr Lintas will attend to it.'

'Jake Lintas is the last guy who'll attend to it!'

'I am not going to interfere.'

Alain knew when his mother was in an obdurate mood; one might as well talk to the faces on Mount Rushmore. 'I'm bringing her out to Souillac on Sunday –'

'If you wish. I take it you'd prefer I didn't ask Polly Jensen.'

'Doesn't make any difference. I think Polly has got the

379

message. I don't know why you still keep trying. You're like one of those 18th century European Queen Mothers, always match-making!'

He went back downstairs to his own apartment, slamming the front door of the penthouse as he went out. She sat very still for a while, debating to what lengths she would go to discourage her son from marrying the Spearfield girl. Then she picked up the phone and called the Pierre.

'Jack? Ah, I wondered if you were back from Charleston. I feared you might have decided to go straight back to London. Can you come to luncheon Sunday at my place in the country?'

'Well ... To tell you the truth, Claudine, I'm hoping to see Cleo tomorrow, Saturday. I haven't spoken to her yet, I want to talk to her away from the *Courier* –'

'I think she is out of town on an assignment, Jack. I heard my son mention it.' She wondered if Queen Mothers had lied and intrigued like this. It seemed so much more suburban than being an Empress. 'I'll send a car to pick you up on Sunday.'

There was silence for a moment, then he chuckled. 'How come a woman has never been elected President of this country?'

'We women know that men make better figureheads.'

2

'I am now at the Pentagon,' said Roger Brisson. He and Louise had driven up from Washington on Friday evening and yesterday they had had Souillac to themselves but for the servants. Strolling round the grounds he had, for the first time, begun to see himself as the lord of the manor. Or as Claudine would have put it, the *seigneur*. 'It is just the civil service in uniform, a division of bureaucrats, but it is a change after a lifetime of army posts.'

'We have an apartment in Watergate,' said Louise, 'but I dare not have address cards printed. We have our mail delivered to a box number. I feel like one of those mail order confidence men.'

'You're being ridiculous,' said Claudine. 'The scandal and Richard Nixon are well behind us. Watergate is a perfectly respectable address again, though I shouldn't want to live there myself. It looks like an annexe to the Pentagon.'

'Then it's appropriate for us,' said Roger, tolerant of his sister this weekend. She had invited some very pretty women to Sunday lunch, or luncheon, including the very attractive Miss Spearfield. 'Cleo, why don't you get them to transfer you to the *Courier*'s Washington bureau?'

Cleo saw Louise, ten feet away and in another group, raise her head like a US cavalryman riding point. 'There's too much to write about in New York.'

'All that crime? Don't you tire of it? There's probably as much skulduggery in Washington, but it's much more civilized.'

'I thought President Ford had raised the moral tone down there,' said Stephen Jensen. With his daughter not present to curb him, he was enjoying himself immensely with the women, old and young.

'He seems to be falling over himself to be honest,' said Claudine, 'but hardly upright.'

Everyone laughed at the President who had had a couple of unfortunate stumbles, both of them photographed and widely distributed. What snobs they are, thought Cleo, they are just like the English Establishment. At dinner parties in St James's Place and at St Aidan's House she had heard the same sort of laughter at the expense of certain lower middle class politicians who had risen to power in the Tory Party; they tolerated gaucheries and even indiscretions in the Labour Party, but suspected Tory ministers who showed too much of the common touch. These Americans are just the same, Cleo thought, still voting for the ghosts of George Washington and John Adams.

'I've been reading about your Prime Minister, Mr Whitlam,' said Roger. 'He sounds rather patrician.'

'Thank you,' said Cleo, resenting the patronizing tone in

381

his voice. 'Maybe I should suggest he move to Washington. He'd raise the level of debate there.'

'When Australia becomes the fifty-first State, we'll nominate him,' said Alain, then saw the look on Cleo's face. 'Sorry, I was only joking. You're still a true-blue Aussie, aren't you?'

'A dinky-di Aussi is the phrase. Yes, I am, especially when I hear suggestions like that. You should hear my father on the subject.'

'He is anti-American?' said Roger.

'Yes. But he's fair-minded. He's anti-British, too.'

'Then I've chosen the wrong moment to arrive,' said Jack Cruze right behind her. 'Hello, Cleo.'

Later Cleo would believe that she was more shocked at that moment than she had been four years ago when Jack had tried to shoot her. There had been warnings of violence then, if only recognized too late; his appearance today was totally unexpected, there had been no hints at all. She looked first at Alain, because he was closest, but he looked as shocked as she felt. Then she glanced at Claudine and recognized the perpetrator of this cruel joke.

'Lord Cruze –' She put out her hand and they shook hands like a trade union official and an employer sealing a recent agreement; it would hold good until the next disagreement. 'You haven't changed. Still surprising people.'

He made an awkward gesture; he knew he had been set up by Claudine. He would bide his time and get even. 'You look well.'

'So do you. You look exactly as you did – when was it? Four years ago?'

Put the knife in, Cleo. He knew he did not look exactly as he had four years ago. He saw the evidence in the mirror every morning; on bad days he had taken to shaving without looking in the mirror at all. He was fifty-seven now or, as he thought of it on the really bad days, within three years of sixty. He no longer made love three times a night, the scoring rate had slowed. Yet he knew he wasn't *old*. He just sometimes felt that way.

'Hello, Mr Roux. I don't believe we've met.'

Alain put out a tentative hand, as if he were expecting a gun to be put into it. 'Lord Cruze, this is a pleasant surprise. Mother must have forgotten to mention you were coming –'

'My mind must be wandering,' said Claudine, whose mind had never been on a tighter rein. 'I'm just so glad I could get you two old *Examiner* hands together.'

I'll bet, thought Cleo. Two old *Examiner* hands: she must have lain awake half the night dreaming up that one. 'I'm sure Lord Cruze doesn't want to spend his Sundays talking newspapers, not even his own.'

'There you go –' said Jack Cruze, then shut up. He didn't want to get off on the wrong foot, though she was treading on his toes just the way she used to.

'We'll leave you to talk over old times,' said Claudine. 'And maybe even new ones. Come on, Alain, help me break up some of these gossiping groups.'

Alain looked at Cleo, asking silently if she needed help. But she was not going to be shot at again, not in New Jersey and with so many witnesses. 'I'll see you at lunch, Alain. I'll take Lord Cruze for a walk and show him Souillac.'

Alain left them reluctantly, limping away, and Jack looked after him. 'He thinks I'm still carrying that gun.'

'Did you know I was going to be here?'

'No.'

'That bloody Claudine!'

'Yes.' But now he was grateful for the way Claudine had pitched him into this meeting. If he had called Cleo and she had hung up on him, he was not sure what he would have done next. He felt as uncertain of himself as he had felt seven years ago at their first meeting at the Windsor horse show. 'I was going to call you anyway.'

'Did she know that?'

'I suppose so.' They were walking down a gravelled path beside a long line of trimmed hedges. This was not a Capability Brown garden; it had the formality of a Le Nôtre design. The French were always more formal, even in their intriguing. 'I've bought into the *Courier*.'

383

She walked in silence but for the crunch of gravel; then she looked sideways at him. 'So I'm working for you again?'

'Not quite. I'm only a minority stockholder compared to the Brisson holdings. But I'm entitled to two seats on the board.'

'So you'll be coming to New York regularly?'

'Not necessarily. I can't sit on the board – officially I have nothing to do with the company that bought the shares. No, Jerry Kibler will be one of the directors.'

'Who'll be the other?'

They stopped beside a row of cumquats in white tubs. He picked one of the small yellow fruits and flicked it away like a large marble. Bugger it, he thought, why can she make me feel like some bloody sixteen-year-old? 'I'd like it to be you.'

She shook her head without thinking. 'No, Jack. I don't want to start anything between us, not again –'

He hid his disappointment, told himself to be patient. 'No strings. I want someone who knows newspapers on the board. It's just commonsense to ask you.'

'Jack, the paper is dying on its feet, you must know that.'

'I think it can be saved.' He wasn't sure that it could be; but he hadn't bought into the paper to save it. He had spent the money in the hope of saving himself from loneliness. 'I want to change the editorial side, too.'

'How?'

'I think there should be a managing editor. That chap who's editor, Lintas, has too much say. It's *his* paper, or so he seems to think.'

'That's true.' All at once she knew what he was leading up to, but she kept hold of the sudden excitement that gripped her.

'The job's yours if you want it.'

'Have you talked to Claudine about it?'

'No. But I know more about running a newspaper than she does. If I had Jerry Kibler bring it up at an open shareholders' meeting, I mean about reorganizing the editorial side, I think we'd have the other minority shareholders on

384

our side. Especially if it meant the chance of some dividends. The paper hasn't paid any for the past two years.'

'Claudine would never give me that sort of opportunity. She'd like nothing better than for me to go back home to Australia. She thinks I'm trying to marry into the family.'

'Are you?'

'No.'

He picked another cumquat, tossed it high into the air and caught it with his hand twisted round backwards: a sixteen-year-old's trick. 'I think you're wrong about her. She likes to have people around her she can either put down or fight with, preferably the latter. In a nice civilized way, of course. You're a bit like her, Cleo, or you will be some day. You'll die of boredom the day you can't take the mickey out of someone.'

Am I really like that? But she didn't believe him; he had been wrong about her before. 'I'm surprised you came back if I'm like that ... No, Jack. It would be too much of a hassle.' She meant fighting with him as much as fighting with Claudine. The thrill of his offer had already started to fade; she could see the payments he would demand. 'No, get someone else.'

'Your contract with the *Courier* is almost up. What are you going to do for a work visa?'

She squinted at him, shook her head. 'I shouldn't be surprised, but I am. How do you know about that?'

'I have my sources. Cleo – take the jobs, on the board and as managing editor. You'll have a visa to stay as long as you like in America – that's what you want, isn't it?'

'Where will you be – in London?'

'I'll come over regularly –'

'How regularly?'

He laid his last card on the table, a blank one. 'As often as you want me to.'

At least he hasn't pleaded with me: she would have found that humiliating, for both of them. She turned away, walked slowly back along the path. Her legs felt unsteady, she could feel the gravel, like a dump of old discarded teeth, biting into her feet through the thin soles of her shoes. She had faced hard decisions before: to go to London, to become his mistress, to leave him ... sections of her road had been very smooth and comfortable, but she had always had to make that first step as she had begun each new lap. She was beginning to think that life was made up of laps, that it was a circular road that led to no horizon.

'How is Emma?'

He was not prepared for that question. 'Emma? She's all right – I think. She still doesn't talk to me. If she wasn't all right, I suppose I'd hear.'

'So you're still not divorced?' She didn't wait for his answer but walked on ahead of him. 'Jack, I don't think you and I could start over again. We couldn't pick up where things were before. . . . You know what I mean. Too much water has flowed under the bridge.'

'You used to go out of your way not to use clichés.'

'I'm older now. You come to realize that sometimes they say it better than all the original phrases can.'

He sighed, another cliché. 'All right, as I said, no strings. But take the job. I don't like to see someone with your talent wasted.'

'Let me sleep on it. I'll call you tomorrow.'

They walked back up to the house, watched from the terrace by Alain. He was experiencing his own spasm of cliché: he was burning with jealousy. He looked along the terrace and saw his mother watching the couple coming up the path and suddenly he hated her. She was part of the plot if not the originator of it. She had told him that Cruze was now a part-owner of the *Courier*.

He limped quickly along the terrace, almost grabbed Cleo's hand as she came up the steps. 'We're going in for lunch.'

He dragged her across the terrace. 'Alain, you're hurting my hand!'

He let her go, slowed down. 'For Christ's sake, what have you been talking about? Jesus, he appears out of nowhere, takes you over as if nothing had happened –'

'Shut up, Alain.'

386

'Was he trying to make up for what he tried to do that night in London? Did he say he was sorry for trying to kill you?'

'He told me that four years ago, that same night.'

She pulled him into a side room as Claudine and Jack came in off the terrace; it was the billiards room. She saw Claudine glance into the room at them, pause just a moment, then turn back to Jack and walk on. She began to get a glimpse of what would face her if she accepted Jack's offer on the *Courier*. The Roux forces were lining up against her, though they would not be on the same side. Dad must feel like this back home in the Party, she thought; and wished he were here to give her advice. Political advice; not parental, at which he would probably be hugely incompetent.

'Alain, don't get possessive –'

'Who said I was?' He was genuinely shocked; he had looked only at her and not at himself. Even conquering armies see themselves as liberators of some sort.

'Jack was talking to me about business.'

'Has he offered you a job back in London? Or is he going to give you the *Courier*?'

She looked around the billiards room. 'I should take one of those cues down off the rack and belt you over the head with it. Let's go into lunch.'

Luncheon, as Claudine insisted on calling it, was a sit-down affair, though there were twenty guests. She did not believe in balancing a plate on her lap; that was for jugglers and peasants in refugee camps. Because she and Alain were the last to sit down, Cleo found herself sitting next to Roger and opposite Jack. Feeling Alain still simmering on her right, she turned to Roger, almost glad of him.

'I wish you'd come down to Washington some time,' he said. 'I could show you around. We're not overworked at the Pentagon.'

'I'd rather Mrs Brisson showed me around. I'd like the women's view on Washington.' She smiled across the table at Louise, trying to tell her she had nothing to fear. 'And on the Pentagon, too.'

387

Louise was polite, but she was not going to help put temptation in her husband's path. At long last her forbearance was wearing thin. Attrition had never been a major tactic in American warfare, but Roger had (unwittingly, she was prepared to concede) raised it to a fine art. It had taken twenty-five years, but the war was coming to an end. She would be the loser, but she was going to lose with dignity.

'The Pentagon doesn't recognize women,' she said.

'Just like the *Courier*,' said Cleo.

'You should repeat that to Claudine,' said Roger, in high good humour amongst the ladies. 'She has the illusion that she *is* the *Courier*.'

'Do you think a newspaper is the true image of its publisher, Lord Cruze?' said Alain.

Jack smiled, sure now that the younger man was no real rival. He had studied Cleo well enough when they had been lovers, he knew when she showed real interest in a man. He had seen it only once, with Tom Border. Who, his sources told him, was safely out of the way now, married and living in Paris.

'Sometimes, not always. I don't see any of my papers back in Britain as an image of me.'

'Is that true, Cleo?' Alain was prepared to cross swords with her or Cruze, though he would be handicapped by more than just his limp.

She could see he might make a fool of himself, which, for his sake, she did not want. 'A cracked image. Would you agree with that, Lord Cruze?'

He saw that she was being diplomatic and he smiled, as proud of her as he had been in the good old days. 'I'll accept that.'

After lunch he sought out Claudine. He did not believe in wasting time; a Sunday without some business being done was a sterile day. The Anglican minister who had conducted the services at the church in Chalfont St Aidan had a lot to answer for: he had preached too strongly on the work ethic. Claudine, on the other hand, believed that to work too hard was a sin. Rich Catholics have a separate faith.

'Jack, leave it till tomorrow –'

'I've got a full day tomorrow. Let's talk now.' Which he proceeded to do without her permission. '... So that's what I want. I'll have Jerry Kibler put it officially to the board this week.'

'There's no board meeting this week. We don't meet till the fifteenth of next month.'

'I want a board meeting this week, preferably no later than Wednesday. You Americans are always accusing us Brits of not getting off our bums. Let's see a little quick action on this side of the Atlantic.'

'Try not to be rude, Jack.'

'You're rude all the time, Claudine. You just don't use rude words.'

'I wish I saw you more often. I'd cut you down slice by slice to your boot-tops.'

'We'll see. You're going to be seeing more of me from now on. Well, you've heard what I want. What do you say?'

They were in her study, one of the smaller rooms of the great house. It was a woman's room: none of your heavy desks and leather chairs and panelled walls. The walls were hung with pale pink and grey silk, her desk was one of Riesener's later pieces, the chairs were by Sené; it had not escaped her that she had surrounded herself with furniture from the last great period before the French Revolution. But she would never lose her own head; the guillotine was a piece of furniture she would have used for her own ends if necessary.

'I can't stop you putting Miss Spearfield on the board, that's your prerogative. But as long as I'm publisher of the *Courier*, there'll be no managing editor over Mr Lintas. He would walk out.'

'She wouldn't be *over* him. But from what I see of the paper, if Lintas walked out it wouldn't be any great loss.'

'He edits a very respected newspaper.'

'The *Observer* in London is even more respected, but it's losing money. I haven't bought into the *Courier* to watch it go on dying. It'll be stone dead in five years, Claudine, if you don't change it.'

389

'You want something like your dreadful *Examiner*.'

He grinned. 'It doesn't have to be like the *Examiner*. But the way it is, it makes the *Congressional Record* look like lively reading. I think Cleo could help change that image.'

She shook her head, in another of her obdurate moods. 'Not as managing editor. I won't allow that title.'

'As what then?'

'The furthest I would go would be to create the position of associate editor, junior to Jake Lintas. And he will have the final say.'

'Whom are you against? Me or Cleo?'

'Both of you,' she said with French candour.

'Well, we know where we stand.' He got up, offered her his arm as they went out of the study. 'You and I shouldn't fight Claudine. Together, we could set up our own dynasty.'

'That would necessitate our going to bed. I don't think we could ever agree who should be on top.'

'Who's being rude now?'

3

Monday morning Cleo rang P.J. at *International*. 'P.J., you've dropped some hints that I might come to work for your magazine –'

'Darling, has the *Courier* fired you? Those goddam male chauvinists over there – I've heard about them –'

'No, I haven't been fired. I just wondered if a job was still going with you.'

'Darling, there's nothing I'd like better than to have you here with us. But Francine gave us the word only last week – we're cutting back. We've been taken over, didn't you know? One of those huge conglomerates with a name that makes them sound like they belong to the UN. They have ordered rationalization, *love* that word –'

It seemed that everyone was being taken over. 'Thanks, P.J. How's your love life?'

'Anything but rational. The man is still going home each weekend to his wife and I'm still nursing my guilt. How's yours? I've seen you around several times with that divine Alain Roux.'

'We're just good friends.' Or were.

'That's what I tell my man. I wish to hell I could tell him something else.'

Cleo hung up, sat at her desk in the *Courier's* newsroom. She looked around it, remarked once again its shabbiness compared to the bright spick-and-span atmosphere she remembered from the *Examiner*. It was like comparing the New York subway with the London underground, though she had read lately that the London system had begun to look dirty and rundown. If she took over here as managing editor she would have the room smartened up as one of her first priorities, as a first sign that the paper itself was going to be smartened up.

Coming back from Souillac last night, under pressure from his questioning, she had told Alain about Jack's offer. 'I haven't made up my mind yet –'

He drove in silence for a while. He no longer had the Aston-Martin and now drove a dark blue Volvo; she had noticed a certain conservatism creeping into him in other small ways. She did not mind. She knew that in everyone, including herself, there was a conservative struggling to vote. Her father, the radical, had told her that.

'It won't work, Cleo,' Alain said at last, concentrating as he took the car onto Route 3 for the run in to Manhattan. The Sunday evening traffic was thick but moving steadily, the cars full of people who had the glazed look of those who had just had their parole revoked. 'Jake Lintas would undermine you every chance he got. There are at least a dozen guys who have worked in the news-room over twenty years. How do you think they'll respond to a woman, a comparative Jane-come-lately and a foreigner to boot, coming in over them?'

'A foreigner to boot – that sounds just like *Courier* editorial writing. That's one thing I'll change if I take the job.'

'There'll be a lot of other things changed, too. You and me, for instance.' He was still staring straight ahead.

'Probably.' She tried not to sound indifferent. She still liked him, but he could not expect any more of her than that.

'I thought we were heading somewhere. You and me, I mean.'

'Why did you think that?' She might as well have him bring it out in the open, though she had already made her guess.

'Well, we've been going out together regularly. Not as much as I'd like, but enough. We've been going to bed. You haven't been doing that with anyone else.' Then he did look at her. 'Have you?'

'If you weren't driving, I'd belt you over the head for that. No, I haven't. You've been to bed with other girls, some of them regularly, I'll bet.'

'I wasn't in love with those girls.'

'Oh, stone the crows!' The expression slipped out, one of her father's old clichés to prove he was a dinki-di Aussie to the voters. But here she was being a foreigner to boot. 'I've never once said I was in love with you. So what's different about my going to bed with you and you going to bed with all those girls you weren't in love with? You're as bad as Jake Lintas and all those twenty-year men on the paper – one rule for you and another for the ladies. You make me sick!'

'Okay, I'm guilty of the double standard. I'm wrong and I'll admit it. But if you take the job, who gets first call on you? Me or Cruze? He's sure as hell not giving you the job because he thinks you're some sort of miracle worker, that you can put the *Courier* back on its feet.'

She could see that his anger was making him say things that he might later regret; but that didn't lessen her own anger. 'I'll tell you who gets first call on me – *me!* I've told him that and now I'm telling you. And as for the *Courier*, there's no one else in sight, including you, who's likely to get it back on its feet! Pull up, I want to get out!'

'We're in the Lincoln Tunnel, for Christ's sake!'

So they sat there at a distance from each other, steaming

392

in the tinfoil of their anger. He dropped her outside her apartment, curtly said goodnight and drove off with a screech of tyres. She stood in the almost-dark street watching him, angry at him but now sorry for him. She turned and saw Mr Kugel standing in the doorway of his store. Sausages hung behind him like fossilized blossoms, an aroma of spices floated out but gave up against the gritty air of Second Avenue. But Mr Kugel had a dolorous humour, he would greet Armageddon with a wry grin and sell salami-on-rye to the camp followers.

'A lovers' tiff, Miss Spearfield? Never worry. The guy always comes back. So the wife tells me.'

'I just sent him packing, Mr Kugel. Why should I want him to come back? How's the apple strudel?'

'Stale. The cherry is fresher. There, a big slice. Never eat your heart out over a man, that's what the wife says. Eat a big meal instead.'

She had gone up to her apartment, eaten the extra large slice of cherry strudel, lain awake half the night with indigestion, got up this morning and come to the office, called P.J., and now here she was making up her mind whether to step off yet another cliff. She picked up the phone and called the Pierre.

'Jack, I'll have dinner with you tonight.'

'Good. We'll have it up here in my suite –'

With the bedroom right off the living-room … 'No, Jack. I know a restaurant where they serve good sensible English cooking. The Tower of London – got that? I'll meet you there at eight.'

'I don't want to talk in a restaurant –' But she had hung up on him.

She hadn't been to the restaurant since the killing of Apollo and Sirio. When she walked in the head waiter recognized her and quickly glanced over his shoulder, as if looking for some more of his guests who were about to be bumped off. She gave him her most dazzling smile, walked past him and down to the table where Jack was already seated. He rose, took her hand and kissed her on the cheek. We might be

393

father and daughter having dinner together, she thought. But knew that if the same thought had occurred to him, it would have been wiped out at once.

'I hate talking business in a public place –'

'Relax, Jack. The good thing about this is that the tables aren't cramped together. And another thing – most Americans in restaurants talk loudly. They won't hear our discreet Commonwealth voices.'

'I've got the feeling you're going to take the mickey out of me again.'

Her hand got away from her again in another of those instinctive gestures; it pressed his affectionately. 'No, we're the best of friends tonight. I'll enjoy myself better than I did last time I was here.'

'What happened then?'

'I was dining here with two gangsters when they were shot.'

'I read about that.' He shook his head, looked around for more assassins; he was as nervous as the head waiter. 'You're always sticking your neck out.'

She nodded. 'One way or the other.'

He caught her meaning. 'Well, about the *Courier*. If you say yes, you go on the board. But Claudine won't buy you as managing editor. The most she will go for is you as associate editor.'

'That would mean Jake Lintas still ran the paper.'

'I know. You'd just have to be persuasive.'

'That would never work with Mr Lintas, not if I seduced him every night. He'd rather put the paper to bed than me.'

'Must be more wrong with the man than I thought. Well, do you want to give it a go?'

She was given time to think while the head waiter took their order. He didn't know who Jack was, but he recognized an Englishman, though this one looked much more untidy than most of them who came here. Jack ordered the liver and bacon, then looked up from the menu at Cleo.

'What's their bread-and-butter custard like?'

'I never got to taste it. They shot my last host just as I was

394

about to take my first mouthful.' She looked at the head waiter, who seemed to have gone a little green. 'Lord Cruze is a connoisseur of bread-and-butter custard. It had better be good.'

The head waiter bent his knee as if he were about to be knighted when he heard the title. 'Of course, your lordship.'

He went away and Jack said, 'He sounded like you that first time we met. He's never been closer to the Tower of London than Brooklyn Bridge.'

'Don't laugh. There's a posh Chinese restaurant in London that has all Italian waiters . . . I'll take the job.'

'Good. We'll drink to that. Do they serve English champagne here?'

He was suddenly in a light-hearted mood, throwing off his nervousness with her, and Cleo threw off her own restraint towards him. The rest of the evening passed enjoyably; even the bread-and-butter custard came up to Jack's hopes. They discussed what changes were needed to brighten up the *Courier* and were in agreement on them. Then they left the restaurant, bowed out by the head waiter and the Beefeater doorman as if they were Henry VIII and his current, if temporary, wife.

He had hired a limousine and took her home to Second Avenue. On the way he said, 'How's your father?'

'He tries to sound happy in his letters, but he's not. I think he knows it's all over for him now.'

'Well, it's not all over for you. Some day he may be proud to be known as Cleo Spearfield's father.'

'Maybe. But for his sake, I hope I don't ever hear anyone say it.'

The car pulled up outside the shut and darkened delicatessen. He got out and looked around him. 'You mean you live *here*?'

'Didn't your sources tell you?' She said it without malice.

'All I had was your address. We'll have to get you out of here.'

'Don't rush me, Jack. I'll move in my own good time.' She kissed him on the cheek, glad that she still lived above Kugel's

Deli. He would never try to go to bed with her in such surroundings. He had his snobberies, about rendezvous. 'Thank you for the job. I shan't let you down.'

'Good luck, Cleo. Let's be the best of friends.' He got back into the car, not pushing his own luck at the moment, and was driven away.

Cleo watched him go, then heard the car start up on the other side of the Avenue. She glanced across the street and saw what looked like a Volvo driving away. It was impossible to see who was in it.

FIFTEEN

1

It seemed that Cleo's fortunes on the *Courier* were in the same time slot as those of certain Presidents, though their fortunes were not the same. She had joined the *Courier* on the day Richard Nixon left the White House; she became associate editor of the paper on the day that Jimmy Carter was given the Democratic nomination for President. She did not go up to Madison Square Garden to cover the convention, though she would dearly have loved to; but she knew that Jake Lintas's and the *Courier*'s sympathies were Republican and she did not want to get off on the wrong foot by showing where her own political sympathies might lie. She was not sure where they did lie because she believed that only by being apolitical could a newspaperman or woman be truly objective.

'You weren't objective when you worked for the *Examiner*,' Jack said.

'I was a columnist then, not an editor. I don't want to be a biased one.'

'A biased editor is one who's blind in one eye, Quentin used to say. An objective editor is one who's blind in both. Keep both eyes open, be biassed if you believe in something, and you can't go wrong.'

The day after Cleo took over as associate editor, Alain resigned. Within a week he had closed up his apartment, sold the Volvo and left for Europe. He did not say goodbye to Cleo; indeed, he had not spoken to her since he had brought her home from that Sunday in the country. She was upset because she knew he would be unhappier than she was. She hoped his disappointment in her was inflated and could be let down in Europe by a girl who went to bed regularly and felt no commitment. Like so many women she thought that men got over their rejected love quicker and less painfully than women did. She had her own double standard.

Jake Lintas did not welcome his new associate. A new office, a tiny storeroom that had been converted for her use, was set up for Cleo. It looked out on to the newsroom and she kept the door wide open both for ventilation and to let it be known that she was available for anyone to consult her; at the end of the first day she wondered if she should not shut the door against the Arctic air drifting in from the Eskimos at their typewriters. When she went into the big room next to Jake Lintas's for the conference of editors on the make-up of tomorrow's paper she might just as well have hung herself on the wall as a decoration. But she kept her mouth shut and bided her time.

At the end of the second week she made her first suggestion. She chose to make it to Lintas himself in his office rather than to the editorial conference.

'You can run the paper when I depart,' Jake Lintas said. 'Till then things stay as they are.'

'I'm sorry you feel that way, Mr Lintas.' He had not asked her to call him Jake and she stuck stiffly to the formal. 'I hoped you would be open to a suggestion or two. I don't think my ideas will mean changing the paper's policy too much.'

'Getting rid of Bill Brenner *would* mean a change of policy, at least to most of our readers. He has been our editorial cartoonist for almost forty years. If you knew anything about American newspapers, you'd know that cartoonists are probably the longest surviving of all of us who work on them.'

'I do know that. But Bill Brenner is still drawing 1930s cartoons – his style is old-fashioned and so's his humour. And he never concedes that we have women readers, that the things he comments on affect them as much as they do men. I think it's time we had someone with more *bite*. There's a

398

girl who does freelance work for the Denver *Post* – '

'A woman cartoonist?' It was as if Cleo had suggested a woman quarterback or, worse, a woman President. 'What makes you think the public would take note of a woman's comment on the political scene? That her stuff would have more bite, as you call it, than Brenner's?'

'You're a bachelor, Mr Lintas. Maybe you haven't come up against a woman's bite. No, I take that back. I'm sure you've had your experiences with Mrs Roux. If she could draw, don't you think her cartoons would have plenty of bite?'

Lintas had no answer to that other than to say, 'There'll be no woman cartoonist or political columnist on this paper while I run it.'

He's medieval, she thought. 'You never read Dorothy Thompson or Rebecca West?' He didn't answer and she stood up. 'I'm not going to give up offering suggestions, Mr Lintas. I'm here to stay.'

She went back to her own office and a little later Hal Rainer wandered in. 'I miss you down at the police shack, Miss Spearfield.'

'Thank you, Mr Rainer. Now cut out the bull. You're the only friend I have around here, Hal. No one comes into this office unless it's pure business. And then they only come in because Jake is tied up and they're in a hurry.'

'It's heavy going, I can see that.'

'Do people know how or why I got the job?' As far as she knew, Jack's name was not known around the office. Unless Alain, out of spite, had spread the word.

'There are rumours,' Hal said, but didn't elaborate. 'You going to stick it out?'

'What's the alternative? How's crime – still paying?'

'Better than newspapers do. You remember your friend Tony Rossano? I got the word in from Kansas City. He's popped up out there and guess what? He's taken over Frank Apollo's territory. He's the front man for the Chicago top Family. Mafia family.'

'So he did set up the Apollo killing?'

'He also set up you and me.'

'Would you like to follow him up? Go out to Kansas City and see what you can make out of him?'

'Jake Lintas and Carl Fishburg would never agree to that. The expense, for one thing – you know what they're like about that. Any day now I'm expecting them to sell all the company cars and put us on bicycles.'

'Leave it with me.'

At the editorial conference that afternoon she waited till the make-up of the paper had been decided, then she said, 'There's a story out in Kansas City that I think Hal Rainer should be sent to cover.' She explained the re-emergence of Tony Rossano and the implications of his new status. 'I think we should run a series on how the Syndicate, or the Families, whatever we like to call them, still go their own way, putting their front men wherever they choose. It makes a mockery of all those crime commissions.'

Jake Lintas said nothing, sitting at the head of the table and looking coldly at her, certain that the lesser executioners around the table would deal with her. One of them, Carl Fishburg, said, 'That's a story for the Kansas City papers, not ours. Forget it.'

'I think it's a national story.' Cleo looked directly at Joe Hamlyn, the national news editor. She knew that he had a wife and four daughters and, by circumstances and subjugation, was less a male chauvinist than any of the others at the table. He was, however, a man who had never been known to rock Jake Lintas's boat. 'What do you think, Joe?'

He looked at Lintas and her heart sank: she knew she was going to get the brush-off she had come to expect. Then surprisingly he said, 'It's a good idea. Let's send Hal out there for a week and see what he can dig up. Every paper in the country but us is running an exposé of some sort. Maybe we can try for a Pulitzer.' He laughed to show everyone it was a joke, but Cleo noticed he was no longer looking at Jake Lintas. 'We haven't won one since the 1950s'.

The editor's boat had indeed been rocked: he looked seasick. 'Prizes aren't the yardstick of a paper's true worth.'

400

'Maybe not,' said Joe Hamlyn, 'but the guys like to win 'em.'

Cleo was doodling on her notepad with the gold pen the St Martin sisters had given her. It was a moment before she realized she had drawn a stout man with a knife sticking out of his back. She screwed up the piece of paper before her pen drew a homburg on the man. She sat forward, glancing at Hamlyn to thank him for his support, then looked directly at Jake Lintas. It was the first time she had seen a crack in that bland, sleek exterior. His boat had not only been rocked, it had run onto rocks.

'Give Hal Rainer a week out there, no more.' He stood up, ending the day's conference; but also ending any further rebellion. 'That's it for today.'

Cleo followed Joe Hamlyn out of the room. 'Joe, could you come into my office for a moment?'

'I have to get my guys started – '

'It will take only a moment.'

She went into her office and sat down behind her desk. He did not sit, but stood with one foot in front of the other, as if about to run, the notes in his hand held out like a relay baton about to be passed on. She smiled at him.

'Relax, Joe. Jake isn't going to have your head, I'll see to that. I'm on the board, remember.'

He tried to look relaxed and succeeded only in looking as if he might fall over. He was a balding, unathletic man who peered out at the world through thick glasses; he no longer had any drive, any ambition, but he had once been a very good reporter. 'Cleo, he's still editor. I don't really know why I spoke up for your idea – '

'Because you know it's a good story, if Hal handles it right. And I'm sure he will. How old are you, Joe?'

'Forty-eight. What's that got to do with it?'

'You've got another ten or twelve years here, maybe more. Between you and me and no one else, I'll be editor of the paper before then. When Jake retires, I intend to take over. You and I and one or two others could make the *Courier* as good as it used to be back in the Twenties. I've looked up old copies in the morgue. It was a good newspaper then, one of the best.'

He sat down, took off his glasses and absent-mindedly cleaned them with his notes. Then he put them back on and looked at her carefully. 'You sound just like my wife, only you think bigger. Are you asking me to be on your side against Jake?'

'No, I don't want the paper divided like that. It would get nowhere if that happened. But I want any ideas I have to be considered on their merits and for you to back them if you think they are any good. I don't want to be ignored because I'm a woman and because you all resent my having been jumped over the top of you. That happens all the time in America. General Eisenhower was the classic example. If it's good enough for men to be promoted that way, it's good enough for a woman.'

'It's not just that. The men see you as the thin end of the wedge of women's lib.'

'Dammit, I'm not a women's libber!' She slapped her desk. 'I support some of the things they want, things we should have had years ago. But I'm not interested in all their petty flag-waving. Burning bras, calling themselves Ms, insisting on non-sexist terms like spokesperson – that's juvenile stuff. I am against the double standard and you men here had better face up to it. The point you all have to accept is something I've already told Jake – I'm here to stay!'

He stared at her through the thick glasses, then he stood up. 'I've never seen you excited before. I'm seeing a new side to you.'

'No, Joe, it's always been there. Not the excitable bit, the standing up for what I think is right. You men just never let yourselves notice it.'

'I feel sorry for Jake.'

'Don't. I've never yet cut the balls off a man.' She had never spoken as crudely as that to him before, but it was the best way of saying it. It sometimes paid not to be a lady. 'If and when Jake goes, I'll be fairer to him than he's been to me.'

Hal Rainer went out to Kansas City and rang Cleo after three days. 'I'll need more time. But there's a story here.'

'Call me at the end of the week and I'll see Jake then. I'll see you get the extra time.'

When she came into the newsroom next afternoon Jake Lintas was waiting at the door of his office. He gestured to her as soon as he saw her come in at the far end of the huge room. Cleo walked down between the long rows of desks, aware at once that everyone had stopped work and was watching her. She felt a sudden apprehension and she thought at once of Jack Cruze. Had something happened to him, was Jake Lintas about to take advantage of it and put her in her place? It was not common knowledge that Jack was a real, if not nominal, stockholder in the *Courier*, but she knew that Jake Lintas knew who had put her on the board and in the room next to his own.

She went into his office and he nodded. 'Shut the door.' She did so, then sat down across from him at his desk. 'The *Kansas City Star* has just called me. Hal Rainer's body has been fished out of the Missouri River. He had two bullets in his head.'

She thought for a moment that she was going to vomit. Then the queasiness passed and she felt faint. She leaned back in her chair and then Jake Lintas did the first considerate thing he had done since she had joined the paper. He pushed his water jug and a glass towards her.

She drank some water, waited till she felt a little better. 'Any details on who killed him?'

'None.'

She waited a little longer, then said, 'We should follow it up. We can't let whoever did it get away with it. He told me yesterday he was on to something.'

'It's the Kansas City police's job. Let them do it.'

'It's the *Courier*'s story, for God's sake! We owe it to Hal – '

'We've lost Hal. I'm not going to let the same thing happen to another of our men.'

'I'll go out there myself – '

'You'll do nothing of the sort. I'm sorry Hal has been

403

murdered – I'll miss him as much as you. I'm not going to risk anyone else from the *Courier*, and that includes you. I'll tell A.P. and the *Star* why he was out there and they can follow it up if they want to. From now on we'll stick to New York and Washington stories. We'll run an obit. on Hal. I'll write it.'

'Has anyone told his wife yet?'

'I thought you could do that. A woman would do it better.'

You bastard. 'Naturally.'

She went out of his office hating him, convinced now that the time could not come soon enough for him to retire or be retired. She went to the personnel office, got Hal Rainer's home address and rang down to the garage for one of the office cars to meet her at the front door. Then she was driven out to Long Island, to a tree-lined street in Great Neck. She told the driver of the car why she was making the journey and he, a young black, sensed she was upset and kept his remarks to a minimum.

The Rainer house was an old one, built before World War One but still in good repair. A big elm stood in the yard at the side and Cleo remembered Hal's telling her that he liked to spend his summer weekends beneath it, reading all the books he could find on the Twenties, a golden decade, as he called it, that he had been too young to know. She rang the front doorbell and a pretty grey-haired woman opened it.

She was smiling and friendly, the sort of trusting woman who opened doors to salesmen, evangelists, muggers and rapists: she still trusted the world. Oh God, thought Cleo; and dealt her a far worse blow than any mugger or rapist could have. Liz Rainer retreated into her home weeping, shaking her head at the one news story she had never wanted to hear.

'I shouldn't be shocked,' she said when she had regained some control of herself. 'I was always telling him to be careful. He knew some dreadful characters, he'd been threatened half a dozen times – '

'I sent him on the story, Mrs Rainer. I'll never forgive

myself for that. I was the one who started this whole chain of events.'

'Hal would never let you say that, if he could hear you. He believed that so long as a reporter was on a story, it was *his* story. Where is his – his body?'

'Still out in Kansas City. We'll bring it home. If you could let me know where you'd like it taken to – I mean, what undertaker – '

Liz Rainer smiled and it struck Cleo that there was something of Hal in the smile. This couple had been very close. 'We call them funeral homes here. Hal used to say that anyone who worked in a funeral home had never known what a real home was.'

Cleo stayed till the Rainers' elder daughter, on a phone call from her mother, came over from Roslyn. Then she left, taking a last look back at the old house and the elm tree that would never throw its shade over Hal Rainer again.

'Back to the office, Miss Spearfield?'

'Please, Henry.' She would work late tonight, putting off going home to the apartment on Second Avenue. She often felt lonely there and, though Hal had never been her closest friend, she knew she would feel lonely tonight. In his own cynical way he had been her only supporter on the *Courier*.

2

Claudine was troubled. She was still adjusting herself to Alain's abrupt departure for Europe when she was given the news of Hal Rainer's murder. Then, a little later, that man Carter was elected President. To cap it all Louise had left Roger in Washington and moved back to their home at Sands Point. She was not accustomed to her well-ordered mind being jolted off its tracks so often in such a short period. A crisis, preferably a small one, a year was enough test for anyone.

Uninvited, a breach of manners she would never expect anyone to inflict on her, she went out to see Louise. The dark

405

blue Rolls-Royce went over the Queensboro Bridge and out along Queens Boulevard to pick up the Long Island Expressway. Her chauffeur, a black man as old as herself, drove cautiously; like his mistress, he was not a regular traveller on Long Island. Claudine sat upright in the back and glanced out at the shabby stores and apartment buildings in Long Island City; but her imagination did not run to impressions of what lay behind the windows and walls that bordered the streets through which she was being driven. She was travelling through a foreign country only a few miles from her home; she knew that most of the population had to struggle to live and she was generous with her donations to charities, but all her life she had been insulated against the reality of other people's deprivation. She looked at people standing at bus queues, staring resentfully at her as she was driven past them, and she knew that neither she nor they would ever understand each other. She was not heartless, just rich.

Roger and Louise's house had been built at the beginning of the century by Louise's grandfather. Teddy Roosevelt and his family had come across here from Sagamore Hill for tea on Sunday afternoons; it suggested a world of slower motion than today's. It was a big white-painted timber house that sat on a slope looking out towards the Sound; it reminded Claudine of photographs of stout matrons of the period who looked as if they could never rise from the chairs in which they lolled. It had a dignity of its own and she always looked for that in houses as well as people.

Louise was not surprised to see her sister-in-law. 'I wondered how long it would take you to come out here.'

There was an independent note in Louise's voice that surprised Claudine. 'I did wait to be invited, but nothing was forthcoming.'

'Forthcoming? I must see in future that all my invitations are forthgoing. That is, when I send them.'

'Are you telling me this is none of my business, you and Roger separating?'

'Well, is it, Claudine?'

She led the way into a sitting-room that, to Claudine's eye, looked like a junk store about to have a jumble sale. She wondered how a person could live in such disorder. It was no wonder Louise's life was such a mess.

'I came to help, Louise, not to interfere.' It was the same thing, since her helping meant her taking over.

'How can you help? Would you like tea or coffee or what?'

'Tea. Perhaps I can bring Roger to his senses. I presume the blame is his and not yours?'

'What do you think?' There was a calm resignation about Louise that Claudine had not expected; she had come anticipating tears and hand-wringing. Perhaps even the hurling of some of the bric-à-brac. 'He's always had his affairs, I've known of them for years. But he never flaunted his women, not like he is now.'

'I don't believe he would *flaunt* them. He has more discretion and breeding than that.'

'Oh Claudine –' It was the first time in her life Louise had ever sounded patronizing; it shocked even herself that she should sound that way towards Claudine of all people. 'The world has changed. Shacking up is a way of life now.'

'Are you trying to tell me that Roger is – is shacking up with some woman?'

'He might just as well be. He spends every weekend with her. Maybe every night with her, now that I've left him. Her name is Mary Tripp. She's a Congresswoman.'

'Does she have a husband?' As if having a spouse was a necessary qualification for being a Member of Congress. 'Where is he?'

Louise shrugged. 'Not in Washington, certainly. Ah, here is the tea.'

Claudine smiled at the old black woman who had brought in the tray. 'Hello, Lena. You're looking well.'

'It's very peaceful out here, Miz Roux.' Lena Jinks had worked for the family since she had come to them as a girl straight out of school. For the past ten years she had been part-caretaker, part-housekeeper here at Sands Point. 'I never want to come back to Manhattan to live. I dunno how you still live there, all that noise and stuff.'

'I'm still young, Lena.' The two old ladies smiled at each other. 'Take care of yourself.'

Lena shuffled out of the room and Louise said, 'She's a comfort to have around. Not to talk to, just to have her here in the house.'

Claudine all at once felt sorry for her sister-in-law, reduced to needing the presence of an old servant as comfort. 'I think you'd do better to get away from here, go somewhere you can have distraction. Paris, for instance.'

Louise had poured tea for Claudine, but was having a gin and tonic herself. 'I've been thinking of shooting Roger. That would be a distraction.'

'That sort of thing is no solution at all.' Claudine did not take the threat seriously. It was not civilized, shooting was something done by mobsters out in Kansas City.

They sat there in the museum of a room looking out at the autumn light reflected from the waters of the Sound. Gulls glimmered in the air like drifting stars and a sail-boat sliced the breeze with a white scythe. A small dry kernel was forming in Claudine's breast, as if her life itself was shrinking, putting itself away inside her just as Louise had put away in this room the reminders of the nomadic life she had led.

'Why did Alain go off so suddenly?' said Louise, sipping her gin, forgetting about murder.

'I'm not sure. He never was one to confide in me,' Claudine admitted. She had never exchanged any intimacies with Louise, but today she felt she owed her one or two. Otherwise she was not going to learn enough about the trouble with Roger and thus be able to help. 'It has something to do with Cleo Spearfield.'

'He is sweet on her, one could see that. Have they broken up?'

'I never really understood their relationship. But I do believe he wanted to marry her.'

'Would you have accepted that?'

'No.' It was safe to say it, now the danger had passed.

'Did she want to marry him? No, obviously not, otherwise

he wouldn't have gone off to Paris. Perhaps I should go over there and keep an eye on him. Comfort him.'

'I think that would be a very good idea,' said Claudine, though she could not imagine Louise with a watchful eye. She had been blind for so long towards Roger, or at least turned her gaze away. 'I'll have Mr Nevin at our Paris bureau look for an apartment for you.'

'Perhaps I could move in with Alain.'

'You'll do no such thing!' What had got into Louise? 'I'll see Mr Nevin gets you a good apartment –'

'Don't organize me, Claudine. I'll go in my own good time and in my own way.' She put down her empty glass. 'I'm not going to donate Roger to that Congresswoman, like some campaign contribution.'

This Louise was a stranger. Abruptly the talk of shooting looked real. 'You're not going to do something foolish?'

'What's foolish?' Louise grinned slyly, as a madwoman might; but Claudine had only seen actresses playing mad-women. She was uncertain whether Louise was acting or not. 'I think Roger is the one who's being foolish.'

'Stupid is the word I'd use. I'll tell him so.'

'No!' Louise stood up quickly and for a moment Claudine thought she was going to throw a fit, she looked so angry and distraught. 'For Christ's sake, Claudine, stay out of our lives! Stop being the fucking *Empress*!'

The language hit Claudine as hard as the dismissal. She pulled on her gloves, gathered up her handbag and stood up. She knew how to beat a retreat, though she had never had to do it before. 'I shall wait for you to call me when your language and your mood are more temperate.'

'Oh shit,' said Louise intemperately. 'Why didn't you say it in French? It would have sounded less pompous.'

Claudine sailed out of the house, looking no less graceful than the yacht out on the Sound, though she felt momentarily rudderless. She was fortunate to have her chauffeur: he pointed the car, if nothing else, in the right direction.

Over that winter events brewed across the world; life is a kitchen where something is always simmering, cooking or burning. So said the *Courier*'s cooking columnist, lost for a recipe and turning philosophical. Cleo, in New York with her own problems, did not know how the widely-spread ingredients were slowly being mixed together.

One day Bill Puskas stopped her as they were coming out of the editorial conference. 'That kid Hurlstone is waiting outside to see you.'

'Hurlstone? Who's he?'

'The spotty-faced kid you used to get those pix of Frank Apollo that day up in Gracie Park. He's been plaguing me ever since with his candid camera stuff – he won't believe we don't run that sort of thing. He's also got no idea what's news.'

'What's he want with me?'

'I dunno. Maybe he thinks he can by-pass me.'

'I shan't do that. Send him in and I'll get rid of him for good.'

George Hurlstone didn't appear to have changed; perhaps he was a little plainer, a little thinner, perhaps the acne had bored deeper. He looked both tentative and aggressive, a rabbit that had suddenly found itself with fangs. He stood just inside Cleo's doorway, hung with cameras like a Kodak porter, a large envelope held in one hand.

'I been getting nowhere with your picture editor, Miss Spearfield, he just keeps giving me the brush-off all the time, everything I bring him –'

'Not just you, Mr Hurlstone. Mr Puskas has I don't know how many pictures submitted to him every day. We have our own photographers, the agencies, freelancers like yourself –'

'I did you a favour once, Miss Spearfield –'

'You were paid for it. You got the going rate, as I remember it.'

'Well, I'm gonna do you another one.'

'Another what?' She was instantly suspicious, she could see the sabre-teeth coming down out of the rabbit's mouth.

'Another favour.' He took a ten by eight photograph out of the envelope and dropped it on Cleo's desk. 'I been down in Washington. You know who that is? The price this time is gonna be well and truly above the going rate, you know?'

Roger Brisson was sitting at a table with a blonde woman in her mid-thirties; she was wearing a low-cut dress and Roger's right hand looked as if he were finger-testing the depth of her cleavage. She was leaning forward as if to help him; their smiles were salacious, almost ugly. It was a good photograph, the technical standard excellent. It was news, too. Or would be in certain publications.

Cleo looked up. 'What's the rate?'

'A thousand dollars.' The fangs showed, though Cleo guessed the hindquarters were trembling.

Cleo sat for a moment looking at the photograph. 'Who's the lady?'

'Representative Tripp, from California. She's a Republican, I think.'

'She would have to be,' said Cleo, but it was really no moment for a joke and Hurlstone missed it anyway. She continued to look at the photo, then she took out her personal cheque book and wrote out a cheque for one thousand dollars. She held out her hand. 'Everything, Mr Hurlstone. The negative, the lot.'

'I haven't got it with me – there's other stuff on it I need –'

'Come back when you have it. No negative, no money.'

'I could sell it to another paper. The *National Enquirer* –'

'Try selling it to anyone else and I'll see the Guild about you, have you barred from every newspaper, respectable one, that is, in the country.'

Hurlstone hesitated, then reached into his camera-bag and took out a batch of negatives. Cleo checked them, then handed him the cheque.

'Don't ever try that with me again, Mr Hurlstone. If you do, I'll let Frank Apollo's friends out in Kansas City know who took that picture of him here in New York, the one that set his killers on him.'

'Jesus Christ! You mean you – ?'

411

'Set him up?' She shook her head. 'Not me, Mr Hurlstone. But someone must have seen that picture ...' It was a bluff, but George Hurlstone was suddenly toothless, was now a frightened rabbit easily cowed. 'Don't splurge that thousand dollars. You may need it some day for an emergency. Good-bye and don't ever come in here again. And stay away from General Brisson.'

Hurlstone fled, rabbit-quick, and Cleo sat gazing at Roger being middle-aged and stupid. She felt angry at him and sorry for Louise; she had recognized the blind love that Louise had for her husband. But above all she felt a certain disgust with herself. She hadn't bought the picture and negatives to protect Roger; she could have done that with the *Courier*'s money, though it would have meant taking Bill Puskas into her confidence. She had paid out her own money for her own ends, though she was not sure what those ends would eventually be.

Conscience pricked her. Should she send the picture, with no covering note, to Roger to warn him of his foolishness? Then she put the thought and her conscience aside; she put the photo and negatives into the envelope Hurlstone had left on her desk. She felt that she had just disarmed Hurlstone only to find that the gun was even more dangerous in her own hands.

When she went home that evening to Second Avenue she put the envelope away beneath her underwear in a drawer. She had once saved her first love letters, from the boy from Riverview, in the same way. She had not, however, been thinking of possible blackmail in those days; there was not much blackmail material in a letter that compared love-making to a two-man rugby scrum. She was not consciously thinking of extortion now, but she had to prepare her de-fences. She had become aware how vulnerable she was now that she was in the middle of Brisson territory.

A week later there was a board meeting. The board-room was one of two rooms in the *Courier* building that had not been allowed to deteriorate: the panelled walls were oiled regularly, the long table polished weekly, the upholstery of the heavy chairs never allowed to become shabby. It was Claudine's throne room and everyone knew better than to allow patches in the seat of power. The other well-preserved room was the publisher's office, which Claudine rarely used.

At all the board meetings she had attended Cleo had sat at the bottom of the table and kept her ears open and her mouth mostly shut. She was still learning about finance, but she had gained a good knowledge of administration; editorial policy was rarely discussed in this room. She had one friend on the board, Jerry Kibler, and a half-friend, Stephen Jensen, who gave her a warm smile before each meeting opened. But it looked more like a personal approach, the wink of a man suggesting dinner afterwards, and she always gave him a cool, wary smile in return. She had the feeling, however, that he appreciated what influence she had been able to use on the paper.

She had seen Claudine only at these meetings since she had become associate editor. Claudine had been cool and distant, an elegant iceberg on the horizon; she had somehow managed to convey the impression that the board table was the size of a county. Cleo had sat quietly, prepared to let the older woman make the first move.

The meeting was about to close. 'Any further business?' said Claudine.

'Yes,' said Jerry Kibler. He had established his place half-way up the table, opposite Stephen Jensen; new money looking directly at old money, as Cleo had remarked to herself. He, like Cleo, had played the game softly so far, but now he looked as if he was about to bang a drum. 'We think it is time the paper itself underwent some refurbishing.'

Cleo had come to note that Jerry occasionally used such phrases; to her it always sounded like the vocabulary of someone whose education had been delayed and who was trying to make up for lost time. She saw Stephen Jensen, who had probably been born already educated, barely hide a smile.

'We?' said Claudine, looking first at Jerry, then down the table at Cleo.

'The people I represent,' said Jerry and Cleo wondered why Jack had asked the banker, and not herself, to bring up the matter. Then, looking up the table at Claudine, she saw the wisdom of Jack's move. He was leaving her to fight the battles in the newsroom, while Jerry fought with Claudine and the board. 'Advertising space has dropped still further. It's not going to improve unless the paper itself is improved.'

'Hear, hear,' said Stephen Jensen unexpectedly, and smiled at Cleo. 'Have you any ideas, Cleo?'

'I have one,' said Jerry, not giving up the floor. 'Retire the present editor, Mr Lintas.'

'Is that what – the people you represent have in mind?' said Claudine, looking at Cleo rather than at Jerry.

'Yes,' said Jerry, still holding the floor. When he was at the board table there was no sign of the giggle that handicapped him at the dinner table. He looked ready to call the tune, or anyway twenty-two per cent of it. 'There's something else we have in mind. That Miss Spearfield take over the editor's chair.'

'I thought you might have that in mind,' said Claudine, who could have started a library of the minds she had read.

Cleo sat quiet. Jack had said nothing to her of this move, though she had always known it would come some day. It was like him to spring it on her through Jerry. He had been meticulous about the distance he had kept between them, as if he were going out of his way to show her that, though no longer lovers, they could be the best of friends.

Claudine went on, 'Mr Lintas still has two years to go before our compulsory retiring age.'

'I didn't think we had a compulsory retiring age for editors,' said Stephen Jensen. 'I've had the impression Jake Lintas had been with the paper since your great-grandfather bought it.'

Claudine ignored his sarcasm. 'The retiring clause is there in the books. But we've never applied it if the man has been doing a good job.'

'Which Jake Lintas hasn't been doing,' said Jerry. 'Not in today's terms.'

One of the other directors looked at Cleo. His name was Beaton, he owned seven per cent of the stock, he was Claudine's age and he was in her camp. 'What do you think of Mr Lintas?'

'I wear two hats in this corporation,' said Cleo carefully. 'None of you does that. I'll put them both on now. I agree with Jerry. Jake Lintas may once have been a good editor, but he's twenty years out of date now. We need someone else in his chair.'

'Yourself?' said Beaton.

'If you vote for me, yes. But we definitely need *someone*, otherwise it won't be long before we're meeting here to wind up the paper.'

'You think you could do the job?' said Beaton.

'Yes.' She knew that she could, though she also knew that there would be major problems, not least the matter of her sex. There were several women publishers throughout the United States, but no major city newspaper had a woman editor.

'You show a lot of confidence,' said Claudine, who had learned the value of it. 'But I don't think our other editors will accept a woman over them.'

'They can always look for jobs elsewhere,' said Stephen Jensen. 'If they can find them.'

'I think you should be backing Cleo, Mrs Roux,' said Jerry Kibler. 'There is a lot of criticism about the lack of opportunity for women in business. You as a woman should be delighted to have someone as competent as Cleo to take over as editor.'

Claudine smiled at Kibler's naïveté. Whatever gave him the idea that she divided the world into male and female? It was a matter of the survival of the fittest, preferably the most powerful and the richest. Cleo had neither riches nor power and Claudine was reluctant to give her any of the latter. But she was pragmatic, a word she had never known when she was Cleo's age.

'Perhaps Cleo is our answer to Rupert Murdoch,' said Jensen. 'An Australian to fight an Australian.'

415

Claudine ignored that, horrified by the idea that Cleo might try to make the *Courier* into a morning edition of the *Post*. 'I'll talk to Jake Lintas. He may be prepared to resign if he knows he no longer has the confidence of some of the directors.'

'We'll give him a golden handshake,' said Jensen. 'If we can dig up the cash.'

He's becoming impossible, thought Claudine, ignoring Jensen again. She suddenly had the same drying-up feeling she had experienced out at Sands Point: she was losing control of things. 'I'll talk to him and we'll have another meeting on Friday. This meeting is now closed. Cleo, will you have luncheon with me?'

Cleo saw Jerry Kibler give her an almost imperceptible nod. *It's your battle now*, it said. She looked up the table at Claudine. 'It will be a pleasure, Mrs Roux.'

Claudine took her to the Colony Club on Park Avenue at sixty-second Street. The big blue flag above the entrance whipped back and forth in the wind and Cleo, glancing up at it as they got out of Claudine's Rolls-Royce, wondered if the atmosphere at the luncheon table would be as disturbed.

In her on-again, off-again studies of American social history, Cleo had learned that the club had once been New York society women's answer to the exclusive men's clubs. It no longer had the grand exclusiveness it had once had; in its earliest days it had once been reckless enough to admit an actress or two as members, but they had been ladies of such high standing as Ethel Barrymore and Maude Adams; a musical comedy star would not even have been allowed to use the bathroom if she had been carried in from the street with a bursting bladder. These days younger women joined other clubs such as the Cosmopolitan, but the Colony's stuffiness somehow suited a woman who was publisher of the *Courier*, even if it did not fit Claudine personally.

'There's nothing worse than an aviary of chattering women at their birdseed,' said Claudine, looking around the room at the well-dressed women, 'but here at this club there is a nice sense of security. It is very reassuring to come here occasionally.'

'Do you need reassuring?' said Cleo.

'No. I thought *you* might. You are amongst women who feel very secure because of their position. If you are going to be editor of the *Courier*, these are the women you will be talking to.'

Not if I have my way, Cleo thought. 'I don't mean to be rude, Mrs Roux, but isn't this club something like a female equivalent of the House of Lords in Britain? A lot of hereditary titles that have no influence at all. There's Mrs Fairman over there –' She nodded discreetly across the room at a white-haired woman presiding at a window table. 'I recognize her from pictures on our social pages. She's the wife of a banker, one of our biggest. I don't think she would have two cents' influence outside her own home.'

'Mrs Fairman owns sixty per cent of the stock in that particular bank,' said Claudine. 'When her husband goes home he bends his knee when he enters the front door – if he has any sense.'

'Perhaps so. But Mrs Fairman will still buy only one copy of the *Courier*. I want her bank's employees, the five hundred or a thousand or whatever, to buy our paper and not the *Times* or the *News*.'

'I can't object to your ideas for the paper because I don't know what they are. I do object to your becoming editor because I don't think you should be thrown into the deep end so soon.'

'When a ship is sinking, Mrs Roux, there is no shallow end.'

Claudine smiled, safe on dry land, secure in the Colony Club. She knew the girl was right, but she was not going to go off the deep end and agree with her at once. Instead she said, 'I hope eventually you will not try to emulate Mr Murdoch on the *Post* and buy me out.'

'The columnists will mention my name with Rupert's because we're both Australians. I'll ignore that. I didn't come to New York to be in his shadow.' Not now, when she was

417

about to step out into the bright sunshine again. 'His is an afternoon paper and ours is a morning one. I don't see us as competitors.'

'I think you'll always be a competitor,' said Claudine, taking up a spoonful of the salmon mousse. 'What do you hear from Alain?'

Does she think I'm going to compete against him somehow? 'Nothing. What do you?'

'He seems to be enjoying Paris. He has met up with your friend Mr Border. Do you ever hear from *him*?'

'Never.' It was her turn to change the subject: 'I'm having dinner with Lord Cruze this evening. He gets in from London this afternoon. Shall I tell him you're talking to Jake Lintas?'

'You may as well. Are you and Jack back on good terms?'

'Is that Colony Club for, Are we sleeping together again? No, we're not. It is still a business arrangement.'

She had begun to feel the urge again for sex, but she was giving no encouragement to Jack, still afraid of the demands that would follow. There was plenty of sex available, but she could not bring herself to think of one-night stands. She had gone out one lonely evening and visited several of the better-known singles bars and felt she might have been visiting a cattle market where the bulls and cows did their own bidding. She had gone home convinced there was more Irish puritanism in her than she had admitted. Brigid Spearfield, had she known, would have said another chorus of Hail Marys in thanks.

'I'll talk to Lord Cruze myself tomorrow,' said Claudine. 'He, I suppose, will decide how soon he wants you in as editor. You owe him a lot, don't you?'

'We all have our debts. Even those of us who inherit what we have.'

'I don't think I shall put you up for membership here. I think you may feel more at home in one of the lesser clubs.'

418

4

When Tom Border, who paid a weekly visit to the *Courier*'s Paris bureau to read the paper, was told by Chuck Nevin of Hal Rainer's murder in Kansas City he was greatly upset. He had never been a close friend of Hal's, but he had been closer to him than to anyone else on the paper. Hal had been his mentor when he had joined the *Courier*, though they had never worked on police rounds together; it had been a case of the old-timer out-of-towner helping the newly-arrived feel at home. Hal had been the sort of newspaperman Tom admired, the solid, hard-working reporter who kept his integrity and believed, under all his cynicism, that he was working for the public good. His death made Tom feel no better than he had felt for the past year.

Though they were still married, he and Simone were only living together. They made love and they went to cinemas and entertained friends, but Tom had come to feel, with an unsettling sense of guilt, that it was all only temporary; nothing, not even the marriage vows, really bound them. He blamed himself; Simone was blameless. She was everything a loving wife should be; but she was French and in France. She had never really been an adventurer: she had explored the world, but always on an Air France schedule. She did not want to drift, that led nowhere. They should buy an apartment here in Paris, settle down, start a family, build their future so that in old age they would be secure and comfortable. Had he ever seen a really happy *old* bohemian?

'*Chérie*, I'm not a bohemian, for crissake! I just don't want to be tied down to the one place all my life, that's all. And I'm a long way from being *old*.'

'I didn't say you were.' Then she said in French, 'Let us speak French. I can argue better then.'

That would be the end of him in the argument. His French had improved in the time they had been living in Paris, but when he used it in public the café waiters and the storekeepers winced and did not stop to listen to him. The French think their language is the most beautiful and precise of all

419

languages and they do not like foreigners abusing it. They would prefer the rest of the world to be as dumb as they often think the rest of the world is.

'We'll have to move out of this apartment,' he said in stubborn English. 'We can't go on paying this rent.'

'Exactly what I said when we moved in here,' she said in French. 'We should not be paying money to landlords, but should own our own home.'

'We don't have that sort of capital.' The returns from *The Vacant Mirror* had been good, but not as good as those from his first novel.

'We do. Your latest royalty statement came in yesterday from Gus Green, for both your books. One hundred and thirty-eight thousand dollars.'

'We're going downhill.' Success had taught him new standards of penury.

They went on arguing, something they had been doing regularly for some months. The arguments were never bitter; neither wanted to hurt the other. Everything usually ended in an embrace, but it worried him that they had started to bicker.

Then the phone rang and he reached for it gratefully. It was Alain Roux. 'I want to take you both to lunch. Pick you up in an hour.'

He liked Alain, but they had seen too much of him lately. 'I have an appointment, Alain –'

'Then lend me Simone, I'll take her to lunch.'

Simone liked Alain. She was full of the mothering instinct; whenever Tom had a cold she put him to bed and fussed over him as if he had yellow fever. When Alain, limping on his stick, had first come to their apartment her heart had overflowed: he had to be looked after. She said she would go to lunch with him, kissed Tom, their argument forgotten at once, and went into the bedroom to make herself look pretty for poor crippled Alain.

'He's not poor, he's a hundred times richer than I am, and don't mention the word cripple in front of him.'

'Don't be stupid, *chéri*.' She was speaking English again, he had been forgiven. 'I am a very discreet mother-figure.'

420

'He has a mother back in New York.'

'She sounds like an ogress, from what you've said.'

He went out to the appointment he had invented on the spur of the moment, wandered around like a lost tourist and finished up in the *Courier* bureau. Chuck Nevin had become accustomed to his dropping in like this and waved him to the beat-up visitor's chair. The Paris office still looked as if New York had forgotten it existed. Tom didn't mind. It put him back in the Twenties, he felt he might look out the window and see Hemingway or Fitzgerald passing by on the other side of the street. With nothing else to occupy him, nostalgia, even for a time he had never known, was as good as getting drunk. Something he had not yet attempted.

'You should go back to New York,' said Chuck Nevin, who would never go back, 'and go to work on a paper again. You're not an author, Tom, you're a newspaperman. You've made your money. Stash it away and go back to real work.'

He had been thinking about it, but only idly. He picked up the press wire sheets lying on Nevin's desk and ran his eye down the items. The world was still fraying at the seams; he sometimes wondered why it didn't fall apart. America was embarrassed by the number of postwar Vietnamese refugees. Oil prices were still rising and motorists in the West were angry about greedy camel-riding Arabs who didn't care how necessary gasoline was to motorists in the West who didn't have camels as support transport. Political leaders were hinting that they had promised the voters too much and now knew they couldn't deliver. Bolivia had had its annual *coup*. Two English footballers had been sacked by their club manager for kissing in the shower instead of on the field. Then he saw the item datelined Hamburg.

He looked up. 'Rosa Fuchs has escaped from jail.'

'It looks quite a story. A gang getting a prisoner out of a top security German prison.'

'Are you sending anyone to follow it up?'

Chuck Nevin spread his hands, a gesture he had learned from his Gallic family. 'Who to send? I've got one other

421

man beside myself. He's down in Italy waiting for the latest Premier to fall or be pushed.'

'I'll cover it for you. Freelance rates and expenses.'

'I was hoping you'd volunteer – you'll have a personal angle on it. Freelance rates and minimum expenses. Find a nice *gasthof* and eat at McDonalds. They should have a McDonalds in Hamburg of all places.'

'You want me to go on foot or can the *Courier* afford the plane fare?'

'You wouldn't settle for a hang-glider?'

Tom went home to pack an overnight bag and to tell Simone where he was going. He could not tell her why he was going; he was afraid of exposing his guilt. She was not at home, she had already gone out to lunch with Alain; he left a loving note and said he would call her from Hamburg. Then he went out to the airport, bought a first-class ticket to Hamburg and, when he landed in that city, booked into the Vier Jahreszeiten, a nice *gasthof* but with no McDonalds attached. He still cared nothing for clothes; but he wasn't going to wear a hair-shirt. Comfortable guilt was better, but when he called Simone tonight he wouldn't tell her where he was staying. She was sure to counsel thrift, and in French too.

He felt a certain excitement when he went out to start work on the story. An odd memory dropped into his mind of an old game dog that he and his father would take with them when they went duck-shooting over by Table Rock Lake. The dog would sit around the house all summer like an old man waiting to die, only paying attention to the family when it was fed; then autumn would come and the dog would seemingly cock one eye towards the sky, looking for southbound ducks, then get up and walk around, getting its creaky limbs greased for the hunting that was sure to come. He felt like that old dog now, felt his limbs being greased and his sense of smell sharpened.

The police remembered him and were not glad to see him. Germans hated failure even more than Americans did, he thought; and none more than the police. The world's criticism of what it thought of as police incompetence at the Munich Olympics massacre in 1972 still rankled with the authorities; the Hamburg police did not appreciate the return of one of Rosa Fuch's kidnap victims to report on her escape from custody. It had been an amazing escape, full of imagination and daring.

A vanload of prison officers, returning from a football match against a police team, had been ambushed by six terrorists. The terrorists had taken charge of the van after gassing the prison officers, who had been relieved of their uniforms and then transferred to a truck which had driven them away to be held on the outskirts of the city for several hours. The van, with the terrorist now disguised as the officers, had been driven to the prison and admitted by a less-than-alert gatekeeper, the one chancing to luck that the terrorists had taken. Once inside they had overpowered guards, got Rosa Fuchs out of her cell and shot their way out of the prison, killing four guards and wounding two others on the way. Rosa Fuchs had been a model prisoner up till her escape.

'She will not like reading any story you may write on her, Herr Border,' said the inspector in charge of the case, meaning the police would also not like reading it. 'You were a strong witness against her at her trial.'

'I won't be writing for German newspapers, Herr Inspector. I doubt very much if she'll care what's in the *New York Courier*.'

The inspector looked relieved; he wouldn't have to read what Herr Border wrote. He gave Tom all the facts of the escape; or almost all. One didn't help journalists draw cartoons of one's colleagues ... 'And we have hopes of an early re-capture of the Fuchs woman and the arrest of those who organized her escape.'

Tom had never met a policeman who didn't have hopes of an early arrest. He went back to the hotel, wrote his piece on what he had and phoned it through to Chuck Nevin, giving it extra depth with his own reactions to the escape of the girl who had kidnapped him and Cleo all that time ago. He hung up after talking to Nevin, then called Simone. She was upset, almost distraught.

'I called M. Nevin and he told me why you had gone to Hamburg. What are you doing? Trying to get yourself killed?'

'*Chérie*, they don't even know I'm in town. They're not interested in me.'

'That girl, what's her name? Fuchs? She'll be interested, if she finds out you're in Hamburg. You're a fool, you don't understand women.'

You can say that again. 'I'll take care, *chérie*, I promise. I'll tidy up the story tomorrow and I'll be home in the evening. How was Alain?'

'More sensible than you.' She was silent a moment, then she said, 'I love you. Please be careful.'

He hung up, guilt hanging on him like an iron overcoat. Having tasted news again, he knew that this was not going to be the last time he would go off on his own; he would be pestering Chuck Nevin for further stories to cover, at free-lance rates and minimum expenses; he would be spending his novelist's royalties to satisfy himself as a newspaperman. The old game dog was hoping for a permanent season out there in the swamps where news fell. The Rosa Fuchs escape was as big an event for him as it was for the German prison authorities.

The phone rang. He picked it up, expecting to hear Simone again; then remembered he had not told her where he was staying. It was not Simone, though it was a woman. 'Herr Border?'

'Yes.'

'This is Rosa Fuchs.'

How the hell had she known where to find him? Was there some leak in the police department? 'How did you know I was here? What do you want?'

'Never mind how I knew where to contact you – that doesn't concern you. I want to warn you, Herr Border. I have other things to do right now, but some day, if you come back to Germany, I shall kill you. You and Fräulein Spearfield.'

424

'She is not here with me.' His voice seemed to be shaking in his throat, but it sounded steady enough in his ears.

'Pass on the warning,' said Rosa Fuchs. Then her voice lightened, she laughed, as if freedom were taking hold of her like a drug. '*Auf wiedersehn*, Herr Border. Take care, as you Americans say.'

She hung up and Tom wondered if he should call the police. Then he decided against it: he would tell no one of Rosa Fuchs's threat, not Simone, not even Cleo.

Sensibly he left Hamburg next morning, going no further with the story. Simone welcomed him back as if he were from a war returning: 'Oh, I was worried for you! Don't volunteer again for such dangers –'

He tried to sound convincing. 'There was no danger. I went after a story, I got it and now it's all over. Relax.'

'You promise me there won't be other stories? Sit down and write another novel.'

Just like that. 'I'll write one after lunch. Let's make love.'

She was always willing to do that. Then, as they lay in bed afterwards, she said, 'I think I am pregnant. Isn't that marvellous?'

'Great,' he said, and knew he must sound like a cheerleader whose team had just lost the ball game 52-nil. He hastened to sound better: 'I mean really great! If it's a boy, I want him born in the United States, so he can grow up to be President.'

'What's wrong with being President of France?' She was building up to start speaking in French.

'Nothing, darling,' he said, keeping English in the bed with them. 'Let's make love again. We may get a President for each side of the Atlantic.'

'It doesn't work like that,' she said, and he wasn't sure whether she was trying to give him a lesson in politics or biology.

A week later, when he dropped in once more at the *Courier* bureau, a note was waiting for him from the associate editor in New York: *An excellent story. It brought back memories. We ran*

425

it on Page One and dug up an old pic of you to head it – I hope you haven't changed. Love, Cleo.

Love, Cleo: that meant nothing these days, when everyone was everyone's *darling*. And what memories had it brought back to her? Memories of them together in bed or in danger? And no, he hadn't changed; at least not in his feelings for her. He wrote back, a note as short as hers, polite but distant. But he knew he could never be distant enough from her.

Two months later Simone had a miscarriage. He felt sicker and more distressed than she, but his condition was caused by guilt. Relief does not always make a person feel better.

SIXTEEN

1

Jake Lintas had agreed to retire as editor; he could read the writing on the wall at any distance you cared to name. He put on his homburg, got his golden handshake, gave no wishes at all to Cleo and went out of the newsroom and the *Courier* without a backward glance. Cleo watched him go and felt badly. She was ambitious but she had squeamish feet; she found it hard to keep her balance walking over others as she climbed the ladder. Suddenly she wished Jake Lintas had waited till he had reached the proper retiring age. But by then, of course, the *Courier* might have sunk and a ladder is of no use in a sea.

Two other senior editors, both on the verge of retirement, both of them not wanting to blight their newspaper careers by finishing up working under a woman, also resigned. One of them was the Washington bureau chief.

Cleo sent for Joe Hamlyn and Carl Fishburg. She had waited a couple of days before she had moved into Jake Lintas's office; she wanted his chair bottom cold before she sat on it. It was only a small tactic, but she hoped all those in the newsroom had taken note of it. She might have to resort to such small tactics for quite some time.

Joe Hamlyn sat down, looking relaxed and easy with her. But Carl Fishburg was wary, as if he expected her to ask for *his* resignation. She had no intention of doing that: she knew how good a newspaperman he was and she wanted him on her side. He just had to be shaken out of the rut he had fallen into.

'I want one of you to take over the Washington bureau.'

'Isn't that something the paper's publisher should decide?' said Fishburg.

'Carl, you know that Mrs Roux has been no more than the nominal publisher for years. Jake was the one who decided who got what jobs were going. If you want to take the matter to Mrs Roux, I shan't disagree –'

'Let's hear what you have to say first,' said Joe Hamlyn.

Cleo gave them a quick summary of what she had in mind. 'I want more *punch*. In every department and particularly from Washington. From now on the *Courier* is going to be non-party –'

'The Empress won't like that.'

'I think she'll accept it, if we don't go over to being a propaganda sheet for the Democrats. I want someone down in Washington who can shake them up – the bureau as well as the politicians –'

Carl Fishburg suddenly relaxed. 'It's not for me, Cleo. I'm a New Yorker born and bred. I'll stay on the city desk, if you don't mind. I'd be lost down in Washington. I still think there's Indians out there west of the Hudson River. Have they got inside toilets yet out in Los Angeles? May Jesus Christ and Sam Houston forgive me, I've never seen Texas and don't want to. I could care less about the rest of America. I could care less for the guys who represent it.'

Cleo smiled at him in surprise. 'You're human, Carl.'

He smiled at her, the first time he had ever done so. 'I'm beginning to think you may be, too.'

'I'm intruding on this love affair,' said Joe Hamlyn. 'I think I better go to Washington.'

'Do you mean that? Your wife won't mind moving?'

'She'll probably raise hell. But if I tell her she might get to have tea and grits with Rosalynn Carter ...' Then he turned serious: 'I think you're so damned right, Cleo. The paper's got to be re-vamped, otherwise we'll be out on our asses, no jobs at all, Washington or New York or anywhere. Maybe it's time I got off my bony ass and went out and did something

428

about it. Anyhow, I've always wanted to shoot down a few of those smug sons-of-bitches in Washington.'

So Joe Hamlyn went to Washington and within a month the news and comment coming out of the bureau showed there was a new gun in town. Cleo retired Bill Brenner and brought in the girl from Denver whom she had recommended to Jake Lintas. Ruby Milford was in her mid-twenties, a brown mouse with a soft voice and a dagger-like pen. There were protests from readers, including women readers, but Cleo ignored the letters and over the next six months Ruby Milford was accepted in the company of Herblock and Paul Conrad and other top political cartoonists; being a woman she was, of course, never considered to be quite as good as any of them. The editorials were sharpened, the wind cut out of them. More pictures were featured, giving Bill Puskas new enthusiasm. The *Courier* slowly began to change, a fact that brought no new readers and lost some of the older, more devoted ones.

Jack came over from London on his usual fortnightly trip. He took her to dinner at the Tower of London, certain now that it was a safe rendezvous and that the food, too, was safe.

'How's it going?'

'Not too well, I'm afraid. Circulation's down.' Cleo had felt dispirited when the circulation manager had given her the figures yesterday.

'Don't worry.' He patted her hand, being fatherly but not recognizing it. 'It's bound to happen. You'll lose the dead-wood readers before you attract the new ones. It was the same way when I took over the *Examiner*. Readers aren't out there on street corners panting for a new-look *Courier*. They'll discover you in their own good time.'

'How long will that be? Jack, I'm spending money while circulation is dropping. If circulation goes down again next month, so will the advertising lineage. I'm supposed to be saving the paper, not hurrying it into bankruptcy.' For the first time she had other people's jobs resting on her and the responsibility weighed her down.

'I've never seen you like this. If there was anyone I knew

429

with confidence, it was you.' Other than himself, of course, but he assumed she would take that for granted.

'Up till now I've always had a buffer between me and the public – an editor like myself. All I really had to do was write to please him and trust to his judgement. I was lucky I had such a good man in London as Quentin.'

'He couldn't help you here. This is a different country, different tastes. You'll do all right. Start swaggering again.'

She didn't know she had stopped. She must look as dispirited as she felt.

'I'll take you home. I'm glad you moved from that dump over that shop. That would be no place to be going back to, not when you feel like this.'

She had been going back to it for four years, sometimes feeling every bit as low as she did tonight. The night after Tom had told her he was married, the night her father and the Labour government had been kicked out of office, the night of Hal Rainer's death ... Did Jack think she had been nothing but happy for the past four years?

She had moved out of the apartment above Kugel's Deli the week after she had moved into the editor's chair. She had been afraid that Mr Kugel would be offended, but he had presented her with a goodbye bouquet of mixed sausage, salami, knackwurst, grutzwurst, the fruit of his Second Avenue garden.

'Your age, Miss Spearfield, you oughta be moving up in the world, it's only right. The editor of a big newspaper sleeping over a salami store, people will think it can't be a very classy newspaper.'

'Maybe I'll come back occasionally, Mr Kugel. You can tell me what the man in the street is thinking.'

'Who cares what the man in the street is thinking? He's an ignoramus. All those public opinion polls, you ever heard a constructive thought from the man in the street? He's a complainer, nothing more. Take no notice of him,' said the man in the street from Second Avenue.

'You sound like an autocrat, Mr Kugel.'

'What better to be? In the store I'm a hypocrite, you gotta

be, you want the customers coming back. Between friends, I'm an autocrat. Good luck up on 89th Street. It's nice neighbourhood. I win the lottery, I'll move up there and be an autocrat all the time.'

The apartment on East 89th Street was not as large as the one Jack had provided for her in London; but it suggested more luxury than the one on Second Avenue and it did not smell of fresh bread, sausages and other odours that she had never identified. A Puerto Rican woman came in every day and kept the place immaculate and Cleo was pleased to come home to it every evening. But it wasn't *home:* that was still the old house in the street above the beach in Coogee. When she thought about it, which wasn't often, she was surprised that her roots were still tangled in the soil she thought she had deserted forever.

Since she had moved into the new apartment Jack had taken to coming up with her for a goodnight drink. His behaviour was still that of a good friend. He would kiss her goodnight, but always on the cheek: he was being avuncular, as if trying to avoid being fatherly. She did not encourage him to be anything else: they were partners, not lovers.

This evening he sat down, made himself comfortable; she knew at once he was planning to stay the night. She sat down beside him, instead of opposite him as she usually did, and put her hand on his.

'Jack, what would be our future – well, my future – if we start up all over again? I'd walk out again if you started trying to *own* me the way you used to in London.'

'I'm not like that any more. I learned my lesson.'

'You'd still be jealous. That isn't something you can educate yourself out of.'

'Probably. But if I didn't love you so much, I shouldn't be so jealous. One comes with the other. You're lonely, Cleo – I can see it plain as day. So am I, perhaps more than you. There's been no one in London to replace you and Quent.'

She lay back against the sofa on which they sat. She was lonely, he was right about that. The note to Tom months ago on the Rosa Fuchs story had been written as much out of

431

personal loneliness as editorial approval; she had felt guilty about it after she had posted it. His reply had been cooler than she had expected, though she did not know why she should have expected more. He was married and happily so, she supposed: why should he care about her any more? Working on a morning newspaper solved the problem of lonely nights; by the time she was finished it was time to come home and fall into bed. But Saturdays had become empty days, holes in her life.

'It's no use saying I'll give it a trial. That sort of thing never works. It's all the way or not at all with me.'

'I shouldn't want it any other way. That's why I've held back. I didn't want to be coming over here for a bit on the side, as they say.'

'How often will you come to New York if –?' It was as if they were working out some business deal, making sure of all the option clauses.

'I shan't move here – I can't afford to do that. I don't mean money-wise, I mean because of all I own in England. I have to live there to keep an eye on it. I have the company in the Bahamas that owns the stock in the *Courier*, but that's nothing, it was just something I set up to buy into the paper.'

'You were taking a long bet on me, weren't you?'

'I had to, Cleo. I needed you. I'll come over more frequently than now, perhaps every weekend.'

'You won't ask me whom I've been out with from Monday to Friday?' She smiled, but it was a serious question.

He smiled, too. 'I told you, I've learned my lesson. What I don't know, I shan't grieve about.' And he would do his best not to imagine.

She stood up, took his hand. 'I can't promise you a good sensible breakfast. All I have is croissants and coffee.'

'I'll survive.' He suddenly seemed to have shed years, he looked like the man she had met so long ago in England.

They went to bed like old lovers, with a mixture of caution and skill; love is as much a craft as an art and they were like craftsmen called back after a long lay-off. It wasn't entirely satisfactory, but the pay was good. They woke in the morning

432

and both of them, no matter how temporary the feeling might be, felt it was good to be back in harness. If nothing else, they had both forgotten their loneliness.

2

Roger Brisson rose from the body of the Congresswoman on a point of order. 'Do you mind if I do this my way?'

'Get on with it, you waste so much time.' Representative Tripp was crisp and Californian, she liked things, herself included, done with quick efficiency. Foreplay was something only the unemployed could afford.

He sighed and rolled over on his back. He was losing his touch; or his sense of choice. Mary Tripp was not the only woman he had had in this bed since Louise had left him and gone back to Sands Point. So many of his affairs had begun to take on a slightly ludicrous note, as if he had somehow strayed into a French farce. No doors were opening and shutting, with characters popping in and out (though he would not be surprised if some night Louise popped in through a door); but some of the dialogue sounded as if it might have been written by an ultra-frank Neil Simon. It was a pity that heterosexuals like himself needed women to make love to.

'You're starting to lose your muscle definition.' Mary Tripp was sitting up in bed, looking critically at him. She had just come back from California and, he presumed, a day at Muscle Beach or whatever they called it.

'I'm getting old,' he said, not meaning it.

He got up and went into the bathroom. Making love, he had always felt, was like attacking an enemy hill: if you lost the momentum, the best thing was to retreat and wait for a better opportunity. When he came back into the bedroom Representative Tripp was getting dressed.

'I better go. I'm late for a reception at the White House.'

'I thought you couldn't stand the Carters? You keep calling him that peanut farmer.'

433

She was a Santa Barbara Republican, which meant she didn't even eat peanuts; macadamias perhaps, but never peanuts. 'It's only in the course of duty. The whole town's gone downhill since he arrived. Appearing on TV in his cardigan, for God's sake!'

He was ambivalent about his feelings towards President Carter. He had admired Gerald Ford for his decency: the man from Michigan had been just the man to succeed Nixon. But decency was not enough: the world beyond Washington and Congress was too big for Ford. It might prove too big for Jimmy Carter; but Carter had talked to Roger about nominating him for the chairmanship of the Joint Chiefs of Staff. The man from Georgia might not know what his foreign policy should be, but he knew a good man when he saw one. Or so the good man himself thought.

'Weren't you invited to the reception?'

'I was,' he said, though he hadn't been. He was learning the rules of the game in Washington, that you never allowed anyone to think you had been excluded from anything. 'I have to go to the Indian embassy. I was committed to them first.'

They went out of Watergate separately, knowing the value of discretion in a town where gossip was as much a product as paperwork. They had been indiscreet once or twice early in their affair. He dimly remembered an evening at a charity ball, when he had had too much to drink, when he had been blinded by the sudden glare of a photographer's flash; by the time his eyes had cleared of the glare, the photographer had vanished. He wondered if the photo had ever appeared in any scandal sheet, but he had heard nothing of it. Since Louise had left him he had tried to be less public in his affairs.

As soon as he walked into the Indian embassy Joe Hamlyn, from the *Courier* bureau, came up to him. 'Hello, General. Is the Pentagon currying favour with India?'

He smiled. 'Don't use that, Mr Hamlyn.'

'Are you going to India with the President in the new year?'

'Why should I be doing that?'

434

'Latrine rumours, General. They say you've been approached to head the Joint Chiefs of Staff.'

He would never get over how much classified information was leaked in Washington. The KGB men at the Russian embassy must think theirs the plum posting of any in the world capitals; he wondered why they would bother to buy information when they could get so much free. Unless, of course, they were like all bureaucracies and had to spend this year's budget or they would have next year's reduced.

'There are four or five men senior to me, Mr Hamlyn.'

'Ah yes, but President Carter seems to delight in making surprise appointments.'

'I believe he's looking around in Georgia to see if he can find a disused Confederate general. But don't quote me,' he added hastily. It did not pay to joke with newspapermen.

Joe Hamlyn grinned. 'I'd lose my job if I did. My boss is here this evening.'

'My sister?' said Roger in surprise.

Hamlyn's grin widened. 'I never think of Mrs Roux as the boss – but don't quote me. No, I mean my editor, Miss Spearfield.'

Cleo materialized out of a cluster of saris: the Indian women drifted away like water lilies. 'Hello, General. Is Mrs Brisson here with you?'

He was instantly on guard. *She knows damn well Louise hasn't been in Washington in over a year.* That was classified information he knew would have leaked out. 'My wife doesn't particularly like Washington. It is not really a town for army wives.'

'I suppose not,' said Cleo, wondering in what sort of town army wives would feel at home. They were still camp followers, even if the camp was the Pentagon. 'I must give Mrs Brisson a ring when I get back to New York and ask her opinion of Washington.'

'Do that.' But he hoped she would not. He could imagine the flak if Louise gave her true opinion of Washington and the Pentagon; she would make Martha Mitchell sound like a soft-voiced diplomat. She had stopped being a good army

435

wife and now had the potential threat of an enemy missile. 'What are you doing here?'

'Just looking over our bureau, checking that Joe doesn't have his hand in the petty cash.'

'Do we have petty cash?' said Hamlyn, happy with Washington and with his boss. 'Nobody told me that. I thought we were supposed to pay our own way.'

'Is the *Courier* still strapped for money?' said Roger.

'Still,' said Cleo, closing the subject.

'How long have you been in town?'

Cleo looked at her watch. 'Two hours.'

'Then you must be ready for dinner. Let me take you.'

'I'm sorry, General. I'm having dinner with Joe at his home. Some other time.'

They fell into the torpid talk of cocktail parties and after a while Roger, spotting the Indian military attaché as a good excuse, drifted away. He felt the old uneasiness with Cleo, as if she carried a gun in her handbag, a gun issued in Vietnam. The higher he had climbed in the Pentagon hierarchy, the more the memory of An Bai had come back to trouble him. It was like climbing a mountain and looking back to see the smoke still thick on the far horizon. An Bai might never be mentioned again, at least not publicly, but it was still an echo in his memory. And Cleo Spearfield was a constant reminder.

Driving out to Joe Hamlyn's apartment in Friendship Heights, Cleo said, 'Friendship? How did it get the name?'

'I've never bothered to find out. Why?'

'Nothing.' Just that Tom Border came from a town called Friendship; she too had echoes in her memory. 'How's the General behaving himself?'

'With the women? He's the greatest ass-chaser since Don Juan Hourigan.'

'I know I shouldn't ask – who was Don Juan Hourigan?'

'An amorous Irishman. He laid girls right across the State of Colorado, north to south, east to west and diagonally – I'm talking about the State, not the position of the girls. The General has covered Washington, DC, with his own grid. He's a damn fool, but who's to tell him?'

436

'He should pull his head in if he's going to be head of the Joint Chiefs of Staff.'

'His trouble is he's over-sexed. I'd like to be the same, but don't mention that to Kitty during dinner – she'd hang me up by them if she thought I was displaying them around town the way he does. I've been talking to some of the guys who were here in Jack Kennedy's day. They knew all about his women, but they kept quiet – you don't print that sort of stuff about the President, not while he's in office. But some of them might be tempted to write about our Roger. Army brass is always fair game.'

'Do you think you should have a word with him? Tell him you've heard some of the other newspapermen talking.'

'Are you kidding? Cleo, he's a general. I'm just a working newspaper stiff – what's more, I work for his sister. Begging your pardon on that latter count. He'd turn his howitzer, or whatever it is they use these days, on me. Cleo, I don't think he's a guy who'd take advice even from one of his girl friends. Forget him, let him take care of himself.'

They drew up outside the apartment block in Friendship Heights. They went in and Kitty Hamlyn, twice as wide as her husband, a motherly blonde who, it seemed to Cleo, was never off her feet during the whole evening, welcomed her as if she were a long-lost cousin instead of her husband's editor. Three of the Hamlyn girls, two of college age and the other in high school, were at home for dinner and Cleo felt herself drawn into the warmth of the family circle. It occurred to her that she had not been in this sort of atmosphere since her own days in the house in Coogee when her mother had been alive and Alex and Perry and, occasionally, her father had been at home.

'This has been a year for Australian women,' said Jane, the eldest of the Hamlyn girls. 'You taking over the *Courier*. Colleen McCullough. Olivia Newton-John. Helen Reddy.'

'Don't forget Rupert Murdoch,' said Joe Hamlyn.

'How did he get in here?' said Cleo.

Joe, and Rupert Murdoch, were voted out: it was a women's night. When Cleo left two hours later she felt more

437

womanly than if she had just climbed out of bed after sleeping with the man she loved. Then, going back to the Mayflower Hotel in the cab she had insisted Joe call for her, not wanting to take him away from his family even for half an hour, she told herself that she was being sentimental and cockeyed. One did not have to be surrounded by a family to be womanly.

But in bed in the hotel room, before she dropped off to sleep, she remembered the look on Kitty Hamlyn's face as she had gazed down the table at her husband and daughters. It had been full of a contentment that she had once seen on Brigid's face at a family Christmas dinner. She had never seen it on her own face, but then how often did one look in a mirror for contentment?

3

Cleo was back in Washington a week later, this time with Jack. He had come over on the Thursday night, slept all day to get over jet lag and, though he didn't mention it to her, get himself ready for a weekend of love-making. Then on Friday night, after the paper had been put to bed, he and Cleo had flown down to Washington and checked into a suite in the L'Enfant Plaza Hotel as Mr and Mrs John Cruze. They went to bed at once, slept comfortably with each other like an old married couple and woke to make love before breakfast like a newly-married couple. Then they rented a car and, with Cleo at the wheel, drove out into Maryland to a horse show.

The American horse set, Cleo decided, was very much a colonial cousin of the English horse set, though its money was more apparent and the women were far better dressed. But she wasn't here this time to write a tongue-in-cheek piece on how the Maryland silvertails spent their weekends. Here, Jack and she were not Mr and Mrs Cruze but Lord Cruze and Miss Spearfield, and if their hosts wondered why they were here together, they were too polite to remark on it.

Jack was a guest competitor and, though he was driving a

team with which he had had only half an hour's practice in the morning, in the afternoon he showed he still had all his old skill: he came second in his event. The weather was beautiful and Cleo enjoyed the day, not least Jack's delight in showing off in front of her. She enjoyed the company of their hosts and their friends and once again, as she had in England, thought of the doors that Jack had opened for her. She knew, of course, that doors would be opened for her because she was the editor of a New York newspaper, but the door to the editor's room itself had been opened for her by Jack.

Jack declined to stay on for a dinner party and they drove back to Washington. 'I didn't have anything to wear, but I'd liked to have stayed for dinner, Jack. There were some interesting people there.'

'I know I'm being selfish. But I have to fly back tomorrow.'

'You usually stay till Monday. Business?'

'No.' He hesitated, then said, 'Rose St Martin died yesterday. I got the news when I phoned London last night. She's being buried on Monday.'

Cleo instantly felt sad. She had not seen the sisters in almost six years and her correspondence with them had been intermittent; but they had always been clear and warm in her memory. They, in a way had opened the door to Jack himself. 'I wish I could come with you.'

'I wish you could, too.' But he didn't press it; he knew the demands of running a daily newspaper. 'If you like, I'll order flowers for you. Cromwell will see they get there in time.'

'How's Dorothy?'

'I don't really know. I spoke to her on the phone and she sounded all right. But I haven't seen them in years. But I've always been grateful to them. Indirectly, they sent you to me.'

They sent you Emma, too. 'Will Emma be at the funeral?'

He had thought of that and was afraid of the prospect. 'I suppose so. She loved them both.'

'So did I, in a way. I'll phone Dorothy at the end of the week. I'll give her time to get over the loss of Rose.'

439

He put his hand on her shoulder. 'You really are affectionate, aren't you? I wish I were.'

She didn't flatter him by saying that he was. 'Maybe it's because I'm a woman.'

'Bull,' he said. 'Men can be just as affectionate as women and you know it. Don't be soft on me, Cleo. I know my faults. I couldn't afford to be affectionate when I was battling my way up. While you're helping a blind man across the street, you've missed the bus you were trying to catch.'

'Helping a blind man across the street isn't affection, that's being kind and considerate.'

'Well, I didn't have time for that, either.' He looked back down the years for missed opportunities to be kind and considerate; but couldn't remember any. He had the clear vision of a non-hypocrite; but he knew no one would ever give him credit for that. He had learned long ago that hypocrisy was a social asset.

They had dinner in their suite, watched television for a while, then went to bed. After they had made love, she went to the bathroom, came back, put on a robe and sat in a chair. He remained in the bed, propped up against the pillows. He still looked as fit as ever and he still made love with the same energetic passion and stamina, as if being with the woman he loved had revived him; but he no longer got out of bed after it and strutted around like a boxer who'd just won the decision in a close-fought match. She wondered if women ever strutted around like that after making love. Maybe women wrestlers did, out of habit.

'Jack, there's a bit of a problem. Roger Brisson is in the running for Chairman of the Joint Chiefs of Staff.'

'That's his problem, not yours.' He had the successful man's opinion that service chiefs should be able to look after themselves. After all, that was what they were trained for, at the taxpayers' expense, too.

'No, it's my problem, too. As an editor. If he gets the job, there's likely to be a lot of dirty gossip flying around. There is also a distinct chance that the husband of a certain Congresswoman would sue for divorce, naming Roger as co-respondent.

He saw her editor's viewpoint at once. 'You mean if that happened, you'd have to back-pedal on the story?'

'If I didn't, there'd be a hell of a fight with Claudine. She is still the publisher.'

'Do you want me to talk to her?' Then he shook his head. 'No, I swore I wouldn't put my oar in when it came to running the paper. If I do it once, she'll expect me to go on doing it. That will only weaken your position.'

She had always thought she was long-sighted, but she wasn't in his class. He not only saw things beyond the horizon, but he had short-focus and peripheral vision.

'How true is the gossip?'

'It's all fact. I have a photo I bought from a snide candid photographer over a year ago, of Roger with his hand down the cleavage of the Congresswoman I've just mentioned. He has several other women on the side.'

'Then you'd better go to him and tell him what you have and what you know. Tell him that if any of the papers run the story, you won't be able to lay off. You couldn't afford to, anyway. People would rush to buy the *Courier* to see how you're handling it. They'd never come back if you funked it.'

'How do I approach him? Being kind and considerate or just protecting our circulation?'

She had meant it as a half-joke, but she should have known he never joked about business. 'He doesn't deserve any kindness and consideration. All you have to think about is whether the *Courier* is beaten to the story if it breaks. When does the service job come up?'

'Another couple of months.'

'Righto then, Brisson has a couple of months to clean up his image. Give him the photo and scare the hell out of him, tell him you know at least one other paper has a copy. Don't pussyfoot around with him.'

For a moment she wondered if it had occurred to him there was not much difference between him and Roger: both of them were married men going to bed with women other than their wives. Perhaps he felt that, in his case, true love was an absolution

441

She didn't love him, but she felt affectionate towards him. He might never stop to help a blind man across a street, but he would stop the traffic on a freeway to help her. She threw off her robe and climbed on top of him. Love-making, among other things, is a gesture of thanks.

4

Louise had been on jury duty. She had been surprised when she was called; the other eleven members of the jury confessed the same when they all met. All their lives they had been passing judgement on their relatives, friends and fellow citizens; but this was different, one didn't expect to be asked to pass an official opinion on a fellow human being. Back-biting and calumny were reasonable, but jury duty was asking a bit too much.

The jury was a good cross-section. Five men, seven women, one rich, several middle class, four working class, two pensioners, eight whites, four blacks. The defendant, a young woman, looked at them sullenly, recognizing that they were all different from her: they were all innocent, or professed to be.

The girl was charged with murdering her *de facto* husband. All the evidence was against her and Louise sensed after the first hour that at least half the jury were against her on another count: she was young, attractive, and she had been living in sin not only with the man she had allegedly killed but three other men before him. She also had a sullen aggressive personality and the prosecuting attorney knew how to bring out all her aggressiveness. Louise recognized that the jury was going to convict on prejudice as much as anything else; but the fact that the girl had murdered her lover was uncontestable. Louise in her own mind could not dispute that, though she wondered why the girl had killed him if she had had three other lovers with whom she had been able to live. All the girl had in her defence was that she had loved the dead man, but she made no attempt to explain any

442

further. Louise understood her and, though she did not ask, she felt that certain of the women in the jury room also understood. Nevertheless, after only an hour's discussion, the twelve decided on a verdict of guilty.

They filed back into the court and the judge, an elderly man who had given up trying to understand today's generation and its morals, sentenced the girl to thirty years with a non-parole term of twelve years. Louise looked at the girl, but there was no expression on her face; she looked sullen and blank, as if she had decided that her intelligence would be of no further use to her. Louise wondered if the girl would have preferred to die instead of spending so many years locked away.

She went back to Sands Point depressed and exhausted by the experience. She felt burdened with a sense of guilt, as if, in some remote way she could not explain to herself or anyone else, she was part of the reason the girl stood in the dock.

She wandered about the big house, her depression growing every minute. Lena, the housekeeper, had gone over to Jackson Heights to spend the night with her sister, so even her company was not available. Louise rang two women friends; both of them were out. She had a moment of aberration: she would call Roger, ask if she could come down to Washington for the night. She could not remember the number of the apartment in Watergate; she had shut her mind against so many things. She had to look it up in an old address book; her hand was shaking by the time she dialled the number. Then a woman answered.

'Yes, General Brisson is here. Who is calling?'

Louise hung up at once. She looked at her watch: it was 10.20. The woman had probably answered from the bedside phone. All at once she wanted to scream, throw things, smash everything that surrounded her, the bric-à-brac that had been the replacement for the children she had never been able to have. Instead she went to bed and writhed all night on a nail-bed of memories. Her clearest memory was the most recent, that of the face of the girl who had killed the man she loved.

Next morning she rang her doctor and went to see him. Dr Guilfoyle had been seeing her once a month for the past three months.

'Louise, you're heading into the menopause. I sympathize with you. We men never have to go through it, though some of my colleagues, probably closet fags, are trying to say that men *do* go through it. Personally, I think what they're saying is a lot of mullarky, they're just trying to give another name to the seven-year itch. Ever since I first started medicine I've always thought God was a misogynist, the way He's loaded things against you women. I once mentioned that to the Cardinal and he threatened to have me excommunicated if I ever said it in public.'

She looked at him frankly, her lips twisted in a wry smile. He was not good-looking, he was too bony and sallow for that, but he was always beautifully groomed and he *looked* good: there was a difference. Claudine, who also came to him, had once said that he looked as if he had graduated from Sulka & Co. rather than from NYU. Louise wondered what he would be like in bed and then wondered why she should have had such a thought. She had never been to bed with anyone but Roger and she was not going to start now.

'How many middle-aged women's hands have you held, Peter?'

'Too many,' he said: and hurt her with what was meant to be sympathy: 'It's a pity all you women can't remain young forever. Especially those of you who couldn't have children.'

He gave her some tablets, but she knew that taking them, like taking another lover, was not really going to help her. She left him and went down into Park Avenue. She was only a few blocks from where Claudine lived, but she brushed aside the thought that she might drop in and surprise (no, shock) her sister-in-law. Claudine had phoned several times after her visit to Sands Point, but Louise had not taken the calls nor returned them; they had not seen each other since that afternoon. To drop in now, unannounced, and then announce that she was going down to Washington to kill Roger would only result in Roger's being alerted. She would be met

444

at the airport or at Union Station by him and probably an entire division of Special Strike troops as back-up. Roger was no coward, but he never took risks, except with his love affairs.

She drove home to Long Island in the peak hour traffic; life was doing everything it could to torture her. Her attention wandered and several times she drifted out of her lane on the parkway; horns blared at her and drivers, all men, blasted her with abuse. They made no impact on her except, by threatening driving, to push her back into her own lane. She was closing a door on the world.

Lena was not at the house; there was a note on the kitchen table saying she had gone shopping. Louise went upstairs to what she still thought of as Roger's dressing-room. She went through the drawers and found the old Smith & Wesson .38 and the box of cartridges. She loaded the pistol, went into her own room and put on a new face, got a handbag large enough to carry the gun in and went downstairs and out to her car. She took no luggage because she had no destination in mind after she had killed Roger.

She had paused by the phone on her way out, wondering if she should ring Dr Guilfoyle. But he could do nothing about the despair in which she was drowning; nor, she reasoned with a sort of fuzzy lucidity, did she want him to. There is a depth of depression like that of a sea, where drowning suddenly becomes welcome. Love pities, she had once read, and pities most when it loves most. She would kill Roger with pity, taking him with her.

She headed the car south and drove in a semi-trance; somehow she caused no accidents to others, did not run herself off the road. She hurried as she always had: some habits can never be changed. She did not think of friends to whom she might have turned for help: she had closed the door on them, too. She thought only of Roger and herself, her world. Though it did not occur to her to analyse her feelings, she felt no rage or hatred.

445

Cleo had left the *Courier*, for that day, to Carl Fishburg. She had called Roger Brisson at the Pentagon and told him she would be in Washington that evening and wanted to see him.

'Come to the apartment,' he had said and, since she did not want to show him the photograph in a public place such as a restaurant, she had agreed. After what she intended saying to him, she knew she would be safe from him.

When she arrived at Watergate and he opened his apartment door to her, he was in dress uniform. 'I'm sorry about this. I've just come from a reception at the White House and I haven't had time to change.'

She wondered if what he said was true or whether he was trying to impress her; or intimidate her. She was neither impressed nor intimidated: she was impervious to uniforms. 'Perhaps it's appropriate, General.'

He looked at her quizzically. 'General?'

She took the drink he offered her and followed him out on to the terrace that overlooked the Potomac. The apartment was large and luxurious, just the bunker for a rich beleaguered general. Though, of course, he didn't yet know that he was to be attacked.

She wasted no time. She opened the large envelope she carried, gave him George Hurlstone's photograph. 'Have you ever seen that?'

She saw no reaction at all on his handsome face. 'No. I dimly remember the occasion. I'd had a little too much to drink.'

'Representative Tripp looks as if she may also have had a little too much.'

'Are you going to run it in the *Courier*?'

'Roger, you misunderstand why I've come down here. I'm not here to blackmail you.'

He had put down his drink and was holding the photograph in both hands, looking at it as if it were a picture of a military rout. 'This was well over a year ago. What's its significance now?'

'The rumour is you're in the running to be Chairman of the Joint Chiefs of Staff. Is it true?' He said nothing, face still blank, and she added impatiently, 'Come on, Roger – I'm trying to help you!'

He nodded. 'Yes, I've been told I'm the favourite to get the post.'

'If you do, then you'd better watch out. Every newspaper-man in this town, so I'm told, knows all about you and Mrs Tripp and your other women. One or two of them also know that Mr Tripp, wherever he happens to be, is seriously considering suing his wife for divorce.'

His expression did change then. 'Where did you get that bit of garbage? Mrs Tripp and her husband haven't lived together since she came to Washington.'

'She's still married to him. Or he to her, whichever way you like to put it. You're a rich man, Roger and a prominent one. Mr Tripp is not rich – his wife is the one with money.'

She had had Joe Hamlyn do a lot of legwork and he had done it well. He had sent her a sealed dossier on the Tripps that contained information that she was sure Roger did not know and, up till now, would probably have not been interested in. Only she and Joe knew what was in the dossier.

'Are you implying that Tripp might sue me for damages?'

'Possibly. You could well afford the money. I don't think you could afford the damage to your reputation. That fancy uniform would look pretty soiled after a day or two in court.'

He smiled: he still had some humour left in him. 'I don't think the Army would consider a divorce court a dress occasion. You still haven't told me why you've come down here with this warning. Did Claudine send you?' Then he shook his head. 'No, she wouldn't deny herself the chance to put me in my place. Was it Louise?'

'I haven't seen Louise in over a year. I came down here as a newspaperwoman. If any of the other papers run a story about you and Mrs Tripp and your other women, then I'll have to run it, too.'

'What are you suggesting I do?'

'That you let the White House know you don't want the

447

job on the Chiefs of Staff. Maybe you can put yourself forward for it in a couple of years –'

'You don't put yourself forward for a post like that. You may work towards it, but you don't volunteer for it.' He looked out across the Potomac. Below him traffic was moving towards the Kennedy Center for the Performing Arts; the people in the cars were heading for an evening's entertainment of synthetic drama. He had always had a sense of the dramatic, but only in his own head; he had never indulged himself in public. He had the feeling that he was now in a drama building to a climax that he had avoided contemplating. 'Is this connected in your mind with what happened at An Bai?'

She was not surprised by the question: sooner or later An Bai would have been mentioned. 'No, it isn't. I'll be honest with you – I haven't forgotten that. But this is a more personal matter. I don't want my paper beaten on a story that, in a way, belongs to it more than it does to any other paper.'

'So you really care about my reputation? Or the President's, if he appointed me? He's already made one or two poor judgements.'

'If you accepted the post, would you care about his reputation? You should have thought about all that before you started playing around.'

'Don't start moralizing –'

'Don't pull rank on me, General. I came down here to do you a favour as much as look after my paper –'

'You keep calling it *your* paper. It's always been looked on as the Brisson paper –'

Suddenly she was angry and lost patience with him. It was a mistake to think one could help the arrogant: it would be a weakness on his part to admit that he needed help. 'Oh, get stuffed! Forget it!'

She started back in off the terrace and was halfway across the big living-room before he caught her and grabbed her by the arm. 'Cleo, forgive me! Please stay –'

Then they were both aware of the woman standing in the

open front doorway. Louise held a gun in both hands and, like a good army wife, was taking careful aim.

6

She had parked the car in the garage below. There was a new attendant on duty and she had had to produce her driving licence to prove that she was Mrs Louise Brisson, wife of General Brisson and co-owner of the apartment on one of the top floors.

'I'll have to call up and check, Mrs Brisson.'

'You do and I shall report you.' She had lived in the shadow of Brisson and army authority for years; now she used some of it, acted like a general's wife. 'I want to surprise my husband – I've just come back from abroad. You won't call him, understand?'

The attendant was young, black and it was his first job in two years. 'Ma'am, we have to be careful –'

She relented. It hurt her to ride roughshod over anyone; killing a husband was a different matter. 'I'm sorry I was sharp. I'm a little tired – it's been a long journey –'

'You look a little pooped, ma'am.'

She left the car with him and went up in the elevator. She was planning no perfect crime; it was as imperfect as it could possibly be, except that the victim would be dead. And herself, too. Which would make it a complete crime, if not a perfect one.

She had read once (she also collected the bric-à-brac of information) that the mind was divided into two sections, the logical and the emotional. So far the logical side of the brain had got her here safely from Long Island; as she rose in the elevator emotion took over. By the time she stepped out of the elevator, took her key and the gun out of the handbag and had opened the apartment door, her mind was nothing but a dark whirling cloud of emotion. She felt as if she were about to blow up, as if she had been mined for years and now she was about to be triggered.

449

She saw Roger with his hand on the woman's arm, heard him say, '– forgive me! Please stay –'

She had the gun raised, held with both hands as she had seen men trained to do on the practice range. She sighted along the barrel, aiming first at Roger: she would kill him before she killed the woman. Then her finger on the trigger turned into dead bone; she could not bend it. She let out a sob of frustration; she stared at the two lovers, hating them. Up till that moment only Roger had been clear in her vision; the woman had been a faceless shape, a stranger. Now she saw who the woman was: Cleo Spearfield.

The shock was like a cold wind storming through her mind: the dark cloud was gone. She whimpered like a child, then abruptly she turned and ran blindly back towards the elevator. But the elevator was several floors below her. She banged at the call-button; then she stumbled towards the door to the emergency stairs. She dragged it open, almost fell down the stairs in her haste to get away. She had no idea where she was running to. If the stairs went down far enough she would run into the bowels of the earth, into Hell itself.

Then she heard the footsteps running down the stairs after her. She ran faster, stumbled and crashed headlong on to a landing. She was stunned, lay there just wanting to die. Then Roger was trying to lift her up, uttering words of comfort; even in her dazed mind they sounded hypocritical. She fought him, striking at him with both hands. She had dropped the gun and her handbag; if she had still had the gun, she would indeed have killed him. Her fingers were no longer dead bone, they clawed at him with a venom that was utterly foreign to her.

Then Cleo, carrying the gun and the handbag, was squatting beside the struggling husband and wife. 'Roger, go back upstairs. Leave me with Louise.'

'No, no!' Louise thought she was shouting, but her voice was only a hoarse whisper magnified in the funnel of the narrow stairwell. 'Both of you – leave me alone! Go – I don't want you to touch me –'

Roger let her go, sat back on the steps. There was a red mark and bloody scratches on his face; somehow Louise's fingers had even clawed the ribbons from the chest of his uniform. His hair hung down and he looked so distraught as to be unrecognizable. He had lost command of the situation and of her.

Cleo was in command: she had been in this situation before. She felt far from calm, but on the surface she looked more matter-of-fact than Louise or Roger. She tapped him on the shoulder and nodded back up the stairs. He sat for a moment staring at Louise; he could not believe what she had tried to do. He had been affronted as well as threatened. Then he stood up and, noticing the gun in Cleo's hand, reached for it.

'No, I'll keep it.'

'It's mine.' It was army issue, so his.

'Go upstairs, Roger.' Cleo spoke as if she were his wife, while his wife still lay like a drunk on the landing. 'Don't argue.'

He looked for a moment as if he would take command again; then he went meekly. When the door, two landings above, had closed behind him, Cleo sat down on the steps and put out a hand, the one without the gun, to Louise.

'It's not what you think, Louise. I'm not one of his women.'

Louise lay on her back staring at her; then, becoming aware of the indignity of her position, she sat up. She was returning to normal: caring about appearances was part of being normal. She was still an army wife, no matter how much she might want to desert. Cleo handed her her handbag, but kept the gun.

'Freshen up. How did you come here?'

Louise did not want to look at herself; she kept her mirror in the closed handbag. 'I drove down.'

'Where's your car?'

'Downstairs, in the garage.' She was like a child answering a teacher, one she was wary of. But she recognized that Cleo was trying to help her and, after all, there was no one else who would. She looked down through the railings into the deep hole of the stairwell. Far below was a concrete floor waiting for her like a morgue slab.

'That's not the answer, Louise, so don't think about it.'

Louise looked at her; then abruptly she started to weep. Cleo drew her head into her lap, stroked the disordered hair. She said nothing till Louise had cried all her tears out of herself: the tears ran out but the bitter shame was still there.

'Oh God –' Louise began to shiver and she crumpled against Cleo's legs. But she was no longer drowning nor wanting to drown; she came back up to the ugly, futureless surface of the world she had to go on living in. She struggled within herself for a moment, not wanting to stay afloat, but it was useless. 'Save me, Cleo – please –'

'Let's go back to New York,' said Cleo. 'I'll drive.'

Like a good editor she wondered how the *Courier* would have handled the story if Louise had shot both her and Roger. But she could never debate it, not even with Jack. He would not want to be reminded of another murder attempt.

She drove Louise back to Sands Point. She stayed the night with her, insisting that she take a sleeping pill. In the morning, while Louise was still asleep, she went downstairs and introduced herself to Lena Jinks. The elderly housekeeper gave her a warm smile.

'You welcome here, Miss Spearfield. Miz Brisson, she had nobody stay here for too long. She all right? I got scared I come back yesterday and she ain't here, no note, nothing. She ain't looked well lately.'

'She's fine. A little tired, that's all. Where is a phone I can use?'

She called Roger at Watergate, told him where she was. 'Louise is not awake yet, but I think she'll be all right. We talked on the way back last night. She's had a lot cooped up inside her for far too long.'

'Why didn't she talk to me?'

'Oh Roger –!' Men, even the most intelligent of them, could be so bloody dumb. 'Call her later this morning. I don't know if you want to get back together – I don't even

452

know if she wants to. That's between the two of you. But call her and ask her how she is. And don't bugger up things by trying to put yourself in the right. She's been through far more than you have.'

'Jesus –' He was silent for a moment, then he said, 'I'll recommend to the President that he make you Chairman of the Joint Chiefs of Staff.'

'Just so long as he doesn't give the job to you. Goodbye, Roger. Be kind to her when you call. That won't cost you any pride.'

She hung up before he could reply, then called Carl Fishburg at his home. 'Any problems at the office last night?'

'No more than usual. There's some male chauvinism in the editorials, but we had to grab our opportunity while you were away. How was Washington?' He was the only one in New York who knew why she had gone to see Roger, though he didn't know all the story.

'Amenable.'

'A pity. It would have made a great story.'

You don't know, mate, the story you might have had. 'I'll see you this afternoon.'

She had breakfast, glanced through the *Courier* that had been delivered to the front porch, then went up to see Louise. She was sitting up in bed, her hair done, a breakfast tray across her lap. She looked pale, almost gaunt, but she managed a smile.

'I was pleased when Lena said you were still downstairs. I'll never be able to thank you, Cleo.'

'I've talked to Roger. If he calls you, don't apologize or say you're sorry for what you tried to do. I'm glad it didn't happen, but he had it coming to him.'

Louise shook her head. 'Not murder! I just don't know how I could have –'

'Don't get yourself upset again. It'll take time, but eventually you'll put it behind you. I once covered a story like this,' she lied. 'It all worked out okay in the end.'

'I get so depressed –'

She guessed Louise was going through the menopause: at

least Jack hadn't been going through *that*. 'Call me any time you feel depressed. Any time.'

'You're busy. I envy you. Perhaps if I were busy I wouldn't have time to feel the way I do.'

There's always time to feel low. 'I'll call you this evening from the office. And remember – don't apologize to Roger. He's a general. They never apologize for starting wars. And he started this one.'

Louise smiled, the gauntness slipping out of her face. 'I'm glad I didn't shoot you.'

'So am I. Incidentally, this is between you, me and Roger. Claudine is never to know.'

SEVENTEEN

1

Claudine did ask Roger why he had been passed over as Chairman of the Joint Chiefs. 'I thought you were favourite for it.'

'You better ask the President.'

There were levels to which decent Republicans did not descend. She let the matter drop; she had other things on her mind. Alain was still in Europe, still at what seemed to her a loose end: she liked people to be tied up, preferably to herself. She had gone across twice to see him, travelling once by TWA and once by Air France to show what she liked to think of as her dual nationality. Neither airline quite met her standards, but one couldn't ask for the QE2 to be airborne.

Alain told her he would come home when he had his personal affairs sorted out. It was on her second visit that she discovered his personal affairs were in the singular: he was having an affair with the wife of Tom Border. He had tried to explain to her that he was not breaking up a marriage; Tom and Simone had been separated for six months and originally, as a family friend, he had been interested only in consoling Simone. Tom, who did not need consoling, was wandering around Europe and the Middle East writing free-lance pieces for the *Courier* and several magazines.

'If Simone divorces Tom, I want to marry her.'

'If? That sounds as if she's hoping he will come back to her.'

'He won't do that. I've talked to him about it.'

455

'He doesn't resent you, a family friend, having an affair with his wife?'

'You make it sound so sordid, Mother.'

A year or so ago she would have put him in his place for that remark. But she was losing her touch, her tongue had slowed down. She never read the sports pages in any newspaper, but she had heard some of her men friends talking about how their reflexes had slowed down on the tennis court. They now called themselves veterans, a word she would never, no matter what the condition of her tongue, apply to herself.

'What will you do if you and what's-her-name –'

'Simone, Mother,' he said patiently.

The slip had been deliberate, a testing of *his* reflexes. 'What will you do if she does marry you? Stay on here?'

He had rented an apartment just off the Avenue Montaigne; she was glad he still had a sense of place if not of behaviour. Weekends and for a month in summer he went down to the château at Souillac; she was pleased that he lived as a Brisson should. She did not, however, want to keep crossing the Atlantic to visit him. She wanted a more comfortable umbilical cord than TWA or Air France.

'No, we'll come back to New York. I've had enough of doing nothing. I'd have been home before this if I hadn't been waiting on Simone to make up her mind. I want to go back to the *Courier*.'

'Won't that be awkward for you? Cleo now runs the paper.'

He smiled at her. 'You mean you let her?'

'Between you and me, she is doing a far better job than I expected. We are now making a little money instead of losing a lot. I don't like some of her innovations, but I just ignore them if they disturb me too much. That girl cartoonist Milford, for instance – she goes too far sometimes.'

'Not with Carter. As far as I'm concerned, no one can go too far with him.' His conservatism was growing, like an early case of hardening of the arteries. He had been pleased and relieved when Simone had told him she was an admirer of Giscard d'Estaing. She could be radical in bed, but that was

456

a different matter. 'But I agree with you – Cleo has improved the paper. What we have to watch is that it doesn't become *her* paper.'

We: she did not miss that. 'She may not have a place for you. Have you thought of that?'

'I think we could arrange that between us, couldn't we?'

He's still my son, she thought; collusion helped make blood thicker than water. Her French blood began to course, she hadn't indulged in any intrigue for God knew how long. She had far too little to occupy her these days. 'In what way?'

'The paper could do with an associate publisher. Someone there to handle the day to day stuff.'

'Cleo appears to do that.'

'It's too much for her, especially if she's editor.'

'You won't come back now?'

'No, not till things are settled between me and Simone.'

Then Simone arrived at the apartment. Claudine had not met her before and she treated the girl to wary inspection. Simone, with a thrifty woman's respect for money and position, was on her best behaviour. After an hour Claudine told herself that the girl, though a little rough round the edges, which was probably due to her experiences as an airline stewardess, had potential. She had no family, which was a plus: families, unless one was marrying into the best of them, were often the biggest handicap to a successful marriage. She took them to dinner at Lassere and was further pleased to see that Simone knew her food and wine. That meant she had at least worked in first class on Air France.

She delicately raised the subject of Simone's husband; that is, she waited till they were having coffee: 'I understand you and Mr Border are contemplating divorce?'

They were speaking French, which has the proper formality for delicate subjects. 'One has to think seriously about such a matter. I have explained to Alain that I do not treat marriage, or divorce, lightly.'

'A proper attitude. One wishes all young people thought that way.'

'It's why I've never rushed into marriage,' said Alain.

457

What a pious hypocrite, thought Claudine; and loved him for his good sense. 'Well, we shall just have to wait and see what happens. Will you take care of the bill, Alain?'

The girl had to be taught early that, if she married into the family, her mother-in-law was not going to be Madame Cornucopia. The look in Simone's eyes told her that the girl had got the message. The women smiled at each other, half-way to being friends.

Claudine had returned to New York and kept in touch with both Alain and Simone by a weekly phone call. She never talked for long on the phone: the instrument, she had always said, was meant for communication not conversation. The Bell Telephone Company, aware of profits, might have disagreed with her, but she knew that the best conversation only came when the speakers were face to face. She was not going to converse with her probable daughter-in-law and not be able to read the girl's face.

Now, talking with Roger, she read his face and pondered on how much he was keeping from her. He appeared to have quietened down over the past couple of months; not in his appearance, which seemed as confident and arrogant as ever, but in an inner atmosphere which he seemed to carry with him. As if, at the age of fifty-six, he had decided to be responsible and middle-aged. She began to think, perversely, that she had preferred him when he had been irresponsible and dashingly young.

'What is happening between you and Louise?'

'We are friends again.'

'A husband and wife who are friends? Ridiculous!'

'I'm on trial. She may take me back.'

This humility was sickening; what's more, she didn't believe it. He had been too long in Washington with that born-again Christian who thought prayer might help save the nation. A regular churchgoer, she believed prayer should be kept in its proper place, in church.

'What's come over you, Roger? You sound as if you couldn't lead in a waltz, let alone a cavalry charge.'

'I was never in the cavalry. I've always been what the

458

British call the Poor Bloody Infantry. Claudine, I'm retiring from the Army. Unless a war breaks out, I've gone about as far as I can.'

'War can break out at any time.' She did not mean to sound encouraging but did.

'Not with this man in the White House.' He did not mean to be critical of President Carter. Though he would not have confessed it to anyone at the Pentagon, nor even to Claudine, he was no longer interested in war either as a profession or a sport. He had always, even when he had been enjoying battles in Korea and Vietnam, looked upon the Army as his self-imposed discipline; it had worked when he was young and it had worked up till a few years ago. Then he had come home to the Pentagon, risen to the rank of lieutenant-general: it had been left to himself to discipline himself and he had failed. He could not court-martial himself, so he would retire and aim higher.

'I am going to study foreign affairs.'

'You want to be an ambassador? You would be ideal for the Paris embassy.'

'No. I should like to be Secretary of State.'

She was not surprised by the extent of his ambition. She had never had any ambition of her own. If one was at the top, even only in one's own estimation, what was there to aspire to? As a girl she had dreamed of being royal; but look at what had happened to Wallis Simpson. She looked at Roger shrewdly, assessing him. They loved each other, but there had always been restraint; ego got in the way of total unselfishness. Each wanted the best for the other, but only if it did not mean too much sacrifice on his or her part. Their trouble was (though the thought did not occur to her) that neither of them had ever been bruised by real suffering; true sorrow might have bound them closer, pushed the egos aside. She tried now to be objective about him and decided he had the material to be a good Secretary of State. Lately, with the exception of Henry Kissinger, she found it difficult to remember who the Secretaries of State were or had been.

'I could help there. With the *Courier*, I mean.'

459

He shook his head: the last thing he wanted at the moment was any further help from Cleo. 'All in good time. First, I have to get out of the Army.'

'Is Louise necessary for your plans?' That might account for his humility in his marriage.

'Not necessary, but helpful.'

'I suppose so. But one never knows in this day and age ... I hope I'm dead before we have a married homosexual couple in the White House. I can't see myself paying my respects to a First Lady named Fred.'

'I'll stay on in Washington after I leave the Army. It will be the best base of operations.' He still thought militarily: the politics would come later.

'You're looking a long way ahead, are you not? There may not be a Republican President next time around. They are talking about that actor as the candidate.' An actor to follow a peanut farmer: she wondered what the acid-penned Miss Milford would make of that in her cartoon.

'He won't be the only candidate. I shall just have to be careful how I play my cards.'

'If I can be of any help ...' She would be, of course: she would see to that. In the meantime Alain was coming home with his new bride. Well, Simone might not be *new*, but so much these days was discounted.

2

Tom Border, divorced but not really feeling free, still shackled by guilt, came home a month ahead of Alain and Simone. Plucking up courage and dampening his love, he went to see Cleo. He walked into the newsroom, which looked much brighter than he remembered it. Video display terminals seemed to have taken the character out of the people who sat in front of them; or was it that they seemed hidden behind the machines? The old copy editors' horseshoe desk had gone and with it the men who had manned it; then Tom saw one or two of the old hands behind VDTs, pecking away at the keys like prisoners tapping out a message for help. He slowly made his way down the long room; despite the new atmosphere, the old feeling began to flow through him. He was like a gardener, banished for years to a hothouse, who had come back to a beloved garden that he had expected to find neglected and overgrown, only to see it blooming. The blooms might be force-fed with all the new equipment, but they were recognizable. He wanted to be part of the staff again.

He stopped by Carl Fishburg's desk. When he had left here Carl had been faded and wilted; now he was a whole bouquet of welcome in himself. 'Are you coming back to us, Tom?'

'If Cleo has a place for me.' He hoped that didn't sound too personal. Then he remembered that no one in the office would know how he felt about Cleo.

'We need a feature writer, Tom. There are plenty of young guys around, kids out of journalism school, but they all want to write like Tom Wolfe. The one in the white suit, not my Tom Wolfe. They drive the old guys who used to be on the copy desk nuts. The paper's livened up under Cleo, you've seen that, but she likes to stick to old-fashioned punctuation. Some of these young guys, they sit down at a machine and write a five hundred-word piece without drawing breath. They have to use *hopefully* every second line, misusing it every time, and no one ever taught them the difference between *who* and *whom*. How's the novel-writing or shouldn't I ask?'

'You shouldn't ask.' But Tom grinned, unoffended.

Cleo rose from her desk as he went into her office. She shook hands with him, then gestured at her open door and the glass wall that separated them from the newsroom. 'I'd kiss you hello, but it might make the rest of the boys jealous. You look great, Tom. You haven't changed. Is that the old Harrods suit or are you being tailored by St Vincent de Paul?'

It was the old Harrods suit and he thought it still looked all right: it had been dry-cleaned only yesterday especially for this interview. 'If you give me a job, I'll go out and buy a new one.'

They were like a couple trying to walk towards each other

461

across thin ice-floes. 'There's a job for you, Tom. I've talked about you with the other editors. Unfortunately the pay's not as high as I'd like to give you.'

'The money doesn't matter.' Then he gestured awkwardly. 'Sorry. That sounds smug. I'm all right, I mean. I've still got something left of what I made out of my books.'

That added to the guilt he still felt about Simone. She (at Alain's insistence, he had guessed) had refused to take any settlement. He knew that Alain had more money (or anyway the promise of it) than he would ever have; but he had wanted Simone to take half their assets, if only as his penance. She had been adamant, however, and given him a sisterly kiss and told him she was sorry she had been such a failure. Women really knew how to wound you, even if they did it unwittingly.

'I understand Alain is coming back, too,' he said, giving himself a breather.

'I didn't know that. How is he?'

'It hasn't been announced yet? His marriage?'

'No.' Cleo knew at once that Claudine would have engineered that; her timing was always perfect. She just wondered why such an announcement had to be delayed till the proper moment. 'I'm glad to hear it. Who's he marrying?'

He drew a deep breath: he must be short of wind. 'My ex-wife. Simone.'

The ice-floes met, crumbled at the edges and drifted apart. There was silence in the room. Outside in the newsroom it seemed to Tom that everyone was listening; then he realized he had been waiting for the clattering, clacking sounds of the old newsroom. Then once again he remembered that nobody out there knew anything of what he had felt for Cleo. Still felt: as soon as he had walked into her office, saw her looking barely different from when he had last seen her, the old feeling had come tumbling back, almost throwing him off balance.

She, for her part, felt as if she might fall apart at any moment. Since he had called her yesterday and asked could he come see her, she had been preparing herself, as if she, and not he, was the one to be interviewed. She did not feel at all comfortable offering him a job; it gave her a dominance she did not want. She wondered why he had not gone to any of the other papers in town, but did not ask.

'It's a small world,' she said at last; then provided her own example: 'I suppose you know who owns a fair parcel of stock in the *Courier*?'

'Lord Cruze. Alain told me that.'

'What else did he tell you, Tom?'

But he could see people hovering outside the glass wall. He half-rose. 'I'm taking up your time, Cleo. It's getting close to conference time, isn't it?'

She knew he had retreated; at once she had her doubts that anything could ever work between them again. She beat her own retreat, became the editor: 'Tom, if you come to work I'll want to hold you to a contract. A two-year one. I don't want you drifting off again when you feel like it, not if I give you the job over the heads of some of the younger guys here.'

He was thirty-nine: suddenly she was telling him he was no longer young. He smiled as he stood up. 'Cleo old girl – remember when I used to call you that? Are we both growing old? Do you still swagger?'

'I'd fire any of the men who said so.' But she smiled, aware that he was trying to ease things for both of them. He was not ready yet for personal questions; she should not have asked him what Alain had told him about Jack Cruze. 'Will you sign a contract?'

'I'll think about it.' Then, realizing that sounded churlish, he added, 'I hope you'd want me around that long.'

'Yes, I would. You'll fit in very well on the paper the way it is now.'

Three people were standing in the doorway. He edged his way out past them: 'I'll call you tomorrow morning.'

She was impatient to see him before then, almost asked him to have supper with her after she left the office tonight. But they still had no solid ground beneath them and she trod carefully: 'Have lunch with me. Where are you staying?'

463

'The Tuscany.'

A good middle-priced hotel: he was glad he had chosen it, it didn't sound too ostentatious in front of the people he would be coming to work amongst. He walked back up the newsroom, feeling weaker than when he had come in; he was more in love with her than he had ever been. It was frightening to find, more than halfway through your allotted span, that there were depths of feeling you had never plumbed.

Cleo attended to the matters brought to her; then had five minutes to herself before the four o'clock editorial conference. In her mind's eye she saw Tom as clearly as if he were still sitting across the desk from her. He was older and, she guessed, wiser: the withdrawn look in his eyes now suggested a reserved wisdom rather than a wariness. She wondered if she was any wiser herself; and doubted it. She should have told him there was no job for him on the paper and sent him away. She should not have allowed him to drift back into her life, though, to be sure, he did suggest that he might now carry an anchor.

The phone rang: it was Jack, watching her from across the Atlantic. Or so she thought, feeling guilty. 'Dear girl –' He had taken to calling her that, sounding paternal. She tolerated it because she did not want to offend him. 'I can't come over this weekend. Doc Hynd thinks I need to rest up a bit –'

'Jack – are you all right?' She was genuinely concerned for him. He was almost sixty, but still lived a programme that would have tired a man twenty years younger. She was angry with him because she was worried for him: 'Dammit, I've been telling you to take it easy –'

'So now I'm doing it.'

'Are you sure it's nothing serious? Don't lie to me, Jack. I can always call Dr Hynd.'

She had noticed over the past couple of months that he seemed lacking in his old vitality. It took him longer to get over the flight from London; there would be no love-making his first night in New York. They would go to an occasional dinner party or out to Souillac to one of Claudine's luncheons; sometimes they would go to the theatre or the ballet,

464

though he went to the latter only to please her. More often than not he was content to, as he said, potter around. It was as if he flew the Atlantic each weekend to spend the sort of quiet two days that tired businessmen spent at home in the Home Counties.

'Dear girl, I'm all *right*. I'll be as right as pie next weekend. I'll miss you, Cleo. I wish you were here.'

'I wish I were, too.' She meant it, but for a different reason from the one he would take for granted. She was all at once afraid of what she was going to do to fill the suddenly empty weekend. If she were in London she would be that much farther from temptation. 'Take care, Jack. I'll call you to-morrow. Tell Mrs Cromwell to stuff you with sensible food.'

'There you go . . .' But he chuckled. 'I love you, Cleo.'

3

She took Tom to lunch next day in the restaurant in Rocke-feller Center. She had at first thought of taking him some-where grander; but, like him, she had her own fear of osten-tation. She did not want to show off in front of him, not even on the *Courier*'s expense account. But Tom smiled at the deference shown to her by the *maîtresse d'* who took them to their table.

'I think I'll go back to Paris. New York is being taken over by women.'

'You can't give up without a fight.'

They were a little more at ease with each other today. But they took their time, looking at other people before they looked carefully at themselves. 'That's a girl named P. J. Lagerlof over there. She works on *International*.'

'One of those, eh?'

'One of those – you mean a liberated woman? No, she's not. She has her problems.' Then she noticed that P. J.'s companion was someone she had not seen before, a handsome boy who could be two or three years younger than P. J. Maybe she no longer had a problem, maybe the married

465

lover had gone back to his wife for good. Or bad. 'What are you smiling at?'

Tom had sighted his own diversion. 'Those two guys over there in the corner. They're both writers. I can guess what they're saying to each other, telling each other lies about their advances and their sales.'

'Is that what writers do?'

'It's all fiction to them.'

'You don't say *to us*.'

'I'm a newspaperman, Cleo. I just strayed from the True Path. Now I'm glad to be back. I'll take the job.'

'You don't want to discuss terms?'

'I'll trust you.'

She turned away abruptly and looked out of the window. The towers of the Center had collected the breezes and turned them into a cauldron of wind; the flags on the line of poles outside flapped like the wings of birds of paradise whose bodies had been squeezed into the hollow staffs. She lowered her own flag, looked back at him.

'What are you doing this weekend?'

He hid his surprise at her direct approach. 'Looking around for an apartment. I don't like hotel living.'

'I'll help you,' she said enthusiastically. Then she backed off, not wanting to force herself on him: 'May I?'

'Of course.' If he was going to put down anchor, then he had to come to terms with the harbour-master. Or mistress.

P. J. and her companion stopped by the table on their way out. 'Cleo, this is Colin Bygraves. We're being married next month.'

Cleo pressed her hand and kissed her cheek, feeling suddenly full of emotion. 'All the happiness in the world for both of you. Will you live in New York?'

'Colin's from California – who in New York ever has a tan like that? I'm retiring, Cleo. I'm going to be a housewife and mother.'

She took away the sun-tanned bridegroom-and-father-to-be. He hadn't said a word, just stood there smiling in his Hollywood handsomeness, proud to be shown off.

'Is he what you women call a living doll?' Tom said.

'He didn't sound as if he had much to offer, did he? But I can't blame P. J. for marrying him.' She didn't explain what she meant by that and he didn't ask. Marriage, anyone's, was a subject to be avoided.

That afternoon she rang Jack at the flat in St James's Place. He told her he had just had dinner – 'liver and bacon' – and tomorrow he would be going down to St Aidan's House. 'I'm taking it easy, just as Doc Hynd said to.'

They talked for a few more minutes, then she hung up and immediately called Dr Hynd. He told her that she was fortunate to catch him, that he was just about to go out to dinner.

'I hope you'll be eating something sensible.'

'Not at all. I'm going to Le Gavroche at someone else's expense. I shall gorge myself on the richest dishes on the menu. I suppose you're calling me about Lord Cruze?'

'He says you've told him to rest up.'

'He drives himself too hard, he has a workload he should have shed ten years ago. He has an angina condition, a severe one. He will be all right if he slows down, takes care of himself and doesn't continue jetting across the Atlantic as if he were some airline pilot half his age. To put it bluntly, Miss Spearfield, that's the message you should try to get across to him. To be his age.'

'I'll do that.' She hung up with the feeling that Dr Hynd, on his way to gorge himself at someone else's expense, did not approve of her. Perhaps he thought she was too rich and indigestible for a man like Jack who wouldn't act his age.

She put the *Courier* to bed that night with a feeling of excitement, not at what the paper contained but because it was the end of the week and tomorrow she would have her mind all to herself, to occupy it any way it cared to lurch. She was determined to have no plan, to let herself drift in the current that surrounded Tom.

They went looking at apartments. It was obvious that Tom had no real idea of what he wanted and he let Cleo take over.

The rents, to him, sounded like purchase prices; she soon realized that Simone must have done all their flat-hunting; his mind was still in the price-bracket of the furnished two rooms he had lived in five or six years ago. On what was still a very healthy bank balance and the promise of thirty thousand dollars a year, he still had a welfare state anticipation of subsidized housing. Like her father, he thought inflation was criminal and therefore not to be encouraged. She would not ask him to write any pieces for the financial pages.

'Does it hurt you to spend money?' she asked.

'I guess it does. I never look at bank statements, so I don't think you could accuse me of hoarding it. I just hate spending it, that's all. Nine hundred bucks a month for this!'

They had looked at seven apartments so far. Finally they came to one in Kips Bay Plaza. It had a view (the Con Edison smokestacks, the New York University Medical Center, four square inches of the East River), the rent was $612 a month and it was immediately available. It had the added advantage of not being in the neighbourhood of her own apartment on East 89th Street.

'Now we'll go and look at furniture. Just the essentials, a bed and a chair and a table. You can do the rest at your leisure.'

'You're just like Simone, a real manager.'

'Don't let's make comparisons.' But she said it lightly, glad in a way that he could bring his ex-wife into the conversation without too much embarrassment. She knew she would feel more awkward herself when she had to mention Jack.

She took him to W & J Sloane's, spending his money with all the profligacy of a woman not married to him, telling him (though not convincing him) that in the long run expensive furniture was the best buy. Then the expedition was finished, daylight was gone and evening, the dangerous time, was upon them.

'I'll take you to dinner,' he said. 'McDonald's. Since you haven't left me any cash for anything better.'

'No, I'll save your last few cents. We'll buy a take-home gourmet dinner and go back to my place.'

468

'A take-home gourmet dinner – they'll be freeze-packing sex next. Can't you cook?'

It struck her then how little they really knew about each other. *We've been in love for all these years and we know nothing of the everyday things that go to make us what we are.* Long distance pen pals who had never met probably knew more about each other.

'I'm the world's worst. Put my cooking alongside a TV dinner and Craig Claiborne would take the TV dinner every time.'

He shook his head. 'The illusions I've had about you all these years.'

They were as easy with each other now as ten-year lovers should be. She took his hand and led him to a French delicatessen whose owner, showing how the French could be corrupted when they emigrated, made up take-away dinners. Tom, showing his own taste, bought a bottle of Corton Renardes – 'though maybe a six-pack of Budweiser would be more appropriate'.

The food was filling, if nothing else; the wine was mood-inducing. When he put down his glass, came round the table and kissed her, it was the natural end of the day. She felt no guilt or concern, because it was as if the walls of her apartment were those of a time capsule. The past and the future had nothing to do with this joyously full Saturday.

They went to bed as if they had been doing it every Saturday for the past ten years: but it was not the Saturday night routine love-making of a married couple. Nor was it a roll in the hay, as it had been for him all that time ago in Saigon. They showed the value of experience to each other, not just of the mechanics but of the emotion of love-making. When she wept after her climax he understood and did not ask her why.

Then the phone rang, a pistol-shot from London.

She knew at once who it would be. She got out of bed, went out to the kitchen and took the call there.

'You didn't phone,' Jack said accusingly.

469

'My phone has been out of order. I haven't been able to call out.' She was more ashamed of how easily she lied than she was of what she had been doing with Tom. 'I didn't want to go out – it's raining cats and dogs here.' That, at least, wasn't a lie. 'How are you?'

'Lonely.' He sounded so self-pitying she wanted to laugh; not cruelly, but because he sounded genuinely funny. 'What are you doing?'

'I'm about to wash up my dinner dishes and go to bed. I watched TV for a while.'

'What did you see?'

'*Barney Miller.*' She had no idea if the show ran on Saturday night or what time it was screened: she didn't care, at least not tonight. She was standing naked in her kitchen being quizzed about her every idle moment: she could feel all the old chains being linked together around her. 'You shouldn't be calling me now. What time is it over there?'

'The middle of the night.'

She knew that the middle of the night was not an hour marked on any clock: it was a state of mind. Suddenly she was not angry with him for what she had thought was his old possessiveness. He was genuinely lonely.

'I've been lying here thinking –' He sounded tentative, as if apprehensive of her answer. 'What would you say if I came to live in New York for six months of the year?'

Oh God, she thought, what a time to ask me! She could see her nakedness reflected faintly in the glass front of the old-fashioned kitchen dresser; she could feel Tom's semen drying on the inside of one of her legs; then Tom, naked as herself, was standing in the kitchen doorway. Yet another pistol, not Tom's, was being pointed at her.

'We'll talk about it.' She did not call him by name, not with Tom standing only three feet from her. 'In the meantime do what Dr Hynd said and take it easy. I'll call you tomorrow. Not in the middle of the night.'

'I love you.' It sounded plaintive, but three thousand miles can do ventriloquial tricks with a person's voice.

'I know that.' She could say no more, could not tell him

470

that she loved him. Not with Tom's hand squeezing her bare buttock. 'I'll call you tomorrow.'

She hung up and Tom, letting go of her buttock, said, 'I know who that was.'

Something of her mother came out in her: she needed to be modestly covered if she was going to talk seriously. Even whores, she guessed, put on something before they discussed price. She brushed past Tom, went into the bedroom and put on a robe. She picked up Tom's boxer shorts, came out into the living room and tossed them to him.

'A little decorum, I see.' He pulled on the shorts and sat down in what, over the time he had been coming to the apartment, had become Jack's favourite chair. 'You're right. I've never been able to understand how nudists can have serious conversations. For about ninety-eight per cent of his time, a man's genitals must be about the most ridiculous, useless appendages ever hung on him. They tend to lower the tone of any serious conversation.'

'Oh shut up!' she said angrily.

There was silence between them for a while, then he said quietly, 'I'm not going to share you with him.'

'I hadn't thought that far.' But the time capsule had been shattered.

'Well, you better.'

She shook her head in despair; she could not argue with him now. 'I know. I tried not to think about it – all I wanted was to have some time with you that wouldn't be spoiled. Every time we've been together . . .' Her voice trailed off. She stared at him in Jack's chair, looking as if he – *belonged* there. Which he did. 'We can't break up again, not now.'

'No.' He knew it would be torture to stay in New York, but there was a certain amount of masochism in all love. 'But you'll have to tell him.'

She nodded, afraid of the prospect.

'When?'

'Oh God, I don't know!' Then she quietened down. 'He'll be over next weekend, if he's well enough. He has a heart condition.'

471

'Oh Jesus!' It was Tom's turn to shake his head. 'He stacks everything in his favour, doesn't he?' She gave him a hard reproachful look and he threw up his hands resignedly. 'Okay, that's not fair. He can't help his health. But he has everything else going for him.'

'I'm as much to blame as he is. Maybe more.'

He didn't argue with her on that point. Abruptly he stood up. 'Do you want some coffee?'

Coffee had become a prop, like the telephone in stage plays. Brazil, the saviour of emotional situations. She followed him into the kitchen, looked at him in surprise as he searched for bread, found it and dropped two slices into the toaster.

'I always get hungry in situations like this,' he said.

'Have you had many of them?'

'Three times. In Saigon, in Hamburg and that day I told you I was married to Simone. I put on weight when I'm unhappy. Watch me over the next few weeks.'

She turned him towards her, kissed him on the lips. 'I'm the opposite, I get thin.'

'Well, we should balance things out.'

The talk was flip, a smokescreen. Suddenly he pulled her into him and kissed her savagely. She responded, then pulled away from him and dredged up a laugh.

'Just as well we don't wear dentures.' The laugh was another smokescreen; but life, she knew, was like that. 'They'd be halfway down our throats choking us.'

The smokescreen lasted the rest of the weekend till she had to leave for the office on Sunday afternoon. Occasionally they came out into the open with each other, to sustain their love. If everything else had been out of kilter, their love-making hadn't. Sex is heartless, so to be enjoyed.

4

Cleo had made some changes to the staffing. She had conferred with Claudine, as the publisher, and been a little surprised at the latter's co-operation.

472

'I am not stupid,' said Claudine, 'I know that Jake Lintas tried to run a one-man band. If you feel we need a managing editor, we'll have one. Titles really don't mean anything.' Not unless they were hereditary and noble. She would rather have been a princess than a publisher, though not of some small principality.

'No, I don't want a managing editor.' Cleo, since coming to America, a land of no nobility, had learned the value of titles. 'I want to make Joe Hamlyn *assistant* managing editor.'

'What happens to the post of managing editor?'

'I'll fill that myself, though I prefer to be called editor.'

Claudine smiled. She knew the public would never appreciate what a managing editor was, the man responsible for all news operations except the editorial pages. But they understood the term *editor*, or thought they did, and Cleo wanted the public to know who she was.

'You are ambitious, aren't you?'

'Only for the paper,' said Cleo. Their smiles were white lies.

So Joe Hamlyn was brought back from Washington to be assistant managing editor, a title he had the grace not to question. Other editors were given more responsibility in their departments. By the time Tom came to work on the *Courier*, there was more team-work on the paper than there ever had been under Jake Lintas.

Tom came to the office on Monday afternoon. 'When do I start?'

'As soon as you like.'

'There's a national story I'd like to do, about organized crime. I know it's been done before, several times. But I'd like to go out to Kansas City and find out why Hal Rainer was murdered.'

'No!' Then she regained control of herself. 'I blame myself for Hal's death. I'm not going to have you risking your life for the same story. Hal was killed because he'd found out too much about Tony Rossano. Let it rest at that.'

'Cleo old girl –' He was totally relaxed, he sounded like the Tom Border she had known in the dangerous days in

473

Vietnam. 'You'll have to separate the editor from that other girl. I don't want any favours.'

'I'm not doing you a favour trying to stop you from being killed!' Her voice rose again, then she looked up as Carl Fishburg knocked on her open door and came into the office.

'You two fighting already?'

'This damfool wants to go out to Kansas City and risk getting what Hal got.'

'It'd be a good story,' said Carl, safe at the city desk. 'It wouldn't be mine, but I'd be glad to lend him to Joe.'

Joe Hamlyn stood in the doorway, one hand cupped to his ear. 'Someone going to loan me something?'

Tom explained what he had in mind. 'But Cleo wants to be protective. Have you ever heard of an editor being protective towards his reporters?'

'I've never been guilty of it myself,' said Joe.

'Me neither,' said Carl.

'Bloody men!' said Cleo. 'It's no joking matter. Tom could go out there and get his head blown off as soon as that man Rossano found out he was in town.'

'If we held back the story till I was back here in New York, the Mob out in K.C. wouldn't know I was working for the *Courier*, that I had any connection with Hal. My by-line hasn't been a regular one in the paper. I could be just a hometown boy come home to visit my folks.'

'Your folks live down in Friendship.'

He was surprised that she remembered. 'Sure, but I once worked in Kansas City. Anyone who works in K.C. for one pay-day, they claim him forever. Count Basie was born in New Jersey and spent, I don't know, no more than two or three years of his entire life in K.C. But out there he's a native son. That's what I'll be, a native son come home for a few weeks.'

'Don't be too conspicuous,' said Joe, suddenly serious.

Cleo saw now that Tom wanted to go to Kansas City for more than just a story. He wanted to be out of New York when Jack came over from London. Perhaps it was cowardice, perhaps it was wisdom: in any event he was putting her out on the limb she herself had grafted on to the tree. She could not blame him for deserting her. But he didn't have to go out into Indian, or gangster, terr'tory.

Woman-like, which was what she knew they all expected of her, she looked at Joe Hamlyn. 'What do you think, Joe?'

'I'd like to know who killed Hal and why,' said Joe. 'I've never really worried myself about whether justice has been done or been seen to be done. But in this case...'

'The sons-of-bitches should be flushed out,' said Carl, and Tom nodded.

Then Cleo realized that, though Tom may have brought up the idea only as an excuse to escape the next week or two, the reminder of Hal Rainer's murder had taken hold of the three men. It was the kinship of the newsroom, the police shack, the locker room: it did not occur amongst all men, but it had with these three men and Hal. It was something that women, even one in a man's game, were locked out of.

She sighed, tossed her gold pen on her desk. 'Righto, you win. You're on the payroll as of now – I'll tell Personnel. You may as well get started right away. Catch a plane out to-night.'

All three men looked surprised. Tom said, 'I'd like to read the files first –'

'Take them with you. Ring Joe every day to let him know how you're going. And don't take any stupid bloody risks!'

Joe Hamlyn and Carl Fishburg, married men, recognized that something else besides the safety of one of her reporters was on Cleo's mind. They suddenly found they had work to do back at their own desks, got up and left Cleo's office.

Tom stood up slowly. 'Honey, I thought I was doing the right thing. I don't want to be around when you tell Cruze –'

'I guessed that. But why the hell can't you choose some-where safe to retreat to? Go – go and do a piece on the national parks!'

He grinned, then was sober. 'I'll take care, I promise. You do the same. I offered to stay here and be with you when you talk to him –'

475

'No.' She had refused the suggestion when he had made it as they lay in bed on Sunday morning. 'That wouldn't be fair to him. Ring me tonight and let me know where you're staying.'

'Do I kiss you or just shake hands?'

'Neither. In this office I'm your editor.' But she wanted to grab him, feel the bone and muscle and flesh of him in her hands. Her hands actually seemed to itch. 'You'd better go.'

He stopped at the door. 'Cleo old girl –'

She shook her head, reading his mind. 'No, it's better that you're out of the way when I see him. There are some things a woman does better on her own.'

5

Jack flew in on Thursday afternoon. She left Joe and Carl to conduct the editorial conference and took a limousine out to meet him at Kennedy Airport. As he came towards her, walking behind the red cap carrying his one bag, she knew that telling him the news of herself and Tom was going to be so much harder than she had thought. He had aged, put on five years or more in the two weeks since she had seen him last. He had aged, but what was worse, she could see the sad defiance in his grey face, he had refused to accept it.

She kissed him on the cheek, took his hand, felt him holding hers as if he were blind and she was leading him through a hostile crowd. But his eyes were not blind and she read the delight in them at seeing her. She felt sicker by the minute at what lay ahead. Bad news is always the easiest news for reporters to write and editors to feature; but none of her training and none of Jack's experience was going to make the personal bad news easy to bear. She held his hand and chattered.

'What's the matter?' he said, good-humoured, already looking a year younger. 'You haven't stopped talking.'

They were in the limousine heading into Manhattan to the

Pierre. Though he occasionally stayed the night at her apartment, he had not made it a habit; for business reasons he always booked into the Pierre. Cleo knew there was gossip about the two of them, but no one ever mentioned it to her face.

'It's been a busy week. I guess I'm still keyed up. It gets like this sometimes.'

'The world's falling apart.' But he didn't look too disturbed. 'I've been thinking about retiring. How'd you like to go and live in the Bahamas or the Virgin Islands?'

'I couldn't edit the *Courier* from there.' She smiled, trying to keep the mood between them light. 'Let's talk after you've rested.'

She settled him into his suite at the hotel, told him she would come by for a late supper. Then she went back to the paper and spent the next few hours agonizing over how she was going to give him the bad news. She looked at the make-up of Page One: disaster covered it. Tomorrow's paper would be chock-full of history in the making, most of which readers would prefer not to read. She had begun to believe that the man in the street, the object of Mr Kugel's scorn, did not want to know about the diseases of his world: he had enough of his own. The curing of them was beyond his power and so he gave up; if he cared at all, he wrote cynical letters to the paper that were as depressing to read as the subjects that made him so discouraged and bitter. Some day she must look for Benjamin Franklin's comments on the man in the streets of Philadelphia.

She finished at the office at ten and took a cab to the Pierre. Jack had slept, then bathed and also washed his hair; the grey was almost white, adding to his aged look. He was dressed in silk pyjamas, a paisley silk dressing-gown and a white silk cravat; but suavity was not his long or his best suit. He looked like Noël Coward's gardener.

The talk was light, like their supper. But there was a heavy feeling in her chest, as if she had stuffed herself with one of his sensible dinners. At last she said, 'Jack, there's something I have to tell you.'

477

'I thought there might. Is it the paper?'

That would be a simple problem. 'No. Jack – I'm in love with someone else.' The words were like a bubble in her mouth, they were straight out of soap opera. 'I wish I didn't have to tell you now – I mean while you're not well –'

He sat very quietly looking at the shreds of smoked salmon on his plate. His cravat had slipped down, exposing his stringy throat, and even his dressing-gown seemed to have slipped off his shoulders. One might have thought he was suddenly falling apart, except that sartorially he had always been on the verge of doing just that. His voice was hoarse: 'Is it someone I know?'

'Not very well. Tom Border.'

'Aah.' It was difficult to tell whether it was a sigh of understanding or of pain. 'How long has it been going on?'

'Only since last weekend. Two days, that's all. He's now out in Kansas City.'

He looked at her quizzically, as if to say, *Pull the other leg.* 'You've known him for years.'

'Only at a distance. He was married for years. Five or six, anyway. He's just been divorced. Alain Roux is marrying his ex-wife.'

'What a bloody merry-go-round!' He pulled the cravat away from his throat, began rolling it up as if it were a bandage.

She waited impatiently, unable to tell whether he was shocked or angry or indifferent. In the old days he would have flown into a rage, accused her of treachery, told her she was ungrateful for everything he had done for her. If he still felt any of that he was either afraid to let it spill out of him or he hadn't energy any more to express it.

He was now pulling the cravat tightly round one hand, like a tourniquet. She was surprised, almost let down, when he said quietly, 'I suppose it had to come. I was always too old for you.'

'It wasn't that.' It was, but only partly so. It was deeper: she had never loved him and, though it was specious honesty

478

on her part, she had never told him she did. But she could not hurt him further now by telling him she had never been in love with him. Though, being shrewd, he had probably known the truth of that. 'There were always too many other things between us.'

'Emma?'

She was glad to accept that excuse if he was. 'Yes. But other things.'

'What?'

Men, she thought, are just like women: they liked to be tortured when in love. She was more composed now that he was not going to fly into a rage and precipitate a heart attack. 'Jack, you've always wanted me to play second fiddle. Look at what you suggested tonight. I'm only thirty-four and you want me to retire, give up everything I've achieved, and go and live with you in the Virgin Islands.'

'Bloody ambition!'

'You had it. Why not me?'

He gestured in frustration, because he had no answer. Then after a while he conceded: 'It really takes hold of you, doesn't it?'

She knew what he meant, had recognized the symptoms in herself. She had not been ambitious as a girl growing up; that had only come when she had grown tired of being nobody but Sylvester Spearfield's daughter. Now she had discovered that ambition had its own momentum; and suddenly, afraid, wondered if Tom, the least ambitious of men, would understand. They hadn't talked of the future beyond her telling Jack that it was all over between them.

She reached across the small table, put her hand on his. She still had affection for him, even love: but not the sort of love he wanted from her. 'I'm sorry, Jack. You haven't made very good choices with your women, have you?'

'You don't *choose* whom you fall in love with. Christ, you should know that!' For a moment he flared, like the old Jack.

She nodded: indeed she did know it. She sat back in her chair, all at once felt hungry and began to nibble at the smoked salmon. The heaviness in her chest had gone: talk, sometimes, is a good antacid.

He watched her with sour admiration. 'You women have remarkable powers of recovery. If a man reacted like some of you do, you'd say he was unfeeling.'

She smiled, unoffended. They were back on safe ground, the war between the sexes. 'I'd never say that about you. You were selfish and demanding and a hundred other things, but you were never unfeeling.'

'There you go again –' Then he grinned, though the humour had difficulty rising in him. He watched her eat and she watched him watching her, knowing that his mind hadn't stopped working. Only when she had finished what was on her plate and sat back, did he say, 'You won't be wanting to see me again, I take it?'

'Do you think it would be wise? It would only make us both more unhappy.'

'There's the paper...'

Abruptly another fear struck her: 'Do you want to get rid of me as editor?'

'No-o.' He didn't sound emphatic. 'But once I sell out, Claudine might not want you.'

He was threatening her, getting his own back in no uncertain way. 'Would you do that to me? Sell your interest in the *Courier*?'

'I bought it for you. You know that, though we never said anything. You've done a good job and the paper's making money for me. But not enough to really interest me, not even enough to pay for these trips I've been making across here to see you. But that's not the point. It's been a fight all along with Claudine – you and Jerry Kibler know that. She's fought every innovation every inch of the way. I'm not interested in that sort of fight any more. Dr Hynd told me to take it easy. So did you,' he added after a proper pause for effect. 'The more I can relieve myself of headaches, the longer I'll live.'

She was angry and hurt; but she couldn't blame him for his attitude. She tried the first argument that came to her tongue: 'If I left, so would a lot of the other editors. The paper would fall apart and a lot of people would be thrown out of work.'

'If I hadn't bought into the paper they'd have all been out of jobs a couple of years ago. Don't start playing hearts and flowers on your second fiddle.'

She couldn't help smiling, though sourly. 'Where did you get that one?'

'I pinched it from Jane Kempton.' She was the columnist who had replaced Cleo when she had gone home to Australia. Whether that was his source or not, it was a nice touch. He had become subtler in the baiting game.

She put it to him directly: 'Will you sell out?'

'I'll think about it.'

The evening had ended as badly as she had feared, but in a different way. She just wondered why she hadn't considered the possibility of what he was suggesting: he owed her nothing. She stood up, looking at her watch. 'I have to go back to the office. With stories breaking the way they have been this past week, I keep an eye on it right down to the last edition.'

That was a lie, he knew. 'Yes,' he said. 'It's been a bad week all round.'

When she had gone he sat in his chair staring at the remains of the meal on the table: the last supper, he guessed. He put a hand to the top of his head where she had kissed him goodnight: it had been like a niece's kiss. He felt anything but avuncular; he felt murderously jealous. Bugger younger men! They did not run the world, that was still the province of older, wiser men; but they were the women's choice in love and sex and that, if it did not run the world, made it go round. Or so the poets, all young ones, he'd bet, had said.

He felt the twinge in his chest; there was a sudden pain in his left arm. He took a pill-box from the pocket of his dressing-gown and swallowed a tablet. He continued to sit, willing himself to relax, opening himself, as it were, to let the emotion drain out of him. Then he began to weep.

He remembered some lines from a Roman poet, one whose

481

name he couldn't recall. The lines had been on the fly-leaf of a political biography:

I shall go quietly
merely shutting my eyes.

But he could not close his eyes, they were too full of tears.

EIGHTEEN

1

Tony Rossano lived in a sprawling house in Mission Hills in Kansas City. The large grounds were surrounded by an eight-foot high spiked railing fence; every fifty feet there were signs on the fence, like armorial bearings, warning that the grounds were patrolled by security men. The security men were not uniformed, unless dead-pan faces and bulges under their armpits were a uniform. Tony Rossano had been black-balled by the three nearby country clubs and so he had laid out a putting green at the rear of his house. It was rumoured that he could not drive a golf ball straight for more than twenty yards, but he was possibly the best putter in the State of Missouri. His neighbours thought he was the worst resident in the area.

He had lost some hair and gained some weight since he had gone up in the world. The underworld, that is; he was still a long way under the surface in Kansas City's social world. *The Independent*, the city's social magazine, would not have run his name even if he had murdered ten of the top socialites. He had the sleek look of a successful businessman, which indeed he was; he was regional director of laundry for the Mob in Chicago. That he laundered money rather than clothes or linen was neither here nor there in his view. He had a nice tolerance of his own attitudes.

He was on his putting green as the housemaid brought two men out of the house. He finished his putt, put the ball in the hole and looked up with the grimace of his lips that he mistakenly thought was his smile. 'So what'd you learn?'

The bigger of the two men took off his hat, the brim of which he had pulled down over his face like an old-time movie gangster. He was a police detective from over the border in Kansas and he always tried to hide his face when he called on gangsters. He amused Tony Rossano, but he was the best informer on Rossano's pay-roll.

'This guy you told me about, his name's Border. Tom Border. He made a lotta dough as a writer. A book writer,' he explained, as if Rossano might confine his reading to race-books. 'But he's a newspaper guy, too. He used to work for the *New York Courier*. Maybe he still does, I couldn't check on that. But I will,' he added when he saw Rossano's look.

'Where's he staying?'

'The Raphael. He seems to know K.C. pretty good.'

Rossano looked at the other man. He was shorter than the detective but probably weighed more. He was bald and wore no hat and his big red face had the friendly politician's look of a cardinal from one of the richer dioceses. He was the only Irishman who worked for Rossano and, as such, invaluable. An Irish ear to the ground in Kansas City politics was as necessary as having an inside line to the White House in Kennedy's day. He was a practising Catholic and, with the new liberalism in the Church, didn't have to go to confession each Saturday to confess his sins, which were many.

'He knows where to go to ask the questions.' He had a deep rumbling voice, in contrast to the detective's, which was only slightly lower than a high squeak. 'He's been getting answers, too. I think he's working for that New York paper, Tony.'

Rossano had a mind like a filing cabinet; he kept a mental dossier on everyone who had crossed him since he was twelve years old and fighting the other kids on East Missouri in Little Italy. 'I know the dame who's editor of that paper. She was a pain in the ass.'

'They all are,' said the Irishman, but didn't say whether he meant editors or dames.

'What you gonna do?' said the detective.

'Depends what he writes, if he writes anything,' said Rossano. 'The men up in Chicago –' Then he stopped. He liked

484

to think, and he liked those who worked for him to think, that he didn't have to concern himself with the opinions of others.

'Can I make a suggestion, Tony? I don't think anything oughta happen to him, not in K.C. The KCPD weren't very happy about what happened to that other newspaper guy from the *Courier*. They know who put out the contract, they told me that. They told me they even knew who the hit guy was, but they couldn't pin it on him. Something happens to this guy Border in this town, the shit's gonna hit the fan, Tony.'

'Well, we'll see if he writes anything. I might sue him for libel.' He thought he smiled, but neither of the men noticed it. 'Any rate, one thing about a hit man, he'll travel anywhere if the price is right. Even to New York.'

The Irishman polished the top of his head with a ham of a hand. 'Wouldn't it be nice if we all lived and let live?'

'You'd be out of a job,' said Rossano and went back to his putting. Golf was the ideal game. You were only playing yourself and, if you watched yourself, no bastard could cheat you.

2

After a week in Kansas City, Tom went down home to Friendship for a couple of days. After the muck he had dug up in K.C., the dogwood and redbud were soft-focus commercials for spring, now on the road up from the south. Goddam, he thought, I even think in city images now. He had almost forgotten what life could be like here in the quiet countryside. He sat on the front porch and watched the ducks and geese heading north again, drawing their dark lines across the pale blue sky. He went down to the big pond beyond the orchards and saw the mallards taking time out on the water still dark from winter and he marvelled again, as he had as a boy, at the colour in the birds' heads and necks. At night he heard the great horned owl over by the

485

main barn, sounding like an echo of the bird he had heard in his youth.

'Do you ever miss all this?' his father said to him on the last day of his visit.

He picked at the Maltese cross of the dogwood blossom in his hand. 'I'm ashamed to say, Pop, I never really think about it. I think about you and Mom, but never this –' He gestured at the countryside, the landscape of his boyhood. 'I should. This is what made me, generations of the families, yours and Mom's, living here.'

'Will you ever come back?' Clem Border stroked the coat of his favourite dog, a crossbred setter. He had lost the knack of talking to his son and he was glad of the dog to distract him. He watched Tom out of the corner of his eye, remarking how the boy he had been close to had changed to this man who was a near-stranger. The change had all taken place in the last few years, since his marriage to Simone.

'Maybe some day. When I'm your age.' He grinned at his father. 'You'll still be here, even then.'

'I guess so. The Borders have always been a long-living family.' He looked carefully at the dog for ticks, though he knew it had none. 'Your mother and I were sorry you and Simone broke up.'

'It was one of those things, Pop. She's married again, or about to be.'

'What about you?'

'Marry again? I don't know. There's another girl –' He told his father about Cleo, but it was a thumbnail sketch; for some reason he was afraid that his parents would be prejudiced against her. 'We've spent ten years dodging each other.'

'I was down in Australia during the war. World War Two.' It hurt him to have to identify the wars; he had thought his would be the last. 'They're a tight-fisted lot, the Aussies. Short arms and deep pockets. Even their girls thought so.'

'Cleo is generous.' She was in her love-making; but how would he know if she was generous in everything else? Ten

486

years, and he was only at the beginning of really knowing her. 'I think you'd like her, Pop.'

'She's important, though, isn't she? In her job, I mean.'

'Women have come out of the kitchen.'

'Yeah, I been reading about that,' his father said with a grin.

'It hasn't spoiled her,' he said doggedly. 'You'll like her.'

'We liked Simone.'

Dear Christ, Tom thought, make it work between Cleo and me! There were so many people to be convinced. He shut his mind against the thought of whether he, too, had to be convinced.

He went back to New York that afternoon and straight to the *Courier*'s office. He typed a few notes for his story, waited around and then took Cleo home to her apartment and bed. They were hungry for each other; there was no discussion of Jack or of Tony Rossano. In the car taking them uptown she did say, 'Things went okay with you?'

'Yes. The same with you?'

She nodded. It was enough; discussion could wait. It was next morning before they talked about Jack, and not at all about Rossano; crime and its power were not important for the moment. She said, 'He took it badly. No temper or anything like that, just as if I'd kicked him in the stomach. I took it badly, too.'

It had been more than a matter of conscience. One doesn't live with a person, or anyway half-live, without his becoming part of oneself. Almost against her will she had found herself remembering moments with him; part of the perspective was that she remembered no moments at all with Alain. Jack had been part of her life; Alain never had. The trouble with Jack had been that he had been only part of her life; not her whole life, as Tom would be. She screwed that last thought firmly into her mind, securing it against any doubts that might arise.

'He's gone back to London?' Tom said. 'I guess I should feel sorry for him, but I don't. He had you all those years when I didn't.'

'Not all the time. I was pretty lonely sometimes, especially when I'd think about Simone being lucky enough to have you. Incidentally, Alain and Simone are due back tomorrow. They were married in Paris last Thursday. Claudine, I gather, is furious. She wanted a royal wedding. Well, semi-royal.'

'I better send them a present. All three of us are still supposed to be good friends. Maybe you and I could send them a joint gift.'

'I don't really think that would be a good idea.' Men, even this one she loved so dearly, so often did not know when to leave well enough alone. 'I'll send them a best wishes card. They can tear it up if they're offended.'

'Simone won't be. She's a sweet girl.'

'Thanks for telling me.' But she kissed him to show she understood his lack of tact. He mistook it for generosity on her part.

Cleo was in seventh heaven (Was there an eighth or ninth? She had never felt so happy) to have Tom so close to her, to no longer have any barrier between them. But at the *Courier* she kept him at a distance; he worked for her but only through Carl Fishburg or Joe Hamlyn. It was Carl who brought Tom's Kansas City story to the news conference table.

'Tom's done a good job. But there's no angle we can hang it on, nothing that's gonna make the readers sit up and take notice. I don't think New Yorkers are going to get too excited about the fact that Tony Rossano runs Kansas City for the benefit of Sebastiano Giuffre and his Family in Chicago. Maybe Tom's been away from New York too long. People here could care less about what happens in the rest of the USA.'

'Righto, spike the story – we may be able to use it if something breaks in the future. What else have you got?'

'The Mayor says the city's going broke again –'

Cleo had no regrets about spiking Tom's story. He might be upset, but she hoped he would not complain to her. Life was never meant to be easy for lovers who worked together. Especially when one was the boss of the other.

Tom did complain to Carl Fishburg, but shut up at once when Carl told him who had spiked the story. He did not mention his complaint to Cleo, but he wondered if she was going to go out of her way to show him no favouritism. He began to see difficulties ahead as a newspaperman.

At the end of that week there was a board meeting. When Cleo walked into the boardroom she was surprised, and at once on guard, to see Alain and Roger there. Alain was standing by a window, leaning on his stick; it seemed to her that he had put on some weight and some years. The college boy that had lingered in him was gone now.

She walked up to him. 'Congratulations, Alain. I hope you and your wife will be very happy.'

'Thank you. We got your card.' He was not cool and distant, but neither was he all smiles and good cheer. 'I hear you've become famous while I've been away. *Meet the Press*, the Johnny Carson show – it must be like London when you lived there.'

'Not quite.'

'No. I understand Lord Cruze isn't around any more.'

She smiled, knowing now exactly where he stood, right on her toes. 'You sound like your mother, did you know that? The same intonation –'

At that moment his mother called the meeting to order. With all the intonation of an empress she said, 'You will have observed the presence of my son and my brother. They are here to be formally introduced. I am putting the motion, seconded by Stanley Beaton, that two more board posts be created. I nominate Alain Roux and Roger Brisson to be the new directors.'

'Just like that,' said Jerry Kibler. 'No agenda notice, nothing. No offence, Roger. But Claudine – you made that sound like a military government edict. I read AMGOT notices like that on village walls in Italy during the war.'

'I'm delighted to hear the military could be so lucid and to the point. I'd always thought they were exactly the opposite,' said Claudine. 'No offence, Roger.'

489

'Everyone is busy not offending me,' said Roger. 'Would you prefer that Alain and I retired?'

'There's no need for that,' said Stanley Beaton. He looked a trifle embarrassed and harassed, as if he had only just learned the motion he was seconding. 'I think the voting will show you are elected.' He glanced at Claudine, then held up his hand. It looked more like a salute to her than a voting gesture.

Everyone but Cleo and Jerry Kibler held up their hands, though Stephen Jensen held up his only after some hesitation. Claudine looked at Cleo, but then addressed herself to Jerry. 'You object? Why?'

'This isn't US Steel, it's a small newspaper company. Why do we need so many directors?'

'Alain will eventually succeed me and I think it will be good for the company that he gets practical experience before he does take over from me.' When Alain had suggested that he be put on the board she had not been enthusiastic; blood was thicker than water, but she did not want her authority watered down. She had, however, never denied him anything he really wanted and she had recognized that he had set his heart on having some authority on the *Courier*. Cleo was the reason, of course; as soon as she realized that, she agreed to nominate him. Cleo, it seemed, had lately begun to look on the *Courier* as *her* paper. 'We must look to the future.'

'I always thought you had the future under control,' said Cleo.

'What about General Brisson?' said Jerry Kibler, before knife-throwing could turn the meeting into a blood-bath.

'Roger owns ten per cent of the stock. That entitles him to a place on the board. If we don't create an extra post, then it will necessitate someone with a lesser holding retiring.' She looked at Jensen and the other four underprivileged directors. 'I don't think we should sacrifice their experience.'

'Certainly not mine,' said Jensen, winking down the table at Cleo. She had continued to sit at the bottom of the table, always leaving argument to Jerry Kibler. She knew that he enjoyed argument and was good at it.

490

'I'll have to consult my client.' Kibler looked at his watch, then at Cleo. 'Would he be at home now?'

'I don't know what his routine is these days,' said Cleo.

At the far end of the table Claudine's smile was like a knife-edge of wintry sun. Alain's grin was nothing more than a smirk: some college boy still lingered in him after all. Kibler went out of the room and Claudine said, 'We shan't waste time. Let's attend to the less important matters.'

Kibler was back in ten minutes. He came to the door of the boardroom and signalled to Cleo with a hooked finger. She got up and went out to him. They stood in the corridor while secretaries, passing them, looked at them curiously and wondered what was going on in the boardroom that had sent the editor and another director out to a whispered conference in the corridor. The secretaries went on to their own offices and spent the rest of the day munching on rumours.

'Have you and Jack Cruze had a fight?' Kibler said. 'He sounded as if he didn't care a damn about Alain and Roger.'

'There was no fight. We're no longer – well, the best of friends, if you want to put it that way. What did he say?'

Kibler looked carefully at her for a long moment, then decided not to ask any more personal questions. He was a banker, not a lawyer: that, to an extent, kept him out of the intimacy of his clients' lives. He had never wanted it any other way.

'He said to do whatever I thought fit.' Cleo noted the *I*. Had Jack already dismissed her from the *Courier*, just biding his time to tell her? 'I'm all for saying no, at least to Alain.'

Cleo looked up and down the corridor. She remembered the political cliché, the corridors of power. There was no power here or even in the boardroom behind her: it was virtually all in the person of Claudine. Two Roux would be too much; it would be hooroo, Cleo. 'What are you smiling at?' said Kibler.

'A dreadful play on words.' But she didn't enlighten him. 'We'll vote yes for Roger and no for Alain.'

Jerry Kibler nodded approvingly. 'Let's go back in and jerk the finger at the Empress.'

Claudine recognized the jerked finger, though she had never in her life seen the actual physical gesture. 'I hope there is nothing personal in this. There never should be in business,' she said, who conducted everything she did on a personal level.

'I'm sure there's nothing personal in it,' said Stephen Jensen, who was sure there was and wished he knew the reason for it. 'But a top-heavy board is like a top-heavy woman, out of all proportion to her efficiency.'

'Thank you for the analogy,' said Claudine, sitting straighter than ever to show she was not top-heavy. 'That sounds like a Hasty Pudding Club line, about 1923.'

'Before my time,' said Jensen, knowing once again that one could never have the last word with Claudine.

Alain stood up, holding his cane halfway down its length like a club. He ignored Kibler and looked down the table at Cleo. 'I hope this won't prevent us from working together.'

Then he limped out of the room and Claudine looked at Cleo. 'You appear puzzled by what Alain said. That was the next point I was going to raise. The paper, improving as it is every day under Cleo's able editorship –' her smile would have cut a swathe through the besiegers of the Alamo '– needs someone in the publisher's office every day, time that I cannot afford. I nominate Alain to be the associate publisher, to stand in for me.'

Kibler glanced at Cleo, who managed to restrain a shrug, knowing the matter was already decided, and dredged up a smile that matched Claudine's. 'A good idea. It will give him that experience he'll need when he takes over from you.'

'I'm glad you see it that way,' said Claudine, who intended to live forever. Or at least till God would invite her to join Him as an equal.

The meeting eventually finished and Roger followed Cleo out of the room. 'You'll have my support. You've done a marvellous job on the paper. It's a little more sensationalist, but I suppose that's what people want these days.'

492

'I like to think it's nicely balanced. I don't believe in sensationalism for its own sake.' She had encouraged the copy editors to brighten up their headings, but the paper was not strident. 'It will be nice to have you on the board, if you're going to be on my side.'

'Oh, I shall be. I do owe you something.'

'I thought serving army officers couldn't take civilian jobs?'

'I retired from the Army yesterday. The announcement is being put out from the Pentagon this afternoon. It will probably get only two lines in tomorrow's papers.' He looked suitably modest, a self-inflicted wound that deserved a Purple Heart.

'I'll give it more, if you wish. I'll mention it to Joe Hamlyn.'

'No, I want to keep a low profile for a while.'

'You're not going to content yourself with being just a part-time businessman.' It was a statement, not a question.

'No, I'll be doing some studying and some travelling.' But he wouldn't tell her any more, though she knew at once there was something to tell. 'In the meantime you can rely on my support.'

'How's Louise?'

'I'm still living in Washington and she's out at Sands Point. But we have dinner together when I come up here. We're friends. Not like you and Jack Cruze, of course.' He was fishing, having listened to Claudine's suspicions.

'You're wrong. We're very much like you and Louise.'

He watched her walk away down the corridor, wondering why (but knowing only too well) she and he could not have been more than friends. She had that rare quality, a lady-like swagger to her ass. It was not as pronounced as it had been when he had first met her in Saigon, but she still had it, though it was now politely provocative. She had class and style, which one didn't expect of Australians. He was going to be an expert on foreign affairs, but a little selective xeno-phobia never hurt anyone.

Alain moved in as associate publisher the very next day. When Cleo arrived in the office that afternoon Joe Hamlyn strolled in immediately behind her. 'Guess who's sitting up in the publisher's office sharpening his pencils and his mother's knives?'

'So soon?' But Cleo was not surprised. The emanations from the Roux end of the table at yesterday's board meeting had warned her that Alain, whether from his own intentions or his mother's, had come home to make life uncomfortable for her.

'Are we going to have trouble with him?' Joe said.

'How did you get on with him when he worked here before?'

'Okay, I guess. He was never pushy. But he was always his mother's son. You could never forget that.'

'Well, don't let us forget it till we find out what he's got in mind. You and I have got a good paper here, Joe, and we don't want anyone, mother's son or not, lousing it up.'

Alain came to the conference that afternoon, was polite and affable to Cleo and the other editors and sat quietly, offering no suggestions and making no notes, while the paper was put together for tomorrow's edition. When the conference was over he limped after Cleo to the door of her office.

'Cleo, could you come up to my office for a few minutes? There is more privacy there than in this goldfish bowl.' But he was smiling as he described her office.

Biding her time, waiting to see what moves he had in mind, she went up with him to the floor above. The publisher's office was next to the boardroom, had the same panelled walls and the same suggestion that, socially, it was several levels above the newsroom below. Early American prints decorated the walls; a sword that Napoleon had once worn hung in its scabbard above the marble-fronted fireplace; the thick Persian carpet dared one to throw screwed-up copy paper on it. The big room, however, was not entirely masculine; Claudine had added her own touches. The drapes and lamp-shades were pale yellow, the desk was a French writing table; a large mirror, with a Matthias Lock rococo frame, hanging on the opposite wall, reassured whoever was at the desk where authority lay. Alain sat down behind the desk looking slightly uncomfortable.

494

'I hope you and I will work together without any friction between us. As my mother said, there should be nothing personal in business. However –' he paused, as he might before he drew the sword from the scabbard above the fireplace. 'However, I shall have certain points of view I'll be putting forward, some of which you may not agree with.'

'It's possible. We don't all agree at the news conference each day. You didn't disagree with anything that's going into tomorrow's paper?'

'Not disagree, no. Reservations, yes. I think we should tread more carefully with our opinions on what's happening in Iran at present. I don't know whether you know, but Roger is going over to Cairo next week on a private study tour. He has contacts there and I think we might wait for what he can bring back for us.'

'Roger is not a newspaperman. And Iran might be blown off the map by next week, the way things are going there.'

'Nonetheless, I think we should wait till Roger comes back with his impressions.'

'I'll think about it.' She stood up. 'How's your wife settling into New York?'

'Very happily. How's Tom? You know, I never knew there was a thing between you and him.'

'There never was. Not till recently.' But she wasn't going to discuss her love for Tom with him. Nor was she going to discuss every editorial decision with him. She laid down the implied rule that she was not going to be at his beck and call: 'I'll see you at tomorrow's conference.'

When she went downstairs she looked for Tom at the desk he had chosen for himself at the far end of the newsroom. Keeping his distance, as he described it. So far nobody in the newsroom, except possibly Joe Hamlyn and Carl Fishburg, suspected there was a thing between her and him. She wondered how long Alain would keep the knowledge to himself.

When she reached home that night Tom was waiting for her in the lobby of her apartment building. As they rode up in the elevator he said, 'We can't go on meeting like this.'

'Is that a joke or are you serious?'

495

'It was a joke once.' She had not given him a key to her apartment, something Jack had had, and he waited while she opened the front door. Once inside he took her in his arms and kissed her almost savagely. Then he said, 'I think I'm serious.'

She put down her handbag, took her second door-key from it and held it out. 'That makes us serious, I guess.'

They had a light supper, went to bed and after they had made love he turned over to go to sleep. He did not stay at the apartment every night, but she was still so hungry for him, there was so much lost time to be made up, that she never turned him out if he wanted to stay. Tonight she clutched his shoulder and pulled him over on his back.

'Don't go to sleep yet, I want to talk. Did you ever discuss me with Alain?'

He had the bemused look, like that of a half-gassed bull, of a man who had just made satisfying love. Why did women always want to talk after it? Simone occasionally had been the same. 'What? Would I do that?'

'I don't know.' It made her feel cheap that he and Alain might have discussed her, though Tom at the time could hardly have had any confidences to exchange. 'But he knows there is a thing, as he calls it, between you and me.'

Tom stared at the ceiling, frowning; then at last he looked at her. 'It must have been Simone. Right at the end she asked me if there was another woman. I had to be honest with her. I told her there had been nothing between us, but that years ago I'd fallen in love with you.'

'What did she say?' She really didn't want to talk about Simone, but another woman's opinion couldn't be ignored.

'Nothing. I think she understood – Simone was always a very understanding girl –'

'Go to sleep,' she said, cutting off any further accolade; one cheer was enough for an ex-wife. 'I just wish she'd kept it to herself instead of mentioning it to Alain ... No, wake up!'

He rolled on his back again, the bemused look gone to be replaced by one of patient irritation. He looked like a husband. 'What is it now?'

496

'Would you like to go to Cairo next week with Roger Brisson?'

'What for?'

'You're experienced in that region –' Last year, freelancing from the Paris bureau, he had done a piece for the *Courier* on NATO bases in Turkey and then gone on to Israel, from there to Cyprus and then on to Egypt. 'I don't know exactly why Roger is going there, but I think Alain is going to foist some of Roger's opinions on us. I'd rather you wrote them.'

He looked at her warily. 'Are you trying to get rid of me?'

'Don't joke,' she said, hoping he wasn't serious. 'I owe you a good story after spiking the Rossano piece. I'll talk to Roger about it tomorrow.'

'Will you talk to Alain about it?'

'Only after we've bought your ticket. Now you can go to sleep.'

'I'm wide awake now.' He lay for a while staring at the ceiling while she turned over to go to sleep. Then he reached for her shoulder and pulled her over on her back. 'Will you marry me?'

She stared at him, but their faces were too close and she could not get his into focus. Or perhaps it was her mind that had suddenly become astigmatic.

'Will you marry me?'

She buried her face against his neck, closing her eyes, blind with love. 'Yes. Yes.'

3

'No,' said Alain. 'That editorial is *out*.'

'Why do you object to it?' said Cleo.

'It's nothing but a condemnation of the Shah. We need to support him.'

'We?' said Cleo. 'We're a newspaper, not the government. The Shah's record needs to be put in perspective and that editorial of Tom Border's does it.'

'I don't know why you had him write it in the first place. He's a reporter, not an editorial writer.'

'I suggested using him,' said Dan Follett, chief of the editorial page. 'He knows the area.'

'Well, it's out. It suggests we're supporting the Ayatollah Khomeini.'

'It doesn't suggest anything of the sort.' Cleo could feel herself getting angry, but she was determined to remain cool, if only on the surface.

'The support is implied. That's the way I read it and so will a good many of our readers. As the publisher I have some responsibility for what appears in the paper –'

Cleo did not remind him that he was only the associate publisher. She was tempted to suggest they should consult his mother, but though she was angry with him, even beginning to hate him for his obduracy, she could not castrate him by bringing Claudine down to resolve the argument. In any event she knew how Claudine would resolve it.

'Righto, it's out, Dan. If we can't have some honest criticism of the Shah, we'll say nothing at all. For the time being, anyway. We'll wait till Tom comes back from Cairo.'

'Are you sending Tom Border to the Middle East?' said Alain. 'Why?'

'Because he has contacts there. He's going with Roger, who thinks it's a good idea ... Okay, Joe, what else have you got for us?'

She took the conference back under her control. The other editors round the table had sat quietly during the short skirmish between her and Alain, all of them by now aware that there was an animosity, at least on Alain's part, that was going to influence all future conferences. The amiable, dry-humoured but always efficient atmosphere that had prevailed since the departure of Jake Lintas was showing distinct cracks.

Alain made no more objections or suggestions and when the conference was finished he picked up his stick and limped out without a word. He knew who was the odd man out.

Cleo gestured for Joe Hamlyn and Dan Follett to remain

behind and when everyone else had filed out she said, 'We have a problem, as you can see.'

'I think we should have voted on that editorial.'

'Dan, a newspaper isn't a democracy. You know that as well as I do. I don't give you guys a vote when I think I'm right. His Nibs has got it into his head that he has to show some authority. Today was his day for the demonstration. I don't believe he cares two hoots about the Shah.'

Dan Follett nodded morosely. He was the oldest of the editors, a grey-haired stick of a man who could alternate between flights of fancy, in wacky third leaders, and pedantry. He had a savage hatred of the misuse of words such as *hopefully* and *momentarily*. He had once been a survivor in an aircraft that had crashed moments after take-off. He had come back to the office and remarked, 'The flight attendant was correct. She said we'd be airborne momentarily and that was it – we were in the air momentarily.' He was only restrained from writing a sarcastic editorial by the knowledge that over a hundred other passengers had died permanently.

'Okay, I'll save it till Tom Border comes back.'

He went back to his desk and Joe Hamlyn waited while Cleo gathered up her papers. She looked up at him. 'What is it, Joe?'

'Will you have supper with me? Uncle Joe would like to talk to you.'

She saw at once that he had something important on his mind. 'I'm having sandwiches brought in. I'll order some for you.'

'There's no privacy in your office. I'll take you to McDonalds.'

'A real hideaway. Joe, you're not going to tell me you love me?'

'In a way,' he said and went back to his own desk.

The McDonalds was round the corner. It was almost empty when they walked in. A few people sat at the tables, but their eyes had the tired, empty look of people who were not interested in others; they were at the end of their day and some of them looked at the end of their tether. Cleo watched

499

them with a stirring of pity, wondering if she had ever felt as low as these strangers looked, while Joe went and fetched the coffee and hamburgers.

He came back, sat down and without preamble said, 'Cleo, you and Tom Border have got to get yourselves sorted out.'

'What do you mean?' She had been about to bite into the hamburger, but now held it, like a grenade, as if she were about to throw it at him.

'Don't tell me it's none of my business. It is. Because I like you and because of the effect it's going to have on the paper. Editors and reporters should never share the same bed.'

He came close to having the hamburger shoved in his face. 'I don't think it is any of your business, Joe.'

'Come off it, Cleo. Look, you and Tom have been discreet, I'll admit that. But people have seen you around town. We see you in the office – you're almost leaning over backwards not to be noticed together. You're like all women – you think we guys don't notice things like that. You two are in love – right? – and I'm glad for you. But it's not going to make things easy for you or us around the newsroom. Are you thinking of getting married?'

She put down the hamburger, no longer hungry. 'Yes.'

'Then I think Tom had better look for a job on another paper.'

'Crumbs, you're taking a lot on yourself. Or are you speaking for all the guys in the newsroom? And the women, too? Don't let's forget the girls.'

'Eat your hamburger, Cleo, while I give you some fatherly advice.'

Why do I get all my advice from men? she asked herself. Where could she get some motherly counsel? She had been in a state of quiet rapture since Tom had proposed; she was thirty-four years old and she had been seduced, propositioned and loved; but never proposed to. She did not count Jack's proposal of a Mexican marriage; that suggested all the binding ties of a United Nations resolution. She had called her father and told him the news and her own pleasure had

500

increased, if that were possible, at his delight in it. Unwisely, however, he had asked:

'Will you give up your job?'

'Dad! Why should I do that?'

'All right, all right.' It was no longer like the old days, when the women's vote had been blind and trusting. 'But there's always a risk when a man works for his wife. Or vice versa,' he added diplomatically but a trifle late.

Now Joe Hamlyn was telling her the same thing. 'Cleo, it won't work. All the guys – and the women – will be looking for some favouritism of Tom. Or you'll go the other way and finish up not using Tom for what he's worth. Either way the paper's going to suffer. Tell him to find a job somewhere else. The *Times* might be glad to have him.'

'Joe, how do I fire my future husband?'

'I don't know. Use your woman's intuition.' He bit into his hamburger, his hunger unspoiled.

'I hope you choke,' she said.

When she went home that night Tom was already in the apartment. She was hungry by then and she warmed up a TV dinner, poured some wine and fired him after her second mouthful. It was best, she decided, to get it over and done with.

He surprised her by saying, 'I've been thinking about resigning. I've actually talked to the *Times* –'

'You might have told me!'

'Don't be woman-like, be an editor. Does a worker tell his boss in advance what he's got in mind? You should learn something about labour relations. The *Times* will give me a job. I'll resign at the end of the month and then we'll get married. Okay?'

She sighed and sat back, relieved that there was to be no unpleasantness but annoyed that he hadn't told her what he had in mind. 'Why are you always so agreeable and understanding and lovable?'

'It's just my nature.'

It wasn't his nature, at least not totally; he had all the faults of an honest, intelligent man. He had used his intelli-

501

gence to sum up his life-to-be with Cleo. There would be drawbacks, hurdles, fights, obstacles of every kind; it would still be immeasurably better to live with her than without her. Love would give him stamina and patience. He said, 'The first Stoic was a man who married his boss.'

'Bull.' She was still prudish with her language, except in bed where prudery can sometimes tie a tongue. 'Maybe it's for the best. But I'll miss you at your desk down at the end of the newsroom. Every time I see you down there I'm tempted to wave.' She giggled; the ridiculousness of the image suddenly and completely convinced her that he had to leave the *Courier*. An editor fluttering her fingers at her husband would finish up using copy-boys to deliver love notes. 'Do you still want to go to Cairo?'

'Yes. I'd rather keep working than mope about missing you. How how about a little humpin'?'

'You're the boss,' she said and meant it.

4

Jack Cruze was sitting in his library watching Gloria Swanson in *Sadie Thompson* when Emma phoned to tell him that Dorothy St Martin had just died. It was the first time she had called him in more years than he could remember; but he recognized her voice before she named herself. Not only in his films was he more and more living in the past. His head was full of echoes.

'I'll go to the funeral,' he said. 'Will you be there?'

'Yes.'

She had not been at Rose's funeral, the excuse being that she was not well enough to attend. He had been glad he had not had to meet her publicly, but now all at once he wanted to see her again. He was about to ask her to have lunch with him after the funeral, then decided it would be better to wait till he saw her. He did not have to rush headlong back into the past.

They had a short, formal conversation, then she hung up.

502

He sat for a while thinking about the St Martin sisters; he had always enjoyed their company back in the old days, even though they had always made him feel socially inferior. But he should be grateful to them: they had brought him both Emma and Cleo. He debated whether he should call Cleo and tell her of Dorothy's death.

He had been tempted to phone her several times: the desperate cries of a drowning man. But he had resisted the urge; he knew it was all over between them. Occasionally he felt bitter and furious, but there was more acceptance of the loss of her than he had expected; his own resignation surprised him. When he had left New York to come home to London it had not even occurred to him to send her white roses; that would have been too spiteful, something he could not do to the woman he still loved. Now there was an excuse to call her.

He phoned her at the *Courier*, knowing she would still be putting the paper to bed. He knew her professional habits had not changed; she was the sort of editor who might leave the chores to other people but never the responsibility. He was put through to her at once.

He was more awkward with her, whom he had spoken to less than a month ago, then he had been with Emma. 'Don't hang up on me –'

'I wasn't going to, Jack. What is it?'

'Dorothy St Martin has just died. I thought you'd like to know. Do you want me to order flowers or something?' He was willing to run errands, do anything for her.

'Please. I'm sorry to hear about her death. I suppose she gave up after Rose died. I believe that often happens with old people when someone dies whom they've loved –'

Not only old people. But he *was* old; or anyway felt it. 'Are you all right?'

'Yes, thank you. And you?' They were as formal as he and Emma had been.

'As well as can be expected.' He couldn't resist that. Then abruptly, before he spoiled everything, he said goodbye and hung up.

503

Cleo sat with the dead phone against her ear for a moment, then she slowly put it down. She picked up her gold pen, the one the St Martin sisters had given her, and looked at it with guilt. She had neglected both sisters: a couple of short letters a year and a card at Christmas were not enough for what was owed to friends. Her life, she realized, was full of debts, small and big; she had never thought of herself as selfish, but she was. She had not given a thought in years to Pat Hamer, the actress who had told her of the story in the St Martin sisters, the story that had started her career in London. Was Pat still playing the maid in French farces, still showing off her *boom* but still dreaming of playing Lady Macbeth? Did Mr Brearly, the features editor on the *Examiner*, and Roy Holden and Simon Pally on *Scope* ever feel that she owed them something? She felt ashamed: she never thought of them at all. She had never trodden on anyone to get to where she now sat; but she had never looked back to thank any of them. Suddenly she wanted to rush across the Atlantic to be at Dorothy St Martin's funeral; then she would go looking for all the others, invite them to a grand reunion of the Cleo Spearfield Progress Association. But the thought was as ridiculous as it was quixotic. And there was no guarantee any of them would appreciate her gesture.

She was only sorry that she could no longer reach Dorothy and Rose.

Two days later Jack went to the funeral. The service was held at the Farm Street church; Jack sat in a rear pew and listened to the priest's eulogy. There was no mention of her as a reformed sinner; the Jesuits were worldly, they knew there were more ways to Heaven than the straight and narrow. There were only a few mourners; Jack recognized some doddering old men as clients from the old bordello days. Emma sat in her wheelchair in a side aisle, her housekeeper by her side. When the service was over Jack walked up the aisle and shook hands with Emma.

'Are you going out to the cemetery?'

'No,' she said. 'Cemetery paths were not made for wheel-chairs.'

She hadn't meant to stab him; but did. He winced inwardly, then said, 'Will you have lunch with me?'

She hesitated, then smiled. 'Only if you take me to the Ritz.'

It was where he had taken her when he was courting her. He was not plunging headlong back into the past, it was creeping up around him. He went out to the street, told Sid Cromwell he would ring him from the Ritz when he wanted to be picked up, then joined Emma in her Rolls-Royce. They drove to the Ritz and once there he took the handles on the back of the wheelchair and steered her himself into the dining-room.

They were almost ceremoniously polite to each other, though he had the feeling she was secretly amused. It is not easy to talk to a wife of long ago; some intimacy remains but it has become saw-toothed. So they talked round themselves, like diplomats at a peace conference held in an arsenal.

At last Emma said, 'And how is Cleo? Dorothy used to tell me how well she was doing in New York.'

'That's all over. I mean between her and me. Yes, she's doing well.'

'Too well, you mean? You should never have chosen a career woman to fall in love with, Jack.'

'I fell in love with you, remember?' He wondered if they could ever become reconciled. But the wheelchair would always come between them. He had slowed down, but he still felt the need for sex; she would not be able to give it to him and he would go off looking for it. She would never countenance that: he knew how much pride she had.

She ignored the memory he had revived. She turned away and looked out through the great window across Green Park. Stallions' manes of white cloud flared in the upper sky; in the park itself trees were green balloons of summer. Lovers walked hand in hand (how times had changed, for the better: she and Jack had never walked hand in hand in public) and a young father played with two children (she could hear their silent laughter in her head, like a pain). She had never really got to know London; city pavements were no better than

505

cemetery paths for the passage of wheelchairs. She stopped thinking for the moment, not wanting to show any self-pity in front of him.

She looked back at him and said out of the blue of her mind, 'You're getting on, Jack. What are you going to do with all your money when you die?'

The question shocked him, though his will was already neat and tidy, if a little out of date. But he did not want to be reminded of death. 'You'll be looked after, I've seen to that.'

'I wasn't thinking of myself – you've always been fair to me. In that way,' she added, for she could never entirely forgive him. 'Have you made any provision for Cleo?'

He hesitated, then nodded. 'Yes. I hope you're not going to object?'

'On the contrary. If she made you happy for so long, she deserves to be remembered in your will. But I'd like the rest of it.'

'*What?!*' It was a loud bark; people at nearby tables looked at him. He tugged at his moustache in embarrassment, suddenly aware of the surrounding stares ... Dammit, Emma was just like Cleo: they could both make him feel awkward. He lowered his voice: 'What would you do with it?'

'I'd set up a charity trust.'

'I was going to do that anyway.'

'Not call it after yourself, I hope?'

'Why not?'

'Jack –' His naïve ego made her feel affectionate towards him. 'One doesn't name a charity trust after oneself. Let me do it. Leave everything to me and then I'll announce that you had expressed a wish for it to be used for charity. I'll set up a trust in your name and you'll lie there in your grave smelling of roses, as they say.'

'Jesus Christ,' he said softly. Then he saw the beginning of a smile on her lips and all at once he burst out laughing. People looked at him again; an Arab sheik wondered what had happened to the manners of the English. But this time he didn't care: 'Can I trust you?'

506

'You can always come back if I doublecross you. I'm sure you have the British rights to resurrection.'

He shook his head in wonder. 'You sound just like Cleo. She was always taking the mickey out of me.'

'I should have done it years ago, Jack,' she said brusquely, not wanting comparison with Cleo or any of his other women. 'Give Cleo something worthwhile and let me handle the rest. We'll make everyone happy. The women of Britain will be smugly pleased to see you had not forgotten your neglected wife after all and the Left wing politicians won't be able to call you a hard-hearted capitalist. Which you are.'

'There you go –' But he smiled, pleased that she seemed almost as calculating as himself. He always looked for the worst in people: it was his easiest way of complimenting them. 'Would you like some champagne?'

'That would be nice. Ask them if they have a Taittinger '61 – that's what I always drink at home. I'm a simple country girl at heart.'

She smiled and he laughed, all at once glad he had invited her to lunch. The nearby diners looked at them again and thought how sweet it was to see two elderly people enjoying each other's company so much.

That afternoon he sent her a single red rose. He knew better than to overdo things.

5

'This region has always been a headache,' said Roger Brisson. 'It will always be, even when the Arabs run out of oil.'

'I suppose Richard Cœur de Lion said that, too.'

Tom Border's French grated on Roger's ear, but the latter nodded in agreement. He was pleased that Cleo had sent Tom with him; he now had to start building up contacts amongst newspapermen and it was safe to start close to home. They were sitting in the lobby of Shepheards Hotel in Cairo watching the passing parade, a suggestion made by Tom.

'If you're going to understand foreign affairs,' he had said;

Roger had confided to him the reason for his trip, though not his ultimate ambition, 'I wouldn't rely entirely on what they tell you in embassies and chancelleries.'

The correspondent from *Al-Asrah* who had interviewed Roger in his suite had said the same thing. 'Everyone is here in this town right now, General. I think it must be like Lisbon was in your war.'

Roger didn't tell him he had missed World War Two by six months. He had glanced in a mirror to check how old he looked and decided that the Egyptian must be suffering from the local disease of glaucoma.

Now he looked across the lobby and said, 'There's Colonel Baskerville – that tall bald-headed man. I wonder what he's doing here? He was one of the British officers at NATO HQ. I thought he'd retired.'

'He works for a British oil company now. He's always been an expert on the Arabs.' Tom had early realized that Roger had done no leg-work as a foreign affairs expert.

A party of American Express explorers came trooping in from their bus, tired and dusty, glad to have seen the Pyramids before they were bombed to rubble. Arab and European and American businessmen sat round in small tight circles, their heads poked into the spoke-holes of their low-voiced conversation. Two whores sat demurely in a corner; being businesswomen, they knew when not to interrupt businessmen. Cleo should be there, Tom thought, the old Cleo and her column, giving the needle to all and sundry.

'What a mixture,' said Roger, waist-deep in *hoi polloi*. He was enjoying life as a civilian, he didn't miss the protocol of army life at all. In a luxury hotel, when you sign in as General, they give you the protocol anyway. 'It would be interesting to know who and what they all are. Some terrorists, for sure.'

'Possibly. But I don't think they hang out in places like this.'

Nor did they. In an apartment overlooking the river four Iranians were having a heated argument with an Italian from the Red Brigade and Rosa Fuchs. She and Poncelli had

508

arrived in Cairo yesterday by way of Beirut. There had been a conference in Vienna of several groups and it had been decided to send two emissaries to Cairo and then on to Teheran to offer any help that was wanted by the Iranian revolutionary movement. Unfortunately, the Iranians they had contacted did not want any help.

'Get it through your thick heads – we don't need you!' The leader of the group had spent two years at Berkeley in California and had come to have contempt for all foreign revolutionaries. They all seemed to think that sex was some part of the revolution. 'Least of all we need a woman!'

Rosa Fuchs wore a black wig to hide her blonde hair; she had thought it would make her less conspicuous amongst the dark heads she had expected to be working with. She wanted to tear off the wig now and throw it in the face of the leader.

'We want no whores in the Islamic revolution –'

Rosa knew she should not have worn the sleeveless sundress with its low-cut front; the weather was hot and she had thought herself modestly dressed. She had not expected to be confronted by someone from the Middle Ages.

She swore in German and hit him hard across the face. He gave her a medieval whack in return. Poncelli, still infected with Italian gallantry and other bourgeois failings, hit him. The fight was only the culmination of the argument that had gone on for over an hour; brotherly love is no more endemic amongst revolutionaries than it is amongst the ruling classes; Poncelli, an Italian realist, knew that. The four Iranians, not burdened by gallantry, attacked Rosa and Poncelli without favouring one or the other and threw them both out of the apartment. Rosa had lost her wig, but the leader threw it out on to the landing after her like a scalp that he did not want. She picked it up and put it on, felt her bruises and cuts and swore loudly in German, screeching at the top of her voice.

'*Stai zitta!*' Poncelli cautioned. 'Be quiet! We don't want the police here –'

But it was already too late. The neighbours had heard the fight and called the police; for once the Cairo police were on hand immediately. They came rushing into the lobby of the apartment building as Rosa and Poncelli came down the stairs. Doors were opening and heads were popping out; curiosity has killed many a Cairene, but south and east of the Mediterranean there is none of the inhibitions of Rosa's Germans; everyone wants to know what is going on. Poncelli was several steps ahead of her and suddenly she slowed, letting him go on down. She had no idea what he had in mind; perhaps he was going to try and bluff his way past the police. She paused by the half-open door on the landing she had reached, looked at the middle-aged woman and the young man who were peering out. She smiled at them, then took the Luger from her handbag and pushed them ahead of her into their apartment. She closed the door behind her and gestured at them with the gun.

'*Sprechen sie Deutsch?*'

'*Ja*,' said the young man. 'A little. I work for Lufthansa out at the airport. I am a mechanic.'

'I shan't harm you if you remain quiet. Is this your mother? Tell her just to be quiet and she won't be hurt. I want to stay here till the police are gone.'

She could hear the hubbub out on the stairs; she thought she heard someone shout *Rosa!* She could hear Poncelli yelling in Italian, then his voice was lost in the general pandemonium. She waited for shots to ring out, but the Iranians evidently were not prepared to fight their revolution here in Cairo. Boots clattered down the stairs and within five minutes all was quiet again.

She nodded to the young man and his mother, put the Luger away in her handbag and thanked them for their hospitality. Then she let herself out of the apartment, went carefully down the stairs and out into the street. There was a small crowd in the street, attracted by the incident and still discussing it; she skirted the crowd and walked down to the corner and hailed a taxi. She went back to the small hotel where she and Poncelli had checked in. She debated whether to wait and see what happened to him, if he might return, then decided she owed him no loyalty, even though he had defended her against the Iranian pig.

An hour later she was at the airport catching a plane for Beirut. She would be back in Vienna tomorrow, safe once again amongst those who believed women had a place in all revolutions.

Next day Tom had a call at Shepheards from the press secretary at the US embassy. 'Weren't you once involved with a girl terrorist named Rosa Fuchs? Well, she's here in Cairo somewhere, unless she skipped out overnight. The police picked up some Iranians yesterday, along with a guy named Poncelli, who's a wanted Red Brigade man. The leader of the Iranians evidently doesn't like women – he put the finger on Rosa Fuchs. She appears to be the only one who got away, which means he probably hates her even more now.'

'Where can I get more on the story?'

'Try Inspector Habib at police headquarters. Mention my name.'

Tom put down the phone and went along to Roger's suite. He had only a small room for himself, but he was still living and travelling better than the *Courier* had ever allowed him to do in the past. It paid to be the husband-to-be of the editor, to be in first class.

'Our girl friend Rosa Fuchs has surfaced again. She's here in Cairo.'

'Do you think she's here looking for me?' A threat to one's life doesn't diminish one's ego.

'I don't think so. Evidently she was here to see some Iranians and got the bum's rush from them. I think there might be a story. I'm going over to police headquarters. Will you be here when I get back? I can tell you what I've found out over lunch.'

'I'm lunching with President Sadat.'

Ah well, Tom thought, there's always a class above first class.

511

NINETEEN

The Iranian leader was willing to talk to Tom and in between propaganda for the revolution in his own country he made a scathing attack on interfering foreigners, especially heathen women. Poncelli would not talk at all, but looked extra sullen when Tom tried to question him about Rosa Fuchs. Then the interview had to end. Inspector Habib, doing a favour for his friend in the American embassy, had broken rules to allow Tom to see the prisoners. Other correspondents, learning of the favouritism, clamoured for the same privilege. Tom went out by a back door and the front door was closed. Tom had an exclusive.

He wrote it, cabled it and Joe Hamlyn, on Cleo's insistence, ran it on Page One: he was favoured everywhere. Within twenty-four hours Rosa Fuchs in Vienna had had every word of the story read to her; the international terrorist network is as good as any newspaper wire service. Tom's story did Rosa a lot of harm with her own group. They did not blame her for being a woman and a heathen, but she was condemned for abandoning Poncelli. He was top brass in the network and, as in any war and any army, the brass should never be left to take care of itself. She should have died to help him escape.

Rosa, the spoiled only child of middle class parents, went away to sulk. Tom stayed on with Roger in Cairo for another four days, then the two of them flew back to New York. Cleo, using some of the political skill she had inherited from her father, knowing the value of numbers, invited both men to the news conference the day after they got back.

512

Roger gave his impressions. 'I don't think we should be blind to the Shah's faults and mistakes. He's finished. Somehow or other we have to make an accommodation with the Ayatollah.'

'That's out of the question,' said Alain, aware at once that he was going to be a minority of one.

'I think it may well be,' said Cleo, already an antagonist of the Ayatollah Khomeini for what he was doing to women in Iran. 'I don't think we have to embrace him. We should try to stay objective. Have you read that editorial I sent you, Roger?'

'Yes, indeed I have.' Roger was assuming the pomposity of the newly expert. He was no longer a general but, in his own mind, an ambassador-at-large. 'I think you should run it.'

Cleo looked down the table at Alain. 'Do you lift your veto?'

Alain had once been gracious, up to a point; now he appeared to have lost that virtue. In a surly tone he said, 'It seems I'm out-voted.'

She resisted the temptation to tell him that he had been out-voted the first time the editorial had been presented but he hadn't let the fact sway him. She showed him a little graciousness of her own: 'No, Alain. I'll still spike it if you wish.'

'No, run it.' He waved a hand as if he no longer cared. 'I just hoped we don't have to regret it.'

Cleo knew that the other editors at the table were silently applauding her for having won her point. She did not look at Tom for his silent approval; she had noticed that Alain had pointedly ignored Tom's presence. She stood up, thanked Roger and Tom and they were shown out. Then she got on with the rest of tomorrow's news, keeping her triumph mute.

When the conference wound up Carl Fishburg stayed behind. 'Something's come up that might give us an angle on that story Tom did on the Mob. Billie Locke is in an upstate hospital dying of cancer. Maybe we could send Tom up to see her. She might have something to say.'

513

When Cleo had got home last night from the *Courier*, Tom had been waiting for her. She was almost dizzy with hunger for him; it was as if he had been away a year instead of only a week. Her hands conquered him like soldier crabs; she had him for supper. Love and lust, she thought, were wonderful when they were the same thing.

'When you go to work for the *Times*, never let them send you out of town. I'll call Abe Rosenthal and tell him that's an order from your wife.'

'You sent me to Cairo.'

'I know I'll never do it again. From now on I shan't even send you up to the Bronx.'

Now she said to Carl Fishburg, 'Carl, Tom is leaving us at the end of the month. Joe Hamlyn knows, but no one else. Tom and I are going to be married and we think it best he doesn't go on working here. He's going over to the *Times*.'

Carl was torn between being an editor and a friend. 'I'll hate to lose him, especially to the *Times*.'

'You'll be losing him to me, too.'

'That'll be bearable,' said Carl, giving her his blessing. 'When do you make the announcement?'

'We thought we'd keep it till the last minute. Next week.'

'The Empress doesn't know? Or Alain?'

'No.'

'Okay, I'll keep my mouth shut. In the meantime I'd like one last good story out of him. Let him try Billie Locke. It may prove a dud, but it'll only take him a day. I'll see he doesn't stay away from you overnight.'

'You're a dirty old man.'

'That's always been my ambition, ever since I was a dirty young man.'

Tom was sent upstate next day to see if he could interview Billie Locke. She was in a hospital on the outskirts of a small town between Saratoga and Utica, a hospital dedicated, it claimed on the peeling sign at the gateless gateway, to the care of the dying. It was an institution built in the days before euphemisms were included in health care as palliatives: dying was dying, by golly, and nothing else. The place looked as out-of-date as its honesty.

Tom had looked up pictures of Billie Locke in the morgue (an inappropriate name for the files in view of his subject) and in the flesh he would not have recognized her except that the name-plate on her bed said that she was indeed Wilhelmina Locke. She was all thin bone and huge dull eyes, a crone thirty years before her proper time. But her eyes took on some shine when she took in that she was being visited by a man. Not a flash, well-dressed one, but still a man all the same.

'None of my gentlemen friends, the bastards, ever come to visit me. Not one a the sons-of-bitches.' Her voice croaked its way out of the tangle of cords that was her throat; two spots of anger appeared in her sunken cheeks like misapplied daubs of rouge. 'I shoulda shit in their beds instead of letting 'em fuck me.'

Two very old ladies in neighbouring beds came awake at the language, determined to live a little longer; one cackled in glee and the other raised a clenched fist that looked like a chicken's elbow. Tom, embarrassed, wondered how often Billie Locke had regaled the old women with stories of her lurid past.

'Billie, I've looked up everything that was written about you when you testified at those crime hearings back in 1974. There was the day you socked a guy named Tony Rossano when you were coming out of the court. Why?'

'That shit Tony Rossano!' There was another cackle from the neighbouring bed. 'He made a rude remark, I can't tell you what he said, it was filthy, and I socked the son-of-a-bitch. I knew he was doublecrossing Frank Apollo – he'd gone to my boy friend, Vito Asaro, and told him I used to go with Frank. So I did, but that was only for a month, maybe two, back in Chicago when I was just starting.' Tom refrained from asking what she had been starting. 'I thought I loved Vito, but he was another shit!'

One of the old ladies had enough life left in her to clap, a sound like two pieces of paper being slapped together. Tom

515

felt more and depressed, suddenly wishing he hadn't come. Death did not upset him unduly; but dying did. He felt he was sitting in the midst of an obscenity far worse than Billie's language.

'Vito, he beat the hell outa me, then he kicked me out. Out on the street! I hadn't been on the street since I was fifteen years old! You know what it's like to have all your friends turn their back on you? They didn't want me in their social circle no more. I give the best years of my life to some of them bastards. I wasn't just Vito's girl friend, I was friendly with some of the others before I met him, big guys people looked up to. I had a heart of gold, like they say, that was my trouble –'

'Billie, why didn't Vito mind you having gone with the other guys if he got so steamed up about Frank Apollo?'

'Because Frank was his enemy, that's why. Frank was trying to muscle in out in Kansas City and Sebastiano Giuffre, up in Chicago, he didn't like that. They were all set to get rid of Frank when that little shitty snitch Rossano told Vito about Frank and me.'

'What happened after Vito kicked you out?'

'They went ahead and done what they was planning to do anyway. Tony Rossano set Frank up for Vito. Vito organized it for Sebastiano Giuffre. They got the hit men to come in from Philly.'

'You're sure of all this?'

'Sure I'm sure. I heard 'em planning it, didn't I, and when I read about it in the papers, it happened just like I'd heard. There was a girl and a guy from some newspaper, they was lucky they didn't get hit, too. I dunno what they was doing there.'

Tom was suddenly aware of the silence on either side of him and Billie. The two old women had fallen asleep; or died. All at once he wanted to be out of here.

'Billie, can I use all this you've told me? I'll have to turn it over to the D.A.'s office. I don't know if they'll try for an indictment on it, but my story could stir up some trouble for the Mob.'

516

'So long as it stirs up trouble for any of the bastards! Sure, write it up. But use one of the old pictures, the good ones, of me, will you?'

'Billie, I've got to warn you – if I use it, some hit man from Philly or wherever, might come looking for you.'

She gestured at herself with a yellow claw. 'He'll do me a favour.'

Tom went back to New York, riding through a summer's day that mocked death. Once back at the *Courier* he went in to see Cleo.

'Can the cash box spare Billie a thousand bucks? She'll be dead in three months, the doc told me. Let her buy herself something that won't last.'

'Have you talked to the D.A.'s office?'

'Just now. I got the feeling they have other things on their mind. Vito Asaro has moved to Chicago anyway. The guy I want is Tony Rossano, for what he did to Hal Rainer.'

'Right, we'll run the story and see what happens. Make it as hard-hitting as you can.'

He paused by the door on his way out. 'Can I make this my last outside story? I didn't enjoy today.'

She understood and loved him for his feeling towards the dying. It seemed that she only gave a thought to the dead. 'Of course. Oh –'

'Yes?'

'My father rang me from London this morning – he's over there on another parliamentary junket. He'll be here Friday. I'd like to be married Saturday, so he can give me away.'

He looked over his shoulder at the busy newsroom, then back at her. 'Sure,' he said, elaborately casual. 'Any time.'

She looked past him; it seemed to her that everyone in the big room was covertly watching them. She smiled widely, as if she were pleased at the story he had just brought in. After Saturday she could give up acting in public how she felt for him.

Rosa Fuchs, in a new dark wig and with a passport that said she was an Austrian named Romy Tischbein, flew into Kennedy Airport that evening. She had an address in Peter Cooper Village and she went there and was welcomed by two girls who were in awe of her reputation. She did not tell them what her mission was, only that she was going on to San Francisco in four days' time and wanted a place to stay over. The two girls were thrilled to have her stay with them; who knew, she might take them with her, allow them at long last to put their theories into practice. She had no intention of doing that. She was here on her own initiative, not the group's.

3

Jack Cruze was not really surprised when he walked into the VIP lounge at Heathrow and saw Sylvester Spearfield sitting by a window. He waited a moment, partly to see if Spearfield was with anyone, partly gathering himself for an encounter that he knew was unavoidable. Around Europe he always flew in the company plane, but on Atlantic flights he flew on a scheduled airline and took his chances that he would not be plagued by some busybody. He protected himself as much as he could by booking the last two seats in first class and putting his brief-case and coat on the spare seat. It sometimes resulted in a little ill-feeling from other passengers, but that never worried him.

Even if he avoided Spearfield now, it was inevitable that, if they travelled on the same plane in the same class, Spearfield would at some time in the six-and-a-half hour journey come up and speak to him. He was an Australian and a politician: one couldn't get a more garrulous combination.

Sylvester saw him coming, was on his feet at once. His smile was genuine, his handshake firm. 'You going British Airways, too? Of course you would be. Got to fly the flag, I suppose. I'm with another all-party committee. The other blokes have gone home the way we came with Qantas, but I'm going right round. I'm spending a few days in New York with Cleo.' Then he quietened for a moment. 'I gather you two no longer speak to each other.'

'Oh, we speak. It's all very civilized.'

'Sure, sure. But it hurts like hell, doesn't it?'

Jack suddenly withdrew all his reservations about the man. 'Yes. But as you once said, I'm old enough to be her father.'

'If you had ever been a father you'd know it's not all beer and skittles.'

But he didn't elaborate and Jack had no time to ask him what he meant; the call came for them to board the aircraft. Jack, taking a chance on being bored but all at once wanting company, asked the flight attendant that Senator Spearfield be seated next to him. He could not have Cleo, but for a few hours he might hear something from her father that would revive sweet, but painful, memories of her.

Once in their seats, however, Sylvester surprised him by being very quiet. They were halfway across the Atlantic before their conversation was flowing freely. Sylvester did not mention Cleo again and Jack was suddenly afraid to bring up her name; instead, they talked about the state of the world in general. Jack found, as he had found so often amongst the socialists of his acquaintance, that Sylvester had drifted, if not to the Right, at least towards the Centre. Nothing mellows a man's belief so much, he thought, as disillusion. Never having had any illusions, except about Cleo, he could be objective.

Sylvester said, 'I remember something Willy Brandt told some of us when we were over in Europe on a junket several years ago. He said all Western politicians had promised the voters too much and we were never going to be able to deliver. I'd add to that. We promised them so much they've now all become greedy. I grew up as a union organizer. In those days we thought about the unemployed as much as we did about the employed – because the unemployed had been our mates. Not any more. All the blokes in work, especially

519

the tradesmen, have become little capitalists interested only in Number One.'

'It's the way of human nature,' said Jack, who had always been interested in Number One. 'I'm surprised it took you so long to realize it.'

Sylvester nodded reluctantly, sipped his scotch: disillusion needed the best of salves. 'I've been spouting off in the Senate for years about rich tax dodgers – they've been getting away with murder back home. Then a couple of months ago I saw some brickies – bricklayers – working on a place next door to my house. They were all being paid in cash at the end of the day. I got the builder on the side and asked him what was going on. He told me if he didn't pay the brickies in cash, they'd go somewhere else and work for a builder who would. They were making five hundred dollars a week and declaring only half of it as income.' He shook his head. 'I've spent more than half my life working for people like that and I find out they're just like the bastards I've been fighting against.'

'People like me?' said Jack.

Sylvester nodded solemnly; then abruptly let out the belly-laugh. Jack grinned at him and the two touched glasses and drank to each other. Jack knew that life was just a Hall of Mirrors: the trick was to recognize that each and every one of the distorted reflections was part of the truth. Sylvester believed that the mirrors were to blame, that they had been put in by some shoddy builder. Jack, who could feel sorry for himself in love but not in business, felt sorry for his new-found, if only temporary, friend.

When they landed at Kennedy, Cleo was waiting for Sylvester. Jack was catching a connecting flight to Charleston, but Sylvester grabbed him by the arm and told him he had to meet Cleo.

'Jack, you're still her boss. Some day you're going to have to meet her again, talk to her. Do it now while I'm with you, it'll be less awkward. If she sees how friendly I am with you, she's got to accept you.'

It's a case of *me* accepting *her*, Jack thought; but didn't

520

voice the thought. Against his own instincts he went out to meet Cleo; and immediately wished he hadn't. She looked as beautiful in his eyes as she ever had; the memories of her flesh enveloped him till he felt he was going to break out in a sweat. But the effect on him wasn't all physical; the presence of her, which had nothing to do with her face or body, weakened him till he felt he was ready to fall at her feet. Her smile, her voice, the occasional sidelong glance from her eyes bruised him like blows; but behind all the surface attraction that was killing him was the core of her. It was indefinable, as it is in any person: it was, he guessed, her deepest nature, the one he had found amongst all the mirrors.

'Emma wished to be remembered to you.' It wasn't what he had meant to say, but the words slipped into the vacuum on his tongue.

'She was at Dorothy's funeral? I felt guilty – I should have been there.'

'Well, we can't be everywhere at once.'

'No.'

It was Sylvester who broke up the meeting, recognizing he had done the wrong thing in bringing them together. He shook Jack's hand warmly, said he would look him up next time he came to London – 'You never know, I might get Malcolm Fraser to put me in the House of Lords. That's the last haven for idealists, isn't it?' – and took Cleo out to the limousine she had waiting for them.

Jack watched them go; it was like watching his life recede. He stood there in the midst of the bustling, careless crowd, an untidy, forlorn multi-millionaire who looked in need of Travellers' Aid.

4

Going into Manhattan in the limousine Cleo said, 'Did he suggest coming out to meet me or did you?'

'I did. It was a mistake, wasn't it? I'm sorry, sweetheart.'

521

'It was harder for him than it was for me. I have Tom. He has no one. I have some news for you, something I hope you'll like. Tom and I are being married Saturday. You can give me away.'

He had always been an emotional man; he could hardly see her for tears as he hugged her. 'Oh sweetheart, I'm so bloody happy for you! I don't know Tom, I can hardly remember what he looks like. But if he's the one for you, then he's all right. You've taken your time, God knows –'

'That's why I know he's the one. He's at my apartment now. You'll like him. You'd bloody well better,' she threatened.

He grinned, kissed her warmly on the cheek. The years fell away, he felt he was embracing the child he had adored all that time ago when he and Brigid would sit and watch their youngest and wonder what traps lay ahead of her. She had negotiated a lot of traps since then, but he was not so cynical as to think that marriage was one. He might no longer believe in the voters but he still believed in love and romance.

'There's just one thing,' Cleo said. 'I made the mistake of mentioning at a board meeting yesterday that you were arriving. Claudine Roux, my other boss besides Jack, the big boss, if you like, is having a dinner party for some Republican senators. I gather it's for her brother's benefit. He's the one who was the general and now he's trying to be a foreign affairs expert. He and Claudine thought it would be a good idea to have a voice from Down Under.'

'Whoever listened to us in Washington? We peed all over the Senate floor back home when Mal Fraser came to Washington and Jimmy Carter introduced him as 'my friend John Fraser'. They had to draw him a map to show him where Australia was, just north of the American base at the South Pole, someone said. Shall I speak English or give them a bit of aboriginal dialect?'

'Be on your best behaviour. I don't want any of your Aussie ocker image. Do you have a better suit than that?'

'No.'

522

'Crumbs, you look worse than Tom. And Jack, too. Why have I always surrounded myself with bums?'

The two bums greeted each other warily, since Sylvester was offering his daughter and Tom was offering only himself. But within ten minutes Sylvester was convinced Cleo had made a good choice; and Tom relaxed, knowing he was accepted. Cleo watched them with the self-satisfied smile of a successful match-maker.

'Are you coming to this dinner tonight?' Sylvester asked.

'No, the help hasn't been invited,' said Tom, relieved that he had not been. Alain and Simone would probably be at the dinner and he did not want to face them, not so close to his wedding day. He would be better prepared to face them, if he had to, when he was properly anchored.

'I've never met this Mrs Roux. I gather she's something worse than Lucrezia Borgia.'

'Only on her good days,' said Cleo. 'Come on, Dad, I'll drop you off at your hotel. I have to go back to the paper for a couple of hours. I'll pick you up at seven-thirty.'

When she picked him up she looked at him in surprise. 'What have you done to yourself?'

'I was kidding this afternoon. When I knew I was coming home this way, I decided I wouldn't disgrace you any more. I went to Harrods and bought this suit.'

'Tom bought a suit there. Once.'

'He is a bit of a bum, isn't he? But it suits him. The same with me. Notice this shirt? I bought it at some pansy shop in Jermyn Street, cost me the bloody earth. The salesman kept trying to make us a couple of consenting adults.'

'You look marvellous. Now behave as well as you look and they will think Australia is civilized.'

Claudine was all regal charm, Catherine greeting a minor prince from Outer Mongolia. 'Is this your first visit to America, Senator?'

'I first came here in 1936. I jumped the rattler – rode the rods, as you call it – from San Francisco to Chicago. I came across to see Harry Bridges – remember him? He was an Aussie who ran your West Coast waterfront. Then I went on

523

to an IWW conference. The Wobblies, you remember? Industrial Workers of the World. They were trying to revive them, but it never came to anything.'

'1936?' said Claudine. 'I think my late husband and I were tiger-shooting in India that year.'

Sylvester didn't let go with the belly-laugh. He smiled and shook his head and Claudine returned the smile. 'I've been heckled many times, Mrs Roux, but never like this. You win.'

'I always do, Senator. Now may I have your arm to go into dinner? You are sitting on my right.' A few moments later, sitting at the head of the table, she looked at her butler. 'What is the main wine this evening?'

'A Margaux, 1937, madame.'

'1937. Was that a good year for the Wobblies, Senator?'

'I don't know,' said Sylvester. 'I was back home shooting rabbits.'

Oh Dad, Cleo thought, I love you! She settled down to enjoy the dinner as much as possible, knowing he was going to hold Australia's end up. She was surprised at her own nationalism; she had never flown the flag except when she felt she was being put down as an Australian. Sylvester had never been anything but what he was tonight, a patriot, and all at once she determined, if only for tonight, to be her father's daughter.

But there was no need to wave the flag. Everyone at the table listened to Sylvester and Roger; not everyone agreed with them and they didn't always agree with each other, but the argument was good-tempered and well-informed. Louise had come with Roger, and Cleo wondered if they were living together again. Several times Louise glanced across the table and smiled at her, but she appeared amused by rather than interested in the talk. She's come to terms with herself, if not Roger, Cleo thought. *Let Tom and me always come to terms with each other.*

From opposite sides of the table Cleo and Simone watched each other carefully. It was the first time Cleo had met Alain's wife, Tom's ex-wife; the two of them, in a way, had more in common than anyone else at the table. Simone was slim and svelte, her hair worn in a chignon; Alain had made her get rid of the bangs. Cleo could see what any man would see in her; she just wondered what was that little extra that, in Tom's and Alain's eyes, put her on a par with herself. She had no vanity, but she liked to put a true value on herself. From further up the table Alain, who might have given her at least half the answer, watched her with the same carefulness. Claudine, not missing a point, open in her gaze, watched them all.

'I liked that story on the terrorists in the *Courier*, Miss Spearfield.' The Senator from the Mid-West, silver-haired and smooth, a Van Cleef and Arpels version of Sylvester, sat on Cleo's right. 'You were properly rough on them. But I thought the editorial on the Shah went too far.'

'So did I,' said Alain.

'Not at all,' said Roger, and Cleo didn't have to defend herself. 'The *Courier* needs to take some definite stands these days.'

'You have a definite enough one on the Mafia,' said the Senator from New England, plump and shiny-skinned, as if New England rock had been pulverized and made into a mud-ball. 'You really named names there. The mobsters out in Chicago and Kansas City can't be too happy.'

'That's our policy now,' said Cleo, aware of Alain's cold stare. 'Naming names.'

When the dinner party broke up Claudine put her hand on Sylvester's arm. 'I hope this won't be the last time you'll visit us, Senator.'

'Now Cleo's settled here I'll be coming over as often as I can. I might even ask Mal Fraser to appoint me Consul-General.'

'Why don't you?'

He laughed, softly; he wouldn't trust her as far as he could throw her with his arthritic shoulder, but he liked her. 'I still have a few old friends back home in the Party. If President Carter made you ambassador to somewhere, would your friends speak to you?'

'I see your point, Senator. Except that I have never worried about what my friends think of me.'

'That's the difference between us. You'd never have felt at home in the Wobblies.'

'I'll try hard not to regret what I've missed.'

Going back to his hotel in the limousine, he said, 'What's wrong between you and Mrs Roux's son?'

'You don't miss much, do you?' She explained what the personal position had been; he made no comment. He was an old-fashioned father who believed in the double standard, especially for daughters. 'Now I'm not sure whether he's being personal, getting his own back on me, or he's suddenly just got plain ambitious. He makes it pretty clear he doesn't like the way I run the paper.'

'Who's winning?'

'I am, so far. But if ever Jack Cruze sold his interest in the paper, I think I'd be out on my neck.'

'Is he likely to do that?'

'I don't know. I could never bring myself to ask him not to sell. He doesn't owe me anything, not any more.'

The limousine drew up outside the Pierre, where Cleo had booked him in. She would have preferred to have had him stay with her in the apartment, but the second bedroom had been converted into a study and it would have meant his sleeping on a couch in the living-room. On top of that Tom was now sleeping every night at her apartment, having virtually abandoned Kips Bay Plaza. It had been easier all round to book her father into the Pierre at her expense and give him some of the luxury that, because of his stubborn ideals, he had dodged all his life.

'Come up for a drink.'

'I'm tired, Dad. And I have to go back to the office for half an hour –'

'I'm tired, too, sweetheart. But I haven't talked to you, really talked, in ages. We've let so many chances go –'

She was suddenly drawn to him. She put her arm in his and they went up to his room, scrutinized by the elevator operator out of the corner of his eye. He wondered how some of these old bastards managed to get some of these younger chicks up to their rooms. She certainly didn't look like a hooker.

As they got out of the elevator Cleo said, 'I'm his daughter. I'm not a hooker.'

'Don't let her fool you,' said Sylvester. 'She is a hooker.'

They both let out the Spearfield belly-laugh as the elevator doors closed and they went down the corridor arm in arm, enjoying their silly joke. It was the sort of joke they had enjoyed together twenty years ago.

Sylvester mixed them a night-cap, then said, 'Did you hear Mrs Roux asking me about whether I was coming back to New York? I didn't want to tell you in front of her, but Mal Fraser *has* offered me the post of Consul-General here.'

'Dad! Why didn't you tell me and Tom earlier?'

He swirled his drink in its glass. 'I don't know. I guess I'm a bit ashamed. It hasn't been announced back home yet, but I'm going to get hell when it is.'

'Meaning the Party will accuse you of selling out?'

'What else? They'll be right. I still can't believe I've accepted the job – it's as if it's someone else, a distant relation. It just sort of happened. I was at a reception and I found myself in a corner with Mal Fraser. I've always got on okay with him, as well as one can with such a shy, stuffy bastard. He asked me about you and I said you were doing fine, but I never saw enough of you. Then he said he was appointing a new Consul-General here and jokingly I asked him, What about me? He laughed and we both thought it was a good joke. Two days later he rang me and asked was I serious. It was one of those days when you'd just phoned me. I was sentimental, I suppose –' He looked at her. 'I get like that, occasionally.'

'Me, too.'

'I added it all up and I decided I wanted to spend my declining years, as they call them, with you. I'd have had only one more term in the Senate and that would have been it. I've given damned near fifty years to the Party and it wouldn't comfort me in my old age. I've seen it happen to

527

other blokes who've retired. I've been a success, a moderate one anyway, and I decided I wanted to come here and bask in your success.'

She put a hand on his. 'I want you here, Dad. But my success has nothing to do with it.'

'Righto, have it your way. But you are successful and I'm proud of you. It wasn't easy, was it?' He smiled at the frown of puzzlement on her brow. 'Sweetheart, I'm not blind, never was. You ran away from home to get away from me. There's a quotation from Milton that begins, *Fame is the spur that the clear spirit doth raise* ... I've forgotten the rest of it. There's something else about fame. It throws a shadow. You wanted to get out of that shadow, right?'

She stood up, wanting to go home to Tom before she broke down and wept like the small child that she felt. 'Come to New York, Dad, and we'll start all over again. You and me and Tom, and no shadow.'

He stood up, kissed her. 'It's not too late. I hope your mother is watching.'

Then she did break down. She leant her face against his chest and wept for all the chances that had been lost.

5

Rosa Fuchs got out of the cab on Fifth Avenue and walked down 89th Street. She was wearing a light tan raincoat; in its pocket was the fully loaded Luger. She had brought no gun to the United States, not wanting to set off any alarm if she were searched; her new American friends, who had not been told why she needed a gun and had not asked, had had no trouble in finding the Luger she had insisted upon. Assassination has become a trade and tradesmen prefer to use tools they have become accustomed to.

She was wearing nothing to disguise herself except the black wig; no dark glasses, since it was eleven o'clock at night, no broad-brimmed hat pulled low down over her face. It was her own wry joke, and she was not much given to humour, that she had chosen to wear a wig that duplicated the hair style of the woman she had chosen to kill.

She had spent the past three days studying Cleo Spearfield's daily routine. She knew now that the Australian bitch came home around this time every night, often with the American Tom Border, with whom she was apparently living. She hoped to find the two of them arriving home together, but if they didn't it wouldn't matter. She would kill whichever one arrived first. Her preference would be the Spearfield woman, since it was she who wielded the power.

On the opposite side of the street Tony Rossano's hit man got out of the black Buick; his companion behind the wheel started up the engine. The hit man crossed the street, walking unhurriedly, the sawn-off shotgun held against his side under his black raincoat. He was from Cleveland and he did not know New York well; he did not like the narrow cross-streets, busy with traffic even at this hour, and he would have preferred to have made the hit somewhere else. He had come into New York two days ago, had studied several photos of the woman he had to kill; last night he had waited across the street to catch a sight of her in the flesh and seen her come home in a limousine. He wondered why, tonight, she should be coming home on foot; he had heard that women walked nowhere in New York at night for fear of muggers and rapists. Well, he was neither of those, thank Christ.

He stopped in front of the woman and, because he always made sure he was killing the right person, he said, 'Miss Spearfield?'

Jack Cruze got out of the limousine where he had been sitting for the past half-hour. He had cancelled his connecting flight to Charleston; the sight of Cleo this afternoon had upset him too much. He had to see her again, make one last attempt to have her come back to him. He had felt ridiculous and juvenile sitting in the limousine and he knew the chauffeur must have been wondering what sort of English fool had hired him and the car. He had no real hope that Cleo would listen to his plea, but he had to make the attempt. If she turned him away, no matter how gently, that would be the end of it. He would sell the *Courier* stock, cut her out of his will and go back and try for a reconciliation with Emma. He did not want to end his days alone and he knew he could never fall in love again.

At first he did not see the man in the black raincoat crossing the street. He was ten yards from Cleo before he saw that it was not her at all, just someone with the same hair style. Then the man in the raincoat stepped in front of the girl, said 'Miss Spearfield?' and took the gun from under his coat and shot her. Jack wasn't sure whether the girl had answered the question the man had put to her; he was already running forward when he saw the gun exposed. He would never know if he was being heroic; perhaps, because the girl did resemble Cleo, he acted on instinct. He ran at the man, shouting a protest that died in his mouth as the killer turned and put two bullets into his chest. He stumbled sideways, hit a parked car and fell to the sidewalk only feet from the dead Rosa Fuchs. In the moment before he died he wondered why he had been rushing to save a stranger, something he had never done in his life before.

TWENTY

Cleo and Tom postponed their wedding; there was no disagreement between them about it. Sylvester could not delay
his return to Australia and went home shocked and disappointed, promising to be back as soon as his appointment as
Consul-General was ratified. A phone call to Tom's parents
told them of the tragedy in the street outside Cleo's apartment
and they were shocked that their future daughter-in-law
should have been the intended target of such a killer. They
said they would come to New York as soon as a new date was
set for the wedding. In the meantime if Tom wanted to bring
himself and Cleo home to Friendship, a safe town, they would
love to have them both.

'You could be married here,' Olive Border said.

'Thanks, Mom. But we both have to stay here in New
York. We still have our jobs to do.'

Tom wanted to write the story on the double killing, but
the night of the murder had been his last at the *Courier* and he
had left the office, was already in Cleo's apartment, when the
shooting took place. He was on hand to get the facts but
Cleo, coming home five minutes later, insisted that his name
could not be on the story. The *Courier*'s chief crime reporter,
Bob Wilkie, came to the scene, put together his story in Cleo's
apartment and phoned it in from there. Cleo had rung the
production manager and told him to hold the presses; she
was then switched through to the newsroom and caught Carl
Fishburg just as he was leaving for home. Page One was
ripped apart and remade. Carl, an old-fashioned newspaper-

531

man, had always been less than enthusiastic about video display terminals, but that night he appreciated the time saved by the VDTs. The last edition of the *Courier* went on the street only forty minutes later, running a bigger spread with its story and pictures than either the *Times* or the *News*.

At one o'clock in the morning Cleo rang Carl, still in the office, to congratulate him. 'I couldn't have held my head up if we'd missed getting out the story. The *Post* would have run it over two or three pages this afternoon and beaten us on our own story.'

'There was no time to remake the editorial page, Cleo. Are you going to run an editorial?'

'We'll have to. And an obit on Lord Cruze. I'll write that. I'll do the editorial too.'

'Cleo –' Carl sounded concerned. 'Why don't you take it easy? You know as well as I do that the Fuchs dame and the hit man, whoever he was, were gunning for you. Something went wrong and it was screwed up. But it doesn't alter the fact you were the target.'

'I'll be all right, Carl. Tom is here with me and so is my father. I'll be in tomorrow at the usual time.'

But she was not as calm as she tried to sound. She had busied herself as a newspaperwomen to keep her mind from blacking out under shock. When she had reached home, the bodies in the street were already covered with sheets and waiting for the ambulances; Tom had been down on the sidewalk and he had told her what had happened. She had not had to look at Jack's body; Tom would go down tomorrow to the morgue to identify it officially. She felt nothing about Rosa Fuchs, not even pity for the girl's death; Tom had told her the police had found the Luger in the German girl's raincoat and it had not been difficult to guess on whom she had intended to use it. But she felt for Jack: pity, love, a sense of loss. He had died for some reason connected with her and he did not deserve to have gone in such a way.

Tom insisted she take a sleeping tablet, something she had always prided herself on not needing; she finally dropped off, but devils walked in the darkness of her mind and Tom came into the bedroom once when she cried out. He and Sylvester kept vigil in the living-room and between long silences came to know each other well enough for respect to be firmly and permanently established. At nine in the morning the phone rang and Tom grabbed it lest it wake Cleo.

'It's me, Mrs Roux. Tom Border. Cleo is still asleep. She was pretty shaken up by what happened last night. Do you want to speak to her father?'

But Sylvester shook his head. He was suffering from his own shock. It had come to him during the night that, if he had not delayed Cleo at his hotel, trying to catch up on all the chances they had let go, she might now be dead.

'No,' said Claudine. 'Tell Miss Spearfield I'm relieved and pleased she is safe. Who is looking after Lord Cruze's remains?'

Remains. Jesus, Tom thought, ashes to ashes, dust to dust . . . More than that remained of a man. 'I don't know. I guess I'll do it. I'll call the *Examiner* in London. Or maybe Mr Kibler will do it.'

'Leave it to me. I'll have Mr Kibler do it. Just see that Miss Spearfield doesn't worry about it. She's been through enough.'

Tom hung up, wondering at the sympathy and understanding one found in the most unlikely places. Claudine hung up her end of the line, thinking of Jack, his life finished, his power gone. Up till not so long ago she had never thought about her own death, but now the thought hovered in her mind, a shadow that had darkened when she had been told of Jack Cruze's death. She would go to Mass this evening, pray for Jack and herself.

'Don't be so surprised,' Sylvester told Tom. 'Women are always better at that than us men. I think they mean it, too. They like to share suffering.'

Tom didn't know whether Sylvester was being cynical or sincere. He was saved from asking by Cleo's appearing from the bedroom.

'Who was that?' She had been sleeping with one ear awake, for gunshots, screams for help.

533

Tom told her, then said, 'There are guys from the other papers and the wire services camped downstairs and enough TV cameramen to shoot *Gone With The Wind*. I really hate those guys, they think they own the world.'

'Go down and tell them I'll see no one till tomorrow.'

'By tomorrow you won't be news.'

'That's what I'm hoping.'

But she was still news even when Sylvester left on the Sunday and she had had to grant interviews. She could have refused, but she knew how she herself would have felt if the editor of some other paper, in similar circumstances, had tried to keep his story exclusively for his own paper. Everyone tried to beat everyone else to a story skulduggery; was part of the game, but there were certain rules that had to be honoured. Two outsiders, working independently, had tried to murder an honest editor and that was everyone's story. The freedom of the press occasionally applied amongst itself.

Sylvester went home; and so did Jack's remains. Cleo had phoned Emma at two o'clock in the morning, three hours after the murder, and told her the news. She had explained she had not wanted Emma to hear of the tragedy on the radio and Emma had thanked her for her thoughtfulness. They talked for a few minutes, two women suddenly missing the man neither of them could live with, then they hung up, neither of them committing herself to any further meeting between them. Each felt they could be friends, but the body of Jack still lay between them.

By Monday the story was dead news. The police traced Rosa Fuchs's New York contacts; but the two girls had fled by the time the police arrived. There was no doubt in anyone's mind as to who had sent the hit man, but there was no evidence to warrant even asking the Kansas City Police Department to pick up Tony Rossano for questioning.

'The Mob may come after you again, Miss Spearfield,' said the captain in charge of the case, 'but we don't think so. That hit man bungled the job and for all we know he may be at the bottom of some river already. If he'd gunned down some innocent nobodies, they might have sent him after you

534

again. But getting Lord Cruze ... All I can say is you were lucky.'

'Yes, wasn't I?' said Cleo and wondered if Jack would have thought the police captain was taking the mickey out of him.

Within a week after the double killing Cleo began to notice a subtle change in Alain's attitude. He had never been more than coolly polite to her since his return to the paper; now he seemed to be going out of his way to avoid her. He had not missed an editorial conference since his first day as associate publisher; now he missed three days in a row. Cleo rang him one afternoon to tell him about a foreign policy editorial she was running next day, only to be told by his secretary that Mr Roux would not be in today and could be contacted at his mother's place out at Souillac.

It was Jerry Kibler who gave her the clue to what was happening. He called her, took her to lunch at Schrafft's. 'You wondering why I brought you here instead of somewhere more expensive?'

'Your bank is going broke?'

He giggled, then was instantly serious. 'Don't knock it, you may need me. I brought you here because I don't think any of my financial friends or any newspaper friends will see us here. I saw Alain Roux having lunch with Dick Hamilton, Claudine's banker, yesterday. I rang Dick and asked him what was going on and he told me to mind my own business. I'd have told him the same. But something is going on. I made a few underhand enquiries – I can be very underhand in the interests of a client –'

'Am I a client?'

'You're going to be, I think. Anyhow, I found out that Alain and Claudine are trying to raise enough cash to buy back Jack Cruze's twenty-two per cent of the stock. If they do that, guess who's going to be shown the door.'

'Me. And you.'

'Don't worry about me. It's you Alain is after. You've put the paper back on its feet and now, with Jack gone, he wants to take over, run it his way with no interference from you. Who would Jack have left his stock to?'

'I don't know. Possibly Emma, his wife. But I could never call her and ask, not something like that.'

'I'll call Jack's lawyers in London. Maybe they won't want to tell me what's in Jack's will, but if I explain the circumstances they may lean a little our way. Not all British lawyers are stuffy. Now what do you want – the Special Plate?'

'I'd better eat up. I may be out of a job soon.'

Two days later he called her. 'The will was read in London this morning. You've got nothing to worry about, at least for the moment. You're the owner of twenty-two per cent. Jack left it to you, no strings attached. Sit tight and leave the next move up to Claudine and Alain. And congratulations. You're a rich woman.'

She hung up the phone and looked at the very faint reflection of herself in the glass that separated her from the newsroom. People came and went through her reflection; she felt as insubstantial as she looked, her head ready to fall off her shoulders. She supposed she had always had a ticket, but she had never really thought of winning the lottery. She had never worried about money and now that she had a lot of it, or the promise of it, she had to count it. She looked up the price of *Courier* stock and punched buttons on her calculator. Then she sat back and her reflection faded away to nothing in the glass opposite her. She was worth slightly more than seven million dollars.

She did not ring Tom, because all at once she did not know how she was going to tell him of her – no, *their* – good fortune. The thought was on her mind all afternoon and she was not in command at the conference. When it was over Joe Hamlyn followed her into her office.

'Something worrying you, Cleo? You were miles away in there at the meeting. You're not pregnant, are you?'

'Joe! Do you ask your daughters that sort of question?'

'All the time. I'm a father.'

'No, I'm not pregnant.' Pregnant with riches, maybe; but she could not tell him that just yet. She hedged: 'I think I'm suffering a reaction to last week. If I hadn't stopped to have a nightcap with my father . . .'

536

He nodded sympathetically. 'Why don't you take a week off? Go away and marry Tom. Carl and I will battle Alain for you while you're away.'

She knew she could not spare even a day away from the *Courier* right now. 'I'll think about it. I'll see what Tom says.'

What Tom said, about her new-found wealth, was very little; so little that it worried her. 'Is that all you're going to say? *That's nice?*'

They were in the living-room of her apartment, finishing the light supper he had prepared. At a loose end, still waiting to start work on the *Times*, Tom had occupied himself with housekeeping for the past week. He was no chef, but he could make a passable *quiche* and a good salad and he made the sort of coffee Cleo had enjoyed in Europe but never found in America. Coffee never kept her awake, but she had the feeling she would not sleep well tonight.

'What do you expect me to say? One of the things you and I had in common was we never talked about money, it didn't worry us. But now ... Seven million dollars! I can't ignore that. It's the same as if you had a wooden leg – I couldn't ignore that. I might get used to it in time, but I sure as hell couldn't ignore it.'

'Money doesn't have to be as obvious as a wooden leg.'

'It is when you're living with it.' He stared morosely into his coffee cup.' Jack Cruze would be living with us, too, even though he's dead.'

'Are you saying that's why he left me the stock, just to come between us?'

'I don't know. How the hell do I know what he had in his mind?'

'We shan't know till we see the date he made his will. Maybe he'd willed me the stock before he and I broke up, before I told him about you and me –' Suddenly she broke down and began to weep.

He looked at her suspiciously, as if she were trying some ploy. He had never seen her weep, except for joy after they had made love. Even a week ago, when she had finally got to bed after the shocking tragedy of Cruze's death and all the intense action that had followed it, she had not broken down and wept. She had always seemed to him to be in control of her tears and it shocked him now to see her weeping as he had seen Simone weep.

He put out a cautious arm and she slid into the crook of it. He said nothing, nor did she. They settled their differences in silence, as lovers so often do; the problem was put aside for another day, to gather interest and be even more difficult to solve. Or so Tom thought, though he did not say so.

At last he said, 'Let's get married *now*. We've got the papers, we can go down to City Hall and take our place in the queue –'

She sat up, saying nothing, and he took her silence for a refusal. But then she said, 'Not down at City Hall. I know a judge or two – I'll ask one of them to come up here and marry us –'

'Okay.' He did not like public weddings, least of all his own.

'There's one thing ... When everything has settled down, I'd like to be married again in a church. A Catholic church.'

It had never occurred to him that she took her religion seriously. 'Okay. But why?'

She could not give him a rational answer. She had never renounced her Catholicism, just drifted away from it; but now all at once she thought of her mother and the example Brigid had tried to set her children, none of whom had followed her. She had said her prayers every night, gone to Mass and Communion every Sunday, tried to be 'a good Catholic'. She had never defined what she thought of as a good Catholic; she had, however, been a good women. The goodness in her had been inherent, but she had always felt she needed the discipline of the Church. She would have wanted her only daughter to start off her marriage in what, for her, was the proper place.

'It would have pleased my mum.' She sounded young; but then she had been young when her mother had died. 'She was an old-fashioned mother.'

'The best kind,' he said, unwittingly unkind. But she let it

538

pass. She had no idea what sort of mother she would prove to be. They had not even discussed their having children.

2

They were married two days later by a District Court judge whom Cleo had met at dinner parties. The ceremony was held in Cleo's apartment and Clem and Olive Border flew in from Missouri to meet their new daughter-in-law for the first time. Carl Fishburg was best man and Cleo was given away by Joe Hamlyn. The only other two guests were Kitty Hamlyn and Ethel Fishburg and no prior announcement was made of the wedding.

The Borders' reaction to Cleo was a mixture of awe and scepticism. They had never met a woman as successful as she and they privately, not even confiding their thoughts to each other, wondered if she would not soon find marriage to their son boring and restricting. Being loving parents, neither of them took into consideration any shortfall in Tom's ability to cope. The marriage if it failed, would be their daughter-in-law's responsibility.

But they were pleasant and made a good fist, if tightly clenched, of looking happy. The judge, after kissing the bride, had to hurry back to his court to sentence a murderer to life imprisonment; life must go on, he joked, thinking he would give the son-of-a-bitch thirty years, and he took his hat and departed. Tom and Cleo took their six guests to lunch at the Four Seasons, but first she rang Jerry Kibler and told him what she and Tom had done.

'Congratulations!' He was genuinely pleased. 'But you should have asked Sara and me to the wedding.'

'I know, Jerry. But then the list would have grown ... We did it in a hurry and we're keeping it quiet, at least for the next week. Till we find out what's happening at the *Courier*.'

'I'll keep an eye on that. Go away on your honeymoon –'

'I can't do that –'

'I promise you, Cleo, I won't let Claudine and Alain knife

539

you in the back. Go away for at least a couple of days. I've got a cottage up in the Berkshires – go there –'

'Jerry, I don't want to lose the paper –'

He was silent for a moment, then he said quietly, 'Cleo, your marriage and Tom are more important than the *Courier*. You better start thinking right now about your priorities.'

More fatherly advice; but she knew her mother would have said exactly the same thing. She hung up and went out to celebrate her first priority, abruptly convinced that Jerry was right. She sat between Tom and his mother, love on one side and stiff pleasance on the other; but she tried hard with Olive Border, mincing words till she felt mealy-mouthed. By the end of the meal Olive had warmed to her and across the table Clem was smiling at her with open appreciation. But they still had their reservations. She was still a stranger, with one foot in their door and that much too well-shod for their standards. Tom had told them she was now not only editor of the *Courier* but part-owner. Mothers dream of rich husbands for their daughters, but sons and rich wives are another matter. A rich daughter-in-law is often harder to bear than a mortgage.

Joe Hamlyn and Carl Fishburg went off to get the *Courier* out and their wives went home with warmly revived memories of their own wedding days. Cleo and Tom, having driven Clem and Olive back to the Pierre, where Cleo had insisted that they stay as her and Tom's guests, went off to the Kibler cottage in the Berkshires. They had a glorious two-day honeymoon, shutting everything out of their minds but the enjoyment of each other. They glutted themselves with sex, where they had equal riches; the disaster in the bed in Saigon was long forgotten. Being news-people they could not shut *everything* out of their minds: they looked at the television news each evening. On the second and last night they switched on to find that hostages had been taken at the US embassy in Teheran.

'I'll have to go back –'

'No,' Tom said. 'Joe knows where you are. If he thought you were needed, he'd have rung you.'

'Darling, I can't sit this out –'

'You can and you will. It's only for tonight. You'll be back in your office tomorrow afternoon.'

'What's got into you? You're a newspaperman –'

'For these two days I'm a husband on his honeymoon. I'm sticking to my priorities.'

Had Jerry spoken to him, too? But she knew that he hadn't. 'You're not trying to tell me, in your own oblique way, that a woman's place is in the marriage bed?'

For a moment she thought she saw the old withdrawn look, something she hadn't noticed in a long time. 'Just for tonight, that's all.'

She argued no further. They went to bed, enjoyed their priorities and went back to New York next morning. The phone was ringing as they came in the front door of their apartment. It was Jerry Kibler.

'There's an emergency board meeting this afternoon. You better come downtown and see me first.'

'Jerry, I have to go to the paper –'

'See me first. Otherwise you're likely to be out on your beautiful ass.' He had never talked to her like that before. 'Get down here!'

She hung up and told Tom of Jerry's urgent command. 'You better go down and see him. You want me to come with you?'

'No, you'd better go and see your parents off. Give them my love and apologies.'

They went their separate ways. Only Tom remarked that Cleo had not asked him to accompany her to the meeting with Kibler; it evidently had not occurred to her that he might *want* to go with her. Lines were drawn that morning that she did not see.

Jerry Kibler's offices were on Pine Street; his New Amsterdam Commercial Bank, despite its whimsical name, had not been able to land a location on Wall Street. Cleo had never visited Jerry in his offices and she was surprised that the bank occupied only three floors of the building.

'Investment bankers don't need that much space. All

541

we carry is paper and what's up here –' He tapped his forehead.

She settled down in the heavy leather chair opposite him. His office was a man's room, all timber and leather and sporting prints, though she knew his only sport was hunting money. A grandfather clock stood in one corner, its golden face brightly polished.

'I've kept my bank small, I like to work the British way. I've got partners, but I'm the boss. I guess I'm like Claudine, I like to run things my way. Like you, too.'

She wondered if she was in for more fatherly advice.

'Stephen Jensen rang me this morning,' he said. 'Claudine and Alain approached him yesterday to sell his stock. They've offered him ten per cent above the market price.'

She frowned. 'That's quite a bid, isn't it? What percentage would that give Claudine?'

'It would give her forty-five per cent. Stephen asked her why she wanted to buy. Evidently she was reluctant to tell him at first, but he said he wouldn't sell till he knew the reason why. So she told him. She wants Alain to take over the running of the paper and they need to be sure of a majority on the board to achieve that.'

'They have a majority now. There's just you and I against them, except for Stephen. Occasionally he's backed us, but not always.'

'This is my opinion –' Jerry said carefully. 'I think Claudine is not quite certain what some of the other directors would do if you were voted out of the editor's chair. They may think more of the viability of the paper than they would of loyalty to her –'

'Vote me out as editor? Who would they put in to replace me?'

'Stephen thinks it will be Alain. He asked Claudine point-blank if she had any editorial changes in mind. She hedged, then said yes. But she wouldn't elaborate. But Alain was there with her and Stephen said he read his answer in Alain's face. Now he may be fooling himself that he's perceptive, but it's a possibility we have to face. You wouldn't be the

542

first one who's been fired for being too successful. Alain has been trying to put the skids under you ever since he moved in as associate publisher.'

'He hasn't succeeded.'

'His mother hasn't owned the majority of the stock. If she's approached Stephen, you can be sure she's been to see the others, Stanley Beaton and the Hargraves family, for instance. They're old friends. And there's Roger with his ten per cent. You're headed for trouble, Cleo. What do you want to do?'

'Fight the bastards.' She was her father's daughter, she knew he would have said the same thing. 'I think everyone of the staff will back me.'

Kibler smiled sympathetically at her naïveté. 'Cleo, in takeovers staff loyalty is worth what it is – a barrel of hot air. Nice words, if you like, but still hot air.'

'I could go to the Guild and ask them to back me.' She knew the clout that some Australian unions had, though she was not sure how successful the newspaper unions had been in fighting takeovers.

'Forget it. If you want to fight, you have to do it on your own. With my help,' he added.

'What do I do then?'

'You increase your own stockholding. I'll raise the money for you. You'll need another twenty per cent at least.' He looked at some figures scrawled on a pad on his desk. 'That will take about seven and a half million dollars, if you're going to match Claudine's bid.'

She couldn't help herself: she laughed, a sound more like that of her throat being trodden on. 'Jerry, where the hell do you think you could raise seven and a half million dollars on my name? I don't even own my own apartment, it's leased. I have money in the bank –'

'How much?'

'I don't know. Something around a hundred thousand – it's drawing bank interest –'

He threw up his hands. Some idiots deserved to be poor. 'Why didn't you come to me? I'd have invested it for you –'

543

'Jerry, I've never been interested in money. I don't know – perhaps it was my father's influence. He was always preaching against people whose only concern was making money. Sorry,' she said as she saw his pained smile, 'I don't feel like that about other people. But I've never thought much about wanting to be rich. Now suddenly I'm worth seven million and you're suggesting I go out and borrow another seven and a half. Something I've always prided myself on – I got this from my mother – is that I've never been in debt. I don't want to start now when I'm supposed to be rich.'

'Well, it's either being rich and out of a job or going into hock to save your job. I guess it's a situation a lot of people wouldn't have any trouble solving. But being editor of the *Courier* means more to you than having all that money, right? You like the power and influence it gives you, right?'

She had never put the question to herself. Now she did, as bluntly as Jerry had put it to her, and the answer didn't surprise her. 'Yes.'

'Okay, then you better decide what you're going to do. Do you want to go home and talk it over with Tom?'

'I don't think that would help.' She knew at once that she was going to make her own decision. She was shocked at her selfishness, but it seemed the natural thing to do. 'What do I need to do to be able to borrow the money?'

'I think I can raise two-thirds of the cash if you put up your own stock as collateral. These days bankers are more cautious with newspapers than they are with other ventures. I'll guarantee another two million. That means we have to find someone who'll lend you a million. That's not much.'

She had to smile. 'Jerry, please talk in my terms –'

'Forget your terms. We're dealing with a woman who's worth two hundred million or more.'

The thought frightened her and suddenly she wanted to give up. She was out of her league on the money battlefield; in her own field it was like a first-year cub reporter trying to take over the editorship of the *New York Times*. Claudine, who seemed never to have lost a battle in her life, would win this one.

Jerry Kibler recognized the surrender in her face. 'Don't give up, Cleo. We'll manage it somehow. I'll see you at the board meeting this afternoon. Be prepared for anything.'

3

The boardroom, Cleo thought, had the atmosphere of a wood-panelled bear garden. But claws were gloved and Claudine greeted her as she might an old friend, one old enough to be buried.

'I hear you and Tom Border are married. There hasn't even been an announcement in our own paper.'

'We didn't think it was news.'

'Surely it was worth a line or two on the back pages?' Her own wedding had been on Page One news, at least in the old *Courier*. 'But perhaps you're right. Marriage shouldn't be such a public thing, unless it is being held up as an example.'

'Ours is a little too new for that.'

Roger came up, handsome and beautifully dressed; Cleo had never seen him less than that, as if he were continually on civilian dress parade. But he sounded sincere, which is not a military habit: 'Congratulations. I hope you and Tom will be very happy. I liked him, that week I spent with him in Cairo.'

Claudine had taken her seat at the head of the table, was calling the meeting to order. 'Some of you may be wondering why this meeting has been called –'

Jerry Kibler, arriving late, slid into his seat beside Cleo. He patted her arm, winked at her and then gave his attention to the chairwoman.

'It is to announce that certain stock transactions have taken place. It is better that you learn of them here than read about them in the *Wall Street Journal*. Or even in our own paper.' She smiled down the table at Cleo.

'We're touched by your sensitivity,' said Jerry and from

545

the tone of his voice Cleo knew at once that he was ready for an argument. For good strong argument: when he had none, he had the wit to remain quiet.

'It's in one's breeding,' said Claudine. 'We want no repetition of the way Lord Cruze bought into the *Courier*.'

'All open and above board then,' said Jerry. 'Good. Tell us what you know or have done, Claudine.'

For a moment Claudine seemed to waver, as if her throne had been placed on water. It had shaken her when she had learned Jack Cruze had left all his *Courier* stock to Cleo; she had known the mistresses of a number of men but none of them, as far as she knew, had ever been so richly rewarded for their services. Somehow it made her feel she had not done enough to merit her own inheritance.

'Stanley Beaton has consented to sell me his seven per cent of the stock – that will make my holdings forty-two per cent. I have also made an offer, at a similar price, for the stock owned by Stephen Jensen and the Hargraves family. I have talked to Mr Parsons, who represents the Galloway family.' The Galloway holding was not represented on the board.

'Have you accepted the offer?' Jerry looked at Jensen.

'Not yet.' Jensen appeared the calmest person at the table, having nothing to lose. He was dressed in a navy blazer and checked shirt and looked as if he had dropped into the wrong room, or the wrong club. 'I should be out sailing this afternoon, not sitting here. Let's say I'm waiting to see which way the wind blows.'

Kibler looked at John Stabler, the lawyer who represented the Hargraves family. He was a bony, bald-headed man on whom the patina of age had been spread too thickly and prematurely. He turned a sour eye on Cleo and gave her, not Jerry, his answer.

'The Hargraves have agreed to sell to Mrs Roux.'

Stabler had never liked her, but then he had never appeared to like Claudine; women had no place in business, they were too emotional. Which was something that could never be said of him. Cleo looked past him and up the table at Claudine.

546

'That gives you forty-eight per cent of the stock. I'm surprised you haven't made me an offer.'

'If you wish to sell, I shall buy you out at the current market price.'

She would not give the girl (for she still thought of her as a girl) a windfall. Jack Cruze had already given Cleo more than she deserved. When Alain had come to her at the weekend with the suggestion that she should buy up enough stock to give her the controlling interest in the paper she had been surprised the idea had not occurred to her first. She must be slowing up, a thought she put out of her mind at once before it could take hold.

She had still asked him, 'Why?'

'I want to be editor.'

She admired candid ambition, so long as it was kept in the family. Outside the family it was vulgar. 'I don't think you would be as good an editor as Cleo.'

He didn't admire *her* candour. 'I think I deserve the chance to show that I could be. It's still the Brisson paper. But it won't be if we let her go on the way she's going. People talk about her and the *Courier* now, not about you.'

'I hadn't heard that.' She had a conveniently deaf ear.

'Who would mention it to you but a loving son?'

She loved him, though he could be annoying. 'Have you discussed this with Simone?'

'Why should I? She's not interested in business.' Simone having married more money than she had ever dreamed of, was no longer thrifty.

'Because I suspect you're using your knife on Cleo for more than just business reasons. Revenge isn't always sweet, Alain.' She had tried it once, on her husband, and it had turned sour in her mouth. She had had to wait till he was dead before the taste had sweetened.

'It's not revenge,' he said, though he thought she might be right. 'It's just that I can't spend the rest of my life working with her. And the *Courier* is my life.' He had become convinced of that, knowing he had no other way to power. He was his mother's son and he wished she would recognize the

547

resemblance without having to have it spelled out for her. 'I want to make it *our* paper again.'

'We can always get rid of her as editor.'

'I don't think so. Stephen Jensen would vote to keep her on. So might Stanley Beaton and even Roger. I don't know about Stabler and Bill Warburg. While the paper's making money they probably wouldn't want to rock the boat.'

'It would cost a great deal of money.'

'We have it.' Actually, he had very little of it; but heirs give themselves airs. 'The paper is a good investment now.'

'Thanks to Cleo.'

But she had said it reluctantly. One did not like to learn that something one had always taken for granted as one's own had been commandeered. She set her mind to being the Empress again.

Now she looked down the table at Cleo and said, 'The offer stands till Friday afternoon. There'll be another board meeting then at three o'clock.'

'We won't be selling,' said Jerry Kibler before Cleo could reply.

'I think it only fair to warn you,' said Claudine, 'that there will be certain changes under the new set-up. You might well be advised to sell.'

Roger, sitting next to his sister, had said nothing so far. He had not been made privy to what Claudine was up to and he resented his exclusion. He had begun to feel lately that his presence on the board was barely tolerated by Claudine, as if she thought he was out of his element out of the army. But now he recognized a small war when he saw one.

'I think we'd all like to know what changes,' he said.

'They'll be announced in due course,' Claudine told him in a voice that implied she was giving him a lesson in tactics.

Jerry said, 'Will you be selling, Roger?'

'Not at present,' he said and was pleased to see his sister look at him sharply, as if she suspected treason.

'Your stock is part of the family's holding,' she said.

'But in my name,' he said.

548

Jerry Kibler turned to the man beside him. 'What about you, Bill?'

Bill Warburg was a big, shambling man with a pleasant face and the air of a man who had always found life pleasant. He was another of those whom Cleo thought of as old money. He was an amiable hedonist and he did not like anything that disturbed his routine. He would sell, if it meant avoiding any fighting.

Jerry knew it, too. 'Never mind, Bill. Ride downtown with me when this is over.'

Claudine saw that she had been out-foxed; short of kidnapping Warburg, she could not keep him away from Kibler. Abruptly she closed the meeting, determined to get to Stephen Jensen before the other side could. Strategic points had to be taken.

As the meeting broke up Jerry put a hand on Warburg's arm. 'Wait here a moment with me and Cleo.'

Warburg looked reluctant, but he was a polite man and he did not know how to be rude. Cleo, on a nod from Jerry, moved up and sat on the other side of Warburg. The others filed out, Claudine the last to go.

'My offer stands, Cleo. Till Friday afternoon.'

'No, thank you,' said Cleo, though Jerry had not yet told her how much money he had raised to fight the battle. 'I've never been for sale, Claudine, despite what you think.'

Claudine whirled and went out. Warburg looked pained and embarrassed; he liked women to be ladies. Jerry smiled appreciatively at Cleo. He liked a fighter, of any sex.

'Things are just starting to warm up.'

'That's what I don't like,' said Warburg.

'You can be out of it, if you like, Bill. Cleo has the money to offer you the same price for your stock as Claudine has been offering.' He glanced at her and nodded: the money was available. 'If you don't like the rough water, now's the time to get out.'

Warburg, like Jensen, belonged to the New York Yacht Club; he smiled at the metaphor used by Jerry, the non-sailor. 'Sailors don't necessarily always like smooth sailing –

it can be dull. But I don't like sailing through muck. Let's talk going downtown.' He took Cleo's hand between his huge paws. 'If you want to buy my stock, Cleo, you're welcome to it. But I hope you're not biting off more than you can chew.'

'Jerry is my adviser. I trust him.'

'I wasn't thinking about the money end. If you take control of the *Courier* away from Claudine – well, personally I'd rather be out in a one-man Finn in a force-nine gale than face up to her.'

'They always name hurricanes after women. Maybe it needs a woman to face up to one.'

He smiled, patted her as if she were mentally ill. 'Good luck.'

Cleo went back downstairs to the news floor, arriving late for the afternoon conference. Alain, sitting at the head of the table, looked up as she took her seat, but she gave him no hint of what had gone on upstairs. Instead she asked at once, 'How much have we done?'

'It's practically wrapped up,' said Joe Hamlyn. 'I'm running the hostage story over on to Page Two. But for the first few days I'm afraid we're going to lose out to the goddam TV wonder boys. All those mobs in the streets are made to order for their cameras.'

'Perhaps we should buy a TV station.'

Cleo had meant it only as a joke, but she saw Alain's head come up as if she were stating a new policy. He made a note on his pad and she determined then that for the next week or two she would be very careful what she said. She was not going to manufacture ammunition for the other side.

When the conference broke up she avoided Alain, then called Joe Hamlyn and Carl Fishburg into her office. 'I have a war on upstairs. I'm having to buy more stock to keep my job.'

The two men listened quietly while she told them what had happened so far and what, she guessed, might happen if she lost out.

Then Joe said, 'I could talk to the staff, if you like. I don't know how much there is in the pension fund, but it might

550

help. It wouldn't be the first time a newspaper's staff has bought a paper to save its jobs. The *Kansas City Star* did it some time back in the Twenties. I, for one, wouldn't want to work with Alain as the editor. In no time at all he'd have us sounding like that guy Loeb up in New Hampshire, campaigning to have Cal Coolidge raised from the dead.'

'Me, neither,' said Carl. 'We'll talk to the guys in finance, see what's in the kitty.'

Cleo shook her head, touched by their loyalty. 'No. This is my fight. I don't want you risking your money on me. I have faith in Jerry Kibler, he'll raise everything we need. If he doesn't, then I'll stay on till they kick me out. Which they'll have to do physically.' Which, she remembered, was what they had almost had to do with Jake Lintas.

She went home that night and told Tom what had happened at the board meeting. 'One thing I have in my favour, all the staff are behind me.'

'It's some story.' He had started work on the *Times* that day. There had been a certain satisfaction at going to work for what he thought of as the Number 1 paper in the United States, but it was a huge organization and he knew he would miss the comparative intimacy of the *Courier*.

'You don't use it,' she said as editor and wife, putting both roles in the right order. 'That's a rule we'd better lay down right now. I never use anything you tell me about inside stuff at the *Times* and you keep your nose out of the *Courier*.'

'Okay.' He saw her point, at least for the moment. 'But I wish I were back on the *Courier* so I could help you.'

'I'll manage,' she said, and Tom felt himself pushed back a step. But she had gone into the bathroom and didn't notice what she had done.

4

Over the next two days Jerry Kibler, enjoying himself immensely, was busy. He bought Bill Warburg's stock and rang Cleo. 'I think I've also just about persuaded Stephen Jensen to sell to you. That will give you a total of thirty-eight per cent.'

'It's not enough.' She had had two sleepless nights and, though she was not prepared to confess it to anyone, not even Tom, she was losing the determination to go on with the battle.

But Jerry was not giving up. 'It's not over yet, dammit! We've lost Beaton's and the Hargraves stock – I rang them and they wouldn't listen to me, not even when I offered to raise the price. That leaves us the Galloway four per cent and Roger's ten per cent.'

She felt even more disheartened. 'Roger would never sell to me.'

'Despite what he said the other day, the stock is held jointly in his and his wife's name. You might try talking to her, see how she feels. I gather she and Claudine have never got on, not really.'

What was it Claudine had said about there should be nothing personal in business? 'What about the Galloway stock?'

'I think I can swing that. I'll have to raise the ante, but it will be worth it.'

'Jerry – how much am I in for so far?'

'If you manage to buy both Roger's and the Galloway stock, you will be up in total for just over eleven million dollars.'

She was sitting up in bed with the breakfast tray Tom had brought her across her lap; it tilted as her body slid down under it. She hadn't fainted, but she felt herself go light-headed and limp. Tom, hearing the rattle of cup and saucer, came to the door of the bathroom.

'What's the matter?'

'Nothing.' She pulled herself up again. 'Jerry –'

'Don't worry, Cleo, don't worry. The assets are there in the company – the *Courier* building, that's prime real estate, the radio station, the paper itself. I haven't raised the cash on thin air.'

'Jerry, how will I ever pay it back?'

'We'll find ways. You can sell the building, for one thing, and then lease it back. You're not going to have any money to spare for the next ten or fifteen years maybe, but you're going to own the *Courier* and run it your way.'

'There's something in the constitution that says if the Brissons lose control, they have to sell out completely. What happens then?'

'You can buy *all* the stock –'

'Jerry, I'm giddy as it is. Don't knock my head right off my shoulders.'

'Okay. But don't worry about that right now. I can always find buyers for Claudine's stock if she has to sell. It would give me the greatest of pleasure to do that and then charge her commission.

Cleo hung up and looked up to see Tom standing in his shorts in the bathroom doorway. 'What was that all about?'

'Jerry Kibler has just told me I may be in debt to the tune of eleven million dollars by the end of the day.'

He didn't whistle or swear, showed no reaction at all. Instead he said quietly, 'Is it worth it?'

'I don't know. What else do I do if I don't want to lose the paper?'

'You could look around for a job running some other paper. There are a lot of papers in trouble – maybe you could try saving one of them. We could do it together,' he added, but his voice was flat and she couldn't tell whether he was enthusiastic or even meant what he said.

'Where? There are no editor's jobs going in New York. It's New York or Washington for me – I don't want to work in any other town. I don't think you do, either.'

'No,' he conceded. 'But I don't want to see us eaten up by the *Courier*.'

'Darling –' She reached out, pulled him down beside her. 'Do you think I'd let that happen? If I thought there was any danger of that, I'd sell my stock and let Claudine and Alain have what they want.'

'Just keep your eyes peeled for the danger signal.' He kissed her and stood up. 'I'm a newspaperman, but the last thing I'd want would be to lose you to a newspaper.'

He began to dress. She was still getting accustomed to

having him here every morning. She had lived alone for so long that to have a man in her bedroom *every* morning was still a novelty. He was untidy but she loved the evidence he left around, since she didn't have to pick it up: the daily maid did that. Yesterday's shirt and shorts were dropped on the floor, his trousers hung from a doorknob; somehow it was all a reminder that he was *permanent*. Lovers, even durable ones like Jack, had somehow never left their mark on her bedroom. She looked at him adoringly, wanting him to strew the room with reminders of himself.

'We'll have to look for a bigger apartment.'

'Sure. Ask Jerry Kibler for another half million.'

He kissed her and went off to a dental appointment; the small pains, as well as the large, had to be attended to. She lay in bed a while longer, trying to get her immediate future into focus. She had not contemplated the alternative if she lost the battle against Claudine and Alain; but she now realized the real possibility that very soon she could be back, if only temporarily, where she had been when she had first come to New York six years ago. She would have money in the bank, a lot of it, and some fame, but those meant little to her: all she could recognize would be that she would have to start all over again. And it would not be easy, at least not in the newspaper field: Tom had been right, newspapers in America were in trouble. She could, of course, go into television, but it didn't appeal to her; at heart she was a newspaperwoman. She decided all at once that she could not leave everything to Jerry Kibler.

She got out of bed, took a hot and a cold shower to wake herself up completely, put on a robe and went back to the bedroom. She phoned Roger at Watergate in Washington, hoping to catch him before he flew up for this afternoon's meeting. She was answered by a woman's voice and she thought, he's at it again. what Congresswoman was it this time?

But it was the cleaning woman, making the General's bed instead of occupying it. 'The General's up in New York, ma'am. At Sands Point, I think.'

554

Cleo dialled the number at Sands Point. 'Louise, I'm trying to get in touch with Roger –'

'He'll be here for lunch. Would you care to come out and have it with us?'

'I don't want to intrude –'

Louise laughed. 'Don't worry, Cleo. I have everything under control, including him. You won't find any awkwardness. Come early, so you and I can have a talk.'

Cleo ordered a car and half an hour later was being driven out to Long Island. It was a beautiful day, a slight breeze coming in off the Sound, and she made up her mind that she and Tom must buy a getaway place somewhere out of Manhattan. Her optimism was returning, she was going to win the war.

Louise came out on to the wide porch of the big house as Cleo got out of the car. She no longer ran but walked sedately, as if she had at last decided that nothing in life was worth chasing. She spent a good deal of her time now looking backwards, at what she had missed, and one can't run safely while looking over one's shoulder.

She greeted Cleo warmly, like a long-lost friend. They had seen very little of each other since the episode in Washington; each had waited on the other to call and as time had gone on the calls had never been made. But there was no awkwardness now.

They sat out on the porch, tossing conversation as light as the breeze that wafted past them. Then Louise said, 'Roger tells me there may be some blood spilled in the boardroom. Is that why you wanted to see him?'

Cleo nodded. 'I understand you and Roger are joint owners of ten per cent of the stock?'

'I think so. I've never been interested in it.' She made a slight gesture of embarrassment. 'I had a mother and father who brought me up to believe that it was – *grubby* – for a woman to concern herself with money. I know that's not the usual case, not in America. Isn't there some statistics that say women own more than half of America? Well, anyway. I've always had more than I needed and I just took it for granted.

Every year I write cheques for charity and I suppose I think that's enough to ease my conscience.' She looked with almost innocent frankness at Cleo. 'It isn't really, is it?'

Cleo felt she was in no position to judge; her own charity ran only to writing cheques. 'Would you back me against Claudine?'

Louise smiled, like a cat that had been offered entrée to a dairy. 'I think I might. But you'd still have to win over Roger. He's a Brisson, whatever else he is.'

'I think he's appreciated the space I've given him on our Op. Ed. page for his articles on foreign affairs.'

'He thinks Alain might give him more space. They're both very conservative, you know.' She herself was conservative because she had never bothered to find out what liberalism was; she was army trained. 'I don't know whether he's told you, but he has his eye on being Secretary of State when we have a Republican President next year.'

Cleo was not surprised at the information. She had become cynical enough to believe that in today's world, when bombast and violence were part of diplomacy, anyone could have aspirations to being a diplomat. Roger was neither bombastic nor violent, but he could learn to be.

'Claudine and Alain would back him for that,' Louise said. 'She would adore to have him President, but unfortunately he was born in France of a French father. She would settle for Secretary of State. *My brother the Secretary* – I can hear it rolling off her tongue in a dozen languages. She would do a crash course at Berlitz in everything they teach.'

Louise had spent too much time alone in the past two years; she had lost her generosity and taken to practising malice. At least towards her sister-in-law.

'Would you back him?' she asked. 'He'll need all the support he can get. But don't tell him I said so. Here he comes now.'

The big black Mercedes came up the driveway. He'll have to change *that*, Cleo thought, if he's to become Secretary of State. Detroit wouldn't want to be represented by a man who drove around in something from Stuttgart. He got out of the car, recognized Louise's visitor at once and bounded up the steps. But not before he had hesitated for a moment as if the two of them might be conspiring against him. He was learning the first defence of a diplomat, suspicion.

He kissed Cleo on the cheek, something he had taken to doing on their last two meetings. 'What a delightful surprise!'

'I'll leave you two together,' said Louise, practising her own diplomacy. 'I'll check with Lena to see how lunch is coming along.'

'Let's go for a walk,' Cleo said and started off down the steps.

Roger looked after her in surprise, then he followed. He attacked at once: 'You're out here to see if I'll sell my stock.'

'Yours and Louise's. I understand it's held jointly.'

'You've been working on her?' He was still affable, if only just.

'No, not *working* on her. I have the feeling she'll do whatever you suggest.'

He nodded; she expected smugness, but there was none. 'We're almost back on our old terms. Not quite, but nearly. About the stock – I've told Jerry Kibler I shan't sell. Why should I?'

'Of course. Why should you?' She, too, was being affable; but she knew it would get her nowhere. 'Roger, Louise has told me you have your eye on State next year if there is a Republican President.'

'Yes,' he said cautiously. 'I've talked to some of those who might be candidates. Governor Reagan, for one.'

'Have they committed themselves?'

'No candidate ever does, not this early. There are several other men who'd like to be Secretary. I shan't be the only runner. Would you back me if I became one of the favourites?'

'I might. I couldn't do it if I were not still the editor of the *Courier*.'

'No-o. But Alain has said he will back me, too. So I shall have the *Courier* behind me, no matter who's in the editor's chair. I'm sorry, Cleo. You're a far better editor than Alain will ever be and the paper can ill-afford to lose you. But blood

557

is thicker than water, isn't that what they say? Blue blood, anyway,' he said, trying some of his sister's snobbery but smiling with it.

She went for the jugular, ashamed of herself; but there was no alternative. She had not consciously thought about the tactic on her way out here; it had been at the back of her mind, hidden, a secret weapon that shouldn't be used in decent warfare. But her father had told her of the chances he had missed because he had never gone for the jugular. She was not going to sacrifice what might be her only chance to stay at the *Courier*.

'Do you ever think about any of the blood that was spilled at An Bai?'

He was shocked at her ruthlessness; he had always thought of her as *decent*. He looked about him, as if wondering how the assassin could have crept up on him here in his own grounds. Sparrows, unfrightened, randomly stapled the lawns with their tiny claws; a gardener abstractedly clipped a hedge down at the bottom of the slope. Cleo, too, looked abstracted, as if she were outside herself, like someone suffering from *petit mal*, not able to believe what the woman in her shape and with her name had just threatened.

'Good God, that was years ago! It's forgotten –'

'Not by me. I never forget it.' Not even if the memory had to be whipped up like a sleeping dog, like now.

He steadied himself, wanting a situation briefing. 'Are you saying you will dig up all that if I don't sell my stock?'

'I don't care whether you sell it to me or not, so long as you back me against Alain as editor. And as publisher,' she added, all at once appreciating that Claudine, too, had to be got rid of. 'I expect to own forty-two per cent of the stock by this afternoon. Your ten per cent, whether I own it or you give me your vote on it, will give me nominal control.'

'If I say no?'

'I'll give all the An Bai stuff – I still have the story I wrote on it in my files –' She hadn't: she kept none of her material. But she knew she could write the story again as clearly as she had eleven years ago. 'I'll give it to several Democrat Senators who I know wouldn't want you as Secretary of State – they're prejudiced against military men in that post. I saved your neck once, Roger. Now it's your turn to save mine.'

He let go a short harsh laugh. 'There's no comparison. You're blackmailing me. I suppose you'll give your Senators that other bit of dirt, too.'

'An Bai will be enough. It's more than a bit of dirt.'

'Jesus Christ –' He looked at her eyeball to eyeball; it never happened in modern warfare, not to generals. 'You must really want the *Courier*.'

'Not the paper itself so much. I just want to run it the way I've been running it. I didn't start this stock-buying. I want to be editor of the *Courier* just as much as you want to be Secretary of State. I'm only sorry I have to do it this way.'

'Horseshit.' He had never been vulgar-mouthed, at least not to ladies. 'You'd do anything to get your own way. All you women are the same.'

She was branded, she could see that; but he had lumped her with her sex. With Claudine, for instance: 'I've never had to fight this way till I met the Brissons. It's just like An Bai, Roger. The end justifies the means. This isn't a moral war, either.'

Louise came out on to the porch and called them to lunch.

'Coming,' Roger said without looking at her. He changed his tactics, turned to pleading, though not abjectly. 'Cleo, I can't just vote Claudine out of her paper. I'm her brother, for Christ's sake she's always looked on the *Courier* as hers –'

She had gone too far for any charity; she couldn't even write a cheque to ease her conscience. Conscience, she decided, had to give way to responsibility; she was fighting to keep other people besides herself in jobs, men like Joe Hamlyn and Carl Fishburg. Guilt, given intelligence, can always invent.

'It's her or me, Roger. Think who deserves your vote the most.'

She turned quickly and went up to Louise on the porch 'I shan't stay for lunch – I have no appetitite. I think I'd better get back to town and get myself ready for this afternoon's shoot-out.'

'Is it going to be bloody?'

'I think it may well be.' She took Louise's hand, then leaned forward and kissed her on the cheek. She felt both hypocritical and sincere; she was genuinely fond of Louise, yet she had just threatened to shoot down her husband in flames. 'But I'll survive.'

She drove away, turning in the car to look back. Roger still stood in the driveway staring after her. It struck her that he probably hated her more than Alain or Claudine did.

5

If the atmosphere in the boardroom had been charged two days ago, it was much worse this afternoon. I'm sitting *inside* a bomb, Cleo thought, one that has to explode within the next half-hour. No one would be able to prolong the suspense any longer than that. All at once she longed for Tom's company; then just as abruptly she was glad he wasn't here. She did not want him ever to learn how she had threatened Roger. If she won this afternoon, Roger would never tell anyone what had made him vote for her. If she lost, she would keep the story to herself forever. It would be cheap charity, like writing a cheque on a bottomless account, but it would help her conscience. No: she had to be honest with herself. It would protect her from Tom's contempt.

Claudine called the meeting to order as soon as the door closed. Cleo looked up the table at Roger, but he avoided her gaze.

'The first point,' said Claudine, looking down the table at Cleo, 'is to repeat my offer to buy your stock.'

'It is not for sale,' said Cleo. 'None of the forty-two per cent I now own.'

Jerry Kibler said nothing. He had told her that the sale of the Galloway stock had gone through; only the papers had to be exchanged. She had then told him she would do all her own talking, that she would look to him for advice only when she needed it. He had not demurred, seeing at once a far more determined woman than he had spoken to this morning. He wondered what had happened to her in the meantime.

Claudine nodded. 'I understand you persuaded the Galloway trustees to sell to you. So it's stalemate as far as the stock situation goes. However, I am still the majority stockholder and I have Roger's support.'

'There's just one point,' said Stephen Jensen, dressed for business and not for sport. 'None of us who has sold his stock has been formally dismissed from the board. We are still directors of the company.'

'Without voting rights,' said Claudine.

'I think I'll stay, anyway,' said Jensen and settled back in his chair. 'As a spectator.'

Beaton, Stabler and Warburg looked at each other; Warburg half rose, then flopped back as the other two remained seated. He looked across the table at Kibler and shook his head as if to say, *This isn't going to be civilized.* Jerry grinned and nodded encouragingly.

'Then I take it there is really only one item of business,' said Cleo, carrying the attack up the table. 'You mentioned some changes, Claudine. I expect that's the item.'

Claudine took her time. All at once she had doubts, something as foreign to her as humility. She could be destroying the *Courier* for the sake of her family pride. Her dignity had been dented by the success of the girl (well, woman) at the far end of the table; the *Courier* had indeed become Cleo Springfield's paper. But that had been her own fault; she had neglected her duties as publisher. If it was to be her paper again, she would have to move in full-time to the office next door. The *Courier* could be Alain's when she was dead. She dispelled her doubts and took out her axe.

'I propose that Cleo Spearfield be asked for her resignation as editor of the *Courier*, effective immediately.' She looked at Roger, who had sat gazing at the blank pad on the table in front of him as if nothing being said interested him. Then she looked down the table, past the spectators, at Cleo and Jerry.

561

'The voting, obviously, will be even, two against two. So I further propose that voting will be decided on the stock held by the respective parties.'

'Highly irregular,' said Stephen Jensen. 'Of course that's only a spectator's opinion.'

'I have never taken any notice of spectators,' said Claudine and looked once more at Cleo. 'Do you?'

'No,' said Cleo. 'We'll vote according to stock held.'

'All those in favour of the motion?' said Claudine and raised a regal finger. Then she looked at Roger, who had not moved. 'Roger, the motion is that Cleo's resignation as editor be asked for.'

Roger looked up, his face pale and strained. He did not look down towards Cleo nor even at Claudine. He just stared straight ahead. 'I vote against the motion. I believe that gives Miss Spearfield a majority of fifty-two per cent to forty-eight.'

TWENTY ONE

'Have you been down to the White House since President Reagan moved in?'

Claudine had been there once and decided she would not go again. She had found it all so *middle class*, all new mink and old quips. She had not found, God forgive her for saying so, the style that had been there in the Kennedy days. Camelot was preferable to Hollywood.

'I'm happy enough here in New York,' said Sylvester. 'I leave all the diplomacy to the embassy in Washington.'

'Aren't consuls-general supposed to be diplomatic?' said Tom.

'Not this one,' grinned Sylvester. 'But so far Mal Fraser hasn't recalled me.'

I'm glad of that, Tom thought. He and Cleo's old man, whom he never thought of as old, had become the firmest of friends; and, God knows, he further thought, I need a friend or two. He looked at Claudine and wished for a moment that he had her impregnability; she seemed as if she needed no one but herself. Then he wondered why she was here at Cleo's party.

It was a party for Emma Cruze, who had come over on her first visit to New York. He did not know, and had not asked, what had gone on after Cleo had won the battle of the *Courier*'s boardroom; but he did know Claudine had sold all her stock and Emma Cruze, courted by Jerry Kibler, had been one of the buyers. Roger was the only Brisson still holding stock, but he had retired from the board, content to

563

be just a stockholder. There was a whole new board these days, but Tom, still a *Times* man, no longer asked questions about the *Courier*.

Emma sat in her wheelchair at the far end of the room by the window that looked out on to Central Park; Cleo sat on a low slipper chair beside. Their heads were close together and they looked what they were: friends. Cleo had invited Emma to New York and she had confessed to Tom that she was not sure if she had done the right thing, that Emma would want to come. But come she had and the two of them had embraced like loving sisters. He, too, liked Emma; but he had left them alone. He did not want to hear them talk of Jack Cruze.

Claudine sat with her arm resting on Sylvester's; she knew they made a handsome couple, though she did not want anyone linking their names. She had brought her own escort, a retired French banker who had handled the Brisson finances in France; he came to New York each year to see the Broadway shows and always called on her. He was a good-looking man, but dull as old pewter in personality. She should have anticipated that Sylvester would be alone at the party. He was better company and, unlike the banker, he did not trail after the young pretty girls like a senile poodle.

She was glad of almost any company these days; that was why she had accepted Cleo's invitation. She had gone off to France, determined to cut all ties with New York; but six months there had shown her she was cutting off her nose to spite a face that the local peasantry didn't pay much heed to. New York was her proper domain, even though she was no longer The Empress. Victory would have been sweet, but she didn't have to make a meal of defeat. She had come home and when Cleo had called her two days ago she had recognized the younger woman's graciousness. Hatchets rusted as much in the open as buried. At her age (the phrase dismayed her) everything should be buried except herself.

'It's a beautiful apartment.' She meant it; she had no reason to be insincere with this pleasant, rough-edged man.' 'And Cleo looks at home in it.'

564

'She does, doesn't she?' Sylvester looked at his daughter, who had left Lady Cruze and was moving amongst the glittering guests. They did glitter: they reminded him of diamonds, hard and expensive. But maybe that was New York at this level. 'But sometimes I feel I'm a bit out of my depth with her. Do you feel like that with your boy Alain?'

'No,' said Claudine, misunderstanding him. 'He's never got out of the shallows.'

Alain and Simone also had gone back to France and, if one was to believe them, they were gloriously happy there. Simone would be, she could believe that; but Alain? They were expecting their first child; soon she would be a grandmother. She would put the thought out of her mind till she was confronted by the child.

On the far side of the room Tom wandered on the edge of the guests, like a limpet looking for an interesting berth. But the talk, smart and empty, repelled him. He and Cleo had moved into the apartment six months ago and once a month Cleo had one of these, by now, famous, parties. The apartment was big enough for such gatherings, God knew. (He had taken to invoking God a lot lately; he would have to watch himself or he might finish up as religious editor of the *Times*.) So far Cleo had not committed them to buying it, but they would have to make a decision on it soon. Jerry Kibler had told them he would have no trouble financing the purchase for them: Cleo was always good for a million with any bank in town. Tom had insisted they use *his* money to furnish the apartment and Cleo had agreed without demur. Then she had gone out and hired an interior designer, who now came to all the parties to admire his own handiwork, and the sleek, henna-haired young man had spent Tom's money with gay abandon. Tom had christened the apartment Fag's Revenge and, perversely, had been annoyed when Cleo had thought the joke was funny.

He passed close by the designer now and heard him say, 'As the intellectual eunuch said, it's mind over matter.'

He drifted on before he lost his temper and redesigned the smart-talking offspring-of-a-bitch. Jesus, he thought, what's

565

happened to me? Where had easy-going Ole Tom Border, the farm boy from Friendship, disappeared to?

'Why so unhappy, Tom?' Roger, age (or was it just disappointment?) beginning to blur the edges of his handsomeness, lifted two glasses from a passing tray and handed one to Tom. 'Things not too good at the *Times*? I thought that piece you did on Haig was superb.'

'Tongue in cheek. I borrowed some of Cleo's style from her old London column.'

'He deserved every word you wrote.' He felt no call to be discreet about an ex-fellow officer. Generals, he knew, were usually more complimentary about the enemy brass than their own kind. 'He's out of his element.'

'You might have been too,' said Tom gently. 'You're lucky you missed out. I wouldn't want to be Secretary of State, not now.'

'Maybe,' said Roger, but commonsense could never dim the dream. He *knew* he would have made a good Secretary, one of the best. Cleo had kept her part of the bargain and, because she had, he had forgiven her her blackmail. The *Courier* had run his articles, dropped hints in its columns what he might do at State if Ronald Reagan was elected and chose him. But it had all been to no avail, the other general had moved back into the White House as if he had never been part of the retreat from it back in Nixon's day. Military history, Roger knew, was full of generals who had come back.

Louise joined them, kissed Tom on the cheek and took Roger's arm. 'Come and talk to Lady Cruze. She asked me who that handsome man was and, reluctantly, I had to confess you were my husband.'

Roger smiled at Tom and shrugged. Tom looked after them as they moved through the crowd. They looked happy and, after thirty years or so of marriage, to *look* happy is in itself an achievement. She was his *aide-de-camp* and, God knows, he probably needed her. *Jesus, why am I so sour?*

'Why so sour-looking?' Cleo kissed him, pressed his upper arm.

He hadn't seen her coming towards him and he turned, so

566

highly pleased to have her beside him that one might have thought she had just come into the room after a week or a month or a year away from him. He would never lose the feeling: he loved her, in the same obsessive way that Jack Cruze had. But he did not make the comparison himself.

'There are too many people here. They keep getting in the way, stopping me from looking at you.'

She squeezed his arm again, loving him as much as ever. She was on top of the world; but he was there beside her. She felt a sense of triumph, but it was in her happiness with him as much as anything else she had achieved.

'I love you,' he said.

She kissed him again, wanting to weep with love for him. He was still not handsome, not in the way that Roger was, but there was a growing craggy dignity to him. His thick hair was turning grey along the temples; his slow smile still could charm women; occasionally his eyes still had the old withdrawn look, but it no longer worried her. If he had secrets, so did she.

'I have to go and mingle.'

'Don't mingle. Clear a path and swagger. Nobody does it better than you.'

She smiled and left him, giving an exaggerated swagger to her hips as she did so. She went back across the room to where Sylvester had now joined Emma Cruze. She passed behind Claudine and her French banker without their seeing her. Then she heard the banker say: 'Who is that tall man over there by the door?'

She stopped and, it seemed to her, that her heart stopped too.

Claudine, sowing seeds for the future, said, 'He's Cleo Spearfield's husband.'